"In terms of ideas, intellectual scope, detail, inventiveness, risk taking and sheer scale, McDonald's novel is one of the most ambitious I have read in recent years. It is also a staggering achievement, brilliantly imagined and endlessly surprising, the characters intriguing and psychologically convincing, their dialogue brisk and naturalistic, the grasp of Indian customs and nuances impressive, the sex scenes unusally spicy, the politics subtle and plausible, and much else besides. . . . *River of Gods* is a brave, brilliant and wonderful novel."

—Christopher Priest, *Guardian*

"*River of Gods* is a big, ambitious novel envisioning India's high-tech future which combines intelligent cynicism about the political realm with an idealism about ordinary people which avoids heroics."

—*Time Out*

"A brilliant novel."

—*Waterstones Books Quarterly*

"Imagine William Gibson's *Neuromancer* or *Mona Lisa Overdrive* set in India."

—*Focus*

"With concepts exploding from every page, McDonald has crammed in reams of social detail, conjuring up a convincing picture of the future that melds myth and politics alongside speculation about the development of artificial intelligence."

—*SFX*

"One big concept story . . . Ian McDonald can do this sort of thing in style. It gathers pace quite superbly. The subject of emergent intelligences in a world of genetic engineering is well-trodden territory, but McDonald adds strong new twists to it. He also throws in the brilliant but entirely reasonable idea that CG-actors will need scandalous off-screen lives if they're ever to replace the real thing. It's not merely window-dressing—it's an effective reminder that, even in this globalised world, there are large parts of our present-day globe that are more 'different' and paradigm-shifting than the futures that have become familiar from dozens of novels and films."

—*Starburst*

"A triumphant panorama of mid-21st Century India . . . hugely adventurous and entertaining, sumptuously inventive and full of heart."

—*Locus*

RIVER OF GODS

RIVER OF GODS

IAN McDONALD

an imprint of Prometheus Books
Amherst, NY

Published 2006 by Pyr®, an imprint of Prometheus Books

Inquiries should be addressed to
Pyr
59 John Glenn Drive
Amherst, New York 14228–2197
VOICE: 716–691–0133, ext. 207
FAX: 716–564–2711
WWW.PYRSF.COM

11 10 09 08 07 6 5 4 3 2

Library of Congress Cataloging-in-Publication Data

McDonald, Ian, 1960–.
River of gods / by Ian McDonald.
p. cm.
Originally published: London : Simon & Schuster, 2004.
ISBN 978–1–59102–436–1 (hardcover. : alk. paper)
1. India—Fiction. I. Title.

PR6063.C38R58 2005
823'.914—dc22

2005035110

Printed in the United States on acid-free paper

CONTENTS

PART ONE: GANGA MATA 9

1 Shiv 11
2 Mr. Nandha 17
3 Shaheen Badoor Khan 30
4 Najia 38
5 Lisa 50
6 Lull 61
7 Tal 67
8 Vishram 77

PART TWO: SAT CHID EKAM BRAHMA 89

9 Vishram 91
10 Shiv 96
11 Lisa, Lull 106
12 Mr. Nandha, Parvati 130
13 Shaheen Badoor Khan, Najia 144
14 Tal 160
15 Vishram 173

PART THREE: KALKI 191

16 Shiv 193
17 Lisa 200
18 Lull 212
19 Mr. Nandha 228
20 Vishram 244
21 Parvati 257
22 Shaheen Badoor Khan 271
23 Tal 285
24 Najia 301
25 Shiv 309

PART FOUR: TANDAVA NRITYA 319

26 Shiv 321
27 Shaheen Badoor Khan 330
28 Tal 338
29 Banana Club 348

30 Lisa 350
31 Lull 363
32 Parvati 373
33 Vishram 377
34 Najia, Tal 387
35 Mr. Nandha 394
36 Parvati, Mr. Nandha 401
37 Shaheen Badoor Khan 409
38 Mr. Nandha 417
39 Kunda Khadar 424
40 Vishram 427
41 Lisa 436
42 Lull 442
43 Tal, Najia 449
44 Shiv 455
45 Sarkhand Roundabout 461

PART FIVE: JYOTIRLINGA 465

46 Ensemble 467
47 Lull, Lisa 581

Glossary 589

PART ONE
GANGA MATA

1

SHIV

The body turns in the stream. Where the new bridge crosses the Ganga in five concrete strides, garlands of sticks and plastic snag around the footings; rafts of river flotsam. For a moment the body might join them, a dark hunch in the black stream. The smooth flow of water hauls it, spins it around, shies it feet first through the arch of steel and traffic. Overhead trucks roar across the high spans. Day and night, convoys bright with chrome work, gaudy with gods, storm the bridge into the city, blaring filmi music from their roof speakers. The shallow water shivers.

Knee-deep in the river, Shiv takes a long draw on his cigarette. Holy Ganga. You have attained moksha. You are free from the chakra. Garlands of marigolds coil around his wet pant legs. He watches the body out of sight, then flicks his cigarette into the night in an arc of red sparks and wades back towards where the Merc stands axle-deep in the river. As he sits on the leather rear seat, the boy hands him his shoes. Good shoes. Good socks, Italian socks. None of your Bharati shit. Too good to sacrifice to Mother Ganga's silts and slimes. The kid turns the engine; at the touch of the headlights wire-thin figures scatter across the white sand. Fucking kids. They'll have seen.

The big Merc climbs up out of the river, over the cracked mud to the white sand. Shiv's never seen the river so low. He's never gone with that Ganga Devi Goddess stuff—it's all right for women but a raja has *sense* or he is no raja at all—but seeing the water so low, so weak, he is uncomfortable, like watching blood gush from a wound in the arm of an old friend that you cannot heal. Bones crack beneath the SUV's fat tires. The Merc scatters the embers of the shore kids' fire; then the boy Yogendra throws in the four-wheel drive and takes them straight up the bank, cutting two furrows through the fields of marigolds. Five seasons ago he had been a river kid, squatting by the smudge-fire, poking along the sand, sifting the silt for rags and pickings. He'll end up there, too, some time. Shiv will end up there. It's a thing he's always known. Everyone ends up there. The river bears all away. Mud and skulls.

Eddies roll the body, catch streamers of sari silk and slowly unfurl. As it nears the low pontoon bridge beneath the crumbling fort at Ramnagar, the corpse gives a small final roll and shrugs free. A snake of silk coils out before it, catches on the rounded nose of a pontoon and streams away on either side. British sappers built this bridge, in the nation before the nation before this one; fifty pontoons spanned by a narrow strip of steel. The lighter traffic crosses here; phatphats, mopeds, motorbikes, bicycle rickshaws, the occasional Maruti feeling its way between the bicycles, horn constantly blaring: pedestrians. The pontoon bridge is a ribbon of sound, an endless magnetic tape reverberating to wheels and feet. The naked woman's face drifts centimetres beneath the autorickshaws.

Beyond Ramnagar the east bank opens into a broad sandy strand. Here the naked sadhus build their wicker and bamboo encampments and practise fierce asceticisms before the dawn swim to the sacred city. Behind their campfires tall gas plumes blossom skyward from the big transnational processing plants, throwing long, quivering reflections across the black river, highlighting the glistening backs of the buffaloes huddling in the water beneath crumbling Asi Ghat, first of the holy ghats of Varanasi. Flames bob on the water, a few pilgrims and tourists have set diyas adrift in their little mango leaf saucers. They will gather kilometre-by-kilometre, ghat-by-ghat, until the river is a constellation of currents and ribbons of light, patterns in which sages scry omens and portents and the fortunes of nations. They light the woman on her way. They reveal a face of middle-life. A face of the crowd, a face that would not be missed, if any face could be indispensable among the city's eleven million. Five types of people may not be cremated on the burning ghats but are cast to the river: lepers, children, pregnant women, Brahmins, and those poisoned by the king cobra. Her bindi declares that she is none of those castes. She slips past, unseen, beyond the jostle of tourist boats. Her pale hands are soft, unaccustomed to work.

Pyres burn on Manikarnika ghat. Mourners carry a bamboo litter down the ash-strewn steps and across the cracked mud to the river's edge. They dip the saffron-wrapped body in the redeeming water, wash it to make sure no part is untouched. Then it is taken to the pyre. As the untouchable Doms who run the burning ghat pile wood over the linen parcel, figures hip-deep in the Ganga sift the water with shallow wicker bowls, panning gold from the ashes of the dead. Each night on the ghat where Brahma the Creator made the ten-horse sacrifice, five Brahmins offer aarti to Mother Ganga. A local hotel pays them each twenty thousand rupees a month for this ritual but that does not make their prayers any less zealous. With fire, they puja for rain. It is three years since the monsoon. Now the blasphemous Awadh dam at Kunda Khadar turns the last blood in the veins of Ganga Mata to dust. Even the irreligious and agnostic now throw their rose petals on the river.

On that other river, the river of tires that knows no drought, Yogendra steers the big Merc through the wall of sound and motion that is Varanasi's eternal chakra of traffic. His hand is never off the horn as he pulls out behind phatphats, steers around cycle rickshaws, pulls down the wrong side of the road to avoid a cow chewing an aged vest. Shiv is immune to all traffic regulations except killing a cow. Street and sidewalk blur: stalls, hot-food booths, temples, street shrines hung with garlands of marigolds. *Let Our River Run Free!* declares a hand-lettered banner of an anti-dam protestor. A gang of call-centre boys in best clean shirts and pants out on the hunt spill into the path of the SUV. Greasy hands on the paint job. Yogendra screams at their temerity. The flow of streets grows straiter and more congested until women and pilgrims must press into walls and doorways to let Shiv through. The air is heady with alcofuel fumes. It is a royal progress, an assertion. Clutching the cold-dewed metal flask in his lap, Shiv enters the city of his name and inheritance.

First there was Kashi: firstborn of cities; sister of Babylon and Thebes and survivor of both; city of light where the Jyotirlinga of Siva, the divine generative energy, burst from the earth in a pillar of radiance. Then it became Varanasi; holiest of cities, consort of the Goddess Ganga, city of death and pilgrims, enduring through empires and kingdoms and Rajs and great nations, flowing through time as its river flows through the great plain of northern India. Behind it grew New Varanasi; the ramparts and fortresses of the new housing projects and the glassy, swooping corporate headquarters piling up behind the palaces and narrow, tangled streets as global dollars poured into India's bottomless labour well. Then there was a new nation and Old Varanasi again became legendary Kashi; navel of the world reborn as South Asia's newest meat Ginza. It is a city of schizophrenias. Pilgrims jostle Japanese sex tourists in the crammed streets. Mourners shoulder their dead past the cages of teen hookers. Skinny Westerners gone native with beads and beards offer head massages while country girls sign up at the matrimony agencies and scan the annual income lines on the databases of the desperate.

Hello hello, what country? Ganja ganja Nepali Temple Balls? You want to see young girl, jig-a-jig; see woman suck tiny little American football into her little woman? Ten dollar. This make your dick so big it scares people. Cards, janampatri, hora chakra, buttery red tilaks thumbed onto tourists' foreheads. Tween gurus. Gear! Gear! Knock off sports-stylie, hooky software, repro Big Name labels, this month's movie releases dubbed over by one man in one voice in your cousin's bedroom, sweat-shop palmers and lighthoeks, badmash gin and whiskey brewed up in old tanneries (John E. Walker, most respectable label). Since the monsoon failed, water; by the bottle, by the cup, by the sip, from tankers and tanks and shrink-wrapped pallets and plastic litrejohns and backpacks and goatskin sacks. Those Banglas with their iceberg, you think they'll give us one drop here in Bharat? Buy and drink.

Past the burning ghat and the Siva temple capsizing slowly, tectonically, into the Varanasi silts, the river shifts east of north. A third set of bridge piers stirs the water into cats' tongues. Lights ripple, the lights of a high-speed shatabdi crossing the river into Kashi Station. The streamlined express chunks heavily over the points as the dead woman shoots the rail bridge into clear water.

There is a third Varanasi beyond Kashi and New Varanasi. *New Sarnath*, it appears on the plans and press releases of the architects and their PR companies, trading on the cachet of the ancient Buddhist city. *Ranapur* to everyone else; a half-built capital of a fledgling political dynasty. By any name, it is Asia's biggest building site. The lights never go out. The labour never ceases. The noise appalls. One hundred thousand people are at work, from chowkidars to structural engineers. Towers of great beauty and daring rise from cocoons of bamboo scaffolding, bulldozers sculpt wide boulevards and avenues shaded by gene-mod ashok trees. New nations demand new capitals and Ranapur will be a showcase to the culture, industry, and forward-vision of

Bharat. The Sajida Rana Cultural Centre. The Rajiv Rana conference centre. The Ashok Rana telecom tower. The museum of modern art. The rapid transit system. The ministries and civil service departments, the embassies and consuls, and the other paraphernalia of government. What the British did for Delhi, the Ranas will do for Varanasi. That's the word from the building at the heart of it all, the Bharat Sabha, a lotus in white marble, the Parliament House of the Bharati government, and Sajida Rana's prime-ministership.

Construction floods glint on the shape in the river. The new ghats may be marble but the river kids are pure Varanasi. Heads snap up. Something here. Something light, bright, glinting. Cigarettes are stubbed. The shore kids dash splashing into the water. They wade thigh-deep through the shallow, blood-warm water, summoning each other by whistles. A thing. A body. A woman's body. A naked woman's body. Nothing new or special in Varanasi but still the water boys drag the dead woman in to shore. There may be some last value to be had from her. Jewellery. Gold teeth. Artificial hip joints. The boys splash through the spray of light from the construction floods, hauling their prize by the arms up on to the gritty sand. Silver glints at her throat. Greedy hands reach for a trishul pendant, the trident of the devotees of Lord Siva. The boys pull back with soft cries.

From breastbone to pubis, the woman lies open. A coiled mass of gut and bowel gleams in the light from the construction site. Two short, hacking cuts have cleanly excised the woman's ovaries.

In his fast German car, Shiv cradles a silver flask, dewed with condensation, as Yogendra moves him, through the traffic.

2

MR. NANDHA

Mr. Nandha the Krishna Cop travels this morning by train, in a first-class car. Mr. Nandha is the only passenger in the first-class car. The train is a Bharat Rail electric shatabdi express: it piles down the specially constructed high-speed line at three hundred and fifty kilometres per hour, leaning into the gentle curves. Villages roads fields towns temples blur past in the dawn haze that clings knee-deep to the plain. Mr. Nandha sees none of these. Behind his tinted window his attention is given over to the virtual pages of the *Bharat Times*. Articles and video reports float above the table as the lighthoek beats data into his visual lobes. In his auditory centre: Monteverdi, the Vespers of the Blessed Virgin performed by the Camerata of Venezia and the Choir of St. Mark's.

Mr. Nandha loves very much the music of the Italian renaissance. Mr. Nandha is deeply fascinated with all music of the European humanist tradition. Mr. Nandha considers himself a Renaissance man. So he may read news of the water and the maybe war and the demonstrations over the Hanuman statue and the proposed metro station at Sarkhand Roundabout and the scandal and the gossip and the sports reviews, but part of his visual cortex the lighthoek can never touch envisions the piazzas and campaniles of seventeenth-century Cremona.

Mr. Nandha has never been to Cremona. He has never visited Italy. His imaginings are Planet History Channel establishing shots cut with his own memories of Varanasi, the city of his birth, and Cambridge, the city of his intellectual rebirth.

The train slams past a rural brickworks; kiln smoke lying on top of the mist. The ranks of stacked bricks are like the ruins of an unborn civilization. Kids stand and stare, hands raised in greeting, dazed by the speed. After the train has passed, they scramble up on to the track and look for paisa coins they have wedged into the rail joints. The fast trains smear them flat into the rail. There's stuff you could buy with those coins but none would be as good as seeing them become stains on the high-speed express line.

The chai-wallah sways down the carriage.

"Sahb?"

Mr. Nandha hands him a tea bag, dangling from a string. The steward bows, takes the bag, drapes it over a plastic cup, and releases boiling water from the biggin. Mr. Nandha sniffs the chai, nods, then hands the wallah the wet, hot bag. Mr. Nandha suffers badly from yeast infections. The chai is Ayurvedic, made to his personal prescription. Mr. Nandha also avoids cereals, fruit, fermented foods including alcohol, many soy goods, and all dairy produce.

The call had come at four AM. Mr. Nandha had just fallen asleep after enjoyable sex with his beautiful wife. He tried not to disturb her but she had never been able to sleep when he was awake and she got up and fetched her husband's Away Bag which she had the dhobi-wallah keep fresh, changed, and folded. She saw him off into the Ministry car. The car bypassed the station approach crowded with phat-phats and rickshaws waiting on the Agra sleeper and brought Mr. Nandha through the marshalling yards on to the platform where the long, sleek electric train waited. A Bharat Rail official showed him to his reserved seat in his reserved carriage. Thirty seconds later the train ghosted out of Kashi Station. All three hundred metres of it had been held for the Krishna Cop.

Mr. Nandha thinks back to that sex with his wife and calls her up on the palmer. She appears in his visual cortex. He's not surprised to find her on the roof. Since the work on the garden began, Parvati has spent increasing amounts of time on top of the apartment block. Behind the concrete mixer and the piles of blocks and sacks of compost and pipes for the drip irrigator, Mr. Nandha can see the early lights in the windows of the tenements leaning close across the narrow streets. Water tanks, solar panels, satellite dishes, rows of potted geraniums are silhouettes against a dull, hazy sky. Parvati tucks a strand of hair behind her ear, squints into the bindi cam.

"Is everything all right?"

"Everything is fine. I will arrive in ten minutes. I just wanted to call you."

She smiles. Mr. Nandha's heart frays.

"Thank you, it's a lovely thought. Are you worried about it?"

"No, it's a routine excommunication. We want to nip it before panic spreads." Parvati nods, sucking in her lower lip in that way she does when she thinks about issues. "So what are you doing today?"

"Well," she says, with a turn of her body indicating the nascent garden. "I've had an idea. Please don't be cross with me, but I don't think we need so many shrubs. I'd like some vegetables. A few rows of beans, some tomatoes and peppers—they'd give lots of cover—maybe even some bhindi and brinjal. Herbs—I'd love to grow herbs, tulsi and coriander and hing."

In his reserved first-class seat, Mr. Nandha smiles.

"A proper little urban farmer."

"Oh, nothing you would be ashamed of. Just a few rows of things until we move out to the Cantonment and get a bungalow. I could grow those salad vegetables you need. It would save money, they fly them in from Europe and Australia—I've seen the labels. Would that be all right?"

"If you wish, my flower."

Parvati claps her hands together in soft delight.

"Oh good. This is a bit cheeky, but I'd already arranged to go with Krishan to the seedsman."

Mr. Nandha often questions what he has done, bringing his lovely wife into Varanasi's rip-throat society, a country girl among cobras. The games among the Cantonment set—his colleagues, his social peers—appall him. Whispers and looks and rumours, always so sweet and well mannered, but watching, weighing, measuring. Virtues and vices in the most delicate of balances. For men it's easy. Marry as well as you can—if you can. Mr. Nandha has married within jati—more than Arora, his superior at the Ministry, more than most of his contemporaries. A good solid Kayastha/Kayastha marriage but the old rigours no longer seem to matter in new Ranapur. That wife of Nandha's. Would you listen to the accent? Would you look at those hands? Those colours she wears, and the styles. She can't speak, you know. Not a word. Nothing to say. Opens her mouth and flies buzz out. Town and country, I say. Town and country. Still stands on the toilet bowl and squats.

Mr. Nandha finds his fists tight with rage at the thought of Parvati caught up in those terrible games of my husband this, my children that, my house the other. She does not need the Cantonment bungalow, the two cars and five servants, the designer baby. Like every modern bride, Parvati made her financial checks and genetic scans, but theirs was always a match of respect and love, not a desperate lunge for the first available wedding-fodder in Varanasi's Darwinian marriage-market. Once the woman came with the dowry. The man was the blessed, the treasure. That was always the problem. Now after a quarter of a century of foetal selection, discreet suburban clinics and old-fashioned Kashi back stair car aerial joints, Bharat's middle-class urban male population outnumbers the female fourfold.

Mr. Nandha feels a slight shift in acceleration. The train is slowing.

"My love, I'm going to have to go, we're coming into Nawada now."

"You won't be in any danger, will you?" Parvati says, all wide-eyed concern.

"No, no danger at all. I've performed dozens of these."

"I love you, husband."

"I love you, my treasure."

Mr. Nandha's wife vanishes from inside his head. I'll do it for you, he thinks as the train draws him into his showdown. I'll think of you as I kill it.

A handsome woman jemadar of the local Civil Defence meets Mr. Nandha with a sharp salute on the down line platform. Two rows of jawans hold onlookers back with lathis. Outriders fall in fore and aft as the convoy swings into the streets.

Nawada is a strip city, a name cast over the union of four cow-shit towns. Then out of the sky came a fistful of development grants, a slapped-down road grid, speed-built metal shed factories and warehouses stuffed with call centres and data-farms. String together with cable and satellite uplinks, hook into the power grid and let it grind out crores of rupees. It's among the corrugated aluminium and construction carbon go-downs of Nawada, not the soaring towers of Ranapur, that the future of Bharat is being forged. In the big heavy army hummer Mr. Nandha slips past the single unit stores and motor part workshops. He feels like a hired gun, riding into town. Scooters with country girls perched side-saddle on the pillion sway out of his path.

The outriders steer into an alley between spray-concrete go-downs, clearing a path for the hummer with their sirens. An electricity pylon slumps beneath illegal power-taps and siphons. Squatting women share chai and breakfast roti outside a huge windowless concrete box; the men gather as far from them as the geometry of the compound will allow, smoking. Mr. Nandha looks up at the outspread blessing hands of the Ray Power solar farm. Salutation to the sun.

"Turn off the sirens," he orders the handsome jemadar, whose name is Sen. "The thing has at least animal-level intelligence. If it receives any advance warning, it will attempt to copy itself out." Sen winds down the window and shouts orders to the escort. The sirens fall silent.

The hummer is a steel sweat-box. Mr. Nandha's pants stick to the vinyl seat-covers but he's too proud to squirm free. He slips his 'hoek over his ear, settles the bone transducer over the sweet spot on his skull and opens his box of avatars.

Ganesha, Lord of Auspicious Beginnings, Remover of Obstructions, throned upon his rat-vehicle, rears over the flat roofs and antenna farms of Nawada, vast as a thunderhead. In his hands are his qualities: the goad, the noose, a broken tusk, a rice flour dumpling, and a pot of water. His pot belly contains universes of cyberspace. He is the portal. Mr. Nandha knows the moves that summon each avatar by heart. His hand calls up flying Hanuman with his mace and mountain; Siva Nataraja, Lord of the Dance, one foot away from universal destruction and regeneration; Durga the Dark One, goddess of righteous wrath, each of her ten arms bearing a weapon; Lord Krishna with his flute and necklace; Kali the disrupter, the belt of severed hands around her waist. In Mr. Nandha's mindsight the aeai agents of the Ministry bend low over tiny Nawada. They are ready. They are eager. They are hungry.

The convoy turns into a service alley. A scatter of police tries to part a press of bodies to let the hummer through. The alley is clogged with vehicles down the entry; an ambulance, a cop cruiser, an electric delivery jeepney. There's something under the truck's front wheel.

"What is going on here?" Mr. Nandha demands as he walks through the scrum of police, Ministry warrant card held high.

"Sir, one of the factory workers panicked and ran out into the alley, straight under," says a police sergeant. "He was shouting about a djinn; how the djinn was in the factory and was going to get all of them."

You call it djinn, Mr. Nandha thinks, scanning the site. I call it meme. Non-material replicators; jokes, rumours, customs, nursery rhymes. Mind-viruses. Gods, demons, djinns, superstitions. The thing inside the factory is no supernatural creature, no spirit of flame, but it is certainly a non-material replicator.

"How many inside?"

"Two dead, sir. It was the night shift. The rest escaped."

"I want this area cleared," Mr. Nandha orders. Jemadar Sen flicks orders to her jawans. Mr. Nandha walks past the body with the leather jacket draped over its face and the shaking truck driver in the back of the police Maruti. He surveys the locus. This bent metal shed makes pasta-tikka. An emigrant family run it from Bradford. Bringing the jobs back home. That's what places like Nawada are all about. Mr. Nandha finds the concept of pasta-tikka an abomination but British-Diaspora Asian cuisine is the thing this season. Mr. Nandha squints up at the telephone cable box.

"Have somebody cut that cable."

While the rural police scramble for a ladder, Mr. Nandha locates the night shift line manager, a fat Bengali pulling nervously at the tag-skin beside his nails. He smells of what Mr. Nandha presumes must be pasta-tikka.

"Do you have a cellular base-port or a satellite uplink?" he asks.

"Yes, yes, a distributed internal cell network," the Bengali says. "For the robots. And one of those things that bounces signals off meteor trails; to talk to Bradford."

"Officer Sen, please have one of your men take care of the satellite dish. We may yet be in time to stop it out-copying."

The police finally drive the basti folk back to the ends of the alley. A jawan waves from the roof, job done.

"All communications devices off please," Mr. Nandha instructs. Jemadar Sen and Rural Sergeant Sunder accompany him into the possessed factory. Mr. Nandha straightens his Nehru-cut jacket, shoots his cuffs and ducks under the roller shutter into the combat zone. "Stay close and do exactly as I instruct." Breathing in the slow, stilling pranayama technique the Ministry teaches its Krishna Cops, Mr. Nandha makes his initial visual survey.

It is a typical development-grant job. Plastic barrels of feedstuff on one side, main processing in the middle, packaging and shipping on the other. No safety guards, no protective wear, no noise abatement equipment, no air-conditioning; one bathroom male, one restroom female.

Everything stripped down to accountancy-minimum. Minimal robotics: human hands have always been cheaper in the strip cities. On the right, a row of glastic cubes house the offices and aeai support. Water coolers and fans, all dead. The sun is well up. The building is a steel oven.

A forklift is run into a wall to his extreme left. A body is just visible between the truck and the corrugated metal bulkhead, half-erect. Blood, glossy and furious with flies, is coagulated beneath the wheels. The man has been bayoneted at belly height by the forklift's tines. Mr. Nandha purses his lips in distaste.

Camera eyes everywhere. Nothing to be done about it now. It is watching.

In his three years as a rogue-aeai hunter, Mr. Nandha has seen a sizeable number of the bodies that result when humans and artificial intelligences cross. He draws his gun. Jemadar Sen's eyes widen. Mr. Nandha's gun is big, black, heavy and looks as if it were cast in hell. It has all the knobs and details and bits a Krishna Cop needs on his weapon, it is self-targeting and dual action. The lower barrel kills the flesh: low-velocity explosive bullets. One hit in any part of the body is an impact trauma sure kill. Dum-Dum, after all, is a district of Kolkata. The upper barrel destroys the spirit. It is an EM pulse gun; a google-watt of power poured into a three-millisecond directed beam. Protein chips crisp. Quantum processors heisenberg out. Carbon nanotubes vaporise. This is the gun that annihilates rogue aeais. Steered by GPS-oriented gyroscopes and controlled by a visual avatar of Indra, lord of the thunderbolt, Mr. Nandha's gun always kills and never misses.

The reek of Bradford pasta-tikka tugs urgently at the base of Mr. Nandha's stomach. How can this muck, this pollution, be all the thing? One of the big stainless steel industrial cooking pots is tipped over, its contents spilled on the floor. Here the second body lies. Its upper half is smothered in pasta-tikka. Mr. Nandha smells cooked meat, flicks out his handkerchief to cover his mouth. He notes the corpse's good trousers, fine shoes, pressed shirt. That will be the IT wallah, then. In Mr. Nandha's experience, aeais, like dogs, turn on their masters first.

He beckons Sen and Sunder in. The rural policeman looks nervous, but the jemadar raises her assault rifle resolutely.

"Can it hear us?" Jemadar Sen asks, circling.

"Unlikely. Level One aeais seldom possess language skills. We're dealing with something with about the intelligence of a monkey."

"And the attitude of a tiger," Sergeant Sunder comments.

Mr. Nandha summons Siva out of the spatial dimensions of the food factory, moves his hands into a mudra, and the go-down springs to life with a glowing nervous system of information conduits. It's the work of a moment for Siva to access the factory intranet, trace the server; a small featureless cube in a corner of a desk, and insinuate himself through the firewall into the factory system. File registers blur across Mr. Nandha's back-brain. There. Password protected. He summons Ganesha. At once the Remover of Obstacles runs into a quantum key. Mr. Nandha is vexed. He dismisses Ganesha and sends in Krishna. There could be a djinn hiding behind that quantum wall. Equally, there could be three thousand pictures of Chinese girls having sex with pigs. Mr. Nandha's fear is that the rogue aeai has reproduced. One mail-out and it will take weeks to grub it all up. Krishna reports the outgoing traffic log as clean. It is still in the building, somewhere. Mr. Nandha disconnects the wireless web, unplugs the server, and tucks it under his arm. His people back at the Ministry will pry out its secrets.

He pauses, sniffs. Is the reek of pasta-tikka stronger, more acrid? Mr. Nandha coughs, something has caught at the back of his throat, burning chilli. He sees Sen sniff, frown. He hears a hum of heavy electrical drain.

"Everyone out!" he shouts and at that moment the chain drive on the roller shutter jerks into action just as the number two cooking vat bursts into choking black chilli smoke. "Quick quick!" he commands, blinking away searing tears, handkerchief pressed to mouth. "Out, out." He follows the others out under the descending shutter with millimetres to spare. In the alley he irritably dusts street grime from his ironed suit.

"This is most annoying," says Mr. Nandha. To the pasta-tikka workers he calls, "You, there. Is there another way in?"

"Round the side, sahb," replies a teen with a skin-condition Mr. Nandha would not want near anything human-consumable.

"No time to lose," he says raising his weapon. "It may have already used the diversion to escape. With me, please."

"I'm not going back in that place," Sunder says, hands on thighs. He's a middle-aged man, putting on middle-body fat and none of this is in the Nawada district police procedure manual. "I'm not a superstitious man, but if you haven't got djinn in there, I don't know what you have."

"There are no djinns," says Mr. Nandha. Sen falls in behind him. Her suit camouflage is the exact shade of pasta-tikka. They cover their faces, squeeze down the fetid side alley paved with cigarette butts and in through the fire exit. The air is acrid with chilli smoke. Mr. Nandha can feel it claw the back of his throat as he delves into his avatars for his most potent programme, Kali the Disrupter. He taps into the factory net and releases her into the system. She'll go through the web, wire and wireless, copy herself into every mobile and stationary processing unit. Anything without a licence she will tag, trace, and erase. There will be only rags left of Pasta-Tikka Inc. by the time Kali has done. She is a reason Mr. Nandha isolated the factory. Let loose on the global web, Kali could wreak crores of rupees of havoc across the continental net within seconds. No better hunter of an aeai than another aeai. Mr. Nandha cradles his gun. The mere scent of Kali, a mongoose after a snake, has often been enough to flush a laired aeai from cover.

On full lighthoek resolution Kali is a startling sight, girdled with severed hands, scimitars raised, tongue out and eyes wide, towering up through a slowly settling pall of chilli smoke as data constellations go out around her, one by one. This is what death must be like, thinks Mr. Nandha. One by one the delicate blue glows of information flow flicker and go out. One by one the nerve impulses fail, the sensations fade, consciousness disintegrates.

Spooked by machine sounds falling silent all around her, Sen draws close to Mr. Nandha. There are forces and entities here she cannot comprehend. When nothing has made a noise or gone dark for a full minute, Sen says, "Do you think they're all gone now?"

Mr. Nandha checks a report from Kali.

"I have deleted two hundred suspect files and programs. If even one percent of those are aeai copies . . ." But something more than chilli throat is tugging at his sensibilities.

"What makes them do this? Why do they turn rabid all of a sudden?" Sen asks.

"I've always found that the root of a computer problem is human frailty" Mr. Nandha says, turning slowly, trying to identify what it is that has provoked his suspicions. "I suspect our friend has been buying in illegal aeai hybrids from the sundarbans. In my experience, no good ever comes out of the data-havens."

Sen has another question but Mr. Nandha hushes her. Very faint, very distant, he hears a movement. Kali has left just sufficient of the office ware for Siva to be able to link into the security system. Nothing on the cameras, as he suspected, but in the diffuse world of infrared, something stirs. His head snaps to the crane gantry at the rear of the go-down.

"I can see you," he says, gesturing to Sen. She goes up one end of the gantry. Mr. Nandha takes the other. The thing seems to be somewhere up in the ceiling. They walk towards each other.

"At some point, it will break for it," warns Nandha.

"What will break?" Sen whispers, cradling her powerful weapon.

"I suspect it has copied itself into a robot and intends to escape by that means. Expect something small and fast-moving."

Mr. Nandha can hear it now between the clanks of the human footsteps; something scrabbling at the roof, trying to tear a way out. Mr. Nandha raises a hand for Jemadar Sen to proceed with caution. He feels as if he is right under it. Mr. Nandha squints up into the nest of wires and ducting. A camera-eye on a boom stabs down at him. Mr. Nandha starts back. Sen raises her weapon; before thought, she lets off a burst into the ceiling. An object drops out so close to Mr. Nandha it almost strikes him, a thing all limbs and thrashing and skittering movement. It's an inspection robot, a little clambering spider-monkey thing. Individual companies usually can't afford them but development corporations keep one to service all the clients in a block. The thing will have access to every unit in this industrial zone. The machine rears, darts at Mr. Nandha, then turns and zigzags pell-mell down the gantry towards Sen. All it knows is that these creatures want to kill it and it wants to exist. Panicked by her wild firing, all military sense flies from Sen as the thing bounces towards her. She fumbles at her assault rifle. Mr. Nandha can see with perfect, still clarity that her panic will kill him.

"No!" he shouts, and draws his gun. Indra targets, aims, fires. The pulse momentarily overloads even his 'hoek. The world goes flash-blind. The robot freezes, spasms, goes down in fat yellow sparks. Its legs twitch, its eye booms slide out. It goes still and quiet. Smoke wisps from its vents. Mr. Nandha is not yet satisfied. He stands over the dead aeai, then kneels down and hooks the Avatar Box into its hotwire socket. Ganesha interfaces with the operating system: Kali stands by, swords raised.

It's dead. Excommunicated. Mr. Nandha stands up, dusts himself down. He tucks his gun away. Messy one. Unsatisfactory. Questions left hanging. Many will be answered when the Fifteenth Floor Gang open up the server, but a man does not become a Krishna Cop without sensitivities and Mr. Nandha's are telling him this tangle of metal and plastic is the opening letter of a new and long story. He will say that story, he will unravel its intricacies and characters and events and bring it to its right conclusion, but at this moment, his most pressing problem is how to get the stink of burned pasta-tikka out of his suit.

3

SHAHEEN BADOOR KHAN

Shaheen Badoor Khan looks down on to the Antarctic ice. From two thousand metres it is less ice than geography, a white island, Sri Lanka gone rogue. The ocean-going tugs hired from the Gulf are the biggest and strongest and newest but they look like spiders tackling a circus big top, hauling away at silk thread guy ropes. Their role is supervisory now; the Southwest Monsoon Current has the berg and the whole performance is running north-by-northeast at five nautical miles per day. Out here on the ocean five hundred kilometres south of the delta the only visual referents are ice and sky and the dark blue of deep water, nothing that gives any sense of motion. How long and hard must those tugs pull to bring it to a stop? Shaheen Badoor Khan thinks. He imagines the berg rammed deep into the Gangasagar, the mouth of the holy river, ice cliffs rising sheer from mangroves.

With a manifest of Bengali politicians and their diplomatic guests from neighbour and erstwhile rival Bharat, the States of Bengal tilt-jet lurches in the chill microclimate spiralling up from the ice floe. Shaheen Badoor Khan notices that the surface is grooved and furrowed with crevasses and ravines. Torrent water glitters; ice-melt has gouged sheer canyons in the ice walls, spectacular waterfalls arc from the berg's cliff edges.

"It's constantly shifting," says the energetic Bangla climatologist across the aisle. "As it loses mass, the centre of gravity moves. We have to maintain equilibrium, a sudden shift close in could prove catastrophic."

"You do not need another tidal wave in your delta," Shaheen Badoor Khan says.

"If it ever makes it," says Bharat's Water and Energy Minister, nodding at the ice. "The rate it's melting . . ."

"Minister," Shaheen Badoor Khan says quickly, but Bengal's official climatologist snaps up the opportunity to shine.

"It has all been worked out to the last gram," he says. "We are well within the parameters for microclimatic shift." This with a flash of expensively dentistried teeth, and a precision purse of thumb and forefinger. Flawless. Shaheen Badoor Khan feels deep shame when one of his ministers opens his mouth and lets his ignorance walk out in public, especially before the smooth Banglas. He long ago understood that politics needs no extraordinary talent, skill, or intelligence. That's what advisors are for. The skill of a politician is to take that advice and make it look as if he made it up himself. Shaheen Badoor Khan hates that someone might think he has not properly briefed his charges. *Go with them, Shah*, Prime Minister Sajida Rana had asked. *Stop Srinavas making a tit of himself.*

The Bengali Minister With Iceberg lumbers up the aisle smiling his big bear smile. Shaheen Badoor Khan knows from his sources of the territory wars between Bengal's government departments over whose bailiwick ten-kilometre chunks of Amery ice shelf fall into. Tension between the joint capitals is always something that can be worked to Bharat's advantage. Environmental Affairs gave way in the end to Science and Technology, with a little help from Development and Industry to secure the contracts and now its Minister stands in the aisle, arms braced on the seat backs. Shaheen Badoor Khan can smell his breath.

"So, eh? And all our own work, too, we didn't run to the Americans to sort out our water supply, like those ones in Awadh, and their dam. But you'd know all about that."

"The river used to make us one country," Shaheen Badoor Khan observes. "Now we seem to be the squabbling children of Mother Ganga; Awadh, Bharat, Bengal. Head, hands, and feet."

"There are a lot of birds," Srinavas says, peering out the window. The berg trails a pale plume like smoke from a ship's stack: flocks of seabirds, thousands strong, hurling themselves into the water to hunt silver sardine.

"That just proves the cold current gyratory is working," says the climatologist, trying to make himself seen past his Minister. "We're not so much importing an iceberg as a complete ecosystem. Some have followed us all the way from Prince Edward Island."

"The Minister is curious about how soon you expect to see benefits," Shaheen Badoor Khan inquires.

Naipaul starts to bluster and blow about the daring and reach of Bengali climatic engineering but his weather wizard cuts him off. Shaheen Badoor Khan blinks at the unforgivable interruption. Have these Banglas no protocol at all?

"The climate is not an old cow to be driven where you will," the climatologist, whose name is Vinayachandran, says. "It is a subtle science, of tiny shifts and changes that over time build to vast, huge consequences. Think of a snowball rolling down a mountain. A half-degree temperature drop here, a shift in the ocean thermocline by a handful of metres, a pressure shift of a single millibar . . ."

"No doubt, but the Minister is wondering how long before these little effects from this . . . snowball . . ." Shaheen Badoor Khan asks.

"Our simulations show a return to climate norms within six months," Vinayachandran says.

Shaheen Badoor Khan nods. He has given his Minister all the clues. He can draw his own conclusion.

"So all this," Bharati Water and Energy Minister Srinavas says with a wave of the hand at the alien ice out there in the Bay of Bengal, "All this will come too late. Another failed monsoon. Maybe if you were to melt it and send it to us by pipeline, it might do some good. Can you make the Ganga flow backwards? That might help us."

"It will stabilise the monsoon for the next five years, for all of India," Minister Naipaul insists.

"Minister, I don't know about you, but my people are thirsty now," V. R. Srinavas says right into the eye of the news camera peering like a vulgar street boy over the back of the seat row in front. Shaheen Badoor Khan folds his hands, content that that line will head every evening paper from Kerala to Kashmir. Srinavas is almost as great a buffoon as Naipaul, but he's a stout man for a good one-liner in a pinch.

The new, beautiful, state-of-the-market tilt-jet banks again, swivels its engines into horizontal flight, and heads back for Bengal.

Also new, beautiful, and state-of-the market is Daka's new airport, and so is its recently installed air-traffic control system. This is the reason a high-priority diplomatic transport is stacked for half an hour and then put down on a stand way on the other side of the field from the BharatAir airbus. An interface problem; the ATC computer are Level 1 aeai, with the intellect, instinct, autonomy, and morals of a rabbit, which is considerably more, as one of the *Bharat Times* press corps comments, than the average Daka air-traffic controller. Shaheen Badoor Khan conceals a smile but no one can deny that the Joint States of East and West Bengal are technologically savvy, bold, forward-looking, sophisticated, and a world player—all those things Bharat aspires to in the avenues and atria of Ranapur, that the filth and collapse and beggary of Kashi deny.

The cars finally arrive. Shaheen Badoor Khan follows the politicians down on to the apron. Heat bounces from the concrete. The humidity sucks out every memory of ice and ocean and cool. Good luck to them with their island of ice, Shaheen Badoor Khan thinks, imagining those urgent Bangla engineers clambering around on the Amery berg in their cold-weather parkas and fur-fringed hoods.

In the front seat of Minister Srinavas's car, Shaheen Badoor Khan slips his 'hoek behind his ear. Taxiways, planes, airbridges, baggage trains merge with the interface of his office system. The aeai has winnowed his mail but there are still over fifty messages requiring the attention of Sajida Rana's Parliamentary Private Secretary. A flick of the finger *yeses* that report on the Bharat's combat readiness problem, *nos* that press release on further water restrictions, *laters* that video conference request from N. K. Jivanjee. His hands move like the mudras of a graceful Kathak dancer. A curl of a finger; Shaheen Badoor Khan summons the notepad out of thin air. *Keep me advised of developments re: Sarkhand Roundabout*, he writes on the side of an Air Bengal airbus in virtual Hindi. *I have a feeling about this one.*

Shaheen Badoor Khan was born, lives, and assumes he will die in Kashi but still cannot understand the passion and wrath Hinduism's scruffy gods command. He admires its disciplines and asceticisms but they seem to him pledged to such poor security. Every day on his way to the Bharat Sabha the government car whisks him past a little plastic shelter on the junction of Lady Castlereagh Road where for fifteen years a sadhu has held his left arm aloft. Shaheen Badoor Khan reckons the man could not put this twig of bone and sinew and wasted muscle down now even if his god willed it. Shaheen Badoor Khan is not an overtly religious man, but these gaudy, cinematic statues, brawling with arms and symbols and vehicle and attributes and supporters as if the sculptor had to cram in every last theological detail, offend his sense of aesthetics. His school of Islam is refined, intensely civilised, ecstatic and mystical. It is not painted day-glo pink. It does not wave its penis around in public. Yet every morning thousands descend the ghats beneath the balconies of his haveli to wash away their sins in the withered stream of Ganga. Widows spend their last rupees that their husbands might burn by the holy waters and attain Paradise. Every year young males fall beneath the Puri Jagannath and are crushed—though nowhere near as many as by the juggernaut of Puri rush hour. Armies of youths storm mosques and take them to rubble with their bare hands because they profane the honour of Lord Rama and still that man sits on the kerb with his arm lifted like a staff. And on a traffic roundabout in new Sarnath, a stained concrete statue of Hanuman not ten years old is told it must relocate to make way for a new metro station and there are gangs of youths in white shirts and dhotis punching the air and banging drums and gongs. There will be deaths out of this, thinks Shaheen Badoor Khan. Little things snowballing. N. K. Jivanjee and his Hindu fundamentalist Shivaji party will ride this juggernaut to death.

There is further confusion at the VIP reception centre. It seems two very important parties are both booked into the business section of BH137. The first Shaheen Badoor Khan knows of it is a tussle of reporters and sound booms and free-fly mikes outside the executive lounge. Minister Srinavas preens himself but the lenses are looking elsewhere. Shaheen Badoor Khan forces himself politely through the crowd to the dispatcher, credentials held high.

"What is the problem here?"

"Ah, Mr. Khan, there seems to be some mix-up."

"There is no mix-up. Minister Srinavas and party are returning to Varanasi on your flight. Why is there any reason for confusion?"

"Some celebrity . . ."

"Celebrity," Shaheen Badoor Khan says with scorn that would wither an entire harvest.

"A Russian, a model," says the dispatcher, flustered now. "A big name model. There's some show in Varanasi. I apologise for the mix-up, Mr. Khan." Shaheen Badoor Khan is already motioning his own staff down to the gate.

"Who?" Minister Srinavas says as he passes the scrum.

"Some Russian model," Shaheen Badoor Khan says in his soft, precise voice.

"Ah!" says Minister Srinavas, eyes widening. "Yuli."

"I'm sorry?"

"Yuli," Srinavas says, craning for a look at the celeb. "The nute."

The word is like the toll of a temple bell. The crowd parts. Shaheen Badoor Khan sees clear and true into the executive lounge. And he is transfixed. He sees a tall figure in a long, beautifully cut coat of white brocade. It is worked with patterns of dancing cranes, beaks intermeshing. The figure has its back to him, Shaheen Badoor Khan cannot make out a face but he sees curves of pale skin; long hands delicately moving; an elegantly curved nape, a smooth perfect curve of hairless scalp.

The body turns towards him. Shaheen Badoor Khan sees a line of jaw, an edge of cheekbone. A gasp goes out of him, unheard in the press corps tumult. The face. He must not look at the face, he would be lost, damned, stone. The crowd shifts again, the bodies close across the vision. Shaheen Badoor Khan stands, paralysed.

"Khan." A voice. His Minister. "Khan, are you all right?"

"Ah, yes, Minister. Just a little dizzy; the humidity."

"Yes, these bloody Banglas need to get their air-conditioning sorted."

The spell is broken but as Shaheen Badoor Khan ushers his Minister down the airbridge, he knows he will never know peace again.

The gate controller has gifts for all from Minister Naipaul; vacuum flasks bearing the crest of the Joint States of East and West Bengal. When he is belted in and the curtains are closed on economy and the

BharatAir airbus is bumping out over the uneven concrete, Shaheen Badoor Khan uncaps his flask. It contains ice: glacier cubes for Sajida Rana's gin slings. Shaheen Badoor Khan caps the flask. The airbus makes its run and as its wheels leave Bengal, Shaheen Badoor Khan presses the flask to him as if the cold might heal the wound in his belly. It can't. It never will. Shaheen Badoor Khan looks out the window at the steadily greying land as the airbus heads west to Bharat. He sees the white dome of a skull; the sweep of a neck; pale, lovely hands elegant as minarets, cheekbones turning towards him like architecture. Cranes dancing.

So long he had thought himself safe. Pure. Shaheen Badoor Khan hugs his glacier ice to him, eyes closed in silent prayer, heart luminous with ecstasy.

4

NAJIA

Lal Darfan, number one soap star, grants interviews in the howdah of an elephant-shaped airship navigating the southern slopes of the Nepali Himalayas. In a very good shirt and loose pants he reclines against a bolster on a low divan. Behind him banners of high cloud stripe the sky. The mountain peaks are a frontier of jagged white, a wall across the edge of sight. The tasselled fringe of the howdah ripples in the wind. Lal Darfan, Love God of Indiapendent Production's biggest and brightest soap, *Town and Country*, is attended by a peacock that stands by the head of his divan. He feeds it fragments of rice cracker. Lal Darfan is on a low-fat diet. It's all the talk in the gossip chati magazines.

The diet, Najia Askarzadah thinks, is a fine conceit for a virtual soapi star. She takes a deep breath and opens the interview.

"In the West we find it hard to believe that *Town and Country* can be so incredibly popular. Yet here there's maybe as much interest in you as an actor as in your character, Ved Prekash."

Lal Darfan smiles. His teeth are as improbably and gloriously white as the tivi chat channels say.

"More," he says. "But I think what you're asking is why an aeai character needs an aeai actor. Illusions within illusions, is that it?"

Najia Askarzadah is twenty-two, freelance and fancy-free, four weeks in Bharat and has just landed the interview she hopes will seal her career.

"Suspension of disbelief," she says. She can hear the hum of the airship engines, one in each elephant foot.

"It is simply this. The role is never enough. The public have to have the role behind the role, whether that is me"—Lal Darfan touches his hands self-deprecatingly to his going-to-bulge midriff—"or a flesh and blood Hollywood actor, or a pop idol. Let me ask you a question. What do you know about, say, some Western pop star like Blóchant Matthews? What you see on the television, what you read in the soap magazines and the chati communities. Now, what do you know about Lal Darfan? Exactly the same. They are no more real to you than I am, and therefore no less real, either."

"But people can always bump into a real celebrity or catch a glimpse at the beach or the airport, or in a shop . . ."

"Can they? How do you know anyone has had these glimpses?"

"Because I've heard . . . Ah."

"You see what I mean? Everything comes through one medium or another. And, with respect, I am a real celebrity, in that my celebrity is indeed very real. In fact these days, I think it's only celebrity that makes anything real, don't you agree?"

Half a million person-hours have gone into Lal Darfan's voice. It's a voice calculated to seduce and it is laying orbits around Najia Askarzadah. It says, "Might I ask you a personal question? It's very simple; what is your earliest memory?"

It's never far, that night of fire and rush and fear, like a geological iridium layer in her life. Daddy scooping her out of her bed, the paper all over the floor and the house full of noise and the lights waving across the garden. That she remembers most; the cones of torchlight weaving over the rose bushes, coming for her. The flight across the compound. Her father cursing under his breath at the car engine as it turned and turned and turned. The flashlights darting closer, closer. Her father, cursing, cursing, polite even as the police came to arrest him.

"I'm lying in the back of a car," Najia says. "I'm lying flat, and it's night, and we're driving fast through Kabul. My Dad's driving and my Mum's beside him, but I can't see them over the backs of the seats. But I can hear them talking, and it sounds like they're very far away, and they've got the radio on; they're listening for something but I can't make the voices out." The news of the raid on the women's house and the issue of their arrest warrants, she knows now. When that bulletin came, they knew they would have only minutes before the police closed the airport. "I can see the streetlights passing over me. It's all very regular and exact, I can see the light start, go over me, and then up the back of the rear seat and out the window."

"That's a powerful image," Lal Darfan says. "How old would you have been, three, four?"

"Not quite four."

"I, too, have an earliest memory. This is how I know I am not Ved Prekash. Ved Prekash has scripts, but I remember a paisley shawl blowing in the wind. The sky was blue and clear and the edge of the shawl was blowing in from the side—it was like a frame, with the action out of shot. I can see it quite clearly, it's flapping. I'm told it was on the roof of our house in Patna. Mama had taken me up to get away from the fumes down at the ground level, and I was on a blanket with a parasol over me. The shawl had been washed and was hanging on the line; odd, it was silk. I can remember it as clear as anything. I must have been two at the most. There. Two memories. Ah, but you will say, yours is manufactured but mine is experience. How do you know? It could be something you've been told that you've made into a memory, it could be a false memory, it could have been artificially manufactured and implanted. Hundreds of thousands of Americans believe they've been spirited away by grey aliens who stick machines up their rectums; utter fantasy, and undoubtedly false memories each and every one, but does that make them fake people? And what are our memories made of anyway? Patterns of charge in protein molecules. We are not so different there, I think. This airship, this silly elephant gimmick I've had built for me, the idea that we're floating along over Nepal; to you it's just patterns of electrical charge in protein molecules. But so is everything. You call this illusion, I'd call it the fundamental building blocks of my universe. I imagine I see it very differently from you, but then, how would I know? How do I know what I see as green looks the same to you? We're all locked up inside our little boxes of self; bone or plastic, Najia; and none of us ever get out. Can any of us trust what we think we remember?"

I do, computer, Najia Askarzadah thinks. I have to trust, because everything I am comes from those memories. The reason I am here, talking in this ludicrous virtual-reality pleasure dome to a tivi soap star with delusions of significance, is because of those memories of light, moving.

"But in that case are you—as Lal Darfan—sailing pretty close to the wind? I mean, the Hamilton Acts on Artificial Intelligence . . ."

"The Krishna Cops? McAuley's hijras," Lal Darfan says with venom.

"What I'm saying is, for you to say you're self-aware—sentient, as you seem to be claiming—is signing your own death warrant."

"I never said I was sentient, or conscious, whatever that is. I am a level 2.8 aeai and it's done very nicely for me. I'm only claiming to be real; as real as you."

"So you couldn't pass a Turing test?"

"Shouldn't pass a Turing test. Wouldn't pass a Turing test. Turing test, what's that prove anyway? Here, I'll give you a Turing test. Classic setup, two locked rooms and a badmash with an old style print-display screen. Let's put you in one room and Satnam from PR in the other—I presume it's him giving you the tour, they always give him the girls. He fancies himself a bit. The badmash with the display types in questions, you type back answers. Standard stuff. Satnam's job is to convince the badmash he's a woman and he can lie, cheat, say anything he wants to prove it. I think you can see it's not going to be that hard for him to do. So, does that make Satnam a woman then? I don't think it does; Satnam certainly doesn't think it does. How then is it any different from a computer to pass itself as sentient? Is the simulation of a thing the thing itself, or is there something unique about intelligence that it is the only thing which cannot be simulated? What does any of this prove? Only something about the nature of the Turing test as a test, and the danger of relying on minimum information. Any aeai smart enough to pass a Turing test is smart enough to know to fail it."

Najia Askarzadah throws up her hands in mock defeat.

"I'll tell you one thing I like about you," Lal Darfan says. "At least you didn't spend an hour asking me stupid questions about Ved Prekash as if he's the real star. Speaking of which, I'm due in make-up . . ."

"Oh, sorry, thank you," Najia Askarzadah says, trying to do the gushy girl journo thing while the truth is she's glad to be out of the pedantic creature's headspace. What she intended to be light and frothy and soapi has turned into existential phenomenology with a twist of retro po-mo. She wonders what her editor will say, let alone the passengers on the TransAm Chicago-Cincinnati red-eye when they pull their inflights out of the seat-back pocket. Lal Darfan merely beams beatifically as his audience chamber comes apart around him until all that's left is pure Lewis Carroll *grin* that fades into the Himalayan sky and the Himalayan sky rolls up into the back of Najia's head and she's back in the render farm, in the rocky swivel chair with the racked cylinders of the protein processors tramlining into the perspective: sci-fi bottled brains in jars.

"He's quite convincing, isn't he?" Satnam-Who-Fancies-Himself's aftershave is a little assertive. Najia slips off the lighthoek, still a little mazy from the total immersion of the interview experience.

"I think he thinks he thinks."

"Exactly the way we programmed him." Satnam has media style, dress, and easy confidence but Najia notes a little Siva trident on that platinum chain around his neck. "Truth is, Lal Darfan's as tightly scripted as Ved Prekash."

"That's my angle, appearance and reality. If folk can believe in virtual actors, what else'll they swallow?"

"Now don't be giving the game away," Satnam smiles as he shows her into the next section. He's almost cute when he smiles, Najia thinks. "This is the meta-soap department, where Lal Darfan gets the script he doesn't think he follows. It's got to the stage where the meta-soap's as big as the soap itself."

The department is a long farm of workstations. The glass walls are polarised dark, the soap-farmers work in the umbral light of low-level spots and screen-glow. Designers' hands draw in neurospace. Najia suppresses a shudder at the thought of spending her working years in a place like this, shut off from the sun. Stray light on high cheekbones, a hairless head, a delicate hand catches her attention and it's her turn to cut Satnam off.

"Who's that?"

Satnam cranes.

"Oh, that's Tal. He's new here. He heads up visual wallpaper."

"I think the pronoun is 'yt,'" Najia says, trying to catch a better glance at the nute through the hand-ballet. She can't say why she is surprised to find a third-sex in the production office—in Sweden nutes tended towards the creative industries and India's premier soap undoubtedly exerts a similar gravity. She realises she has assumed that India's long history of trans- and non-genders has always been hidden, veiled.

"Yt, him, whatever. Yt's full of it today, some invite to a big celebi party."

"Yuli. The Russian model. I tried to get invited to that, to interview him. Yt."

"So you settled for Fat Lal instead."

"No, I really am interested in the psychology of aeai actors." Najia looks over at the nute. Yt glances up. Yts eyes meet hers for a moment. There is no recognition, no communication. Yt looks back into its work again. Yts hands sculpt digits.

"What Fat Lal doesn't know is the characters and plot are basic packages," Satnam continues, ushering Najia along between the glowing workstations. "We franchise them out and different national broadcasters drop their own aeai actors in on top of them. There are different actors playing Ved Prekash in Mumbai and Kerala and they're as mega down there as Fat Lal is up here."

"Everything's a version," Najia says, trying to decipher the beautiful dance of the nute's long hands. Out in the corridor, Satnam tries the chat.

"So, are you really from Kabul?"

"I left when I was four."

"It's not a thing I know very much about. I'm sure it must have been . . ."

Najia stops dead in the corridor, turns to face Satnam. She's half-a-head shorter, but he takes a step back. She grabs his hand, scrawls a UCC across his knuckles.

"There, my number. You call it, I may answer. I may suggest we go out somewhere, but if we do, I choose where. Okay? Now, thanks for the tour, and I think I can find my way back to the front door."

He's where and when he said he would be as she cruises in to the kerb in the phatphat. He's dressed in nothing he's too fond of, as Najia requested, but he still wears his trishul. She's been seeing a lot of those, on the streets, around men's necks. He settles in the seat beside her; the little autorickshaw rocks on its home-brew suspension.

"My shout, remember?" she says. The driver pulls out into the swarm of traffic.

"Mystery tour, okay, that's fine," Satnam says. "So, did you get your article written?"

"Written, done, off," Najia says. She banged it out this afternoon on the terrace at the Imperial International, the Cantonment backpackers hostel where she has a room. She'll move out when the payment comes in from the magazine. The Australians are getting to her. They moan about everything.

The thing is, Najia Askarzadah has a boyfriend. He's called Bernard. He's a fellow Imperialist, a gap-yearer whose twelve months turned into twenty, forty, sixty. He's French, indolent, overly convinced of his own genius and has atrocious manners. Najia suspects he only stays at the hostel to pull fresh girls like her. But he practises Tantric sex, and can keep his dick up any woman for an hour while chanting. So far Tantra with Bernard has involved her squatting on his lap for twenty, thirty, forty minutes tugging on a leather thong looped around his cock to keep it hard hard hard until his eyes roll up and he says Kundalini has risen, which means the drugs are finally kicking in. It's not Najia's idea of Tantra. He's not Najia's idea of a boyfriend. Neither is Satnam, and for many of the same reasons, but it's an idea, a game, a *why not?* Najia Askarzadah has steered as many of her twenty-two years as she's been allowed responsibility for by *why nots?* They steered her to Bharat, against the advice of her tutors, friends, and parents.

New Varanasi runs into old Kashi in a series of discontinuities and juxtapositions. Streets begin in one millennium and end in another. Vertiginous corporate spires lean over shambles of alleys and wooden houses unchanged in four centuries. Metro viaducts and elevated expressways squeeze past the sandstone *linga* of decaying temples. The cloy of rotting petals permeates even the permanent jizz of alcohol-engine fumes, dissolving into an urban perfume that cities dab behind their cloacal bits. Bharat Rail employs sweepers with besoms to keep flower petals off the track. Kashi generates them by the billion and the steel wheels can't cope. The phatphat turns down a dark laneway of clothing shops; pale plastic dummies, armless and legless but smiling nevertheless, swing from racks overhead.

"Am I allowed to ask where you're taking me?" Satnam says.

"You'll find out soon enough." Truth is, Najia Askarzadah has never been, but ever since she heard the Australians crowing about how bold they were in going to it and they weren't grossed out, not at all, she's looked for an excuse to find this back-of-backstreet club. She has no idea where she is, but she reckons the driver is taking her in the right direction when dangling shop dummies give way to hookers in open storefronts. Most have adopted the Western standard uniform of lycra and overemphatic footwear, a few cling to tradition, in the steel cages.

"Here," says the phatphat driver. The little wasp-coloured plastic bubble rocks on its suspension.

Fight! Fight! exclaim the alternating neons above the tiny door between the Hindu icon shop and the hookers drinking Limka at the chai stall. A cashier sits in a tin cubby by the door. He looks thirteen, fourteen, and already he's seen everything from under his Nike beanie. Beyond him, stairs lead up into stark fluorescent light.

"One thousand rupee," he says, hand out. "Or five dollar."

Najia pays local.

"This isn't exactly what I imagined for a first date," Satnam says.

"Date?" Najia says as she leads him up the stairs that climb, turn, dip, turn again, and finally empty on the balcony over the pit.

The large room had once been a warehouse. Sick green paint, industrial lamps and conduiting, louvred skylights all tell its history. Now it's an arena. Ranged around a five-metre hexagon of sand are ranks of wooden pews, tiered as steeply as a lecture hail. Everything's new built from construction timber stolen from the cash-starved

Varanasi Area Rapid Transit. The stalls are faced with packing case panels. When Najia lifts her hand from the railing it comes away sticky with resin.

The warehouse is heaving, from betting booths and fighters' stalls down at the ringside to the back row of the balcony where men in check workshirts and dhotis stand on their benches for a better look. The audience is almost entirely male. The few women are dressed to please.

"I don't know about this," Satnam says but Najia has the scent of close packed bodies, sweat, primal fluids. She pushes to the front and peers down into the pit. Money changes owners over the betting table in a blur of soft, worn notes. Fists wave fans of rupees and dollars and euros; the sattamen keep track of every paisa. All eyes are on the money, except for one man, diagonally opposite her on the ground floor, who looks up as if he has felt the weight of her regard. Young, flashy. Obvious Hood, thinks Najia. Their eyes meet.

The barker, a five-year-old boy in a cowboy suit, stalks the pit hyping up the audience as two old men with rakes turn the bloody sand into a Zen garden. He has a bindi mike on his throat; his weird little voice, at once old and young, rattles from the sound system through a wash of tabla-and-mix anokha. From his tone of innocence and experience, Najia wonders if he might be a Brahmin. No: that's the Brahmin in the front row booth, a seeming ten-year-old dressed twentysomething flanked by tivi-wannabe girlis. The barker is just another street boy. Najia finds she's breathing fast and shallow. She no longer knows where Satnam is.

The din, already staggering, ratchets up a level as the teams go out on the sand to parade their fighters. They hold them high over their heads, stalking around the ring, making sure everyone can see where their money is going.

The microsabres are appalling creatures. A small California gentech company owned the original patent. Cut standard *Felis domesticus* with reconstructed fossil DNA from *Smilodon fatalis*. Result: bonsai sabretooth, something the size of a large Maine Coon with Upper Palaeolithic dentistry and manners to match. They enjoyed a brief star-pet celebrity until their owners found them taking out their and their neighbours' cats, dogs, Guatemalan domestics, babies. The engineering company filed for bankruptcy before the writs took to the air, but the patent had already been massively infringed in the battle clubs of Manila and Shanghai and Bangkok.

Najia watches an athletic girl in cropped muscle top and parachute baggies parade her champion head-high around the ring. The cat is a big silver tabby, built like a strike aircraft.

Killing genes, gorgeous monster. Its fangs are sheathed in leather scabbards. Najia sees the girl's pride and love, the crowd's roaring admiration redirected on to her. The barker retires to his commentary podium. The bookies issue a rush of slips. The competitors slide back into their boxes.

Muscle-top girl jabs a needle of stimulant into her cat while her male colleague waves a bottle of poppers under its nose. They hold their hero. They hold their breaths. Their opponents drug up their contender, a low lean black microsabre, mean as midnight. There is absolute silence in the arena. The barker gives a blast on his air horn. The combatants let slip the leather guards and throw their battle cats into the pit.

The crowd rises in one voice and one blood. Najia Askarzadah howls and raves with them. All Najia Askarzadah knows is two fighting cats leaping and slashing at each other down in the pit as the blood surges in her eyes and ears.

It's terrifyingly fast and bloody. Within seconds the beautiful silver tabby has one leg hanging from a rope of gristle and skin. Blood jets from the open wound, but it screams defiance at its enemy, tries to dodge and dart on the flapping triangle of meat; slashing with its terrible, killing teeth. Finally it's down and spinning spastically on its back, ploughing up a wave of bloody sand. The victors have already hooked their champion with a neck loop and are wrestling the furious, shrieking thing towards the pen. The silver tabby wails and wails until someone from the judge's pew walks over and drops a concrete breeze-block on its head.

Muscle-top girl stands staring sullenly as the mashed, twitching thing is shovelled away. She bites her bottom lip. Najia loves her then, loves the boy whose glance she caught, loves everyone, everything in this wooden arena. Her heart is quivering, her breath burning, her fists clenched and trembling, her pupils dilated, and her brain blazing. She is eight hundred percent alive and holy. Again she makes eye contact with Obvious Hood. He nods but she can see he has had a heavy loss.

The victors step into the ring to receive the adulation of the crowd. The barker screams into the sound system and on the bookies' bench hands push money money money. This is what you came to Bharat for, Najia Askarzadah, she tells herself. To feel this way about life, about death, about illusion and reality. To have something burn through bloody reasonable, sane, tolerant Sweden. To taste the insane and raw. Her nipples are hard. She knows she's damp. This war, this war for water, this war that she denies brought her here, this war that everyone fears will come. She doesn't fear it. She wants that war. She wants it very much.

5

LISA

Four hundred and fifty kilometres above Western Ecuador, Lisa Durnau runs through a herd of bobbets. They scatter from her, hiking up on their powerful legs and hoofing it, semaphore crests raised. The canopy forest echoes their warbling alarms. The young look up from their grazing, forelegs pawing at air in dread, then shrill and dive for their parents' pouches. The waist-high sauro-marsupials peel away from Lisa in her running tights and top and shoes in two wings of fright, hatchlings trying desperately to stuff themselves headfirst into belly flaps. They're one of Biome 161's most successful species. The forests of Simulated Year Eight Million Before Present throb black with their herds. Alterre is running a hundred thousand years a Real World day, so by tomorrow they could be extinct; this high, humid cloud forest of umbrella-shaped trees desiccated by a climatic shift.

But in this ecological moment, this timeslice of what, in another age, another earth, will be northern Tanzania, today belongs to them.

The rush and dash of bobbets disturbs a group of tranter, reared up on their hind legs, sucking leaves from a trudeau tree. The big slow tree feeders drop to their longer forelegs and canter disjointedly away. Their internal armour plates move like machinery under willow-striped hides. Camouflage by William Morris, Lisa Durnau thinks. Botany by René Magritte. The trudeau trees are perfect hemispheres of leaves, regularly spaced across the plain like an exercise in statistical distribution. Some of the branches bear seed buds, penduluming on the breeze. They can scatter seed across a hundred-metre radius, like a riot-control flechette gun. That's how they achieve their mathematical regularity. No trudeau will grow in the shade of another, but the forest canopy is a cornucopia of species.

Flickers of moving shadow between the trees; a flock of parasitic beckhams darts from the dead tranter in which they have injected their eggs. An ystavat stoops from its high glide path, darts and weaves and scoops up a laggard sauro-bat in the net of skin between its hind legs. A flip, a duck of the tearing beak, and the hunter climbs away again. Invulnerable, inviolable, Lisa Durnau runs on. No god is mortal in his own world and for the past three years she has been director, sustainer, and mediator of Alterre, the parallel Earth evolving in accelerated time on eleven and a half million Real-World computers.

Beckhams. Tranters. Trudeaus. Lisa Durnau loves the mischief of Alterre taxonomy. It's the principles of astronomy applied to alternative biology; you find it lurking in your hard-drive, you name it. Mcconkeys and mastroiannis and ogunwes and hayakawas and novaks. Hammadis and cuestras and bjorks.

So very Lull.

She's settled into her rhythm now. She could move like this forever. Some listen to music when they run. Some chat or read their mail or the news. Some have their aeai PAs brief them on the day. Lisa Durnau checks out what's new across the ten thousand biomes running on eleven and a half million computers participating in the biggest experiment in evolution. Her usual route is a loop around the University of Kansas campus, her marvellous and mysterious bestiary laid over the Lawrence traffic. There's always something to surprise and delight, some new phone-directory name hanging off a fantastical creature that's fought its way out of the silicon jungle. When the first arthrotects had appeared out of the insects by pure evolutionary leap on a Biome 158 host in Guadalajara, she had experienced that thrilled satisfaction you feel when a plot twist hits you that you didn't expect. No one could have predicted the lopezs, but they had lain there, latent, in the rules. Then, two days ago the parasitogenic beckhams evolved from an elementary school in Lancashire and it hit her all over again. You never see it coming.

Then they fired her into space. She hadn't seen that coming, either.

Two days ago she had been running her loop of the campus, past the honey stone faculty buildings, Alterre laid over Kansas summer. She turned by the student halls to run back to shower, shampoo, and office. In which a woman in a suit had been waiting as Lisa came in screwing water out of her ears with twists of tissue. She'd shown identifications and authorisations for responsibilities Lisa hadn't known her nation ever needed and three hours later Lisa Durnau, Director of the Alterre Simulated Evolution Project, was on a government hypersonic transport seventy-five thousand feet over central Arkansas.

The G-woman had told her luggage was strictly mass-limited but Lisa packed her running gear anyway. It felt like a friend. Down in Kennedy she took it out on to the space centre roads to unwind, to explore, to try to get some perspective on where she was and what her government was doing to her. With the sun setting across the lagoons, she ran past sentry rows of rockets, old boosters and missiles and heavy lift launchers. Glorious, perilous machines, now jammed like pikes into the earth, their purpose defeated, their shadows long as continents.

Forty-eight hours on, Lisa Durnau runs orbits of the centrifuge wheel of the ISS, wheeling over Southern Colombia. In her Alterre-sight she sees a krijcek castle rising in the distance above the trudeau tree cover. The krijcek are evolutionary *arrivistes* from Biome 163 in southeast coastal Africa. They're a species of finger-sized dinos that have developed a hive culture, complete with sterile workers, breeders, egg laying queens, a complex social order based on skin colour, and herculean architecture. A new colony will work outwards from a small underground bunker, converting anything and everything organic to pulp, moulding it with dextrous tiny hands into soaring piers and towers and buttresses and vaulted egg chambers. Sometimes Lisa Durnau wishes she could override Lull's naming policy. 'Krijcek' has a nice tone of lethality, but she would have loved to call them 'gormenghasts'.

A chime in her auditory centre tells her her pulse rate has hit the required digits for the requisite amount of time. She has caught up with herself. Alterre's un-reality has anchored her. She jogs to a stop, goes into her cool-down regime, and flicks out of Alterre. ISS's centrifuge is a hundred-metre diameter ring, spun to give a quarter gravity. It rises sheer in front and behind her, she's forever at the bottom of a spin-gravity well. Plant racks lend a gloss of green but nothing can conceal that this is aluminium, construction carbon, plastic, and nothing beyond. NASA doesn't build its ships with windows. Outer space for Lisa Durnau has thus far been crawling from one sealed room to another.

Lisa stretches and flexes. Low grav puts different loads on new muscle groups. She slips off her runsoles, flexes her toes against the metal honeycomb. As well as an intensive NASA exercise regimen she takes calcium supplements. Lisa Durnau's at the age a woman starts to think about her bones. ISS virgins have puffy faces and upper limbs as body fluids redistribute; sophomores a stretched, light, cat-look, but the long-termers eat their own bones. They spend most of their time up in the old core from which ISS has grown chaotically over its half-century in the sky. Few ever come down to dirty gravity, centrifugal or otherwise. Legend is they never can. Lisa Durnau wipes herself down with a moist towelette, seizes a wall rung, and hand-over-hands up the spoke towards the old core. She feels her weight dropping exponentially; she can grab a rung and swoop herself upwards two, five, ten metres. Lisa has a meeting with her G-woman up in the hub. A long-termer dives towards her, executing a neat midcourse somersault to point his feet downwards. He nods and he tumbles past Lisa. His flexibility makes her look like a walrus, but the nod encourages her. It is as warm a welcome as ISS has offered. Fifty people is small enough for first names, big enough for politics. Just like the faculty, then. Lisa Durnau loves the physicality of space but she does wish the budget had stretched to windows.

Shock number one came on the first Kennedy morning as she sat on her verandah with the ocean view and the maid poured coffee. That was when she realised that Dr. Lisa Durnau, Evolutionary Biologist, had been vanished by her own state. She had been unsurprised to learn from the woman in the suit that she was to be sent into space. The State Department did not fly people down to Kennedy in a hypersonic shuttle to study the bird life. When they confiscated her palmer and gave her a lookie-no-talkie model it had been a displeasure but not a shock. Startlement but no shock to find the hotel had been cleared for her. The gym, the pool, the laundry. All for her, alone. Lisa felt good Presbyterian guilt about calling room service until the Nicaraguan maid told her it gave her something to do. That is, the maid said she came from Nicaragua. She poured the coffee and in that same moment of vertiginous paranoia came the second shock: Lull had vanished, too. Lisa had never thought it anything other than a reaction to his marriage disintegrating.

At their next meeting Lisa Durnau confronted Suit Woman, whose name was Suarez-Martin, pronounced the Hispanic way.

"I have to know," said Lisa Durnau, shifting her weight from foot to foot, unconsciously recapitulating her warm-up routine. "Was this what happened to Thomas Lull?"

The government woman Suarez-Martin kept the executive suite as her office. She sat with her back to the panoramic of rockets and pelicans.

"I don't know. His disappearance was nothing to do with the United States government. You do have my word on that."

Lisa Durnau chewed the answer over a couple of times.

"Okay then, why me? What's this about?"

"I can answer that first part."

"Shoot then."

"We got you because we could not get him."

"And the second part?"

"That will be answered, but not here." She slid a plastic bag across the desk to Lisa. "You'll need this."

The bag was marked with NASA logos and contained one standard issue one-size-fits-all flight-suit liner in hi-visibility yellow.

When next she saw Suarez-Martin the G-woman was not wearing her suit. She lay strapped into the acceleration couch on Lisa Durnau's right with hints of NASA yellow peeking through her flight gear at wrists and throat. Her eyes were closed and her lips formed silent prayers, but Lisa had the idea that these were the rituals of familiar terror rather than stark novelty. Airport rosaries.

The pilot occupied the couch on the left. He was busy with pre-flight checks and communications and treated Lisa as he would any other cargo. She shifted on her couch and felt the gel flow and conform to her body contours, a disturbingly intimate sensation. Beneath her, down in the launch pit, a thirty-terawatt laser was charging, focusing its beam on a parabolic mirror underneath her ass. I am about to be blasted into space on the end of a beam of light hotter than the sun, she thought, marvelling at the cool with which she could contemplate this insane notion. Perhaps it was self-defensive disbelief. Perhaps the

Nicaraguan maid had slipped something in the coffee. While Lisa Durnau was trying to decide the count hit zero. A computer in Kennedy flight control fired the big laser. The air ignited under Lisa and kicked the NASA lightbody orbitwards at three gravities. Two minutes into flight a thought so ridiculous, so absurd hit her that she could not help giggling, sending laughter ripples through her gel bed. Hey ma! Top of the world. The most exclusive travel lounge on the planet, the Five-Hundred-Mile-High Club! And all this in something that looks like a designer orange squeezer.

It was there that the third shock crept up and mugged her. It was the realisation of how few people would ever miss her.

The ident patch on the yellow suit liner reads *Daley* Suarez-Martin. The G-woman is one of those people who will set up office anywhere, even in a cubby full of film-wrap astronaut food. Palmer, water bottle, television patch, and family photos are velcroed in an arc on the wall: three generations of Suarez-Martins arrayed on a big house porch with palms in large terracotta pots. The TV patch is set to timer and tells Lisa Durnau she's at 01.15 GMT. She does a subtraction. She'd be at Tacorofico Superica with the Wednesday night gang on her third Margarita.

"How are you settling in?" Daley Suarez-Martin asks.

"It's, uh, it's okay. Really." Lisa still has a small back-of-skull headache, like you get the first few times you use a lighthoek. She suspects it's the ash of the launch trauma drugs she hasn't run out of her system in the rat wheel. And zero-gee leaves her feeling horridly exposed. She doesn't know what to do with her hands. Her breasts feel like cannons.

"We won't keep you long, honest," Daley Suarez-Martin says. In orbit she smiles more than in Kennedy or Lisa Durnau's Lawrence office. You can only do so much authority wearing something that looks like an Olympic luge suit. "First, an apology. We have not exactly told you the *actualité*."

"You've told me exactly nothing," Lisa Durnau says. "I presume this is to do with the Tierra project, and it's a great honour to be involved on the mission, but I really work in a completely different universe."

"That's our first tactical misdirection," Daley Suarez-Martin says. She sucks in her bottom lip. "There is no Tierra mission."

Lisa Durnau feels her mouth is open.

"But all that Epsilon Indi stuff . . ."

"That's real enough. There's a Tierra all right. We're just not going to it."

"Wait wait wait, I've seen the light sail. On television. Hell, I even eyeballed the thing when you sent it out to the L-five point and back on that test run. Friends of mine had a telescope. We had a barbecue. We watched it on a monitor."

"You certainly saw that. The light sail is perfectly real and we did run it out to the Lagrange-five point. Only, that wasn't the test. That was the mission."

In the same year that Lisa Durnau made the Fremont High soccer team and found out that rock boyz, pool parties, and sex are not a good combo, NASA found Tierra. Extra-solar planetary systems had been popping out of the big black faster than the taxonomists could thumb through their dictionaries of mythology and fable for names, but when the Darwin Observatory's rosette of seven telescopes turned back for a closer look at Epsilon Indi, ten light-years away, they found a pale blue dot hugged up close to the warmth of the sun. A waterworld. An earthworld. Spectroscopes peeled the atmosphere and found oxygen, nitrogen, CO_2, water vapour, and complex hydrocarbons that could only be the result of biological activity. There was something living out there, close to the sun in Epsilon Indi's shrunken habitable zone. It might be bugs. It might just be people with scopes watching our own little blue spot on the sun. The discovery team christened the planet Tierra. A Texan immediately filed a claim to the planet and everything that dwelt upon it. It was this story that broke Tierra through the celebrity gossip and crime-of-the-month scandal into checkout chitchat. Another Earth? What's the weather like? How can he own a planet? He just has to file a claim, that's all. Like half your DNA's owned by some biotech corporation. Every time you have sex, you break copyright.

Then came the pictures. Darwin's resolution was high enough to resolve surface features. Every school in the developed world carried a map of Tierra's three continents and vast oceans on its wall. It alternated with Emin Perry, reigning Olympic five thousand metres champion, as the screen saver on Lisa Durnau's A-life project in her first year at UCSB. NASA put an interstellar space probe proposal together with First Solar, the orbital power division of EnGen, using its experimental orbital maser array and a light sail. Transit time was two hundred and fifty years. As development schedules grew ever longer Tierra receded into the wallpaper of public perception and Lisa Durnau found it easier and more satisfying to explore strange worlds and discover new lifeforms in the universe inside her computer. Alterre was as real as Tierra and much cheaper and easier to visit.

"I don't understand what's going on here," Lisa Durnau says, up in space.

"The Tierra probe project is a presentational solution," Suarez-Martin says. Her hair is pinned back with an array of glitter clips. Lisa's short bob of curls hovers around her like a nebula. "The real mission was to develop a space propulsion system sufficiently powerful to move a large object to the Lagrange-five point of orbital stability."

"What kind of large object?" Lisa Durnau cannot connect anything that has happened in the past fifty hours to any part of accumulated thirty-seven years of experience. They tell her this is space, but it's hot, stinks of feet, and you can't see anything. Your government pulls off the biggest sleight-of-hand in history but no one notices because they were watching the pretty pictures.

"An asteroid. This asteroid." Daley Suarez-Martin palms up a graphic on the screen. It's the usual deep-space potato. The resolution is not very good. "This is Darnley 285."

"This must be some very special asteroid," Lisa says. "So is it going to do a Chicxulub on us?"

The G-woman looks pleased. She palms up a new graphic, coloured ellipses crossing each other.

"Darnley 285 is an Earth-crossing asteroid discovered by NEAT skywatch in 2027. Please watch this animation." She taps a yellow ellipse, close in to Earth, far out to the back side of Mars. "Its nearest approach to earth is just inside lunar orbit."

"That's close for a NEO," Lisa Durnau says. See, I can do the speak, too.

"Darnley 285 is on a thousand-eighty-five-day orbit; the next one would have brought her close enough to pose a statistical risk." The animation passes within a hair of blue earth.

"So you built the light sail to move it out of harm's way," Lisa says.

"To move it, but not on account of safety. Please look carefully. This was the projected orbit in 2030. This is the actual orbit." A solid yellow ellipse appears. It's exactly the same as the 2027 orbit. The woman continues. "Close interaction with Near Earth Object Sheringham Twelve on the next orbit would bring Darnley 285 to its closest approach, one twelve thousand miles. Instead, in 2033 . . ." The new dotted parabola switches place with the observed course: exactly the same trajectory logged in 2027. "It is an anomalous situation."

"You're saying . . ."

"An unidentified force is modifying Darnley 285's orbit to keep it the same distance from Earth," Daley Suarez-Martin says.

"Jesus," whispers Lisa Durnau, preacherman's daughter.

"We sent a mission out for the 2039 approach. It was in the highest confidentiality. We found something. We then embarked on an extended project to bring it back. That's what the light sail test mission was about, all the Epsilon Indi cover story. We had to get that asteroid to somewhere we can take a long, close look at it."

"And what did you find?" Lisa Durnau asks.

Daley Suarez-Martin smiles. "Tomorrow we'll send you out to see for yourself."

6

LULL

Eleven thirty and the club is jumping. Boom-mounted floods define an oval of sand. The bodies cluster to the light like moths. They move, they grind, eyes shut in ecstasy. The air smells of used-up day, heavy sweat, and duty-free Chanel. The girls wear this summer's shift-Dresses, last summer's two pieces, the occasional classic V-string. The boys are all bare-chested and carry layers of neck jewellery. Chin wisps are back, the Mohican is *so* '46, tribal body-painting hovers on the edge of the terminally unhip, but scarification seems to be the coming thing, boys and girls alike. Thomas Lull is glad the Australian penis-display thongs have cycled out. He's worked the parties for the Ghosht Brothers for the past three seasons, cash in hand, and he's seen the fast tide of planet youth culture ebb and flow, but those things, strapping it up like a periscope . . .

Thomas Lull sits on the soft, tired grey sand, forearms resting on drawn-up knees. The surf is unusually quiet tonight. Hardly a ripple at the tide line. A bird cries out over the black water. The air is still, dense, tired. No taste of monsoon on it. The fishermen have been saying that since the Banglas brought their ice up past Tamil Nadu the currents have been out of kilter. Behind him, bodies move in total silence.

Figures resolve out of the dark, two white girls in sarongs and halter-tops. They're dirty beach-blonde with that exaggerated Scandinavian tan emphasised by pale Nordic eyes, hand in hand, barefoot. How old are you, nineteen, twenty? Thomas Lull thinks. With your sunbed top-up tans and bikini bottoms under those travel-ironed sarongs. This is your first stop, isn't it, somewhere you saw on a backpacker site, just wild enough to see if you're going to like it out in the raw world. You couldn't wait to get away from Uppsala or Copenhagen and do all the fierce things in your hearts.

"Ho there," Thomas Lull hails softly. "If you're planning on attending tonight's entertainment there are a couple of preliminaries. Purely for your own safety." He unfolds his scanning kit with a gambler's flick.

"Sure," says smaller, goldier girl. Thomas Lull runs her fistful of pills and patches through his scanner.

"Nothing here going to leave you like a plate of Vichysoisse. Soup of the day is Transic Too, it's a new emotic, you can get it from anyone up on the stage area. Now, madam . . ." This to bug-eyed beach-Viking who has started the party early. "I need to see if it'll ab-react with anything you're already running. Could you . . . ?" She knows the drill, licks her finger, rolls it across the sensor plate. Everything goes green. "No problem. Enjoy the party, ladies, and this is a no-alcohol event."

He checks their asses through their sheer sarongs as they insinuate themselves into the quiet writhe. They're still holding hands. That's so nice, Thomas Lull thinks. But the emotics scare him. Computer emotions brewed on an unlicensed Level 2.95 Bharat sundarban aeai, chain-bred up in some Coke-bottle bedroom factory and stuck onto adhesive patches, fifty dollars a slap. It's easy to tell the users. The twitchings and grinnings and bared teeth and uncanny noises of bodies trying to express feelings with no analogue in human need or experience. He's never met anyone who could tell him what this feeling makes you feel. Then again, he's never met anyone who can report what a natural emotion makes you feel. We are all programme ghosts running on the distributed network of Brahma.

That bird's still out there, calling.

He glances over his shoulder at the silent beach party, every dancer in his or her private zone, dancing to his or her custom beat beamed through 'hoek link. He lies to himself that he only works the club nights because he can use the cash, but he's always been drawn to mass humanity. He wants and dreads the self-loss of the dancers, merged into an unconscious whole, isolate and unified. It's the same love and loathing that drew him to the dismembered body of India, one of the planet's hundred most recognisable faces, shuffled into the subcontinent's appalling, liberating, faceless billion and a half. Turn around, walk away, disappear. That ability to dissolve his face into a crowd has its flip-side: Thomas Lull can detect the individual, the unusual, the countervailing out of the herd.

She moves across the currents of the crowd, through the bodies, against the grain of the night. She is dressed in grey. Her skin is pale, wheat, Indo-Aryan. Her hair is short, boyish, very glossy, with a tinge of red. Her eyes are large. Gazelle eyes, like the Urdu poets sang. She looks impossibly young. She wears a three-stripe Vishnu tilak on her forehead. It doesn't look stupid on her. She nods, smiles, and the bodies close around her. Thomas Lull tries to angle himself to look without being seen. It's not love, lust, fortysomething hormones. It is simple fascination. He has to see more, know more of her.

"Hey there." An Australian couple want their gear checked. Thomas Lull runs their stash through his scanner while watching the party. Grey is the perfect party camouflage. She has melted into an interplay of silently moving limbs.

"Fine, you're whistling Dixie. But we do have a zero-tolerance policy on penis-display suits."

The guy frowns. Get out of here, leave me to my recreation. There, close by the decks. The bhati-boys are flirting with her. He hates them for that. Come back to me. She hesitates, bends low for a word. For a moment he thinks she might buy something from the Bangalore Bombastic. He doesn't want her to do that. She shakes her head and moves on. She vanishes into the bodies again. Thomas Lull finds he is following her. She does blend well; he keeps losing track of her amongst the bodies. She isn't wearing a 'hoek. How is she getting it then? Thomas Lull moves to the edge of the dance space. She only looks like she is dancing, he realises. She is doing something else, taking the collective mood and moving to it. Who the hell is she?

Then she stops in her dance. She frowns, opens her mouth, swallows for breath. She presses a hand to her labouring chest. She can't breathe. The gazelle eyes are scared. She bends over, trying to release the grip in her lungs. Thomas Lull knows these signs well. He is an old familiar of this attacker. She stands in the middle of the silent crowd, fighting for breath. No one sees. No one knows. Everyone is blind and deaf in their own private dancescapes. Thomas Lull forces a path through the bodies. Not to her, but to the Scandie girls.

He has their stash read-out on his scanner. There's always someone doing a quick, dirty lift on the salbutamol/ATP-reductase reaction.

"I need your wheezers, quick." Goldie girl peers at him as if he's some incredible alien elf from Antares. To her, he could be. She fumbles open her pink Adidas purse. "Here, those." Thomas Lull scrapes out the blue and white caplets. The grey girl is panting shallowly now, hands on thighs, very frightened, looking round for help. Thomas Lull bulls through the party people, cracking the little gelatin capsules and shaking them into his fist.

"Open your mouth," he orders, cupping his hands. "Inhale on three and hold for twenty. One. Two. Three."

Thomas Lull claps his cupped hands over her mouth and blows hard between his thumbs, spraying powder deep into her lungs. She closes her eyes, counting. Thomas Lull finds he's looking at her tilak. He's never seen one like it before. It looks like plastic fused to the skin, or raw bone. Suddenly he has to touch it. His fingers are millimetres away when she opens her eyes. Thomas Lull snatches his hand back.

"You all right?"

She nods. "Yes. Thank you."

"You should've brought some medication with you. You could have been in a lot of trouble; these people, they're like ghosts. You could have died and they'd've danced right over you. Come on."

He leads her through the maze of blind dancers to the shadowed sand. She sits, bare feet splayed out. Thomas Lull kneels beside her. She smells of sandalwood and fabric conditioner. Twenty years of undergraduate expertise pins her at nineteen, maybe twenty. Come on, Lull. You've saved a strange little driftwood girl from an asthma attack and you're running your prepull checks. Show some self-respect.

"I was so scared," she says. "I am so stupid, I had inhalers but left them back at the hotel . . . I never thought . . ."

Her soft accent would sound English to less experienced ears but Thomas Lull's recognises a Karnatakan twang.

"Luck for you Asthma Man picked up your wheezing on his super-hearing. Come on. Party's over for you tonight, sister. Where are you staying?"

"The Palm Imperial Guest House." It's a good place, not cheap, more popular with older travellers. Thomas Lull knows the lobby and bar of every hotel for thirty kays up and down the coconut coast. Some of the bedrooms too. Backpackers and gap-yearers tend toward the beachshacks. He's seen a few of those too. Killed a few snakes.

"I'll get you back. Achuthanandan will look after you. You've had a bit of a shock, you need to take it easy."

That tilak: he's certain it's *moving*. Mystery girl gets to her feet. She offers a hand shyly, formally.

"Thank you very much. I think I would have been in very bad trouble without you." Thomas Lull takes the hand. It is long and aesthetic, soft and dry. She cannot quite look at him.

"All in a day's work for Asthma Man."

He walks with her toward the lights among the palms. The surf is lifting, the trees grow agitated. The lamps on the hotel veranda dance and glimmer behind the veil of fronds. The beach party behind him is suddenly weary and stale. All the things that seemed valuable and confirming before this girl now taste thin and old. Perhaps the monsoon is coming; the wind that will blow him on again.

"If you want, there's a technique I can teach you. I used to suffer asthma bad when I was young; it's a breathing trick; to do with gas exchange. It's quite easy. I haven't had an attack in twenty years, and you can throw away those inhalers. I could show you the basics; you could call round tomorrow . . ."

The girl pauses, gives it thought, then nods her head. Her tilak catches a light from somewhere.

"Thank you. I would value that very much."

The way she talks; so reserved, so Victorian, such regard for the stress of words.

"Okay well, you can find me . . ."

"Oh, I will just ask the gods, they will show me. They know the way to everywhere."

Thomas Lull has no answer to that, so he sticks his hands in the pockets of his cut-off baggies and says, "Well, gods permitting, I'll see you tomorrow, ah?"

"Aj." She gives her name a French pronunciation: *Ah-zjh*. She looks to the hotel lights, coloured bulbs jigging in the rising wind. "I think I will be all right from here, thank you. Until tomorrow then, Professor Lull."

7

TAL

Tal travels tonight in a plastic taxi. The little bubble phatphat rattles over the pocks and pots of a rural road as the driver steers nervously by his single headlamp. He's already narrowly missed one wandering cow and a column of women with bundles of firewood on their heads. Shade trees loom out of the deep, thick rural night. The driver scans the verge for the turn-off. His instructions are taped to the dash where he can read them by instrument light. So many kays along this road, through this number of villages, second left after the wall ad for Rupa underwear. He's never been out of the city before.

Tal's special mix plays big anokha breaks with Slav Metal death chords, in honour of the host. Celebrity occasions demand extra-special mixes. Tal's life can be chronicled by a series of soundtrack files. Tal's DJ aeai wove up a set of top grooves between drafting the wedding pavilion for the Chawla/Nadiadwala match. There's much happening in *Town and Country*'s actors' lives right now.

A sudden lurch throws Tal from the bench seat. The phatphat bounces to a stop. Tal rearranges yts thermal scatter coat, tuts at the dust on yts silk pants, then notices the soldiers. Six of them phase out of rural night camouflage. A chubby Sikh officer has his hand raised. He steps up to the taxi.

"Didn't you see us?"

"You are kind of hard to spot," the driver says.

"No chance of a licence, I suppose?" the jemadar asks.

"None whatever," the driver says. "My cousin . . ."

"Do you not know we are in a state of heightened vigilance?" the Sikh soldier admonishes. "Awadhi slow missiles could already be moving across our country. They are stealthy things, they can conceal themselves in many ways."

"Not as slow as this old crock," the driver jokes. The Sikh suppresses a smile and bends down to glance in at the passenger. Tal hastily shuts off the bpm. Yt sits very still, very upright, heart betrayingly loud.

"And you sir? Madam?"

His soldiers titter. The Sikh has been eating onions. Tal thinks yt might pass out from the reek and the tension. Yt opens yts evening bag, slips out the thick, gilt-scallop-edged invitation. The Sikh looks at it as if it could be grounds for a full body-cavity search, then snaps it back to Tal.

"You're lucky we're out here tonight. You missed your turn a couple of kilometres back. You must be about the seventh or eighth. Now, what you do is . . ."

Tal breathes again. As the driver turns the cab Tal can clearly hear the soldiers' nasty laughter over the purr of the alcohol motor.

Hope there are slow missiles a-creeping up on you, Tal thinks.

The half-ruined Ardhanarisvara temple stands among trees on a country track that strikes right from the main road. The party organisers have lit the drop-off zone with biolume patches. The green light draws faces from the tree trunks, spook-lights the slumped statues and yakshis, bedded in the ancient soil. The reception is themed around polar opposites: sakti and purusa; female and male energies; sattva and tamas; spiritual intelligence and earthy materialism. The yoni-shaped tanks have been extravagantly flooded. Tal thinks of yts party preparations, a frugal lick-wash with a bottle of warmed mineral water. The mains water in the White Fort—the mammoth agglomeration of housing projects where Tal has yts two-room apartment—has not been working for two months now. Day and night a procession of women and children carry water cans up and down the stairs past yts front door.

Gas flames blaze from nozzles in the centres of the yoni tanks. Tal studies the twin temple guardian dvarapalas while the taxi driver runs yts card through his reader. The ruined arcade is dominated by the image of Ardhanarisvara; half male, half female. A single full breast, an erect penis sliced down the middle, a mono testicle, a curl of labius, a hint of a slit. The torso has a man's broadness of shoulder, a woman's fullness of hip, the hands sensitively held in ritual mudras but the features are genetic, androgynous. The third eye of Siva is closed on the forehead. Inside, the music is banging. Invitation clutched in hand, Tal passes between the guardian deities, into the party of the season.

Even when Tal showed them the invitation, the department told yt yt had faked it. It was an automatic supposition to make in a section designing visual wallpaper for the fake lives of the aeai actors of India's favourite soapi. Tal hadn't believed it ytself when yt found the thick, creamy wafer card resting in yts intray.

FASHIONSTAR PROMOTIONS on behalf of
MODE ASIA invites TAL,
27 Corridor 30, 12th Floor, Indira Gandhi Apartments
(as White Fort was known only to the post office,
the tax department, and the bailiffs) to a
RECEPTION
to welcome YULI to Varanasi for BHARAT FASHION WEEK.
LOCATION: Ardhanarisvara Temple, Mirza Murad District
CELEBRATION: 22 bells.
NATION: NuTribe.
RSVP.

The card felt warm and soft as skin. Tal had shown it to Mama Bharat, the old widow woman whose front door shared yts stair head. She was a soft soul incarcerated by her family in a silk prison. The modern way: an independent old age. Three months ago Tal had moved in and become Mama Bharat's family. No one would talk to yt, either. Tal accepted the daily chai and snack visits and twice weekly cleaning calls and never asked what kind of family yt was to her, daughter or son.

The aged aged woman ran her fingers over the invitation, stroking and cooing softly, like a lover.

"So soft," she said. "So soft. And will they all be like you?"

"Nutes? Most. We're a theme."

"Ah, a great great honour, the best in the city, and all the tivi people."

Yes, Tal had thought. But why this one?

Tal walks through the shadowy temple mandapa lit by flambeaux held by four armed Kali avatars and feels a little gnaw of awe in yts nadi chakra. *There* is a Big Name Film Director talking rather uncomfortably to a Well Respected New Young Woman Writer underneath a startlingly pornographic statue. *Here* is an international circuit tennis star looking relieved to have found not just a Big Pro golfer, but an

All-India League footballer and his radiant wife so they can all talk strokeplay and handicaps. And *that's* Mr. Interstellar Pop Promoter Man and he's his latest piece of pop engineering with a debut song bound to go to Number One on prerelease bookings already while the girl in the too-short skirt clutching the cocktail a little too hard and laughing a little too loud has to be FASHIONSTAR PROMOTIONS PR. That's not counting the three under-twenty-five wetware rajas, the two edgy games designers, and the deeply shady Lord of the Sundarbans, the Cyberjungle entrepreneur of the Darwinware hot zone, all on his ownio, at ease and sleekly tigerish as only a man with his own pandava legion of aeai bodyguards can. Plus the overdressed overmouthed faces Tal doesn't recognise but who advertise their fashion magazine origins, the fortysomething tivi commissioning editors looking sweaty and over-familiar with each other, the gossip journos with the very wide and active peripheral vision, and the Varanasi society have-to-haves, ruffled and sullen at being outshone by a gaggle of *nutes*. There are even a couple of generals, gorgeous as parakeets in their full dress. Army is *trés trés* hip in this time of edge-play with Awadh. Not forgetting that clutch of sullen seeming-ten-year-olds looking daggers over the tops of their gyro-stabilised cocktail glasses: the Golden, the Brahmin sons and daughters.

Tal's been given a checklist by Neeta, boss Devgan's PA. Most of the metasoap unit find Neeta's perfect vacuity oppressive but Tal likes her. Her unfeigned banality throws up unexpected, Zen-like juxtapositions. She wanted to know what yt was wearing, what makeup yt was going to put on, where yt was going for pre-club drinks and the after-party bash. You have to make an effort for the biggest brashest celeby gotta-go bash of the season. Along the colonnade yt clicks thirty Big Names off Neeta's list.

Two rakshasas guard the entrance to the sanctuary and the free bar. The groove is Adani, Biblical Brothers remix. Scimitars swing down. The actors are flesh but the lower set of arms is robotic. Tal admires the full-body makeup. It really is seamless. They scan the invitation. The swords go up. Tal steps into wonderland. Every nute in the city has turned out. Tal notes that yts ankle-length shag-fibre optical shatter coat is still the thing, but since when have ski goggles pushed high on the forehead become the accessory? Tal hates missing a move. Heads turn as yt progresses to the bar, then bend together. Yt can feel the wave of gossip spread behind yt like a wake: *Who's that nute, yt's new, where's yt been hiding ytself, Stepped Away or stepped in?*

I disregard your regard, Tal declares to ytself. Tal is here for stardom. Yt stakes a pitch at the end of the curving luminous plastic bar and scans the talent. Four-armed barmen shake acrobatic cocktails. Tal admires the dexterity of their robotics. "What's this?" yt asks of the fluorescent cone of golden ice balanced on its point on the bar.

"Non-Russian," says the barman as his lower arms lift another glass and scoop up ice. Tal sips cautiously. Vodka-based something vanilla-syrupy, a fistful of crush and a slash of German cinnamon schnapps, flakes of gold foil drifting down through the interstices in the ice. The thrum of the microgyros tickle Tal's fingers.

Then party dynamics opens a momentary corridor of clear eyeline and in pure white polar bear shag and gold-tinted ski goggles Tal glimpses the Star Ytself: YULI.

Tal can't speak. Yt is paralysed by the presence of celebrity. All media pretensions and sophistications fly. Even before yt Stepped Away, Tal idolised YULI: Superstar as a construct, a manipulation like the cast of *Town and Country*. Now yt's here, in flesh and clothes and Tal's awestruck. Yt has to be near Yuli. Yt has to hear yt breathe and laugh and feel yts warmth. There are only two real objects in the temple tonight. Guests, nutes, staff, music, all are indeterminate, in the domain of Ardhanarisvara. Tal is behind Yuli now, close enough to reach and touch and reify. The angle of the cheekbone shifts. Yuli turns. Tal smiles, big dumb grin. Oh Gods, I look like a drooling celebrity idiot, what am I going to say? Ardhanarisvara god of the dilemma, help me. Gods; do I smell, I only had a half bottle of water to wash in . . . Yuli's gaze washes over yt, looks right through yt, annihilates yt, swings to focus on a figure behind yt. Yuli smiles, opens yts arms.

"Darling!"

Yt sweeps past, a warm wash of fur and gold tan and cheekbones like razors. The entourage follows. A hip jostles Tal, knocks the glass from yts hand. It falls to the floor, teeters wildly before coming to centre, spinning on its point. Tal stands stunned, stone as any of the temple's alien sex statues.

"Oh, you seem to have lost your drink." The voice that breaks through the wall of chatter is neither man's nor woman's. "Can't have that dear, can we? Come on, they're a pack of bloody bitches, sib, and we're just wallpaper."

Yt's a head shorter than Tal, dark skinned, a hint of epicanthine fold: Assam or Nepali genes down in the mix. Yt carries ytself with shy pride of those peoples. Yt's dressed in simple, fashion-denying white, the shaved scalp dusted with gold-flecked mica the only concession to contemporary style. As with all yts kind, Tal can't begin to guess yts age.

"Tranh."

"Tal."

They curtsey and kiss in greeting. Yts fingers are long and elegant, French manicured, unlike Tal's stubby, nail-bitten keypad-stabbers.

"Bloody awful thing, isn't it?" Tranh says. "Drink, dear. Here!" It raps the bar. "Enough of that Non-Russian piss. Give me gin. Chota peg, by two. Chin chin." After the cloying, theatrical house cocktail, the pure clear glass with the twist of lemon is very good and very pure and very cold and Tal can feel it shooting up yts spinal column like cold fire straight to the brain.

"Bloody marvellous drink," Tal says. "Built the Raj, it did. All that quinine. Here!" This to the bar avatar. "Actor wallah! Two more of these."

"I really shouldn't, I've got work in the morning and I've no idea how I'm even getting back," Tal says but the nute slides the dew-slick glass into yts hand and the music hits that perfect beat and a flaw of wind runs through the half-ruined temple drawing flames and shadows in its wake and everyone looks up at its touch, wondering if it could be the first caress of the monsoon. It blows a touch of mad into the terrible party and in its wake Tal finds ytself dizzy and full of talk and life and wonder at finding ytself in a new town, in a new job, in the eye of the social vortex with a small and dark and beautiful nute.

It all runs like calligraphy in the rain then. Tal finds yt dancing with no memory of how yt got out on the floor and there are a lot more people standing around watching than dancing, in fact no one is dancing, only Tal, alone dancing wonderfully, flawlessly, like all the wind that blew through the temple gathered into one place and one restlessness; like unaccustomed chota pegs, like light, like night, like temptation, like a laser focused on Tranh, illuminating yt alone, saying *I want I need I will, come on*, beckoning, *come on*, drawing Tranh out, step by step, yt smiling and shaking yts head, *I don't do this sort of bloody thing dear*, but yts being pulled into the circle by this play of shakti and purusha until Tal sees Tranh shiver, as if something has come out of the night and passed into yt, some possessing, abandoned thing, and Tranh smiles a little, mad smile, and they come together in the circle of music a hunter and the thing yt hunts and every eye is on them and from the corner of one eye Tal sees YULI, brightest star in heaven, stalking away with yts entourage. Upstaged.

The meeja all expect them to kiss and make the drama perfect, but, despite the cascade of erotic sculpture tumbling from every pillar and buttress, they are Indian nutes, and the time and place for the kiss is not here, not now.

Then they're in a taxi and Tal doesn't know how or where but the dark is very big and yts ears are humming from the music and yts head is thudding from the chota pegs but things are gradually becoming more broken up and discrete. Tal knows what yt wants now. Yt knows what's going to happen. The certainty is a dull, crimson throb at the base of yts belly.

On the back seat of the jolting phatphat, Tal lets yts forearm fall, soft inner flesh upwards, on Tranh's thigh. A moment's hesitation, then Tranh's fingers stroke yts sensitive, hairless flesh, seek out the buried studs of the hormone control system beneath the skin and delicately tap out the arousal codes. Almost immediately, Tal feels yts heart kick, yts breath catch, yts face flush. Sex strums yts body like a sitar, every cord and organ ringing in its harmonic. Tranh offers yts arm to Tal. Yt plays the subdermal inputs, tiny and sensitive as goose flesh. Yt feels Tranh stiffen as the hormone rush hits. They sit side by side in the back of the jolting taxi, not touching but shivering with lust, incapable of speech.

The hotel is by the airport, comfortable, anonymous, internationally discreet. The bored receptionist hardly looks up from her romantic magazine. The night porter stirs, then identifies these guests and hides behind the cricket highlights on the television. A glass elevator takes them up the side of the hotel to their fifteenth-floor room, the patterned airport lights spreading themselves ever wider around them, like jewelled skirts. The sky is mad with stars and the navigation lights of troopships, flying in to support the state of heightened vigilance. All in heaven and earth tonight is trembling.

They fall into the room. Tranh reaches for yt, but Tal slips away, teasing. There is one thing necessary; Tal finds the room system and plugs in a chip. FUCK MIX. Nina Chandra plays and Tal sways and closes yts eyes and melts. Tranh comes towards yt, moving into the rhythm, stepping out of the shoes, slipping off the pure white coat, the linen suit, the Big Name Label mesh underwear. Yt offers yts arm.

Tal runs yts fingers over the orgasm keys.

Everything is soundtrack.

The ghost of departing chota pegs wakes Tal and sends yt to the bathroom for water. Yt stares, still drunk, vertiginous with what has happened, at the never-ending stream from the mixer tap. There is a grey predawn light in the room. Tranh looks so very small and breakable on the bed. The aircraft never stop. Something in this morning lights makes every surgical scar on Tranh's body stand out. Tal shakes yts head, suddenly needing very much to cry, but slips in beside Tranh and shivers when yt feels the other nute move in yts sleep and fold an arm around yt. Tal dozes and only wakes to the chambermaid banging on the door wondering if she can service the room. It's ten o'clock. Tal has a wretched hangover. Tranh is gone. Yts clothes, yts shoes, yts shredded underwear. Yts gloves. Gone. In yts place is a card, with a street name, an address and two words: *non-scene.*

8

VISHRAM

The compere has the audience really laughing now. Down in the green room, Vishram can feel it like waves on a shore. Deep laughter. Laughter you can't help, you can't stop even though it hurts you. Best sound in the world. Hold that laugh for me, people. You can tell an audience by the sound of its laugh. There are the thin laughs down south and the flat laughs from the Midlands and the resonant laughing that's like church singing from way up in the islands, but that's a good Glasgow laugh out there. A home crowd laugh. Vishram Ray taps his feet and puffs out his cheeks and reads the yellow reviews tacked to the green room wall. He's within *this* of a cigarette.

You know your stuff. You can do this material forwards and backwards, in English, in Hindi, on your head, dressed as a lettuce. You know the hook points and the builds, you've got your three topical referents, you know where you can improv and then on-ramp without shifting gear. You can take out a heckler with a single shot. They'd laugh at a cat up behind the mike tonight so why do you feel like there's a fist up your ass slowly hauling your guts out? Home crowds are always hardest and tonight they have the power. Thumbs-up, thumbs down, vote with your throat in the Glasgow region heat of the Funny Ha-Ha contest. It's the first hurdle to Edinburgh and a Perrier Award, but it's the first one trips you up.

Compere is doing the slow build up now. People on the right put your hands together. People on the left do the really penetrating two-finger whistles. People in the balcony start a titanic roar. For. Mr. Vishram! Raaaaayyyl And he's out of the blocks, running for the bright stage lights, the roar of the audience and his metal mistress, the slim steel torso of the lone microphone.

With his party eye he glimpses her leave her coat at the club check and decides, I'll have a crack at that. Meerkatting. Head up high, looking left right, all over. She heads for the bar clockwise around the room. He heads widdershins, tracking her through the jungle of bodies. She has the gang of friends, the scary professional one, the one who's into her body but you try touching, the dumpy one who'll go with anything. He can cut her out, round her up. Vishram times his run and gets to the bar that split second before she does. The bar girl does a double take, left, right.

"Oh, sorry, go ahead there," Vishram yells.

"No, you were here . . ."

"No no, you go on . . ."

Glasgow accent. Always good to go native. She wears a strap-back V-top and hipsters so low cut he sees the twin curves of her fit nates as she bends over the bar to roar an order at the bar girl.

"Here I'll get this." To the bar girl: "Throw in a vodka black dog."

"We should be buying you . . ." she shouts in his ear. He shakes his head, chancing a glance round to see if his mates are looking. They are.

"My shout. I'm feeling flush."

The bottles come. She hands them round to her mates, arrayed behind her, and clinks with him.

"Congratulations. So, is that you through?"

"To the Edinburgh final, yes. After that, fame, fortune, my own sitcom . . ." Time for manoeuvre one. "Listen, I can't hear myself think, let alone attempt witty and scintillating conversation. Can we move away from the speakers?"

The corner by the cigarette machine under the balcony is not significantly quieter than anywhere else at the party, but it's away from her friends and dark.

She says, "You got my vote."

"Thank you. I owe you that drink then. Sorry, I didn't catch your name."

"I didn't throw it," she says. "Anye."

"Anye, good . . ."

"Gallic."

"Yeah, Gallic name. Good Gallic solidity."

"Thank my parents for that. Good solid Galls, the pair of them. You know, I think Bharat and Scotland have a lot in common. New nations, all that."

"I still think we've got you beat when it come to good old-fashioned religious violence."

"You clearly haven't seen an Old Firm game."

While Anye talks Vishram has been moving his body around, closing off her access to the dance floor, her friends. Manoeuvre two—the isolation—complete, he moves on to manoeuvre three. He pretends to recognise the music.

"I like this one." He detests it but it's a good solid 115. "You fancy a wee boogie?"

"I fancy a wee boogie very much," she says, coming out of the corner at him with a low light in her eyes. The regulation five dances later, he's found out that she's a Law Major at Glasgow U, an SNP party worker and likes mountains, new nations, going out with her mates, and coming home without them. This sounds flawless to Vishram Ray, so he buys her another— her friends have receded into a glum huddle at the end of the bar nearest the women's toilets—necks it quick and dirty and hauls her out for another couple on the floor. She dances heavy but enthusiastic, all limbs. He likes them meaty. Halfway through the mid-tempo shift-of-pace number his hip pocket starts calling his name. He ignores it.

"Aren't you going to answer that?"

He hauls out the palmer hoping it'll be someone wanting to talk to him about comedy. It's not. *Vishram, it's Shastri*. Not now, old servant. Absolutely not now.

But he's getting bored with the party. Cut to manoeuvre four.

"Do you want to stay here, or shall we go on somewhere else?"

"I'm easy," she says.

Right answer.

"Do you fancy coming back to mine, wee coffee?"

"Aye," she says. "I would."

Outside on Byres Road there's still lingering magic hour blue over the rooftops. The car lights look unnatural, theatrical, a scene shot day for night. The taxi slo-mos through a midnight twilight. Anye sits close on the big leather seat. Vishrani slips the hand. She slides back on the seat to open up the front of her hipsters. He hooks panty elastic. Manoeuvre five.

"Funny man," she says, guiding his fingers.

The golden stone of the tenements seem to glow in the half dark. Vishram can feel the stored warmth from the stonework on his face. There's still a smell of cut grass from the park.

"This is nice," Anye says. "Expensive."

Vishram still has his hand down her pants, guiding her up the steps with his hot finger. His groin, his breathing, his belly muscles all tell him he's going to have her big and heavy and naked on his floor. He's going to find out the noises she makes. He's going to see the dirt in her head, the things she wants another body to do to her. Vishram almost tumbles through the door in a rush of want. His foot sends the thing waiting for him skittering across the lobby. He thinks about leaving it. The automatic lights pick out the green and silver logo of The Company.

"Just a wee second."

Already his proto-stiffie is subsiding.

The plastic priority mail wallet is addressed to Vishram Ray, Apartment 1a, 22 Kelvingrove Terrace, Glasgow, Scotland. Sick, sober and de-aroused, Vishram opens the envelope. Inside, two items: a letter from Shastri the wrinkled retainer and a ticket from Glasgow via LHR to Varanasi, first class, one way.

He began the thing with the woman in the very good suit in the BharatAir Raja Class lounge because he's still glowing on the winning high and the booze but mostly frustrated libido.

He had the zip just pulled on his jam of travel essentials when the limo arrived. He'd offered Anye a ride back to hers. She'd given him a freezing, solid Gallic SNP-activist look.

"I'm sorry, it's family."

She looked very cold, in those pants, that much bare skin, hurrying through the early August Glasgow predawn. Vishram made it to check-in with ten minutes to spare. He was the sole occupant of the sharp end of the short shuttle flight to London. He came down the air-bridge slightly vertiginous from the velocity of it all and headed straight to the first-class lounge with a determination for vodka. The shower, the shave, the change of clothes, and a shot of Polish restored his Vishram Ray-ness. He felt good enough about himself to try to hook the woman in the comfortable-for-flying suit into casual chat. Just to pass the time. Lounge reptile.

Her name is Marianna Fusco. She is a corporate lawyer. She has been summoned to Varanasi to attend to a complex trusteeship issue.

"Me, I'm just the black sheep, the court jester. The youngest brother sent to England to study law at some 'bridge university; except he ends up in Scotland aspiring to stand-up. The highest human art form, incidentally. And not all that different from law, I suspect. We're both creatures of the arena."

She doesn't rise to that one. Instead, she asks,

"How many brothers?"

"Big bear, middle bear."

"No sisters?"

"Not many sisters in Varanasi, or at least, my bit of it."

"I've heard this," she says, turning her body comfortably on the leather couch towards him. "What's it like, a society with four times as many men as women?"

"Not too many lady lawyers," Vishram says, settling back on the creaking upholstery. "Not too many ladies anything professional."

"I shall remember to press home my advantages," the lawyer says. "Can I get you another vodka? It is going to be a long flight."

Shortly after the third they are called to board. Vishram's seat goes all the way back. After years of budget airlines, the legroom is incredible. There is such play value in the buttons and toys that he doesn't notice the passenger strapping in beside him.

"Well, hello there, isn't this a coincidence?" he says.

"It isn't," Marianna Fusco says, slipping off her jacket. She has good arm definition under her stretch-brocade top.

The first armagnac comes over Belgium as the hypersonic plane climbs steeply towards its thirty-three kilometre cruising altitude. It's not a drink Vishram has ever considered. He's a vodka boy. But now he thinks armagnac rather suits the personality he's playing here. He and Marianna Fusco talk through the indigo sky about their childhoods, hers in a vast nation of family spread out across marriages and remarriages—her *constellation family*, she calls it, his in the bourgeois patriarchy of Varanasi. She finds the emergent social stratification fascinating and horrifying, as the

English always have. It's what they perennially love about Indian culture and literature. The guilt and thrill of a really good class system.

"I do come from rather a well-off family." Play it up. "Not Brahmins, though. Capital 'B' Brahmins, I mean. My father's a Kshatriya, quite devout in his wee way. Tinkering with the DNA would be blasphemous."

Two more armagnacs and the conversation sags into a doze. In full luxurious recline, Vishram pulls his airline blanket up around his neck. He imagines the chill of near-space beyond that nanocarbon wall. Marianna moves against him under her blanket. She is warm and far too close and breathing in time with him.

Manoeuvre six. Somewhere over Iran he cups a breast. She moves against him. They kiss. Armagnac tongues. She wiggles closer. He slides her breasts out of her white stretch top. Marianna Fusco has big areolar patches with raised pores and nipples like bullets. She hitches up her comfortable-but-businesslike skirt as the shockwave rider hits Mach 3.6. He licks and tries the slip but Marianna Fusco intercepts him and guides his finger to that other, pert hole. She gives a little gasp, rides his finger up to the hilt and slickly unzips. Vishram Ray's heavy dick tumbles out into the gap between the seats. Marianna Fusco rubs her thumb over the glans. Vishram Ray tries not to be overheard by the stewardess and thumbs her clitoris.

"Fuck," she whispers. "Rotate it. Fucking rotate."

She hooks a leg over, settles deeper on to his digit. Sutra at thirty-three kay. A quarter of the way to orbit, Vishram Ray comes carefully into a BharatAir Raja Class napkin. Marianna Fusco has an airline pillow half stuffed into her mouth, making tiny muffled mewling screams. Vishram rolls back, feeling every centimetre of altitude beneath him. He just made it into the most exclusive club on the planet, the Twenty-Five-Mile-High Club.

They clean off in the bathroom, separately, giggling uncontrollably at each glance of the other. They straighten their clothes and return soberly to their seats and shortly after they feel the shift in pitch as the aerospacer enters descent, plunging like a burning meteor towards the IndoGangetic plain.

He waits for her on the far side of customs. He admires the cut of her cloth, how her height and the solid way she moves stand out among the Bharatis. He knows there will be no phone calls or e-mails or comeback. A professional relationship.

"Could I offer you a lift?" he asks. "My father will have sent a car—I know, it's cheesy, but he's old-fashioned about things like that. It's no problem to drop you at your hotel."

"Thank you," Marianna Fusco says. "I don't like the look of the taxi rank."

It's easy to spot the limo. The chauffeur is actually flying little Ray Power company flags from the wings. He doesn't miss a beat as he takes Marianna Fusco's bag, sticks it in the trunk, and chases a small posse of beggars and badmashes. The few seconds of heat between airport and air-conditioned car stun Vishram. He's been too long in a cold climate. And he had forgotten the scent, like ashes of roses. The car pulls into the wall of colour and sound. Vishram feels the heat, the warmth of the bodies, the greasy hydrocarbon soot against the glass. The people. The never failing river of faces. The bodies. Vishram discovers a new emotion. It has the blue remembered familiarity of homesickness but is expressed through the terrible mundane squalor of the people that throng beneath these boulevards. Home nausea. Nostalgic horror.

"This is near the Sarkhand Roundabout, isn't it?" Vishram says in Hindi. "I'd like to see it."

The driver waggles his head and takes the next right.

"Where are we going?" Marianna Fusco asks.

"Somewhere to tell that constellation family of yours about," Vishram says.

Police barricades block the main road so the driver takes a way he knows through intestinally narrow back streets and turns out of them straight into a riot. He hits the brakes. A young male tumbles over the bonnet. He picks himself up, more shaken than damaged, a chubby post-teen with a wisp of a holy moustache, but the impact has rocked the car and its passengers. Instantly, the crowd's attention switches from the gaudy statue of Hanuman under his shady concrete chhatri to the car. Hands drum the hood, the roof, the doors. They bounce the limo on its springs. The crowd sees a big Merc, tinted windows, company flags, a thing allied to the forces that would demolish their sacred place and turn it into a metro station.

The driver slams the car into reverse, smokes rubber as he backs down the alley beneath the banners of laundry and rickety wooden balconies. Bricks lob through the air, crack off the metal work. Marianna Fusco gives a small cry as the windscreen suddenly stars into a white spider web. Steering by rear-view cam, the driver slots his car between two flanking bamboo scaffold towers. The young karsevaks chase the car, striking at it with lathis and calling curses on the faithless Ranas and their demonic Muslim spin-doctors. They wave the torn-off company flags. One petrol bomb in these alleys, and hundreds are dead, Vishram Ray thinks. But the driver navigates the maze to his point of entry, finds a momentary gap in the constant torrent of traffic, and throws his car backwards into it. Trucks buses mopeds slam to a halt. The driver handbrakes it. The holy boys follow them through the traffic, slipping between phatphats and Japanese pick-ups painted with Hindu iconography. Slipping, jogging, gaining. The driver raises his hands in desperation. Nothing to be done in this traffic. Glancing over his shoulder, Vishram can read their shirt-buttons. Then Marianna Fusco cries out *Oh Jesus God!* and the car slams to a halt hard enough for Vishram to jar the bridge of his nose off the back of the driver's seat. Through tears and stun he sees a steel demon drop out of the sky before him; Ravana the devourer, demon-lord, squatting on hydraulic-loaded titanium hams, ten blades spread like a fan. The tiny mantis-head looks right at him, unfolds a dentist's arsenal of sensor pods and probes. Then it leaps again. Vishram feels clawed toes rake the limo's roof. He whirls, looks out the back to see it land beside a bus stop. Traffic freezes, karsevaks scatter like goats. The thing stalks away down the street, quartering the boulevard with gatling pods. It wears the stars and bars on its carapace. A US combat robot.

"What the . . . ?" They've started a war while he was in immigration. The driver points to the street across the intersection to a street of neon shop fronts and glowing umbrellas where a man in dark, expensive clothing yells imprecations at the departing machine. Behind him are two fillets of Mercedes SUV. The man picks up lumps of circuitry and metal and shies them after the battle-bot. "I still don't . . ."

"Sahb," the driver says as he engages drive. "Have you been so long gone you have forgotten Varanasi?"

The journey to Marianna Fusco's hotel is in grim silence. She thanks him politely, the Rajput doorman salutes and lifts her bag, and she goes up the steps without a look back.

Not looking good for a follow-up fuck, then.

The battered limo turns into the gates between the motor parts shop and the IT school through the screen of ashok trees. At once he is in a different world. The first thing money buys in India is privacy. The street roar is hushed to a pulse. The insanity of his city is shut out.

The house staff has lit naphtha flares all along the drive to welcome the returned prodigal. Drummers greet Vishram Ray with a tattoo and escort the car, and there is the house, wide and proud and unbelievably white in the floods. Vishram finds uninvited tears in his eyes. When he was beneath its roof he had always been ashamed to acknowledge that he lived in a palace, cringing at its pillars and pediments and wide portico screened with honeysuckle and hibiscus, its bloody whiteness, its interior of swept marble and old quaint, pornographic wood carvings and ceilings painted in the Nepali style. A family of merchants had built it in the British days in a style to remind them of home. The

Shanker Mahal, they named it. Now that adolescent contempt, that embarrassment at being privileged, is swept away as he steps out and the house assails him with the old remembered smells of dust and neem trees and the musk of the rhododendrons and the faint reek of the sewage system that never really worked.

They await him on the steps. Old Shastri, on the lowest rung, already namasteing. Flanking him, the house staff, in two wings, the women to his left, the men to the right. Ram Das the venerable gardener is still there, an incredible age now but still zealous as ever, Vishram doesn't doubt, in his eternal war against the monkeys. On the middle rank, his brothers. Eldest Ramesh seems taller and thinner than ever, as if the gravity of the interstellar objects he studies is drawing him into the sky, spinning him into a rope of inquiry. Still no significant female. Even in Glasgow, Vishram heard Bharati diaspora rumours about weekend specials to Bangkok. Next, perfect brother, Govind. Perfect suit perfect wife perfect twin heirs Runu and Satish. Vishram sees the middle body fat piling around his chest. The stellar DiDi, former breakfast-tivi presenter and trophy bride, is at his side. At her side the aya cradles the latest line in the dynasty. A girl. How 2047. Vishram coos and chuckles little Priya but something about her gives him the idea that she's a Brahmin. Something primal, pheromonal, a shift in the body chemistry.

His mother holds the top step; superior in her deference, as Vishram always remembers her. A shadow among the pillars. His father is not present.

"Where's Dadaji?" Vishram asks.

"He will meet us tomorrow at the head office," is all his mother will say.

"Do you know what this is about?" Vishram asks Ramesh when the greetings and cryings and look-at-you-haven't-you-got-bigs? are done. Ramesh shakes his head as Shastri motions with a finger for a porter to carry Vishram's case up to his room. Vishram doesn't want to answer questions about the limo, so he begs jet lag and takes himself off to bed. He'd expected to be given his old room, but the porter guides him to a guest bedroom on the sunrise side of the house. Vishram is affronted at being treated as a stranger and sojourner. Then, as he settles his few things in the huge mahogany wardrobes and tallboys, he is glad not to have his childhood possessions watching him as he returns from his life beyond them. They would drag him back, revert him to teenage again. The old place never had air-conditioning worth a damn so he lies naked on the sheets, appalled by the heat, reading faces in the foliage of the painted ceiling, and listening to the rattle of monkey hands and feet in the vines outside his window. He lies on the edge of sleep, slipping towards unconsciousness and reawakening with a start as some half-forgotten sound breaks through from the city beyond. Conceding defeat, Vishram goes naked on to the iron balcony. The air and the perfume of the city of Siva powder his skin. Clusters of winking aircraft lights move over the hazy yellow skyline. The soldiers who fly in the night. He tries to imagine a war. Robot killing machines running through the alleys, titanium blades in all four hands, avatars of Kali. Aeai gunships piloted by warriors half a planet away coming in across the Ganga on strafing runs. Awadh's American allies fight in the modern manner, without a single soldier leaving home, without a single body bag. They kill from continents away. He fears that strange tableau he had seen enacted on the streets was prophecy. Between the water and the fundamentalists, the Ranas have run out of choices.

A crunch of gravel, a movement on the silver lawns. Ram Das appears from the moon shadows under the harsingars. Vishram freezes on his balcony. Another Western way he has slipped into: casual nakedness. Ram Das steps on to the shaved lawn, parts his dhoti, and takes a piss by the lazy moon of India, lolling on its side like a temple gandava. He cleans himself, then turns around and waggles his head slowly at Vishram, a salutation, a blessing. He goes on his way. A peacock shrieks.

Home at last.

PART TWO

SAT CHID EKAM BRAHMA

9

VISHRAM

Until thirty minutes ago, Vishram Ray had boasted that he had never owned a suit. He has always recognised that some day he might need one and that when he did he really would so he keeps a set of measurements with a family of Chinese tailors in Varanasi together with choice of fabric, cut, lining, and two shirts. He's wearing that suit now in his seat at the teak boardroom table of Ray Power. It arrived at the Shanker Mahal half an hour ago by bicycle courier. Vishram was still adjusting the collar and cuffs as the flotilla of cars arrived at the steps. Now he's on the twentieth floor of the Ray tower with Varanasi a smoggy brown stain at his feet, the Ganga a distant curl of sullied silver, and still no one will tell him what the hell this is about.

Those Chinese really understand fabric. The collar fit is perfect. He can hardly see the stitches.

The boardroom doors open. Corporate lawyers file in. Vishram Ray wonders what the collective noun is for corporate lawyers. A fleece? A fuckover? Last in line is Marianna Fusco. Vishram Ray can feel his mouth sag open. Marianna Fusco gives him the smallest of smiles, certainly less than you would expect from someone you (a) had first-class sex with and (b) embroiled in a street riot, and sits down opposite him. Under the teak table, Vishram flicks on his palmer and types invisible text.

WHAT THE HELL ARE YOU DOING HERE?

The staff open the double doors to now admit the board members.

I TOLD YOU IT WAS A FAMILY BUSINESS MATTER.

Marianna's message appears to Vishram to be hovering over her breasts. She's in that great and eminently practical suit.

But he's not so bad himself. The bankers and representatives from the credit unions and grameen banks take their seats. Many of the members from the rural micro-credit banks have never been so far off the ground in their lives. As Vishram coolly pours himself a water with his left hand while his right texts IS THIS A GAME? his father enters the room. He wears a simple round-collared suit, the length of the jacket his only concession to fashion, but he turns every head. There is a look on his face Vishram hasn't seen since he was a boy when his father was setting up the company, the determined serenity of a man certain he is doing right. Behind him is Shastri, his shadow.

Ranjit Ray goes to the head of the table. He doesn't take his seat. He salutes his board and guests. The big wooden room hums with tension. Vishram would give anything to make an entrance like that.

"Colleagues, partners, honoured guests, my dear family," Ranjit Ray begins. "Thank you all for coming today, many of you at considerable inconvenience and expense. Let me say at the outset that I would not have asked you to come if I did not feel it was a matter of the utmost importance to this company."

Ranjit Ray's voice is a soft, deep prayer that carries to every part of the big room without loss. Vishram recalls that he has never heard it raised.

"I am sixty-eight years old, three years past what Westerners consider in their business ethos the end of economically useful life. In India it is a time for reflection, for the contemplation of other paths that might have been taken, that yet might be taken." A sip of water.

"In the final year of my engineering degree at the Hindu University of Varanasi I realised that the laws of economics are subject to the laws of physics. The physical processes that govern this planet and the continued life upon it place as stringent an upper limit on economic growth as the speed of light does on our knowledge of the universe. I realised that I was not just an engineer, I was a Hindu engineer. From these understandings I concluded that if I was to use my abilities to help India become a strong and respected nation, I must do it in an Indian way. I must do it in a Hindu way."

He looks at his wife and sons.

"My family has heard this many times, I trust they'll forgive one more. I went on a year of pilgrimage. I followed bhakti and did puja at the seven sacred cities, I bathed in the holy rivers and sought the councils of swamis and sadhus. And of each of them, at each temple and holy site, I asked this same question."

How may this engineer lead the right life? Vishram says to himself. He has indeed heard this homily more times than he cares to remember: how this Hindu engineer used a crore of rupees from a micro-credit union to build a low-cost, no-maintenance domestic-scale carbon nanotube solar power generator. Fifty million units later, plus alcohol fuel refineries, biomass plants, wind farms, ocean current thermal generators, and an R&D division pushing Indian—*Hindu*—minds into the void of zero-point energy, Ray Power is one of Bharat's

—India's—leading companies. One that has done it the Indian way, sustainably, treading lightly on the earth, obeying the wheel. A company that steers resolutely around the maelstrom of the international markets. A company that commissions exciting new Indian architectural talent to build a corporate headquarters from sustainable wood and glass and still welcomes Dalits into its boardroom. It is a great and inspiring story, but Vishram's attention is wandering all over Marianna Fusco's stretch-brocaded breasts. A message appears cross them in cheeky lilac. PAY ATTENTION TO YOUR FATHER!

BAA BAA BLACK SHEEP he thumbs back.

PUNS ARE THE LOWEST FORM OF COMEDY, she returns.

WELL EXCUSE ME, I ALWAYS THOUGHT IT WAS SARCASM, he emblazons in quick-riposte blue across the lapels of his really fast suit. Which is how he almost misses the punch line.

"That is why I have decided it is time to once again take up that inquiry into how the right life may be lived."

Vishram Ray looks up, nerves electric.

"At midnight tonight, I will resign my directorship of Ray Power. I will give up my wealth and influence, my prestige and responsibilities. I will leave my house and family and once again take up the sadhu's staff and bowl."

The boardroom of Ray Power could not be any more quiet or still if it had been nerve gassed. Ranjit Ray smiles, trying to reassure. It doesn't work.

"Please understand that this is not a decision I undertake lightly. I have discussed this at length with my wife and she is in agreement with me. Shastri, my aide and help of more years than I care to remember, will be joining me on this journey, not as a servant, for all such distinctions end tonight, but as a fellow seeker after right life."

The shareholders are on their feet, shouting, demanding. A Dalit woman bellows in Vishram's ear about her clients, her sisters, but Vishram finds himself cool, detached, anchored to his seat by a sense of inevitability. It is as if he knew from the moment the ticket arrived on his Glasgow doorstep this would happen. Ranjit Ray quiets the board.

"My friends, please do not think I have abandoned you. The first requirement of the man who would follow the spiritual life is that he leaves the world responsibly. As you know, other corporations seek to buy this company but Ray Power is first and last a family business and I will not give it to alien and immoral systems of management."

Don't do it, Vishram thinks. Don't say it.

"Therefore, I am passing control of the company to my sons Ramesh, Govind, and Vishram." He turns to each of them, hands held out as if blessing. Ramesh looks freshly shot. His big veiny hands are flat on the table like flayed animals. Govind fluffs himself up and looks around the table, already dividing the room into allies and enemies. Vishram is numb, a player caught up in a script.

"I have appointed trusted advisors to guide you through the transitional period. I have put great trust in you. Please try to be worthy of it."

Marianna Fusco leans across the wide table, hand extended. A sheaf of ribbon-bound papers rests on the polished surface beside her. Vishram can see the dotted lines at the bottom of the page, awaiting his signatures.

"Congratulations, and welcome to Research and Development, Mr. Ray."

He takes the hand he remembers so firm and dry and soft around his dick.

Suddenly he knows this script.

"Lear," he breathes.

10

SHIV

Yogendra leaves the SUV in the middle of the street outside Musst. Police and thieves alike recognise a raja's parking space is where he leaves his motor. Yogendra opens the door for Shiv. Cycle rickshaws detour around him, bells jingling.

MUSST, feat. TALV announces the neon. Now everyone's got personalised aeai DJs and grooves to their own mix, clubs sell themselves by their barmen. It's too early in the week for the salary-men, wife hunting, but the girls are in. Shiv slips on to his stool. Yogendra takes the seat behind him. Shiv sets the flask of ovaries on the bar. The subsurface lighting turns it into some alien artefact in a Hollywood sci-fi movie. Barman Talv slides a glass dish of paan over the plane of fluorescent plastic. Shiv pops a pinch, rolls it round inside his cheek, lets the bhang percolate through him.

"Where's Priya?"

"Down the back."

Girls in knee boots and short skirts and cling-silk tops cluster around a table where the club polychrome begins. At the centre, haloed by cocktail glasses, is a ten-year-old boy.

"Fuck, Brahmins," Shiv says.

"Contrary to appearances, he is legal age," Talv says, pouring two glasses from a shaker that looks treacherously similar to Shiv's stainless steel prize.

"There's good men out there, give a woman everything she wants, good home, good prospects—she'd never have to work—good family, children, a place up the ladder, and they hang off that ten-year-old like a calf from a teat," Shiv says. "I'd shoot the lot of them. It's against nature." Yogendra helps himself to paan.

"That ten-year-old could buy and sell this place ten times over. And he'll be bouncing around long after you and me've gone to the ghats."

The cocktail is cool and blue and deep and chases the red paan into the deep dark places. Shiv scans Club Musst. None of his girls will catch his eye tonight. Those who aren't laughing with the Brahmin are fixed intently on the tabletop tivi.

"What got them so wrapped up?"

"Some fashion thing," Talv says. "They've brought this Russian model in, some nute, Yuri, something like that."

"Yuli," Yogendra says. His gums are scarlet from paan. The light is blue and the string of pearls he always wears knotted around his neck glows like souls. Red, white, blue. American grin. As long as Shiv has worked with him he has always worn those pearls.

"I'd shoot them, too," Shiv says. "Deviates. I mean Brahmins; okay, they fuck around with the genes, but they are men and women."

"I read the nutes are working on ways to get cloned," Talv says mildly. "They'd pay normal women to carry their kids."

"Now that is just plain disgusting," Shiv says and when he turns back to set down his empty glass there's a slip of paper on the luminous blue bar.

"What is this?"

"This is what they call a bill," Talv says.

"I beg your pardon? Since when have I paid for drinks in this establishment?"

Shiv unfolds the little docket, glances over the number. Double takes.

"No. What the fuck is this? Is my credit no good here? Is this what you're saying, Shiv Faraji, we don't trust him any more?"

The tivi girls look up at a raised voice, lit blue like devis. Talv sighs. Then Salman's there. He's the owner, he has connections Shiv doesn't. Shiv holds up the bar tab like a charge sheet.

"I was telling your star here . . ."

"I've been hearing things about your bankability."

"My friend, I have status all over this city."

Salman lays a cold finger on the cold canister.

"Your stock is no longer as ascendant as it used to be."

"Some fucker is undercutting me? I'll have his balls in dry ice . . ."

Salman shakes his head.

"This is a macroeconomic issue. Market forces, sir."

And Musst Club Bar goes into long zoom, so that its walls and corners seem to rush away from Shiv except the Brahmin's head, which is huge and inflated and rocking like a painted helium balloon at a festival, laughing at him like a rocking fool.

Some see the red haze. For Shiv it has always been blue. Deep, vibrant, intense blue. He snatches up the plate of paan, smashes it, pins Talv's hand to the bar-top, a long blade of glass poised over his thumb like a guillotine.

"Let's see him shake and make with no thumbs," Shiv hisses. "Bar. Star."

"Shiv; now," Salman says very slowly and remorsefully and Shiv knows that it's the hiss of the cobra, but it's blue, all blue, quivering blue. A hand on his shoulder. Yogendra.

"Okay," Shiv says, not looking at anyone or anything. He sets the sliver down, puts his hands up. "It's okay."

"I will overlook this," Salman says. "But I do expect payment, in full, sir. Thirty days. Standard business terms."

"Okay, there is something very wrong here," Shiv says, backing away. "I will find out what it is and I will be back for your apology."

He kicks over his bar stool but doesn't forget the body parts. At last, the girls are looking at him.

The Ayurvedic restaurant closes promptly at eight because its philosophy dictates you should eat no later. From the scene in the alley, Shiv guesses that it won't be opening again. There's a hire van, two pony carts, three delivery trikes, and a gaggle of pay-by-the-hour gundas running cardboard boxes in a chain out the door. Headwaiter Videsh, dismantling tables, barely looks up as Shiv and boy wonder storm in. Madam Ovary is in the office cherry-picking the filing cabinet. Shiv bangs the vacuum flask down on the battered metal.

"Going somewhere?"

"One of my laddies is on his way to your lodgings as we speak."

"I was taken away. On business. I have got one of these, you know?" Shiv flips out his palmer.

"Shiv, nonsecure communications. No."

Madam Ovary is a small, fat, almost globular Malayam and wears a greasy pigtail down to the small of her back that hasn't been released from its bonds in twenty years. She is Ayurvedic Mother to her laddies and plies them with tinctures and papers of powder. Those who believe credit her with genuine healing powers. Shiv gives his to Yogendra, who hawks them to tourists coming off the riverboats. Her restaurant has an international reputation, especially among Germans. The place is always full of pale Northern Euros with that gauntness of facial features you get from thirty days of constant gastro problems.

Shiv says, "Explain then: you're firing everything into handcarts and all of a sudden this"—his cool, stainless flask—"has got leprosy in it."

Madame Ovary consigns a few balance sheets to her plastic briefcase. No leather, no animal produce at all. Human products for human consumption, that is Ayurvedically sound. That includes embryonic stem cell therapy.

"What do you know about nonblastular stem cell technology?"

"Same as our normal foetal stem cell technique except they can use any cell in the body to grow spare parts and not embryos. Only they can't get it to work."

"It's been working perfectly since eleven AM Eastern US Standard Time. What you have in there isn't even worth the flask."

Shiv sees again the body caught by the stream. He sees the woman's sari bubble up behind her. He sees her on the scrubbed enamel tabletop in the All-Asia Beauty plastic surgery clinic, open under the lights. Shiv hates waste. He especially hates it when an inexperienced surgeon turns a routine egg-harvest into a bloodbath.

"There're always going to be people can't afford American technology. This is Bharat . . ."

"Laddie, do you know the first rule of business? Know when to cut your losses. My overheads are enormous: doctors, couriers, policemen, customs officials, politicians, city councillors, all with their hands out. The crash is coming. I do not intend to be underneath it."

"Where are you going?" Shiv asks.

"I'm certainly not telling you. If you've any sense, you'll have diversified your assets long before now."

Shiv has never had that luxury. At every stage of his journey from Chandi Basti to this Ayurvedic restaurant, there was only ever one choice to make. Morality was for those who lived somewhere else than the basti. There had been one choice that night he raided the pharmacy. Any badmash could get a gun in the years of the Separation, but even then Shiv Faraji had been a man of style. A stylist uses a stolen Nissan SUV, rammed through the pharmacy steel shutter. His sister had recovered from the tuberculosis. The stolen antibiotics had saved her life. He had done what his father would not, could not. He had shown them what a man of courage and determination could achieve. He had not touched a paisa of the pharmacist's money. A raja takes only what he needs. He had been twelve. Two years younger than his lieutenant Yogendra. Every step, the only step. It's the same now the ovaries have come apart in his fingers. An action will present itself to him. He will take it. It will be the only action he can take. The one thing he will not do is run. This is his city.

Madam Ovary snaps shut her valise.

"Make yourself useful. Give me your lighter."

It's an old US Army model from the time they went into Pakistan. The days when they sent soldiers who smoked rather than machines. Madam Ovary applies fire. The papers catch and burn.

"I'm done here now," she says. "Thank you for your work. I wish you well, but do not try to contact me, ever. We will not meet again, so good-bye for this life."

In the car Shiv slaps on the radio. Jabber. All these DJs do: jabber, as if the only way to tell them from aeais is by the constant flow of garbage from their mouths. Like the Ganga; this constant flow of shit. You're a DJ, you play music. Music people want to hear, that makes them feel good or think of someone special or cry.

He leans against the window. By the dash glow he sees his face in half profile, ghosted over the people in the street. But it is as if every one of those people over whom his image falls takes ownership of part of him.

Fucking jabber.

"Where are you taking me, boy?"

"Fighting."

He's right. There's nowhere else to go where it comes down. But Shiv doesn't like the boy being that close, watching, observing, second-guessing.

Fight! Fight! is thumping. Shiv walks down the shallow steps and straightens his cuffs and the smell of blood and money and raw wood and the adrenaline kicks in under his breastbone. He loves this place above all places on earth. He checks the clientele. Some new faces. That girl, up by the rail in the balcony, the one with the Persian nose, trying to look so cool. Shiv catches her eye. She holds him, long enough. Some other night. Now the barker is calling the next bout and he goes down to the bookies' table. Down on Sonarpur Road fire engines are putting out a restaurant blaze started in a filing cabinet while something with the anatomy of a ten-year-old boy and appetites twice that is sliding chubby fingers towards the shakti yoni of his girl and a woman dead without profit drifts in the Ganga flow towards moksha, but here are people and movement and light and death and chance and fear and a girl parading a superb silver tabby battle cat around a sand ring. Shiv flips his crocodile wallet out of his jacket, fans notes, and lays them out on the table. Blue. He's still seeing that blue.

"One lakh rupees," Bachchan says. Beyond which there are no more, nor hope of more. Bachchan's scribe counts the cash and writes the docket. Shiv takes his place by the pit and the barker calls *fight! fight!* The crowd roars and rises and Shiv with them, pressing against the wooden rail to hide his hard on. Then he is out of the deep blue with the silver tabby microsabre meat on the sand and his one hundred thousand notes scraped into the sattaman's leather satchel. He wants to laugh. He realises the truth of the sadhus: there is blessing in having nothing.

In the car the laughter breaks out of him. Shiv beats his head against the window again and again. Tears run down his face. Finally he can breathe. Finally he can talk.

"Take me to Murfi's," Shiv orders. He is ravenously hungry now.

"What with?"

"There's change in the glovebox."

Tea Lane embraces its smokes and miasmas under domed umbrellas. They serve no meteorological purpose: Murfi claims his protects him from moonlight, which he feels to be baleful. Murfi has many claims, not the least of which is his name. Irish, he says. Irish as Sadhu Patrick.

Tea Lane has grown up to serve the men who build Ranapur. Behind the ranks of hot food and spice and fruit sellers, the original chai-houses open their wooden shutters on to the street and spill their tin tables and folding chairs on to the road. Over the gentle roar of gas burners and wind-up radios pushing Hindi Hits, a never-ending surf of soapi dialogue plays from hundreds of wall-screen televisions. Ten thousand calendars of soapi goddesses hang from drawing pins.

Shiv leans out the window counting loose change into Murfi's monkey hand.

"And some of those pizza pakoras for him." Shiv regards these as he would monkey turd pakora, but Yogendra has this idea they are the epitome of Western snack cool. "Murfiji, you say you pakora anything. Try these."

Murfi unscrews the top of the flask, waves away the clouds of dry ice, tries to scry inside.

"Eh, what you got in there?"

Shiv tells him. Murfi screws up his face, thrusts the flask back at Shiv.

"No, you keep 'em. You never know someone may get the taste."

It is no comment on Murfi's cooking but between one bite and the next, Shiv's appetite vanishes. The people are all looking in the same direction. Behind Shiv. Shiv drops his newspaper of fried things. Street dogs descend on it. He snatches Yogendra's dung from him.

"Leave that shit and get me away."

Yogendra boots the pedal, wheel-spins into the suddenly empty street as something comes down on the roof so hard it bows the Merc to the axles. A shock absorber detonates like a grenade, there's a flash of blue and a smell of burning electrics. The car rocks on its remaining three suspension points. Something moves up there. Yogendra flogs and flogs and flogs the engine but it will not catch.

"Out," Shiv commands as the blade comes down through the roof. It is long, scimitar curved, serrated, bright as a surgeon's steel and stabs the Merc from roof plate to transmission tunnel. As Shiv and Yogendra tumble out into Tea Lane, it rips forward and guts pressed steel like a sacrificial kid.

Now Shiv can see what's hit the roof of his sixty million rupees of German trash metal and though it is the absolute death of him, he's as paralysed by the sheer spectacle as any of the frozen people on Tea Lane. The windscreen shatters as the fighting robot's blade completes the first pass. The lower grasping arms seize the raw edges and peel the roof open. The blunt phallus of the E-M gun seeks Shiv out on the street, fixes him with its monocular stare. That can't hurt him. Shiv is transfixed by the big blade as it withdraws from the wreck formerly known as a Series 7 Mercedes and swivels into horizontal slash. The fighting machine rises up on its legs and steps towards him. It still has the serial number and little stars and stripes on its side but Shiv knows that the pilot will not be some late-teen with game-boy reactions and a methamphetamine habit wired twenty levels under Plains States America. This will be someone in the back of that panel van down by the twenty-four-hour cinema, smoking a bidi and weaving his hands through cyberspace in the dance of Kali. Someone who knows him.

Shiv does not try to run. These things can hit one hundred kph in a gallop and once they have the scent of your DNA, that blade will cut through any obstacle until it meets the soft flesh of your belly. The Urban Combat Robot rears over him. The vile little mantis head lowers, sensor rigs swivelling. Now Shiv relaxes. This is a show for the street.

"Mr. Faraji." Shiv almost laughs. "For your information; as of this moment, all debts and fiscal encumbrances owed to Mr. Bachchan have been assigned to Ahimsa Collections Agency."

"Bachchan is calling in my account?" Shiv shouts, looking at the remains of his last vestige of value, gutted on the street, bleeding alcofuel.

"That is correct, Mr. Faraji," the hunter-killer robot says. "Your account with Bachchan Betting currently stands at eighteen million rupees. You have one week from today to settle this account or action for recovery will ensue."

The machine spins on its hind heels, gathers itself, and leaps over the tea-vendors, cows, and hookers towards the intersection

"Hey!" Shiv calls after it. "What's wrong with an invoice?" He picks up shards and orts of German precision engineering and shies them after the debt collector.

11

LISA, LULL

"So, Ms. Durnau, your best idea," Thomas Lull said across the wide desk with her CV and presentation file on it and beyond the picture window, wider Kansas in the hottest June this century. "Where were you when it came to you?"

(She flashbacks to this, twenty-two hours out from ISS, twenty-six to Darnley 285, stuffed full of flight drugs and zipped up in a bag vel-croed to the wall of the transfer pod so she doesn't get in the way of Captain Pilot Beth who has a slightly blocked right nostril and whose breath whistles rhythmically until it is the biggest thing in Lisa Durnau's universe.)

No one had known a June like it; the airport staff, the car rental girl, the university security man she asked for directions. This was more than hot water off the coast of Peru or the dying thrash of the Gulf Stream. Climatology had run into the white zone where nothing could be predicted any more. Thomas Lull had flipped through her CV, glanced at the first page of her presentation and when she flashed up the first slide, stopped her with that curve-ball question.

Lisa Durnau can still recall the surge of anger. She pressed her hands palm-down on to the thighs of her good pant suit to push the rage down. When she lifted them she had left two palm-shaped sweat marks like warnings against the evil eye.

"Professor Lull, I'm trying to be professional here and I think you owe me the professional courtesy of your attention."

She could have stayed in Oxford. She had been happy in Oxford. Carl Walker would have sold body parts to keep her at Keble. Better doctorates than hers had returned shattered from this cow town where the schools by law still taught Intelligent Design. If the world's pre-eminent centre for cyberlife research sat on a hill in the Bible Belt, Lisa Durnau would come to that hill. She had rejected her father's Christian universe before he and her mother separated, but Presbyterian stubbornness and self-reliance were twined around her DNA. She would not let this man shake her. He said, "You can earn my attention by answering my question. I want to know about your inspiration. Those moments when it hit you like lightning. Those moments when you ran for seventy hours on coffee and Dexedrine because if you let go of it, even for an instant, you'd lose it. The moments when it came out of the void and was all there, perfect and entire. I want to know how and when and where it hit you. Science is creation. Nothing else interests me."

"Okay," Lisa Durnau said. "It was the women's toilet in Paddington Station in London, England."

Professor Thomas Lull beamed and settled back in his chair.

The Cognitive Cosmology group met twice monthly in Stephen Sanger's office at Imperial College London. It was one of those things that Lisa Durnau knew she should get round to some time but probably never would, like balancing her cheque book or having children. Carl Walker would cc. her its notes and abstracts. It was intellectually thrilling and she had no doubt that membership of the group would advance her name and career, but theirs was a quantum informational approach and Lisa's thoughts moved in topological curves. Then the bimonthly reports began to stray from quantum informational judder into speculation that Artificial Intelligence could indeed be a parallel universe mapped out in computing code as Oxford's cloisters and choristers were in elementary particles and DNA. This was her bailiwick. She resisted for a month, then Carl Walker took her out for a Friday lunch that ended up in a Jamaican restaurant at midnight drinking Triple-X Guinness and swaying to the towers of dub. Two days later she was in a fifth-floor conference room breakfasting on chocolate croissants and smiling too much at the country's leading thinkers on the place of mind in the structure of the universe.

Everyone recharged coffee cups and the discourse began. The speed of debate left Lisa slipstreamed and breathless. The transcripts gave no indication of the breadth and diversity of discussion. She felt like a fat kid at a basketball match, clutching and darting too late, too slow. By the time Lisa got to speak she was responding to things said three ideas ago and the climate of the conversation had raced on. The sun moved across Hyde Park and Lisa Durnau felt herself settling into despair. They were fast and quick and dazzling and they were wrong wrong wrong but she couldn't get a word in to tell them. They were already becoming bored with the subject. They had milked it for what they thought it could yield and were moving on. She was going to lose it. Unless she told them. Unless she spoke now. Her right forearm lay flat on the oak table. She slowly raised her hand to the vertical. Every eye followed it. There was a sudden, terrible hush.

"Excuse me," Lisa Durnau said. "Can I say something here? I think you're wrong." Then she told them about the idea that made life, mind, and intelligence emerge from the underlying properties of the universe as mechanically as physical forces and matter. That CyberEarth was a model of another universe that could exist in the polyverse, a universe where mind was not an emergent phenomenon but a fundamental like the Fine Structure constant, like Omega, like dimensionality. A universe that *thought*. Like God, she said and as she said those words she saw the gaps and the flaws and the bits she hadn't thought through and she knew that every face around the table saw them, too. She could hear her own voice, hectoring, so so certain, so so sure she had all the answers at twenty-four. She tailed off into an apologetic mumble.

"Thank you for that," Stephen Sanger said. "There are a lot of interesting ideas in there . . ."

They did not even let him finish his sentence. Chris Drapier from the Level Three Artificial Intelligence Unit at Cambridge sprang first. He had been the rudest and loudest and most pedantic and Lisa had caught him trying to size up her ass in the queue for the coffee flask. There was no reason to invoke some *deus ex machina* argument when quantum computation had the whole thing sewn up pretty nicely. This was vitalism—no, this was *mysticism*. Next up was Vicki McAndrews from Imperial. She picked a loose theoretical thread in her modelling, tugged it, and the whole edifice unravelled. Lisa didn't have a topological model of the space or even a mechanism for describing this universe that thought. All Lisa could hear was that high-pitched whine behind her eyes that is the sound when you want to cry but must not. She sat, annihilated among the coffee cups and chocolate croissant smears. She knew nothing. She had no talent. She was arrogant and stupid and shot her mouth off when any sensible postgrad would have sat and nodded and kept everyone's coffee cups filled and the cookies coming round. Her star was at its absolute nadir. Stephen Sanger passed some encouragement as Lisa crept out, but she was destroyed. She cried her way back across Hyde Park, up through Bayswater to Paddington Station. She downed a half bottle of dessert wine in the station restaurant as that seemed the menu item that would get her whacked really quickly. She sat at her table shuddering with shame and tears and the certainty that her career was over, she could not do this thing, she didn't know what they meant. Her bladder called ten minutes before her train. She sat in the cubicle, jeans around her knees, trying not to sob out loud because the acoustics of London station toilets would take it and amplify it so everyone could hear.

And then she saw it. She could not say what it was she saw, staring at the cubicle door, there was no shape, no form, no words or theorems. But it was there, whole and unimaginably beautiful. It was simple. It was so simple. Lisa Durnau burst from the cubicle, rushed to the Paperchase store, bought a pad and a big marker. Then she ran for her train. She never made it. Somewhere between the fifth and sixth carriages, it hit her like lightning. She knew exactly what she had to do. She knelt sobbing on the platform while her shaking hands tried to jam down equations. Ideas poured through her. She was hardwired to the cosmos. The evening shift detoured around her, not staring. It's all right, she wanted to say. It's so all right.

M-Star Theory. It was there all along, right in front of her. How had she not seen it? Eleven dimensions folded into a set of Calabi-Yau shapes, three extended, one time-like, seven curled up at Planck length. But the handles, the holes in the shapes, dictated the winding energies of the superstrings, and thus the harmonics that were the fundamental physical properties. All she had to do was model CyberEarth as a Calabai-Yau space and show its equivalence to a physical possibility in M-Star theory. It was all in the structure. Out there was a universe with its onboard computer built in. Minds were part of the fabric of reality there, not shelled in evolved carbon as they were in this bubble of the polyverse. Simple. So simple.

She cried with joy all the way home in the train. A young French tourist couple sat across the table, nervously touching every time Lisa shuddered to a new attack of bliss. Joy bursts would send her wandering out of her room and through Oxford in the week she wrote up her insights. Every building, every street, every shop and person filled her with fierce delight at life and humanity. She was in love with every last thing. Carl Walker had flicked through the draft, grin growing wider with every page. Finally he said, "You've got them. Fuckers."

Sitting in Thomas Lull's over-air-conditioned office, Lisa Durnau could still catch the emotional afterglow of that outburst, like the microwave echo of the fires of the big bang. Thomas Lull swivelled his chair, leaned towards her.

"Okay," he said. "Well, two things you should know about this place. It's got a fucking awful climate, but the people are mighty friendly. Be polite to them. You may need them."

For Thomas Lull's amusement today, Dr. Darius Ghotse has a set of recordings of the English comedy classic "It's That Man Again" in the boot of the tricycle that he labours along the sand tracks of Thekkady. He is anticipating slipping the file into Professor Lull's machine and the plummy voice blaring out the signature tune. "One hundred and five years old!" he will say. "When the bombs were falling on London, this was what they were listening to in their underground railway tunnels!"

Dr. Ghotse collects antique radio programmes. Most days he calls around for breakfast with Thomas Lull on his boat and they sit under the palm-thatch awning to sip chai and listen to the alien humour of the Goons or the hyperreal comedy of Chris Morris's *Blue Jam*. Dr. Ghotse has a particular fondness for BBC Radio. He is a widower and former paediatrician but in his heart of hearts, he is an Englishman. He wishes Thomas Lull could understand cricket. He could then share his classic Aggers and Johnners Test commentaries with him.

He rattles down the rutted lane that runs beside the backwater, kicking at chickens and insolent dogs. Without braking, he swerves the aged red trike off the track, up the gangplank, and on to a long, mat-roofed kettuvallam. It is a manoeuvre he has performed many times. It has never yet ended him in the water.

Thomas Lull has Tantric symbols painted on his coconut thatch and a name on the hull in white: *Salve Vagina*. They offend local Christians mightily. The priest has informed him thus. Thomas Lull counterinformed him that he (priest) could criticise him (Lull) when he could do so in as good Latin as his boat title. A small high-power satellite dish is gaffer-taped to the highest point of the sloped roof-mats. An alcohol generator purrs in the stern.

"Professor Lull, Professor Lull." Dr. Ghotse ducks under the low eave, fileplayer held high. As usual, the houseboat smells of incense, alcohol, and stale cooking. A Schubert quintet plays, mid-volume. "Professor Lull?"

Dr. Ghotse finds Thomas Lull in his small, neat bedroom that is like a wooden shell. His shirts and shorts and socks are laid out on pristine cotton. He folds his T-shirts the proper way, sides to the middle, then triple-crease. A lifetime spent among suitcases has made this second nature.

"What has happened?" Dr. Ghotse asks.

"Time to move on," Thomas Lull says.

"A woman, then?" Dr. Ghotse asks. Thomas Lull's appetite for, and success with, the girlis from the beach circuit has always baffled him. Men should be self-contained in later life, without attachments.

"You could say. I met her last night at the club. She had an asthma attack. I saved her. There's always someone frying their coronary arteries on salbutamol. I offered to teach her some Buteyko tricks and she turned round and said, I will see you tomorrow, Professor Lull. She knew my name, Darius. Time to go."

When Dr. Ghotse met Thomas Lull, Lull had been working in an old record shop, a beach bum among the ancient compact discs and vinyls. Dr. Ghotse had been a recently bereaved pensioner, chipping away at his grief laugh by antique laugh. He found a kindred soul in this sardonic American. Afternoons passed in conversation, recordings shared. But it was still three months before Dr. Ghotse invited the man from the record shop for afternoon tea. Five visits later, when the afternoon tea turned into evening gin watching the astonishing sunsets behind the palms,

Thomas Lull confided his true identity. At first Dr. Ghotse felt sullied, that the man at the record shop he had got to know was an effigy of lies. Then he felt burdened: he did not wish to be the receptor of this man's loss and rage. Then he felt privileged; owner of a world-class secret that could have netted him a fortune from the news channels. He had been entrusted. In the end, he realised that he had approached Thomas Lull with the same agenda, for someone to entrust and listen.

Dr. Ghotse slips the file player into his jacket pocket. No ITMA today. Or any other day, it seems. Thomas Lull picks up the hardback copy of Blake that has sat beside every bed he has ever made home. He weighs it in his hands, then puts it into the case.

"Come on, I've coffee on the go."

The rear of the boat opens in an impromptu veranda, sheltered by the ubiquitous coir matting. Dr. Ghotse lets Thomas Lull pour two coffees, which he does not much like, and follows him out to the two accustomed seats. Swimming kids splash in water two degrees lighter and cooler than the coffee.

"So," Dr. Ghotse says. "Where you will go?"

"South," Thomas Lull says. Until he said it he hadn't an idea of a destination. From the day he had moored the old rice-kettuvallam to the backwater shore, Thomas Lull has made it clear he was only here until the wind blew him on. The wind blew, the palms beat, the clouds passed and dropped no rain, and Thomas Lull remained. He had come to love the boat, the sense of beachcombing rootlessness that would never have to prove itself. But she knew his name. "Lanka, maybe."

"Island of demons," Dr. Ghotse says.

"Island of beach bars," Thomas Lull says. Schubert reaches his allotted end. The waterkids dive and splash, drops clinging to their dark grinning faces. But the idea is in his head now and will not leave. "Maybe even get a boat over to Malaysia or Indonesia. There're islands there where no one will ever know your face. I could open a nice little dive school. Yeah. I could do that . . . Hell, I don't know."

He turns. Dr. Ghotse feels it too. Living on water makes you as sensitive to vibrations as a shark. *Salve Vagina* rocks subtly to a tread on the gangplank. Someone has come aboard. The kettuvallam shifts as a body moves through it.

"Hello? It is very dark in here." Aj ducks out from under the coir awning on to the rear deck. She is dressed in the same loose, flowing grey of the night before. Her tilak is even more prominent in the daylight. "I'm sorry, Dr. Ghotse is with you, I can come back later . . ."

Say it, Thomas Lull thinks. Her gods have given you this one chance, send her away and disappear and never look back. But she knew his name without meeting him, and she knows Dr. Ghotse's name and Thomas Lull has never been able to walk away from a mystery.

"No no, you stay, there's coffee."

She is one of those people whose smile transforms their entire face. She claps her hands in small delight.

"I'd love to, thank you."

He's lost now.

The hour clicks over to thirty and Lisa Durnau bubbles up from deep memory. Space, she decides, is the dimension of the stoned.

"Hey," she croaks. "Any chance of some water?" Her muscles are beginning to twist and wither.

"Tube to your right," Pilot Captain Beth says without looking up from her board. Lisa cranes round to suck warm, stale distilled water. The woman pilot's men friends back on the station are chattering and flirting. They're never done talking and flirting. Lisa wonders if they ever get round to anything, or are they so frail and attenuated that anything approaching a fuck would snap them in two? New memory steals up on Lisa.

She was back in Oxford again, running. It was a city she loved to run in. Oxford was generous with paths and green spaces and the students had a culture of physical activity. It was an old route from her

Keble time, along the canal path, through the meadows of Christ Church, up Bear Lane on to the High and then dodge pedestrians to the gate of All Souls and through on to Parks Road. It was good, physically secure, familiar to the foot. Today she turned right past the back of Merton through the Botanic gardens to Magdalen where the conference was being held. Oxford wore summer well. Groups of students were encamped on the grass. The flat thump and yell of soccer carried over the field, a sound she missed at KU. She missed the light also, that peculiar English gold of early evening with its promise of seductive night. Set in her evening were a shower, a quick squint at the completely unsuspected mass extinction in Alterre's marine biosphere, and dinner at High Table, a formal thing of frocks and jackets to conclude the conference. Much better to be out in the streets and people places with the gold light moth-soft against bare skin.

Lull was waiting in her room.

"See you, L. Durnau," he said. "See you in those ridiculous, clingy little lycra shorts and that tiny tiny top and your bottle of water in your hand." He stepped towards her. She was glossy and stinking with woman sweat. "I am going to take those ridiculous little shorts right off of you."

He seized two fistfuls of elastic waistband and jerked down shorts and panties. Lisa Durnau gave a small cry. In one motion she peeled off her running top, kicked off her shoes, and jumped him, legs around waist. Locked together, they reeled back into the shower. While he struggled with his clothing and cursed his clinging socks, she showered down. He barged in, pinned her against the tiled wall. Lisa swivelled her hips, wrapped her legs around him again, trying to find his cock with her vulva. Lull took a step back, pushed her gently away. Lisa Durnau flipped back into a handstand, locked her legs around his torso. Thomas Lull bent down, went in with the tongue. Half drowned, half ecstatic, Lisa wanted to scream but fought it. More enjoyable to fight it, half asphyxiated, inverted, drowning. Then she pinned Lull again with her thighs and he took her dripping and wrapped round him, threw her on to her bed, and fucked her with the quad bells ringing curfew.

At High Table she sat next to a Danish postgrad, starry eyed at actually talking to an originator of the Alterre project. At the centre of the table Thomas Lull debated the social Darwinism of geneline therapy with the Master. Other than glancing up at his words, "kill the Brahmins now, while there aren't that many of them," Lisa did not acknowledge him. Those were the rules. It was a thing of conferences. It had begun at one, it found its fullest expression at them. When it came to its allotted end, the rules and terms of disengagement would be drawn up between conference items. Until then, the sex was glorious.

Lisa Durnau had always thought of sex as something that was all right for other people but was never part of her lifescript. It wasn't that fantastic. She could live pretty happily without it. Then, with the most unexpected of people, in the most inconvenient relationship, she discovered a sexuality where she could bring her own natural athleticism. Here was a partner who liked her sweaty and salt-flavoured in her beloved running gear, who liked it *al fresco* and *al dente* and seasoned with the things she had locked up in her libido for almost twenty years. Pastor Durnau's sporty daughter didn't do things like play-rape and Tantra. At the time her confidante was her sister Claire in Santa Barbara. They spent evenings on the phone going into all the dirty details, whooping with laughter. A married man. And her boss. Claire's theory was because the relationship was so illicit, so secret, Lisa could unfold her own fantasy.

It had begun in Paris in the departure lounge at Charles de Gaulle Terminal 4. The flight to O'Hare was delayed. A fault in Brussels air traffic control had backed up planes as far out as the East Coast. BAA142 was on the board with a four-hour delay. Lisa and Lull had come off an intellectually gruelling week defending the Lullite argument that real and virtual were meaningless chauvinisms against heavy attack from a cadre of French neorealists. By now Lisa Durnau just wanted to climb her porch steps and check if Mr. Cheknavorian next door had watered the herbs. The board clicked over to six hours delay. Lisa groaned. She had done the e-mail. She had updated her finances. She had looked in on Alterre, going through a quiescent phase between bursts of punctuated evolution. It was three o'clock in the morning and in the boredom and the tiredness and the dislocation of the limbo of the brightly lit lounge between nations, Lisa Durnau leaned her head against Thomas Lull's shoulder. She felt his body move against hers and she was kissing him. Next thing they were sneaking into the airport showers, with the attendant handing them two towels and whispering *vive le sport*.

She liked to be round Thomas Lull. He was fun, he could talk, he had a sense of humour. They had things in common; values, beliefs. Movies, books. Food; the legendary Mexican Friday lunches. All that was a long way from fucking doggie style on the wet tiles of a Terminal 4 shower cubicle, but in a sense not so far. Where else does love start but next door? You fancy what you see every day. The boy across the fence. The water-cooler colleague. The opposite-sex friend you've always been especially close to. She knew she had always felt something for Thomas Lull; she had just never been able to give it a name or an action until exhaustion and frustration and dislocation took her out of her Lisa Durnau-ness.

He'd had them before. She knew all the names and many of the faces. He'd told her about them when the others went back to their partners and families and it was just the two of them with the jug of margarita and the oil lamps burning down. Never student flings, his wife was too well known on campus. Usually one nighters on the conference circuit, once an e-mail affair with a woman writer from Sausalito. And now she was a notch on the bedpost. Where it would end she could not say. But they still kept the thing about the showers.

After the dinner and the drinks reception they extricated themselves from the knot of conversation and headed over the Cherwell bridges to the cheaper end of town. Here were student bars that had not succumbed to corporatisation. One pint turned into two, then three because they had six guest real ales.

Halfway down the fourth he stopped and said, "L. Durnau." She loved his name for her. "If anything should happen to me, I don't know what, whatever happens when people say, 'should something happen': would you look after Alterre?"

"Jesus, Lull." Her name for him. Lull and L. Durnau. Too many Ls and Us. "Are you expecting something? You haven't got . . . anything?"

"No no no. Just, looking ahead, you never know. I could trust you to look after it right. Stop them sticking fucking Coke banners on the clouds."

They never made it through the rest of the guest ales. As they walked back to the halls through the warm, noisy night, Lisa Durnau said, "I will, yes. If you can swing the faculty, I will look after Alterre."

Two days later they came in to Kansas City on the last flight of the night and the staff closed up the airport behind them. It was only jet lag that kept Lisa Durnau awake on the drive to the university. She dropped Thomas Lull at his sprawling green place out in the burbs.

"See ya," she whispered. She knew better than to expect a kiss even at three in the morning. By the time she got up her steps and through her screen door and dumped her bag in the hall the accumulated body-shock rolled over her like a semi. She aimed herself for the big bed. Her palmer called. She thought about not answering it. Lull.

"Could you come over? Something's happened."

She had never, ever heard his voice sound like that before. Terrified, she drove through the greying predawn. At every intersection her imagination cranked up a new level of dreads and possibilities but back of them all was the master fear; they had been found out. The lights were all on and the doors stood open.

"Hello the house?"

"In here."

He sat on the old rollback leather sofa she knew from faculty barbecues and Sunday sports days. It and two tall bookcases were the only pieces of furniture in the room. The rest had been stripped. The floor was bare, the walls carried picture-hooks like hanging Spanish question marks.

"Even the cats," Thomas Lull said. "Right down to the toy mice. Can you believe it? Toy mice. You should see the den. She took her time over that one. She went through every single book and disk and file. I suppose it's not so much losing a wife as getting rid of a collection of Italian opera favourites."

"Had you?"

"Any idea? No. I walked in and all was as you see it. There was this." He held up a piece of paper. "The usual stuff, hadn't been working, sorry, but it was the only way. Don't try to get in touch. You know, she has the gumption to get up and lift everything without a word of warning, but when it comes to the fond farewell, she comes out with every fucking cliché in the book. That is so her. That is so her."

He was shaking now.

"Thomas. Come on, you can't stay here. Come on back to mine."

He looked puzzled then nodded.

"Yes, thank you, yes."

Lisa picked up his bag as she steered him to her car. He suddenly seemed very old and uncertain. At her house she made him hot tea which he drank while she made up the spare bed, out of sensitivity.

"Would you mind?" Thomas Lull asked. "Could I come in with you? I don't want to be on my own."

He lay with his back to Lisa Durnau, folded in on himself. Photo-sharp images of the desecrated room and Lull tiny as a boy on his big man's sofa startled Lisa awake each time she approached the drop into sleep. In the end she did sleep, as the grey of predawn filled up her big bedroom.

Five days later, after everyone telling him she was a cow and how well he was doing and he would get over it and he would be happy again and there's always your work/friends/self, Thomas Lull walked out of the worlds real and virtual without a word, without a warning. Lisa Durnau never saw him again.

"You'll forgive me, but this seems a somewhat unorthodox way of curing asthma," says Dr. Ghotse. Aj's face is red, her eyes bulge, her fingers twitch. Her tilak seems to throb.

"Couple of seconds longer," Thomas Lull says. He waits until she can take no more, and one second beyond. "Okay, and in." Aj opens her mouth in an ecstatic, whooping inhalation. Thomas Lull clamps his hand over it. "Through the nose. Always through the nose. Remember, the nose for breathing, the mouth for talking."

He removes his hand, watches the slow belling out of her little round belly.

"Would it not be simpler taking medication?" Dr. Ghotse opines. He holds a little coffee cup very delicately in his two hands.

"The whole point of this method," says Thomas Lull, "is that you don't need medication, ever again. And hold."

Dr. Ghotse studies Aj as she again empties her lungs in a long, whistling exhalation through her nostrils and holds.

"This is very like a pranayama technique."

"It's Russian; from the days when they had no money to buy anti-asthma drugs. Okay, and out." Thomas Lull watches Aj exhale. "And hold again. It's a very simple theory if you accept that everything you've been taught about how to breathe is dead wrong. According to Dr. Buteyko, oxygen is poison. We rust from the moment we're born. Asthma is your body's reaction to try to stop you taking in this poison gas. But we go around like big whales with our mouths open taking great searing lungfuls of O_2 and tell ourselves it's doing us good. The Buteyko method is simply balancing your O_2 and your CO_2, and if that means you have to starve your lungs of oxygen to build up a healthy supply of carbon dioxide, then you do what Aj here is doing. And in." Aj, face pale, throws her head back and expands her belly as she inhales. "Okay, breathe normally, but through the nose. If you feel panicky, do a couple of rounds of breath retention, but don't open your mouth. The nose, always the nose."

"It seems suspiciously simple," Dr. Ghotse says.

"The best ideas are always the simplest," Thomas Lull says, the Barnum of breathology.

After he has seen Dr. Ghotse creaking off on his tricycle, Thomas Lull walks Aj back to her hotel. Trucks and Maruti micro-buses roll along the straight white road tootling their multiple horns. Thomas Lull raises a hand to the drivers he recognises. He should not be here. He should have sent her off with a wave and a smile and when she was out of sight taken his bag straight to the bus station. And why does he say, "You should come back tomorrow for another session. It takes a while to get the technique right."

"I don't think so, Professor Lull."

"Why?"

"I do not think you will be here. I saw the case on your bed, I think you will be leaving today."

"What makes you think that?"

"Because I found you."

Thomas Lull says nothing. He thinks, can you read my mind? A dug-out carrying neatly dressed schoolchildren crosses the backwater to the landing, alcofuel engine burbling.

"I think you want to know how I found you," Aj says mildly.

"You do?"

"Yes, because it would always have been easier for you to leave, but you are still here." She stops, head following a dagger-billed, wild-eyed bird that glides down from the pastel blue Church of St. Thomas through the palms, their trunks banded red and white to warn traffic, to settle at the edge of a raft of copra husks softening in the water. "Paddy-bird, Indian pond-heron, *Ardeola greyii*," she says, as if hearing the words for the first time. "Hm." She moves on.

"You obviously want me to ask," says Thomas Lull.

"If that is a question, the answer is, I saw you. I wanted to find you but I did not know where you were, so the gods showed me you here in Thekaddy."

"I'm in Thekkady because I don't want to be found by gods or anyone."

"I am aware of that, but I did not want to find you because of who you were, Professor Lull. I wanted to find you because of this photograph."

She opens her palmer. The sunlight is very strong even through the palm-dapple, the picture is washed-out. It is taken on a day as bright as this, three Westerners squinting in front of the Padmanabhaswamy temple in Thiruvananthapuram. There is a slight sallow-skinned man and a South Indian woman. The man's arm is around the woman's waist. The other is Thomas Lull, grinning in Hawaiian shirt and terrible shorts. He knows the picture. It was taken seven years ago, after a conference in New Delhi when he took a month to travel the states of newly sundered India, a landmass that had always fascinated, appalled, and attracted him in equal measures. Kerala's contradictions held him a week longer than planned; its perfume of dust, musk, and sun-seared coconut matting, its sense of ancient superiority to the caste-ridden north, its dark, fetid chaotic gods and their bloody rituals, its long and successful realisation of the political truth that Communism was a politics of abundance not scarcity; its ever-shifting flotsam of treasures and travellers.

"Can't deny it, that's me," Thomas Lull confesses.

"The other couple, do you recognise them?"

Thomas Lull's heart kicks.

"Just tourists," he lies. "They've probably got a photograph exactly the same. Should I?"

"I believe they may be my natural parents. It is them I am trying to find; it is because of them that I asked the gods to show me you, Professor Lull."

Now Thomas Lull stops up short. A truck decorated with images of Siva and his wife and sons rolls past in a wave of dust and Chennai filmi music.

"How did you come by this photograph?"

"It was sent to me on my eighteenth birthday by a firm of lawyers in Varanasi, in Bharat."

"And your adoptive parents?"

"They are from Bangalore. They know what I am doing. They gave me their blessing. I always knew I had been adopted."

"Have you any photographs of them?"

She scrolls up an image of a coltish teen sitting on a verandah step, knees pressed chastely together, hands wrapped around shins, barricading virginity. She doesn't wear the Vishnu tilak. Behind her stand a South Indian man and woman in their late forties, dressed in the Western style. They look like people who would be always open and honest and Western with their daughter and never try to interfere with her journey of self-discovery. He thumbs back to the temple photograph.

"And these you say are your natural parents?"

"I believe so."

Impossible, Thomas Lull wants to say. He keeps silent, though silence binds him in lies. No, you bind yourself in lies wherever you turn, Thomas Lull. Your life is all lies.

"I have no recollection of them," Aj says. Her voice is flat and neutral, like the shade she wears. She might be describing a tax return. "When I received the photograph, I felt nothing. But I do have one memory; so old it is almost like a dream. It is of a white horse galloping. It comes to me and then it rears up with its hooves in the air, as if it is dancing, just for me. Oh, I can see it. I love that horse very much. I think it is the only thing I have from that time."

"No explanation from these lawyers?"

"That is correct. I had hoped that you could help me. But it seems you cannot, so I will go now to Varanasi and find these lawyers."

"They're about to start a war up there."

Aj frowns. Her tilak creases. Thomas Lull feels his heart turn.

"Then I shall trust the gods to keep me safe from harm," she declares. "They showed me where you were from this photograph, they will guide me in Varanasi."

"These are mighty handy gods."

"Oh yes, Professor Lull. They have never failed me yet. They are like an aura around people and things. Of course, it took some time before I realised that not everyone could see them. I just thought it was manners, that they had all been taught not to say what they knew, and that I was a very rude and unmannerly girl, who blurted out everything she saw. Then I understood that they couldn't see and didn't know."

As a ragged-assed seven-year-old William Blake had seen a London plane tree churning with angels. Only his mother's intercession prevented a thrashing from his father. Presumptions and lies. A lifetime later the visionary had looked into the eye of the sun and seen an innumerable company of the Heavenly Host crying *Holy Holy Holy is the Lord God Almighty*. Thomas Lull had squinted at the Kansas sun every morning of his working life and seen nothing but nuclear fusion and the uncertainties of quantum theory. Tension coils at the base of Thomas Lull's stomach but it is not the old serpent of sexual anticipation he knows from the affairs and the sun-warmed backpacker girls. It is something other. Fascination. Fear.

"Any person or thing?" Aj cocks her head, a gesture between a Western nod and an Indian head-roll. "Who's that, then?" Thomas Lull points to the tin toddy-stall where Mr. Sooppy sits waving away flies with a tattered copy of the *Thiruvananthapuram Times*.

"That is Sandeep Sooppy. He is a toddy-seller and he lives at number 1128 Joy of the People Road."

Thomas Lull feels his scrotum slowly contract in fear.

"And you've never met him before in your life."

"I have never met him at all. I never met your friend Dr. Ghotse before, either."

A green and yellow bus rolls past. Aj does the head-cock thing again, frowning at the hand-painted licence number. "And that bus belongs to Nalakath Mohanan, but it could be someone else driving. The bus is well past its service date. I would not recommend riding on it."

"It'll be Nalakath," Thomas Lull says. His head is wheeling as if he had taken an eighth of the Nepali that Mr. Sooppy sells out the back of his toddy stand. "So, how come these gods of yours can tell the state of Nal's brakes just by glancing at his licence-plate, but they can't tell the first thing about these people you say are your natural parents?"

"I can't see them," Aj says. "They are like a blind spot in my vision, every time I look at them, everything closes up around them, and I can't see them."

"Whoa," says Thomas Lull. Magic is spooky, but a hole in the magic; that's scary. "What do you mean, you can't see them?"

"I can see them as human beings but I can't see the aura around them, the gods, the information about them and their lives."

A rising wind rattles the palm blades, rattles Thomas Lull in his spirit. Forces are drawing around him, penning him inside a mandala of lives and coincidences. Blow on, away out of here, man. Don't get involved in this woman and her mysteries. You've lied to her, what you could not bear is if she is not lying to you.

"I can't help you," Thomas Lull says. They are at the gate of the Palm Imperial. He can hear the satisfying crisp twang of a tennis rally. The wind confesses in the bamboo, the surf is high again. He will hate to leave this place. "I'm sorry your trip has been wasted."

Lull leaves her in the lobby. When she has gone to her room he calls in a long-term favour from Achuthanandan the hotel manager and pulls her account details from the register. Ajmer Rao. 385 Valahanka Road, Silver Oak Development, Rajankunte, Bangalore. Eighteen years young. Paid for with an industrial-grade Bank of Bharat black card. A high-calibre financial weapon for a girl working the Kerala Bhati-club circuit. Bank of Bharat. Why not First Karnatic or Allied Southern? A small mystery among the hosts of luminous gods. He tries to spy them as he trails back the straight white road to his home, catch them out of the corner of his eye, fix them in his fleeting vision like floaters. The trees remain trees, the trucks obdurately trucks, and the Indian pond-heron stalks among the floating coir husks.

Aboard *Salve Vagina* Thomas Lull swiftly sets a stack of folded beach-shirts on top of Blake and closes the bag. Leave and don't look back. The ones who look back are turned to salt. He leaves a note and some money for Dr. Ghotse to find a local woman and pack the rest into boxes. When he arrives where he's meant to be he'll send for his stuff.

On the road he flags down a phatphat and rides in to the bus station, bag clutched on his lap. Bus station is a generosity: the battered Tatas use a wide spot in the road as a turning circle, which they do without regard for buildings, pedestrians, or any other road user. The gaudily decorated buses lounge beside sewing repair stalls and hot snack vendors and the ubiquitous toddy-men. Marutis with interior fans rattling and open-back Mahindra pickups honk their way through the bustle. Five bus sound-systems compete with hits from the movies.

The bus for Nagercoil won't leave for an hour so Thomas Lull buys himself a toddy and squats on the oily soil under the seller's umbrella to watch the driver and conductor argue with their passengers and grudgingly wedge their luggage on to the roof rack. The Palm Imperial's microbus arrives at its usual breakneck speed. The side door slams open and Aj steps out. She has a small, grey bag with her and wears shades and a wrap-round over her pants. Boys mob her, clutching at her bag; informal porters. Thomas Lull gets up from under his shady umbrella, strolls over to her, and lifts her bag.

"All connections to Varanasi this way, ma'am."

The Nagercoil bus driver sounds his horn. Last call for the south. Last call for peace and dive schools. Thomas Lull steers Aj through the skinny boys towards the Thiruvananthapuram express coach, firing up its biodiesels.

"You have changed your mind?"

"Gentleman's prerogative. And I've always wanted to see a war close up."

He jumps up on to the steps, pulls Aj up after him. They squeeze down the aisle, find the back seat. Thomas Lull puts Aj by the window grille. Shadows bar her face. The heat is incredible. The driver sounds his horns a last time, then the bus for the north draws away.

"Professor Lull, I do not understand." Aj's short hair stirs as the bus picks up speed.

"Nor do I," Thomas Lull says, looking at the cramped bus seat with distaste. A goat squirms against him. "But I do know if sharks ever stop moving they drown. And sometime gods are not enough to keep you right. Come on."

"Where are you going?" Aj says.

"I'm not spending five hours cooped up in here on a day like this." Thomas Lull raps on the driver's glass partition. He rolls his paan into his left cheek, nods, stops the bus. "Come on, and bring your bag. They'll have everything out of it."

Thomas Lull climbs the roof ladder, extends a hand down to Aj.

"Throw that up here."

Aj slings the bag up. Two roof-rider boys grab it and stash it safe among the bales of sari fabric. One hand holding her dark glasses in place, Aj scrambles up on to the roof and sits down beside Thomas Lull.

"Oh, this is wonderful!" she exclaims. "I can see everything!"

Thomas Lull bangs on the roof. "To the north!" With a fresh gust of biodiesel smoke, the driver draws off. "Now, Buteyko method, advanced class."

Lisa Durnau's not sure how many times Captain Pilot Beth's called her but the board is lit up, there's chatter on the com channels and an air of imminence in the atmosphere.

"Are we coming in?"

"Final approach adjustments," the little shave-headed woman says. Lisa feels a soft nudge; the attitude jets burping.

"Can you patch this up on my 'hoek?" She's not going in blind to a rendezvous with a certified, genuine Mysterious Alien Artefact. Captain Pilot Beth hooks the device behind the immobilised Lisa's ear, seeks the sweet spot in the skull, then touches a few lighted panels on the board. Lisa Durnau's consciousness explodes into space. Under full prope, the sensation that her body is the ship, that she is flying skin to vacuum, is overwhelming. Lisa Durnau hovers like an angel in the midst of a slowly rotating ballet of space engineering: the laddered wings of a solar power array, a rosette of film-mirrors like a halo of miniature suns; a high-gain antenna loops over her head, an outbound shuttle flashes past. The whole array basks in baking light, webbed by cable to the spider at the dark heart, Darnley 285. Millions of years of accumulated dust have coloured the asteroid only a shade less black than space itself. Then the mirrors shift and Lisa Durnau gasps as a rayed trefoil blazes silver on the surface. Astonishment turns to laughter; someone has stuck a Mercedes logo on a space rock. Someone not human. The triskelion is vast, two hundred metres along an arm. The huge waltz slows as Pilot Captain Beth matches rotation with the rock and Lisa Durnau forces a mental reorientation. She no longer drifts face-forward towards a crushing dark mass. The asteroid is under her feet and she settles like an angel on to it. Half a kilometre off touchdown, Lisa picks out the clusters of lights of the human base. The domes and converted drop-off tanks are coated in a thick layer of dust attracted by the static thrown up by the construction. The alien triskelion alone shines clear. The shuttle settles towards a cross-target of red navigation beacons. A procession of manipulator arms works diligently dusting the lamps and the launch laser lens. Looking up, she can see them marching hand-over-hand up and down the power and com cables. Preacherman's daughter Durnau thinks of Bible stories of Jacob's ladder.

"Okay, I'm going to shut you down now," the voice of Captain Pilot Beth says. There is a moment of dislocation and she is back and blinking in the cramped cockpit of the transfer boat. Counters scroll down to zero, Lisa feels the lightest of touches, and they are down. Nothing happens for quite a long time. Then there are clanks and clunks and hissings, Pilot Captain Beth unzips her, and Lisa Durnau tumbles out in a wash of cramps and truly astonishing body odour. Darnley 285 possesses insufficient gravity to pull, but enough to give Lisa a sense of direction. This is down. This is left and right and forwards and backwards and up. Another mental reorientation. She is hanging head-down like a bat. Down, in front of her face, the hatch dogs spin and opens out into a short tube narrow as a birth canal. A further hatch rotates and opens. A chunky, crew-cut man sticks his head and shoulders through. His nose and eyes hints at Polynesian genes not too many branches down his family tree and the suit-liner shoulder flashes say *US Army*. But he has a great smile as he reaches a hand out to Lisa Durnau.

"Dr. Durnau, I'm Sam Rainey, project director. Welcome to Darnley 285, or as our archaeological friends like to call her, the Tabernacle."

12

MR. NANDHA, PARVATI

The traffic is worse than ever now the karsevaks have a permanent encampment around the imperilled Ganesha statue and Mr. Nandha the Krishna Cop's yeast infections are punishing him. Worst, he has a briefing with Vik in Information Retrieval. Everything about Vik irritates Mr. Nandha, from his self-crowned nickname (what is wrong with Vikram, a fine, historical name?) to his MTV fashion sense. He is the inverse of the fundamentalists camped out on the roundabout. If Sarkhand is atavistic India, Vik is a victim of the contemporary and fleeting. But what has set Mr. Nandha's day foul was the almost-argument with Parvati.

She had been watching breakfast television, laughing in her apologetic, hand-lifting way at the hosts gushing over their chati, soapi, celebriti guests.

"This invoice. It seems . . . it is, quite a lot."

"Invoice?"

"Ah, the drip irrigation."

"But it is necessary. You cannot hope to grow brinjal without irrigation."

"Parvati, there are people do not have water to cook their rice."

"Exactly, that is why I went for the drip irrigation. It's the most efficient way. Water conservation is our patriotic duty."

Mr. Nandha held the sigh until he was out of the room. He authorised payment through his palmer and his aeai informed him that Vik had requested a meeting and gave him a new, unfamiliar route to work avoiding Sarkhand Roundabout. He returned to bid Parvati good-bye and found her watching the top-of-the-hour news.

"Have you heard?" she said. "N. K. Jivanjee says he will get up a rath yatra and ride across the country like Rama until a million peasants march on Sarkhand Roundabout."

"That N. K. Jivanjee is a rabble-rouser, and his party, too. What we need is national unity against Awadh, not a million karsevak louts marching on Ranapur."

He kissed Parvati on her forehead. The day's ills sweetened.

"Good-bye, my bulbul. You will be working on the garden?"

"Oh yes, Krishan will be here at ten. Have a good day. And don't forget to pick up your suit from the laundry, we've that durbar at the Dawars tonight."

Now Mr. Nandha rides up the outside of the Vajpayee tower in a glass elevator. Stomach acid gnaws at him. He imagines it dissolving him from within, cell by cell.

"Vikram."

Vikram is not particularly tall nor particularly well shaped but he has not let these deter his fashion sense. The style being: baggy sleeveless T with random text messages flashing up on the smart fabric—they achieve the condition of accidental Zen, so the doctrine goes—square-cut below-the-knee ketchies with athletic tights worn underneath.

Finish with Nike Predators at the equivalent of the monthly salary of the upright Sikh on the front door. To Mr. Nandha this looks merely undignified. What he cannot tolerate is the strip of beard from lower lip to Adam's apple.

"Coffee?"

Vik always has one, in a never-cool cup. Mr. Nandba cannot drink coffee. His acid reflux hates it. He gives his Ayurvedic tea bag to Vikram's quiet assistant, whose name Mr. Nandha can never remember. The processor unit stands on Vik's desk. It's an industry-standard translucent blue cube, charred inside from Mr. Nandha's EMP assault. Vik has it hooked into an array of probes and monitors.

"Okay," he says and cracks his fingers. *Theater of Bludd* whispers from the speakers, muted from its usual thunder out of respect for Monteverdi-loving Mr. Nandha. "It would be a lot easier if you occasionally left us something to work on."

"I perceived a clear and present danger," Mr. Nandha says and is struck by revelation. Vik, cool Vik, technological Vik, trance-metal Vik, is jealous of him. He wants the missions, he wants the reserved first-class bogies and the well-cut Ministry suits and the gun that can kill two ways and the pocketful of avatars.

"You left even less than usual," says Vik, "but there was enough to get a few nanoprobes in and unravel what's been going on. I presume the programmer . . ."

"He was the first victim."

"Aren't they always? Would have been nice if he could have told us exactly why his home-brew satta aeai was running a background programme buying and selling on the international ventures market."

"Please clarify," says Mr. Nandha.

"Morva up in Fiscal will explain it better, but it looks like Pasta-Tikka was unconsciously trading crores of rupees for a venture capital company called Odeco."

"I shall indeed speak with Morva," Mr. Nandha decides.

"One thing I can tell you right off." Vik stabs a line of code on his thin blue screen with his forefinger.

"Ah" says Mr. Nandha with a thin smile.

"Our old friend Jashwant the Jain."

Parvati Nandha sits in a bower of amaranthus on the roof of her housing block. She shields her eyes with her hand to watch another military transport slide in from the east and disappear over New Varanasi's corporate towers. They and the high-circling black kites are the only interruptions of the peace of her garden in the heart of the city. Parvati goes to the edge, peers over the parapet. Ten stories down the street is thick with people as an arm with blood. She crosses the tiled patio to the raised bed, gathers her sari around her as she stoops to inspect the marrow seedlings. The plastic evaporation tent is opaque with moisture. Already the air on the roof is thirty-seven degrees and the sky is heavy, impenetrable, close, caramel yellow from the smog. Peering between the sheeting and the soil, Parvati inhales the smell of soil and mulch and moisture and growing.

"Let them get on with it themselves."

Krishan is a big man who can move very quietly, as many big men can, but Parvati felt the cool of his shadow on the soft hairs on the nape of her neck, like the dew on the marrow leaves.

"Oh, you gave me a shock!" she says, demure and flustered, which is a game she likes to play with him.

"Forgive me, Mrs. Nandha."

"So?" Parvati says.

Krishan takes his wallet and hands Parvati a hundred rupee note.

"How did you guess?"

"Oh, it's obvious," Parvati says. "It has to be Govind, otherwise why would he track her down to that bad house in Brahmpur East just to mock and deride her? No no no, only a true husband would find his wife, no matter what she had done, and forgive her and bring her home. I knew it was him from the moment he turned up on the doorsteps of that Thai Massage house. That airline pilot disguise did not fool me. Her family may cast her out, but a true husband, never. Now, all he has to do is get his revenge on the director of that SupaSingingStar Show . . ."

"Khursheed."

"No, he runs the restaurant. Arvind is the director. Govind will get his revenge, if the Chinese do not get him first about the casino project."

Krishan throws his hands up in surrender. He is no devotee of *Town and Country* but he will watch and bet on its improbably complex plot lines if it makes his client happy. It is a strange commission; this farm on top of a downtown apartment block. It hints at compromises. They can be hard, these town and country marriages.

"I will have cook fetch you chai," Parvati says. Krishan watches her call down the stairs. She has the grace of the country. The city for gloss, the village for wisdom. Krishan wonders about her husband. He knows that he is a civil servant and that he settles his accounts promptly and without argument. With only half a picture, all Krishan can do is speculate on the relationship, the attraction. Not such a speculation, the attraction. He sometimes wonders how he can ever find a wife for himself when even a low-caste girl can catch herself a solid middle-class husband with a glance and a turn of the hand. Garden well. Make money, plant it, grow it into more money. Buy a Maruti and move out to Lotus Gardens. You will marry as well as you can, out there.

"Today," Krishan announces when he has finished his chai and set the glass down on the wooden wall of the raised bed, "I am thinking, perhaps beans and peas there, to give some kind of screen. You're open on the left. And here, a quarterbed for Western-style salad vegetables. Western-style salad is the thing at dinner parties; when you entertain, cook can cut fresh."

"We do not entertain," Parvati says. "But there is a big reception out at the Dawar house tonight. It will be quite an occasion. It is so lovely out there. So many trees. But Mr. Nandha says it's inconvenient, too far out. Too much driving. I can have everything here they have out there, and so much more convenient."

It takes two runs down to the street for Krishan to bring up the old wooden railway sleepers he uses to build the retaining walls for the beds. He lays them out in rough order, then cuts and moulds the damp-proof sheet and lays it in position. Parvati Nandha sits on the rim of the tomato and pepper bed.

"Mrs. Nandha, are you not missing *Town and Country*?" Krishan asks.

"No no, it is delayed until eleven thirty today, it's the final day of the test against England."

"I see," says Krishan, who adores cricket. When she goes, he might bring up the radio.

"Well, don't mind me." He sets to drilling the drain holes in the sleepers but all the time he is aware that Mrs. Nandha is still perched there, watching.

"Krishan," she says after a time.

"Yes, Mrs. Nandha?"

"It's just, it's such a lovely day, and when I'm down there, I hear all the dragging and bumping and hammering up here, but I never see it until it's finished."

"I understand," Krishan the mali says. "You won't disturb me."

But she has, and she does.

"Mrs. Nandha," he says as he bolts the last railway sleeper into place. "I think you are missing your programme."

"Am I?" Parvati Nandha says. "Oh, I never noticed the time. Not to worry, I can catch the early evening repeat."

Krishan hefts a sack of compost, slashes it open with his gardening knife, and sprinkles rich brown earth food down through his fingers on to the rooftop.

The burning dog gives off a vile oily smoke. Jashwant the Jain, his broom-boy before him, stands eyes closed. Whether they are closed in prayer or outrage Mr. Nandha cannot say. Within moments the dog is a small intense fireball. The other dogs still surge yipping around Mr. Nandha's feet, too stupid in their small programmed obsessions to recognise danger.

"You are a vile, cruel man," says Jashwant the Jain. "Your soul is black as anthracite, you will never attain the light of moksha."

Mr. Nandha purses his lips and levels his gun at a fresh target, a cartoon scoobi with lugubrious eyes and yellow/brown Friesian-patterned fur. Sensing attention, the thing wags its tail and waddles towards Mr. Nandha through the frenzied sea of robot dogs, tongue lolling. Mr. Nandha considers Animal Welfare charities a ludicrous social affectation. Varanasi cannot feed its children, let alone its abandoned cats and dogs. Sanctuaries for cyberpets occupy an altogether higher level of scorn.

"Sadhu," Mr. Nandha says. "What do you know of a company called Odeco?"

It is not the first time the Ministry has called on the Mahavira Compassion Home for Artificial Life. It is an ongoing debate in Jainism whether cyberpets and artificial intelligences are soul or non-soul. But Jashwant is old school, a Digambara. All things that live, move, consume, and reproduce are jiva, and so when the kids have tired of the cyberscoobi and the Faithful Friend cyberguard-dog calls the cops out eighteen times a night, there's a place other than the rubbish piles of Ramnagar to go. More than the occasional harried aeai finds shelter there, too. Mr. Nandha and his avatars have been here twice in the past three years to carry out mass excommunications.

Jashwant had been waiting outside the scruffy Janpur business district pressed-aluminium warehouse to greet him. Someone or thing had tipped him off. There would be nothing here for Mr. Nandha. As Jashwant walked forward to greet the man from the Ministry, his sweeper, a ten-year-old boy, doggedly brushed insects and crawling things from the holy man's path with a long-handled besom. A

Digambara, Jashwant did not wear clothes. He was a big man, heavy with fat around his middle body and constantly flatulent from his holy high-carb diet.

"Sadhu, I am investigating a fatal incident involving an unlicensed aeai. Our research indicates it was downloaded from a transfer point on these premises."

"Indeed? I find that hard to believe; but, as you are entitled, feel at liberty to check our system. I think you will find all is in legal order. We are an animal welfare charity, Mr. Nandha, not a sundarban."

Broom boy led the way. He wore only a very brief dhoti and his skin seemed to shine, as if it had been rubbed over with oil flecked with gold. There had been similar boys on his previous visits. All with those dull eyes and too much skin.

Inside the warehouse, the din was as Mr. Nandha remembered, and then some. The concrete floor heaved with thousands of cyberdogs, constantly circling from charge point to charge point. The metal shell rang to their creaking, yapping, humming, singing.

"More than a thousand in the past month," Jashwant said. "I think it is fear of a war. In sinful times, people reconsider their values. Much is cast off as worthless encumbrance."

Mr. Nandha drew his gun and aimed it at a stumpy little lap dog sitting up on its back legs, front paws and tail waving, pink plastic tongue waggling. He shot the dog. Now Indra the Thunderer has the slowly advancing *scoobi*-pet in his sights.

"Sadhu, did you supply an unlicensed Level One Artificial Intelligence to Pasta-Tikka of Nawada?"

Jashwant twists his head in pain but that is not the correct answer. The em-bolt sends the cartoon dog a metre and a half into the air. It lands on its back, thrashes once, and starts to smoke.

"Bad, evil man!"

The sweeper has his little besom raised, as if he might whisk Mr. Nandha and his sin away. It is not beyond the bounds of possibility that there are infected needles among the bristles. Mr. Nandha stares the catamite down.

"Sadhu."

"Yes!" Jashwant says. "Of course I did, you know that. But it was only resting in our network."

"Where did it come from, sadhu?" Mr. Nandha says, raising his weapon. He draws aim on a waddling steel dachshund, all smiles and clog-feet, then swings the barrel to bear on a beautiful, top-end cyber-collie, indistinguishable from the flesh right down to the live-plastic coat and fully interactive eyes. Jashwant the Jain lets slip a small squeak of spiritual anguish.

"Sadhu, I must insist."

Jashwant works his mouth.

Indra targets, aims, and fires in one flick of Mr. Nandha's intention. The cybercollie lets out a long, shrieking keen that silences every other yap and wuff in the warehouse, snaps head to tail in an arc that would crack any flesh dog's spine, and spins on its side on the concrete.

"Well, sadhu?"

"Stop it stop it stop it, you will go to hell!" Jashwant shrills.

Mr. Nandha levels the gun and one shot puts the thing out of its misery. He picks a gorgeous tiger-stripe vizla.

"Badrinath!" Jashwant screams. Mr. Nandha clearly hears him fart in fear. "Badrinath sundarban!"

Mr. Nandha slides his gun into his jacket pocket.

"You have been of great assistance. Radhakvishna. Most interesting. Please do not attempt to leave the premises, police officers will arrive shortly."

As he departs, Mr. Nandha notices that the broom boy is also quite quick with the fire extinguisher.

Ram Sagar Singh, Bharat's Voice of Cricket, burbles the tail-end batting order on the solar-powered radio. Dozing in the shade of the hibiscus-trellis, Krishan is lulled into memory. All his life, that slow voice has spoken to him, closer and wiser than a god.

It was a school day but his father had woken him before light.

"Naresh Engineer bats today at ul-Huq."

Neighbour Thakur was taking a load of shoe leather up to his buyer in Patna and had been only too happy to give Kudrati father and son a ride in his pickup. A low-caste lift, but this was in all likelihood the last time Naresh Engineer would ever take the bat.

The Kudrati land had come from the hands of Gandhi and Nehru; taken from the zamindar and given to the tillers of Biharipur. Its history was his pride, not just the Kudrati inheritance but the heritage of the nation itself; its name was *India*, not Bharat, not Awadh or Maratha or States of Bengal. That was why Krishan's father must see the greatest batsman India had produced in a generation step to the crease; for the honour of a name.

Krishan was eight years old and his first time in a city. The StarAsia sports channels were no preparation for the crowds outside the Moin ul-Huq stadium. He had never seen so many people in one place. His father led him surely through the crowd that swirled, patterns within patterns, like printed fabric.

"Where are we going?" Krishan asked, aware that they were moving against a general gyre towards the turnstiles.

"My cousin Ram Vilas, your grandfather's nephew, has tickets."

He remembers looking around at the hive of faces, felt his father's sure tug on his hand. Then he realised that the crowd was bigger than his father had imagined. Dreaming wide green spaces, stands in the distance, polite applause, he had forgotten to arrange a meeting place with cousin Ram Vilas. Now he was going to spiral his way around the ul-Huq ground, if necessary checking every face.

After an hour in the heat the crowd was thin but Krishan's father ploughed on. Inside the concrete oval bursts of loudspeaker cackle introduced the players; the Indians greeted them with bursts of applause and cheering. Father and son both knew now that his grandfather's nephew had never been here. There never were any tickets. In the sloping shadow of the main stand was a nimki seller. Mr. Kudrati seized his son's hand again and hauled him across the concrete. When they got within smelling distance of the rancid, hot oil, Krishan saw what had galvanised his father. Balanced on the glass display counter was a radio, blatting stupid pop.

"My son, the test match," his father gibbered at the vendor. He thrust a flutter of rupees at the hot snack seller. "Tune, tune, retune! And some of those pappadi, too."

The vendor reached in to the hot eats with a cone of newspaper.

"No no no!" Krishan's father almost screamed with frustration. "First, retune. Then the food. 97.4." Ram Sagar Singh came through in his BBC Received Pronunciation and Krishan sat down with the paper cone of hot pappadi, back against the warm steel cart to listen to the match. And that is how he remembers Naresh Engineer's last innings, sitting by a nimki vendor's cart outside the Moin ul-Huq cricket ground, listening to Ram Sagar Singh and the faint, half-imagined crack of the bat, and then the rising roar of the crowd behind him; all day as the shadows moved across the concrete car park.

Krishan Kudrati smiles in his doze under the climbing hibiscus. A darker shadow moves across his closed eyelids, a waft of cool. He opens his eyes. Parvati Nandha stands over him, looking down.

"I should really be telling you off, sleeping on my time."

Krishan glances at the clock on his radio. He still has ten minutes of his time but he sits up and flicks the radio off. The players are on lunch and Ram Sagar Singh is trawling through his compendious tallboy of cricket facts.

"I just wanted to see what you thought of my new bracelets for the reception tonight," Parvati says, one hand on hip like a dancer, the other weaving in front of him.

"If you held it still, I might actually see it."

Metal catches light, dazzling Krishan. Instinctively, he reaches out. Without thought, his hand is around her wrist. Realisation paralyses him for a moment. Then Krishan releases his grasp.

"That's very fine," he says. "Is it gold?

"Yes," Parvati says. "My husband likes to buy me gold."

"Your husband is very good to you. You will be number one star attraction at this party."

"Thank you." Parvati ducks her head, now ashamed at her forwardness. "You are most kind."

"No, I am just speaking the simple truth." Made bold by the sun and the heavy scent of soil, Krishan dares: "Forgive me, but I don't think you get to hear that as much as you should."

"You are a very forward man!" Parvati scolds, then, gently, "Is that the cricket you are listening to?"

"The second test from Patna. We are two hundred and eight for five."

"Cricket is not a thing I understand," Parvati says. "It seems very complex and hard to win."

"Once you understand the rules and the strategies, it is the most fascinating of sports," Krishan says. "It is the nearest the English come to Zen."

"I should like to know about it. It's all the talk at these social events. I feel stupid, standing there not able to say anything. I might not know about politics or the economy, but I might be able to learn cricket. Perhaps you could teach me?"

Mr. Nandha drives through New Varanasi to *Dido and Aeneas*, English Chamber Opera recording, which Mr. Nandha notes for its rough approach to the English Baroque. On the edge of his sensory envelope, like a rumour of monsoon, is this evening's durbar at the Dawars. He would welcome an excuse not to go. Mr. Nandha fears Sanjay Dawar will announce the happy conception of an heir. A Brahmin, he suspects. That will start Parvati again. He has repeatedly made his position clear, but all she hears is a man telling her he will not give her babies. This depresses Mr. Nandha.

A discord in his auditory lobes: a call from Morva, in Fiscal. Of all of his people in the Ministry, Morva is the only one for whom Mr. Nandha has any respect. There is a beauty and elegance to the paper trail. It is detection at its purest and holiest. Morva never has to leave his office, never faces the streets, never threatens violence or carries a weapon, but his thoughts go out from his desk on the twelfth floor across the whole wide world with a few gestures of his hand and blinks of the eye. Pure intellect, disembodied as he flits from shell company to tax haven, off-shore datahaven to escrow account. The abstraction of his work excites Mr. Nandha: entities with no physical structure at all. Pure flow; the movement of intangible money through minute clusters of information.

He has chased down Odeco. It is a secretive investment company sheltered in a Caribbean tax haven, much given to throwing megadollars into blue sky. Its investments in Bharat include the Artificial Intelligence unit at the University of Bharat, Varanasi; Ray Power Research and Development division, and a number of Darwin-ware hothouses hovering on the edge of legality breeding low-level aeais. Not the aeai that leaped out of the backyard betting scheme in Pasta-Tikka and ran amok, Mr. Nandha thinks. Even a high-risk venture company like Odeco would not risk dealing with the sundarbans.

Americans fear these jungle places as they fear everything outside their own borders and co-opt Mr. Nandha and his kind to wage their unending war against the wild aeais, but much of Mr. Nandha admires the datarajas. They have energy and enterprise. They have pride and a name in the world. The sundarbans of Bharat and the States of Bengal, Bangalore and Mumbai, New Delhi and Hyderabad resound globally. They are the abodes of the mythical Generation Threes, aeais sentient beyond sentience, as high over human intelligences as gods.

The Badrinath sundarban physically occupies a modest fifteenth-floor apartment on Vidyapeeth. Dataraja Radhakrishna's neighbours doubtless never suspect that next door live ten thousand cybernetic devis. As he hoots his way in to park through the mopeds Mr. Nandha summons his avatars. Jashwant had been warned. Datarajas have so many feelers, trembling to the vibrations in the global web, that is almost as if they are prescient. As he locks the car Mr. Nandha watches as the streets and skyline fill with gods, huge as mountains. Siva scans the wireless traffic, Krishna the extra- and intranet, Kali raises her sickle above the satellite dishes of New Varanasi to reap anything copying itself out of Badrinath. *Harm's our delight and mischief all our skill*, sings the English Chamber Orchestra Chorus.

And it all goes white. A shout of static. The gods are wiped from the skyline. *Dido and Aeneas* shorts in mid-continuo. Mr. Nandha rips the 'hoek from his ear.

"Make way, make way!" he shouts at the pedestrians. In his first week with the Ministry Mr. Nandha experienced firsthand a full-strength EM pulse. There is no mistaking its signature. As he sprints up the steps to the foyer, thumbing for police support on his sputtering palmer, he thinks he sees a something, too big for a bird, too small for an aircraft, loop away from the apartment building and vanish into the Varanasi sky-glow. Seconds later the fascia of the fifteenth-floor apartment explodes in a gout of flame.

"Run, flee!" Mr. Nandha shouts as the smoking debris rains down on the gawpers but the one, huge, gagging thought in his head is that he won't get his suit from Mukherjee's now.

13

SHAHEEN BADOOR KHAN, NAJIA

Prime Minister Sajida Rana wears gold and green today. Her cabinet knows to expect matters of national pride when she is dressed in the flag. She stands at the east end of the long teak table in the luminous marble cabinet room of the Bharat Sabha. Gilt framed oils of forebears and political inspirations line the long wall. Her father, Diljit Rana, in his judge's robes, father of the nation. Her grandfather, Shankar Rana, in his English Queen's Counsel silk. Jawarhalal Nehru, aloof and vaguely fearful in his sweetly cut suit, as if he had seen the price future generations would pay for the quick, dirty deal he did with Mountbatten. The Mahatma, father of all, with his bowl and wheel. Lakshmi Bai, warrior Rani, standing in the stirrups of her Maratha cavalry horse commanding the charge on Gwalior. And the autocrats of that other mighty Indian dynasty to share the name Gandhi, Sonia; assassinated Rajiv; Indira the martyr, Mother India.

The marble walls and ceiling of the cabinet chamber have been worked into an intricate filigree of Hindu mythology. Yet the acoustic is dry and resonant. Even whispers ring and carry. Sajida Rana places her hands on the polished teak, rests her weight on them, a fighter's stance.

"Can we survive if we strike at Awadh?"

V. S. Chowdhury, Defence Minister, turns his hooded, hawk eyes to his leader.

"Bharat will survive. Varanasi will survive. Varanasi is eternal."

There is no doubt in the echoing hall what he means.

"Can we beat them?"

"No. Not a hope. You saw Shrivastava on the White House shaking hands with McAuley on his Most Favoured Nation status."

"It'll be the Shanker Mahal next," says Energy Secretary Vajubhai Patel. "The Americans have been sniffing around Ray Power. The Awadhis won't need to invade, they can just buy us up. Last I heard, old Ray was down at Manikarna ghat doing his surya namaskar."

"Then who's running the bloody shop?" Chowdhury asks.

"An astrophysicist, a packaging salesman, and a self-styled comedian."

"Gods save us, we should surrender right now," Chowdhury mutters.

"I cannot believe what I am hearing around this table," says Sajida Rana. "Like old women around a pump. The people want a war."

"The people want rain," says Biswanath, Minister of Environmental Affairs, stiffly. "And that is all they want. A monsoon."

Sajida Rana turns now to her most trusted aide. Shaheen Badoor Khan is lost in marble, his attention seduced by vulgar pagan deities scrambling over each other's bodies, up the walls and across the roof. Then he mentally erases the grosser contours, the sculpted cones of the breasts, the crude jut of the linga, reduces them to an androgynous blur of marble flesh, flowing into and through and out of itself. Vision jumps to an angle of cheekbone, an elegantly curved nape, a smooth perfect curve of hairless scalp glimpsed in an airport corridor.

"Mr. Khan, what did you get from Bengal?"

"It is fantasy," Shaheen Badoor Khan says. "As always, the Banglas want to demonstrate they can engineer, a high-tech solution to a problem. The iceberg is a PR stunt. They are almost as thirsty as we are."

"This is it precisely." Interior Minister Ashok Rana speaks now. Shaheen Badoor Khan has no issue with nepotism, but it should at least aspire to fitting the man to the job. In pretence of making a point, Ashok will deliver a short speech in support of his sister's policy, whatever it is. "What the people need is water and if that takes a war . . ."

Shaheen Badoor Khan gives the slightest of sighs, enough for the brother to catch. Defence Minister Chowdhury chimes in. He has a high and querulous voice that strikes unpleasant harmonics from the squabbling marble apsaras.

"The Land Forces Strategic Development Unit's best model involves a preemptive strike on the dam itself. Send a small commando force in by air, take the dam, hold it until the last moment, and then withdraw across the border. Meanwhile we press the United Nations for an international peace-keeping force on the dam."

"If the Americans do not call for sanctions first," Shaheen Badoor Khan comments. A murmur of agreement rolls around the long dark table.

"Withdraw?" Ashok Rana is incredulous. "Our brave jawans strike a mighty blow against Awadh and they turn tail and run? How will that look on the streets of Patna? This Strategic Development Unit, have they no izzat?"

Shaheen Badoor Khan feels the climate in the room change. This balls-talk of pride and brave soldiers and cowardice is stirring them. "If I might offer an opinion," he says into the perfect, resonant silence.

"Your opinions are always welcome here," Sajida Rana says.

"I believe that the greatest threat this government faces comes from the orchestrated demonstrations at Sarkhand Roundabout, not our dam dispute with Awadh," he says carefully. Voices on every side of the table raise objection. Sajida Rana lifts her hand and there is quiet.

"Continue, Secretary Khan."

"I am not saying there will not be war, though I think my position on aggression towards Awadh is clear to everyone by now."

"Woman's position," Ashok Rana says. Shaheen hears Ashok whisper to his aide, "Muslim's position."

"I am talking about threats to this government and clearly, the biggest threat we face is internal division and civil unrest fomented by the Shivaji. As long as our party enjoys mass popular support for any military action against Awadh, any diplomatic negotiations will come through this cabinet. And we are agreed that military force is purely a tool to get the Awadhis to the negotiating table, despite Ashok's high regard for our military prowess." Shaheen Badoor Khan holds Ashok Rana's eyes long enough to tell him he is a fool appointed above his competence. "However, if the Awadhis and their American patrons see a political alternative with wide popular support in Bharat, then N. K. Jivanjee will set himself up as peacemaker. The man who stopped the war, made the Ganga run again, and brought down the proud Ranas who shamed Bharat. We will not see the inside of this room for a generation. This is behind that play-acting over Sarkhand Roundabout. It is not the moral outrage of the Honest Hinduvavadi of Bharat. Jivanjee plans to raise the mob against us. He is going to ride that Chariot of Jaggarnath right up Chandni Boulevard into this room."

"Is there anything we can arrest him on?" Foreign Minister Dasgupta asks.

"Back taxes?" Vipul Narvekar, Ashok Rana's PA, suggests to a murmur of laughter.

"I have a suggestion," Shaheen Badoor Khan says. "Let N. K. Jivanjee have what he wants, but only when we want him to have it."

"Explain please, Mr. Khan." Prime Minister Rana leans forward now.

"I say, give him his head. Let him call up his million staunch believers. Let him ride his war chariot with his Shivaji dancing behind him. Let him be the voice of Hindutva, let him make the war-mongering speeches and stir up the offended Bharati pride. Let him drive the country into war. If we show ourselves to be doves, then he will become the hawk. We know he can stir a mob to violence. That could be directed against Awadhis in the border towns. They'll appeal to Delhi to protect them, the whole thing will escalate. Mr. Jivanjee needs no persuasion to ride his rath yatra right up to the Kunda Khadar dam. The Awadhis will strike back; then we move in as the injured party. The Shivaji are discredited as the ones who started the whole thing; the Awadhis are on the back foot with their Americans; and we go to the negotiating table as the party of reason, sanity, and diplomacy."

Sajida Rana stands upright.

"Subtle as ever, Secretary Khan."

"I am a mere civil servant . . ." Shaheen Badoor Khan dips his head obediently but catches Ashok Rana's eye. He is furious. Chowdhury speaks up.

"With respect, Secretary Khan, I think you underestimate the will of the Bharati people. There is more to Bharat than Varanasi and problems with its Metro stations. I know that in Patna we are simple, patriotic people. There, everyone believes a war will unite popular opinion and marginalise N. K. Jivanjee. It is a dangerous tactic, playing subtle games at times of national danger. The same Ganga flows through us as flows through you, you are not the only thirsty ones here. As you say, Prime Minister, the people need a war. I do not want to go to war, but I believe we must, and strike fast and strike first. Then we negotiate from a position of strength and when there is water in the pumps, that is when Jivanjee and his karsevaks will be seen as the rabble they are. Prime Minister, when have you ever misjudged the mood of the people of Bharat?"

Nods, grunts. The climate is shifting again. Sajida Rana stands at the head of her table of ministers, looking over her ancestors and influencers as Shaheen Badoor Khan has seen at so many cabinet meetings before, calling on them to sanctify the decision she is about to make for Bharat.

"I hear you, Mr. Chowdhury, but there is merit in Mr. Khan's proposal. I am minded to try it. I will let N. K. Jivanjee do our work for us, but keep the army on three-hour standby. Gentlemen, reports to my office mail by sixteen hundred today, I will circulate directives by seventeen hundred. Thank you, this meeting is closed."

Cabinet and advisors rise as Sajida Rana turns and strides out in a furl of colours, her secretarial staff falling in behind her. She is a tall, thin, striking woman, no trace of grey in her hair despite a first grandchild imminent. Shaheen Badoor Khan catches a ghost of Chanel as she sweeps past. He glances once at the sex divinities crawling all over the walls and roof, suppresses a shudder.

In the corridor, a touch at his cuff: the Defence Minister.

"Mr. Khan."

"Yes, how can I help you, Minister?"

Chowdhury draws Shaheen Badoor Khan into a window alcove. Minister Chowdhury leans towards him, says quietly and without inflection, "A successful meeting, Mr. Khan, but might I remind you of your own words? You are a mere civil servant."

He tucks his briefcase under his arm and hurries on down the corridor.

Hungover on blood, Najia Askarzadah wakes late in her backpackers' berth at the Imperial International. She staggers into the communal kitchen in search of chai, steers past Australians complaining about how flat the landscape is and that they can't get decent cheese, makes a glass and gets back to her room, mobbed by horrors. She remembers how the microsabres leaped for each other and she had risen with the crowd with the blood roar in her throat. It's a viler and dirtier feeling than she ever had from any drugs or sex but she's addicted.

Najia has thought much about her attraction to danger. Her parents had brought her up a Swede, permissively educated, sexually liberal, Westward-looking. They brought no photographs into their exile, no souvenirs, no words or language or sense of geography. The only Afghan thing about Najia Askarzadah is her name. Her parents' opus was so complete that it was not until her first term at university, when her tutor had suggested she research an essay on post–Civil War Afghan politics that Najia understood that she had an entire, buried identity. That identity opened up beneath Najia Askarzadah the little liberal arts Scandinavian poly-sexual and swallowed her for three months in which the essay became the foundation of the work that would become her final thesis. There is a life she could have led and her career so far has been foreplay with it. Bharat on the edge of water war is the preparation for her return to Kabul.

She sits on the cool cool veranda of the Imperial and checks her mail. The magazine likes the story. Likes the story a lot. Wants to pay her eight hundred dollars for the story. She thumbs agreement to the contract through to the United States. One step on the path to high Kabul, but only one step. She has a next story to plan. It will be a politics story. Her next interview will be Sajida Rana. Everyone's after Sajida Rana. What's the angle? It's woman to woman. Prime Minister Rana, you are a politician, a leader, a dynastic figure in a country divided over a traffic roundabout, where men are so desperate to marry *they* pay the dowry, where monster children who age half as fast as baseline humanity assume the privileges and tastes of adults before they are biologically ten, that is dying of thirst and about to start a war because of it. But before any of that, you are a woman in a society where women of your class and education have vanished behind a new purdah. What was it that enabled you, virtually alone, to escape that silk cage of cherishing?

Not a bad line that. Najia flips her palmer open. As she is about to thumb it in her palmer chirps. It'll be Bernard. Not very Tantra, going to a fighting club. Not very Tantra, going with another man. Not that he's possessive, so he doesn't need to forgive her, but what she needs to ask herself is, is this going to advance me down the path to samadhi?

"Bernard," says Najia Askarzadah, "fuck off and stay fucked off. I thought you didn't do jealousy or is that just another thing you tell women like the Tantric thing with your dick?"

"Ms. Askarzadah?"

"Oh, I'm sorry, I thought you were something else."

She's listening to a lot of air noise.

"Hello? Hello?"

Then: "Ms. Askarzadah. Be at the Deodar Electrical warehouse, Industrial Road, within the next half hour." An educated voice, lightly accented.

"Hello? Who are you, look, I'm sorry about . . ."

"The Deodar Electrical warehouse, Industrial Road."

And he's gone. Najia Askarzadah looks at the palmer as if it is a scorpion in her hand. No call back, no explanation, no identification. She taps in the address the voice gave her, the palmer displays a route map. She's out the gate on her moped within the minute. Deodar Electrical is part of the old *Town and Country* studio lot, broken up into small businesses when the series went virtual and moved into Indiapendent's Ranapur headquarters. The map leads her to the huge double doors of the main studio, where a teen in a long kurta and waistcoat sits at a table listening to cricket on the radio. Najia notices he wears a Shivaji trident medallion, like the one she had seen around Satnam's neck.

"Someone called me, told me to come here. I'm Najia Askarzadah."

The youth looks her up and down. He has an attempted moustache.

"Ah. Yes, we were told to be expecting you."

"Told? By who?"

"Please come with me."

He opens a small access door in the gates. They duck through.

"Oh, wow," says Najia Askarzadah.

The rath yatra stands fifteen metres high under the studio floods, a red and gold pyramid of tiers and parapets, riotous with gods and adityas. It is a mobile temple. At its apex, almost touching the studio girders is a plexiglass cupola containing an effigy of Ganesha, throned, the people's god, claimed by the Shivaji. The base, a wide balcony for party workers and PR, rests on the backs of twin flatbeds.

"The trucks are ganged together," the guide says enthusiastically. "They will always move in tandem, see? We will fit ropes if people want to be seen pulling, but Shivaji is not about exploiting anyone."

Najia's never seen a space launch, never even been close to rocketry, but she imagines the launcher assembly buildings share this buzz and industry: embraced in cranes and gantries, workers in coveralls and spray masks working up and down the golden flanks, light joinery robots poking their glue-gun probosces into crannies and corners. The air is dopey with paint and glass fibre fumes, the steel shed rings with power staplers, drills, and buzz saws. Najia watches a Vasu go up on a hoist. Two workers with Shivaji stickers on their coveralls glue it into position at the centre of a rosette of dancing attendants around a throned Vishnu. And at the centre, the golden ziggurat of the holy vessel. The chariot of Jaggarnath. The juggernaut itself.

"Please, feel free to take photographs," the teen aide says. "There is no charge." Najia's hands shake as she calls up the camera on the palmer. She goes in among the workers and machines and clicks until her memory is full.

"Can I, I mean, the papers?" she stammers at the Shivajeen, who seems to be the only person at the studio in any form of authority.

"Oh yes," he says. "I am presuming that is why you were brought here."

The palmer calls softly. Again, an anonymous number. Najia answers carefully.

"Yes?"

It is not college-voice. It's a woman.

"Hello, I have a call for you from N. K. Jivanjee."

"Who? What? Hello?" Najia stammers.

"Hello, Ms. Askarzadah." It's him. It really is him. "Well, what do you think?"

She has no words. She swallows, mouth dry.

"It's, um, impressive."

"Good. It's supposed to be. It cost a damn pile of money, too, but I do think the team has done an outstanding job, don't you? A lot of them are ex–television set designers. But I'm glad you like it. I think a lot of people are going to be equally impressed. Of course, the only ones that really matter are the Ranas." N. K. Jivanjee's laugh is a deep, chocolate gurgle. "Now, Ms. Askarzadah. You do understand you've been given a highly privileged preview that will make you a goodly sum of money from the press? No doubt you're asking, what's this about? Simply that the party I have the honour to lead occasionally has information it does not wish to release through conventional channels. You will be this unconventional channel. Of course, you do realise that we may suspend this privilege at any time. My secretary has a short prepared statement that she will forward to your palmer. It's a piece from me on the pilgrimage; my loyalty to Bharat, my intention that the pilgrimage be a focus for national unity in the face of a common enemy. It's all checkable back to my press office. Can I expect to see something in the evening editions? Good. Thank you, Ms. Askarzadah, bless you."

The prepared statement comes through with a discreet chime. Najia scans it. It is as N. K. Jivanjee said. She feels as if she has been hit across the front of the head with a big, soft, heavy bat. She hardly hears the Shivaji boy ask, "Was that him? Was it really him? I couldn't make it all out, what was he saying?"

N. K. Jivanjee. Anyone can get Sajida Rana. But N. K. *Jivanjee.* Najia Askarzadah hugs herself with joy. Scoop! Exclusive! Pictures copyright Najia Askarzadah. They'll be syndicated around the planet before the ink's dry on the contract. She's on the bike, course set for the *Bharat Times* office, swinging out through the wire gates into the path of an oncoming school bus before the thought penetrates the amazed numbness.

Why her?

Mumtaz Huq the ghazal singer will perform at ten. Shaheen Badoor Khan intends to be well away by then. It is not that he dislikes

Mumtaz Huq. She features on several compilations on his car system, though her tone is not as pure as R. A. Vora. But he does dislike parties like these. He clutches his glass of pomegranate juice in two hands and clings to the shadows where he can peek at his watch unseen.

The Dawar garden is a cool, moist oasis of pavilions and canopies among sweet-smelling trees and precision-pruned shrubs. It speaks of money and bribes to the water department. Candle lanterns and oil torches provide barbarous illumination. Waiters in Rajput costume move among the guests with silver trays of eats and alcohol. Musicians saw and tootle to an electric bass from a pandal under a harsingar tree. Here Mumtaz Huq will perform and afterwards there will be fireworks. That is what Neelam Dawar has been telling all her guests. Ghazals and fireworks. Rejoice!

Bilquis Badoor Khan seeks her husband out in his place of concealment.

"Darling heart, at least try and make an effort."

Shaheen Badoor Khan deals his wife a society kiss, one on each side.

"No, I'm staying here. Either they recognise me and all they want to talk about is war, or they don't and it's schools, share prices, and cricket."

"Cricket—that reminds me." Bilquis touches Shaheen's sleeve lightly, an invitation into conspiracy. "Shaheen, this is priceless . . . I don't know where Neelam gets them. Anyway, this terrible grubby little country wife, you know the sort of thing, straight off the Bihar bus, married up and everyone's got to know about it. There she is, over there. Anyway, we're standing around talking and she's hovering, obviously wanting to get her two rupees in, poor thing. We get round to the cricket and Tandon's century and she says, wasn't it marvellous, on the eighth and final ball, just before tea. I mean to say. Eight balls an over. Just priceless!"

Shaheen Badoor Khan looks at the woman where she stands alone under a pipal tree, a beaker of lassi in hand. The hand around the silver mug is long and slender, patterned with henna. Her wedding ring is tattooed on her finger. The woman carries herself with country elegance, tall, refined in an unaffected, unsophisticated way. She looks unutterably sad to Shaheen Badoor Khan.

"Priceless, yes," he says, turning away from his wife.

"Ah, Khan! I thought you'd show your heathen face here."

Shaheen Badoor Khan had tried to steer himself away from Bal Ganguly but the big man can smell news like a Luna moth. It is his purpose and passion as proprietor of Varanasi's premier Hindi news site. Though he is never without his posse of unmarried stringers—the kind of parties he is invited to draws the kind of women they hope to marry—Ganguly is an obdurate bachelor. *Only a fool works his life away building his own cage*, he says. Shaheen Badoor Khan also knows that Ganguly is a big giver to the Shivaji.

"So, what's the word from the Sabha? Shall I start digging a shelter or just stockpile rice?"

"I'm sorry to disappoint, but no war this week." Shaheen Badoor Khan glances around for escape. The bachelors circle around him.

"You know, it wouldn't surprise me if Rana declares war and half an hour later sends the bulldozers into Sarkhand Roundabout." Ganguly laughs at his own joke. He has a big, gurgling, infectious laugh. Shaheen Badoor Khan finds himself smiling. The devotees compete for who laughs loudest. They check to see if any women are looking. "No, but come on, Khan. War is a serious matter. It sells serious amounts of advertising space." The unattached women in their own private pavilion glance past their chaperone, smiling but shy of eye contact. Shaheen Badoor Khan's attention is again on the country wife under the pipal tree. Between worlds. Neither one nor the other. That is the worst place to be.

"We won't go to war," Shaheen Badoor Khan says smoothly. "If five thousand years of military history has taught us anything, it's that we aren't good at wars. We like the pretence and the posturing, but when it comes to battle, we'd rather not. That's how the British rolled right over us. We sat in our defence positions and they kept coming, and they kept coming and we thought, well; they'll stop sometime soon. But they just kept coming, bayonets fixed. It was the same in 'oh-two and 'twenty-eight up in Kashmir, it will be the same at Kunda Khadar. We'll pile our troops on our side of the dam, they'll pile theirs on their side, we'll exchange a few mortar rounds and then everyone can march away, izzat satisfied."

"They weren't dying of drought in 'twenty-eight,'" one of the paperboys says angrily. Ganguly pulls up, next witticism aborted. Bachelor reporters do not speak out of turn to Prime Ministerial Private Secretaries. Shaheen Badoor Khan uses the embarrassment to duck out of the conversation. The low-caste girls follow him with their eyes. Power has the same smell, town or country. Shaheen Badoor Khan dips his head to them, but Bilquis is on an intercept course with her former lawyer friends. The Ladies Who Used to Litigate. Bilquis's career, like a generation of educated working women, has vanished behind a veil of social functions and restrictions. No law, no imam, no caste tradition took them out of the workplace. Why work, when five men claw for every job and any educated, socially adept woman can marry into money and prestige? Welcome to the glass zenana.

The clever women are talking now about a widow of their acquaintance; an accomplished woman, a Shivaji activist, quite intelligent. No sooner back from the burning ghat and what do you know? Bankrupt. Not a paisa. Every last stick of furniture gone as surety. Twenty forty-seven, and still an educated woman can be turned out on to the streets. At least she hasn't had to go to, you know. The "O" people. Has anyone heard from recently? Must look her up. Girls need to stick together. Solidarity, all that. Can't trust men.

Musicians take up positions in their pandal, tuning, striking notes off each other. Shaheen Badoor Khan will make his getaway when Mumtaz Huq comes on. There is a tree near the gate, he can hide in its shadows and when the applause starts, slip out and call a taxi. Another has seen the opportunity, a man in a rumpled, civil servant's suit holding a full flute of Omar Khayyam. His hands around the glass are quite refined, as are his features, but he carries a heavy five o'clock shadow. He has great dark, animal eyes, with animal fear in them, in the way that animals instinctively first fear everything.

"Do you not fancy the music?" Shaheen Badoor Khan says.

"I prefer classical," the man says. He has an English-educated voice.

"I've always thought Indira Shankar very underrated myself."

"No, I mean Classical; Western Classical. Renaissance, Baroque."

"I'm aware of it but I don't really have the taste for it. I'm afraid it all sounds like hysteria to me."

"That's the Romantics," says the man with a private smile but he has decided Shaheen Badoor Khan shares some kindred feeling with him. "So, what line are you in yourself?"

"I am a civil servant," Shaheen Badoor Khan says. The man gives his answer consideration.

"So am I," he says. "Might I ask what area?"

"Information management," Shaheen Badoor Khan says.

"Pest control," the man says. "Congratulations then to our hosts." He raises his glass and Shaheen Badoor Khan observes that the man's suit is smudged with dust and smoke.

"Yes, indeed," Shaheen Badoor Khan says. "A fortunate child indeed."

The man grimaces.

"I cannot agree with you there, sir. I have considerable issues with geneline therapy."

"Why so?"

"It is a recipe for revolution."

Shaheen Badoor Khan starts at the vehemence in the man's voice. He continues, "The last thing Bharat needs is another caste. They may call themselves Brahmins, but in fact they are the true Untouchables." He remembers himself. "Forgive me, I know nothing about you, for all I know . . ."

"Two sons," Shaheen Badoor Khan says. "The old way. Safely at university, God be praised, where no doubt they're at things like this every night, prowling for wedding material."

"We are a deformed society," the man says.

Shaheen Badoor Khan wonders if this man is a djinn sent to test him for everything he speaks is in Shaheen's own heart. He was remembering a young married couple, their careers dazzling, their path luminous, the parents so proud, so delighted for their children. And, of course, the grandchildren, the grandsons. Everything you have, save this one thing, a son. A son and spare. Then the appointments with the doctors they had not asked to see, and the families poring over the results. Then the bitter little pills, and the bloody times. Shaheen Badoor Khan cannot count how many daughters he flushed away. His hands have twisted the limbs of Bharati society.

He would talk more with the man, but his attention is turned to the party. Shaheen follows his direction: the woman Bilquis had derided, the good-looking country woman, makes her way through the excited crowd. The arrival of the diva is imminent.

"My own wife," the man says. "I am summoned. Do excuse me. A pleasure to have met you." He sets his champagne down on the ground and goes to her. Applause as Mumtaz Huq arrives on the stage. She smiles and smiles and smiles to her audience. Her first song tonight will be a tribute to the generous hosts and a hope for joy, long life, and prosperity for their graced child. The players strike up. Shaheen Badoor Khan leaves.

Shaheen Badoor Khan's raised hand fails to stop any of the infrequent taxis in this private-mobility suburb. A phatphat drums past, turn at a gap in the concrete central reserve, and pulls over to the verge. Shaheen Badoor Khan starts towards it but the driver twists the throttle and surges away. Shaheen Badoor Khan glimpses a shadowed figure in swathes of voluminous clothing beneath the plastic canopy. The phatphat again crosses the median strip, rattles towards Shaheen

Badoor Khan. A face peeks out from the bubble, a face elegant, alien, fey. Cheekbones cast shadows. Light glints from the hairless, mica-dusted scalp.

"You are welcome to share my ride."

Shaheen Badoor Khan reels back as if a djinn has called the secret name of his soul.

"Not here, not here," he whispers.

The nute blinks yts eyes, a slow kiss. The engine races, the little phatphat pulls into the night traffic. Streetlight catches on silver around the nute's neck, a Siva trishul.

"No," Shaheen Badoor Khan pleads. "No."

He is a man of responsibilities. His sons have grown and left, his wife is all but a stranger to him these years but he has a war, a drought, a nation to care for. Yet the directions he gives to the Maruti driver who finally stops for him are not to the Khan haveli. They are to another place, a special place. A place he hoped he would never need go to again. Frail hope. The special place is down a gali too narrow for vehicles, overhung by intricately worked wooden jharokas and derelict air-conditioning units. Shaheen Badoor Khan opens the cab door and steps out into another world. His breath is tight and shallow and fluttering. There. In the brief light of a door's opening and closing, two silhouettes, too slim, too elegant, too fey for mundane humanity.

"Oh," he cries softly. "Oh."

14

TAL

Tal runs. A voice calls yts name from the cab. Yt does not look. Yt does not stop. Yt runs, shawl pluming out behind it in a blur of ultra-blue paisleys. Horns blare, sudden looming faces yell abuse; sweat and teeth. Tal reels back from a near miss with a small fast Ford; music thud-thud-thuds. Yt spins, dodges the shocking blare of truck horns, slips between a rural pickup and a bus pulling out from a halt. Tal halts a moment on the median strip for a glance back. The bubble cab still purrs on the footpath. A figure stands there, glimpsed through the headlight glare. Tal plunges into the steel river.

Tal tried to hide that morning, behind work, behind huge wrap-round tilt-jet pilot shades, behind the Lord of the Hangovers, but everyone had to come and get the goss on the *faaa*bulous people at the *faaa*-bulous party. Neeta was celebstruck. Even the cool guys circulated past

Tal's workstation, not of course asking directly, but accessing hints and suspicions. The goss-nets were full of it, the news channels, too, even the headline services were beaming pictures from the night to palmers all over Bharat. One of which was two nutes going at it on the floor and A-listers cheering and clapping.

Then a neural Kunda Khadar burst behind Tal's eyes and it all came gushing back. Every. Little. Detail. The taxicab fumblings, the airport hotel mumblings and profanities. The morning light flat and grey with the promise of another merciless day of ultra-heat, and the card on the pillow. *Non-scene.*

"Oh," Tal whispered. "No." Yt crept home as early as the impending wedding of Aparna Chawla and Ajay Nadiadwala would permit, a shaking, paranoid wreck. Huddled up in the phatphat yt could feel the card in yt's bag, heavy and untrustworthy as uranium. Get rid of it now. Let it flutter out the window. Let it slip down the seat lining. Lose and forget. But yt could not. Tal was terribly, terribly afraid yt had fallen in love and yt didn't have a soundtrack for this one.

The women were on the stairs again, winding their way up and down with their plastic water carriers, their conversation dying as Tal squeezed past, mumbling apologies, then resuming in titters and low whispers. Every rattle, every snatch of radio seemed a weapon thrown at yt. Don't think about it. In three months you will be out of here. Tal plunged into yts room, tore off yts stiff, smoke-reeking party clothes and dived naked into yts beautiful bed. Yt programmed two hours of non-REM sleep but yts agitation and heart-hurt and wonderful, mad bafflement defeated the subdermal pumps and yt lay watching the nibs of light cast by the window blind bindings move across the ceiling like slow worms and listening to the voiceless, choral roar of the city moving. Tal unfolded that last insane night again, smoothed out its creases. Yt hadn't gone out to get involved. Yt hadn't even gone out to get fucked. Yt had gone out for a simple mad time with famous people and a bit of glam. Yt didn't want a lovely person. Yt didn't want an entanglement. Yt didn't want involvement, a relationship. And the last thing yt wanted was *love at first sight*. Love, and all those other dreadful things yt thought yt had left in Mumbai.

Mama Bharat was slow answering Tal's knock. She seemed in pain, her hands uncertain on the door locks. Tal had washed in a cup of water, removing surface layers of sleep and grime but the smoke, drink, and sex were engrained. Yt could smell them off ytself as yt sat on the low sofa watching the turned-down cable news while the old woman made chai. She was slow about her making, visibly frail. Her aging scared Tal.

"Well," Tal said. "I think I'm in love."

Mama Bharat rocked back on her seat, swaying her head in understanding.

"Then you must tell me everything about it."

So Tal began yts tale, from stepping out of Mama Bharat's front door to the card on the pillow in the numb morning.

"Show me this card," Mama Bharat said. She turned it over in her leathery, monkey hand. She pursed her lips.

"I am not convinced about a man who leaves a card with a club address rather than a home address."

"Yt's not a man."

Mama Bharat closed her eyes.

"Of course. Forgive me. But he is acting like a man." Dust motes rose in the hot light slanting through the slatted wooden blind. "What is it you feel about him?"

"I feel I'm in love."

"That is not what I asked. What do you feel about him? *Yt*."

"I feel . . . I think I feel . . . I want to be with yt, I want to go where yt goes and see what yt sees and do what yt does, just to be able to know all those little, little things. Does that make any kind of sense?"

"Every kind of sense," Mama Bharat said.

"What do you think I should do?"

"What else can you do?"

Tal stood up abruptly, hands clutched.

"I will, then, I will."

Mama Bharat rescued Tal's discarded tea-glass from the rug before yt could flood it with hot, sweet *chai* in yts excited determination. Siva Nataraja, Lord of the Dance, watched from his place on the tallboy, annihilating foot eternally raised.

Tal spent the remains of the afternoon in the ritual of *going out*. It was a formal and elaborate process that began with laying down a mix. STRANGE CLUB was yts mental title for yts venture to Tranh. DJ aeai sourced an assortment of late-chill grooves and Viet/Burmese/Assamese sounds. Tal stripped off yts street clothes and stood in front of the mirror, raising yts arms over yts head, relishing yts round shoulders, child-slim torso, full, parted thighs free of any sexual organ. Yt held yts wrists up, studied in reflection the goose flesh of the subdermal control studs. Yt contemplated yts beautiful scars.

"Okay, play it."

The music kicked in at floor-shaking volume. Almost immediately Paswan next door began banging on the wall and shouting about the noise and his shifts and his poor wife and children driven demented by freaks perverts deviates. Tal namasted ytself in the mirror, then danced to the wardrobe cubby and swept back the curtain in a balletic twirl. Swaying to the rhythm, Tal surveyed yts costumes, weaving permutations, implications, signs and signals. Mr. Paswan was beating on the door now, vowing he would burn yt out, see if he did not. Tal laid out yts combo on the bed, danced to the mirror, opened yts makeup boxes in strict right to left order and prepared to compose.

By the time the sun set in glorious polluted carmines and blood, Tal was dressed, made up and geared-in. The Paswans had given up hammering an hour ago and were now treating Tal to half-heard sobbing. Tal ejected the chip from yts player, slipped it into yts bag and was out into the wild wild night.

"Take me, here."

The phatphat driver looked at the card and nodded. Tal hooked up yts mix and slumped back on to the seat in ecstasy.

The club was off an unprepossessing alley. In Tal's experience, the best clubs usually were. The door was carved wood, grey and fibrous from years of heat and pollution. Tal guessed it had been there even before the British. A discreet camera bindi blinked. The door swung open to the touch. Tal unhooked yts mix to listen. Traditional dhol and bansuri.

Tal took a breath and walked in.

A great haveli had once lived here. Balconies in the same weathered grey wood rose five floors around the central courtyard garden, now glassed over. Vines and climbing pharm bananas had been let run and ramble up the carved wooden pillars to spread across the ribs of the glass dome. Clusters of biolume lamps hung from the centre of the roof like strange fetid fruit; terracotta oil lanterns were arranged across the tiled floor. All was flicker and folded shadow. From the recesses of the wooden cloisters came low conversation and the musical burble of nute laughter. The musicians sat facing each other on a mat by the central pool, a shallow rectangle dappled with lilies, intent on their rhythms.

"Welcome to my home."

The small, birdlike woman had appeared like a god in a film. She wore a crimson sari and a brahmin's bindi and carried her head cocked to one side. Tal guessed her at sixty-five, seventy. The woman's gaze darted over yts face.

"Please, make yourself at home. I have guests from every walk of society, from Varanasi and beyond." She pulled a thumb-sized banana from its broad-leafed vine, peeled it open, and offered it to Tal. "Go, eat eat. They grow wild."

"I don't want to appear rude, but . . ."

"You want to know what it does. It will get you into the way we are here. One to start, that is the way we do it. There are many varieties, but the ones by the door are the ones to start with. The rest you will discover on your journey. Relax, my lovely. You are among friends." She offered the banana once again. As yt took it, Tal noticed the curl of plastic behind the aged woman's right ear. That tilt of the head, that dodge of the eyes, were explained now. A blindhoek. Tal took a bite from the banana. It tasted of banana. Then yt became aware of the details in the woodcarving, the pattern of the tiles, the colours and weave of the dhuris. The individual parts of the music became distinct, stalking and twining around each other. A sharpness of focus. A lifting of awareness. A glow in the back of the head like an inner smile. Tal ate the rest of the banana in two bites. The old blind woman took the skin and deposited it in a small wooden bin already half-full of blackening, fragrant peels.

"I'm looking for someone. Tranh."

The old woman's black eyes hunted over Tal's face.

"Tranh. Lovely thing. No, Tranh is not here, yet. But Tranh will be, sometime." The old woman clasped her hands together in joy. Then the banana kicked in and Tal felt a relaxed warmth spread down from yts agnya chakra and yt hooked up yts music and explored the strange club. The balconies held low divans and sofas, arranged intimately around conversation tables. For those who did not do bananas there were elegant brass hookahs. Tal drifted past a knot of nutes, slo-moed in smoke. They inclined their heads towards yt. There were a lot of gendered. In the corner alcove a Chinese woman in a beautiful black suit was kissing a nute. She had the nute down yts back on the divan. Her fingers played with the hormonal gooseflesh on yts forearm. Somewhere Tal reasoned yt should be leaving, really, but all yt felt was a warm dislocation. Another banana, yt thought, would be good.

The crop from the far left pillar gave a short, sharp rush of well-being. Tal stepped carefully to the edge of the pool to look up at the tiered balconies. The higher you went, the fewer clothes you needed, yt concluded. That was all right. Everything was all right. The blind woman had said.

"Tranh?" Tal asked of a knot of bodies gathered around a fragrant hookah. An achingly young and lovely nute with fine East Asian features peered out of a press of male bodies. "Sorry," Tal said and drifted on. "Have you seen Tranh?" yt asked a nervous looking woman standing by a sofa of laughing nutes. They all turned to stare at yt. "Is Tranh here yet?" The man stood by the third magic banana vine. He was soberly dressed in a semiformal evening suit; Jayjay Valaya, Tal guessed from the cut. A smart man, thin, middle-aged but took care of his flesh. Fine, aesthetic features, thin-lipped, a look of intelligence in his darting eyes. The eyes, the face, were nervous. His hands, Tal observed through the marvellous power of the banana that put everything into significant focus, were well manicured, and shaking.

"I beg your pardon?" the dapper man said.

"Tranh. Tranh. Is yt here?"

The man looked nonplussed, then plucked a banana from the fist beside his head. He offered it to Tal.

"I'm looking for someone," Tal said.

"Who is this?" the man said, again offering the banana. Tal brushed it away with yts hand.

"Tranh. Have you? No . . ." Tal was already walking away.

"Please!" the man called after yt, clutching the banana between yts fingers like a linga. "Do stay, and talk, just talk . . ."

Then yt saw. Even in the flicker-lit shadows beneath the balcony, there was no mistaking the profile, the angle of the cheekbones, the way yt leaned forward to talk animatedly, the play of the hands in the lantern light; the laughter like a temple bell.

"Tranh."

Yt did not look up from yts intent conversation with yts friends, all huddled over the low table, deep in shared memory.

"Tranh." This time, yt was heard. Tranh looked up. The first thing Tal read on yts face was blank incomprehension. I do not know who you are. Then, recognition, then remembrance, then surprise, shock, displeasure. Last: embarrassment.

"Sorry," Tal said, stepping back from the alcove. All the faces were looking at yt. "I'm sorry, I've made a mistake . . ." Yt turned and fled, discreetly. A need to cry pumped through Tal's skull. The shy man still stood in the greenery. Feeling enemy eyes still on yt, Tal took the banana from his soft fist, peeled it, bit deep. Then the pharm piled in and Tal felt the dimensions of the courtyard inflate to infinity around yt. Yt offered the strange fruit to the man.

"No, thank you," he stammered but Tal had him by the arm and was marching him to a vacant sofa dock. Yt could still feel those eyes hot on the back of yts skull.

"So," Tal said, sitting sideways on the low sofa and draping yts thin hands over yts folded knees. "You want to talk to me, so let's talk." A glance back. They were still looking. Yt finished the banana and the fluttering lanterns opened up and yt fell into their gravity and yts next clearly focused thought was of the facade of a Kurdish restaurant. A waiter whisked yt past tables of startled customers to a small booth at the back partitioned by a fragrant carved cedar screen.

The blind woman's bananas, like good guests, came promptly and departed early. Tal felt the carved geometric patterns on the wooden screens rush in from celestial distance to claustrophobia. The restaurant was hot and every customer voice, kitchen noise, and street sound was intolerably sharp and close.

"I hope you don't mind me bringing you here, but I don't like it back there," the man was saying. "It's no place to talk, really talk. But it's discreet here; the owner is in my debt." Mezze were brought, and a bottle of clear liquor with a jug of water. "Arak," the man said, pouring a measure. "I don't drink myself, but I'm told it is a great instiller of courage." He added water. Tal marvelled as the clear liquid turned to luminous milk. Tal took a sip, recoiled at the alien aniseed, then had a slower, more considered measure.

"Yt's a chuutya," Tal declared. "Tranh. "Yt's a chuutya. Yt wouldn't even look at me; just sat mooning all over yts friends. I wish I'd never come now."

"It's so hard to find someone to listen to," the man said. "Someone who doesn't have an agenda, who isn't asking me for something or trying to sell me something. In my work everyone wants to hear what I have to say, what my ideas are, every word I say is treated like gold. Before I met you, I was at a durbar in the Cantonment. Everyone wanted to hear what I had to say, everyone wanted something from me, except this one man. He was a strange man and he said a strange thing; he said that we are a deformed society. I listened to that man."

Tal sipped yts arak.

"Cho chweet, we nutes have always known that."

"So tell me the secrets you know. Tell me what you are. I'd like to hear how you came to be."

"Well," Tal said, conscious of every scar and implant under the man's attentive gaze, "my name's Tal, and I was born in Mumbai in 2019 and I work in Indiapendent on the metasoap design team for *Town and Country*."

"And in Mumbai," the man said, "in 2019 when you were born, what . . ."

Tal laid a finger to his lips.

"Never," yt whispered. "Never ask, never tell. Before I Stepped Away, I was another incarnation. I am only alive now, do you understand? Before was another life, and I am dead and reborn."

"But how . . ." the man asked. Again, Tal laid its soft, pale finger against the man's lips. Yt could feel them trembling, the flutter of warm, sweet breath.

"You said you wanted to listen," Tal said and gathered yts shawl around yt.

"My father was a choreographer in Bollywood, one of the top. Did you ever see *Rishta*? The number where they're dancing across the roofs of the cars in the traffic jam? That was him."

"I'm afraid I don't much care for films," the man says.

"It got too camp in the end. Too self-referential, too knowing. It always gets like that, things become superexaggerated, then they die. He met my mother on the set of *Lawyers in Love*. She's Italian, she was a hovercam trainee—at the time, Mumbai was the best, even the Americans were sending people out here to learn technique. They met, they married, six months later, me. And before you ask, no. An only. They were the toast of Chowpatty Beach, my parents. I got to all the parties; I was a real accessory. I was a gorgeous kid, baba. We were never out of the filmi mags and the gossip rags; Sunny and Costanza Vadher, with their beautiful child, shopping on Linking Road, on the set of *Aap Mujhe Acche Lagne Lage*, at the Chelliah's barbecue. They were the most incredibly selfish people I think I have ever met—but they were totally unselfconscious about it. That's what Costanza accused me of when I Stepped Away; how incredibly selfish I was. Can you believe it? Where did she think I learned it?

"They weren't stupid. They might have been selfish, but they weren't stupid, they must have known what was going to happen when they started to bring in the aeais. It was the actors first—one day *Chati* and *Bollywood Masala* and *Namaste!* are full of Vishal Das and Shruti Rai at an opening at Club 28, next *Filmfare*'s running centre page triple pullouts without a single cubic centimetre of living flesh. It really was that quick."

The man murmurs polite amazement.

"Sunny could have a hundred people dancing on a giant laptop, but now it was one touch and you'd have them dancing from here to the horizon, all in perfect synch. They could get a million people dancing on clouds, just with one click. It hit him hardest first. He got bad, he got ratty, he would take it out on people around him. He was mean when it turned against him. I think that's maybe why I wanted to get into soapi; to show him there was something he could have done, if he'd tried, if he hadn't been so strung up by his own image and status. Then again, maybe I just don't care enough. But it hit Costanza soon after, too; you don't need actors or dancers, you don't need cameras, either. It's all in the box. They would fight: I must have been ten, eleven, I could hear them screaming so loud the neighbours would come banging on the door. Two of them in that apartment all day, both of them needing work, but jealous as hell in case the other actually got something. In the evenings they'd go to the same old parties and durbars to schmooze. Please, *a job*. Costanza coped better. She adjusted, she got a different job in the industry in script development. Sunny, he couldn't. Walked right out. Fuck him. Fuck him. He was a waste anyway."

Tal snatched up the arak, took a bitter draft.

"It all ended. I'd say it was like a film, the credits roll, the lights came up, and we were back in the real again, but it wasn't. It didn't have a third act. It didn't have an against-all-the-odds-happy-ever-after. It just got worse and worse and then it just ended. It stopped, like the film snapped and I wasn't living in a Manori Beach apartment and I wasn't at the John Connon School and I wasn't going round the parties with all the stars saying, *oh look, isn't it sweet and look how big it's getting?* I was in a two-room apartment in Thane with Costanza, going to the Bom Jesus Catholic School, and I hated it. I hated it. I wanted it all back again, all the magic and the dancing and the fun and the parties and this time I wanted it to go on after the credits rolled. I just wanted everyone to look at me and say, wow. Just that. Wow."

Tal sat back, inviting admiration but the man looked afraid, and something more Tal could not identify. He said, "You are an extraordinary creature. Do you ever feel that you're living in two worlds, and that neither of them is real?"

"Two worlds? Honey, there are thousands of worlds. And they're as real as you want them to be. I should know; I've lived all my life between them. None of them are real, but when you get into them, they're all the same."

The man nodded, not in agreement with anything Tal had said, but at some inner dialogue. He summoned the bill, left a pile of notes on the little silver tray.

"It's getting late, and I do have affairs to attend to in the morning."

"What sort of affairs?"

The man smiled to himself.

"You are the second person to ask me that tonight. I work in information management. Thank you for coming with me here and the pleasure of your company; you really are an extraordinary human, Tal."

"You didn't give me your name."

"No, I don't believe I did."

"That's so male," Tal said, sweeping along behind the man on to the street where he was already waving down a taxi.

"You could call me Khan."

Something has changed, Tal thought as yt slid in to the back seat of the Maruti. The man Khan had been nervous, shy, guilty at the Banana Club. Even in the restaurant he had not been at ease. Something in yts story had worked on his mind and mood.

"I don't go to White Fort after midnight," the driver said.

"I will pay you treble," Khan said.

"I'll get as close as I can"

Khan leaned his head against the greasy rest.

"You know, it really is an excellent little restaurant. The owner came here about ten years ago in the last wave of the Kurdish diaspora. I . . . helped him. He set the place up, he's doing well. I suppose he's a man trapped between two worlds as well."

Tal was only half listening, curling up in the arak glow. Yt leaned against Khan, for warmth, for solidity. Yt let yts inner arm roll into the space between them. The row of buds were puckered like bitch-nipples in the street glow. Tal saw the man start at the sight. Then a hand was stabbing down the front of yts lounging pants, a face loomed over yt, a mouth clamped over yts. A tongue pressed entrance to yts body. Tal gave a muffled scream, Khan recoiled in shock, which gave Tal space to push and shout. The phat-phat bounced to a halt in the middle of the highway. Tal had the door open and was out, shawl flapping behind yt, before yt was fully conscious of what yt was doing.

Tal ran.

Tal stops running. Yt stands, hands on thighs; panting. Khan is still there, peering through the headlight blur, calling out futilely into the traffic roar. Tal stifles a sob. Yt can still smell the aftershave on yts skin, taste tongue in yts mouth. Shaking, yt waits a safe few minutes before flagging in a cruising phatphat. DJ Aeai plays MIX FOR A NIGHT TURNED SCARY.

15

VISHRAM

New day, new array. Everyone from cleaners to Centre Director turned out under the canopy of the Ranjit Ray Research Centre. They look nervous. *Not nearly as nervous as your unexpected and unprepared CEO*, Vishram Ray thinks as the car crunches sensuously up the raked gravel drive. Vishram checks cuffs, tugs collar.

"You should have worn a tie," says Marianna Fusco. She is cool, immaculate, creases all geometrical.

"I've done my tie-wearing for this lifetime," Vishram says, lick-slicking down hair in the vanity mirror in the chauffeur's headrest. "Anyway, as any historian of costume will tell you, the sole purpose of the tie is to point to your dick. That's not very Hindu business, that."

"Vishram, everything points to your dick."

Vishram thinks he hears the driver snigger as he opens the door.

"Don't worry, I've got you," Marianna Fusco whispers in Vishram's ear as he walks purposefully up the steps. His 'hoek comes to life in his head. A moment's visual blur as the aeai deletes the junk and filters the ads, then he is striding forwards to meet the director, hand held out in greeting. GANDHINAGAR SURJEET say the blue words hovering in front of him. D.O.B 21/02/2009. WIFE SANJUAY, CHILDREN: RUPESH (7); NAGESH (9). JOINED RAY RESEARCH AND DEVELOPMENT 2043 FROM UNIVERSITY OF BANGALORE RENEWABLE RESOURCES RESEARCH DEPARTMENT. FIRST DOCTORATE . . . Vishram blinks off the supplementary information.

"Mr. Ray, you are very welcome to our division."

"It's a pleasure to be here, Dr. Surjeet."

It's all playing a role, really.

"You do find us in something of a state of unreadiness," he says.

"Not half as unready as me." The joke seems to go down well. But then they would laugh, wouldn't they? Dr. Surjeet moves to his department heads.

INDERPAL GAUR, says the relentless palmer. 15/08/2011, CHANDIGARH. RESEARCH SUBDIVISION: BIOMASS. MARITAL STATUS: SINGLE. EMPLOYMENT HISTORY AT RAY POWER: JOINED R&D 2034 FROM UNIVERSITY OF THE PANJAB, CHANDIGARH CAMPUS.

LET HIM DO THE INTRODUCTIONS, Marianna warns in lilac over Director Surjeet's head. Dr. Gaur is a toothy, plump woman in traditional dress, through there is nothing old-fashioned about the anodised aluminium 'hoek curled against the side of her pigtail. He wonders what is her 'hoek graffiting about him? VISHRAM RAY: WASTER SON. FAILED LAWYER. ASPIRANT STAND-UP. THINKS HE'S PRETTY DAMN FUNNY.

"It's a great honour," she says, namasteing.

"All mine, I assure you," Vishram says.

And on, down the row of department heads and senior researchers and team leaders and those who have had important papers published.

"I am Khaleda Husainy," says a small, intense woman in a Western-style suit and a headscarf chador. "It is a great pleasure to meet you, Mr. Ray." Her discipline is microgeneration. Parasitic power.

"What, people generate power just walking up and down?"

"Pumps in the pavement, yes" she enthuses. "There is immense energy being wasted out there, waiting for us to capture it. Everything you do and say is a source of power."

"You should hook it up to our legal department."

It gets a laugh.

"And what do you do to help make Ray Power A-Number One?" Vishram says to a young, almost-good-looking woman whose lapel badge identifies her as Sonia Yadav.

"Nothing," she says with a smile.

"Ah," Vishram says, moving on. Hands to shake. Faces to remember. She calls after him.

"When I said nothing, I meant, energy from nothing. Endless free power."

"You've got my attention now."

"I'm taking you to the zero-point lab," Sonia Yadav explains as she leads Vishram and his entourage to her research unit. She looks at him closely.

"Your eyeballs are moving. Is someone messaging you?"

Vishram shuts off Marianna Fusco's silent commentary with a twist of a finger.

His father's engineers have designed a building more furniture than architecture. All is wood and fabric, curved into bows and arches, translucent and airy. The place smells of sap and resin and sandalwood. The floors are strip maple inlaid with marquetry panels of scenes from the *Ramayana*. Sonia Yadav looks pointedly at Marianna's heels. She slips them off and closes them in her bag. It feels right to Vishram to be barefoot here. It's a holy place.

At first sight the zero-point lab disappoints Vishram. There are no humming machines or looping power conduits, just desks and glass partitions, paper piled unsteadily on the floor, whiteboards on the walls. The white boards are full of scrawls. They continue onto the walls. Every square centimetre of surface is crammed with symbols and letters wedged at crazy angles to each other, lassoed in loops of black felt marker, harpooned by long lines and arrows in black and blue to some theorem on the other side of the board. The brawling equations spread over desks, benches, any flat surface that will take felt marker. The mathematics is as unintelligible to Vishram as Sanskrit, but the cocoon of thought and theory and vision comforts him, like being inside a prayer.

"It may not look like much but the research team at EnGen would pay a lot of money to get in here," Sonia Yadav says. "We do most of the hot stuff over on the University collider, or at the LHC in Europe, but this is where the real work gets done. The headwork."

"Hot stuff?"

We're following two approaches, hot and cold, we call them. I won't bore you with the theory but it's to do with energy levels and quantum foam. Two ways of looking at nothing."

"And you're hot?" Vishram asks, studying the hieratic glyphs on the wall.

"Absolutely," Sonia Yadav says.

"And can you do what you say; generate power from nothing?"

She stands firm with a light of belief in her eyes.

"Yes, I can."

"Mr. Ray, we really should be moving on," Director Surjeet urges.

As his party leaves, Vishram picks up a felt marker and quickly writes on the desktop: DNNR, 2NITE?

Sonia Yadav reads the invite upside down.

"Strictly professional," Vishram whispers. "Tell me what's hot and what's not."

OK she writes in red.

8. PICK-UP HERE.

She underlines the OK twice.

Immediately outside in the corridor is a sight that instantly detumesces Vishram's good humour: Govind, in his too-tight suit, with his phalanx of lawyers, bowling down the corridor as if he owned the place. Govind spies his younger brother, opens his mouth to greet, damn, bless, chide—Vishram doesn't care, never hears because he calls out, loudly,

"Mr. Surjeet, could you please call security." Then, as the Director talks into his palmer, Vishram holds up one single, commanding finger in front of his brother and his crew. "You, say nothing. This is not your place. This is my place." Security arrives; two very large Rajputs in red turbans. "Please escort Mr. Ray from the building and scan his face for the security system. He is not to return without my express, written permission."

The Rajputs seize Govind, one on each arm. It gives Vishram's heart a pile of pleasure to watch them march him at a fast trot down the corridor.

"Hear me, hear me!" Govind shouts back over his shoulder. "He will wreck it like he has wrecked everything else he has ever been given. I know him of old. The leopard cannot change his spots, he will ruin you all, destroy this great company. Don't listen to him, he knows nothing. Nothing!"

"I'm so sorry about that," Vishram says when the doors have sealed behind his still-protesting brother. "Anyway, shall we continue, or have I seen everything?"

It had begun at breakfast.

"Just what have I inherited?" Vishram asked Marianna Fusco through mouthfuls of kitchiri at his breakfast briefing on the east balcony.

"Basically, you've got the research and development division." She laid out the documents around his greasy plate like tarot cards.

"So, no money and a pile of responsibility."

"I don't think this is something your father thought up on a whim."

"How much did you know about this?"

"What, who, where, and when."

"You're missing a 'w' there."

"I don't think anyone understands that 'w.'"

I can, Vishram thought. I know how good it is to walk away from expectations and obligations. I know how frightening and freeing it is to go out there with nothing but a begging bowl, chancing people's laughter.

"You could have told me."

"And breach my professional confidentiality?"

"You are a cold, hard woman, Marianna Fusco."

He forked down another load of kitchiri. Ramesh wandered into the geometrical planting of English roses, now crisped and withering in their third year of alien drought. His hands were folded behind him, a posture as ancient and familiar as any other element of the Shanker Mahal. Vishram-aged-six had mocked his older brother, stalking after him, hands clamped behind back, lips sucked in in abstract concentration, head up looking around for wonder in the world.

What about those East Asian trips? he wondered. Those Bangkok girls who could do and be anything you imagined. He felt a small stirring beneath his navel, a twitch of hormone. But it would be too easy. No hunt there, no play, no testing of the will and wit, no unspoken contract of mutual recognition that both were engaged on a game with its ploys and stages and rules. A warm wind with the smell of the city on it tugged at the documents of incorporation. Vishram deployed cups and saucers and cutlery to hold them in their proper places. Ramesh, who had been trying to smell the desiccated roses, looked up at the warm touch on his face and was genuinely surprised to see his kid brother and his lady lawyer on the terrace.

"Ah, there you are, I was half-hoping to find you."

"Wretched coffee?"

"Oh, please, yes. And there wouldn't be any more of that, would there?"

Vishram nodded to the servant. Wonderful, how quickly you settle back into the way of service. Ramesh poked at his plate of kitchiri with his fork. "Why did he give it to me?" he said abruptly. "I don't want it, I don't even understand it. I never did. Govind was always the one with the head for business; still is. I'm an astrophysicist; I know deep space organic molecular clouds. I do not know electricity generating."

The split was clever, Shakespearean. Ramesh would have wanted the unworldliness of blue-sky thinking. He had been given the meat and muscle of the generating division.

Govind's ambitions would have been for the core infrastructure. Instead he had been handed control of the distribution network. Wires and cables and pylons. And Number Three Son, the attention seeker, the grab-ass, had gear so arcane he didn't even know if it did anything. Casting against type. Evil old sadhu.

The old man had left before the dawn. His clothes were neatly hangered in the wardrobe. His palmer and 'hoek sat square on the pillow with his wallet and his universal card beside them. His shoes, well polished, were arranged toe-to-footboard at a perfect right angle. His silver-backed hairbrush and comb were caught together in their final kiss on the dressing table. Kukunoor, khidmutgar now Old Shastri had left on the pilgrim path, showed all this to Vishram with the same dispassionate sense of disposable history he had seen in Scotland's historic homes and castles. He did not know where his master had gone. Their mother did not know, either, though Vishram suspected some secret conduit of communication to monitor his legacy. The company would always be the company.

"What are you telling me, Ram?"

"It's not for me."

"What do you want, Ram?"

He toyed with his fork.

"Govind has made me an offer."

"He didn't waste much time."

"He thinks it's disastrous, splitting generation from transmission. The Americans and Europeans have been competing for years to get their hands on Ray Power. Now we are divided and weak and it's only a matter of time before someone approaches one of us with an irresistible offer."

"I'm sure he made a very convincing case. I can't help but wonder where his money's coming from for this great display of fraternal solidarity."

Marianna Fusco's palmer was already open.

She said, "His annual reports are filed with Companies House but his profits are down for the fifth quarter in a row and his bankers are getting edgy. I would say he's looking at protective bankruptcy in the next couple of years."

"So if it's not Govind's, I think you have to ask yourself, whose money is it?"

Ramesh pushed the plate of kitchiri away from him.

"Could you buy me out?"

"Govind at least has a company and a credit rating. I have a jokebook and pile of unopened envelopes with little cellophane windows."

"What can we do?"

"We will run the company. It's a strong company. It's Ray Power, we've grown up with it, we know it like we know this house. But I'll tell you one thing, Ram; I will not let you blame me for what happens. Now if you'll excuse me, I've got employees to meet."

Marianna Fusco rose with him, nodded to Ramesh as they entered the cool dark of the house. Monkeys came skirling down the trees hungry for leftover kitchiri.

Vishram smelled Govind before he saw him reflected in the vanity mirror.

"You know, I could have got you any God's amount of decent aftershave from London duty free. You still on that *Arpal* stuff? Is it some national loyalty thing, the national smell of Bharat?"

Govind slid into the reflection beside Vishram as he adjusted the hang of his cuffs. Good suit. Looking better than you, fat boy.

"And since when did we start to walk in without knocking?" Vishram added.

"Since when has family needed to knock?"

"Since they all became big businessmen. And by the way, I won't be staying here tonight. I'm moving out to a hotel." Cuffs right. Lapels right. Collar right. Bless those Chinese tailors. "So, make your offer."

"Ramesh has spoken to you, then."

"Did you really think he wouldn't? I hear you've a liquidity problem."

Uninvited, Govind seated himself on the edge of the bed. Vishram noticed in the mirror that his brother's feet did not quite reach the ground.

"You may find this hard to believe, but all I want to do is keep the company together."

"You're right."

Still Vishram kept his back turned.

"EnGen have made no secret that they want Ray. Even when our father was CEO, they had made approaches. They will have it, sooner or later. We cannot hope to stand against the Americans. They will have us in the end, and what we, between us, have to decide is if they pick us off one by one, or take us in one big mouthful. I know what I prefer. I know what is better for the company our father built. There is strength in unity."

"Our father built an Indian business in an Indian way."

"My brother, the social conscience?" In those five words Vishram knew that he and his brother were eternal enemies. Rama and Ravanna. "Those old women and Grameen bankers will be the first to turn on you when the offers come in," Govind continued. "They speak fine and noble but offer then a purseful of dollars and see the solidarity of the poor then. They know business better than you, Vishram."

"I don't think so," Vishram said softly. His brother frowned.

"I'm sorry, I didn't hear you."

"I said, I don't think so. In fact, you can say whatever you like now, and I will go against you. That's the way it's going to be from now on. Whatever you do, whatever you say, whatever offer you make or deal you strike, I will oppose it. You may be wrong, you may be right, it may make me a billion dollars, but I am going to oppose it. Because now I can, and now you can't do anything or run to anyone or issue any older-brother orders, because I will still own one-third of Ray Power. Now, you're in my bedroom and you didn't knock and you're certainly not here by invitation, but I'm going to overlook it because this is the last night I stay in this room, in this house and I have work to do now."

It was only as he settled into the airco-cooled leather of the car that Vishram noticed the little crescents of blood in his palms; the stigmata of clenched nails.

It's a dire Italian but it's the only Italian. Nostalgic already for the cooking of the Glasgow Italians, a mighty race, Vishram had lit upon the prospect of pasta and ruffino before he remembered that Varanasi has no rooted Italian community, has no Italian in its genes at all. The staff is all local. The music is compiled from the charts. The wine is overheated and tired from the long drought. There is something on the menu called pasta-tikka.

"I'm sorry it's so terrible," he apologises to Sonia Yadav.

She struggles with overcooked spaghetti.

"I've never eaten Italian before."

"You're not eating Italian now."

She has made an effort for this dire dinner. She has done something with her hair, hung a little gold and amber around her. *Arpege 27*: that'll have been some European duty-free somewhere. He likes it that she has worn a business sari and not an ugly Western-style suit. Vishram sits back in his chair, touches his fingertips together, then realises he looks too much like a James Bond villain and unfolds.

"How much could you reasonably expect a liberal arts boy to understand about zero-point power?"

Sonia Yadav pushes her plate away from her with evident relief.

"Okay, well for starters, it's not strictly zero-point as most people think of it." Sonia Yadav has a slight pucker between the eyes when she is saying or thinking or contemplating something difficult. It's very cute. "Do you remember what I said back in the lab about cold and hot? The classic zero-point theories are cold theories. Now, our theories suggest they won't work. Can't work: there's a ground-state wall you just can't get around. You don't beat the second law of thermodynamics."

Vishram lifts a breadstick, breaks it theatrically in two.

"I got the cold and hot bit . . ."

"Okay. I'll try. And by the way, I saw that thing with the breadstick in the remake of the *Pyar Diwana Hota Hai*."

"Little more wine, then?"

She takes the refill but doesn't touch it. Wise woman. Vishram settles back with the traumatised Chianti in the ancient ritual of listening to a woman tell a story.

It's a strange and magical tale as full of contradictions and impossibilities as any legend from the Mahabharata. There are multiple worlds and entities that can be two contradictory things at the same time. There are beings that can never be fully known or predicted, that once entangled remain linked though they be removed to opposite ends of the universe so that what happens to one is instantly felt by the other. Vishram watches Sonia's demonstration of the double-slit experiment with a fork, two capers, and ripples in the tablecloth and thinks, what a strange and alien world you inhabit, woman. The quantum universe is as capricious and uncertain and unknowable as the triple world that rested on the back of the great turtle, ruled by gods and demons.

"Because of the uncertainty principle, there are always virtual particle pairs being born and vanishing again at all possible energy levels. So, in effect, in every cubic centimetre of empty space, there is theoretically an infinite amount of energy, if we can just stop the virtual particles disappearing."

"I have to tell you, this liberal arts boy doesn't understand a word of this."

"No one does. Not deep down; understand as we understand understanding. All we have is a description of how it works, and it works better than any theory we've ever come up with, and that's including M-Star theory. It's like the mind of Brahma; no one can understand the thoughts of a creator deity, but that doesn't mean that there is no creation."

"For a scientist, you use a lot of religious metaphors."

"This scientist believes we live in a Hindu universe." Sonia Yadav presses her point. "Don't get me wrong, I'm not like those Christian fundamentalist creation scientists—that's not science; it denies empiricism and the very fact the universe is knowable. Creationists adapt the empirical evidence to suit their particular scriptural interpretation. I think what I think because of the empirical evidence. I'm a rational Hindu. I'm not saying I believe in actual gods, but quantum information theory and M-Star theory teach you the connectedness of all things and how properties emerge that can never be predicted by any of the constituent elements and that the very large and the very small are two sides of the same superstring. Do I need to tell a Ray about Hindu philosophy?"

"Maybe this Ray. So you'll not be pulling N. K. Jivanjee on his rath yatra." He'd seen the photographs on the evening news. Hell of a scoop.

"I'll not be pulling, but I might be in the crowd. And anyway, it's got a biodiesel engine in it."

Vishram sits back in his chair, pulls at his lower lip as he does when observations and turns of phrase come flocking and cawing into a comedy routine.

"So tell me; you haven't got a bindi and you're out without a chaperone; how does this all sit with N. K. Jivanjee and the mind of Brahma?"

Sonia Yadav does the pucker again.

"I will say this straight and simple. Jati and varna have benighted our nation for three thousand years. Caste was never a Dravidian concept—it was those Aryans and their obsession with division and power. That's why the British loved it here—they're still fascinated with anything to do with this country. The class divide is their national narrative."

"Not the bit of Britain I was in," Vishram asides.

"For me, N. K. Jivanjee is about national pride, about Bharat for Bharat, not sold by the kilo to the Americans. About Hindu zero-point energy. And in the twenty first century, no woman needs a chaperone; and anyway, my husband trusts me."

"Ah," Vishram says, hoping his crestfallenness doesn't carry. "So, M-Star theory?"

As far as he can get it, it's like this. First there was string theory, which Vishram has heard of, something to do with everything being notes from vibrating strings. Very pretty. Very musical. Very Hindu. Then there was M-theory, which attempted to resolve the contradictions of string theory but which reached in different directions, like the legs of a starfish. The theoretical centre arrived last, in the late twenties in the shape of M-Star theory . . .

"I can see the star, but what's the M for?"

"That's a mystery," Sonia Yadav smiles. They're on Stregas now. The liqueur holds up well against the climate.

In M-Star theory the wrappings and foldings of the primal strings in eleven dimensions into membranes create the polyverse of all possible universes, all with fundamental properties differing from those experienced by humans.

"Everything is there," says Sonia Yadav. "Universes with an extra time dimension, two-dimensional universes—there's no gravity in two-dimensional universes. Universes where self-organisation and life is a basic property of space-time . . . An infinite number of universes. And that's the difference between cold and hot zero-point theory."

Vishram calls for another round of Stregas. He doesn't know if it's the Sip that Charms or the physics, but his brain is at the Swaddled in Cottonwool stage.

"What stops cold zero-point theory in its tracks is the second law of thermodynamics." The waiter serves the second round. Vishram studies Sonia Yadav through the gold in the little bubble glass. "Stop that, and pay attention! To be useful, energy has to go somewhere. It's got to flow from higher to lower, hot to cold, if you like. But in our universe the zero point, the quantum fluctuation, is the ground state. There's nowhere for the energy to flow; it's all uphill. But in another universe . . ."

"The ground state, whatever you call it, might be higher . . ."

Sonia Yadav claps her hands together in a silent namaste.

"Exactly! Exactly! It would naturally flow from higher to lower. We could tap that infinite energy."

"First find your universe."

"Oh, we found one a long time ago. It's a simple manifold of the M-Star theoretical structure of our own universe. Gravity is more powerful there; so is the expansion constant, so there's a lot more vacuum energy tied up in the stressed space-time. It's quite a small universe, and not too far away."

"I thought you said the universes were all inside and outside each other."

"They are, topologically. I'm talking about energy distance, how much we need to warp our 'branes to the geometry of that one. In physics, ultimately, everything is energy."

Warped brains, all right.

Sonia Yadav sets her empty glass firmly on the gingham tablecloth, leans forwards, and Vishram cannot refuse the physical energy in her eyes, her face, her body.

"Come with me," she says. "Come and see it."

After Glasgow, the University of Bharat Varanasi at night is unusually well mannered. No discarded polystyrene trays of rain-soaked chips or dropped beer glasses or vomit pizzas to dodge in the brownout. No sounds of coitus from the halls or urination from the shrubberies. No sinister drunk reeling out of the peripheral vision with a racial curse. No gangs of half-naked girls arm in arm streeling across the dusty, withered lawns. What there is is a lot of heavy security, a few dons on big clunky bicycles with no lights, the rattle of a solitary night-radio and a sense from the shut-up faculty buildings and student residences of curfew.

The driver heads towards the only light. The experimental physics building is an orchidlike confection of luminous plastic sheeting and pylons, daring and delicate. The name on the marble plinth is the Ranjit Ray Centre for High Energy Physics. Buried beneath the delicate, flowery architecture is a grunt engineering pulse laser particle collider.

"He seems to have been a man of many parts, my father," Vishram says as the night security nods them through the lobby. His face is known now.

"He's not dead," Sonia Yadav says and Vishram starts.

An elevator bank at the end of the lobby takes them down a tube to the root of the beast. It is a mythological creature indeed, a world-devouring worm curled in a loop beneath Sarnath and Ganga. Vishram looks through the glass observation window at electrical devices each the size of a ship engine and tries to imagine particles forced into strange and unnatural liaisons.

"When we run it to full power to open an aperture, those containment magnets put out a field strong enough to suck the haemoglobin out of your blood," Sonia Yadav says.

"How do you know this?" Vishram asks.

"We tried it with a goat, if you really want to know. Come on."

Sonia Yadav leads the way down a long flight of concrete steps to an air-lock door. The security panel eyeballs her, opens into an airlock.

"Are we going into space or something?" Vishram asks as the lock cycles.

"It's just a containment device."

Vishram decides he doesn't want to know what's being contained, so he fluffs, "I know my father's rich—was rich—and there's rich buys private jets, rich buys private islands, but rich that buys private particle colliders . . ."

"There are other backers involved," Sonia Yadav says. The inner hatch spins and they enter an unspectacular concrete office, headachingly lit with neon and flatscreen flicker. A young, bearded man rocks back on a chair, feet on the desk, reading the evening paper. He has an industrial thermos of chai and a Styrofoam cup; the computers bang out old-school bhangra from a Bengali station. He jumps up when he sees his late-night visitors.

"Sonia, I'm sorry, I didn't know."

"Deba, this is . . ."

"I know, pleased to meet you, Mr. Ray." He has an overemphatic handshake. "So, you've come to take a look at our own little private universe?" Beyond a second door is a small concrete room into which the visitors fit like segments of an orange. A heavy glass panel is level with Vishram's head. He squints but can make nothing out of it. "We only need numbers really, but some people have this atavistic urge to eyeball things," Deba says. He's brought his chai with him, he takes a sip. "Okay, we're in an observation area beside the confinement chamber, which we in our humorous physicists' way call the Holding Cell. It's basically a modified tokamak torus—does this mean anything to you? No? Think of it as an inverse donut; it's got an outside, but inside is the hardest vacuum you can imagine. It's actually harder than any vacuum you can imagine, all there is in there is space-time and quantum fluctuation. And this."

He hits the lights. Vishram's blind for an instant, then he becomes aware of a gaining glow from the window. He remembers a physics student he once took home telling him that the retina can detect a single photon and therefore the human eye can see on the quantum scale. He leans forwards; the glow comes from a line of blue, sharp as a laser; Vishram can see it curve off around the walls of the tokamak. He presses his face to the glass.

"Uh oh, panda eyes," Deba says. "It throws off a lot of UV."

"This is . . . another universe?"

"It's another space-time vacuum," Sonia Yadav says. She stands close enough for Vishram to fully appreciate her *Arpege 27*. "It's been stable for a couple of months. Think of it as another nothing, but with a vacuum energy higher than ours . . ."

"And it's leaking into our universe."

"It's not much higher, we're only getting a two percent above input return from it, but we hope to use this space to open an aperture into a yet higher energy space, and so on, up the ladder until we get a significant return."

"And the light . . ."

"Quantum radiation; the virtual particles of this universe—we call it Universe two-eight-eight—running into the laws of our universe and annihilating themselves into photons."

Not it's not, Vishram thinks, looking into the light of another time and space. And you know it's not, Sonia Yadav. It is the light of Brahma.

PART THREE
KALKI

16

SHIV

A boyz always got his mother.

It had been almost a homecoming, walking through the narrow galis between the shanties, ducking under the power cables, keeping the good shoes on the cardboard paths because even in the driest of droughts the alleys of Chandi Basti were piss-mud. The runways constantly realigned themselves as shanties collapsed or additions were built on, but Shiv steered by landmarks: Lord Ram Indestructible Car Parts where the brothers Shasi and Ashish were taking a VW apart into tiny parts; Mr. Pilai's Sewing Machine under its umbrella; Ambedkar the child-buyer's agent sitting on his raised porch of forklift pallets, smoking sweet ganja. Everywhere, people looking, people stepping aside, people making gestures to ward off the eye, people following him with their gaze because they had seen something from outside their existence, something with taste and class and great shoes, something that was *something*. Something that was a *man*.

His mother had looked up at his shadow across her doorway. He pushed money on her, a wad of grubby rupees. He had a little cash in hand from the man who hauled away the remains of the Merc. It left him short, but a son should repay some of the debt he owes his mother. She pretended to tsk it away, but Shiv saw her tuck it behind the brick by the fire.

He's back. It's only a charpoy in the corner but there's a roof and a fire and dal twice a day and the secure knowledge that no one, no thing, no killing machine with scimitars for hands will find Shiv here. But there is a danger here, too. It would be easy to sink back into the routine of a little eating, a little sleep in the noon-day sun, a little thieving, a little hanging around with your friends, talking this and that and looking at the girls and that is a day, a year, a life gone. He must be thinking, talking, pulling in his debts and his favours. Yogendra goes out running through basti and city, listening to what the streets are saying about Shiv, who has turned his collar against him, who still has a thread of honour.

And then there is his sister.

Leela is a reminder that a son and brother should not leave it from Diwali to Guru Poornima to see his family. What had been a nice-looking, quiet, shy but solid-minded seventeen-year-old—could have married up—has turned Bible Christian. She went out one night with a friend to a religious thing run by a cable television station and came back born again. But it is not enough that she has found the Lord Jesus Christ. Everyone else must find him, too. Especially her baaaadest of baaaadmash brothers. So round she comes with her Bible with the whisper-thin paper that Shiv knows makes the very best spliffs and her little tracts and her cumbersome zeal.

"Sister, this is my time of rest and recreation. You disrupt it. If your Christianity means as much as you say, you would respect your brother. I think it says that somewhere, respect and honour your brother."

"My brothers are my brothers and sisters in Christ. Jesus said that because of me, you will hate your mother and father, and your brother, too."

"Then that is a very foolish religion. Which one of your brothers and sisters in Christ got you drugs when you were dying of tuberculosis? Which one of them rammed that rich man's pharmacy? You are making yourself no one, nothing. No one will marry you if you are not properly Indian. Your womb will dry up. You will cry out for those children. I don't like to say this, but no one else will tell you this truth but me. Mata won't, your Christian friends won't. You are making a terrible mistake, put it right now."

"The terrible mistake is to choose to go to hell," Leela says defiantly.

"And what do you think this is?" Shiv says. Yogendra bares his ratty teeth.

That afternoon Shiv has a meeting: Priya from Musst. Good times there are not forgotten. Shiv watches the chai stall for fifteen minutes to be sure it is her and her alone. She is pain to his heart in her pants that cling to the curve of her ass and her wispy silk top and her amber shades and her pale pale skin and red red sucking lips that pout as she looks around impatiently for him, trying to pick his hair, his face, his walk out of the thronging, staring bodies. She is all the things he has lost. He must get out of here. He must raise himself up again. Be a raja again.

She bounces on her boot heels and gives little squeaks of delight to see him. He gets her tea, they sit on a bench at the metal counter. She offers to get the bill but he pays with some of his dwindling wad. Chandni Basti will not see a woman buy Shiv Faraji tea. Her legs are long and lean and urban. The men of Chandni Basti measure them with their eyes, then catch the hem of the leather coat on the man beside her. They go on their way then. Yogendra sits on an upturned plastic fertiliser barrel and picks at his teeth.

"So, are my women and bartender missing me?" He offers her a bidi, takes a light from the gas burner under the rattling water boiler.

"You are in such trouble." She lights hers off his, a Bollywood kiss. "You know who Ahimsa Debt Collection Agency is?"

"Some gang of hoods."

"The Dawood Gang. It's a new line of work for them, buying debts. Shiv, you have the Dawoods after you. These are the men skinned Gurnit Azni alive in the back of his limo."

"It's all bargaining; they go in high, I go in low, we meet in the middle. That is the way men do business."

"No. They want what you owe them. Not a rupee less."

Shiv laughs, the free, mad laugh breaking up inside. He can see the blue around the edge of his field of vision again, the pure, Krishna blue.

"No one has that kind of money."

"Then you are dead and I am very sorry." Shiv lays his hand flat on Priya's thigh. She freezes.

"You came here to tell me that? I was expecting something from you."

"Shiv, there are a hundred big dadas like you on every street corner, all expecting . . ." Her sentence snaps off as Shiv seizes her jaw, pressing his fingers hard into the soft meat, rubbing his thumb over the bone. Bruises. He will leave bruises like blue roses. Priya yelps. Yogendra bares his incisors. Pain arouses that boy, Shiv thinks. Pain makes him smile. The people of Chandni Basti stare. He feels eyes all around him. Stare well.

"Raja," he whispers. "I am a raja."

He lets her go. Priya rubs her jaw.

"That hurt, madar chowd."

"There's something, isn't there?"

"You don't deserve it. You deserve the Dawoods to cut you up with a robot, behen chowd." She flinches as Shiv reaches for her face again. "It's a little thing but it could lead to more. A lot more. Just a drop off. But if you do it right, they say . . ."

"Who says?"

"Nitish and Chunni Nath."

"I don't work for Brahmins."

"Shiv . . ."

"It is a point of principle. I am a man of principle."

"It's principle to get chopped up into kabob by the Dawoods?"

"I do not take orders from children."

"They aren't children."

"They are here." Shiv cups his hand over his groin, jerks. "No, I will not work for the Naths."

"Then you won't need to go here." She snaps open her little bag and slides a piece of paper across the greasy counter. There is an address, out in the industrial belt. "And you won't need this car." She parks a rental chitty beside the address slip. It's for a Merc, a big Kali-black four-litre SUV Merc, like a raja would drive. "If you don't need any of that, I guess I'll go now and pray for your moksha."

She scoops up her bag and slides off the high bench and pushes past Yogendra and strides off over the cardboard in those high heel boots that make her ass go wip-wop side-a-side.

Yogendra is looking at him. It's that wise-kid look that makes Shiv want to smash his head against the tin counter until he hears things crack and go soft.

"You finished that?" He snatches the kid's can of tea, splashes its contents over the ground. "You have now. We have better business."

The kid is right in his fuck-you silence. He is as old as any Brahmin, inside there in the skull. Not for the first time Shiv wonders if he is a rich boy, a son and heir to some pirate lord, tumbled out of the limo under the neons of Kashi to learn how the world really works. Survive. Thrive. No other rules apply.

"You coming or what?" he shouts at Yogendra. Somewhere the kid has found himself a chew of paan.

Leela comes around again that night to help her mother make cauliflower puris. They are a treat for Shiv but the smell of hot ghee in the confined, dark house makes his skin crawl, his scalp itch. Shiv's mother and sister squat around the little gas cooker. Yogendra sits with them draining the cooked *puris*, on crumpled newspaper. Shiv watches the boy, squatting with the women, scooping the smoking hot breads into their paper nests. This must have meant something to him once. A hearth, a fire, bread, paper. He looks at Leela clapping out the puris into little ovals and throwing them into the deep fat.

She says into the peace of the house, "I'm thinking of changing my name to Martha. It is from the Bible. Leela is from Leelavati who is a pagan goddess but is really a demon of Satan in hell. Do you know what hell is like?" She casually ladles cauliflower puris out on the chicken-wire scoop. "Hell is a fire that never goes out, a great dark hall, like a temple, only greater than any temple you have ever seen because it has to hold all the people who never knew the Lord Jesus. The walls and the pillars are tens of kilometres high and they glow yellow hot and the air is like a flame. I say walls, but there is no outside to hell, only solid rock going on forever in every direction, and hell is carved inside it, so that even if you could escape, which you can't, because you're chained up like a package, there would be nowhere else to go. And the space is filled with billions and billions of people all chained up into little bundles, piled on top of each other, a thousand deep and a thousand wide and a thousand high, a billion people in a pile, and a thousand of those piles. The ones in the centre cannot see anything at all but they can hear each other, all roaring. That is the only sound you hear in hell, this great roaring that never stops, from all the billions of people, chained and burning but never being burned up. That is the thing, burning in flame, but never eaten up."

Shiv shifts on his charpoy. Hell is one thing Christians do well. His dick lifts in his pants. The torment, the screaming, the bodies heaped up in pain, the nakedness, the helplessness, have always stirred him. Yogendra sifts the drained puris into a basket. His eyes are dead, dull, his face animal.

"And the thing is, it goes on forever. A thousand years is not even a second. An age of Brahma is not even one instant in hell. A thousand ages of Brahma and you are still no nearer the end. You haven't even begun. That is where you are going. You will be taken down by the demons and chained up and set on top of the pile of people and your flesh will begin to burn and you will try not to breathe in the flame but in the end you will have to and after that nothing will ever change. The only way to avoid Hell is to put your trust in the Lord Jesus Christ and accept him as your personal Lord and Saviour. There is no other way. Imagine it: hell. Can you even begin to imagine what it will be like?"

"Like this?" Yogendra is fast as a knife in an alley. He grabs Leela's wrist. She cries out but she cannot break his hold. His face is the same feral blank as he pushes her hand towards the boiling ghee.

Shiv's boot to the side of his head knocks him across the room, scattering puris. Leela/Martha flees shrieking to the back room. Shiv's mother flies back from the stove, the hot fat, the treacherous gas flame.

"Get him out of here, out of my house!"

"Oh, he's going," Shiv says as he crosses the room in two strides, lifts Yogendra by two fistfuls of T-shirt and drags him out into the gali. Blood wells from a small cut above his ear but Yogendra still wears that numb, animal smile. Shiv throws him across the alley and follows in with the boot. Yogendra doesn't fight back, doesn't try to defend himself, doesn't try to run or curl into a ball, takes the kicking with a fuck-you smile on his face. It is like striking a cat. Cats never forgive. Fuck him. Cats you drown, in the river. Shiv kicks him until the blue is gone. Then he sits back against the shanty wall and lights a bidi. Lights another, passes it to Yogendra. He takes it. They smoke in the gali. Shiv grinds the butt out on the cardboard beneath the heel of his Italian shoe.

Raja of shit.

"Come on, we've got a car to pick up."

17

LISA

Hand over hand, Lisa Durnau hauls herself up the tunnel into the heart of the asteroid. The shaft is little wider than her body, the vacuum suits are white and clinging, and Lisa Durnau cannot get the thought out of her head that she is a NASA sperm swimming up a cosmic yoni. She pulls herself up the white nylon rope after Sam Rainey's receding gripsoles. The project director's feet come to a halt. She pushes back against a knot on the rope and floats, halfway up a stone vagina, a quarter of a million miles from home. A robot manipulator arm squeezes past her on its way down from the core, outstretched and creeping on little manipulator fingers. Lisa flinches as it brushes past her compression suit. Japanese King Crabs are a childhood horror; things chitinous and spindly. She used to dream of pulling back the bed cover and finding one lying there, pincers weaving up towards her face.

"What's the delay?"

"There's a turning hollow. From here on, you'll begin to feel the effects of gravity. You don't want to be heading facedown."

"This Tabernacle doofus has its own gravity field?"

Sam Rainey's feet tuck up, he vanishes into the gloom between the lume tubes. Lisa sees vague whiteness tumbling and manoeuvring, then his face looks through its visor into hers.

"Just be careful not to get your arms trapped where you can't use them."

Lisa Durnau gingerly draws herself up into the turning space. It's just wide enough to fit a hunched body in a vacuum suit and, as Sam warns, get yourself inextricably trapped. She grimaces at the rock grating on her shoulders.

It's all been cramming and jamming and slamming since she was excreted through the pressure lock into Darnley 285 Excavation Headquarters. If ISS had smelled rancid, Darnley Base was that distilled and casked for a year. Darnley was an unstable trinity of space scientists, archaeologists, and oil rats from the Alaska north slope. Darnley's greatest surprise was what the drill-crews discovered when their bits punched through raw rock and the spycams were lowered in. It was not a propulsion system, a mythical space-drive. It was altogether other.

The suit she had been given was a tight-fitting skin, a microweave smaller than a molecule of oxygen, flexible enough to move in the confined spaces of Darnley's interior, yet with the strength to maintain a human body against vacuum. Lisa had clung, still vertiginous from the transfer from the shuttle, to a handhold in the pressure lock as she felt the white fabric press ever-tighter against her skin and one by one the crew upended themselves and dived down the rabbit hole that was the entrance to the rock. Then it was her turn to fight the claustrophobia and go down into the shaft. Clocks were ticking. She had forty-five minutes to get in, get done with whatever it was dwelt in the heart of Darnley 285, get out, and get on to Captain Pilot Beth's shuttle before she made turnaround.

In the gullet of the asteroid, Lisa Durnau folds her arms across her chest, pulls up her legs, and neatly somersaults. Pushing herself down the rope she feels a little extra assistance pulling at her feet. Now there is a distinct sensation of down and up and her stomach starts to gurgle as it reverts to its natural orientation. She glances between her feet. Sam Rainey's head fills the shaft; around it is a halo. There's light down there.

A few hundred knots downshaft and she can kick off and glide in hundred-metre swoops. Lisa whoops. She finds microgee more exhilarating and liberating than bloated, nauseous free fall.

"Don't forget, you have to come back up again," Sam says.

Five more minutes down and the light is a bright silver shine. Lisa's body says *half a gravity* and getting stronger by the metre. Her mind rebels at the outrage of weight in absolute vacuum. Suddenly Sam's head vanishes. She clings fingers and toes to the wall and squints through her feet into a disk of silver light. She thinks she sees a spider web of ropes and cables.

"Sam?"

"Climb down until you see a rope ladder. Grab a good hold of that, you'll see me."

Feet first, in a too-tight sperm-suit, Lisa Durnau enters the central cavity of Darnley 285. Beneath her feet is the web of cables and ratlines strung around the roof of the cavern. Clinging to the guy ropes, Lisa catwalks across the net towards Sam Rainey, who lies prostrate on the netting.

"Don't look down," Sam warns. "Yet. Come over here and lie beside me." Lisa Durnau eases herself prone on to a sling of webbing and looks down into the heart of the Tabernacle.

The object is a perfect sphere of silver grey. It is the size of a small house and hangs perfectly at the centre of gravity of the asteroid twenty metres beneath Lisa Durnau's faceplate. It gives off a steady, dull, metallic light. As her eyes become accustomed to the chromium glow she becomes aware of variations, ripples of chiaroscuro on the surface. The effect is subtle but once she has the eye for it, she can see patterns of waves clashing and merging and throwing off new diffraction patterns, grey on grey.

"What happens if I drop something into it?" Lisa Durnau asks.

"Everyone asks that one," says Sam Rainey in her ear.

"Well, what does happen?"

"Try it and find out."

The only safely removable object Lisa Durnau can find is one of her nametags. She unvelcroes it from the breast of her suit, drops it through the web. She had imagined it would flutter. It falls straight and true through the tight vacuum inside Darnley 285. The tag is a brief silhouette against the light, then it vanishes into the grey shimmer like a coin into water. Ripples race away across the surface to clash and meld and whirl off brief vortices and spirals. It fell faster than it should, she thinks. Another thing she noticed: it did not pass through. It was annihilated as it intersected the surface. Taken apart.

"The gravity increases all the way down," she observes.

"At the surface it's about fifty gees. It's like a black hole. Except . . ."

"It's not black. So . . . stupid obvious question here . . . what is it?"

She can hear Sam's intake of breath through his teeth on her suitcom.

"Well, it gives off EM in the visible spectrum, but that's the only information we get from it. Any remote sensing scans we perform just die. Apart from this light, in every other respect, it is a black hole. A light black hole."

Except it isn't, Lisa Durnau realises. It does to your radar and X-rays what it did to my name. It takes them apart and annihilates them. But into what? Then she becomes aware of a small, beautiful nausea in her belly. It isn't the embrace of gravity or the worm of claustrophobia or the intellectual fear of the alien and unknown. It's the feeling she remembers from the women's washroom in Paddington Station: the conception of an idea. The morning sickness of original thought.

"Can I get a closer look at it?" Lisa Durnau asks.

Sam Rainey rolls across the mesh of webbing to the technicians huddled together in a rickety nest of old flight chairs and impact strapping around battered instrument cases. A figure with a woman's shoulders and the name *Daen* on an androgynous breast passes an image amplifier to Director Sam. He hooks it over Lisa Durnau's helmet and shows her how to thumb up the tricky little controls. Lisa's brain reels as she zooms in and out, in and out. There's nothing to focus on here. Then it swims into vision. The skin of the Tabernacle fizzes with activity. Lisa remembers elementary school lessons where you popped a slide of pond water under the video camera and it was abuzz with microbeasts. She ratchets up the scale until the jittering, Brownian motion resolves into pattern and action. The silver is the newsprint grey of atoms of black and white, constantly changing from one to the other. The surface of the Tabernacle is a boil of patterns on fractal scales, from slow wave-trains to fleeting formations that scuttle together and annihilate each other or merge into larger, briefer forms that decay like trails in a bubble chamber into exotic and unpredictable fragments.

Lisa Durnau ratchets the vernier up until the graphic display says X1000. The grainy blur expands into a dazzle of black and white, flickering furiously, throwing off patterns like flames hundreds of times a second. The resolution is maddeningly short of clarity but Lisa knows what she would find at the base of it if she could go all the way in; a grid of simple black and white squares, changing from one to the other.

"Cellular automata," whispers Lisa Durnau, suspended above the fractal swirls of patterns and waves and demons like Michelangelo in the Sistine, inverted. Life, as Thomas Lull would know it.

Lisa Durnau has lived most of her life in the flickering black and white world of cellular automata. Her Grandpa Mac—geneful of Scots-Irish contrariness—had been the one to first awaken her to the complexities that lay in a simple pattern of counters across an Othello board. A few basic rules for colour conversion based on the numbers of adjacent black and white tokens and she had baroque filigree patterns awaken and grow across her board.

On-line she discovered entire bestiaries of black-on-white forms that crawled, swam, swooped, swarmed, over her flatscreen in eerie mimicry of living creatures. Downstairs in his study lined with theological volumes, Pastor David G. Durnau constructed sermons proving the earth was eight thousand years old and that the Grand Canyon was carved by waters from the Flood.

In her final High School year, while girlfriends deserted her for Abercrombie, Fitch and skaterboyz, she concealed her social gawkiness behind glitterball walls of three-dimensional cellular automata. Her end-of-year project relating the delicate forms in her computer to the baroque glass shells of microscopic diatoms had boggled even her math teacher. It got her the university course she wanted. So she was a nerd. But she could run fast.

By her second year she was running ten kay a day and probing beneath the surface dazzle of her black-and-white virtual world to the bass-line funk of the *rules*. Simple programmes giving rise to complex behaviour was the core of the Wolfram/Friedkin conjecture. She had no doubt the universe communicated with itself but she needed to know what it was in the fabric of space-time and energy that called the counterpoint. She wanted to eavesdrop on the Chinese whisper of God. The search spun her off the chequerboard of Artificial Life into airy, dragon-haunted realms: cosmology, topology, M-theory and its heir, M-Star theory. She held universes of thought in either hand, brought them together, and watched them arc and burn.

Life. The game.

"We've got a few theories," Sam Rainey says. Thirty-six hours of drugged sleep later, Lisa Durnau is back on ISS. She, Sam, and G-woman Daley form a neat, polite trefoil up in the free-gee, an unconscious recapitulation of the steel symbol pointing the way to the heart of Darnley 285. "Remember when you dropped your name badge."

"It's a perfect recording medium," Lisa says. "Anything it interacts with physically is digitised to pure information." Her name is now part of it. She isn't sure how she feels about that. "So, it takes stuff in; has it ever given anything out? Any kind of transmission or signal?"

She catches a transmission or signal between Sam and Daley. Daley says, "I will address that momentarily, but first Sam will brief you on the historical perspective."

Sam says, "She says historical; it's actually archaeological. In fact even that's not close. It's the cosmological perspective. We've done isotope tests."

"I know some palaeontology, you won't blind me with science."

"Our table of U238 decay products gives it an age of seven billion years."

Lisa Durnau's a clergy child who doesn't like to take the Lord's name in vain but she says a simple, reverent, "Jesus." Alterre's aeons that pass like an evening gone have given her a feel for Deep Time. But the decay of radioactive isotopes opens on the deepest time of all, an abyss of past and future. Darnley 285 is older than the solar system. Suddenly Lisa Durnau is very aware that she is a mere chew of gristle and nerve rattling round inside a coffee can in the middle of nothing.

"What is it," Lisa Durnau says carefully, "that you wanted me to know this *before?*"

Daley Suarez-Martin and Sam Rainey look at each other and Lisa Durnau realises that these are the people her country must rely on in its first meeting with the alien. Not super-heroes, not super-scientists, not super-managers. Not super-anything. Workaday scientists and civil servants. Working through, making it up as they go along. The ultimate human resource: the ability to improvise.

"We've been videoing the surface of the Tabernacle more or less since day one," Sam Rainey says. "It took us some time to realise we had to run the camera at fifteen thousand frames per second to isolate the patterns. We're having them analysed."

"Trying to pick out the rules behind the automaton."

"I don't think I'm betraying any secrets, but we don't have the capacity in this country."

This country, thinks Lisa Durnau, orbiting at the L-5 stable point. Screwed by your own Hamilton Act. She says, "You need high-level pattern-recognition aeais; what, 2.8, higher?"

"There are a couple of decrypting and pattern-recognition specialists out there," Daley Suarez-Martin says. "Regrettably, they aren't in the most politically stable of locations."

"So you don't need me to try and find your Rosetta Stone. What do you need me for?"

"On occasions we have received an incontrovertible, recognisable pattern."

"How many occasions?"

"Three, on three successive frames. The date was July third, this year. This is the first."

Daley floats a big thirty by twenty glossy through the air to Lisa Durnau. Etched in the grey on grey is a woman's face. The cellular automaton's resolution is high enough to show her slight, puzzled frown, her mouth slightly open, even the hint of her teeth. She is young, pretty, racially indeterminate and the scuttling blacks and whites, frozen in time, have caught a tired frown.

"Do you know who she is?" she asks.

"As you can imagine, determining that is a primary priority," Daley says. "We've already interrogated FBI, CIA, IRS, Social Security, and passport databases. No matches."

"She doesn't have to be American," Lisa Durnau says.

Daley seems genuinely surprised by that. She skims the next glossy to Lisa face down. Lisa Durnau turns over the sheet of paper and reaches instinctively for something not falling to cling to. But everything falls here, all together, all the time.

He's changed his glasses, trimmed the beard to a rim of stubble;

he's grown out his hair and lost a pile of weight, but the little grey cells have captured the sardonic, self-conscious, get-that-camera-away-from-me look. Thomas Lull.

"Oh my good God," she breathes.

"Before you say anything, please look at this last image."

Daley Suarez-Martin sets the final photograph floating, framed in space.

Her. It is her face, drawn in silver but clear enough to make out the love spot on her cheek, the laugh-lines around the eyes, a shorter, sportier haircut, the open-mouthed, eyes-wide, muscle-straining expression she cannot quite read: Fear? Anger? Horror? Ecstasy? It is impossible and unbelievable and mad; it is mad beyond madness, and it is her. Lisa Leonie Durnau.

"No," Lisa says slowly. "You're making this up, it's the drugs, isn't it? I'm still on the shuttle. This is out of my head, isn't it? Come on, tell me."

"Lisa, can I assure you that you are not suffering from any post-flight delusions. I'm not showing you fakes or mock-ups. Why should I? Why bring you all the way up here to show you fake photographs?"

That soothing tone. That G-woman MBA-speak. Peace. Be calm. We are in control here. Be reasonable, in the face of the most unreasonable thing in the universe. Clinging with one hand to a webbing strap on the quilted wall of ISS's hub, Lisa Durnau understands that it has all been unreasonable, a chain of ever larger and heavier links, from the moment the people in suits turned up in her office. From before; from the moment her face swirled out of the seethe of cells, without her knowledge, without her permission, the Tabernacle chose her. It has all been foreordained by this thing in the sky.

"I don't know!" Lisa Durnau shouts. "I don't know why . . . it throws up nothing and then comes up with my face. I don't know, right? I didn't ask it to, I didn't want it to, it has nothing to do with me, do you understand me?"

"Lisa." Again, the gentling tone.

It is her, but a her she has never seen. She's never worn her hair like that. Lull has never looked like that. Older freer guiltier. No wiser. And this girl; she has never met her, but she will, she knows. This is a snapshot of her future taken seven billion years ago.

"Lisa," Daley Suarez-Martin says a third time. The third time is Peter's time. The betraying time. "I'm going to tell you what we need you to do."

Lisa Durnau takes a deep breath.

"I know what it is," she says. "I'll find him. I can't do anything else, can I?"

The earth has the little lightbody firmly in its grip. It's three minutes—Lisa's been counting seconds—since the roll jets last fired. The aeai has made its mind up, it is all now in the hands of velocity and gravity. Back-first, Lisa Durnau screams along the edge of the atmosphere in a thing that still looks like an over-gymmed orange squeezer, only now, with the hull temperature climbing towards three thousand cee, it's not as funny as it was down in Canaveral. One digit out either way and thin air becomes a solid wall that ricochets you off into space and no one to catch you before your airco runs flat, or you fireball out and end as a sprinkle of titanium ions with a seasoning of charred carbon.

When she was a teen in her college hall room, Lisa Durnau had given herself one of the great scares of her life, alone in the dark among the noisy plumbing, by imagining what it will be like when she dies. The breath failing. The rising sense of panic as the heart fights for blood. The black drawing in from all sides. The knowledge of what is happening, and that you are unable to stop any of this and that after this meagre, unworthy last instance of consciousness, there will be nothing. And that this will happen to Lisa Durnau. No escape. No let-off. The death sentence is incommutable. She had woken herself up, frozen cold in her stomach, heart sick with certainty. She had stabbed on her light and tried to think good thoughts, bright thoughts, thoughts about guys and running and what she would do for that term paper and where the girls could go for Friday lunch club, but her imagination kept returning to the awful, delicious fear, like a cat to vomit.

Reentry is like that. She tries to think good thoughts, bright thoughts, but all she has is a pick of evils and the worst is out there, heating the hull beyond that padded mesh wall to cremation temperatures. It burns through the drugs. It burns through everything. You are the woman who fell to earth. The lightbody jolts. Lisa gives a small cry.

"It's okay, it's routine, just an asymmetry in the plasma shield." Sam Rainey is strapped in the number two acceleration couch. He's an old hand, been up and down a dozen times but Lisa Durnau smells bullshit. Her fingers have cramped around the armrest; she frees them, touches her heart for brief reassurance. She feels the flat square object in the pocket with her name written on it.

When she finds Thomas Lull she is to show him the contents of her right breast pocket. It is a memory block containing everything known or speculated about the Tabernacle. All she has to do then is persuade him to join the research project. Thomas Lull was the most prominent, eclectic, visionary, and influential scientific thinker of his day. Governments and chat-show hosts alike heeded his opinions. If anyone has an idea, a dream, or a vision of what this thing is, spinning in its stone cocoon, if anyone has a way of unravelling its message and meaning, it will be Thomas Lull.

The block is also guru. Its special power is that it can scan any public or security camera system for recognised faces. It's such a piece of gear that if it's away from Lisa Durnau's personal body odour for more than an hour, it will decompose into a smear of protein circuitry. Be careful with the showers, swims, and keep it close by you when you're in bed, is the instruction. Her one lead is a semiconfirmed sighting of Thomas Lull three and a half years ago in Kerala, South India. The revelation of the Tabernacle hangs from a single, uncorroborated old backpacker story. The embassies and consuls are on Render-All-Assistance alert. A card has been authorised for expenses; it is limitless, but Daley Suarez-Martin, who will always be Lisa Durnau's handler, in orbit or earthbound, would like some record of outgoings.

The little lightpusher hits the air hard, a fist of gravity shoves Lisa Durnau deep into her gel couch and everything is jolting and rattling and shaking. She is more afraid than she has ever been and there is nothing, absolutely nothing she can hold on to. She reaches out a hand. Sam Rainey takes it. His gloved hand is big and cartoonish and one tiny node of stability in a falling, shuddering universe.

"Some time!" Sam shouts, voice shaking. "Some time! When we! Get down! How about! We go out! For a meal! Somewhere?"

"Yes! Anything!" Lisa Durnau wails as she hurtles Kennedy-wards, drawing a long, beautiful plasma trail across the tall-grass prairies of Kansas.

18

LULL

How Thomas Lull knows he is un-American: he hates cars but loves trains, Indian trains, big trains like a nation on the move. He is content with the contradiction that they are at once hierarchical and democratic, a temporary community brought together for a time; vital while it lasts, burning away like early mist when the terminus is reached. All journey is pilgrimage and India is a pilgrim nation. Rivers, grand trunk roads, trains; these are sacred things across all India's many nations. For thousands of years people have been flowing over this vast diamond of land. All is riverrun, meeting, a brief journey together, then dissolution.

Western thought rebels against this. Western thought is car thought. Freedom of movement. Self-direction. Individual choice and expression and sex on the back seat. The great car society. Throughout literature and music, trains have been engines of fate, drawing the individual blindly, inexorably towards death. Trains ran through the double gates of Auschwitz, right up to the shower sheds. India has no such understanding of trains. It is not where the unseen engine is taking you; it is what you see from the window, what you say to your fellow travellers for you all go together. Death is a vast, crowded terminus of half-heard announcements and onward connections on new lines, new journeys. Changing trains.

The train from Thiruvananthapuram moves through a wide web of lines into the great station. Sleek shatabdis weave over the points on to the fast uplines. Long commuter trains whine past festooned with passengers hanging from the doors, riding the boarding steps, piled onto the roofs, arms thrust through the barred windows, prisoners of the mundane. Mumbai. She has always appalled Thomas Lull. Twenty million people live on this onetime archipelago of seven scented islands and the evening rush is upon her. Downtown Mumbai is the world's largest single building; malls and housing projects and office and leisure units fused together into a many-armed, many-headed demon. Nestled at the heart of it is Chattrapati Shivaji Terminus, a bezoar of Victorian excess and arrogance, now completely domed over with shopping precincts and business units, like a toad entombed in a nodule of limestone. There is never a moment when Chattrapati Shivaji is still or silent. She is a city within a city. Certain castes boast they are unique to it; families claim to have raised generations among the platforms and tracks and red brick piers who have never seen daylight. Five hundred million pilgrim feet pass over the Raj marble each year, tended to by citiesful of porters, vendors, shysters, insurance sellers, and janampatri readers.

Lull and Aj descend among the families and luggage onto the platform. The noise is like a mugging. Timetable announcements are inaudible blasts of public address roar. Porters converge on the white faces; twenty hands reach for their bags. A skinny man in a red MarathaRail high-collar jacket lifts Aj's bag. Quick as a knife, her hand stabs out to arrest him. She tilts her head, looks into his eyes.

"Your name is Dheeraj Tendulkar, and you are a convicted thief."

The ersatz porter recoils as if snake-bit.

"We'll carry our own." Thomas Lull takes Aj by the elbow, guides her like a bride through the press of faces and smells. Her gaze darts from face to face to face in the torrent of people.

"The names. All the names; too many to read."

"I still can't understand this gods thing," he says.

The red-jackets have gathered around the rogue. Raised voices, a cry.

There is an hour's wait until the Varanasi shatabdi. Thomas Lull finds haven in a global coffee franchise. He pays Western prices for a cardboard bucket with a wooden stirrer. There is a tightening in his chest, the asthmatic's somatic reaction to this claustrophobic, relentless city beneath a city. Through the nose. Breathe through the nose. The mouth for talking.

"This is very bad coffee, don't you think?" Aj says.

Thomas Lull drinks it and says nothing and watches the trains come and go and the people mill through on their pilgrimages. Among them, a man bound for the last place a man of his age and sentiments should go, a dirty little water war. But it's mystery, allure, it's mad stuff and reckless deeds when all you expect to feel is the universal microwave background humming through your marrow.

"Aj, show me that photograph again. There's something I need to tell you."

But she is not there. Aj moves through the crowd like a ghost. People part around her, staring. Thomas Lull throws cash on the table, dives after her, waving down a couple of porters to heft the bags.

"Aj! Our train is over here!"

She moves on, unhearing. She is the Madonna of Chattrapati Shivaji Terminus. A family sits on a dhuri underneath a display board drinking tea from thermos flasks: mother, father, grandmother, two girls in their early teens. Aj walks towards them, unhurried, unstoppable. One by one they look up, feeling the whole attention of the station turned upon them. Aj stops. Thomas Lull stops. The porters trotting behind him stop. Thomas Lull feels, at some quantum level, every train and luggage van and shunter stop, every passenger and engineer and guard freeze, every signal and sign and notice board halt between the flip and the flop. Aj squats down before the frightened family.

"I have to tell you, you are going to Ahmedabad, but he will not be there to meet you. He is in trouble. It is bad trouble, he has been arrested. The charge is serious; theft of a motorbike. He is being held in Surendranagar District police station, number GBZ16652. He will require a lawyer. Azad and Sons is one of the most successful Ahmedabad criminal law practices. There is a quicker train you can catch in five minutes from Platform Nineteen. It requires a change at Surat. If you hurry you can still catch it. Hurry!"

Lull seizes her arm. Aj turns; he sees emotions in her eyes that frighten him but he has broken the moment. The terrified family are in various states of alarm; father fight, mother flight, grandmother hands raised in praise, daughters trying to gather up the tea things. A hot wet stain of spilled chai spreads across the dhuri.

"She is right," Thomas Lull calls as he drags Aj away. Now she is unresisting, leaden, like the ones he would escort from the beach parties, stumbling over the sand, the ones on the evil trips. "She's always right. If she says go, you go."

Chattrapati Shivaji Terminus exhales and resumes its constant low-intensity scream.

"What the fuck were you thinking of?" Lull says, hurrying Aj to Platform Five where the Mumbai-Varanasi Raj shatabdi has been called, a long scimitar of green and silver glistening in the station floods. "What did you tell those people? You could have started anything, anything at all."

"They were going to see their son but he is in trouble," she says faintly. He thinks she might collapse on him.

"This way sir, this way!" The porters escort them through the crowd. "This car, this car!" Thomas Lull overpays them to take Aj to her seat. It's a reserved two-person carrel, lamp-lit, intimate. Leaning into the cone of light, Thomas Lull says, "How do you know this stuff?"

She will not look at him, she turns her head into the padded seat-back. Her face is ash. Thomas Lull is very afraid she is going to have another asthma attack.

"I saw it, the gods . . ."

He lunges forward, takes her heart-shaped face between his two hands, turns it to look at him.

"Don't lie to me; nobody can do this."

She touches his hands and he feels them fall away from her face.

"I told you. I see it like a halo around people. Things about them; who they are, where they're going, what train they're on. Like those people going to see their son, only he wouldn't be there for them. All that, and they wouldn't have known, and they would have been waiting and waiting and waiting at the station and trains would come and trains would go and still he wouldn't come and maybe the father would go to his address but all they would know is that he went out that morning to work and that he'd said he would meet them all at the station and they'd go to the police and find out that he'd been arrested for stealing a motorbike and they would have to bail him and they wouldn't know who to go to get him out."

Thomas Lull slumps in his seat. He is defeated. His anger, his blunt Yankee rationalism fail before this girl's pale words.

"This son, this prodigal, what's his name?"

"Sanjay."

Automatic doors close. Up the line a whistle shrills over the station roar.

"Have you got that photograph? Show me that photograph, the one you showed me down by the backwater."

Silently, smoothly, the train begins to move. Station wallahs and well-wishers keep pace for a last chance sale or farewell. Aj unfolds the palmer on the table.

"I didn't tell you the truth," Thomas Lull says.

"I asked you. You said: 'Just other tourists on the trip. They've probably got a photograph exactly the same.' That was not the truth?"

The fast electric train rocks over points; picking up speed with every metre it dives into a tunnel, eerily lit by flashes from the overhead lines.

"It was a truth. They were tourists—we all were, but I know these people. I've known them for years. We were all travelling together in India, that's how well we knew each other. Their names are Jean-Yves and Anjali Trudeau; they're Artificial-life theoreticians from the University of Strasbourg. He's French, she's Indian. Good scientists. The last time I heard from them they were thinking of moving to the University of Bharat—all the closer to the sundarbans. That was where they thought the real cutting research was being done, unhampered by the Hamilton Acts and the aeai licensing laws. Looks like they did, but they are not your real parents."

"Why is that?" Aj asks.

"Two things. First, how old are you? Eighteen? Nineteen? They didn't have a child when I knew them four years ago. But that all falls at the second. Anjali was born without a womb. Jean-Yves told me. She could never have children, not even in vitro. She cannot be your natural mother."

The shatabdi bursts out from the undercity into the light. A vast plane of gold slants through the window across the small table. Mumbai's photochemical smog has blessed it with Bollywood sunsets. The perpetual brown haze renders the ziggurats of the projects ethereal as sacred mountains. Power gantries strobe past; Thomas Lull watches them flicker over Aj's face, trying to read emotions, reactions in the dazzling mask of gold. She bows her head. She closes her eyes. Thomas Lull hears an intake of breath. Aj looks up.

"Professor Lull, I am experiencing a number of strong and unpleasant sensations. Let me describe them to you. Though I am at relative rest, I experience a sense of vertigo, as if I am falling; not in a physical sense, but inwards. I experience a sense of nausea and what I can only describe as hollowness. I experience unreality, as if this present is not happening to me and I am dreaming in my bed in the hotel in Thekkady. I experience a sense of impact, as if I have been struck without a physical blow being landed on me. I imagine that the physical substance of the world is frail and fragile like glass and that at any moment I will fall through into a void, yet at the same time I find a thousand different ideas rushing through my head. Professor Lull, can you explain my contradictory sensations?"

The swift sun of India is now setting, staining Aj's face red like a devotee of Kali. The fast train blurs through Mumbai's vast basti-lands. Thomas Lull says, "It's what anyone feels when their life turns to lies. It's anger and it's betrayal and it's confusion and loss and fear and hurt but those are only names. We have no language for emotions other than the emotion itself."

"I feel tears starting in my eyes. This is most surprising." Then Aj's voice breaks and Thomas Lull helps her to the washroom to let the alien emotions work themselves out away from the stares of the passengers. Back at his seat he calls a steward and orders a bottle of water. He pours a glass, adds a high-grade tranq from his small but efficacious travelling apothecary, and marvels at the simple complexity of the ripple patterns on its surface transmitted from the steel beat of the wheels. When Aj returns he pushes the trembling glass across the table before any more of her questions can tumble out. He has enough of his own.

"All of it."

The tranq is not long taking effect. Aj blinks at him like a drunk owl, curls up as cat-comfortable as she can in the seat. She is out. Thomas Lull's hand moves to her tilak, stops. It would be a violation as monstrous as if he slipped his hand down the front of her loose grey tie-waist pants. And that is a thought he hadn't verbalised until this second.

Strange girl, curled up like a gangly ten-year-old in her seat. He told her truths to scarify any heart and she treated them like propositions in philosophy. As if they were strange to her, new. Alien. Why had he told her? To break her illusion or because he knew how she would react? To see the look on her face as she fought to comprehend what her body was experiencing? He knows that fearful bafflement from the faces of the beach-club kids when emotions brewed up in the protein processor matrices of the cyberabads hit them. Emotions for which their bodies have no needs or analogues; emotions they experience but cannot understand. Alien emotions.

He has much work to do. As the fast train plunges past the empty, stepped reservoirs of the purifying Narmada, hurling itself into the night past the villages and towns and drought-blighted forests, Thomas Lull goes far-fetching. An old down-home expression of Lisa Durnau's for blue-skying; sitting back and letting your mind roam the furthest bounds of possibility. It is the work he loves best and the closest heathen old Thomas Lull comes to spirituality. It is, he thinks, all of spirituality. God is our selves, our true, preconscious selves. The yogis have had it right all these millennia. The working out of the idea is never as thrilling as the burn of creation, the moment of searing insight when all at once, you know absolutely. He studies Aj as ideas tumble and collide and shatter and are drawn together again by intellectual gravity. In time they will coalesce into a new world, but there is enough for Thomas Lull to guess its future nature. And he is afraid. The train ploughs on, peeling a bow-wave of night from its streamlined prow as it eats two hundred and eighty kilometres of India every hour. Exhaustion struggles with intellectual excitement and eventually subdues it. Thomas Lull sleeps. He wakes only at the brief halt at Jabalpur as Awadhi customs make a perfunctory border check. Two men in peaked caps glance at Thomas Lull. Aj sleeps on, head cradled on arm. White man and Western woman. Unimpeachable. Thomas Lull dozes again, waking once to shiver with an ancient, childhood pleasure at the rumble of the wheels beneath him. He falls into a long and untroubled sleep terminated by an untimetabled jolt that throws him out of unconsciousness hard against the table.

Luggage crashes from the overhead racks. Passengers in the aisles fall. Voices cry, merge into a jabber of panic. The shatabdi jars hard, jars again; comes to a screaming, shuddering halt. The voices peak and fall silent. The train sits motionless. The com crackles, goes dead. Thomas Lull cups his hands around his face, peers out of the window. The rural dark is impenetrable, enfolding, yonic. He thinks he sees distant car headlights, bobbing lights like torches. Now the questions start, everyone asking at once is everyone all right what happened?

Aj mumbles, stirring. The tranqs are more effective than Thomas Lull thought. Now he is aware of a wall of voices advancing down the train and with it a stench of burning polycarbon from the air-conditioning ducts. With one hand he snatches up Aj's bag, with the other he drags her upright. Aj blinks thickly at him.

"Come on, sleeping beauty. We're making an unscheduled disembarkation." He pulls her, still quasi-conscious, into the aisle, seizes the bags, and pushes her towards the rear sliding doors. Behind him the black picture window explodes in a spray of glass-sugar as a concrete block trailing a sling-rope bursts through. It bounces off the table, strikes a woman in the seat across the aisle. She goes down, spraying blood from a smashed knee. The press of fleeing passengers trip over her and fall. She is dead, Thomas Lull realises with a terrible, intimate chill. The woman, or anyone else who goes down in this surge.

"Get the fuck moving!" Thomas Lull bounces the dazed Aj down the aisle with slaps of his hands to her back. He glimpsed flames through the empty window; flames and faces. "Go go go." Behind them the jam is hideous. Low vanguards of smoke steal from the vents and under the uptrain carriage door. The voices rise to a chorus of dread.

"To me! To me!" roars a Sikh steward in railway livery standing on a table by the inner carriage door. "One at a time, come on, there is plenty of time. You. Now, you. You." He uses his passkey to turn the sliding door into a people-lock. One family at a time.

"What the hell is going on?" Thomas Lull asks as he takes his place at the head of the line.

"Bharati karsevaks have fired the train," the steward says quietly. "Say nothing. Now, you go."

Thomas Lull shoves Aj into the door section, blinks into the dark outside.

"Fucking hell." A ring of fire encircles the small encampment of dazed, fearful passengers and their goods. Decades of working with the digits of cellular automata have made Thomas Lull skilled at estimating number from a single glance. There must be five hundred of them out there, holding burning torches. Sparks blow back from the front of the train; orange smoke, luminous in half light, is a sure signifier of burning plastics. "Change of plan. We're not getting off here."

"What's going on, what's happening?" Aj asks as Thomas Lull forces open the doors to the next carriage. It is already half empty.

"The train's been stopped, some Shivaji protest."

"Shivaji?"

"I thought you knew everything. Hindu fundamentalists. Who are pretty pissed with Awadh right now."

"You're very glib," Aj says and Thomas Lull cannot tell if it is the end of the tranqs or the start of her weird wisdom. But the glow from outside grows stronger and he can hear the slam and shatter of objects hurled against the carcass of the train.

"That's because I'm very very scared," Thomas Lull says. He pushes Aj past the next door open on to the night. He does not want her to register the screams and the sounds he recognises as small-arms fire. The bogies are almost empty now, they plough their way through one, two, three, then the car staggers sending Thomas Lull and Aj reeling as a deep boom rocks the train. "Oh Jesus," Thomas Lull says. He guesses that a power car has exploded. A roar of acclamation goes up from the mob outside. Thomas Lull and Aj press on. Four carriages back they meet a wide-eyed Marathi ticket inspector.

"You cannot go on, sir."

"I am going on whether it's past, over, or through you."

"Sir, sir, you do not understand. They have fired the other end, too."

Thomas Lull stares at the inspector in his neat suit. It is Aj who pulls him away. They reach the intercarriage lobby as smoke forces its fingers between the inner door seals. The lights go out. Thomas Lull blinks in darkness, then the emergency floor-level lighting kicks in casting an eerie, Gothic footlight glow into the crannies and crags of human faces. The outer door remains fast. Sealed. Dead. Thomas Lull watches the smoke fill up the carriage behind the inner door. He tries to find purchase on the rubber seal.

"Sir, sir, I have a key."

The inspector hauls a heavy metal Allen key out of his pocket on a chain, fits it to a hex nut, and begins to crank the door open. The inner carriage door is blackened with soot and beginning to buckle and blister. "A few more moments, sir . . ."

The door cranks wide enough for six hands to haul it open. Thomas Lull flings the luggage into the dark and himself after it. He hits awkwardly, falls, rolls on rocks and rails. Aj and the railwayman follow him. He pulls himself upright to see the interior of the carriage they have abandoned light startling yellow. Then every window detonates outwards in a hail of crumbed glass.

"Aj!" Thomas Lull shouts through the tumult. He has never heard noise like it. Screaming voices, wailing, a jagged tangle of cries and roars and language multilayered and shattered into incomprehensibility. Revving engines, a steady hammer of missiles. Children's fear-stricken shrieks. And behind all, the sucking, liquid roar of the burning train, steadily consuming itself from both ends like vile incense. Hell must sound like this. "Aj!"

Bodies move everywhere in every direction. Thomas Lull has a sense of the geography of the atrocity now. The people flee from the head of the train, now a series of actinic detonations as electrical switchgear blows, where a deep line of men in white advances on them like a Raj army. Most are armed with lathis, some carry edged mattocks, hoes, machetes. An agricultural army. There is at least one sword, raised high above the horizon of heads. Some are naked, white with ash, naga sadhus. Warrior priests. All carry a scrap of red on them, the colour of Siva. Flames glint from missiles; bottles, rocks, pieces of smashed train superstructure hailing down on the passengers who crouch and scurry, not knowing where to look for the next attack, dragging bundles of luggage. Gunsmoke plumes up into the air. The ground is strewn with abandoned, burst baggage, shirts and saris and toothbrushes trampled and scuffed into the dust. A man clutches a gashed head. A child sits in the middle of the rush of feet, looking around in terror, mouth wide and silent with a terror beyond cries, cheeks glossy with tears. Feet trample a crumpled pile of fabric. The pile quivers, struck by hurrying shoes. Bones crack. Thomas Lull now senses a purpose and direction in the flight: away from the men in white, towards a low line of huts that has become visible as eyes adjust to the dark of Bharati countryside. A village. Sanctuary. Except a second wave of karsevaks runs from behind the burning rear of the train, cutting off the retreat. The stampede halts. Nowhere to run. People go down, piling up on each other. The noise redoubles.

"Aj!"

And then she is there in front of him, like she's come up off the ground. She combs glass crumbs out of her hair.

"Professor Lull."

He seizes her hand, hauls her back towards the train.

"It's all cut off on this side of the train. We're going the other way."

The two wings of attackers hook towards each other, closing a half-encirclement. Thomas Lull knows anything in that arena is dead. There is only a small gap to the dark, desiccated fields. The families flee into it, dropping everything and running for their lives. Ash swirls and storms in the updrafts from the train fire; Lull and Aj are now within missile range. Rocks and bottles start to clang off the carriages, shattering into glassy shrapnel.

"Under here!" Thomas Lull ducks under the train. "Watch out for this." The undercarriage is lethal with high-voltage cables and drums of pressurised hydraulic fluid. Thomas Lull crawls out to find himself looking at a wall of car headlights. "Fuck." The vehicles are parked in a long line a hundred metres from the train. Trucks, buses, pickups, family cars, phatphats. "They're right round us. We're going to have to try it."

Aj snaps her head up to the sky.

"They're here."

Thomas Lull turns to see the helicopters roar over the top of the train, fast, hard, low enough to swirl the flames up into a fire tornado. They are blind insects, combat bots slung from their dragonfly thoraxes like eggs. They carry the green and orange yin-yang of Awadh on their noses. Counterinsurgency pulse lasers pivot in their housings seeking targets. Deep under Delhi, helicopter jockeys recline on gel beds watching through their pineal eyes, moving their hands a centimetre here, a flicker there to instruct the pilot systems. The three helicopters turn in the air above the parked cars, bow to each other in a robot gavotte, and swoop down on their drop runs. Gunfire cracks out from beyond the line of headlights, bullets smack, and white from the spun-diamond carapaces. From ten metres they release their riot control bots, then climb, spin, and open up with the pulsers. The bots hit the ground and immediately charge. Cries. Shots. Men come running from between the cars into the open space. The helicopters lock on and fire. Soft bangs, dull flashes, bodies go sprawling, crawling. The pulse lasers flash the first thing they touch to plasma and pump it into an expanding shock wave, whether clothing or the ash-daubed skin of a naked naga. The karsevaks go reeling, stripped bare-chested by laser-fire. The counterinsurgency bots clear the vehicles in a leap like something from a Japanese comic and unfold their riot control shock-staves.

"Down!" Thomas Lull yells, shoving Aj's face to the dust. The men flee but the springing bots are faster, harder, and more accurate. A body crashes beside Thomas Lull, face scorched in second-degree sunburn. Steel hooves flash, he covers his head with his arms, then rolls to see the machines hurdle the train. He waits. The helicopters are still up there. He plays dead until they pass over, frail craneflies never intended for human occupancy. "Up! Go, now! Run!" A prickle of suspicion on the back of his neck makes Thomas Lull look up. A helicopter turns a sensor cluster on him. A gatling pulser swings to bear. Then smoke billows between man and machine, the aeai loses tracking and the helicopter dips over the train, turrets stuttering laser fire. "Get behind the cars, down behind a wheel, that's the safest place," Thomas Lull shouts over the tumult. Then they both freeze in their flight as the air between the cars seems to shiver and the wash of light from the massed headlights breaks into moving shards. Men in combat gear fade into visibility. Thomas Lull pulls his passport from his pocket, holds it high like an Old Time preacher of the gospel.

"American citizen!" he shouts as the soldiers slip past, their suits now camouflaged in mirror and infrared. "American citizen!" A subadar with an exquisitely groomed moustache pauses to survey Thomas Lull. His unit badge bears the eternal wheel of Bharat. He casually cradles a multitask assault gun.

"We have mobile units to the rear," the subadar says. "Make your way there. You will be cared for." As he speaks the helicopters reappear over the train, now half ablaze. "Go now, sir." The subadar breaks into a run; the lead helicopter locks its belly turret onto him and fires. Thomas Lull sees the officer's uniform glow as it absorbs the laser, then the Bharati soldier brings his weapon to bear and fires off a Sam. The helicopter pulls up and peels away in a spray of chaff, the little missile zig-zagging after it, a line of fire across the night. A rain of tinsel the colour of burning shatabdi falls around Thomas Lull and Aj. Recognising a more potent threat, a squad of riot control bots has taken position along the top of the train attempting to hold off the Bharati troops with stun lasers and riot control chaff. The fire-light catches on the chromed joints and sinews. The humans take them one at time with EMP fire. As each bot tumbles from the train it releases a clutch of fist-sized subdrones. They bounce, unfold into scurrying scarabs armed with spinning strimmer-wires. They swarm the soldiers; Thomas Lull sees one man go down and turns Aj away before the wire flays him to the bone. He sees the subadar kick one off the toe of his boot, raise his weapon butt, and smash it to pieces. But there are always too many of them. That is the tactic. The subadar calls his men back. They run. The scarabs skitter after. Thomas Lull still clutches his passport, like a tract waved in the face of a vampire.

"I think it will take more than that," the subadar says, snatching Thomas Lull by the arm and dragging him in his wake. Beyond the line of vehicles men with flamethrowers fade out of stealth into visibility. And Thomas Lull realises that Aj has slipped his grip. He yells her name. He does not know how many times this night he has called that name in that lost, crippled by fear tone. Thomas Lull tears himself away from the Bharati officer.

Aj stands before the scurrying, bounding line of combat bots. She goes down on one knee. They are metres, moments away, flay-wires shrilling. She raises her left hand, palm outward. The onslaught of robots halts. By ones, then by two, tens, twenties, they spin down their weapons, curl up into their transit spheres. Then a Bharati jawan darts in and whirls her away and the flamethrower men open up, fire on fire. Thomas Lull goes to her. She is shivering, tearful, smoke-smeared with the strap of her small luggage still twisted in her hand.

"Has somebody got a blanket or something?" he asks as the soldier moves them through the line of cars. A foil spaceblanket unfolds from somewhere, Thomas Lull pulls it around Aj's shoulders. The soldier backs away; he has seen aeai strike helicopters and fought robots, but this scares him. You do well, Thomas Lull thinks as he guides Aj towards the laager of troop carriers. We would all do well.

19

MR. NANDHA

Each of the five bodies has its fists raised. Mr. Nandha has seen enough death by fire to understand that it is a thing of biology and temperature but an older, pre-Enlightenment sensibility sees them fighting swirling djinns of flame. It would have been demonic at the end. The apartment is still sooty with floating polycarbon ash, drifts of vaporised computer casing. When they settle on Mr. Nandha's skin they smear to the softest, darkest kohl. It takes a temperature of over a thousand degrees to reduce plastic to pure carbon soot.

Varanasi, city of cremations.

The morgue crew zip black bags shut. Sirens from the street; the firefighters pulling out. The scene is now in the hands of the law agencies, last of which is the Ministry. SOCO boys brush past Mr. Nandha, recording videos on their palmers. He is trespassing on another's bailiwick. Mr. Nandha has his own comfortable methodology and for him simple observation and the application of imagination yield insights and intuitions police procedural might never apprehend.

The first sense the crime assails is smell. He could smell the burned meat, the oily, sweet choke of melted plastic from the lobby. The stench so overpowers all other senses that Mr. Nandha must focus to extract information from it. He opens his nostrils for hints, contradictions, subtle untogethernesses that might suggest what has happened here. An electrical fault among all the computers, the fire investigation officer had immediately suggested. Can he pick that unmistakable prickle of power out of the mix?

Sight is the second sense. What did he see when he entered the crime locus? Double doors forced open by fire department hydraulics, the outer the standard apartment block fascia door; the inner, heavy green metal, dogged and barred, the latches warped by fire service jacks. They could not open the door? They trapped themselves in their own security? The paint is seared from the inside of the inner door, blackened raw metal. Proceed. The short lobby, the main lounge, the bedrooms they had been using as their memory farm. Kitchen; skeletons of cupboards and racks on the wall, melamine peeled away but the woodchip intact. Chipboard survives. Ash and blackness, one thing fused into another. The windows have blown inwards. A pressure drop? The fire must almost have exhausted itself. It would have burned smoky and black. They would have asphyxiated before the windows blew and fresh oxygen kindled the fire djinn. Melted stubs of computer drives flow into each other. Vikram will rescue what is rescueable.

Hearing. Three thousand people in this apartment pile yet the quiet on the fire floor is absolute. Not even the chirp of a radio left burbling. The firemen have withdrawn their cordon but residents are reluctant to return to their homes. There are rumours that the blaze was a revenge attack by the Awadhis for the shatabdi massacre. The neighbours on either side only knew what was happening when the wall grew hot and the paint started to blister.

Touch. The greasy, coagulating smut of soot in the air. A black floating cobweb settles on to Mr. Nandha's sleeve. He goes to wipe it, then remembers that it is ten percent human fat.

Taste, the fifth test. Mr. Nandha has learned the technique from cats, a flaring of the nostrils, a slight opening of the mouth, a rasping of the air across the palate. It is no elegance but it works for little hunters and Krishna Cops.

"Nandha, whatever are you doing?" Chauhan the State Pathologist bags up the penultimate corpse and slaps the despatch notice on the plastic sack.

"A few preliminaries. Have you anything for me yet?"

Chauhan shrugs. He is a big bear of a man with the callous joviality of those who work among the inner doings of the violently killed.

"Call by me this afternoon, I may have something for you by then."

Vaish, the police inspector in charge, looks up, disapprovingly, at the trespass.

"So, Nandha," Chauhan says as he steps back and his white-suit team lift the bag on to the stretcher. "I hear your good woman is rebuilding the hanging gardens of Babylon. She really must be missing the old village."

"Who is saying this?"

"Oh, it's all the word," Chauhan says, noting down comments on the fourth victim. "Doing the rounds after the Dawar's party. This one's a woman. Interesting. So, green fingers then, Nandha?"

"I am having a roof-top retreat constructed, yes. We're thinking of using it for entertainments, dinners, social get-togethers. It's quite the thing in Bengal, roof gardens."

"Bengal? They've all the fashions, there." Chauhan regards himself as Mr. Nandha's equal in intellect, education, career, and standing; everything but wedlock. Mr. Nandha married within jati. Chauhan married below subcaste.

Mr. Nandha frowns at the ceiling.

"I presume this place would have a halon fire extinguisher system as a matter of course?"

Chauhan shrugs. Inspector Vaish stands up. He understands.

"Have you found anything that looks like a control box?" Mr. Nandha asks.

"In the kitchen," the inspector answers. The box is under the sink beside the U-bend, the most inconvenient place. Mr. Nandha rips off the seared cupboard door, squats down, and shines his pencil torch all around. These people used a lot of multisurface cleaner. All those hard cases, Mr. Nandha presumes. The heat has penetrated even this safe cubby, loosening the plumbing solder and sagging the plastic cover. A few turns of the multitool unscrews it. The service ports are intact. Mr. Nandha plugs in the avatar box and summons Krishna. The aeai balloons beyond the tight constraints of the under-sink cupboard. The god of little domesticities. Inspector Vaish crouches beside him. Where before he had radiated spiky resentment, he now seems in mild awe.

"I'm accessing the security system files," Mr. Nandha explains. "It will take no more than a few moments. Ironic; they'll protect their memory farm with quantum keys but the extinguisher system is a simple four-digit pin. And that," he says as the command lines scroll up on his field of vision, "seems to have been their downfall. Do we have an estimated time of the fire?"

"The oven timer is stopped at seven twenty-two."

"There's a command from the insurance company—it's certainly false—logged at seven oh five shutting down the halon gas system. It also activated the door locks."

"They were sealed in."

"Yes." Mr. Nandha stands up, brushes himself down, noting with distaste the soft black smears of ten percent human fat where floating soot has gravitated on to him. "And that makes it murder." He folds his avatars back into their box. "I shall return to my office to prepare an initial scene of crime report. I'll need the most intact of the processors in my department before noon. And Mr. Chauhan." The pathologist looks up from the last corpse, burned down to bones and a grin of bloody white teeth in black char. He knows those teeth; Radhakrishna's impudent monkey-grin. "I will call on you at three and I expect you to have something for me by then."

He imagines the SOCO's smile as he quits the incinerated shell of the Badrinath sundarban. Like him, they have neither the money nor the patience to marry in jati.

At breakfast the talk had all been of the Dawar's reception.

"We must have one," Parvati said, bright and fresh with a flower in her long, black hair and the Fifth Test burbling in male baritones behind her. "When the roof garden is finished, we'll have a durbar and invite everyone and it'll be the talk for weeks." She pulled her diary from her bag. "October? It should be looking best then, after the late monsoon."

"Why are we watching the cricket?" Mr. Nandha asked.

"Oh that? I don't know how that came to be on." She waved her hand at the screen in the gesture for *Breakfast with Bharti*. An in-studio dance-routine bounced upon the screen. "There, happy? October is a good time, it is always such a flat month. But it might seem a bit of an anticlimax after the Dawars, I mean, it's a garden and I love it very much and you are so good to let me have it, but it is only plants and seeds. How much do you think it cost them to get a Brahmin baby?"

"More than an Artificial Intelligence Licensing Investigations Officer can afford."

"Oh, my love, I never thought for a moment . . ."

Listen to yourself, my bulbul, he thought. Babbling away, letting it fall from your lips and presuming it will be golden because you are surrounded by colour and movement and flowers every second of every day. I heard the society women you so envy and said nothing because they were right. You are quaint and open and say what is in your heart.

You are honest in your ambitions and that is why I would keep you away from them and their society.

Bharti on the Breakfast Banquette chattered and smiled with her Special! Morning! Guests! Today: *Funki Puri* Breakfast Specials from our Guest Chef, Sanjeev Kapur!

"Good day, my treasure," Mr. Nandha said pushing away his half-empty cup of Ayurvedic tea. "Forget those snobbish people. They have nothing we need. We have each other. I may be late back. I have a scene of crime to investigate." Mr. Nandha kissed his beautiful wife and went to look at the incinerated remains of Mr. Radhakrishna in his sundarban wedged unassumingly into a fifteenth-floor apartment in Diljit Rana Colony.

Dangling his damp tea bag from its string, Mr. Nandha looks out over Varanasi and tries to make sense of what he has seen in that charred apartment. The fire was savage but contained. Controlled. An engineered burn. A shaped charge? An infrared laser fired through the window?

Mr. Nandha flicks Bach violin concertos on to his palmer, sits back in his leather chair, puts his fingers together like a stupa, and turns to the city outside his window. It has been an unfailing and unstinting guru to him. He scrys it like an oracle. Varanasi is the City of Man and all human action is mirrored in its geography. Its patterns and traumas have yielded insights and wisdoms beyond reason and rationality. Today his city shows him fire patterns. On any given day there will be at least a dozen coils of smoke from domestic conflagrations. Among the jostling middle classes the habits of bride-burning have been extinguished, but he does not doubt that some of those further, paler smoke ribbons are "kitchen fires."

You are safe with me, Parvati, he thinks. You can forever trust that I will not hurt you or tire of you, for you are rare, a pearl without price. You are protected from the sati of boredom or dowry envy.

The military troopships cut down across the skyline in the same regular rhythm. How many lakhs of soldiers now? In the police cruiser he had scanned the day's headlines. Bharati jawans had driven back an Awadhi incursion along the railway line into western Allahabad. Awadhi/American robots were attacking a sit-down demonstration blocking a Maratha shatabdi on the mainline from Awadh. Mr. Nandha knows the reek of Rana spin, stronger than any incense or cremation smoke. Ironic that the Americans, engineers of the Hamilton Acts, chose to wage war through the machines they so mistrusted. If high-generation aeais ever gained access to the fighting robots . . .

Mr. Nandha's fingers part. Intuition. Enlightenment. A movement at his side: a chai-boy whisks his used bag away on a silver saucer.

"Chai-wallah. Send Vikram down here. Quick now."

"At once, sahb."

Military aeai counter-countermeasure gunships. Trained to fly down and assassinate cyber-war craft like hunting falcons. Armed with pulse lasers. The murder weapon is out there, cutting patrol arcs through the sacred city's sacred airspace. Someone cut into the military system.

Mr. Nandha smells Vik before any other sense announces his arrival.

"Vikram."

"How can I please you?"

Mr. Nandha turns in his chair.

"Please get me a movement log of every military aeai drone over Varanasi for the past twelve hours."

Vikram sucks in his upper lip. He's dressed in vast running shoes and pseudo-shorts hitting midcalf today, with a clingtop someone of his carbohydrate intake should never contemplate.

"Doable. Why for?"

"I have an idea that this was no conventional arson. I have an idea that it was a sustained, high-energy infrared laser pulse from a military aeaicraft." Vik's eyebrows lift. "Anything on the source of the lock-down on the security system?"

"Well, it didn't come from Ahura Mazda Mutual of Varanasi. Its ass is well covered but we'll follow it home. We've got some initial data back from what we could salvage from Badrinath. Whatever it was they wanted gone, they took a lot of high-rental property out with it. We lost bodhisofts of Jim Carrey, Madonna, Phil Collins."

"I don't believe it was bodhisofts, or even information they were after," Mr. Nandha says. "I think it was the people."

"How come we're the Aeai Licensing Department but it always ends up humans every time?" Vikram says, bobbing on his big padded jog boots. "And next time you need me so badly, a simple message will suffice. Those stairs kill me, man."

But that would not be seemly for a Senior Investigator, Mr. Nandha wants to say. Order, propriety, smudge-free suits; varna. On his tenth Holi his mother dressed them up as little Jedi with swirling robes and the new super-soaker guns from Chatterjee's store, the ones with five separate barrels, Gatling-style and a different festival colour in each one. He had watched his younger brother and sister go through their moves in their hooded cloaks made from old sheets with their tubes of brightly coloured festival liquid, going zuzh, zuzh, zuzh as they cut down the forces of the dark side. He feels again the nausea of embarrassment, that they were expected to go in public in these humiliating rags, with these cheap toys, with everyone looking. That night he had crept from his room and taken the lot to Dipendra the nightwatchman's brazier and fed them to the coals. His father's fury had been terrible, his mother's incomprehension and disappointment worse, but he bore the emotions and the privations stoically for he knew he had prevented a more terrible thing altogether: shame.

Mr. Nandha's fingers scrabble for his lighthoek. He will call Parvati now, about that Brahmin baby talk, he will tell her what his opinion really is about those *things*. He will set her straight, she will know, and there will be no more of this. He slides the 'hoek over his ear, unconsciously adjusts the inducer, and has the number up as an unexpected call comes through from outside.

"Umph," says Mr. Nandha, discommoded. It is Chauhan.

"Here's a novelty, me calling you. Something to show you, Nandha."

"It was an infrared laser, wasn't it?" Mr. Nandha says as he walks into the morgue. The bodies are laid on ceramic tables, black, shrivelled mummy-corpses and snapping teeth.

"Well guessed," says jolly, brutal Chauhan in his morgue greens with his demure forensic nurses around him. "Short, high-intensity burst from a high-power infrared laser, almost certainly air-capable, though I wouldn't rule out a lined-up shot from Shanti Rana Apartments opposite."

One body, more terribly charred than the rest, is a black stick opening into bare ribs and yellow thigh bones, truncated at the knee. The stench of burned hair, flesh, incinerated bone is worse in Ranapur's pristine new city morgue than masked by the hydrocarbons and polycarbonates of the apartment, but there is nothing in this clean, cool room that is ultimately unfamiliar or disturbing to a Varanasian.

"What happened to him?"

"I suspect he was by the window when the fireball blew out. He's not the interesting one," Chauhan continues as Mr. Nandha bends over the inhuman Y-shape of the Darwinware pirate. "These ones. Nothing to identify them of course—I've only had an initial poke around—but this one was male, this one female. The male is European, anywhere from Palermo to Paris, the female is South Indian-Dravidian. I get the feeling they were a couple. Interesting, the woman was born with a severe deformity of the womb—certainly nothing functional. Good old police procedure'll crack them eventually, but you might be interested in these."

Chauhan slides open a padded drawer and holds up two plastic evidence bags. In each is a small ivory pendant, charred and blackened. The motif is a white horse rearing on its back legs in a chakra circle of stylised flames.

"Do you know what it is?" Chauhan asks.

"Kalki," Mr. Nandha says. He lifts a disc and holds it to the light. The work is very fine. "The tenth and final incarnation of Vishnu."

Veritable shitfuls of holy monkeys pour off the trees and come loping on their soft knuckles to greet the Ministry Lexus as it draws up outside the old Mughal hunting palace. The bot steps out of the scrub rhododendrons to scan the driver's credentials. The staff has let the gardens go to weed and wild again. Few gardeners pass the security vetting and those that do don't work long for Ministry money. The machine squats down in front of the car, drawing a line on Mr. Nandha with its arm-turret. Its left-leg piston vents intermittently, giving it a lopsided bob as it interrogates the clearances. Maintenance slipping also. Mr. Nandha purses his lips as the monkeys swarm the car, prying for crannies with their mannikin fingers. They remind him of the hands of the burned corpses in Chauhan's clean morgue, those black, withered fists. A langur perched over the radiator like a hood ornament masturbates furiously as the St. Matthew Passion swirls around Mr. Nandha.

Lack upon slack upon slop breeds lapse. It was scruffy maintenance and shoddy security that let the prisoner escape those other two times. That, and stealthy robots the size and agility of cockroaches.

The security bot completes its check, stalks away into the shrubbery like some late Cretaceous hunter. Mr. Nandha jerks the car forward to scare off the monkeys. He has a horror of one getting trapped in his wheel-arch. Lord High Masturbator takes a tumble from the bonnet. Mr. Nandha peers to see if it has left a vile squiggle of monkey-jizz on the paintwork.

When he was thirteen and hammered flat by hormones and doubt, Mr. Nandha had entertained a fantasy about catching a sacred monkey, keeping it in a cage, and slowly and excruciatingly breaking every one of its tiny, birdlike bones. He can still feel a glow of the joyous anger of that delight.

A persistent few monkeys ride the Ministry Lexus all the way up the curving drive to the lodge. Mr. Nandha kicks them away as he steps out on to the crunching red gravel and slips on his dark glasses. The white Mughal marble is dazzling in the afternoon light. Mr. Nandha steps away from the car to enjoy the uninterrupted view of the palace. It is a hidden pearl, built in 1613 by the Shah Ashraf as a game retreat. Where hunting cheetahs rode atop howdahs and Mughal lords hawked over the marshes of Kirakat, now factory units and pressed-aluminium go-downs nudge up to the low, cool lodge on every side. But the genius of the architect endures: the colonnaded house remains enfolded, separate in its jungled gardens, unseen by any of them, unseeing in return. Mr. Nandha admires the balance of the pillared cloister, the understatement of the dome. Even among the English Perpendicular and Baroque triumphs of Cambridge, he had still considered the Islamic architects the masters of Wren and Reginald of Ely. They built as Bach composed, strong and muscular, with light and space and geometry. They built timelessly and for all time. Mr. Nandha thinks that he might not mind confinement in such a prison as this. He would have solitude, here.

Sweepers bow around him, twig besoms busy as Mr. Nandha goes up the shallow steps to the cool cool cool of the cloister. The Ministry staff greet him at the door; discreetly scanning him down with their palmers. Mr. Nandha commends their thoroughness but they look bored. They are EO1 civil servants, but they did not join the Ministry to guard a mouldering pile of Mughal masonry. Mr. Nandha waits for the warder to cycle the transparent plastic lock that sits like an ugly sex-toy yoni in the wall of exquisitely carved alabaster. The last security check lights green. Mr. Nandha steps into the banqueting hall. As ever, he catches his breath at the white stone jalis, the banded masonry, the low generous spaciousness of the onion arches, the geometries of the azure roof tilings, the tall pointed windows shaded by fabric blinds. But the true focus of the room is not the radiant harmony of the design. It is not even the Faraday cage painstakingly woven into the fabric of the architecture. It is the transparent plastic cube that stands in the centre. It is five metres long and five metres high, a house within a house divided by transparent plastic partitions into see-through rooms, with transparent plumbing and wiring and chairs and tables and a transparent bed and a transparent toilet. In the midst of this transparency sits a dark, heavily bearded man, running to fat. He is dressed in a white kurta and is barefoot and reads a paperback book. His back is turned to Mr. Nandha but hearing his footfalls on the cool marble he rises. He peers short-sightedly, then recognises his visitor and drags his chair to the transparent wall. He pokes the broken-backed paperback with a toe. He wears a transparent toe ring.

"The words still don't move."

"The words don't need to move. It is you who is moved by them."

"It is a very effective way of compressing a virtual reality experience, I'll give it that. All this for one-point-four megs? It's just so non-interactive . . ."

"But it is different for everyone who reads it," says Mr. Nandha.

The man in the plastic cube nods his head, pondering.

"Where's the shared experience in that? So, what can I do for you, Mr. Nandha?"

Mr. Nandha glances up as he hears the mosquito drone of a hovercam. It rolls its lens-eye at the plastic cage, climbs away towards the fantasia of the domed roof. Light falls in dusty shafts through the mullions. Mr. Nandha takes the plastic evidence bags out of his jacket pocket, holds them up. The man in the plastic chair squints.

"You're going to have to bring them closer, I can't see anything without my glasses. You could at least have left me them."

"Not after last time, Mr. Anreddy. The circuitry was most ingenious."

Mr. Nandha presses the bags against the plastic wall. The prisoner kneels down. Mr. Nandha sees his breath mist the transparency. He gives a small, hushed gasp.

"Where did you get these?"

"From their owners."

"They're dead, then."

"Yes."

J. P. Anreddy is a short, dumpy asthmatic in his midtwenties with too little hair on his head and far too much around his soft jowls and he is Mr. Nandha's greatest professional triumph. He was Dataraja of the Sinha sundarban, a major station on the aeai underground railway when Awadh ratified the Hamilton Acts and outlawed all artificial intelligences above Level 2.0. He had made a cosmological amount of money rebranding high-level aeais as low and faking their licence idents. Man-machine fusion had been his peccadillo, an extension of his one hundred and fifty kilos of mostly middle-body fat into lither, nimbler robot bodies. When Mr. Nandha came to arrest him for licence violations, he had cut his way through charge after charge of service robots. He remembers the clicking plastic peds, conflates them with the little black monkey hands besieging his Ministry car. Mr. Nandha shivers in the bright, warm, dust-fragrant room. He had run the dataraja down through his suite of chambers until Indra locked on to the protein matrix chips seeded across the underside of Anreddy's cranium that allowed him to interface directly with his machine extensions and fused them all with a single EM pulse. J. P. Anreddy had lain in a coma for three months, lost fifty percent of his body mass, and regained consciousness to find that the court had confiscated the house and turned it into his prison. Now he lived at the centre of his beautiful Mughal architecture in a transparent plastic cube where every move and breath, every mouthful and motion, every scratch and flea and insect crawling upon it could be monitored by the hovercams. He had twice escaped with the help of bug-sized robots. Though he could no longer control them by will alone, J. P. Anreddy had never lost his love for little scuttling sentiences. Here he would remain under house arrest until he expressed remorse for what he had done. Mr. Nandha confidently expected he would die and rot in his plastic wrap. J. P. Anreddy genuinely had no comprehension that he had done anything wrong.

"How did they die?" the dataraja asks.

"In a fire, on the fifteenth floor of . . ."

"Stop. Badrinath? Radha?"

"No one survived."

"How?"

"We have theories."

Anreddy sits on the transparent plastic floor, head bowed. Mr. Nandha shakes out the medallions, holds them up by the chain.

"You knew them, then."

"Knew of them."

"Names?"

"Something French, though she was Indian. They used to work at the University but got into the free world. They had a big-name project, there was a lot of money behind them."

"Have you ever heard of an investment company called Odeco?"

"Everyone's heard of Odeco. Everyone out in the wild, that is."

"Did you ever receive funding from Odeco?"

"I'm a dataraja man, big and wild and fierce. Public enemy number one. Anyway, I wasn't their particular shade of blue sky. I was into nanoscale robotics. They were high-level aeai; protein circuitry, computer-brain interfaces."

Mr. Nandha holds the amulets against the plastic. "You know the significance of this symbol?"

"The riderless white horse, the tenth avatar."

"Kalki. The final avatar that will bring the Age of Kali to an end. A name from legend."

"Varanasi is a city of legends."

"Here is legend for our times. Might Badrinath, with funding from this Odeco organisation, have been developing a Generation Three aeai?"

J. P. Anreddy rocks back on his coccyx, throws his head back. Siddha of the scuttling robots. He closes his eyes. Mr. Nandha lays out the amulets on the tiles in Anreddy's full view. Then he goes to the window and slowly pulls up the blind. It folds up on itself in a wide concertina of sun-bleached fabric.

"I will tell you now our theory about how they died at Badrinath. We believe it was a deliberate attack by a laser-armed drone aircraft," Mr. Nandha says. He draws up the next blind, admitting the blinding sun, the treacherous sky.

"You bastard!" J. P. Anreddy shouts, leaping to his feet. Mr. Nandha moves to the third window.

"We find this theory convincing. A single high-energy shot." He crosses the room to the opposite set of mullions. "Through the living-room window. A precision attack. The aeai must have targeted, identified, and fired in a few milliseconds. There's so much traffic in the air since the train incident no one is ever going to notice a drone slip out of its patrol pattern."

Anreddy's hands are spread on the plastic, his eyes wide, scanning the white sky for flecks of betrayal.

"What do you know about Kalki?"

Mr. Nandha furls another blind. Only one remains. Buttresses of light slant across the floor. Anreddy looks in pain, a cyber-vampire burned by the sun.

"They'll kill you, man."

"We shall see about that. Is Kalki a Generation Three aeai?"

He takes the soft cotton cord of the last blind and hauls it in, hand over hand. A wedge of light expands across the tiles. J. P. Anreddy has retreated to the centre of his plastic cage but there is no hiding from the sky.

"So?"

"Kalki is a Generation Three aeai. It exists. It's real. It's been real and existent for longer than you think. It's out there. You know what

Generation Three means? It means an intelligence, measured on standard assessment scales, between twenty and thirty thousand times human baseline. And they're only the start. These are emergent properties, man. Evolution is running a million times faster in there. And if they want you, you cannot run, you cannot hide, you cannot lie down and hope that they will forget about you. Whatever you do, they can see you. Whatever identity you take, they know it before you do. Wherever you go, they'll be there ahead of you, waiting, because they'll have guessed it before you even think it yourself. These are Gen Threes, man. These are the gods! You cannot license gods."

Mr. Nandha lets the rant ebb before he collects the cheap, heat-tarnished Kalki amulets and returns them to their bags.

"Thank you. I now know the name of my enemy. Good day."

He turns and walks away through the shafts of dusty white light. His heels resound on the fine Islamic marble. Behind him he hears the soft woof of fists on flexible transparent plastic, Anreddy's voice, distant and muffled.

"Hey, the blinds man! Don't leave me, don't leave the blinds! Man! The blinds! They can see me! Fuck you, they can see me! The blinds!"

20

VISHRAM

He has a desk big enough to land a fighter on. He has a top-level wood and glass office. He has an executive elevator and an executive washroom. He has fifteen suits made to the same design and fabric as the one he wore when he inherited his empire, with matching hand-tooled shoes. And he has for his personal assistant Inder who has the disconcerting ability to be physically in front of him and at the same time manifesting herself on his desk-top organiser and as a ghost in his visual cortex. He's heard about these corporate PA systems who are part human, part aeai. It's modern office management.

Vishram Ray also has a raging Strega hangover and an oval of sunburn around his eyes where he looked too deep and too long into another universe.

"Who are these people?" asks Vishram Ray.

"The Siggurdson-Arthurs-Clementi Group," says Inder-on-the-carpet while Inder-in-the-desk opens her lotus-hands to show him a schedule and Inder-in-the-head dissolves into mugshots of well-fed white men with good suits and better dentistry. Inder-on-the-carpet has a surprisingly deep voice for someone so very Audrey Hepburn. "Ms. Fusco will brief you further in the car. And Energy Secretary Patel has requested a meeting, as has the Shivaji's energy spokeswoman. They both want to know your plans for the company."

"I don't even know them myself, but the Honourable Secretary will be the first to find out." Vishram pauses at the door. All three Inders wait inquiringly. "Inder, would it be possible to move this whole office right out of Ray Tower, to the Research Facility?"

"Certainly, Mr. Ray. Is it not to your satisfaction?"

"No, it's a lovely office. Very . . . businesslike. I just feel a bit . . . close to the family. My brothers. And while we're at it, I'd like to move out of the house. I find it a bit . . . oppressive. Can you find me a nice hotel, good room service?"

"Certainly, Mr. Ray."

As he leaves Inder's alters are already pricing corporate removal firms and hotel penthouse suites. In the Ray Power Merc, Vishram savours Marianna Fusco's Chanel 27. He can also sense that she is pissed at him.

"She's a physicist."

"Who's a physicist?"

"The woman I had dinner with last night. A physicist. I'm telling you this because you seem a little . . . snippy."

"Snippy?"

"Short. Annoyed. You know. Snippy."

"Oh. I see. And this is because you had dinner with a physicist?"

"Married physicist. Married Hindu physicist."

"I'm interested why you felt you had to tell me that she was married."

"Married Hindu physicist. Called Sonia. Whose pay-cheques I sign."

"As if that makes any difference."

"Of course. We're professional. I took her to dinner and then she took me back to hers and showed me her universe. It's small, but perfectly formed."

"I was wondering how you were going to explain the panda eyes. Is this a universe of sunbeds?"

"Zero-point energy, actually. And you have very elegant ankles."

He thinks he sees a shadow of a smile.

"Okay, these people, how do I deal with them?"

"You don't," says Marianna Fusco. "You shake hands and you smile politely and you listen to what they have to say and you do absolutely nothing. Then you report back to me."

"You're not coming with me?"

"You're on your own on this one, funny man. But be prepared for Govind to make Ramesh an offer this afternoon."

By the time he gets to the airport, Vishram's forehead is starting to flake. The car drives past the drop-off zones and the white zones and picking-up zones and tow-away zones to the bizjet zone through the double barrier security gate on to the field up to a private executive tilt-jet perched on its engines and tail pods like a mantis. An Assamese hostess, immaculate in traditional costume, opens the doors, namastes like a flower budding, and takes Vishram to his seat. He raises a hand to Marianna Fusco as the Merc pulls away. Flying solo.

The hostess's hand lingers as she checks Vishram's seat belt but he doesn't notice for then Vishram feels his belly and balls sag as the tilt-jet leaps into the air, puts its nose down, and takes him up over the brassy towers of Varanasi. An ineluctable part of Vishram Ray registers the close presence of an attractive woman next to him but he keeps his face pressed to the window as the tilt-jet swoops in over the river temples and ghats and the palaces and havelis onto a course following Ganga Devi. The shikara of the Vishwanath temple dazzles gold. The hand on his thigh finally draws his attention as the engines swivel into horizontal flight and the pilot takes the aircraft up to cruising altitude.

"I can get you some ointment for your forehead, sahb," says the perfect, round face full in front of his like a moon.

"I'll survive, thank you," says Vishram Ray. The first of the champagne arrives. Vishram assumes it's the first. He'll make that first last, although he's supposed to abuse the hospitality. It is cold and very very good and drinking airborne has always made Vishram Ray feel like a god. The bastis spread under him, multicoloured plastic roofs so tight together they look like a cloth spread on the ground for a feast. The tilt-jet follows the line of the river to the edge of Patna airspace, then swings south. Vishram should read his briefing but Bharat bedazzles him. The titanic conurbation of slums breaks up in a weave of fields and villages that rapidly turns from tired yellow to drought white as the river's influence diminishes. It would have looked little different two thousand years ago and were Vishram Ray indeed a god passing across holy Bharat to battle the rakshasas of the black south. Then his eyes catch on a power line and a stand of wind-turbines turning sluggishly in the heavy dry air. Ray Power turbines. His brother's turbines. He looks out at the yellow haze of the horizon. Does he imagine a line of shadow in the brown high-atmospheric smog, the skirmish line of an advance of clouds? The monsoon, at last? The burned stone of the plain deepens to beige, to yellow, to outcrops of green trees as the land rises. The tilt-jet rises with the edge of a plateau and Vishram is over high forest. To the west rises a line of smoke, drifting northward on the wind. The green is a lie, this high forest is dry, fire-hungry after three years of drought. Vishram finishes his champagne—flat and hand-warm now—as the seat belt sign lights.

"Shall I take that?" the hostess says, too close again. Vishram imagines a tic of irritation on that perfect, made-up face. I resisted your seductions. The tilt-jet leans into a landing spiral. A change in turbine pitch tells him the engines are swivelling into landing mode but looking down Vishram can see nothing that appears like an airport. The tilt-jet drifts across the forest canopy, so low its jet-wash sends the leaves raving and storming. Then the engine roar peaks, Vishram drops into the canopy, birds scatter on every side in a silent explosion of wings, and he is down with a gentle bounce. The engines ebb to a whine. Assam girl is doing the thing with the door. Heat floods in. She beckons. "Mr. Ray." At the foot of the steps is an old Rajput with a great white moustache and a turban so tight Vishram feels himself developing a sympathetic migraine. Ranked behind him are a dozen men in khaki with bush hats bent severely up at one side and heavy assault rifles at the slope.

"Mr. Ray, you are most welcome to Palamau Tiger Sanctuary," says the Rajput with a bow.

Assam girl stays with the tilt-jet. The hats carrying rifles spread out on all sides as the Rajput guides Vishram away from the 'plane. The ship has come down in a circle of bare dirt in a dense stand of bamboo and scrub. A sandy path leads into the trees. The path is lined with what seems to Vishram an excessive number of solidly built wood shelters. None is more than a panicked sprint away.

"What are they for?" Vishram asks.

"In case of attack by tigers," the Rajput answers.

"I'd imagine anything that could eat us is kilometres away by now, the noise we made coming in."

"Oh, not at all sir. They have learned to associate the sound of aeroplane engines."

With what? Vishram feels he should ask, but can't quite bring himself to. He's a city boy. City. Boy. Hear that you man-eaters? Full of nasty additives.

The air is clean and smells of growing and death and the memory of water. Dust and heat. The path curves so that in a few footsteps the landing pad is invisible. By the same camouflage the lodge conceals itself until the last stride. One moment it is green and leaves and rustling stems; then the trunks turn into stilts and ladders and staircases and there is a great wooden game lodge strung out across the treetops, like a galleon lifted by a monsoon and dropped in the forest.

White men in comfortable and therefore expensive suits hang over the balcony rail, greeting him with waves and smiles.

"Mr. Ray! Come aboard!"

They line up at the top of the wooden companionway as if receiving a boarding admiral. Clementi, Arthurs, Weitz, and Siggurdson. They have firm handshakes and make good eye contact and express Business School bluff cheer. Vishram does not doubt that they would bend you over and stick a mashie niblock up your hoop at golf or any other *muy macho* power game. His theory of golf is, never play any sport that requires you to dress as your grandfather. He can see quite a nice little routine falling together about golf; if his were the kind of life that any longer contemplated stand-up routines.

"Isn't this just the greatest place for lunch?" the tall, academic-looking one, Arthurs, says as he escorts Vishram Ray along wooden walkways, spiralling higher and higher into the roof canopy. Vishram squints down. The men with rifles look up at him. "Such a pity that Bhagwandas here tells us we've almost no chance of seeing a tiger." He has the nasal, slightly honking Boston accent. He'll be the accountant then, Vishram decides. In Glasgow they had said, always have Catholic lawyers and Protestant accountants. They pass between rows of elegantly pyjamaed waiters in Rudyard Kipling turbans. Double mahogany doors carved with battle scenes from the Mahabharata are thrown open, a *maitre d'* leads them to the meal, a sunken dining pit with cushions and a low table that would be the acme of kitsch but for the view out under the eaves through the panoramic windows to the waterhole. The verge is puddled to mud but Vishram thinks he sees chital sip nervously from the dirty brown water, ears swivelling on perpetual alert. He thinks of Varanasi, her vile waters and her radar defences.

"Sit, sit," insists Clementi, a wide, dark-haired man, sallow as an Indian and already developing a blue chin. The Westerners adjust themselves with some huffing and laughing. Punkah fans wave overhead, redistributing the heat. Vishram seats himself comfortably, elegantly on the low divan. *Maitre d'* brings bottled water. *Saiganga*. Ganges water. Vishram Ray raises his glass.

"Gentlemen, I am entirely at your mercy."

They laugh overappreciatively.

"We'll claim your soul later," says Weitz, who is the one who obviously never had to try too hard in Junior High, High, College Sports, and Business Law School. Vishram's eye for an audience notes that Siggurdson, the big cadaverous one, finds this marginally less funny than the others. The Born-Again; the one with the money.

Lunch comes on thirty tiny thalis. It is of that exquisite simplicity that is always so much more expensive than any lavishness. The five men pass the dishes between them, murmuring soft alleluias of appreciation at each subtle combination of vegetables and spices. Vishram notices that they eat Indian style without self-consciousness. Their Marianna Fuscos have even drilled them on which hand to use. But for the quiet epiphanies of flavour and mutual encouragements to try a taste of this, a morsel of that, the lunch is conducted in silence. Finally the thirty silver thalis are empty. The *maitre d's* boys flurry in like doves to clear and the men settle back on to their embroidered bolsters.

"So, Mr. Ray, without wasting too many words, we're interested in your company." Siggurdson speaks slowly, a measured tread of words like a buffalo drive, inviting dangerous underestimation.

"Ah, if only it were all mine to sell," Vishram says. He wishes he hadn't taken a side of the table all to himself now. Every head is turned to him now, every body-language focused on him.

"Oh, we know that," says Weitz. Arthurs chips in.

"You've got a nice little middle-size power-generation and distribution company; good build-up, rudimentary semi-feudal ownership model and you really should have diversified years ago to maximise shareholder value. But you guys do things differently here, I recognise that. I don't understand that, but then there's a lot of things about this place that frankly makes no sense to me at all. Maybe you're a little overcapitalised and you do have way too much invested in social capital—your R&D budget would raise eyebrows at home, but you're in pretty good shape. Maybe not planet-beating, not sector-leading, but good Little League."

"Nice of you to say so," Vishram says which is all the venom he can permit himself in this teak arena—he knows that they want to niggle him, nettle him, needle him into a careless comment. He looks at his hands. They are steady on the glass as they were always steady on the mike. It's no different from dealing with hecklers.

Siggurdson rests his big fists on the table, leans forward over them. He means to intimidate.

"I don't think you quite appreciate the seriousness of what we are saying. We know your father's company better than he knows it himself. His move was abrupt but not altogether unexpected: we have models. They are good models. They predict with an acceptable degree of accuracy. This conversation would be happening whatever he decided with regard to you. That this conversation is taking place here is a reflection of how much we know not just about Ray Power, but about you, Mr. Ray."

Clementi draws a cigar case from inside his jacket. He flips it open. Little beautiful black Cuban cigarillos like bullets in a magazine. Vishram's saliva glands stab with hungry pain. Lovely smokes.

"Who's backing you?" he asks with fake nonchalance. He knows they can see through it like a gauze veil. "EnGen?"

Siggurdson deals him a long stupid-son look.

"Mr. Ray."

Arthurs moistens his lip with his tongue, a tiny, delicate pink darting dab, like a tiny snake lodged in the crevices of his palate.

"We are a registered acquisitions arm of a large transnational concern."

"And what is that large transnational's concern in the research division of Ray Power? Might it be anything to do with the results we've been getting in the zero-point lab? Results that are turning in neat little positives where everyone else's are handing back big red negatives?"

"We've heard rumours to that effect," says Weitz, and Vishram decides that he is the cortex behind the whole operation. Arthurs the money man, Siggurdson the baron, Clementi the enforcer.

"More than rumours," Vishram says. "But the zero point is not for sale."

"I think perhaps you may have misunderstood me," Siggurdson says slowly, ponderously. "We don't want to buy your company outright. But if the results you've been getting are reproducible on a commercial scale, this is a very exciting area of potential high yield. This is an area we would be interested in investing in. What we want, Mr. Ray, is to buy a share in your company. It would be enough money to run a full-scale demonstration of the hot-zero-point technology."

"You don't want to buy me out?"

"Mr. Siggurdson said no," says Clementi tetchily. Siggurdson nods. He has a smile like a Minnesota winter.

"Ah. I think I have misunderstood you. Could you excuse me one moment, gentlemen? I have to go to the snanghar."

Enthroned among the exotic wood panels, Vishram slips his 'hoek behind his ear and flicks open the palmer. He's about to call up Inder when the paranoia strikes. Plenty of time for these men in suits to have bugged the gents. He calls up a mail aeai, raises his hand like a pianist, ready to type air. They could have bindicams. They could have movement sensors that read the flexing of his fingers. They could have nanochips that read the gurglings of his palmer; they could have sanyassins looking into the corners of his soul. Vishram Ray settles on the polished mahogany ring and zips off a query to Inder. Inder-in-the-head is back within seconds; head and shoulders materialising over the toilet paper holder on the back of the door.

She reels out names and connections Vishram knows only from the pink pages and money sections he would click past on his way to the entertainment listings, attention only caught by the unintentionally ridiculous corporate titles. He thinks of the khaki men with the straitly tilted bush-hats and assault rifles. Hey guys, you're in the wrong place. The tigers are up here.

He types, HYPOTHETICAL: WHY WOULD THEY WANT MY COMPANY?

There is an un-aeaily pause. When Inder speaks next, Vishram knows that it is the flesh and bone.

"To tie you up forever in due diligence clauses, with the eventual aim of gaining full control of the zero-point project."

Vishram sits on the warm mahogany seat and the wood beneath and around him seems sweltering and oppressive, a coffin buried in summer earth. It is going to be like this from now on.

"Thank you," he says aloud. Then he washes his hands to fix his alibi and walks back to the men around the table.

"Sorry to be so long; funny, but I haven't readjusted to the diet yet." He sits down, crosses his legs nimbly, comfortably. "Anyway, I've had a think about your offer . . ."

"Take your time," Clementi suggests. "This isn't the sort of decision to rush. Take a look at our proposal, then get back to us." He pushes a plastic wallet of high-gloss documents across the table. But Weitz sits back, detached, planning permutations. He knows, Vishram thinks.

"Thanks, but I'm not going to need any more time and I don't want to waste any more of yours. I am not going to accept your offer. I realise that I owe you some kind of explanation. It isn't going to make much sense to you; but the main reason is my father wouldn't want me to do it. He was as hard-headed a businessman as any of you here and he wasn't scared of money, but Ray Power is first and foremost an Indian company and because it's an Indian company, it has values and morals and ethics that are quite alien to the way you do business in the West. It's not racism or anything like that, it's just the way we work in Ray Power and our two systems are incompatible. The second reason is that we don't need your money. I've seen the zero-point field myself." He touches a finger to the flaking corner of his eye. "I know you've been politely not staring at this; but that's the seal of approval. None genuine without this mark. I've seen it, gentlemen. I've seen another universe and I've been burned by its light." Then the rush comes, that moment when you go off script. Head reeling with adrenaline, Vishram Ray says, "In fact, we're going public with a full-scale demonstration within the next two weeks. And by the way, I gave up smoking three weeks ago."

After that there is coffee and very good armagnac, a drink Vishram knows he will never be able to take again without a freight of memory, but the talk is polite and mannered and dies quickly in the way of enemies with etiquette. Vishram wants to be out of there, out from the wood and the glass and the hunting creatures. He wants to be on his own in a place he can enjoy the fierce, intimate burn of a fine deed well done. His first executive decision, and he knows he made it right. Then hands are shaken and leaves taken but as the Major and his jawans escort Vishram back to the tilt-jet he imagines he is walking differently, and that they can all see, and understand, and approve.

The hostess doesn't try to come on to him on the flight home.

At Ray Tower a gang of coolies shifts corporate furniture to a flotilla of removal trucks. Still glowing on adrenaline afterburn, Vishram rides the elevator up to his former office. The executive lift makes an unscheduled stop at the third floor, where a small, dapper, birdlike Bangla in a black suit steps in and smiles at Vishram as if he has known him all his life.

"Might I say, Mr. Ray, that you made the correct decision," says the Bangla, beaming.

The glass elevator climbs the curving wooden cliff of the Ray Tower. Fires still burn out on the cityscape. The sky is a precious velvety apricot colour.

"Just who," says Vishram Ray, "the hell are you?"

The Bangla beams again.

"Oh, a humble servitor. A name, if you must, would be Chakraborty."

"I have to tell you, I'm not really in the mood for obfuscation," Vishram says.

"Sorry, sorry. To the point. I am a lawyer, hired by a certain company to convey a message to you. The message is this: we fully support your announcement to go to a full output demonstration as soon as possible."

"Who is this we?"

"Less who than what, Mr. Ray."

The glass elevator climbs higher into the amber glow of Varanasi's holy smog.

"What then?"

"Odeco is a company that makes a few, carefully chosen, highly specific investments."

"And if you know that I just turned down an offer from a company that at least I'd heard of, what do you think your Odeco could offer me?"

"Exactly what we offered your father."

It is now that Vishram wishes this glass cocoon had the fantasy stop button that is a mandatory feature in Hollywood elevators. But it doesn't and they keep climbing the sculpted wood face of Ray Power.

"My father didn't take partners in the company."

"With respect, Mr. Ray, I differ. Where do you think the investment for the particle collider came from? The budget for the zero-point project would have bankrupted even Ranjit Ray, unassisted."

"What's your cut?" Vishram asks. His Hero of the People warmth has been snuffed out. Games within games, levels of access and secrecy, names and faces and masks. Faces that can get into your elevator and tell you your most secret dealings.

"Only success, Mr. Ray. Only success. To repeat and perhaps amplify my employers' message to you, you intend to run a full-scale demonstration of the zero-point project. Odeco desires this very much. It wishes you to know that it will back you to ensure the success of the project. Whatever that entails, Mr. Ray. Ah. This seems to be my floor. Good day to you, Mr. Ray."

Chakraborty slips between the doors before they fully open. Vishram ascends a full floor before he thinks to drop a level back to where the weird little man got off. He looks out into the curving corridor. Nothing, no one to see. He could have stepped into an office. He could as easily have stepped into another, zero-point universe. The lowering sun beats into the elevator but Vishram shudders. He needs to get out somewhere tonight, away from all this, even for a handful of hours. But which woman is he going to ask?

21

PARVATI

The apricot flies in a high, rising arc out over the parapet, turning slowly, bleeding a trail of juice from its crushed skin. It drops out of sight between the buildings, the long fall to the street.

"So that crossed the boundary in the air, so that makes it?"

"A six!" Parvati exclaims, clapping her hands together.

The crease is a line in gardener's chalk, the wicket, a ply seedling box with three sides knocked off, stood on its heel. Krishan leans on his bat; a spade.

"A six is technically a weak shot," he says. "The batsman has to get under it and he's got no real control over where it's going. Too easy for the fielders to get an eye on it and make the catch. The real enthusiast will always applaud a four more than a six. It's a much more controlled stroke."

"Yes, but it looks so much more bold," Parvati says, then her hands fly to her mouth to suppress giggles. "Sorry, I was just thinking, someone down there . . . and they haven't done anything, but all of a sudden they're covered in apricot . . . and they think, what's going on? Apricots are falling out of the sky. It's the Awadhis! They're bombing us with fruit!" She folds over in helpless laughter. Krishan does not understand the joke but he feels the infection of laughing tug at his rib cage.

"Again again!" Parvati picks up a fresh apricot from the folded cloth, hitches her sari, makes her short run, slings the fruit side-arm. Krishan slices the apricot down into a skittering roll towards the parapet drain slits. Shattered flesh sprays up in his face.

"Four!" Parvati calls, pressing four fingers to her arm.

"Properly, it's a no-ball because it was thrown, not bowled."

"I can't do that overarm thing."

"It's not hard."

Krishan bowls a handful of apricots one at a time, slow up the back, accelerating into the downswing, counterbalancing with his free arm. The soft fruit go bouncing into the shrub rhododendron.

"Now, you try."

He tosses Parvati an underripe apricot. She catches it sweetly, bares the sleeve of her choli. Krishan watches the play of her muscles as she tries to make the run and step and swing in her cumbersome, elegant clothing. The apricot slips from her grasp, drops behind her. Parvati rounds on it, teeth bared in exasperation.

"I cannot do it!"

"Here, let me help you."

The words are spoken before Krishan can apprehend them. Once as a boy in a school lesson he read on the school web that all consciousness is written in the past tense. If so, then all decisions are made without conscience or guilt and the heart speaks truly but inarticulately. His path is already set. He steps up behind Parvati. He rests one hand on her shoulder. With the other he takes her wrist. She catches her breath but her fingers remain curled around the ripe apricot.

Krishan moves her arm back, down, turns the palm upwards. He guides her forward, forward again, pressing the left shoulder down, moving the right arm up. "Now pivot on to the left foot." They hang a precarious moment in their dance, then Krishan sweeps her wrist to the zenith. "Now, release!" he commands. The cloven apricot flies from her fingers, hits the wooden decking, bursts.

"A fine pace delivery," Krishan says. "Now, try it against me." He takes up his position at the crease, sights with his spade-bat, affording Parvati all the sporting courtesies. She retreats beyond the further chalk line, adjusts her clothing, makes her run. She lunges forward, releases the fruit. It hits the deck cleavage first, bounces crankily, spinning. Krishan steps forward with his spade, the apricot hits the top, skips and splatters against the wicket. The flimsy plywood falls. Krishan tucks his spade beneath his arm and bows.

"Mrs. Nandha, you have clean bowled me."

The next day Parvati introduces Krishan to her friends the Prekashs, the Ranjans, the Kumars, and the Maliks. She lays out the magazines like dhuris on the sun-warmed decking. The air is as still and heavy as poured metal this morning, pressing the traffic din and smoke down under a layer of high pressure. Parvati and her husband fought last night. They fought his way, which consists of him making statements and then defending them with lofty silence, sniping down her sallies with looks of high disdain. It was the old fight: his tiredness, her boredom; his remoteness, her need for society; his growing coldness, her ticking ovaries.

She opens the chati mags to the full colour centre spreads. Perfect courtships; glossy weddings; centrefold divorces. Krishan sits in the tailor-position, toes clasped in his hands.

"This is Sonia Shetty, she plays Ashu Kumar. She was married to Lal Darfan—in real life, not in *Town and Country*—but they divorced back in the spring. I was really surprised about that, everyone thought they were together forever, but she's been seen around with Roni

Jhutti. She was at the premiere of *Prem Das*, in a lovely silver dress, so I think it's only a matter of time before we get an announcement. Of course, Lal Darfan's been saying all kinds of things about her, that she is slack and a disgrace. Isn't it strange how actors can be nothing like their characters in *Town and Country*? It's quite changed the way I think about Dr. Prekash."

Krishan flips the thick, shiny pages, aromatic with petrochemicals.

"But they aren't real, either," he says. "This woman wasn't married to anyone in real life, she wasn't at any premiere with any actor. They're just software that believes it's another kind of software."

"Oh, I know that," Parvati says. "No one believes they're real people. Celebrity has never been about what's real. But it's nice to pretend. It's like having another story on top of *Town and Country*, but one that's much more like the way we live."

Krishan rocks gently.

"Forgive me, but do you miss your family very much?"

Parvati looks up from her chati glamshots.

"Why do you ask?"

"It just strikes me that you treat unreal people like family. You care about their relationships, their ups and downs, their lives, if you can call them that."

Parvati pulls her dupatta over her head to protect it from the high sun.

"I think about my family, my mother every day. Oh, I wouldn't go back, not for a moment, but I thought with so many people, so much going on, to be in the capital, I would have a hundred worlds to move through. But it is easier to be invisible than it ever was in Kotkhai. I could disappear completely here."

"Kotkhai, where is that?" Krishan asks. Above him aircraft contrails merge and tangle, spyship and killer, hunting each other ten kilometres above Varanasi.

"In Kishanganj District, in Bihar. You have just made me realise a strange thing, Mr. Kudrati. I mail my mother every day and she tells me about her health and how Rohini and Sushil and the boys are and all the people I know from Kotkhai, but she never tells me about Kotkhai."

So she tells him of Kotkhai, for in telling she tells herself. She can go back to clutches of cracked mud-brick houses gathered around the tanks and pumps; she can walk again down the gently sloping main street of shops and corrugated iron awnings sheltering the stonecutters' workshops. This was the men's world, of drinking tea and listening to the radio and arguing politics. The women's world was in the fields, at the pump and the tanks, for water was the women's element, and the school where the new teacher Mrs. Jaitly from the city ran evening classes and discussion groups and a micro–credit union funded on egg money.

Then it changed. Trucks from Ray Power came and poured out men who put up a tent village so that for a month there were two Kotkhais as they built their wind turbines and solar panels and biomass generators and gradually webbed every house and shop and holy place together with sagging cables. Sukrit the battery seller cursed them that they had put a good man out of business and a good daughter to prostitution.

"We are part of the world now," Mrs. Jaitly had told her women at the evening group. "Our web of cables connects to another web, connects to a greater web, connects to a web across the whole world."

But old India was dying, Nehru's dream bursting at the seams under the pressure of ethnic and cultural division and an environment sagging beneath a billion and a half humans. Kotkhai prided itself that its backwardness and isolation would insulate it from Diljit Rana's idiosyncratic mix of Hinduism and future vision. But the men were talking at the dhaba, reading out columns from the evening news about National Armies and armed militias and lightning raids to seize and hold a fistful of sand-poor villages like Kotkhai in the grab for national territory. *Jai Bharat!* The young men went first. Parvati had seen how her father watched them leave on the country bus. S. J. Sadurbhai had never forgiven his wife for only delivering him daughters. He daily envied the middle classes who could afford to choose the sex of their children. They were building a strong nation, not weak and womanly as old India had been, bickering herself to death. It was almost a relief in the Sadurbhai house when he announced that he and his apprentice Gurpal from the garage were driving off to the war. A good war. A man's war. They drove off and in all Kotkhai there were only two casualties, those two, killed in the truck they were driving by an aeai attack helicopter that could not tell friend from foe. A man's war, a man's death.

Three weeks later a nation was born and war replaced with soap. Within a month of the proclamation of new Bharat, more men brought more cables, fibre-optic cables, down which came news and gupshup and soap. Teacher Jaitly railed against *Town and Country* as mind-gelling propaganda promulgated by the state to stifle real political debate, but week by week her classes dwindled, woman by woman, until in the end she returned to the city, defeated by the affairs of the Prekashs and Ranjans. The new village gathering place was around the state-supplied widescreen. Parvati grew to womanhood in the light of *Town and Country*. From it she learned all the skills needed to become the perfect wife. Within six months Parvati was in Varanasi receiving the final social lacquer that would get her into every best party and durbar on the loop. A half-year later, at a wedding of some cousin of a cousin, she caught a whisper from her second cousin once-removed Deepti, and looked where the whisper pointed, across the lantern-lit gardens, through the glowing awning to the thin, scholarly looking man trying not to be seen looking at her. She remembers that the tree under which he stood was hung with tiny wicker birdcages containing candles. She imagined him haloed in stars.

A further six months and the arrangements were complete, the dowry lodged in Parvati's mother's grameen account and a taxi booked to carry Parvati's few things to the new penthouse flat in the heart of great Varanasi. Except that the things looked like orphans in the cedar-lined closets and penthouse it might be but everyone was now moving out of that dirty, crowded, noisy Kashi to the green soft Cantonment and the thin, scholarly man cloaked with stars was only a policeman. But with a word or a wave of her hand the Prekashs and Ranjans would be there, round to call, who were as happy in Kotkhai as Varanasi, who knew neither snobbery nor caste and whose doings and scandals were always interesting.

On the Thursday Krishan works late on the roof. There are many needling things that require finishing off; the electrical supply to the drip irrigation, the grouting on the path of round stones, the brackets on the bamboo screens around the meditation bowl. He tells himself that he will not be able to move on unless he completes these small niggles, but the truth is that Krishan is curious to see again this Mr. Nandha, this Krishna Cop. He knows from the papers and the radio chat what it is they do but he cannot comprehend why what he hunts down is such a terrifying menace. So he works until the sun swells to a globe of blood in the west beyond the towers of the money town, tightening bolts and cleaning tools until he hears the door close downstairs and Parvati's voice meet the deeper, wordless male rumble. The conversation grows in definition with each step he descends. She is asking, pleading, wanting him to take her out. She wants to go somewhere, get away from this high apartment. His voice is tired and flat and Krishan knows that it will say no to anything she suggests. He sets down his bag and waits by the door. He is not eavesdropping, he tells himself. Doors are thin and words have their natural volume. The policeman is impatient now. His voice hardens, like a parent worn away by an insatiable child. Then Krishan hears the voice bark in anger, a chair scrape back from a table. He seizes his bag, retreats down the main stairs. The door flies open and Mr. Nandha strides down the stair to the lobby door, face set like a carving. He brushes past Krishan as if he were a lizard on a wall. Parvati comes out of the kitchen. She and Mr. Nandha face each other at opposite ends of the stairs. Krishan, invisible, is trapped between their voices.

"Go then!" she shouts. "It is obviously so important."

"Yes," Mr. Nandha says. "It is so important. But I would not trouble you with matters of national security."

He opens the door to the elevator lobby.

"I will be on my own, I am always on my own!" Parvati leans over the chromed railing but the door is closed and her husband is gone without a look. Now she sees Krishan.

"Will you go, too?"

"I should."

"Don't leave me. I'm always on my own, I hate being on my own."

"I really think I have to go."

"I am on my own," Parvati says again.

"You have your *Town and Country*," Krishan ventures.

"That's just a stupid soap!" Parvati shouts at him. "A stupid television programme. Do you really think I believe it? Do you think I'm some country yokel can't tell the difference between a television programme and real life?" She bites back the anger. The women of Kotkhai's training holds. "I'm sorry. I should not have said that. It wasn't you it was aimed at. You should not have had to hear any of that."

"No, I'm sorry," Krishan says. "He should not speak to you like that; like you are a child."

"He is my husband."

"Forgive me, I've spoken out of turn. I should go. It's the best thing."

"Yes," Parvati whispers. She is backlit by the deepening sun, beaming through the apartment windows, turning her skin to gold. "It would be the best thing."

The gold light is amber, trapping the moment. Krishan is sick with tension. The futures balance on a brass pin. Their fall could crush him, crush her, crush them all here in this penthouse apartment. He picks up his bag. But the kick inside takes him.

"Tomorrow," he says, feeling the shake deep in his voice. "Tomorrow there is a cricket match at the Dr. Sampurnanand Stadium. England,

Bharat, the third test. The last, I think. The English will recall their team very soon. Would you . . . could you . . . might you come?"

"With you?"

Krishan's heart thunders, then he realises.

"No, of course not, you could not be seen . . ."

"But I would very much like to see a Test Match, and against England as well. I know! The Cantonment Set ladies go to the Test. We would be in different parts of the ground, you understand. But we would be there together, sharing it. A virtual date, as the Americans would say. Yes, I shall go tomorrow and show the ladies of The Mall that I am not a rural ignoramus about the game of cricket."

The sun has dropped, Parvati is no longer golden-skinned, the amber is broken, but Krishan's heart is in light.

"We'll do that then," Krishan says. "Tomorrow, the Test." Then he picks up his bag and is whirled down the lift out into the eternal traffic.

Dr. Sampurnanand Stadium is a white concrete bowl, simmering under a beige sky, a pan of heat and anticipation circled around a disc of fresh, watered, microclimate-controlled green. Varanasi has never been one of India's great cricketing cities like Kolkata or Chennai or Hyderabad or even her neighbour and former rival for capital city-hood, Patna. The Doctor's stadium had been little more than a bumpy, scorched stretch of withered grass, a crease no bowler of international standing would risk a ball on and no batsman would dare defend. Then came Bharat and the same transfiguring hand of the Ranas that had swept Sarnath into a citadel of audacious architecture and high technology changed the old Sanskrit University sports ground in a hundred-thousand seater. A classic government white elephant, it has never been more than half-full, not even for the 3rd Test of 2038 when Bharat crushed an ailing Australia to win the series, the first and only time. Today its climate-field traps a lens of cool air against forty-degree ambient heat, but the white men out on the field still need plastic bags of water slung on to the pitch. Bharat are 55 for 3, lunch is an hour off and high above the stadium Awadhi and Bharati aeaicraft hunt each other. At the moment the action in the stratosphere is more interesting than the action on the green to the cricketing ladies of canopy-shaded Block 17. The block is owned by Mrs. Sharma's husband, a property developer in Sarnath who bought it as a corporate hospitality tax-break to treat friends and guests and clients. In the season it is a recognised gathering place for society ladies. They make a pretty patch of colour, like an unexpected window-box on the face of a tenement. They squint up through their Western-label sunglasses at the twining helices of contrails. Everything is different since Bharat's brave jawans made their daring move in the night from Allahabad to seize the Kunda Khadar Dam. Mrs. Thakkur opines that they are scouting out an Awadhi attack.

"On Varanasi?" Mrs. Sharma is affronted. Mrs. Chopra thinks that would be typical of Awadh, a vindictive, weasel nation. The jawans took Kunda Khadar so easily because Awadh's troops are already moving on the capital. Mrs. Sood wonders if they are spreading plagues. "You know, like spraying crops." Her husband is a middle-manager in a big biotech firm, booking air-dusting on monocrops the size of entire districts. The ladies hope the Ministry of Health would give enough warning to relocate to their summer bungalows in the hills ahead of the rush.

"I should expect the more important elements in society would be informed first," says Mrs. Laxman. Her husband is a senior civil servant. But Mrs. Chopra has heard another rumour, that the Banglas' ridiculous iceberg is actually starting to work and that the winds are swinging around, drawing the monsoon back to true. This morning as she took tea on the verandah she was certain, certain, she saw a line of shadow along the horizon to the southeast.

"Well then, nobody will need to invade anybody," Mrs. Laxman declares but the Begum Khan, who is married to Sajida Rana's Private Secretary and has the word from the Bharat Sabha, is derisive.

"If anything, it makes war more likely. Even if the monsoon started tomorrow it would take a week for the levels to rise on Ganga. And do you think the Awadhis are going to let us see any of it? They're as thirsty as we are. No, I tell you, pray it doesn't rain, because as soon as the first drop hits, Delhi'll want its dam back. That, of course, is predicated on whether the Banglas' ludicrous iceberg is anything more than a juggernaut of pseudoscience and the opinion, frankly, is no."

The Begum Khan has a reputation as a hard, opinionated woman, with too much learning and too few manners. Muslim traits; but that's not the sort of thing you mention in company. But she is a voice men listen to, in her articles and radio pieces and talks. And there are strange rumours about her quiet, busy little husband.

"Seems we're dammed if we do and damned if we don't," Mrs. Sharma puns in English. The ladies smile and the cricket ground rustles to applause as Bharat hit a boundary. A sport of gentle, distant sounds, cricket; muted handclaps, a click of ball on bat, muffled voices. The umpire lowers his finger, the scoreboard flips over, the ladies turn back to the sky. The confrontation is ended, the contrails blowing ragged on a high wind from the southeast, the monsoon wind. The shy Mrs. Sood wonders who won.

"Why, our side, of course," says Mrs. Chopra, but Parvati can see that Begum Khan is not so sure. Parvati Nandha shades herself with her parasol from the sun that edges under the canopy. It doubles as sunscreen for her palmer on which scores and Test statistics flash up, beamed diagonally across the pitch, through the umpires and the outfield and the infield and the wicket keeper and the batsman and the bowler, from Krishan, down on the boundary line in the day-ticket stands.

The English bowler winds up. TREVELYAN, says the palmer. SOMERSET. PACE. 16TH CAP FOR ENGLAND. CLEAN BOWLED SIX SRI LANKAN WICKETS IN THE SECOND TEST IN COLOMBO, 2046 SEASON.

The batsman steps forward, bat held out in front like a narrow shield. He bears the ball down, his counterpart at the far wicket tenses. No. The ball runs a little way before a fielder (SQUARE SHORT LEG, says the palmer) scoops it up, looks around, sees no one vulnerable out on the wicket, lobs it back to the bowler.

LAST BALL OF OVER, Krishan palms.

"Their square short leg was right on top of that one," Parvati says. The ladies halt in their talk of state, mildly perturbed. But once again she feels outbatted, a Deep Fine Leg watching the ball scurry towards the boundary. She has tried so hard, learned the language and the rules and still they are beyond her; the war, government strategy, the Ranas, international power politics. She persists: "Husainy's up next, he'll take Trevelyan's pace delivery like it's being served to him on a thali."

Her words are less than the jet contrails evaporating in the yellow air above Sampurnanand Stadium. Parvati flips up zoom on her palmer, scans the ranked faces across the pitch. She thumbs WHERE ARE YOU? A message comes back: TO RIGHT OF SIGHT SCREENS. THE BIG WHITE THINGS. She swings her screen over the brown, sweating faces. There. Waving smally, so as not to disturb the players. That would not be cricket.

She can see him. He cannot see her. Fine features, naturally pale skin darkened by his work in the sun on the roof of Diljit Rana Apartments. Clean-shaven; it is only when she contrasts Krishan with the exuberance of moustaches around him that Parvati realises that has always been an important thing for her in a man. Nandha is a shaving man, too. Hair lightly oiled, springing from its chemical confinement, spilling over his forehead. Teeth, when he shouts in delight at some male pleasure from the rules, good and even and present. His shirt is clean and white and fresh, his trousers, as she notices when he stands up to applaud a good two runs, are simple and well ironed. Parvati feels no shame at watching Krishan anonymously. The first lesson she learned from the women of Kotkhai was that men are their most true and most beautiful when they are least conscious of themselves.

A crack of willow. The crowd surges to its feet. A boundary. The scoreboard clicks over. The Begum Khan is saying now that the Ranas have made N. K. Jivanjee look quite the fool since the Awadhi incursion sent him and his silly rath yatra flying back to Allahabad like Ravana fleeing to Lanka.

I SPY YOU, whispers the palmer. The screen shows her Krishan's smiling face. She tilts her parasol in unobtrusive greeting. Behind her the ladies have fallen to chatter of the Dawar's party and why Shaheen Badoor Khan had not stayed for the entertainment. Begum Khan pleads that he is a very busy man, doubly so in this time of Bharat's need. Parvati hears the hooks in their voices. She turns to the game. Now that Krishan has opened up cricket's mysteries, she can see that there is much subtlety and wit in it. A Test Match is not so different from *Town and Country*.

MAZUMDAR WILL TAKE JARDINE, Krishan messages. Jardine walks lazily back from the crease, examining the ball, working at it with his thumb, polishing it. He lines up. The fielders tighten up in their strangely titled positions. Mazumdar, two stripes of anti-dazzle cream beneath his eyes like a tiger's stripes, prepares to receive the delivery. Jardine bowls. The ball bounces, hits a scuff in the grass, bounces high, bounces sweet. Everyone in Sampurnanand Stadium can see how high, how sweet; can see Mazumdar judge it, weight it, shift his position, bring his bat back, get underneath it, send it soaring up, out into the yellow sky. It is a magnificent stroke, a daring stroke, a brilliant stroke. The crowd roars. A six! A six! It must be. All the gods demand it. Fielders run, eyes on heaven. None will ever catch it. This ball is going up, up, out.

Keep your eye on the ball, Krishan had told Parvati when it was spades and apricots on the roof garden. Parvati Nandha keeps her eye on the ball as it reaches the top of its arc and gravity overcomes velocity and it falls to earth, towards the crowd, a red bindi, a red eye, a red sun. An aerial assault. A missile from Krishan, seeking out the heart. The ball falls and the spectators rise but none before Parvati. She surges up and the ball drops into her upheld right hand. She cries out at the sting, then yells "Jai Bharat!" mad on the moment. The crowd cheers, she is marooned in sound. "Jai Bharat!" The noise redoubles. Then, as Krishan showed her, she hooks back her sari and flings the ball out across the boundary. An English fielder catches it, nods a salute, and skims it to the bowler. But it is six, six, glorious six to Mazumdar and Bharat. I kept my eye on the ball. I kept my hand soft, moved with it. She turns to show off her pride and achievement to her ladies and finds their faces rigid with contempt.

Parvati only allows herself to stop when she is outside the ground but even then she can still hear the muttering and feel the burn of shame on her face. A fool a fool a country fool, carried away with the mob, getting up and making an exhibition of herself like someone with no manners, no class at all. She had shown them up. Look at the Cantonment lady who throws the ball like a man! Jai Bharat!

Her palmer has been vibrating, message after message after message. She does not want to see them. She does not want even to look back for fear he might have come after her. She heads across the landscaped area to the road. Taxis. There must be taxis, any time on a match day. She stands by the cracked roadside, parasol raised as the phatphats and city cabs slide past. Where are you going who are you driving this time of day? Can't you see a lady is hailing you?

Hope-to-be lady. Never-was lady. Never-can-be lady.

A moped cab swings through the traffic to the curb. The driver is a buck-toothed youth with a straggle of down for a moustache.

"Parvati!" The voice is behind her. This is worse than death. She climbs into the back and the driver accelerates away, past the startled, staring figure in the pressed black trousers and the sharply ironed pure white shirt. Returning to the empty apartment, shaking with shame and wanting to die, Parvati finds the doors unlocked and her mother with her travelling baggage encamped in the kitchen.

22

SHAHEEN BADOOR KHAN

The dam is a long, low curve of bulldozed earth, huge as a horizon, one end invisible from the other, anchored in the gentle contours of the Ganga valley. The Bharati Air Force tilt-jet comes in over Kunda Khadar from the east. It passes low over the waving jawans, turns above the lake. The aeai strike-copters flock closer than Shaheen Badoor Khan finds comfortable. They fly as birds fly, daring manoeuvres no human pilot could attempt, by instinct and embodiment. The tilt-jet banks, the aeaicraft dart and swoop to cover and Shaheen Badoor Khan finds himself looking down into a wide, shallow bowl of algae-stained water rimmed by dirty, sandy gravel as far as the eye can see, white and toxic as salt. A silty sump not even a cow would drink. Across the aisle Sajida Rana shakes her head and whispers, "Magnificent."

If they had listened, if they had not rushed in the soldiers, heads full of Jai Bharat! Shaheen Badoor Khan thinks. *The people want a war*, Sajida Rana had said at the cabinet meeting. The people shall have one, now.

The Prime Ministerial jet lands on a hastily cleared field on the edge of a village ten kays on the Bharati side of the dam. The aeaicraft flock above it like kites over a Tower of Silence. The occupation force has made its divisional headquarters here. Mechanised units dig in to the east, robots sow a minefield. Shaheen Badoor Khan in his city suit blinks behind his label shades in the hard light and notes the villagers standing at the edges of their requisitioned and ruined fields. In her tailored combats Sajida Rana is already striding purposefully towards the receiving line of officers and guards and V. S. Chowdhury. She wants to be Number One pin-up on the barrack-room walls; Mama Bharat, up there with Nina Chandra. The officers namaste and escort Prime Minister and prime counsellor through the dust to the hummers. Sajida Rana strides out, Minister Chowdhury trotting alongside as he attempts to brief her. Little yipping dog, Shaheen Badoor Khan thinks. As he climbs into the sweatbox of the hummer's passenger compartment he glances back at the tilt-jet, perched on its wheels and engines as if fearful of contamination. The pilot is a black-visored tick plugged into the plane's head. Beneath the sensor-tipped nose the long barrel of an autocannon is like the proboscis of some insect that lives by sucking the juices from another. A dainty killer.

Shaheen Badoor Khan sees the banana club, the blind smile of the old woman, identifying her guests by pheromone; the dark alcoves where the voices mingled and laughed and the bodies relaxed into each other. The alien, beautiful creature, swimming out of the dark and the dhol beat like a nautch dancer.

The hummer smells of Magic Pine air freshener. Shaheen Badoor Khan unfolds blinking into the light that glares from the concrete road surface. They are on the dam-top road. The air is rank with dead soil and stagnant water. Magic Pine is almost preferable. A thin piss of yellow water trickles from the spill-way flume. That is Mother Ganga.

Jawans form up a hasty honour guard. Shaheen Badoor Khan notes the SAM robots and the nervous glances between the lower level officers. Ten hours ago this was the Republic of Awadh and the soldiers wore green, white, and orange triple yin-yangs on their otherwise identical chameleon camous. Easy mortar range from those ghost villages revealed in their architectural nakedness by the dwindling water level. A single sniper, even. Sajida Rana strides on, her hand-tooled boots clicking on the roadbed. The troops are ranked up beyond the dais. Someone is testing the PA with a series of feedback shrieks. The news channel camerapersons spot the Prime Minister in combats and charge her. Military Police draw lathis and brush them aside. Shaheen Badoor Khan waits at the foot of the steps as Prime Minister, Defence Secretary, and Divisional Commander mount the dais. He knows what Sajida Rana will say. He put the final lacquer on it himself this morning in the limo to the military airfield. The general susurrus of men gathered together under a hot sun ebbs as they see their commander-in-chief take the microphone. Shaheen Badoor Khan nods in silent pleasure as she holds the silence.

"Jai Bharat!"

An unscripted moment. Shaheen Badoor Khan's heart freezes in his throat. The men know it, too. The silence hangs, then erupts. Two thousand voices thunder it back. *Jai Bharat!* Sajida Rana gives the call and response three times. Then she delivers the message of her speech. It is not for the soldiers standing easy on the dam top road, sloped at their weapons in the APCs. It is for the cameras and the mikes and the network news editors. Sought a peaceful resolution. Bharat not a nation craves war. Tigress roused. Sheathe her claws. Hoped for diplomatic solution. Still achieve a negotiated peace with honour. Noble offer to our enemies. Water should always have been shared. No one nation. Ganga our common life-vein.

The soldiers don't shift. They don't shuffle. They stand in their battle gear in the tremendous heat with their heavy weapons and take this stuff and cheer at the cheer points and hush down when Sajida

Rana quiets them with her eyes and hands, and when she leaves them on a final killer: "And finally, I bring you another major triumph. Gentlemen, Bharat three hundred and eighty seven for seven!" they erupt and the chanting starts. *Jai Bharat! Jai Bharat!* Sajida Rana takes their applause and strides off while it is still fresh and ringing.

"Not bad, eh, Khan?"

"Mazumdar just went for one hundred and seventeen," Shaheen Badoor Khan says, falling in behind his leader. The hummer convoy whisks them back to the forward command headquarters. This was always going to be an in and out operation. General Staff had counselled in every way against it but Sajida Rana insisted. The offer of conciliation must be made from a posture of might that would not demean the Rana government. The analysts had studied the satellite data and cywar intelligence and given an hour of reasonable confidence before the Awadhis could muster a retaliation. The hummers and APCs rip back along the corrugated country dirt roads. Their dust plumes must be visible from orbit. The aeaicraft flock in behind like a hunt of raptors. Sentries nervously eye the sky as they hurry Prime Minister Rana and her chief advisor to the powering-up tilt-jet. The hatch seals, Shaheen Badoor Khan belts up, and the ship bounds into the air, leaving his stomach down there on the flattened, scorched crops. The pilot climbs at full throttle a hair under stall angle. Shaheen Badoor Khan was not born to fly. He feels every lurch and drop like a little death. His fists grip white on the armrests. Then the tilt-jet flips over into horizontal flight.

"Well that was a bit dramatic, wasn't it?" Sajida Rana says, unfastening her seat belt. "Bloody army never forgets who's the woman here. Jai Bharat! Still, that went well. I did think the cricket score finished it off nicely."

"If you say you, Ma'am."

"I do say so." Sajida Rana writhes in her clinging combats. "Bloody uncomfortable things. I don't know how anyone ever does any serious fighting in them. So, your analysis?"

"It will be frank."

"Is it ever anything else?"

"I think the occupation of the dam is foolhardy. The plan called . . ."

"The plan was good as far as it went, but it had no balls."

"Prime Minister, with respect . . ."

"This is diplomacy, I know. But fuck it, I am not going to let N. K. Jivanjee play the Hindutva martyr. We're Ranas, for God's sake." She lets the little touch of theatre ebb, then asks, "Our position is still salvageable?"

"Salvageable, but international pressure will be a factor when it hits the news channels. It might give the British their excuse to renew calls for an international conference."

"Hopefully not in London, the shopping's gone to hell. But the Americans . . ."

"We're thinking the same thought, Prime Minister. The Special Relationship . . ."

"Is nowhere near as reciprocal as the Brits like to think. I'll tell you one thing gives me joy out of this whole mess, Khan. We stuck it up that chuutya Jivanjee. He thought he was so clever, leaking those photographs of his Holy Shopping Trolley; well, now he's the one running back home with his balls in his mouth."

"Still, Prime Minister, he hasn't gone away, you know. I think we shall be hearing from Mr. Jivanjee if we get our peace conference."

"When, Khan."

Shaheen Badoor Khan dips his head in acquiescence. But he knows that there is no science in this thing. He, his government, and his nation have been lucky thus far. Sajida Rana picks a badly sewn seam in her combat pants, slouches down in her seat, and asks, "Anything about me yet?" Shaheen Badoor Khan flips on his palmer and scans the news channels and agency services. Phantom pages appear before his field of vision. News breaks around him in soft, colourful detonations.

"CNN, BBC, and News International are running it as breaking news. Reuters is just copying to the US Press."

"What's the Great Satan's general tenor?"

Shaheen Badoor Khan flicks through leader articles from Boston to San Diego.

"Mild scepticism to outright rejection. The conservatives are calling for our withdrawal, then maybe negotiations."

Sajida Rana tugs gently at her bottom lip, a private gesture known only to intimates, like her fabulously dirty mouth.

"At least they aren't sending the marines. But then it's only water, not oil. Still, it's not Washington we're at war with. Anything from Delhi?"

"Nothing on the online channels."

Prime Minister Rana drags the lip a little lower.

"I don't like that. They've got other headlines written."

"Our satellite data show Awadhi forces still holding position."

Sajida Rana lets go her lip, sits up in her seat.

"Fuck them. This is a great day! We should rejoice! Shaheen." The first name. "In confidence: Chowdhury, what do you think of him?"

"Minister Chowdhury is a very able constituency member . . ."

"Minister Chowdhury is a hijra. Shaheen, there's an idea I've been pushing around the back of my head. Deedarganj will be up for by-election some time in the next year, Ahuja's putting a brave face on it but that tumour's eating him from the inside out, poor bastard. It's a good staunch seat; hell, they'd elect James F. McAuley if he waved a bit of incense at Ganesha."

"With respect Prime Minister, President McAuley is not a Muslim."

"Well fuck it, Khan, you're hardly Bin Laden. What are you, Sufi, something like that?"

"I come from a Sufi background, that's correct."

"Well, that's my point exactly. Look, truth of it is, you've played a good chukka on this one and I need your abilities out in the open. You'd have to serve out your apprenticeship on the backbenches, but I'd certainly be fast-tracking you for a ministerial portfolio."

"Prime Minister, I don't know what to say."

"Well, you could start with thank you, you fucking parsimonious Sufi. Strictest, of course."

"Of course, Prime Minister."

Deprecating, bowing, acquiescing; a mere civil servant; but Shaheen Badoor Khan's heart leaps. There was a time at Harvard after the freshman results when the tension burst and the summer opened free and wide and he forgot both business school virtues and the disciplines of his school of Islam. Under the lengthy guidance of a liquor store owner he had bought himself a bottle of imported Speyside single malt whisky and, in the shafts of dusty light through his room window, toasted his success. Between the creak of the cork in the bottle-neck and the dry retching in the purple twilight there had been a distinct period when he felt embedded in joy and radiance and confidence and that the world was his without limit or bar. He had gone to his window, bottle in hand, and roared at the planet. The hangover, the spiritual guilt, had been worth it for that one, charged burn of epiphany. Now strapped in beside his Prime Minister in an army tilt-jet, he knows it again. Cabinet Minister. Him. He tries to look at himself, imagine a different seat at the table in the beautiful, luminous council room; imagine himself rising to his feet under the dome of the Sabha. The Honourable Member for Deedarganj. And it will be right. It is his just reward, not for his diligent, unstinting service, but for his ability. He deserves this. Deserves it, will have it.

"How long have we worked together?" Sajida Rana asks.

"Seven years," Shaheen Badoor Khan replies. He thinks, and three months twenty-two days. Sajida Rana nods. Then she does the thing with the lip again.

"Shaheen."

"Yes, Prime Minister?"

"Is everything all right?"

"I'm afraid I don't know what you mean, Prime Minister."

"It's just, well, you've seemed distracted recently. I've heard a rumour."

Shaheen Badoor Khan feels his heart stop, his breath freeze, his brain crystallise. Dead. He is dead. No. She would not have offered him everything she has in this high, private place only to rip it away from him for a trifle of madness. But it is not madness, Shaheen Badoor Khan. It is how you are. Thinking you can deny it, hide it, is the madness. He moistens his lips with his tongue. There must be no faltering, no dryness or failure in these words he has to say.

"Government is the province of rumours, Prime Minister."

"I'd just heard you'd left some do in the Cantonment early."

"I was tired, Prime Minister. That was the day . . ." He is not safe yet.

"Of the briefing, yes, I remember. What I heard, and doubtless it's gross slander, is that there was a bit of . . . tension between you and Begum Bilquis. I know it's bloody cheek, Shaheen, but is everything all right at home?"

Tell her, Shaheen Badoor screams at himself. Better she finds out now than from some party tout, or, God preserve us, N. K. Jivanjee. If she does not know already, if this is not some test of honesty and loyalty. Tell her where you went, who you met, what you almost did with him. *Yt*. Tell her. Hand it over to the mother of the nation, let her manage it and spin it and massage it for the cameras, all those things he has done so long, so loyally, for Sajida Rana.

He cannot. His enemies within and without the party hate him enough as a Muslim. As a pervert, a wife-abandoner, a lover of things most of them cannot even regard as human, his career would be over. The Rana government could not survive. Before everything, Shaheen Badoor Khan is a civil servant. The administration must stand.

"May I be frank, Prime Minister?"

Sajida Rana leans across the narrow aisle.

"That's twice in one conversation, Shaheen."

"My wife . . . Bilquis . . . well, recently, we've been going through a cold period. When the boys left for university, well, we'd never had that much apart from them to talk about. We live independent lives now—Bilquis has her column and women's forum. But you can be assured that we won't let that get in the way of our public duties. We won't embarrass you that way again."

"No embarrassment," Sajida Rana murmurs, then the military pilot makes a terse announcement about landing at Nabha Sparasham Air Force Base in ten minutes and Shaheen Badoor Khan uses the distraction to look out of the window at the great brown stain of Varanasi's monstrous bastis. He allows himself a small twitch of a smile. Safe. She doesn't know. He has spun it. But there are tasks he has to do now. And there, along the very southern edge of the horizon, is that a dark line of cloud?

It was only after his father died that Shaheen Badoor Khan understood how much he hated the house by the river. It is not that the haveli is ugly or overbearing—it is the contrary of all of those things. But its airy cloisters and verandahs and spacious, high-ceilinged white rooms are heavy with history, generation, duty. Shaheen Badoor Khan cannot go up the steps and pass under the great brass lantern in the porch and enter the hall with its twin spiralling staircases, the men's and the women's, without remembering himself as a boy, hiding behind a pillar as his grandfather Sayid Raiz Khan was carried out to the burying ground by the old hunting lodge in the marshes, and again, walking behind his own father as he made that same, swift journey through the teak doors. He will make that journey himself, through his fine teak double doors. His own sons and grandsons will bear him through. The haveli is crowded with lives. There is no cranny away from relatives and friends and servants. Every word, deed, intention is visible, transparent. The concept of *place apart* is one he remembers with tight pleasure from Harvard. The concept of privacy, the New England reserve: reserve, a thing set aside, for another use.

He crosses the mezzanine to the women's half of the house; as always, he hesitates at the door of the zenana. Purdah had been abolished in haveli Khan in his grandfather's time but Shaheen Badoor Khan had always felt a sense of shame of the women's apartments; things here, stories in the walls, ways of living that had nothing to do with him. A house divided, like the hemispheres of the brain.

"Bilquis." His wife has set up her office in the screened balcony with its view over the teeming, tumultuous ghats and the still river. Here she writes her articles and radio speeches and essays. In the bird garden beneath she entertains her clever, disenfranchised friends as they drink coffee and make whatever plans clever, disenfranchised women make.

We are a deformed society, the music-loving civil servant had said as Mumtaz Huq took the stage.

"Bilquis."

Footsteps. The door opens, the face of a servant—Shaheen Badoor Khan cannot remember which one—peeps out.

"The Begum is not here, sahb."

Shaheen Badoor Khan slumps against the sturdy doorframe. The one time he would cherish a few sentences snatched between busy lives. A word. A touch. For he is tired. Tired of the relentlessness. Tired of the appalling truth that even if he sat down and did nothing like the sadhu on a street comer, events he has set in motion will swell behind him, one feeding the other, into a drown-wave. He must always run those few steps ahead. Tired of the mask, the face, the lie. Tell her. She will know what to do.

"Always out, yes."

"Mr. Khan?"

"It doesn't matter."

The door closes on the sliver of face. For the first time in memory, Shaheen Badoor Khan is lost in his own house. He cannot recognise the doors, the walls, the hallways. He is in a bright room now, overlooking the river, a white room with the mosquito nets tied up in big, soft knots, a room filled with slants of light and dust and a smell that calls him back to himself. Smell is the key of memory. He knows this room, he loved this room. It is the old nursery; his boys' room. His room, high over the water. Here he would wake every morning to the salutations of the Brahmins to the great river. The room is clean and pale and bare. He must have ordered it cleared after the boys left the house for university but he cannot remember instructing it so. Ayah Gul died ten years ago but in the wooden slats, the draped curtains he can smell the perfume of her breast, the spice of her clothing though Shaheen Badoor Khan realises with a start that it is decades since he entered this room. He squints up into the light. *God is the light of the Heavens and of the Earth. . . . It is light upon light. God guideth whom He will to His light, and God setteth forth parables to men, for God knoweth all things.* The sura curls like smoke in Shaheen Badoor Khan's memory.

It is only because, for the first time in long memory, he feels there are no eyes watching, that Shaheen Badoor Khan can do what he does now. He reaches his arms out at his side and starts to spin, slowly at first, feet feeling for balance. The Sufi spinning dance, that whirled the dervishes into the God-consciousness within. The dhikr, the sacred name of God, forms on his tongue. A bright flash of child-memory, his grandfather holding perfectly in place on the geometric tiled floor of the iwan as the qawwals play. A Mevlevi had come from Ankara to teach Indian men the sema, the great dance of God.

Spin me out of this world, God-within.

The soft mat rucks beneath Shaheen Badoor Khan's feet. The concentration is intense, every thought on the motion of the feet, the turning of the hands, down to bless, up to receive. He spins back through his memories.

That crazy New England summer when high pressure moored over Puritan Cambridge and the temperature climbed and stuck and everyone opened their doors and windows and went out into the streets and parks and greens or just sat in their doorways and balconies, when Shaheen Badoor Khan, in his sophomore year, forgot what it was to be cold and restrained. Out with friends, coming back late from a music festival in Boston. Then it came, out of the soft, velvet, scented night and Shaheen Badoor Khan was paralysed, fixed like a northern star as he was to be a quarter of a century later in Dhaka airport by a vision of the unearthly, the alien, the unobtainable beauty. The nute frowned at the rush of noisy undergraduates as it tried to sidestep. It was the first Shaheen Badoor Khan had ever seen. He had read, seen pictures, been intrigued, tantalised, tormented by this dream of his childhood incarnate. But this was flesh: real, no legendary beast. He had fallen in love on that Harvard green. He had never fallen out again. Twenty-five years, carrying a thorn in the heart.

Feet move, hands weave, lips shape the mantra of the dhikr. Spinning back.

The wrapping was perfect, simple, elegant. Red, black, and white koi patterned paper, a single strand of cellophane raffia, gold. Minimal. Indians would have prettied it, gaudified it, put hearts and bows and Ganeshas, had it play tunes and spring out confetti blessings when opened. At the age of thirteen, Shaheen Badoor Khan knew when he saw the parcel from Japan that his would never be a true Indian spirit. His father had brought gifts for all the family back from the trade trip to Tokyo. For his younger brothers, Boys Day Carp Kites—proudly flown from the balconies of Haveli Khan ever after. For oldest son, Nihon in a box. Shaheen had goggled at the squeeze tubes of Action Drink, the Boat In the Mist chocolate, the trading cards and Waving Kitty robotpet, the mood-colour scarves and the disks of Nippon-pop. What transformed his life, like a motorbike that turns into an avenging battle-bot, was the manga. At first he had not liked their easy mix of violence and sex and high-school anxiety. Cheap and alien. But what seduced him were the characters; the elongated, sexless teens with their deer eyes and their snub noses and their ever-open mouths. Saving the world, having parent problems, wearing fabulous costumes, sporting fantastic hairstyles and footwear, worrying about their boy-girl-friends as the destroying angel-robots bore down on Tokyo but mostly being independent and cool and fabulous and long-legged and androgynous. He wanted their thrilling, passionate lives so badly he had cried. He envied their beauty and sexy sexlessness and that everyone knew and loved and admired them. He wanted to be them in life and death. In his bed in the loud Varanasi dark, Shaheen Badoor Khan would invent on-stories for them; what happened after they defeated the angels streaming through the crack between the heavens, how they loved and played together in their fur-lined battle-dome. Then they pulled him down into the pink fur-lined bulb of the battle-nest and they rubbed together, indeterminate but passionate, for ever and ever and ever. On those nights when he was made a Mage-rider of a Grassen Elementoi, Shaheen Badoor Khan would wake in the suffocating morning with the front of his pyjama pants stiff.

Years after he would sneak those yellowing, soft, and fraying comics out of the shoebox. Ever young, ever slim, ever beautiful and adventurous, the boy-girl pilots of the Grassen Elementoi stood, arms folded, challenging him with their cheekbones and animal eyes and sullen, kissable mouths.

Shaheen Badoor Khan, whirling on the edge of the transcend, feels his eyes sharp with tears. The sema wheels him back, to the beach.

His mother had complained about the humidity and the socialism and how the fishermen would shit on the sand outside the bungalow. His father had been edgy and stuffy and homesick for the searing north. He had fretted about in creased pants and short-sleeved poplin shirts and open-toe sandals in the smothering Keralese heat and it had been the worst holiday Shaheen Badoor Khan could remember because he had been looking forward to it so much. The south the south the south!

In the evening the fisher kids would come in from the sea. Sun-blackened, naked, smiling, they had played and yelled and splashed while Shaheen Badoor Khan and his brothers sat on their verandah and drank lemonade and listened to their mother tell them how terrible those dreadful children were. Shaheen Badoor Khan did not find them dreadful. They had a little outrigger. They would play all day with that boat, in and out of it. Shaheen Badoor Khan would imagine them sailed in from an adventure out on the big water; piracy, rescue, exploration. When they ran their outrigger up on to the strand and played cricket on the beach he thought he would die from desire. He wanted to sail off with black, grinning Keralese boy-girls, he wanted to slip naked into blood-warm water and wear it like a skin. He wanted to run and yell and be skinny and un-self-conscious and free.

In the next bungalow was a family of civil servants from Bangalore, below the salt in every way, but Shaheen Badoor saw their boy and girl play on the outrigger, jump into the clear water and surface, gasping, dewed with drops, laughing and laughing and laughing to do it all again. A seed of emptiness was planted there, that germinated on the long train journey back up the length of India into an ache, a hope, a desire that had no name or words, but smelled like sunburn lotion, itched like sand between the toes, felt like warm coconut matting, sounded like children cries coming across water.

Shaheen Badoor Khan whirls to a stop. He fights immense, racking sobs heaving up inside him. He wanted it so much but his was not the life that could ever have that kind of freedom. He would give anything to be that beautiful, even for one day.

Feet. Outside. Bare feet. Shaheen Badoor Khan shakes free of the succubus.

"Who's there?"

"Sir? Are you all right?"

"I'm fine. Leave me, please."

Everything is fine, as fine it can be amidst ruins. Shaheen Badoor Khan straightens his suit, smoothes out the rucked up dhuri where he whirled, and God honoured him. He was taken down into the nafs, the desiring core of the soul, and there shown the true nature of the God-within and his cry for aid beyond comprehension was answered.

He knows what he must do now about the nute.

23

TAL

For the rest of the week Tal throws ytself into yts work, but not even the interiors for the haveli into which Aparna Chawla and Ajay Nadiadwala will move after their virtual wedding can quell the demons. A gendered. A *man*. A Khan. Tal tries to shake the image from yts brain but he's strung out along the neurons like Diwali lights. That's the ultimate fear: it's all unravelling in there, all those biochips and hormone pumps dissolving into yts bloodstream. Tal fears yt's pissing yts nuteness away through yts kidneys. Yt can still taste this Khan's lips.

By the end of the week even Neeta is telling yt yt should take time off.

"Get, go on, out of here," Line Producer Devgan orders. Tal gets, goes, out-of-heres to Patna. No one but a nute would think of week-ending in that sprawling, hot, soul-free industrial city. There's someone Tal needs to see there. Yts guru.

Two hours later Tal is down at the river, blinking polarised contact lenses against the brilliants glinting from the water and booking a first return (it is better to travel first class than to arrive, baba) on the fast hydrofoil to Patna. Thirty minutes later yt's curling back into yts seat, closing yts eyes and small, soft fists in pleasure to the opening beats of GURU GRANTH MIX as the industrial plants slip by on the far dry banks. Yt's amazed there's enough water to *float* this thing.

There's a new look on Patna's pollution-soaked streets. Dark and flowing is in. As is *hair*, worn in a single off-centre moheek, flopped over the forehead. And nobody would be seen dead in ski-goggles. Nothing Tal can do about the hair but ClimBunni on Amrit Marg has all the look, racked up and ready to vend. Tops here, bottoms there, unders here, footwear in back. The card takes another weighty blow but half an hour later Tal swings out on to the streets in swathes of soft grey silk and silver-black cow-nute boots with five-centimetre heels and the *essential* bead tassles swaying from the bootstraps. The guys are reeling, the girls are watching enviously, the women in the coffee-shops are leaning together and talking behind their hands, the traffic-cop on point-duty at the roundabout almost spins three sixty as Tal clicks yts contact lenses black against the sun and it's good, so good, so astonishingly unexpected and wonderful and hilarious to be back on Patna streets under Patna sun breathing Patna smog, threading through the Patna bodies and faces, moving to the Patna mix in yts phones. Everything dances to the mix. Everything is a musical, every chance encounter between passersby is murder or an adultery or a robbery or long-lost lovers reuniting. The clothes are brighter and the signs are flashier and everything is about to break into one huge production number, citywide, just for Tal. Yt prays to Ardhanarisvara god of nutes to let yt be the first to bring the noo look back to Varanasi.

Varanasi. And men called Khan. And everything.

For those who know, there is the fast boat down beneath the glass towers of the Commercial Bund that will take you up to the sangam where the guru conducts yts operations. The boat is a mahogany Riva, Tal notes with approval. Twin engines stand the Riva on its tail and take it out past the scuttling little ferries and barge trains. The boat cuts across the main channel and veers left towards the great sand spit where the Gandak joins the sacred Ganga. On and around this wide sand delta stands Bharat's biggest, cheapest, dirtiest, and least regulated free-trade zone. The pressed aluminium larri-gallas and go-downs long ago crowded each other off the available land on to the water: the sangam is fringed by decommissioned lighters twenty deep. Families live here that boast they never set foot on dry land; all they need for birth, for life, for death, they can find running over the maze of gangplanks and companionways, boat to boat.

The Riva takes Tal through ever-narrowing channels between steel hulls painted with improving Hindu texts until it squeezes into a conduit barely wide enough to contain it to pull in beside an old tug with the unlikely name of *Fugazi*. For thirty years she hauled bulk cargo upstream from Kolkata to Patna's new industries. Then White Eagle Holdings bought her up, sailed in to final dock on the Gangak Free Trade Zone and eviscerated her engines. White Eagle Holdings is a deeply respectable fund management company based in Omaha, Nebraska, specialising in pension plans for healthcare workers. It owns several floating factories in Patna that specialise in those medical services the Bible-believing voters of the Midwest vehemently deny their fellow countrymen. Hundreds of high-revenue, low-legality industries have their corporate headquarters in Gangak Eff Tee Zee: custom-pirate radio stations, pharm phakers, fileshare services, datahavens, emotic breweries, genebusters, clonelabs, cell therapists, Darwinware jungles, copy protection strippers, forex shuttle services, label tippers, stem-cell farmers, pornocrats, at least one Gen 3 aeai (mooted), and Nanak the kind doctor, the good nute, the guru of the sweet knives.

Tal climbs the steel ladder, nervously conscious of the looming metal wall of the neighbouring barge at yts back. One eddy in the mingling of waters around this point and the closing walls of steel would burst yt like a dropped egg. A face peeps over the rail: it is Nanak, the good doctor, disreputable as always in a pair of cargo shorts three times too big, a clingy mesh top and big tank-girlie boots, grinning like a holy monkey.

They embrace. They touch. They kiss. They stroke emotions of joy and presents and childhood stay-up-lates and the first bread of the morning and glissandos of baroque into their subdermals, those same neural keys Nanak's robot surgeons fused into the nerve fibres of Tal's flayed body. Then they break and smile and make silly, joyous noises and are happy all over again.

"The style got you, I see," Nanak says. Yt's small and a little shy and coy, and bowed a little lower by gravity but yt's still got the kindest smile. Yts skin is ochre from the sun.

"At least I make an effort," Tal says, inclining yts head at Nanak's dock-wallah gear.

"You just watch your heels around here," Nanak warns. The deck is a fashion assault course of cable ducts and hatch dogs and pipes any of which could send the careless nute crashing against hard steel plate. "You will stay for tea, won't you? Careful here." They scale a steep ladder to the wheelhouse. One step before the top Tal pauses to look out over the city of boats. It is as busy as any bazaar. Beyond making money, there is always work to be done on any ship: painters and deck-swabbers, gardeners, water-engineers, solar power experts, com riggers. Music booms, bass amplified by the copious hollow metal.

"So, what is it?" Nanak asks as yt shows Tal into the wood-panelled, cedar-scented reception room. The smell evokes as powerful an emotional reaction in Tal as any neural keyed response. Yt is back in the wood-lined womb. Yt remembers how the leather sofas creak, how Suniti on the desk hums filmi hits when she thinks no one else is around.

"Just a routine check up," Tal says.

"Well, we'll certainly do that for you," Nanak says and calls the elevator to go down into the empty heart of the ship where yt carries out yts transformations.

"You busy?" Tal asks to hide yts apprehension. The elevator opens on to a corridor of mahogany and brass doors. Tal spent a month behind one of them, crazy on painkillers and immunosuppressives as yts body came to terms with what the robot surgeons had done to it. The real insanity had come when the protein chips wired into yts medulla unpacked and started overwriting four million years of biological imperative.

"I've two in," Nanak says. "One waiting—cute little Malay, really nervy, could bolt at any time, which would be a shame—and one in post-op. We seem to be picking up a lot of old-style transgenders so our reputation is spreading outside the scene but I'm not that keen on it. It's just butchery. No finesse at all."

And they will pay for it, as Tal pays for it still; ten percent down and monthly repayments for most of the rest of yts life. Full body mortgage.

"Tal," Nanak says gently. "Not that one, in here." Tal finds yts hand on the door of the surgery. Nanak swings open the clinic door. "Just checking you over, cho chweet. You don't even need to take your clothes off."

But Tal does kick off yts boots and slips out of yts cool coat before lying back on the white, softly padded table. Yt blinks, self-conscious, up into the lights as Nanak bustles about recalibrating the scanner. This is when Tal remembers that Nanak, the sweet doctor, doesn't even have a nursing qualification. Yts just a broker, a stevedore of surgery. Robots dismembered Tal and put yt back together again, micromanipulators, molecule-thin scalpels guided by surgeons in Brazil. Nanak's talent is in bedside manner and a nose for the sharpest medics at the keenest prices wherever the global market opens an opportunity.

"So, baba, tell Nanak, is this a purely medical call or are you checking out the Patna scene?" Nanak asks as yt slips a 'hoek behind yts large ear.

"Nanak, I'm a career nute now, don't ya know? I've moved up to section head in three months. A year from now, I'll be running the show."

"Then you'll be able to come to me to buy whole new sets of emotics," Nanak says. "I've got some new stuff, fresh from the mixers. Very good. Very strange. Right. Ready. Just breathe normally." Yt lifts a hand in a mudra and semicircles of white metal slide out of the bed base and join in a ring over Tal's feet. Despite Nanak's injunction, Tal finds yt's holding yts breath as the scanner begins its pilgrimage up yts body. Yt closes yts eyes as the ring of light sweeps over yts throat and tries not to imagine that other table, beyond that other door. The table that is not a table, but a bed of gel in a tank of robots. Yt was lain on that table, anaesthetised to within a glimmer of death, autonomic responses wired to a medical aeai that kept yts lungs pumping, heart beating, blood circulating. Tal cannot remember the top of the tank descending, locking in place, filling with more pressurised, anaesthetic gel. But yt can imagine and imagination has become memory, a claustrophobic imaginary memory of drowning. What yt cannot—dares not—imagine are the robots moving through the gel, blades extended, to flay every centimetre of skin from yts body.

That was the first part.

As the old skin was incinerated and the new one that had been seeded three months before from a sample of Tal's DNA and a egg sold by some basti woman grew ripe in its tank, the machines went in. They moved slowly through the viscous, organic gel, driving in under the muscle armouring, peeling back fat, detouring around blood tines and engorged arterials, disconnecting sinews to get to the bone. In their São Paulo offices, the cheap surgeons operated on air with their manipulator gloves and opened up intimate, bloody vistas of Tal's body on their visors. Osteobots sculpted bone, reshaping a cheek here, widening a pelvis, shaving slivers from shoulder blades, dislocating, relocating, amputating, substituting plastic and titanium. As they worked, teams of GUMbots removed all genitalia, replumbed ureter and urethra, and respliced the hormone triggers and neural response pathways to the array of subdermal studs embedded in the left forearm.

Tal hears Nanak laugh. "I can see right inside you," yt giggles.

Three days in that tank Tal hung; skinless, bleeding constantly, a whole body stigmata, while the machines worked slowly, steadily, shift after shift dismantling yts body and rebuilding. Then their task was done and they withdrew and the neurobots went in. Different doctors guided these, a team from Kuala Lumpur. In the three days of Tal's passion, the market had shifted in neurosurgery. This was a different, more refined science than cutting and pasting gobbets of meat. Clicking crab-bots fused protein circuitry to nerve fibre, spliced nerves to gland inducers, rewired Tal's entire endocrine system. While they grafted, big machines took the top off Tal's skull and micromanipulators crept between the tangled ganglia like hunters in a mangrove swamp to spot-weld protein processors to neural clusters in the medulla and amygdala, the deep, dark root-buttresses of the self. Then, on the morning of the fourth day, they brought Tal back from the edge of death and woke yt up. The aeai hooked into the back of Tal's skull now had to run a full autonomic nervous system test that the chip grafts had seated correctly and that the neural firing patterns yt had previously associated with *gender* would trigger the new, implanted behaviours. Skinless, muscles hanging like sacks from disconnected sinews, eyeballs and brain naked to dermal trauma gel, Tal woke up.

"Nearly done, baba," Nanak says. "You can open your eyes, you know."

Only that cocoon of anaesthetic gel kept Tal from dying of pain. The aeai played yts neural network like a sitar. Tal imagined fingers moving, legs running, felt urgings and stirrings where yt never had before, saw visions and wonders, heard choruses and God whistling, was sucked down by washes of sensation and emotion yt had never known before, hallucinated monster striped buzzing insects filling yts mouth like a gag, then, in the same instant, dwindling to the size of a pea, revisited places yt had never been, regreeted friends yt had never known, remembered lives yt had never lived, tried to cry out yts mother's name, yts father's name, God's name, screamed and screamed but yts body had been shut down, mouthless, helpless. Then the aeai shut Tal's brain down again and in the amnesia of anaesthesia yt forgot all the wonders and horrors yt had met in the tank of gel. The helpful machines put the top back on yts head, reconnected everything that had been disconnected and draped Tal in yts new skin fresh from the stem cell vat. Five days more yt hung, merely unconscious, in a wash of cell stimulant medium, dreaming the most astonishing dreams. On the tenth morning the aeai disconnected from Tal's skull, drained the tank, and washed down yts sleek new skin as yt lay there, complete, new, on the transparent plastic, shallow chest rising and falling in the white spotlights.

"Well, that's you," Nanak says and Tal opens yts eyes to see the scanner ring split in two and retract inside the diagnostic bed.

"Am I?"

"Apart from time's usual depredations, you look lovely inside. Full of light. Otherwise, the usual homily about saturated fats, alcohol, tobacco, nonprescription drugs and moderate exercise."

"What about . . ." Tal raises a hand to yts head.

"Not a damn thing wrong with you. I issue you a complete bill of health. Isn't that good? Now, get up and have dinner with me and tell me what this is all about."

Swinging over the side of the diagnostic bed, Tal tries out a dozen excuses to turn down the invitation and then realises that if yt doesn't tell Nanak what's in yts heart, then the entire trip to Patna will have been folly.

"Right then," yt says. "I accept."

Dinner is simple, exquisite vegetarian thalis taken on the flying bridge from which captains once overviewed their flotillas of barges. Nanak's assistant and cook Suniti flits in and out with bottles of cold Kingfisher and advice on how each dish should be eaten, "a mouthful, and hold it until your tongue goes numb," "two bites," "a spoon of this, a bite of that, then the lime." Gandaik FTZ winds down after its day earning dividends for the medical professionals of Nebraska. Music and the smell of ganja coil up from the barges where entrepreneurs emerge from their workshops to lean on the rails and smoke and crack beer in the last of the sun.

"So, now you must pay me," Ninak says and when yt sees the consternation on Tal's face, yt touches it lightly, reassuringly. "No no. Suniti will take care of that. You must pay me what you owe me for this excellent food and fine evening and my exquisite company, with what you have kept from me all day, bad baba."

Tal rolls on to yts back on the soft tatami mat. Above yt, the sky is barred with straps of purple cloud, the first yt has seen in months. Yt imagines yt can smell rain, so long anticipated, an imagination of a memory.

"It's someone, but you knew that anyway."

"I had an idea."

A lone bansuri throws notes out in the softening dark. A musician, down there amongst the badmashes, coiling out an ancient Bihari folk tune.

"Someone who is clever and successful and quiet and deep, with good taste and mysteries and secrets and is scared by it all but wants it so much."

"Isn't that what we're all looking for, janum?"

"Someone who happens to be a man."

Nanak leans forward.

"This is a problem to you?"

"I got out of Mumbai to get away from complicated relationships and I'm in the most complex of them all. I Stepped Away because I didn't want to have to play that game; the man and woman game. You gave me new rules, you put them in my head, down there and now they don't work, either."

"You wanted me to check out that everything was functioning within its operational parameters."

"There has to be something wrong with me."

"There is nothing wrong with you, Tal. I saw right through you to the other side. You are perfectly healthy in body, mind, and relationships. Now you want me to tell you what to do. You call me guru, you think I'm wise, but I won't do that. There's never been a rule of human behaviour that hasn't been broken by someone, somewhere, sometime, in some circumstance mundane or spectacular. To be human is to transcend the rules. It's a phenomenon of this universe that the simplest of rules can give rise to the most complex behaviours. The implants just give you a new set of reproduction-free imperatives, that's all. The rest, thank the gods, is up to you. They wouldn't be worth anything if they didn't give rise to the most troubling and complex problems of the heart. They are what makes all this glory, this madness worthwhile. We are born to trouble as sparks fly upwards, that is what is great about us, man, woman, transgen, nute."

The notes of the flute stalk Tal. Yt smells a rumour of rain on the evening wind that blows up from the river.

"It's who, not what," Suniti comments as she gathers up thalis. "Do you love him?"

"I think about him all the time, I can't get him out of my head, I want to call him and buy him shoes and make him music mixes and find out all the things he likes to eat. He likes Middle Eastern, I know that."

Nanak rocks on yts hip bones.

"Yes yes yes yes yes. My assistant is, of course, right as she always is, but you haven't answered her question. Do you love him?"

Tal takes a breath.

"I think so."

"Then you know what you must do," Nanak says and Suniti scoops the metal dishes up in the tablecloth and whisks them away, but Tal can tell from the set of her shoulders that she is pleased.

After the dinner is the Jacuzzi. Nanak and Tal lap in nipple-deep water in the big wooden tub on the other wing of the flying bridge, dappled with marigold petals and a subtle slick of tea-tree oil, for Nanak's persistent athlete's foot. Incense rises vertically on three sides, the air is preternaturally still, climate in abeyance, waiting.

Patna's airgiow is a golden nebula on the western horizon. Nanak strokes Tal's thighs with its long, articulate big toes. There is no gendered rule of arousal in it. It is touching, what nutes do, friends do. Tal lifts two more Kingfishers from the plastic cool box, uncaps them on the side of the tub. One for yt, one for yts guru.

"Nanak, do you think it will be all right?"

"You, personally? Me? Yes. It is easy for people to have happy endings. This city, this country, this war? I am not so sure. Nanak sees a lot from yts bridge here. Most days I can see the Indian Brown Cloud, I see the water level go down, I see skeletons on the beach, but they don't frighten me. It is those dreadful children, those Brahmins, they call them. Whoever gave them that name knew a thing or two. I tell you what it is scares Nanak about them. It's not that they live twice as long, half as fast as we do, or that they are children with the rights and tastes of adults. What frightens me is that we have reached a stage where wealth can change human evolution. You could inherit crores of money, send your children to American schools—like all those inbred half-mad Maharajahs—but you couldn't buy an IQ, or talents or good looks even. Anything you could do was cosmetic. But with those Brahmins, you can buy a new infrastructure. Parents have always wanted to give their children advantages, now they can hand it down through all future generations. And what parents would not want that for their child? The Mahatma, blessed be his memory, was wise in many many ways, but he never spoke bigger nonsense than when he said about the heart of India was in the villages. The heart of India, and her head, has always been in the middle classes. The British knew this, it's how a handful of them ran us for a hundred years. We are an aggressively bourgeois society; wealth, status, respectability. Now all of those have become directly inheritable, in the genes. You can lose all your money on the markets, go bankrupt, gamble it away, be ruined in a flood but no one can take your genetic advantage away from you. It is a treasure no thief can steal, a legacy they will pass free to their descendants . . . I have been thinking about this a lot, these days."

Tal says, "Nanakji, you mustn't trouble yourself. It's nothing to do with us. We've Stepped Away." Yt feels Nanak stiffen against yts touch.

"But we haven't, baba. No one can. There are no noncombatants in this. We have our beautiful lives and our crushing little things of the heart, but we are humans. We are part of it. Only now it is us divided against ourselves. We will be at each other's throats for our children's futures. All the middle classes have learned from the Lost Women decades is how easy it is to create a new caste, and how we love that, especially when the bindi is in your DNA. It will rule us for a thousand years, this genetic Raj."

It is full dark now. Tal feels cool air from an unexpected quarter on yts skin. Yt shivers, a small thing on a huge continent, sensing a future with no place for yt, Stepped Away, genetically noncombatant. An Australian accent calls up from below.

"Good evening to you up there, Nanakji! Rain in Hyderabad, I've just heard."

Nanak lifts ytself half out of the scented water but the caller in the night cannot be seen.

"Good news indeed!" yt replies. "We shall certainly celebrate that!"

"I'll drink to that!"

There is a soft sound from the hatch to the main bridge. The bathers turn. A nute stands there, wrapped in a crisp blue *yukata*, arms wrapped round itself.

"I heard . . . I thought, could I?"

"All are welcome," Nanak says, fishing in the ice bucket for a Kingfisher.

"Is it true, is the rain really coming?" the nute asks as yt slips out of yts blue cotton robe. Tal experiences a cold shock at the narrow shoulders, the broad child-giving hips, the hormone-injection flattened breast buds, the sacred triangle of the shaven yoni. Pre-op. The shy one, the one Nanak had said might bolt. Yt tries to remember the three years yt had lived as a pre-op, trying to save the deposit on a berth on the *Fugazi*. Like a memory of a nightmare it is a series of disjointed impressions. The three-a-day hormone jabs. The constant shaving. The endless roll of mantras to stop thinking like a gendered, be a nute.

"Yes, I believe it's coming at last," Nanak says as the nute steps down into the water beside yt and all sexual identity is erased. They move together through the blood-warm water, touching, as nutes do. Tal sleeps that night by Nanak's side, curled up and deep, touching, as nutes do, as friends who sometimes sleep together.

"Take care in that Varanasi," Nanak calls to Tal as yt climbs down the scabbed side of *Fugazi* to the waiting Riva, skipping on the filthy water.

"I'll try," Tal calls back, "but it's a crushing little thing of the heart."

Looking out of the window as the hydrofoil pulls away from the astonishing sweep of the Bund waterfront, Tal sees a plane of churned grey cloud spread into the south and east further than yt can see. ROMANCE AND ADVENTURE MIX booms in yts inner ears.

As Tal had hoped, yt wows Varanasi. More specifically, yt wows India-pendent Productions, Meta-Soap Design Department. Precisely, yt wows Neeta on the desk, who claps her hands and tells yt yt looks faaaabulous and yt obviously had a good time in horrid Patna and oh I almost forgot there's a letter for you, special delivery and all.

The Special Delivery wears a plastic wallet with *priority* and *hand deliver* and lightning flash seals and tricky little strings to pull here that released tabs there which in turn enable you to rip a perforated strip and then draw out the inner IMPORTANT DOCUMENT liner on its quick release thumb-pull and tear open the sealed plastic along the marked perforations and only then do you get the message. A single sheet of paper. Handwritten; these words. *Must see you again. Can you come tonight, August 12? The club, whenever. Please. Thank you.* And a single looping initial at the bottom.

"It's like *Town and Country*, but real!" Neeta declares.

Tal reads the letter a dozen times in the phatphat to the White Fort. As yt tarts up *the look* for the big night (if there's anyone else in the club with *the look*, yt'll have their eyes) the television news is all war bores and the entertainment channels are all full of smiling people dancing in echelon and for the first time yt can't watch any of it. Nothing for it. Yt grabs yts bag and dashes. Mama Bharat is out on the landing leaving out trash.

"Can't stop, can't stop, hot hot date," Tal shouts. Mama Bharat namastes, then yt's down the stairs, squeezing past a couple of men in suits who stare just those few seconds too long. Yt watches them pass yts door and up the next flight. Down in the pillared sublevel the cab is waiting and tonight tonight tonight the kids can shout what they like and call names and make animal and sucking noises and they just fall around Tal like marigold petals. On yts system this night of nights are STRANGE CLUB, FUGAZI FLOAT TANK and, dare yt dare yt dare yt? FUCK MIX.

At the entry to the alley of the Banana Club Tal slides up yts sleeve and programmes in *blissfullfloatyanticipationsmoulder*. The protein chips kick in as the grey wood door opens. The blind bird-woman in the crimson sari is there, head tilted back slightly, fingers filled with dwarf bananas. She might not have moved since Tal's last visit.

"Welcome back, welcome back, lovely thing! Here, help, have." She offers her fruit. Tal gently curls her fingers on the bananas.

"No, not tonight." Tal hesitates, shy to ask, "Is there . . ."

The blind woman points to the topmost gallery. No one's in tonight, though it's early in the month. Rumours of war and rain. Down in the central courtyard a nute in a long swirling skirt performs a kathak with a grace beyond classical. The second level is deserted but for two couples talking on the divans. The third level is leather club armchairs and low tables. Brass table lanterns shed a glow-worm ambience. The chill zone. There is only one guest up here tonight. Khan sits in the chair at the end of the gallery, hands resting symmetrically on the armrests in that way that Tal has always thought timelessly classy. Very English. Eyes meet. Tal blinks a blessing. Khan is so sweet, he doesn't know the language. Tal trails yts hand along the wooden rail. Sandalwood has been used in the construction, the handrail leaves a pheromone imprint on Tal's palm.

"Oh, you," Tal says as yt curls ytself into a chair at right angles to Khan. Yt waits for a smile, a kiss, any greeting. Khan starts edgily with a small grunt. There is a white envelope on the low fat-legged table. Tal takes out yts own letter, neatly quartered and sets it beside the envelope. Yt crosses yts smooth thighs.

"Well, at least tell me I look stupendous," Tal jokes. The man starts. This is not going by his script. He nudges the envelope towards Tal.

"Please, take that."

Tal unfolds the flap, peeks inside, then can't believe what yt's seeing and takes a longer, even less believing stare. It's a wad of thousand rupee notes, one hundred of them.

"What is this?

"It's for you."

"What, me? This is . . ."

"I know what it is."

Tal sets the envelope flat on the table.

"Well, it's very generous, but I'd need to know a bit more about it before I accept it. It's a hell of a lot of money."

The man grimaces.

"I can't see you again."

"What? Is it me, what've I done?"

"Nothing!" Then, soft with sorrow, "Nothing. It's me, I should never . . . I can't see you. I shouldn't even be seeing you here." He laughs painfully. "It seemed the most secure place. . . . Take it, it's for you, please have it."

Tal knows yts mouth is open. Yt experiences what yt imagines it might be like to feel your brain slam against the back of your skull after an impact from a cricket bat. Yt also knows, by the smooth sacred skin on the back of yts skull, that there's someone else up on the third level balcony with them, a newcomer.

"You're buying me off? You're handing me a lakh rupees and telling me you never want to see me again, to never cross your path again. I know what this is. This is get out of Varanasi money. You bastard. You bastard. What do you think I'll do? Blackmail you? Tell your wife, or your boyfriend? Run to the papers? Tell all my pervy nute friends and lovers, because we're all over each other, everyone knows that? Who do you think you are?"

The man's face crumples in anguish but Tal will not be stopped. Yt has the red rage in yt. Yt snatches out the money, lunges across the table to shred the treacherous paper in Khan's face. The man lifts his hands, turns his face away, but there is no defence.

"And hold that, Tal," says a voice. A flash of light. Tranh stands at the end of the table, feet apart, a solid brace for the palmer camera in yts right hand. "And another one" Flash. The man hides his face behind his hands, looks for a getaway but Tranh is backed by muscle in suits. "I'll tell you who he bloody thinks he is, cho chweet. He is Shaheen Badoor Khan, Private Parliamentary Secretary to Sajida Rana, that's who. And I am so sorry about this, my lovely, I am so sorry it had to be you. It's nothing personal, please believe me. Politics. Bloody politics. So sorry, Tal." Tranh snaps the palmer shut, hesitates, hand pressed to mouth as if holding in a vomitous secret. "Tal, get out of Varanasi. You were set up from the start. I was sent to find you; you were new, you were innocent, you are absolutely dispensable. Go!" The heavy men guide yt down the stairs, a hummingbird mobbed by crows.

24

NAJIA

Najia Askarzadah, power-walking with her girlfriends. In crop-top and shortie shorts and noo shoes that grope your feet and remember the sensation. She bought them with money from the Rath Yatra shots, and a lot of other things besides. Things for her, things for friends, to keep them friends. Najia Askarzadah's relationships have always been contracts.

The girls have been doing this walking before breakfast every Tuesday and Thursday since Najia joined the Imperial International set. This morning she needs it. They all got destroyed on Omar Khayyam champagne last night. Bernard was present to praise her grudgingly on her journalistic fortune and then talked for the rest of the evening about representation and epistemic polyverses and how the only possible intellectual response was to treat the whole thing as an episode of *Town and Country*, no less and certainly no more, the unfolding soapi that can never be dramatically concluded, had anyone any evidence that Sajida Rana actually set foot on the Kunda Khadar apart from TV pictures? and as for N. K. Jivanjee, well, it's a good political joke that everyone's seen him but no one can remember meeting him; the impending wedding of Aparna Chawla and Ajay Nadiadwala at least had the credibility of the kitsch. But he was glad about her success, glad, because now she was realising the totalising energy of war.

He's going to invite me back, she thought. He's jealous and hasn't had a fuck in a week.

Would she like to come back, work up a theory about all this with him? He'd got some Red Roof Garden Skunk in.

He had got into gauze. It was draped all over his rooms, great swags and drapes, billowing slightly in the rising winds through the louvers. He had heard that the rain was moving up over the Deccan and whole villages were going out to dance. He would love that, to dance in the rain, dance with her. She liked the thought of that. The Red Roof Garden was very fine and within half an hour she was squatting naked, thighs drawn up oyster-pose, on his lap with his penis held straight and hard inside her, clenching and releasing, clenching and releasing in time with the hummed mantra in the light of a dozen terracotta oil-lamps. But it was the bottle-and-a-half of Omar Khayyam that worked the magic so that they achieved what Bernard promised so long, which was to keep his cock inside her for one hour, not moving, breathing and chanting as one, clenching and releasing, clenching and releasing, clenching and releasing until, to Najia's surprise, she felt the slow glow of orgasm light inside her and spread like running lamp oil until they both came in a white blast of semen and Kundalini burning a hole through the tops of their Sahasrar chakras.

The walking girls turn out of the shaded drive of the Imperial International on to the Mall. The greenery is cool and smells damp and growing but out on the boulevard the heat an hour after sunrise is already like a hammer. She's sweating. Sweat out the night things. Najia Askarzadah's gloved fists beat out her walk and her skinny ass rolls in her tight shortie-shorts as two lanes of traffic head inbound to Varanasi, gold and pink in the morning haze. Men whistle and call but power walking expat girlies are faster than Varanasi crush-hour traffic. Those foot-grope sports shoes can have Najia Askarzadah intersections ahead in the time it takes them to jerk one car length. By the new park hawkers are already laying out their plastic tarpaulins and arranging their fruit and car batteries and bootleg pharma in the limp, dusty shade of the dying almond trees. It's going to be the hottest one yet, Najia's pores tell her. It reaches a peak of unbearability just before it breaks, Bernard says. She scans the horizon as she takes a sip from her water bottle, but the sky beyond the towers of Ranapur is an upturned bowl of hammered bronze.

She feels the heat radiate from the big, soft-engined car as it tucks in beside her, a Merc SUV shimmering scarab black. The mirrored window rolls down, the low-level dhol'n'bass thud from the music centre jumps a level.

"Hi! Hi!"

A gap-toothed, dark-faced gunda leers out at her. He wears a string of pearls knotted around his neck.

Head down, fists up. Keep moving. Her ass quivers; her palmer, hooked over her waistband, is being called. Not a voice or video or a text: a direct data-transfer. Then the Merc accelerates past and the driver waves his palmer at her and gives an OK sign. He swings the black car through a gap between a municipal bus and a water tanker with its military escort.

Najia wants to collapse into the cool of the Imperial's leisure pool but her mystery message won't let her. It's a video file. Her journalistic sense whispers caution. She takes the palmer into a shower cubicle and clicks up the video. N. K. Jivanjee is seated in a light, airy pavilion of beautifully patterned kalamkaris. The fabric billows gently, pregnantly. N. K. Jivanjee namastes.

"Ms. Askarzadah, good morning to you. I assume that is when my operatives will deliver this message to you. I trust you have a refreshing walk, I do think exercise first thing in the morning really does get the day off to the best possible start. I do wish I could say that I still greet every dawn with the surya namaskar, but, ah, the years . . . Anyway, my congratulations on the use to which you put my last piece of information. You have exceeded my expectations; I am quite, quite delighted. Therefore I have decided to entrust you with another release of privileged data. You will pick it up from my worker at midnight tonight, at the address which will follow on this screen. This one will be of the utmost sensitivity, I don't think I exaggerate when I say that it will transform the political shape of this nation. All my previous *caveats* are repeated, and amplified. Yet again, I'm sure we can rely on you. Thank you, bless you."

Najia Askarzadah knows the address. She takes care to lock her palmer in her room before joining her walking mates splashing in the blue pool.

Go somewhere once and you will be there again sooner than you think. The noise in the club is an assault. The scrap wood benches are packed with men waving betting slips and roaring down on to the blood spattered sand. Many are in uniform. All war is a bet. The instructions on her palmer direct her down the stairs, into the pit. The sound, the stink of sweat and spilled beer and oxidised perfume, are overpowering. Najia pushes between the shouting, gesticulating bodies. Through the forest of hands she can glimpse the fighting microsabres held high by their owners, parading around the sand ring. She wonders about the handsome, feral boy who caught her eye that first night. Then the cats go down, the owners dive over the side of the ring, and the crowd surges forward with a roar like a hymn. Najia beats through to the satta booths. The bookies measure her with their round, lilac glasses. A fat woman beckons her over.

"Sit, sit here beside me."

Najia squeezes on to the bench beside her. Her clothes smell of burned ghee and garlic.

"Have you something for me?"

The sattawoman ignores her, busy at her book. Her assistant, an old thin man, claws in the cash and sends betting slips skittering across the polished wooden desk. The barker leaps down from his high chair and scuttles into the ring to announce the next bout. Tonight he is dressed as a pierrot.

"No, but I do," a voice says sudden and close behind her. She turns. The man leans over the pew-back. He is dressed in black leather; Najia can smell it, smoky, sensual. The feral boy from the Mercedes is beside him; same shirt same grin same string of pearls. The man holds up a manila A4 envelope. "This is for you." He has dark, liquid eyes, lovely as a girl's. You do not forget eyes like that and Najia knows she has seen them before. But she hesitates to take the envelope.

"Who are you?

"A paid operative," the man says.

"Do you know what this is?"

"I merely deliver. But I do know that everything in there is real and can be verified."

Najia takes the envelope, opens it. Merc-boy's hand strikes over the partition, staying hers.

"Not here," the man says. Najia slides the envelope into her shoulder bag. When she turns back again the stall is empty. She wants to ask that nagging question: *why me?* But the man with lovely eyes would have no answer to that either. She slips her bag over her shoulder and weaves through the crowd as the barker stalks the killing floor, blasting his air-horn and bellowing bet! bet! bet! She remembers where she knows those eyes from. They met across this perspective, her by the balcony rail, he in the satta pit.

Back on the moped, out in the traffic. The city seems close tonight, threatening, knife-bearing. The cars and trucks want her under their wheels. The street jams up around a cow taking a long luxurious piss in the middle of the road. Najia opens the manila envelope, slides out the top third of the first photograph. She pulls out half. Then the whole. Then she takes out the next photograph. Then the next. Then the next.

The cow has wandered on. Vans are hooting, drivers shouting, waving, issuing vivid curses at her.

And the next. And the next. That man. That man is. That man, she recognises him though his is a face that has concealed itself well from the cameras. That man is said to be the will behind Sajida Rana. Her private secretary. Giving money. Wads of cash. To a nute. In a club. Shaheen Badoor Khan.

The entire street is looking at her. A policeman advances waving his lathi. Najia Askarzadah rams the pictures back into the envelope, heart hammering, twists the throttle, revs away, her little alcohol engine going putty-putter-putt. Shaheen Badoor Khan. Shaheen Badoor *Khan*. She's driving by amygdala alone through the blaring, poisonous traffic, seeing the money, seeing the riverside apartment in New Sarnath, seeing the noo clowthz and holidaze and champagne that isn't Omar Khayyam and interviews and the name on the banner headlines Bharat-wide India-wide Asia-wide Planet-wide and in far cool nice Sweden her parents opening the *Dagens Nyheter* and it's their darling daughter's photograph under the foreign news leadline.

She stops. Her heart is beating arrhythmically, fluttering, wowing. Caffeine does it shock does it big sex does it joy does it. Getting everything you ever wanted does it. She can see. She can hear. She can sense. A gyre of noise and colour confronts her. No other place her preconsciousness could bring her than to the heart of Bharat's madness and contradiction. Sarkhand Roundabout.

Nothing with wheels and an engine is getting through this intersection. The radiating roads have swollen like diseased arteries into tent cities and truck laagers, glossy with yellow streetlight and the glow of sidewalk shrines. Najia sets her feet on the ground and walks her little bike into the fringes, drawn to the magnificent chaos. The spinning wall of colour, glimpsed through the mess of trucks and plastic sheeting, is a wheel of people, loping and chanting as they orbit the gaudily painted concrete statue of Ganesha. Some carry placards, some hold lathis by the tips, the ends swaying and bobbing over their heads like a forest of cane in a premonsoon wind. Some wear dhotis and shirts, some are in Western pants, even suits. Some are naked, ash-smeared sadhus. A group of women in red, devotees of Kali, rush past. All have fallen into unconscious lockstep and perfect rhythm. Individuals spin in, spin out, but the wheel turns endlessly. The cylinder of air between the facing buildings throbs like a drum.

A massive red and orange object lumbers into Najia's field of vision: rath yatra, like the one she saw on Industrial Road. Perhaps that same one. N. K. Jivanjee's Chariot of Siva. She walks her bike inward. The syncopated chanting is a mad, joyful hymn. She can feel her breath and pulse fall into rhythm with the dance, feel her womb tighten, her nipples harden. She is part of this insanity. It defines her. It is all the danger and madness she has sought as the antidote to her sane Swedishness. It tells her it is still a life of surprises, worth enduring. *Ribbed and Exciting! Corduroy trousers!* declares a large yellow advertising sign above the crazy mela.

A buck-toothed karsevak thrusts a sheet of A5 at her.

"Read read! Demons attack us, sex-crazed violators of children!" he shouts. The flyer is printed front Hindi, back English. "Our leaders are in thrall to Bible Christians and Demonic Mohammedans! Mata Bharat founders! Read this paper!"

The leaflet features a large cartoon of Sajida Rana as a shadow puppet, dancing in her designer combat fatigues, her sticks held by a hook-nosed caricature Arab in a red and white *shumagg*. His *ogal* reads *Badoor-Khan*. She points the way for an American televangelist who sits at the controls of a big bulldozer, cigar erect in mouth, advancing on a Hindu mother and child cowering in the shadow of the rat-vahana of an enraged Ganesha, trunk uplifted, axe drawn back to strike.

Child-raping paedophile Muslims plan capitulation to Coca-Cola Kultur! First they steal the waters of Mother Ganga, then Sarkhand, then Holy Bharat. Your nation, your soul, are at risk!

They hate him, thinks Najia Askarzadah, still trembling from the accreted human energy. They hate him worse than anything I can imagine. And I can deliver him to them. I can give them what they want, the highest, hardest fall. Child-raping paedophile? No, much much worse: a lover of things not male, not female. Monsters. Nutes. An un-man. A glare of light, a bloom of yellow flame and a thunder of approval from the jogging crowd. A burning Awadhi flag twists into her view, writhing like a soul in fire. She can lift a finger and send all these futures spinning off into unknown dimensions. She has never felt so alive, so potent, so powerful and capricious. All her life she has been the outsider, the refugee, the asylum seeker, the Afghan Swede; wanting to be part, the whole, the core, the blood. She feels a delirious rub of warm damp against the vinyl of the bike saddle.

25

SHIV

Shiv and Yogendra ride up through a cylinder of sound. *Construxx* boasts a crew of architectural surveyors who cruise Varanasi and Ranapur's construction zone jungles looking for the best pre- and post-industrial sites. *Construxx*'s niche is the dips in the cash flow charts. Last month it was the penthouse levels of the Narayan Tower in west Varauna: eighty-eight floors of rentable flexform office space; tenants four. This month it is the vast concrete shaft that, when the money comes on line again after the war, will be University metro station. *Construxx* boasts mighty architecture and word-of-mouth PR. If you want to find it, you must ask the right people in the right places.

Location of *Construxx* August 2047 Site. Take the metro to Panch Koshi Station, last stop on the new South Loop line, all chrome and glass and that concrete that looks oily to the touch. At the end of the platform is a temporary wooden staircase down onto the tracks. This section of the line is deactivated. Follow the tunnel until you see a small circle of flickering light. Two dark shapes will emerge on either side of the expanding circle: they are security. You must either impress them with your looks, your style, your celebrity, or your status. Or be an invited guest of Nitish and Chunni Nath.

Construxx August 2047 Site: for best effect, look up. Blue spots swing and dash down from a lighting gantry rigged under the temporary plastic roof. Catwalks, platforms, rigging wires, steel grilles and meshes shatter the light into a net of shadow and aqua. Moving shadows are bodies, dancing, grooving to the personalised tunes coming through their palmers. The DJ box is halfway up the wall, a rickety raft of scaffolding rods and construction mesh. Here a two-human, fifteen-aeai crew pump out a customised channel of *Construxx* August 2047 mix for every dancer out there on the platforms.

Construxx August 2047 Site obeys a strict and simple vertical hierarchy. Shiv and Yogendra ride the service elevator up through the new meat and the office grrrls who've saved all month for this one night of notoriety and the soapi wannabes and the fine young criminals and the sons and daughters of *something*, all arrayed on their appropriate platforms. The elevator drags them up red spray-bomb letters, each ten metres high: the dogma of *Construxx*, filling half the orbit of the concrete shaft: *Art Empire Industry*. Shiv flicks away his dead bidi. It rolls through the steel grating beneath his feet and falls into the throbbing blue, shedding sparks. The main bar and crush zone is on what will be the ticket concourse. The true gods are up on the vip levels, stacked out over the drop like a fan of playing cards. Shiv moves towards the security. They are two big blonde Russian women in orange coveralls bearing the *Construxx* mantra and bulges that speak of concealed yet easily accessible firepower. While they scan his invitation, Shiv checks out the action up on the vip level. The Naths are two small figures dressed in gold, like images of gods, giving darshan to their supplicants. A Russia grrrl waves Shiv over to the bar. He is far down the social order.

Drinks are served from the ticket counters. Ranks of cocktail-wallahs mix, shake, chill, and pour in a rhythm part dance, part martial art. Cocktail of the night seems to be something called Kunda Khadar. Drop an ice bubble into neat vodka. Ice cracks, seeps a clear liquid that turns red in contact with the alcohol. The blood of Holy Bharat shed on the waters of Mother Ganga. Shiv wouldn't mind trying one, wouldn't mind anything with a shot of grain in it to steady his nerve but he can't even afford the house water. Someone will buy him one. The only eyes that will hold his belong to a girl by the railing, alone, on the edge of the spirals of talk. She is red: short soft terracotta leather skirt, a fall of long, straight crimson hair. An opal nestles in her navel. She has garial skin boots with feathers and bells swinging from the straps, a new look Shiv must have missed in his exile in Shit City. One two three seconds she looks at him then turns away to gaze down into the pit. Shiv leans on the rail and looks out into the motion and light.

"It's bad luck, you know."

"What's bad luck?" the girl asks. She has a lazy, city drawl.

"This." He taps her belly jewel. She flinches but does not recoil. She balances her gyroscopic cocktail glass on the rail and turns to face him. Red tendrils spiral through the clear alcohol. "Opals. Bad luck jewels. That is what the English Victorians believed."

"I can't say I feel particularly unlucky," the girl says. "Are you bad luck?"

"The worst kind," Shiv says. He relaxes and spreads himself along the railing and so knocks her cocktail off the railing. It drops like a god's tear, catching the light like a jewel. A woman's scream comes up from below. "And there's your bad luck. I'm so sorry. I would get you another one . . ."

"Don't worry."

Her name is Juhi. Shiv steers her towards the ticket booths. Yogendra detaches himself from watching pretty things and follows at a discreet distance. The Kunda Khadars really are very cold and very good and very expensive. The red stuff is cinnamon flavoured, with a little THC kick. Juhi chatters away about the club and its people. Shiv glances up at the vip zone. The Nath siblings have moved up to a higher level yet, two gold stars under the rippling plastic canopy. Juhi kicks him gently, foreplayfully with her garial boot. Feathers and everything.

"I see you looking up there, badmash. Who are you working for?" Juhi works closer to him.

Shiv nods towards the Naths, surrounded by their dark fixers. Juhi screws her face up.

"Chuutyas. You have business with them? You be careful. They can do what they like because they have money and their daddy owns the police. They look like angels but inside they are dark and old. They are bad to women. He wants to fuck because he is twenty years old inside his head but he can't get it up so he has to take hormones and things and even then it's nothing. I've seen bigger on a dog. So he uses toys and things. And she is as bad. She watches him play. I know this because a friend of mine went with them once. They are as bad as each other."

Russia grrl catches Shiv's eye, nods him over, and your little monkey too.

"Come up with me," he says to Juhi. "You don't have to meet them." He is thinking about when he has his setup money. There will be more of those Kunda Khadar things and a hotel room and some place with junk food and a television for Yogendra. Shiv begins to feel the glow in his belly. The shoulders go back. The chin up. The step lengthens, lightens. Golden people turn to look, their Kunda Khadars like little murders in their hands. At the centre of them, the golden children. Nitish and Chunni Nath stand side by side. They are dressed identically in gold brocaded sherwanis. Their faces are smooth and puppy-fat and more open and innocent than they should be. The girl Chunni's hair hangs to her waist. Nitish is shaved, his scalp glitters with mica dust. Shiv thinks it makes him look like a cancer kid. They smile. Now he sees where it is hiding. In the old, old smiles. Nitish beckons.

"Mr. Faraji." Nitish Nath's voice is high and pure and cuts through the mix. "And the boy is your . . . ?"

"Personal assistant."

"I see."

Shiv feels sweat bead inside his leather. Every word, nuance, tone, muscle alignment is being scanned and read. He is getting that scent again. He does not know if it is real or his mind, but when he is around Brahmins he can always smell wrongness, genes turned awry. They don't smell human.

"And the . . . female?"

"No one. Just someone I met. She's nothing."

"Very well. Come with me please."

There is a level above all levels, a tiny cage of construction mesh suspended from the main crane. Shiv, Yogendra, and Nitish Nath fit it like segments into an orange skin. All the chatter, the echoes, the shuffle of bodies dancing silently on their tiered platforms are silenced so abruptly Shiv feels their absence as a sharp pain.

"This area has a mute field," Nitish Nath says. His voice is flattened, it sounds to Shiv as if he is speaking in his eardrum. "Clever, isn't it? Most useful for sensitive business. We are pleased with your performance to date, Mr. Faraji. Your businesslike ethos is refreshing. It was intimated to you that if we were satisfied with your work, there would be other tasks. We would like to offer you a new contract. It will be dangerous. There's a distinct possibility you could be killed. In return we will write off your debts to the Dawoods. Their machines will not visit you again. And we will add enough to set you up in this town, or any other."

"What is the job?"

"Abstraction, Mr. Faraji. Background then. This won't make any sense to you, but never let it be said that you weren't fully informed. For some time now the United States government has subcontracted intelligence-related computing that it cannot process under its own Hamilton

Acts. It routinely uses datahavens in countries that are not signatory to the international agreement that have access to high-level artificial intelligence. You know what Generation two-point-five means?"

"A computer you can't tell from a human seventy-five percent of the time."

"A good summary. Anything above two-point-five is banned under the terms of the act. Anything below must be licensed. Bharat is a non-signatory country but self-enforces licensing of everything up to two-point-seven-five—this is to preserve its dominant position in the media market through the likes of *Town and Country*. Our client has ascertained that a Bharati sundarban is carrying out a decryption job for the United States—NASA, the Pentagon, and the CIA are all involved, which is unusual but gives some indication of the importance of the decoding work. Our client wants that decryption key."

"What exactly do you want me to do?" The mute field is making Shiv's molars ache. Nitish Nath claps his small, pudgy hands.

"So businesslike! It is a two-part mission. The first is to find which sundarban is doing the decrypt. The second is to infiltrate and steal the key. We know that this man arrived in Bharat three weeks ago." Nitish Nath holds up his hand. He's wearing a palmer glove. He holds a videoclip of a bearded Westerner in those baggy clothes they wear that never fit them. He's been caught stepping out of a phatphat looking left, right for traffic and pushing through the crowds towards a Kashi bar. The clip loops again. "His name is Hayman Dane, he's an American, a freelance crypto specialist."

Shiv studies the fat man. "I think he is in for a great deal of pain." Nitish Nath giggles. It is not a sound Shiv wants to hear again.

"Once you have the location and a plan for how to arrange the abstraction, our client will cover your legitimate expenses in addition to our generous remuneration package. Now can we leave this place? Your body odour is beginning to nauseate me."

The mute field pops. *Construxx* August 2047 implodes on Shiv. It feels fresh, lithe, breathing, clean. Shiv follows Nitish Nath down the steep steps to the vip zone.

"I have a free hand?"

"Yes. Nothing will be traceable to us or our client. Now, we do need your decision."

It is no decision.

"I'll do it."

"Good good good!" Nitish Nath stops at the foot of the steps to thrust his small, smooth hand into Shiv's. Shiv fights the recoil reflex. The hand feels dead to him. He sees a woman's corpse spilling out of black plastic into the black river. "Chunni! Mr. Faraji is with us!"

Chunni Nath is less than half Shiv's height but when she looks up into his eyes his balls prickle with fear. Her eyes are like spheres of lead.

"You are with us. Good." She spins the word out like cotton. "But are you one of us, Mr. Faraji?" Her brother smiles.

"I'm sorry, Ms. Nath, what do you mean?"

"We mean, you have shown your worth in small things, but any street gunda can do that."

"I am not some street gunda . . ." Blue flickers, down in the dance-shaft.

"Then demonstrate it, Mr. Faraji." She looks at her brother. Shiv feels Yogendra's hand on his sleeve. "That girl you came in with, the one you brought up here. I think you said you met in the bar."

"She's just someone I met, she wanted to see the vip area."

"Your words were, *she's nothing*."

"Yes, I said that."

"Good. Throw her over the railing, please."

Shiv wants to laugh, a vast, coughing bark of a laugh the size and shape of this underground chamber at mad things that cannot possibly be said.

"Much has been entrusted to you, Mr. Faraji. The least we can demand is a demonstration of trustworthiness."

The laugh dies in his lungs. The platform is high and cold and terrifyingly fragile over a vast abyss. The lights look like epilepsy.

"You are joking. You're mad, you are. She said you were mad fuckers, that you liked to do things, play mad games."

"All the more reason then. We don't tolerate insults, Mr. Faraji. It's as much a test for us as for you. Do you trust us that you can do this thing here and no one will touch you?"

It would be easy. She stands by the rail, glancing over at him and the other stellar rich on the platform. Kunda Khadars have relaxed her. A hook of the foot, a push, the pivot around the metal rail would send her over. But he cannot do it. He is a seller of parts, a dealer, a butcher, a spiller of bodies into rivers but he is not a killer. And he is dead now. He might as well get up on that rail, put his arms out, and fall forwards.

Shiv shakes his head. He would speak, tell them this, but Yogendra is faster. Juhi smiles, frowns, opens her mouth to scream all in the instant it takes Yogendra to slam into her. He's a scrawny pup but he's got momentum. The glass flies into the air spilling a spray of bloody vodka. Juhi reels backwards. Yogendra lowers his head and butts her in the face. Her hands fly up. She loses balance. She goes backwards over the rail. Her garial boots kick, her feathers flutter. Her arms windmill. She falls through the slashing lights and silent dancers. The brief scream, the ringing crack as she smashes into the edge of a lower platform echoes up the concrete well of *Construxx* August 2047 Site. She bounces. She spins, a strange, misshapen smashed thing. Shiv hopes it killed her. He hopes it broke her spine quick and clean. Everyone hears the soft splintering thud as she hits the bottom of the shaft. It took very much longer than Shiv had imagined. Peering over the rail he sees the door muscle come running. There is nothing they can do but talk into their collars. They look up the light beams straight at him. The shrieks start from below. *Construxx* August 2047 is a cylinder of panicked screaming.

She came out for a night. That was all. Drinks. Dance. A flirt. A bit of celebrity. Fun. Something to tell the girls the next day.

The empty glass still spins on the floor.

Nitish and Chunni Nath look at each other.

He's not a killer. He's not a killer.

A Russian girl gives him a thick plastic wallet. He can see the wadded bank notes through the smoky vinyl. It seems to float in front of him, he cannot understand what it is. He can see Yogendra standing by the rail, drawn in on himself, pale as bone. He cannot understand what it is.

She came out for a night. A body, spilling into the dark water. Juhi, falling away from him, hands and feet milling.

"By the way." It is Nitish speaking. His voice had never sounded so dead and flat even in the mute field. "In case you ever wonder what the Americans are decoding. They have found something in space and they have no idea what it is."

Art Empire Industry, whispers the red graffiti.

PART FOUR

TANDAVA NRITYA

26

SHIV

The American is a big man and bleeds a lot in the sand ring. Unseen in his box in the shadows under the gallery, Shiv studies him. There is an expression he likes from American crime movies. *Stuck pig*. He has never seen a pig stuck with a blade but he can imagine it, little pig legs lifted up and kicking as it fights against the hands pulling its head back, opening its pig throat to the edge. Then the knife goes into the sweet spot, the blood spot. He imagines the pig's waving legs like this man's pale, hairy hocks sticking out of his baggy shorts. He imagines it might make a sound like this panting wailing, flat and ugly, pushed through layers of fat. It would look around it like this, looking for its killer. He dresses the pig-of-his-mind in these American clothes.

Pigs revolt him.

It had only been a tiny nick, just to get the bleeding started. They are more aggressive when there is blood on the air, the girl in the muscle-top told him. You could even consider it a fashion declaration. The earring looked ridiculous on a grown man. Better no lobe at all.

"I ask you again. Where is the sundarban?"

"Look, I keep telling you, I don't know what the fuck you are talking about . . . I'm not the man you want."

Shiv sighs. He nods to Yogendra. The kid climbs up on the rail, scissors held out to catch the light.

"Don't you fucking cut me, man. You cut me and it's a diplomatic incident. You are so fucked. You hear me?"

Yogendra grins, puts his arms out at his side, wiggles his hips, snips his scissors chip-chop chip-chop. Shiv watches the estuary of blood fan across the American man's neck. Some has already dried and crusted, food for flies. He follows it under the round collar of his surf-shirt—some starting to show through the fabric—down his arm to form a rubbed, red slick around his wrists where he has chafed at the cuffs. Stuck pig, Shiv thinks.

"You are Hayman Dane?"

"No! Yes. Look, I don't even know who you are."

"Hayman Dane, where is the sundarban?"

"Sundarban? Sundarban, what fucking sundarban?"

Shiv stands up. He brushes the dust from his new full-length leather coat. As the tour guides who take the backpackers past the ghats at dawn say, morning light makes all the difference. It shows *Fight! Fight!* for the cheap dirty little back-alley gambling joint it is. It shows up the dust and the cigarette burns and cheap wood. Empty of fighters and sattamen and the gamblers and the ringmaster strutting in his sequin costumes, singing into his microphone, it has no spirit, no atman. He opens the door of his box and steps on to the shallow staircase.

"The sundarban where the United States government is decoding information it received from space."

The big American rolls his head back.

"Man, you fuck off right now. I'm telling you, that little pecker there with the scissors can cut off as much as he likes, but you don't fuck over the White House."

Shiv moves to the row in front. This is the sign he has arranged. The pit doors open and the girl pushes the microsabre cage in on a rubber-wheeled gurney.

It had been sweet, getting back into the car, feeling the leather upholstery, resetting the radio, knowing it wasn't hired now, it was his; his raja's chariot, his own rath yatra. Sweet to have an anthracite black unlimited card in his pocket, nestled right in there with the roll of notes because as any gentleman knows the important transactions are cash only. Sweet to let the streets see that Shiv Faraji was back and untouchable. In Club Musst he peeled off the notes one thousand two thousand three thousand four and slid them across the blue counter in a little fuck-you line in front of Salman.

"You have given me more than you owe me, sir," Fat Salman poked his pudgy finger at the last in line, a big ten K. Bar Star Talvin was with clients around the angle of the bar, but glanced over between cocktail acrobatics.

"That's a tip."

All the girls stared as he left. He looked for Priya, to acknowledge her, tip her the nod of big thanks but she was drinking elsewhere that night.

"You think maybe we should do some work now?"

It was the longest sentence he had ever heard from Yogendra. Shiv sensed a change in the relationship since *Construxx* August 2047. The kid was cocky now. He had the balls to do the things Shiv could not, because he felt something, because he was weak, because he had choked at the moment. Never again. The boy would see. The boy would learn. There was another body beside the woman in the sari rolling into Ganga: Juhi going back over the balcony, heels kicking, hands snatching. What he saw most clearly were her eyes. Long stick-on lashes, semaphoring ultimate, resigned betrayal. It was easier now, and he knew it would get easier still, but it pulled him up. It was bad, bad as it can be, but he was a man again. A raja. And he would do some work now.

Now it is morning and Hayman Dane backs away from the microsabre snarling in its cage, snarling because Sai his cute handler in the big combat baggies and small tight muscle top has shot his ass full of stimulants and hallucinogens so when he looks at fat American he sees enemy bad cat thing he hates kill pussycat faster faster. And oh dear, fat Hayman Dane has forgotten his handcuffs and he goes over heavy like a load falling off a truck, kicking his legs and squirming around trying to get up and you can't when you are that fat and your hands are cuffed behind your back.

"Unfortunate," Shiv says, getting up and walking down one step two three to the row in front.

"The fuck with you, man!" Hayman Dane shouts. "You are in so much trouble. You are dead, you know. You and your butt-boy and your bitch and your little fucking pussy."

"Well, there's not really any trouble here at all," Shiv says taking a seat, resting his chin on his hands on the wooden pew top. "You could tell me what sundarban you're working for."

"How many times do I fucking have to say this?" Hayman Dane bellows. A string of drool lolls from his mouth on to the sand where he lies on his side, face red with rage. For a genius he makes a very fine fool, Shiv thinks. But then that is the Western idea of genius, someone who is inhumanly good at just one narrow thing.

A vast morning was opening in crimson and saffron beyond the swags of power and com cables as Yogendra took the car out to make the lift. Unsettled times coming. Perhaps even the long-promised monsoon. Shiv pulled his jacket around him, suddenly chilled, and went to call on his technical adviser. Anand was an aspirant dataraja who ran a small stable of unlicensed Level 2.5 aeais out of the back of his uncle's shoe repair shop in Panch Koshi. That was how Shiv knew him; he had taken pairs there in the past. He was a good man with leather. He had sewn them sweet and tight as Shiv waited with the finest hand-stitching he had ever seen. Anand served coffee to the customers, good strong Arab style coffee, with a nugget of Nepali Temple Ball melted in the sweet, seething black liquid for those that wanted.

This morning Anand's Gucci wraprounds masked flaky red eye-sockets. Anand kept US time. Shiv folded himself onto the low bolster, lifted a tiny, beautifully aromatic cup, and sipped. Mynahs crackled and commented on the unfolding red morning from their cages hung from the beams of the open wooden balcony. He tilted his head back as the Nepalese kicked in.

"Raiding a sundarban." Anand pursed his lips and bobbed his head in the way aspirant datarajas did to indicate *impressed*. "My first advice is, if you can possibly get away with not doing it, do."

"Your second advice?"

"It's surveillance surveillance surveillance. Now, I can breed you up some ware will probably make you invisible to most common monitoring aeais—few of them are even over Level One, but these guys by definition aren't industry standard. Until I know who you're up against, it's all guesswork." Anand puffed his cheeks out: *bafflement* in aspirant dataraja.

"We're on that right now."

Yogendra would almost be there now. The parking space outside the hotel had been reserved, an agreement with the doorman. He would be powering the window down now, reaching for the stinger on the seat beside him. No guns. Shiv hated guns. You have one shot, boy, make it right.

Shiv sat back on his low embroidered divan. The coffee bubbled on its trivet over the charcoal brazier. Anand poured two fresh cups. He may look like a lavda, but he does things well, Shiv thought.

"My next query?"

"How much faith do you put in conspiracy theory."

"I don't put much faith in any theory."

"Everyone's got a theory, my friend. Theory is at the bottom of everything. My cousin's wife's brother works dataprocessing for the ESA and this is the rumour there. Remember some time back the Americans and the Russians and the Chinese and the Europeans announced they were going to send an unmanned mission to Tierra?"

Shiv shook his head. The second cup was making Anand's voice spread out into a wash of story, like his mother telling him a hero tale of Rama and bold Hanuman.

"The first EXP? Earth-like Extrasolar Planet? No? Anyway, they found this planet Tierra and there was a big tarrah and stuff on the news channels that they were going to build a probe to go there. Listen up, here comes the conspiracy: there is no Tierra mission. There never was. It's all a smokescreen for what they were really doing up there. The rumour is, they found something. Something God didn't make and we didn't put there. Some kind of object, and it's old. Way old. I mean, not just millions, but billions of years old. Can you imagine that? Arahbs of years. Brahma-scale time. It's got them shit-scared—so shit-scared they're prepared to risk their security and take it to the only people can do quantum crypto right. Us." He stabbed his thumbs at his chest.

The American will be coming out now, Shiv thought, floating with the sweet smoke up into the cube of air that filled the courtyard, away from the flat words to the street where the women worked and the big hire car waited with the needle in it. He will be coming out the door, pale and blinking and cold. He will not even look at the car. He will be thinking about his coffee and donut, coffee and donut, coffee and donut. It is the habits that kill us. Shiv heard the spit of the stinger. He saw the fat man's knees crumple as the chemicals overloaded his motor neurons. He saw Yogendra wrestle him into the back of the car. He smiled at the skinny street kid trying to haul the big man up over the tailgate.

Shiv sat, hands draped over knees, on the soft cushion. The bars of early cloud were burning away, the sky blueing. Another death-dry day. He could hear distant radio. The announcer seemed to be very excited about something. Raised voices, arguments, a denouncing tone. He tilted his head back and watched the steam from the coffee curl up until he could, with a squint, merge it with jet contrails. The Nepali Temple Ball said, *believe*: believe nothing is solid, everything is credible. It is a big universe. Shit. The universe was tight and mean and crammed into a wedge of brightness and music and skin a handful of decades long and no wider than your peripheral vision. People who believed otherwise were amateurs.

"And my third query?"

Yogendra would have him by now, would have got him somehow into the back before the spasms wore off, would have turned through the traffic: fuck you to cars cabs phatphats trucks buses mopeds and sacred cows, be bringing him in.

Anand's eyes widened as if taking in a truth too large even for a conspiracy-theorist aspirant dataraja.

"Now this is the mad thing. You don't fucky-fuck with the Naths, but there are rumours about who they're working with, who their *client* might be."

"Conspiracies and rumours."

"If there's no God, they're all you've got left."

"The client?"

"Is none other than Mr. Geniality himself, friend of the poor and champion of the downtrodden, scourge of the Ranas and hammer of the Awadhis: I present, the Honourable N. K. Jivanjee."

Shiv passed on a third cup of the enriched coffee.

Shiv gets up and moves, slowly as the play demands, to the row in front. That is the cue for Yogendra to jump down on to the sand. He saunters up to Hayman Dane, who is panting now. Yogendra turns his head to this side, then to the other, studying him as if he is a new fruit.

Yogendra squats, makes sure Hayman Dane can see what he is doing and picks up the severed earlobe. He dances over to the caged microsabre and daintily drops the ear-tip through the bars. One snap. Shiv can hear the crunch, small but distinct. Hayman Dane starts to shriek, a shrill, pant-pissing keening moan, the shriek of a man in final fear of his life, the shriek of a man who is no longer a man. Shiv grimaces at the ugly, unseemly sound. He remembers his first sight of him as Yogendra brought him down the tunnel into the ring; Yogendra bouncing him before him with shoves from his hands, the fat man taking little tripping, trotting steps for fear of losing his balance, gaping around, blinking to try to understand what manner of place this was. Now Shiv sees the piss stain spreading warm and dark as the waters of birth across his tan shorts and he cannot believe this white Western genius for hire can bring himself to end so stupidly.

Yogendra hops back on to the rail. Sai goes to the cage. She lifts the microsabre above her head and starts her parade, one foot slowly, deliberately in front of the other. Step step step, turn. Step step step, turn. The ritual dance that seduced and mesmerised Shiv the night he saw her, in this ring, on this sand. The night he lost everything. And now, she dances for him. There is something ancient in it, the woman stalking the fighting floor, powerful, a dance of Kali. The microsabre should have her wrist open, the side of her head off. It hangs there, caressed by hands, hypnotised.

Shiv moves to the front row now. Ringside seat.

"I ask you, Hayman Dane. Where is the sundarban?"

Sai crouches in front of him, one leg bent under her, the other outstretched to the side. She fixes Hayman Dane's tearful eyes with her own. She drapes the cat around her neck. Shiv holds his breath. He has never seen that move before. He has a fast, hard, pleasing erection.

"Chunar," Hayman Dane sobs. "Chunar Fort. Ramanandacharya. His name is Ramanandacharya. Let go my hands, man! Let go my fucking hands!"

"Not yet, Hayman Dane," Shiv says. "There will be a file name, and a code."

The man is hysterical now; an animal, no thought or wit.

"Yes!" he shrieks. "Yes, just let go my hands!"

Shiv nods to Yogendra. Crowing like a rooster he scampers up to the American and unlocks the cuffs. Hayman Dane cries out as circulation returns to his wrists.

"Fuck you, man, fuck you," he mutters but there is no defiance in it now.

Shiv raises a finger. Sai strokes the tattered head of her microsabre, millimetres from her right eye.

"The name and the key, Hayman Dane."

The man raises his hands: see, I am unarmed, helpless, no threat or danger. He fishes in the breast pocket of his gaudy shirt. He has bigger tits than some women Shiv has fucked. He holds his palmer aloft.

"See man? It was in my fucking pocket all the time."

Shiv raises a finger. Yogendra snatches the palmer, swings over the rail into the seating. Sai strokes the tattered head of her microsabre.

"You'll let me go now, man. You've got what you want, you'll let me go now."

Yogendra is already halfway up the aisle. Sai is on her feet, moving back towards the tunnel. Shiv climbs the shallow stairs, one by one.

"Hey, what do I do now?"

Sai stands at the gate. She looks at Shiv, waiting. Shiv raises a finger. Sai turns and throws the microsabre into the ring of bloodied sand. Pig time.

27

SHAHEEN BADOOR KHAN

In a white yukata, Sajida Rana leans over the carved stone balustrade and exhales smoke into the scented fore-dawn darkness.

"You have fucked me up the ass, Khan."

Shaheen Badoor Khan had thought he could feel no sicker dread, no tighter guilt, no deeper annihilation as his state car slipped through the three AM streets to the Rana Bhavan. He had watched the thermometer on the dashboard rise. The monsoon is finally coming, he had thought. It is always unbearable just before it breaks. Yet he saw ice, Bangla ice. The States of Bengal and their tame berg had worked ice magic. He tried to imagine it, moored in the Bay of Bengal, blinking with navigation lights. He saw the gulls circling over it. Whatever happens, it will rain down on me and these streets. He thought, I have bottomed out. I am hammered flat. There is no further down to go. On the verandah of the Rana Bhavan he understands that he is not even over the first shelf. The abyssal plain lies tens of kilometres below him, down in the crushing dark. There is ice above him, ice he can never break through.

"I don't know what to say."

It is so weak. And it is a lie. He does. He had rehearsed it as he reeled in the phatphat back to the haveli. The words, the order of the confessions, the drawing out of secrets a lifetime deep, all had come to him in one mass, one rush, perfectly formed in his head. He knew what he must do. But he must be let do it. She must grant him that grace.

"I think I deserve something," Sajida Rana says.

Shaheen Badoor Khan lifts one hand in exquisite pain but there is no placating it, no amelioration. He deserves no mercy.

The lamps had been on in the old zenana. Standing in the cloister, Shaheen had strained to pick out women's voices. Most nights there were guests; woman writers, lawyers, politicians, opinion makers. They would talk all the hours beyond the old purdah. Bilquis should know, before any, before even his Prime Minister, but not in front of guests. Never in front of guests.

Gohil the chauffeur came bleary, hobbling with a rolled-down sock in his boot, stifling a yawn. He turned the official car in the courtyard.

"The Rana Bhavan," Shaheen Badoor Khan ordered.

"What is it, sahb?" Gohil asked as he drove through the automatic gates into the perpetual crawl of traffic. "Some vital affair of state?"

"Yes," Shaheen Badoor Khan said. "An affair of state." By the time the car reached the junction he had written his letter of resignation on the government notepad in the arm-rest. Then he took his 'hoek, set it to audio only, and called the number he had kept next to his heart since the day he was invited to the Prime Ministerial Office and offered the role of Grand Vizier, the number he had confidently expected never to use.

"Shah." He heard Sajida Rana's breath shudder. "Thank gods it's you; I thought we'd been invaded."

Shaheen Badoor Khan imagined her in bed. It would be white;

wide and white. The light would be a small, shallow pool from a lamp. She would be leaning over a bedside cabinet. Her hair would be loose, it would fall darkly around her face. He tried to imagine what she wore in bed. You have betrayed your government, your nation, your faith, your marriage, your dignity, and you are wondering if your Prime Minister sleeps naked. Narendra would be at her side, rolled over into a muffled, white cylinder, go to sleep, affairs of state. It was well known that they still slept together. Sajida Rana was a woman of appetite, but she insisted on her family name.

"Prime Minister, I must tender my resignation with immediate effect."

I should have rolled the partition up, Shaheen Badoor Khan thought. I should have put glass between myself and Gohil. Why bother? In the morning he will see everything. Everyone will see everything. At least he will have a good story, nuggety with gossip and eavesdroppings. You owe him that much, good and faithful driver.

"Shah, what nonsense is this?"

Shaheen Badoor Khan repeated himself verbatim, then added, "Prime Minister, I have put myself in a position that has allowed the government to become compromised."

A soft sigh like a spirit departing. A sigh so weary, so tired. A rustle of fine, crisp, clean-smelling white cotton.

"I think you should get over here."

"I am on my way, Prime Minister," Shaheen Badoor Khan said, but she had already cut the connection and all he heard was the Zen hum of cyberstatic in the sanctuary of his skull.

Sajida Rana rests on the white balustrade, hands firmly gripping the rail.

"How good is the detail?"

"My face is clearly visible. There will be no doubt that it is me. Prime Minister, they photographed me giving money to the nute."

She bares her teeth, shakes her head, lights another cigarette.

Shaheen Badoor Khan had never thought of her as a smoker. Another secret about his Prime Minister, like her vile mouth. That is the reason she must have brought him out here; to keep the smoke out of the Rana Bhavan. Marvellous, the details he notices.

"A nute."

Now the dying within starts. In that one syllable are all her disgust and incomprehension and betrayal and rage.

"They are . . . a gender . . ."

"I know what they are. This club . . ."

Another cube of him is torn away. The tearing is agony but once it is gone the pain vanishes. There is a clean joy in being able say the truth for once.

"It is a place where people go to meet nutes. People who find nutes sexually attractive."

Smoke rises straight from Sajida Rana's cigarette before breaking into lazy, phantom zigzags. The air is wonderfully still. Even the eternal roar of the city is muted.

"Tell me one thing, what did you think you could do with them?"

It was never a doing thing, Shaheen Badoor Khan wants to exclaim. That is what you can never understand, soft from your bed with the smell of your husband still on you. That is what the nutes have always understood. It is not about doing anything. It is about being. That is why we go there, to that club, to see, to be among creatures from our fantasies, creatures we have always longed to be but which we will never have the courage to become. For those brief burning stabs of beauty. Sajida Rana does not let him say these things; she cuts in: "I don't need to know any more. There is, of course, no hope of you remaining in the administration."

"I never thought there might be, Prime Minister. I was set up."

"That's no excuse. In fact, it only makes it . . . What were you thinking? No, don't answer that. How long has it been going on?"

Another wrong, uncomprehending question.

"Most of my life. As long as I can remember. It's always been going on."

"When you said that time we were coming back from the dam, when you said you and your wife were going through a cold period . . . for fuck's sake, Khan . . ." Sajida Rana grinds the dead stub out with the heel of her white satin slipper. "You have told her, haven't you?"

"Not about this, no."

"Then about what?"

"She knows about my . . . predilections. She has known for some time. For a long time."

"How long?"

"Decades, Prime Minister."

"Stop calling me that! You do not call me that. You've been a liability to this government for twenty years and you still have the gall to *Prime Minister* me. I needed you, Khan. We could lose this. Yes, we could lose this war. The generals have all been showing me their satellite pictures and their aeai models and they all say that the Awadhis are moving troops in to the north towards Jaunpur. I'm not so sure. It's too obvious. One thing the Awadhis have never been is obvious. I needed you, Khan, to play against that fool Chowdhury."

"I am sorry, I am truly sorry." But he does not want to hear what his Prime Minister has to say. He has heard it all already, he told it to himself again and again as the car slipped through the stifling morning. Shaheen Badoor Khan wants to talk, to let all the things he has packed down all this lifetime spill out like water from the stone lips of a fountain in some decadent European city. He is free now. There is no secret now, no restraint, and he wants so much for her to understand, to see what he sees, feel what he feels, ache where he burns.

Sajida Rana settles heavily on the balustrade.

"It's raining in Maratha, did you know that? It will be here before the week is out. It's moving across the Deccan. As we speak, there are children dancing in the rain in Nagpur. A few days more, and they will be dancing in the streets of Varanasi. Three years. I could have waited.

I didn't need to take the dam. But I couldn't risk not taking it. So now I'm going to have Bharati jawans patrolling the Kunda Khadar dam in the rain. How will that look to the plain people of Patna? You were right though. We did fuck N. K. Jivanjee up the ass. And now he's paying me back. We have underestimated him. You underestimated him. This is the end of us."

"Prime . . . Mrs. Rana, we don't know . . ."

Who else? You're not as clever as you think, Khan. None of us are. Your resignation is accepted." Then Sajida Rana clenches her teeth and smashes her fist into the carved limestone railing. Blood starts from her knuckles. "Why did you do this to me? I would have given you everything. And your wife, your boys . . . Why do men risk these things? I will condemn you."

"Of course."

"I can no longer protect you. Shaheen, I do not know what is going to happen to you now. Get out of my sight. We shall be lucky if we survive the day."

As Shaheen Badoor Khan crunches back over the raked gravel to the state car, the dark trees and shrubs around him light up with birdsong. For a moment he thinks it is the singing ringing in his inner ear of all the lies that are his life rubbing past each other as they flock to the light. Then he realises it is the overture of the dawn chorus, the herald birds that sing in the darkest of night. Shaheen Badoor Khan stops, turns, lifts up his head, listens. The air is hot but piercingly clean and present. He breathes pure darkness. He senses the heavens a dome above him, each star a pin of light spearing down into his heart. Shaheen Badoor Khan feels the universe wheel around him. He is at once axle and engine, subject and object, turned and turner. A tiny thing, a small song calling out with countless others into the vast dark. Time will smooth out his deeds and misdeeds; history will flatten his name into the general dust. It is nothing. For the first time since those fisher children splashed and adventured in the Kerala sunset he understands *free.*

Joy kindles in the well of his manipura chakra. The Sufi moment of selfessness, timelessness. God in the unexpected. He does not deserve it. The mystery of it is that it never comes to those who think they do.

"Where to, sahb?"

Responsibilities. After enlightenment, duty.

"To the haveli." It is all downhill now. The words having been said once are easy to repeat. Sajida Rana had been right. He should have told her first. The accusation had surprised him: Shaheen Badoor Khan had been reminded, sharply, that his Prime Minister was a woman, a married woman who would not take her husband's name. He polarises the windows dark against prying eyes.

Bilquis doesn't deserve it. She deserves a good husband, a true man who, even if she no longer loved him or shared his bed or his life, would do her no disgrace in public, would smile and talk the right talk and never cause her to cover her face in shame among the Ladies of the Law Circle. He had it all—Sajida Rana had said as much—he had it all and he still could not stop himself from destroying it. How deeply he deserves what has happened to him. Then on the sun-cracked Bharat government leather upholstery, Shaheen Badoor Khan's perceptions turn. He doesn't deserve it. No one deserves it and everyone deserves it. Who can hold his head up, and who would presume to judge? He is a good advisor; the best advisor. He has served his country wisely and well. It still has need of him. Perhaps he can go dark, burrow down like some toad in a drought to the bottom of the mud and wait for the climate to change.

An edge of light fills the streets as the government car whirrs along, soft as a moth. Shaheen Badoor Khan allows himself to smile inside his cube of darkened glass. The car turns the corner where the sadhu sits on a concrete slab, one arm held aloft in a sling strapped around a lamppost. Shaheen Badoor Khan knows that trick. After a time you lose all feeling. The car stops abruptly. Shaheen Badoor Khan has to put out his hands to keep himself from falling.

"What is it?"

"Trouble, sahb."

Shaheen Badoor Khan unpolarises the window. The road ahead of him is blocked with early traffic. People have left their cabs and are leaning against their open doors to watch the spectacle that has stopped them. Bodies stream past the intersection; shadowy men in white shirts and dark pants, young men with first moustaches, moving at a steady, angry jog, lathis jerking up and down in their hands. A battery of drummers passes, a group of fierce, sharp-faced women in Kali red; naga sadhus, white with ash, wielding crude Siva trishuls. Shaheen Badoor Khan watches a vast, pink papier mâché effigy of Ganesha lumber into view, gaudy, almost fluorescent in the rising light. It veers from side to side, steered unsteadily by bare-legged puppeteers. Behind Ganesha, an even more extraordinary sight: the billowing orange and red spire of a rath yatra. And torches. In every hand, with every attendant and runner, a fire. Shaheen Badoor Khan dares open the window a crack. An avalanche of sound falls on him: a vast, inchoate roar. Individual voices emerge, take up a theme; submerge again: chants, prayers; slogans, nationalist anthems, karsevak hymns. He does not need to hear the words to know who they are. The great gyre of protestors around Sarkhand Roundabout has broken out and is streaming across Varanasi. It would only do so if it had a greater object for its hate. Shaheen Badoor Khan knows where they are going with fire in their hands. The word is out. He had hoped for longer.

Shaheen Badoor Khan looks behind him. The road is still clear.

"Get me out of here."

Gohil complies without question. The big car backs up, swings round, hooting savagely at traffic as it mounts the concrete central strip and crunches down on to the opposite side of the road. As Shaheen Badoor Khan blackens the windows, he glimpses smoke coiling up into the sky in the east, oily as burning fat from a funeral pyre against the yellow dawn.

28

TAL

The phatphat is headed nowhere, just driving. Tal had thrust a bouquet of rupees at the taxi driver and told him that: just drive.

Yt has to get away. Abandon job, home, everything yt had made for ytself in Varanasi. Go to a place where nobody knows yts name. Mumbai. Back to Mum. Too close. Too bitchy. Deep south, Bangalore, Chennai. They have big media industries there. There is always work for a good designer. Even Chennai might not be far enough. If yt could change yts name, yts face again. Yt could go via Patna, buy more surgery from Nanak. Stick it on the tab. If yts credit was still good with Nanak. Yt'd need work, soon. Yes, that's yt; get everything, get to the station, get to Patna, get a new identity.

Tal taps the driver.

"White Fort."

"Don't go there this time of night."

"I'll pay you double."

Yt should have taken the money. The cash in yts bag is running out like water through sand. The cards that aren't at the limit are close to it. A crore rupees, untraceable, unstoppable, that could take yt anywhere. Anywhere on the planet. But that would be to accept yts role. Who has written that yt must be punished? What has yt done to deserve global infamy? Tal looks at yts small life, unpicks the terrible vulnerabilities that have turned it into an unthinking political weapon. Alien, alone, isolated, new. They had been watching from the moment yt stepped off the shatabdi. Tranh, the night of burning delirium in the airport hotel—the best sex yt has ever known—the temple party, the creamy gilt-edged invitation it had waved around the office like an icon . . . Every one of those chota pegs poured down yts golden throat . . . Yt had been played like a bansuri.

Tal finds yts fists tight in fury. The heat of yts anger surprises Tal. Safe, sane, wise nute would be to run. But yt wants to know. Yt wants one good, clear look at the face that ordained all this for yt.

"Okay my friend, this is as far as you go." The driver waves his radio. "Those Shivaji lunatics are on the move. They've broken out of Sarkhand Roundabout."

"You're leaving me with them out there?" Tal shouts after the receding phatphat. Yt can hear the rage of Hindutva, swelling and receding in the cavernous streets. And the streets are waking, shop by stall by kiosk by dhaba. A pickup dumps bundles of morning editions in the concrete centre strip. The newsboys descend like black kites. Tal pulls yts collar around yts betraying features. Yts shaved skull feels hideously vulnerable, a fragile brown egg. Two roads to safety. Yt can see the satellite-dish studded revetments of White Fort beyond the rooftop water tanks and solar panels. Tal slips along the line of vehicles, headdown, avoiding eye contact with the shopkeepers rolling up their shutters, the night workers heading back from a shift on Pacific Coast Time. Sooner, not later, someone will see what yt is. Yt eyes the bundles of newspaper. Front page, banner headline, full colour splash.

The sound of the mob moves behind yt, left, then right, then close behind. Tal breaks into a jog, coat pulled tight around yts chin despite the rising heat. People are looking now. One more junction. One more junction. The voiceless roar moves again, seemingly in front now, then leaps in volume and vehemence. Tal glances around. They are behind it. A front of jogging males in white shirts turns out of a side street on to the avenue. There is a moment of silence. Even the traffic falls still and hushed. Then a focused roar strikes Tal with almost physical force. Yt gives a small whimper of fear, throws off yts stupid, encumbering coat and runs. Yips and bays go up behind yt. The karsevaks come leaping in pursuit. Not far. Not far. Not. Far. Not. Far. Not. Far. Close. Close. Close. Tal fires ytself through the forest of pillars that are White Fort's undercroft. Howling shouts echo and dart off the concrete piles. We are closing. We are fast. We are faster than you, unnatural, perverted thing. You are bloated with unnaturalness and vice. We will stamp on you, slug. We will hear you burst beneath our boots. Missiles clatter and bounce around Tal: cans, bottles, pieces of broken circuitry. And Tal is failing, failing. Fading. There's nothing left in yt. The batteries are flat. Zero charge. Tal taps commands into yts subdermals. Seconds later the adrenaline rush hits. Yt'll pay dearly for it later. Yt'll pay anything now. Tal pulls away from the hunters. Yt can see the elevator bank. Let there be one. Ardhanarisvara, Lord of the divided things, let there be one, and let it work. The hunters slap their hands off the oily concrete pillars. We. Are. Coming. To. Kill. You. We. Are. Coming. To. Kill. You.

Green light. Green light is salvation, green light is life. Tal dives towards the green elevator light as the door slides open. Yt squeezes through the dark slit, hits the button. The doors close. Fingers squeeze through, feeling for the sensors, the switches, the flesh within, anything. Centimetre by centimetre, they force the door open.

"There he is, the chuutya!"

Yt! Yt! Tal screams silently as it smashes at the fingers with yts fists, yts sharp boot heels. The fingers reel back. The door seals. The ascent begins. Tal goes two levels low to draw them up, waits while the doors open and the doors close, and then goes up one over. As yt creeps down the stairwell, glossy from the steady tread of bare feet and reeking of dank ammonia even in drought, yt hears a growing babble of voices. Tal edges around the turn. Yts neighbours are crowded into Mama Bharat's open door. Tal edges a step lower. Everyone is talking, gesticulating, some of the women have their dupattas pressed to their mouths in shock. Some bow and bob in the rituals of grief. Men's voices cut through the jabber and keening, a word here, a phrase there. *Yes, the family are coming, right away, who would have left an old woman here on her own, shameful shameful, the police will find them.*

One step closer.

The smashed door to Mama Bharat's apartment lies on the floor. Over the heads of the angry men, Tal can see the desecrated room. Walls, windows, paintings of gods and avatars are full of holes. Tal gapes at the holes, not wanting to comprehend. Bullet holes. It is a gape too long. A cry.

"There he is!"

Neighbour Paswan's querulous voice. The crowd parts, allowing a clear line of connection between Tal and Paswan's accusing finger and the feet on the floor. Every head turns. Their feet are in a slick of blood. The slick of startling, fresh, red blood, fresh with life and oxygen, already drawing in the flies. The flies are in the room. The flies are in yts head.

You're dispensable now, Tranh had said.

The feet in the fresh, oily blood. They are still in the building. Yt turns, runs again.

"There he is, the monster!" Paswan roars. Tal's neighbours take up the cry. The mass voice throbs in the concrete shaft of the stairwell. Tal grasps huge handfuls of steel banister, hauls ytself up the stairs. Everything aches. Everything screams and moans and tells yt it's come to the end, there is no more. But Mama Bharat is dead. Mama Bharat is shot and this August morning with the early light climbing down the sides of the shaft from the grimy cupola far above, all the hatred and despite and fear and anger of Bharat is focused on one nute hauling ytself up a concrete stairwell. Yts neighbours, the people yt lived among so quietly these months, want yt torn apart by their hands.

Yt pushes past two men on the seventh-floor landing. A flicker of memory: Tal glances back. They are young, and lean dressed in baggy pants and white shirts, the Young Bharati Male Street uniform but there is something out of place about them. Something not White Fort. Eyes meet. Tal remembers where yt has seen them before. They wore suits then, fine dark suits. They had passed him on the landing, down there, as Mama Bharat put out the trash and Tal had danced past, blowing a kiss, all excited and bouncing about heading out to the end of it all. They had looked back, as yt looks back now. A good designer never forgets the details.

You're dispensable now.

In the instant it takes them to work out their mistake, Tal has gained a floor and a half but they are young and male and fit and do not wear hi-fashion boots and have not been running for what seems an entire night.

"Out of my way!" Tal yells as yt ploughs into the head of the daily procession of water girls from the upper levels descending the endless staircases with their plastic litrejohns balanced on their heads. Yt must get into the open. White Fort is a trap, a vast concrete killing machine. Yt has to get out. Get into the crowd, get among the people. They will shield you with their bodies. Tal swings off at the next landing, wrenches open the door and plunges out on to the exterior walkway.

Diljit Rana's urban planners, good neo–Le Corbusiens all, had conceived White Fort as a village in the sky and had drafted in wide sunlit terraces for urban farming. Most of the drip-irrigated plots have gone to dirt and dust in the long drought and plumbing crisis or grow stands of GM cannabis, tended with painstaking love and bottled spa water. Feral goats, five generations from their first urbanised forebears, graze the trash-piles and desiccated market gardens. They are as sure-footed on the concrete runways and safety rails of White Fort as their native precipices. The maintenance bots duel them ferociously with high-voltage tasers. The goats have a taste for wiring insulation.

Tal runs. Goats look up, ruminating. Mothers snatch children out of the path of the mad, flying, perverted thing. Old men smoking bidis and solving crosswords in the early sun follow yt with their heads, delighted by action, any action. Young men, idle men cheer and hoot.

The chemical surge is failing, fading. Yt's not built to run. Tal glances over yts shoulder. Guns beat up and down in the men's hands. Black hard guns. That changes everything on the White Fort farm levels. Women whisk children indoors. Old men hide themselves. Young men edge away.

"Help me!" Tal cries. Yt grabs bins, piles of paper, baskets, anything that might cost the men behind yt a second, pulls them down behind yt. Saris and dhotis and lungis, the daily laundry is pinned out along line after line sagging across the wide sky-streets. Tal ducks under the dripping dhobi, sticks out yts arm to knock out clothes prop after clothes prop. Yt hears damp curses, looks back to see the hunters disentangling themselves from a wet green sari. Sanctuary is in sight, a service elevator at the end of the street filling up with the school run. Tal darts through the closing gates, dodges past the fluttering chaperone. The lift jerks and begins its descent. Tal hears voices. Yt looks up to see the two dacoits hanging over the rail. They put their guns up. From the midst of the press of black-eyed primary-school girls in their beautiful neat uniforms, Tal waves up at them.

The sun pours scalding light into the canyon streets of Varanasi as Tal moves through the crush hour. Yt slips between the walking schoolkids and the white-shirted civil servants on bicycles, the street sellers and the shopworkers, the doorway sleepers and the students in their labels and Japanese shoes, the delivery drays piled high with cardboard boxes of Lux Macroman underwear and the fine ladies under the canopies of the cycle rickshaws. Any time, any one in that crowd might recognise yt from the front page of the newspaper tucked under his arm, from the breakfast news bulletin on his palmer, from the news stand headline posters or the scrolling ad-screens on every intersection and chowk. One shout; one hand thrust out to snag a jacket sleeve; one Hey! You! Stop! and that milling motion of individuals would crystallise into a mob, one mind, one will, one intent.

Tal skips down trash-strewn steps into VART. Even if the killers had followed yt through the morning crush, they cannot hope to hunt yt in the labyrinth of Varanasi underground. Tal dodges the line for the iris reader, slips into the women's queue, who do not permit the Varanasi Area Rapid Transit such liberties with their eyes. Yt drops five rupees into the hopper and squeezes through the barrier before the ladies of New Varanasi can complain.

Tal works up the platform to the women's section. Yt scans the crowd for the wake of killers cutting through the press of people. So easy to die here. A hand in the back as the train surges out of the tunnel. And the down-wave is coming, the ashes of the artificial adrenaline hit washing out of yts bloodstream. Tal shivers, alone and small and very very paranoid. A wave of sickeningly hot, electric air; the train slams into the station. Tal rides two stops in the women-only bogie and gets off. Yt counts one train, two, then boards again in the reserved women's section. Yt has no idea if this is the right thing to do, if there is any right thing to do, if there are any self-help books on how to throw killers on the city metro.

The robot train slams through the underpinnings of Varanasi, jolting across the points and switchovers. Tal feels naked among the women's bodies. Yt can hear their thoughts: *this is not your place; we do not know what you were but you are no longer one of us, hijra.* Then yts heart freezes. Jammed in between a stanchion and the fire extinguisher, an office girl has found room to read the *Bharat Times*. Her attention is on the back page, the cricket news. The front shrieks an eighty-point banner headline and a half-page photograph. Yt is looking at ytself, face pale in the flash, eyes wide as moons.

The train rocks across points. The passengers sway like grain in the wind. Tal releases yts straphold and reels across the carriage. Yt pulls ytself up in front of the screaming front page. Newspaper girl folds the top of her morning read down to stare at Tal, then gets back to the gossip about Test hero V. J. Mazumdar and his forthcoming celebrity wedding. The subhead at the bottom of the page reads DEATHS IN PERVERT CLUB FIRE ATTACK.

Varanasi City Station, the aeai announces over the din of radios and conversation. Tal spills out on to the platform, running ahead of the slow spreading stain of commuters. Time to mark and meditate on that headline later, when the shatabdi is up to speed and Varanasi a hundred kilometres behind yt.

The escalator casts Tal up on to the main concourse. Yt's already checked on yts palmer what's going soonest out of here. The Kolkata Hi-Speed. Straight down the steel line to the States of Bengal. Patna and Nanak can wait. What Tal needs more than a new face is a new nation. The Banglas are civilised, cultured, tolerant people. Kolkata shall be yts new home. But the online booking is slow slow slow and the pile of bodies around the ticket office deadly. Unwanted newspapers lie scattered among the discarded mango-leaf bowls of aloo and dal on the concrete concourse. Ragpickers poke and sift. Any one of them would turn yt in for a fistful of rupees.

Thirty minutes to train time.

Again, the online booking is locked out. And the card-ticketing machine have felt-markered Out of Service posters taped over their slots.

Bloody Bharat.

"Hey, hey there friend, you want to buy ticket right quick?" The tout is a barely moustached youth in sports fashion, pressing close, do-a-deal intimate. He spreads a fan of tickets "Safe, sound. Reservation guaranteed. You look, you find your name on the bogie, no questions. We have a hack into the Bharat Rail system." A wave of a beatup palmer.

Come on come on. Yt's not going to make it. Yt's not going to make it.

"How much?"

Sports boy names a price that any other time, any other situation, would have made Tal laugh out loud.

"Here, here." Yt presses a fan of rupees at the ticket tout.

"Hey hey first things first," the boy says, leading Tal towards the platforms. "What train what train?"

Tal tells him.

"You come with me." He hustles Tal through the crowd around the chai stall where morning commuters sip their sweet, milky tea from tiny plastic cups. He slips a ticket blank into the palmer print slot, enters yts ID, thumbs a few icons. "Done. Bon voyage." He hands the ticket to Tal, grinning. The grin freezes. The mouth opens. A tiny ascot of red appears on the neck of his Adidas Tee. The red spreads into a soft gush. The expression goes from smug satisfaction to surprise to dead. The boy slumps on to Tal, a cry goes up from a woman in a purple sari, a cry taken up by the whole crowd as Tal sees over the shot tout's shoulder the man in the neat Nehru suit with the silenced black gun in his hand, caught between getting out after a botched job or taking a clear shot and finishing it here, now, in front of everyone.

Then out of the crowd comes a moped, twisting this way, that, horn blaring; a moped, with a girl on it, aiming straight at the gunman who hears and sees and reacts just that millisecond too late. He brings the gun around as the moped smashes into him. Screams. The gun spins out of his hand. The man in black reels across the platform, slams into the side of the train, slips down between the edge of the platform and the bogie, under the Kolkata Unlimited, on to the tracks.

The girl spins her moped round to face Tal as the crowd rushes to the train to see what has become of the gunman. "Get on!" she cries in English. A hand appears from underneath the bogie. Arms reach down to help it up. "If you want to live, get on the bike!"

Any other option would be a greater insanity. The girl swings Tal around, yt slips on close and clinging behind her. She twists the throttle, tears away through the platform crowd, horn buzzing furiously. She runs off the end of the platform, steers the bouncing moped over the tracks and sleepers, cuts in front of a slow moving local, speeds along the litter-strewn verge, hooting at the pedestrians who use it as a commuter run.

"I should introduce myself," the girl throws back over her shoulder. "You don't know me, but I sort of feel I owe you.

"What?" shouts Tal, cheek pressed against her back.

"My name's Najia Askarzadah. I got you into all this."

29

BANANA CLUB

By eleven o'clock repeated police lathi charges have cleared the streets. Policemen chase individual karsevaks through the galis but they are just the rude boys, trouble boys who are always there for anything on their terrain. The alleys are too narrow for the fire engines so the brigade reels hoses along the streets, bolting them together into longer runs. Water sprays from the seams. Kashi residents peer enviously from their verandas and open storefronts. It is all too late. It is over. The old wooden haveli has fallen in on itself in a pile of glowing, clinking coals. All the firefighters can do is tamp it down and prevent it spreading to neighbouring buildings. They slip and fall on a slick of banana skins.

The attack was thorough and effective. Amazing, the speed with which it caught and held. Dry as tinder. This drought, this long drought. Stretcher parties draw away the dead. Varanasi, city of burnings. The ones who fled out the front ran into the full wrath of the Shivaji. The bodies are strewn up the alley. One wears a car tire around its neck, burned down to the steel wires. The body is intact, the head a charred skull. One has been run through with a Siva trident. One has been disembowelled and the gape filled with burning plastic trash. The police stamp out the flames and drag the thing away, trying to handle it as little as possible. They fear the polluting touch of the hijra, the un-sex.

Hovercams and handhelds come in for close-ups, back in the live-feed studio the news editors read the footage and decide what stance to take: outraged liberal opinion or popular wrath at the hypocrisy of the Rana government. N. K. Jivanjee will issue a statement at eleven thirty. Newsroom editors love a story on the up-ramp. The cricket pulled out before the climax, the war has provided nothing but hours of armoured personnel carriers driving up and down the long curve of the Kunda Khadar dam; but this Rana sex scandal is spiralling out of control into charred bodies and street fighting. One shot in particular makes it on to all the morning bulletins; the poor blind lady, caught up by the rage with the side of her head smashed in by a club. No one can work out why she has a banana in her hand.

30

LISA

Beyond the dripping fringe of coconut thatch, the rain reduces the world to flux. Palms, church, the stalls along the road, the road itself and the vehicles that pass up and down it are shades of grey, washed out, liquid, running into each other like a Japanese ink painting. The truck headlights are wan and watery. Earth, river, and sky are a continuity.

In her shapeless plastic cape, Lisa Durnau can't even see the end of the gangplank. In the next cabin Dr. Ghotse crouches over the gas burner with a promise of chai and cheer. Lisa Durnau can leave the chai. She's tried to get them to make it just with water and nix the sugar but it comes sweet and milky anyway. Iced would be ecstasy. Beneath her stifling rainsheet sweat clings to her. The rain cascades from the eaves.

It was raining when she touched down at Thiruvananthapuram. A boy with an umbrella escorted her across the streaming apron to arrivals.

Coach-class Westerners dashed and cursed, jackets and newspapers held over their heads. The Indians just got wet and looked happy. Lisa Durnau has seen many types of rain; the steely grey rain of north eastern springs; the penetrating drizzle that blows for days on end up in the northwest; the terrifying cloudbursts of the plains states that are like a waterfall opening in the sky, mothers of flash-floods and sheet erosion. Happy rain was new to her. The cab to the hotel had driven axle-deep through streets awash with floodwater and floating trash. The cows stood mired to the hock. Cycle rickshaws ploughed through the dancing brown liquid, throwing up beery wakes. She watched a rat swim across the taxi's path, brave head held high. Today as she dodged between the puddles to the gangplank she had seen a little girl swimming up the backwater, pushing a slim raft no more than three bamboo poles lashed together, a battered metal pot balanced on it. The girl's hair was plastered to her skull like some sleek aquatic mammal but her face was radiant.

The CIA briefing had neglected to tell her it was the monsoon in Kerala.

Lisa Durnau does not like being a government spook. No sooner had the lightbody touched down on a pyre of plasma than the lessons began. She had her first briefing in the bus to the medical centre, still weak and achey from welcoming back gravity. She had not even had time to change before they lifted her and threw her on the flight up to New York. At Kennedy she was briefed on embassy liaisons and security passwords in the limo to the vip suite. There a man and a woman in suits lectured her on the correct use of the location device inside one of the business centre mute fields. At the gate they presented her with a small valise of suitable clothing in her size. Then they shook hands gravely and wished her a pleasant trip and a successful mission. Lisa opened the case as the taxi drew up at the hotel. As she had feared. The sleeves on the T-shirts were all wrong and the underwear was simply unspeakable. Folded at the bottom were two elegant black suits. She half expected Daley Suarez-Martin to climb out of the minibar. The next day Lisa took her bottomless black credit card out to the bazaar and refilled the case for less than the price of a pair of Abercrombie and Fitch panties. Including wet-weather wear.

"Yes, it is a marvellous thing to see," Dr. Ghotse says. Lisa Durnau starts. She has let herself become hypnotised by the fingers of rain on the thatch. He stands with a cup of chai in either hand. It is as she feared but it indeed cheers her. The boat smells damp and neglected. She does not like to think of Thomas Lull ending up here. She cannot imagine it under any other climate than this endless white rain. She had read the Tantric symbols on the roof mats, noted the name in white on the prow: *Salve Vagina*. No doubt that Thomas Lull had been here. But she had been scared at what she would find: Lull's things; Lull's life beyond her, beyond Alterre; Lull's new world. Now that she has seen how little there is, how poor and spare the three thatched cabins are, apprehension turns to melancholy. It is like he has died.

Dr. Ghotse bids her sit on one of the upholstered divans that run the length of the cabin. Lisa Durnau struggles out of her plastic sheet, leaves it dripping on the soft fibre matting. The chai is good, sensual.

"Why, up in the black north they have gone to war over it. They are uncivilised people. Most caste ridden. Now, Miss Durnau; what is it you require from my good friend Thomas Lull?"

Lisa Durnau realises there are two ways she can play this and every other similar scene. She can assume Lull has told his good friend Dr. Ghotse about what he left behind, and who. She can take the line of her intelligence briefings and assume no one knows or can know anything.

You're in India now, LD.

A chip of Schubert piano sonatas has worked its way down the side of the cushion.

"I've been commissioned by my government to find Lull and pass information to him. If possible, I'm to persuade him to return to the United States with me."

"What is this information you are asking?"

"I'm technically not at liberty to disclose that, Dr. Ghotse. Sufficient to say that it's of a scientific nature and requires Lull's unique insight to interpret."

"Lull. Is that what you called him?"

"Did he tell you about me?"

"Enough for me to be surprised that you are about your government's business."

Look after it right. Stop them sticking fucking Coke banners on the clouds, he had charged her. The memory of Lull that night in the Oxford student bar is more fresh, more vital than this house he vacated so recently. She cannot feel him here, beneath this canopy of rain-sound. She imagines running through that rain, pushing like an otter through the blood-warm backwater like the little raft girl with her pewter pot. What have they asked you to become?

Lisa Durnau takes out the datablock and thumbs it open. Dr. Ghotse sits with his legs crossed at the ankles, his chai cup set on the low carved coffee table.

"You're right. This is the truth. You may not believe it, but as far as I know, it is true." She calls up the Tabernacle image of Lull.

"That is Professor Lull," Dr. Ghotse says. "It is not a very good photograph. Excessively grainy."

"That's because that photograph was generated by an extraterrestrial artefact discovered by NASA inside an asteroid called Darnley 285. This artefact is known as the Tabernacle."

"Ah, tabernacle, the sanctuary of the Ark of the Covenant of the Hebrews."

"I'm not quite sure you heard what I said. The Tabernacle is a nonhuman artefact. It's the product of an extraterrestrial intelligence."

"I heard you correctly, Miss Durnau."

"You're not surprised?"

"The universe is a very great place. The surprise would be if it were not so."

Lisa sets the block down on the table between the chai cups.

"There's something else I need you to understand. This asteroid Darnley 285 is extremely old. It's older than the age of our solar system. Can you understand that?"

"Miss Durnau, I am educated in both Western and Hindu cosmologies. It is indeed a wonder that an object has survived the destruction at the end of the Dwapara Yuga; perhaps even ages before that. This Tabernacle might be a remnant of the Age of Truth itself."

"The reason I want to find Thomas Lull, what I want to ask him is: why is his face inside a rock seven billion years old?"

"That would be a question," Dr. Ghotse agrees.

The rain has found its way through the coconut thatch. A small but swelling drip gathers and bursts on the low table carved with entwined Tantric lovers. Monsoon above Lisa Durnau, below her, behind her, before her, dissolving the certainties of Kennedy, of New York, of the hypersonic transport. This rain, this India.

The roar, the rain, the smell of sewage and spice and rot, the ceaseless chaos of the traffic, the burst dog half gone to black bones in the streaming gutter, the circling carrion-eyed kites, the peeling mould-stained buildings, the sweet stench of sugar-cane alcofuel and burning ghee from the puri vendors, the children pressing in around her, clean and fed but asking for rupee rupee, a pen a pen, the hawkers and vendors and fortune tellers and massage artists homing in on a white woman in the rain: the people. The people. Within a hundred metres of her hotel, Kerala felled her. The sounds, the smells, the sights and sensations combined into a massive attack on her sensibilities. L. Durnau the preacherman's daughter. This was Thomas Lull's world. She must meet it on Thomas Lull's terms.

She got her hair cut in the Ganga Devi Booti Salon by a blind hairdresser and only afterwards as she patted the short bob did she realise it was the style in the Tabernacle image. Seal of prophecy. She bought bottled water in the middle of the monsoon and her light, efficacious wet wear and had dozens of photographs of Thomas Lull copied from the datablock—which she was beginning to think of as the Tablet—at a print shop wedged behind a pipal tree hung with red and orange Brahmin threads. Then she began her investigation.

The rickshaw driver looked about twelve. Lisa doubted such a scrawn could ever carry a passenger but he hung on her heel for three blocks, calling "hello, hello lady," as she wove between the umbrellas. She stopped him where the road narrowed at the fort gate.

"You speak English?"

"Indian, American, or Australian, lady?"

"I need boys speak English."

"There are many such boys, lady."

"Here's a hundred rupees. Come back with as many as you can in half an hour to that chai shop there and there are two hundred more for you. I need boys can speak English and know everything and everyone."

He tucked the banknote into a pocket inside his Adidas pants, gave the wiggle of his head that Lisa had learned meant affirmation.

"Hey! What's your name?" she shouted as he pulled into the traffic, bells chiming melodiously. He shot a grin back as he pedalled off through the swirling water.

"Kumarmangalam."

Lisa Durnau installed herself in the chai shop and surfed into Alterre for the half hour. A week was literally an age at twenty thousand years per hour. Algal blooms in Biome 778 in the Eastern Pacific had generating a self-sustaining oceanic microclimate that created a wind reversal similar to RealEarth's El Niño. The montane cloud-forests were dying; the complex symbiotic ecosystems of flowering trees, pollinating colonial birds, and complex arborealsaurian canopy societies was coming apart. Within a couple of days a dozen species and a system of rare, poised beauty would have slipped into extinction. Lisa knew she should hold the Buddha-nature about Alterre; they were only virtual species competing for memory and power resources and a set of mathematical parameters in eleven million host computers, but she grieved for every extinction. She had proved the physical possibility of CyberEarth's reality somewhere in the postexpansion polyverse. It was real death, real annihilation, real forever.

Until now. In a Kerala chai shop, it felt like games, toys. A pocket freak show. The flatscreen was running a soap. Every eye was turned to it. She had read that not only were the characters aeai generated, so were the actors that played them. A vast false edifice threatened to overwhelm the drama, like the huge encrusted towers that dominated the temple architecture of the Dravidians. There is not one CyberEarth, she realised. There are thousands.

Kumarmangalam was back on the half hour. This was a thing she was discovering about this alien world. It only looked like chaos. Things got done and done well. You could trust people to lift your bags, launder your clothes, find your former lover. The street boys jammed into the chai shop. The owner gave the bold Western woman hard looks. The other clients moved their seats and complained loudly that they could not hear the television. Kumarmangalam stood beside Lisa and shouted at this one, then that one, and they seemed to obey him. Already he was making himself her lieutenant. As Lisa had suspected, most of them had only meet-greet-and-fleece English but she fanned the photographs of Thomas Lull across the table.

"One to each," she ordered Kumarmangalam. Hands tore at the prints as the rickshaw boy dealt them out. Some he dismissed without a photograph, some he harangued lengthily in Malayalam. "Okay, I need to find this man. His name is Thomas Lull. He is American. He comes from Kansas, can you get that?"

Kansas, the street boys intoned back. She held up the shot. It was his publisher's PR shot, the sensitive one leaning on one arm with the wise smile. How he'd hated it.

"This is how he looked about four years ago. He may still be here, he may have moved on. You know where the tourists go, where the people who decide to stay go. I want to know where he is or where he has gone. Do you understand?"

An oceanic murmur.

"Okay. I'm going to give Kumarmangalam here some money. There are one hundred rupees now. There are another four hundred if you come back with information. I will check this information before you are paid."

Kumarmangalam translated. Heads nodded. She took her new lieutenant aside and gave him the wad of notes.

"And there's your two hundred, and another thousand if you keep your eye on these people."

"Lady, I will keep them in line, as you say in American English."

In her first year at Keble, Lisa Durnau had taken the crash course in Anglophilia and read the complete Sherlock Holmes. She had always felt that the Baker Street Irregulars never saw enough column inches. Now she had her own. As Kumarmangalam pedalled her back through the rain to the hotel, she imagined them, running out through the city, into a shop here, a café there, a restaurant, a temple, a travel bureau, a money changer, a lawyer, a real estate agent, a leasing factor. *This man this man?* It pleased her greatly. Women make the best private detectives. At the hotel she swam fifty lengths of the outdoor pool with the rain slashing around her and the attendants huddled together under an awning watching her gravely. Then she changed into a sarong and top with gaudy blue gods printed on it and took a phatphat out to the places Thomas Lull would have gone, the tourist bars where the girls are.

The rain added a new glaze of dismal to the upstairs bars and dance clubs. The Westerners who were stupid enough to have been caught in town by the big rain were all corporate or political spooks. The club owners and barristas and restaurateurs who shook their heads and pursed their lips over her photographs were a hundred Lulls-that-might-have-been; overweight and balding in XL beach-shirts that hung off their bellies like square-rigging. The local bar boys stirred from their stools and came round for the chat and an attempted slip of the hand into her V-string. She worked twenty bars and could take no more. Humming home in the phatphat she sat half-hypnotised by the rhythm of the rain through the headlights and wondered how it was that clouds never rained themselves dry. In the hotel she attempted to watch CNN but it seemed as alien and irrelevant as Alterre. One image lodged with her; warm monsoon rain falling on an iceberg in the Bay of Bengal.

Kumarmangalam was circling on his rickshaw when she ventured out the next morning. He swung her out through the traffic in a big U-turn to an Internet shop on the other side of the street. Nobody walked in this country. Just like home.

"This boy has information," he said. Lisa wasn't even sure he was one of the mob from the day before. The boy waved his photograph.

"Four hundred rupees four hundred rupees."

"We check it out first. Then you get your money."

Kumarmangalam glared down the boy's insolence. They rode on his rickshaw. The boy would not ride in the back with a Western woman; he clung on in front of Kumarmangalam, feet on the axle nuts, leaning back against the handlebars, steering the rickshaw-wallah through the traffic. It was a long heavy haul. Kumarmangalam dismounted and pushed several times. The boy helped him. Lisa Durnau clutched her bag beset by Presbyterian work-ethic guilt. Finally they rolled downhill and through an arch scatter-gunned with filmi flyposters into a courtyard framed by wooden balconies and cloisters in the Keralese style. A cow chewed sodden straw. Men glanced up from a battery of sewing machines. The boy led them upstairs past an actuary and an Ayurvedic wholesaler to an open-fronted office unit beneath the peeling sign *Gunaratna Floating Lotus Craft Hirings*. A greying Malayali and a younger Westerner in a surf-brand T-shirt looked up.

"You've come about the gentleman in the photograph?" the local man, Gunaratna, asked. Lisa Durnau nodded. Mr. Gunaratna waved the street boys out of his office. They squatted on the balcony, listening hard.

"This man." She slid the Tablet across the desk like a poker dealer. Gunaratna showed it to his associate. Surf-shirt-man nodded.

"It was a while ago." He was Oceanian—Oz, maybe Enzee; Lisa had never been able to tell them apart but then some folk couldn't distinguish Canucks from Americans.

"Several years," Gunaratna confirmed. Then Lisa realised that they were waiting for the baksheesh. She fanned out three thousand rupees.

"For information retrieval," she hinted. Gunaratna scooped it sweetly away.

"We only remember him because he bought a boat from us," Oz-boy said.

"We run a bespoke vessel chartering service on the backwaters," Gunaratna chimed in. "It is most unusual for someone wanting to buy, but such an offer . . ."

"In cash." Oz-boy was now perched on the edge of the desk.

"In cash, was impossible for us to refuse. It was most excellent craft. It had not one but two certificates of seaworthiness from the State Inspectorate of Shipping."

"You have a record of the transaction?"

"Madam, this is an upstanding business of immaculate repute and all accounts are triple-filed in strict accordance with State Revenue regulations."

Oz-boy hooked up a rollscreen and tapped through a database.

"There's your boy."

July 22, 2043. Ten-metre kettuvallam/houseboat conversion with fixtures and fittings and ten horsepower alcofuel engines last serviced 18/08/42, moored at Alumkadavu. Sold to J. Noble Boyd, US citizen, passport number . . . A true Lull touch; using the name of the Kansas pastor who had made it his religious duty to oppose the evolutionist heresies of Alterre on his false ID. Lisa Durnau jotted the boat's registration details into the Tablet.

"Thank you, you have been most helpful."

Oz-boy pushed a thousand rupees back across the desk.

"If you do find Dr. Lull could you get him to do another series like *Living Universe*? Best science show I've seen in years. Made you think. There's nothing but soap these days."

On the way out she gave the boy his four hundred rupees. In the back of the rickshaw as Kumarmangalam pushed her up the long, slow hill into the city centre Lisa Durnau called for the first time on the full power of the Tablet. By the time Kumarmangalam had slipped back onto his saddle, she had her answer. Ray Power Electric Pallakad District Office had registered a hook-up to kettuvallam *Salve Vagina* registry no: 18736BG at Thekaddy, St. Thomas's Road Mooring. Supplied's name: J. Noble Boyd. Revd.

Salve Vagina.

The coastal hydrofoil did not run in the monsoon months so Lisa Durnau spent four hours leaning against the window of an air-conditioned express coach looking out at the buffalos in the village ponds and the country women swaying beneath their burdens along the raised pathways between the flooded fields and trying not to hear the dsh dshdsh on her neighbour's fileplayer earphone that was as irrefutable and annoying as Captain Pilot Beth's whistling nostril. She could not believe she had been into space. She pulled out the Tablet and thumbed through the data from the Tabernacle. Hey, she wanted to say to her *Hindi-Hits!* aisle-mate, look at this! Have you any idea what this means?

That was the question she must put to Thomas Lull. She found she was dreading that meeting. When his disappearance had crossed the subtle but distinct boundary between temporary and permanent, Lisa Durnau had often imagined what she might say if, Elvis-like, she bumped into Thomas Lull in some hypermarket aisle or airport duty-free. It was easy to come up with smart lines when you knew you would never have to use them. Now every kilometre through the rain and dripping palm trees brought that impossible meeting closer and she did not know what she was going to say. She put it away from her while she found a phatphat in the sodden whirl of people and vehicles at the wide spot in the road that was Thekkady's bus station. But as she bounced around the lagoon-sized puddles on the long straight road past the backwater the dread returned, became a fearful sickness in her stomach. She sped past an elderly man labouring through the rain on an enormous red tricycle. The phatphat driver let her off at the mooring. Lisa Durnau stood in the rain, paralysed. Then the red tricycle creaked past her, executed a right-angle turn, and bounced down the gangplank on to the rear deck.

"Well, Ms. Durnau, even though I am not sure how Professor Lull can help you, you have been frank with me and it is only proper that I should reciprocate," Dr. Ghotse says. He shuffles out into the rain to search in the boot of his red tricycle and returns with a sheet of paper, folded and soggy. "If you please."

It's an e-mail printout. *Amar Mahal Hotel, Manasarovar Ghat, Varanasi. My Dear Dr. Darius. Well, it's not that little dive school I promised myself. Against all your advice, I'm in the black north with Aj. Asthma girl, remember? Deep mystery here—never could resist a mystery. Last place on earth I should be—already been caught up in a small railroad incident you might have read about—but could you ease my sojourn in hell by forwarding the rest of my stuff to this address? I will reimburse you by BACS transfer.*

There followed a list of books and recordings including the Schubert nestling down the side of the cushion.

"Aj?"

Dr. Ghotse corrects her pronunciation. "A young lady Professor Lull met at a club. He taught her a technique to control her asthma."

"Buteyko method?"

"Indeed so. Most alarming. I would not professionally recommend it. He was most perturbed that this young woman knew who he was."

"Stop. I'm not the first?"

"I doubt she was the operative of any government."

Lisa Durnau shivers though it is clammy warm in the humid cabin. She thumbs the first image from the Tabernacle upon the Tablet and turns it on the low table to face Dr. Ghotse.

"Again, it is a poor photograph, but that is the young woman."

"Dr. Ghotse, this is also an image from the artefact inside Darnley 285."

Dr. Ghotse sits back on his divan.

"Well, Miss Durnau, as Professor Lull says in his letter, there is indeed deep mystery here."

Outside the rain finally seems to be lightening.

31

LULL

In the lawyer Nagpal's office the windows and shutters are all thrown open. The din from the street is oppressive.

"Apologies apologies," the lawyer Nagpal says showing his visitors to their cracked leather club chairs and settling himself behind his ornately carved desk. "But otherwise the heat . . . Our air-conditioning system; it is our landlord's duty to keep it in good repair. A strongly worded letter, I think. Please, some chai. Personally, I find hot chai the most refreshing beverage when the heat oppresses."

Thomas Lull disagrees but the lawyer Nagpal has rung his little bell for the office-wallah.

"I have heard it is already raining in Jharkhand." The boy serves the hot, sickly chai from a brass tray. Nagpal picks up his cup and gulps it down. Lawyer Nagpal of Nagpal, Pahelwan, and Dhavan is a man who acts older than his years. Thomas Lull has long subscribed to the theory that every human has an inner spiritual age at which they remain all their lives. He's stuck at twenty-five. This advocate is late fifties, though from his face and hands Thomas Lull pegs him at no more than thirty. "Now, how may I help you?"

"A photograph was sent from this office to my colleague here," he says.

Nagpal frowns, purses his lips in a little *oh?* Aj pushes her palmer across the desk. Thomas Lull puts the temperature in the early forties but she is cool and poised. Her tilak seems to shine in the shadowy office.

"It was sent to me on my eighteenth birthday," Aj prompts.

"Ah, I have you now!" Nagpal opens his palmer in a hand-tooled leather case, taps up briefs. Thomas Lull reads the play of lawyer's fingers, the movements of his pupils, the dilation of his nostrils. What are you scared of, lawyer Nagpal with your degrees and diplomas and certificates on the wall? "Yes, Ajmer Rao. You have come all the way from Bangalore, most extraordinary, and in these troubled times too. The photograph, I believe, is of your natural parents."

"Bullshit," says Thomas Lull.

"Sir, the photograph is of . . ."

"Jean-Yves and Anjali Trudeau. They're well known A-life researchers, I've been working with them for years. And while Aj here was theoretically being conceived, I was in daily contact with Anjali and Jean-Yves in Strasbourg. If anyone had been pregnant I would have known."

"With respect, Mr. Lull, there are modern techniques, surrogacies . . ."

"Mr. Nagpal, Anjali Trudeau never produced a viable egg in her life."

The lawyer Nagpal chews his bottom lip in distaste.

"Our questions then are: who are Aj's natural parents, and who instructed you to send that photograph? Someone is playing head-games with her."

"Much as I feel for Miss Rao's confusion, I am not at liberty to divulge that, Mr. Lull. It is a matter of client confidentiality."

"I can always talk to them directly. I'm only here as a formality."

"I do not think so, sir. Pardon my bluntness, but Mr. and Mrs. Trudeau are deceased."

Thomas Lull feels the dark, sweating, cluttered room turn inside out.

"What?"

"Sir, I regret to inform you that Mr. and Mrs. Trudeau died in an apartment fire yesterday morning. There is a question over the circumstances, the police are investigating."

"Are you saying they were murdered?"

"I can say, sir, that the incident has attracted the attention of the government department known informally as the Ministry."

"The Krishna Cops?"

"As you say. The apartment was alleged to be the location of the Badrinath sundarban."

"They were working with the datarajas?"

Lawyer Nagpal spreads his hands.

"I could not possibly speculate."

Thomas Lull speaks slowly and clearly so the lawyer can make no mistake about what he means.

"Did the Badrinath sundarban instruct you to send the photograph to Aj?"

"Mr. Lull, I have a mother, brothers, a married sister with three children, gods be kind to her. I am a public notary and recorder of oaths in a less than salubrious location. There are forces at work here I do not have to understand to know are powerful. I merely follow my instructions and bank my fee. I cannot help you with any of your questions, please understand. But I can comply with one final instruction from my clients."

Mr. Nagpal rings his bell, chips an order in Hindi at his babu who returns with a book-sized case wrapped in Varanasi silk. Mr. Nagpal unwraps the hand-woven silk square. Inside are two objects, a photograph and a carved wooden jewellery box. He passes the photograph to Aj. It is such a photograph as families take, a mother, a father, a girl, smiling by the waterside with the towers of a bright city behind them. But the man and the woman are dead now, and the girl blinking in the bright morning has a shaved scalp scarred with the evidence of recent surgery.

Aj runs her hand over her hair.

"I am sorry for your trouble," Lawyer Nagpal says. "This is the second part of what they wished you to have." He presents the little jewel box for Aj to open. Thomas Lull smells sandalwood as she unfastens the brass catch.

"My horse!"

Between her thumb and forefinger is the universal circle of the fiery chakra. Dancing in its centre, a white horse rears.

Beyond the cracking towers and tank farms of the East Bank the sky is obsidian, the curtain wall of a fortress ten kilometres high. From where he sits on the upper tiers of Dasashvamedha ghat, Thomas Lull can feel its pressure in his sinuses. Hazy yellow sun covers city and river. The wide sand shoals of the eastern shore where the nagas perform their asceticisms are white against the black sky. A flaw of wind chases marigold petals across Dasashvamedha ghat, sets the boats rocking on the river. Even in Kerala Thomas Lull never knew humidity like it. He imagines the heat, the humidity, the chemicals coiling around his airways, tightening.

The nose for breathing, the mouth for talking.

The mood in the city is tight, coiling. Heat and war. The anger of Sarkhand has boiled over into the streets. Burnings. Deaths. The nutes first; then the Muslims, as ever. Now Mahindra pickups ram-raid American fast-food chains in the New Town and karsevaks pour alcofuel over blasphemous cow burgers. For the first time Thomas Lull feels self-conscious of his accent and skin.

The army officer had taken his passport and left him alone in the windowless storeroom in the small village medical centre that the Bharati Defence Forces were using to process refugees from the train attack. Thomas Lull sat on the metal chair under the single shadeless lightbulb suddenly scared, suddenly naked while in the next room men made loud, rattling phone calls in Hindi about his passport. He had never consciously believed in the American grace, that that little booklet made him a global aristocrat, cloaked him with invulnerability, but he had held it up like a crucifix, caught between incomprehensible clashing forces. He had not thought that it might make him a player, at best a running-dog of hostile power, at worst a spy. Thomas Lull was three hours in the room while keypads rattled as army babus took down testimonies from a torrent of voices and women keened on the street outside. Then a chubby subaltern with a neat blue tilak down the centre of his tongue from licking the point of his pen ripped out dockets, stamped pages, and handed Thomas Lull a rustle of papers, pink blue and yellow, and his solid black passport.

"This is a travel permit, this is your temporary ID, this is your ticket," he pointed out with his pen. "The buses leave from the front of the Durga temple; your bus number is 19. May I express the regrets of the Bharati government for your hardships and wish you a safe onward journey." Then he beckoned with his pen to the women behind him in the line.

"My travelling companion, a young woman, with a Vishnu tilak?"

"All buses, all people in front of the temple. God-speed you sir."

The subaltern flicked Thomas Lull off the end of his pen. The village street was lit by vehicle headlights. Thomas Lull walked between rows of bodies, laid out close as lovers to each other. By the time he was half way to the white buses the army had run out of body bags and the dead lay uncovered. He tried not to breathe in the stench of charred flesh. Army medics were already at work stripping out the corneas.

"Aj!" he shouted. Camera-flashes flickered, camera lights bobbed as news crews sought shots. Behind the forest of sound booms, satellite uplink trucks unfolded dishes like poppies blooming. "Aj!"

"Lull! Lull!" A pale hand waved from a bus window. The tilak caught the light. Lull pushed through the crowd, turning his back to cameras with American logos on them. "You were so long," she said as he piled down beside her.

"They wanted to make sure I wasn't an agent of a foreign power. What about you? I'd've thought, with that display . . ."

"Oh, they let me go at once. I think they were afraid."

The bus drove through the remains of the night and all the next day. Hours blurred into heat and flatness and villages with painted advertisements for water and underwear and the constant blaring of vehicle horns. What Thomas Lull saw were red-eyed corpses laid out on the village street and Aj on one knee, her hand outstretched and the enemy robots obeying.

"I have to ask you . . ."

"I saw their gods and asked them. That is what I told the soldiers. I do not think they believed me, but then they seemed afraid of me."

"Robots have gods?"

"Everything has a god, Mr. Lull. You just have to find it."

At the next toilet stop Thomas Lull bought a newspaper to convince himself that all his shards of impression and experience were real memory. Bharati Hindutva extremists had attacked an Maratha Rail shatabdi in a regrettable excess of patriotic zeal (the editorial said) but the brave jawans of the Allahabad division had driven back the savage and unjustified Awadhi retaliatory strike.

However liberal the Westerner, there is always some part of India that shocks. For Thomas Lull it is this buried stratum of rage and hatred that can one day take a neighbour of a lifetime into his neighbour's house to cut him open with an axe and burn his wife and children in their beds, and then, when it is all done and over, to go back to the neighbourly life. Even on the ghats amongst the worshippers and the dhobi-wallahs and the hawkers chasing the rag-end of the tourist trade, the mob is only a shout away. There is no explanation for it in his philosophy.

"There was a time I thought I might work with the sundarbans," Thomas Lull says. "That was after I testified to the Hamilton Inquiry. They were right to be suspicious; half the idea behind Alterre was to set up an alternative ecosystem where intelligence could evolve on its own terms. I don't think I could have stayed in the States. I like to think I'd have been tough and noble under persecution, like Chomsky in the Bush Wars, but I'm a complete pussy cat when it comes to authority with guns. What I was scared of was being ignored. Writing and speaking and talking and not one blind soul paying attention to me. Locked in the white room. Shouting into your pillow. That's worse than death. That's what did Chomsky in the end. Smothered by inanity.

"I knew what they had over here, everyone who did anything with aeai knew what they were hiding in their cyberabads. In the month before the Hamilton Act came into force they were pushing bevabytes of information out of the United States. Washington had all the Indian states under incredible pressure to ratify the International Agreement on Artificial Intelligence Registration and Licencing. And I thought, they might at least have someone to speak for them, an American voice, making the other side of the argument.

"Jean-Yves and Anjali wanted me to come—they knew that even if Awadh went with Washington the best they could ever get from the Ranas was a halfway house licensing deal to keep the soapis sweet. And then my wife walked out on me with half of my worldly goods and I thought I was together and sophisticated and cool and I was none of those things. I was the opposite of everything I thought I was. I was crazy for some time, I think. I'm not out of it yet. Jesus, I cannot believe they are dead."

"What do you think they were working on in the sundarban?"

Aj sits cross-legged on a wooden level where the priests celebrate the nightly puja to Ganga Devi. Devotees look long at her tilak, a Vaishnavite in the heart of Siva's lordship.

"I think they had a Generation Three in there."

Aj toys with a twist of marigold petals.

"Have we reached the singularity?"

Thomas Lull starts at the abstruse word falling like a pearl from Aj's lips.

"Okay mystery girl, what do you understand by singularity?"

Doesn't it mean the theoretical point where aeais become first as intelligent as humans, then rapidly leave them behind?"

"My answer is yes and no. Yes, there are undoubtedly Generation Three aeais out there that are every bit as alive and aware and filled with sense of self as I am. But they aren't going to reduce us all to slavery or pethood or just nuke us because they perceive we're in competition with them for the same ecological niche; that's Hamilton's thinking, and it's not thinking at all. That's the 'no' part of the answer: they are intelligent but not as humans are intelligent. Aeai is alien intelligence. It's a response to specific environmental conditions and stimuli, and that environment is CyberEarth, where the rules are very very different from RealEarth. First rule of CyberEarth: information cannot be moved, it must be copied. In RealEarth, physically moving information is a piece of piss; we do it every time we stand up, carrying this sense-of-self-ware around in our heads. Aeais can't do that, but they can do one thing we can't. They can copy themselves. Now, what that does to your sense of self, I don't know, and technically speaking, I can't know. It's a philosophical impossibility for us to be in two places at the same time; not for aeais. For them, the philosophical implications of what you do with your spare copy when you move yourself to a new matrix is of fundamental importance. Does a complete self die, or is it just part of a greater gestalt? Already we're getting into a completely alien mind-set. So, even if aeais have hit the singularity and are racing away into IQs in the millions, what does that actually mean in human terms? How do we measure it? What do we measure it against? Intelligence is not an absolute thing, it's always environment specific. Aeais don't need to manufacture stock market crashes or set the nukes flying or trash our planetary web to put humanity in its place; there is no competition, these things have no meaning or relevance in their universe. We're neighbours in parallel universes and as long as we live as neighbours we will live peacefully to our mutual advantage. But the Hamilton Acts mean we've risen up against our neighbours and are driving them into annihilation. At some point they will fight, like anything will when its back's against the wall, and that will be a terrible, bitter battle. There's no battle more terrible than when the gods fight and we are each other's gods. We're gods to the aeai. Our words can rewrite the appearance of any part of their world. That's the reality of their universe; nonmaterial entities that can unsay any part of reality are as much the fabric of it as quantum uncertainty and M-Star theory is of ours. We used to live in a universe that thought like that once; spirits and ancestors and everything was held together by the divine word. We need each other to maintain our worlds."

"Maybe there is another way," Aj says softly. "Maybe there doesn't have to be a war."

Thomas Lull feels a stir of wind on his face, a distant tiger-purr of thunder. It is coming.

"Wouldn't that be something?" he says. "Wouldn't that be a first? No no, this is the Age of Kali." He stands up, dusts wind-blown sand and human ashes from his clothes. "Come on then." He extends a hand to Aj. "I'm going to the Computer Science department at the University of Varanasi."

Aj tilts her head to one side.

"Professor Naresh Chandra is in today but you will have to hurry. You will forgive me if I do not accompany you, Lull."

"Where are you going?" Spoken like a piqued boyfriend.

"The Bharati National Records Office on Raja Bazaar Road is open until five o'clock. As other methods have failed, I feel a mitochondrial DNA profile will tell me who my real parents are."

The rising wind ruffles her boy-short hair, flaps Thomas Lull's pant legs like flags. Down on the suddenly choppy water rowboats swarm for shore.

"Are you sure about this?"

Aj turns her ivory horse over and over in her fingers.

"Yes. I have thought about it and I have to know."

"Good luck then." Without thought, against will, Thomas Lull hugs her. She is slight and bony and so so light that he fears he might snap her like glass rods.

Thomas Lull prides himself on possessing the male gift for visiting somewhere once and forever after being able to navigate infallibly around it. Which is how he is lost within two minutes of stepping out of the phatphat onto the dense green lawns of the University of Bharat Varanasi. It had been eighty percent building site when Thomas Lull delivered his lecture to the nascent Computer Science department.

"Excuse me," he asks a mali inexplicably wearing gumboots in the greatest drought in Bharat's brief history. The clouds pile deep and dark behind the light, airy faculty buildings, flickering with edges of lightning. The hot wind is strong now, the electric wind. It could sweep this frail university up into the clouds. Let it rain let it rain let it rain, Thomas Lull prays as he runs up stairs past the chowkidar and through the double doors into the department office where eight young men and one middle-aged woman fan themselves with soapi magazines. He picks the woman.

"I'd like to see Professor Chandra."

"Professor Chandra is unavailable at present."

"Oh, I have it on the highest authority that he is sitting there in his office. If you could just buzz him."

"This is most irregular," the secretary says. "Appointments must be made in advance through this office and written into the appointments diary before ten AM on a Monday."

Thomas Lull parks his ass on the desk. He's getting his thunderhead on him but knows that the only ways to deal with Indian bureaucracy are patience, bribery, or rank. He leans over and palms on all the intercom buttons at once.

"Would you be so good as to tell Professor Chandra that Professor Thomas Lull needs to talk to him?"

Up the corridor a door opens.

32

PARVATI

It had started at the railway station. The porters were thieves and gundas, the security checks a gross discourtesy to a respectable widow from a loyal village in a peaceable district, the taxi driver had banged her case manhandling it into the boot and when he did drive took the longest route and drove fast and dodged in and out of the buses to terrify an old woman up from the country and then after half frightening her to death demanded an extra ten rupees to carry her bag up all those stairs and she had to give it to him, she could never have managed with the lungs half-coughed out of her with the terrible fumes in this city. And now the chai the cook has given her has a sour tang; there is never good clean water in this city.

Parvati Nandha shoos the sullen cook away, greets her mother with proper daughterly fervour, and has the sweeper carry her bags to the guest room and make all ready.

"I will make you a proper cup of chai, and then we will go up on to the roof."

Mrs. Sadurbhai softens like a ghee sculpture at a mela.

The sweeper announces that the room is ready. As her mother goes to inspect and unpack, Parvati busies herself with the kettle and wipes and tidies and neatens any lingerings of her humiliation at the cricket match.

"You should not have to do that," Mrs. Sadurbhai says, pushing in beside Parvati at the kettle. "The very least you should expect from a cook is that she can make a cup of chai. And that sweeper is cheating you. An exceedingly lazy girl. The dust rabbits I found under the bed. You must be firm with staff. Here." She sets a garish packet of tea on the worktop. "Something with real flavour."

They sit in the semishade of the jasmine arbour. Mrs. Sadurbhai studies the workmanship, then the neighbouring rooftops.

"You are a little overlooked here," she comments, pulling her dupatta over her head. The evening rush has started, conversation competes with car horns. A radio blasts chart hits from a balcony across the street. "It will be nice when it grows up a little. You will have more privacy then. Of course you cannot expect the kind of privacy you would get out in the Cantonment with full-size trees, but this will be quite pleasant of an evening, if you're still here."

"Mother," Parvati says, "why are you here?"

"A mother cannot visit her own daughter? Or is this some new style in the capital?"

"Even in the country it's customary to give some warning."

"Warning? What am I, a flash flood, a plague of locusts, an air raid? No, I came because I am worried about you, in this city, in this current situation; oh you message me every day but I know what I see on the television, all those soldiers and tanks and aeroplanes, and that train burning, dreadful, dreadful. And I sit here, and I look up and I see these things."

Aeaicraft patrol the edge of the monsoon, white wings catching the westering light as they bank and turn kilometres above Varanasi. They can stay up there for years, Krishan had told Parvati. Never touch the ground, like Christian angels.

"Mother, they are there to keep us safe from the Awadhis."

She shrugs.

"Ach. That is what they want you to think, but I know what I see."

"Mother, what do you want?"

Mrs. Sadurbhai hitches up the pallav of her sari.

"I want you to come home with me."

Parvati throws her hands up but Mrs. Sadurbhai cuts in and breaks her protest.

"Parvati, why take needless risks? You say you are safe here and maybe you are, but what if all these wonderful machines fail and the bombs fall on your lovely garden? Parvati, it may only be a risk the size of a grain of rice but why take any risk at all? Come back with me to Kotkhai; the Awadhi fighting machines will never find you there. It will only be for a little time, until this unpleasantness is over."

Parvati Nandha sets down her chai glass. The low sun shines into her face, and she must shade her eyes to read her mother's expression.

"What is this about really?"

"I'm not at all sure what you mean."

"I mean, you've never really thought my husband sufficiently honours me."

"Oh, but I don't, I don't, Parvati. You married within jati and that is a treasure beyond price. It just grieves me when ambitious women—no, we are speaking as we find here this evening, so I shall call them what they are, caste-jumpers: there, that's it said—when caste-jumpers flaunt their wealth and husbands and status to which they have less right than you. It hurts me, Parvati . . ."

"My husband is a highly respected and important civil servant. I know of no one who speaks of him with the slightest disrespect. I want for nothing. See, this fine garden? This is one of the most sought after government apartments."

"Yes, but government, Parvati. Government."

"I have no desire to move to Cantonment. I am content here. I also have no desire to come with you to Kotkhai in some ruse to focus my husband's attention on my needs because you do not think he appreciates me enough."

"Parvati, I never . . ."

"Oh, forgive me." The women fall silent at the third voice. Krishan stands at the head of the stairs in his cricketing best. "I need to, ah, check the drip irrigator."

"Mother, this is Krishan, my garden designer. All this is the work of his hands."

Krishan namastes.

"A remarkable transformation," Mrs. Sadurbhai says grudgingly.

"Often the finest gardens grow from the least promising soils," Krishan says and leaves to fiddle purposelessly with the pipes and taps and regulators.

"I don't like him," Mrs. Sadurbhai whispers to her daughter. Parvati catches Krishan's eye as he lights little terra-cotta oil cups along the bed borders as day ebbs from the sky. The tiny flames gutter and sway in the wind that has sprung up among the rooftops. Thunder growls in the dark east. "He has a familiar way with him. He gives looks. It is never good when they give looks."

He has come to see me, Parvati thinks. He has followed me here to be with me, to keep me safe from the tongues of the caste-jumping women, to be strong for me when I am in need.

The garden is transformed into a constellation of lamps. Krishan bows to the ladies of the house.

"I'll bid you a good night and I hope to find you well in the morning."

"You should have him pick up those apricot stones," Mrs. Sadurbhai throws after Krishan as he goes down the stairs. "They will only attract monkeys."

33

VISHRAM

Marianna Fusco really does have the most magnificent nipples, Vishram thinks as she heaves herself out of the pool and drips across the tiles to the sunlounger. He traces them through wet lycra; round and hand-filling, pores puckered into little subnipples, textured, satisfying. The cold water has brought them up like champagne corks.

"Ah God, that's great," Marianna Fusco declares, shaking out her wet hair and knotting a silk wrap around her waist. She flops weightily into the chair beside Vishram, leans back, slides on shades. Vishram motions for the waiter to pour coffee.

He hadn't meant to move into the same hotel as his legal advisor. War had put suites at a premium; every hotel parking lot in Varanasi was full of satellite uplink vans, every bar full of foreign correspondents catching up on the boring bits between conflicts. He had not even realised it was the same hotel at which he had left her after the disastrous first night limo ride until he saw her descending in an elevator through the glass atrium. He knew the cut of that suit anywhere.

The suite is unexceptionably comfortable but Vishram can't sleep in it. He misses the hypnagogic tendril patterns of his bedroom's painted roof. He misses the morning-glory comfort of Shanker Mahal's erotic carvings. He misses sex. Vishram watches the sweat bead Marianna's arm before the water drops have even dried.

"Vish." She's never called him that before. "I mightn't be staying for much longer."

Vishram sets his coffee cup down carefully so no rattle may betray his dismay.

"Is it the war?"

"I've had calls from head office; the Foreign Office advice is for nonessential British passport holders to leave, and my family's worried too, especially after the rioting . . ." Her family, that brawling constellation of partnerships and remarriages among five different races across the red brick terracelands of South London. The front of her swimsuit has dried in the sun but it's still damp and bodyhugging next to the chair. Vishram has always had a notion for onepieces. Conceal to appeal. Its wet cling emphasises the muscled curve of Marianna Fusco's lower back. Vishram feels his cock stir in his Varanasi silk trunks. He would love to take her there and then down into the pool, legs hooked over in the lapping water with the roar of the morning rush hour bouncing over the wall from the street beyond.

"I have to tell you, Vish, I didn't really want this brief. I had projects I was working on."

"It's not really my idea of a gig either," Vishram says. "I had a good career going as a stand-up comedian. I was funny. I made people laugh. That's not a thing to brush off: oh, Vishram, what silliness are you up to now? Well stop it right now and come here, there's important stuff for you to do. And do you know what the worst part of it is, the part that really makes me choke? I love it. I fucking love it. I love this corporation and the people who work for it and what they're trying to do and the things they've got out at that research place. That's what really annoys me, the bastard didn't give a fuck about my feelings but he was right all along. I will fight to save this company and that's with or without you and if it's going to be without you, if you are going to leave me, I need to clear a couple of things with you and the first is that I adore the sight of your nipples through that swimsuit and the second is there is not a moment at a meeting or a briefing or at the desk or on the phone that I do not think about sex with you in the pointy end of a BharatAir 375."

Marianna Fusco's hands are flat on the armrests. She looks dead ahead, eyes invisible behind her Italian shades.

"Mr. Ray."

Oh fuck.

"Come on then."

Marianna Fusco is professional and roused enough not to coo at the size of Vishram's penthouse as they stumble through the door, quaking with lust. He just about remembers to undress the proper way, the gentleman's way, from the bottom up; then she whips off her silk sarong and comes for him across the room, twisting the translucent fabric into a rope and tying it into a chain of large knots, like a thugee. The stretchy swimsuit fabric takes some ripping but it's what she wants and Vishram is only too eager to oblige and he loves the feel of it in his fists, tearing apart, exposing her. He tries to push into her vagina, she rolls away saying *no no no, I'm not letting that thing in there.* She lets him get three fingers in both orifices and blasphemes and thrashes on the mat by the foot of the bed. Then she helps him fold the silk scarf knot by careful knot up inside her and she straddles him, big nipples silhouetted against the yellow storm-light, handing him until he comes and after he's come she rolls onto her back and makes him wank her clitoris with the ball of his big toe and when she is swearing and beating her fists off the carpet she rolls into the yoga plough position and he wraps the free end of the scarf around his hand and slowly pulls it out, each knot accompanied by a blaspheme and full-body thrash.

By the time either of them can speak again it is twenty past eleven on the Noughties retro wall-clock and they lie side by side on the mat drinking minibar malt from the bottle and thrilling to the flickers and growls of approaching thunder.

"I will never, ever be able to look at that silk wrap the same way," Vishram says. "Where did you learn that from?"

"Who said I had to be taught?" Marianna Fusco rolls on to her side. "It's you Indians have this guru thing."

The room flashlights blue to a stronger pulse of lightning. Vishram thinks of the photograph on the cover page of his morning news-site; the faces white in the camera flash, the man, open mouthed, the alien, sexlessly beautiful nute with the bank notes in yts hand. What do they do? he thinks. What do they think they can do? And whatever they can do, does it deserve the destruction of a man's career and family? He had always thought of and practised sex as one thing, one set of actions and reactions whatever the sexual orientation but on the floor with Marianna Fusco among the shreds of her swimsuit and the knotted snake of a scarf he had lovingly pulled out of her colon he realises it is a nation of many erogenies and responses, as full of languages and cultures as India.

"Marianna," he says, staring at the ceiling. "Don't go."

"Vish." The nick again. "This time there really is something I need to tell you." She sits up. "Vish, I told you I was hired by your father to oversee the transfer of power."

"Hired, ah, right, so what does that make what we've just done?"

"You know, any real comedian I've ever known doesn't try to be funny in real life. Vish, I was hired by another company. I was hired by Odeco."

Vishram feels he is falling into the floor. Muscles go limp, his hands fall open, an unconscious Corpse Asana.

"Well, now it all makes sense, doesn't it? Soften the horny fucker before you knife him . . ."

"Hey!" Marianna Fusco sits up, leans over him. Her hair falls around her face, a soft dark silhouette against the windows. "That is not right and it is not fair. I am not a corporate . . . whore. We did not do this because it was some plot or conspiracy. Fuck you, Vishram Ray. I told you because I trusted you, because I like you, because I like sex with you. You've had your hand up my ass, how much more trust would you like?"

Vishram counts the spaces between the lightning flicker and the thunder growl. One Odeco two Odeco three Odeco four. . . . The rain is almost upon them.

"I have absolutely no idea what the hell is going on," he says to the bland, international-stylie ceiling. "Who's behind what, who's funding what, who's got a stake in what and who is working for what and why."

"You think I know any better?" Marianna Fusco says, rolling on to her side and pressing her thick dense body against Vishram's. He can feel the soft kiss of her pubic hair against his thigh. He wonders at the yonic secrets she keeps from him. "I'm a junior partner in a London corporate law firm. We do mergers, acquisitions, and hostile takeovers. We're not very good at cloak and dagger, skulduggery and conspiracy theory."

"So can you tell me, what is Odeco?"

"Odeco is an international group of venture capitalists based in various tax havens. They specialise in blue-sky technology and in what some might consider the grey economy; industries that aren't strictly illegal but have a dodgy reputation, like Darwinware. They've invested in Silicon Jungles in cyberabads all across the developing world, including a sundarban right here in Varanasi."

"And they came up with the money for the accelerator at the research centre. I met Chakraborty, or rather, Chakraborty met me."

"I know. Mr. Chakraborty is my liaison here in Varanasi. You can believe me or not, but Odeco wants the zero-point project to succeed."

"He told me he was delighted I was going to run a full demo. The only people I told that to were our friends from EnGen."

"EnGen is not Odeco."

"Then how did Chakraborty know about the trial?"

Marianna Fusco chews her top lip.

"You'll have to ask Chakraborty. I'm not authorised to tell you. But believe me, anything EnGen has offered you to shut down the experiment, Odeco will match it to keep it open. Match it and more."

"Good," says Vishram Ray sitting up. "Because I'm minded to take their money. Can you get me a meeting with your liaison? Provided he doesn't know already, like telepathy or something? And can we do this again, real real soon?"

Marianna Fusco tosses back her still-damp and chlorine-perfumed hair.

"Can I borrow a bathrobe? I don't think I should go down in the lift like this."

Forty minutes later Vishram Ray is showered, shaved, suited, and humming to himself as he rides down through the glass roof of the hotel atrium. The car waits among the satellite vans. The silk wrap soaks in the Jacuzzi, still in its knots, all the better to scandalise the prying room staff.

Marigolds on black water. In the open boat Vishram feels the wall of cloud like the hammer of God, raised over him. The wind from the feet of the monsoon stirs the river into a chop. Buffalo press close to shore, nostrils lifted out of the water, flared, sensing the change of the season. Along the ghats women bathers struggle to hold their saris with modesty. It is one of his nation's perennial contradictions that the culture that wrote and illustrated the Kama Sutra should be so glacially prudish. People in cold, wet Christian Glasgow burned more ardently. He suspects what he has just done with Marianna Fusco would get him twenty in chokey in back-country Bihar.

The boatman is a fifteen-year-old with a frozen wide smile, struggling against the frets and flows. Vishram feels unclad and exposed to the lightning. Already the factories across the river have put on their lights.

"I hate to say it but EnGen got me a tilt-jet? To a tiger sanctuary? With armed guards and a really good lunch. And their flight crew was a lot better looking than him."

"Hm?" Chakraborty says. He stands in the middle of the boat absently watching the passing panoply of shore life. Vishram wishes he wouldn't do that. He remembers an old number from the College Dram. Soc. production of *Guys and Dolls*. Sit down you're rocking the boat. *And the devil will drag you under . . .* Heavy on the Christian sin and judgement and damnation today Vishram, he thinks.

"I said, it's kind of choppy."

Rowing-boy grins. He has a clean blue shirt and very white teeth.

"Ah yes, a little turbulent, Mr. Ray." Chakraborty touches a finger to his lips, then shakes it at the gleaming ghats. "Do you not find it comforting, knowing where you will end, on these steps, by this shore, before the eyes of all the people?"

"Can't say it's a thing I've thought too much about." Vishram reaches for the gunwales as the boat rocks.

"Really? But you should, Mr. Ray. I think a little about death every day. It is most focusing. It is a great reassurance that we leave the particular and rejoin the universal. That I think is the moksha of Ganga. We rejoin the river of history like a drop of rain, our stories told and woven into the stream of time. Tell me—you have lived in the West—is it true that they burn their dead in secret, hidden away from everyone as if they are a thing to be ashamed of?"

Vishram remembers the funeral in a grimy sandstone district of Glasgow. He had not known the woman well—she had been a flatmate of a girl he had been having sex with because she had a name as an up-and-coming director in the Dram. Soc.—but he did recall the sense of shock when he learned she had been killed in a climbing accident in Glencoe. And he does recall the sense of horror in the crematorium; the muffled grief, the eulogy by a stranger that had got her friends' names wrong, the taped Bach as the sealed casket lurched on the dais and then slowly sank out of sight to the furnace below.

"It is true," he says to Chakraborty. "They can't look at it because it scares them. For them, it is the end of everything."

On the ash-strewn river steps the process of death and moksha wheels on. By the waterline a pyre has collapsed, the head and shoulders of the dead loll out, strangely untouched by the flames. That is a burning man, Vishram thinks. The wind swirls smoke and ash over the burning ghat. Vishram Ray watches the burning man slump on his pyre, cave in, and collapse in sparks and charcoal and he thinks that Chakraborty is right; it is better by far to end here, death in the midst of life, to leave the particular and rejoin the universal.

"Mr. Chakraborty, I would like a very large sum of money from you," Vishram Ray says.

"How much do you need?"

"Enough to buy out Ramesh's part of the company."

"That will require a sum in the region of three hundred billion rupees. I can give you that in US dollars, if you require."

"I just need to know that that money could be available to me."

Mr. Chakraborty does not hesitate.

"It is."

"One other thing. Marianna told me there was something I should ask you, that only you could answer."

"What is that question, Mr. Ray?"

"What is Odeco, Mr. Chakraborty?"

The boat-boy idles on his oars, letting the current carry the skiff past the burnings to the capsized temple of Scindia ghat, leaning into the cracked mud.

"Odeco is one of a series of shell companies for the Generation Three Artificial Intelligence known informally as Brahma."

"I'm going to ask you that question again," Vishram says.

"And you will receive the same answer."

"Come on, man." The Bengali might as well have said Jesus or James Bond or Lal Darfan. Chakraborty turns to Vishram.

"What is it about my answer that you do not believe?"

"Generation Three aeais, that's science fiction."

"I assure you my employer is quite actual. Odeco is indeed a venture capital holding company, it just happens that the venture capitalist is an artificial intelligence."

"The Hamilton Acts, the Krishna Cops . . ."

"There are spaces where an aeai may live. Especially in something like the international financial markets which demand loose regulation to exploit their so-called market freedoms. These aeais are not like our kind of intelligence at all; they are distributed, in many places at once."

"You're telling me that this . . . Brahma . . . is the stock market, come to life?"

"The international financial markets have used low-level aeais to buy and sell since the last century. As the complexity of the financial transactions spiralled, so did that of the aeais."

"But who would design something like that?"

"Brahma is not designed, no more than you, Mr. Ray. It evolved."

Vishram shakes his head. The heat at the edge of the monsoon is terrible, crazy, draining of all sense and energy.

"Brahma?" he says weakly.

"A name. A title. It means nothing. Identity is a much larger and looser construct in CyberEarth. Brahma is a geographically dispersed entity across many nodes and many subcomponents, lower-level aeais, that may not realise they are part of a larger sentience."

"And this . . . Generation Three . . . is more than happy to give me one hundred million US dollars."

"Or more. You must understand, Mr. Ray, to an entity such as Brahma, making money is the easiest thing there is. It is no harder than breathing is for you."

"Why, Mr. Chakraborty?"

Now the lawyer sits. The boat-boy reaches for the oars to keep the little shell from spilling its passengers into the Ganga water that washes those it receives free from karma.

"My employer wishes to see the zero-point project safeguarded and brought to fruition."

"Again, why?"

Mr. Chakraborty shrugs slowly and expressively inside his well-cut black suit.

"This is an entity with the financial power to destroy entire economies. I am not privy to that kind of intelligence, Mr. Ray. Its understanding of the human world is partial. In the financial markets that are its ecological niche, Brahma as far exceeds human intellect as we do snakes but if you were to speak with it directly, it would seem to you naïve, neurotic; even a little autistic."

"I have to ask this, does . . . did . . . my father know?"

Chakraborty sways his head. Affirmation.

"The money can be transferred into your account within the hour."

"And I have to decide who I trust; a gang of American corporate raiders who want to shred my company or an aeai that just happens to be named after a god and can erase every bank account on the planet."

"Succinctly put sir."

"Not really a choice, is it?"

Vishram gestures to the boat-boy. He leans into his left oar and turns the little skiff on the black water back towards the great Dasashvamedha Ghat. Vishram thinks he feels a spot of rain on his lip.

34

NAJIA, TAL

A whisper: "He can't stay here"

The air is fetid and oppressive but the figure on the mattress sleeps the sleep of Brahma.

"Yt's not a he, yt's an yt," Najia Askarzadah whispers back to Bernard. They stand in the door of the darkened room like parents watching over a colicky child. The light fades by the minute, the humidity climbs. The veils of gauze hang straight, heavy, gravity-bound.

"I don't care, yt's not staying here."

"They tried to kill yt, Bernard," Najia hisses. It had seemed bold and brilliant when she took the moped across the polo lawn past the yelling malis and along the verandah, dodging tables and gap-yearers to Bernard's room. Somewhere to hide. Somewhere they would never connect but was close. Bernard had not said a word as they stumbled through his door. The nute had been half-conscious, raving something about adrenaline in yts strange, heavily accented voice. Yt was out by the time they got it to the bed. Bernard had taken yts boots off, then stepped back, scared. Then they stood in the door and argued in whispers.

"And you make me a target now as well," Bernard hisses. "You don't think. You run in and shout and expect everyone to cheer because you're the hero."

"Bernard, I've always known that the only ass you're ultimately interested in is your own, but that is a new low." But the barb hits and hooks. She loves the action. She loves the dangerous seduction that it all looks like drama, like action movies. Delusion. Life is not drama. The climaxes and plot transitions are coincidence, or conspiracy. The hero can take a fall. The good guys can all die in the final reel. None of us can survive a life of screen drama. "I don't know where else to go," she confesses weakly. He goes out shortly afterwards. The closing door sends a gust of hot air, stale with sweat and incense, through the rooms. The hanging nets and gauzes billow around the figure curled into a tight foetus. Najia chews at scaly skin on her thumb, wondering if she can do anything right.

She feels again the crack of the thugee's ribs as she slammed into him; the recoil through the frame of the bike and her hips as the kar-sevak assassin slid away across the platform. She starts to shake in the stifling, dim room. She cannot hold herself, she finds a chair and sits, hugging her arms close against the cold from within. It is all madness and you walked into it. A nute and a Swedish girl reporter. You can be disappeared from Varanasi's ten million and no one will blink.

She turns her chair to cover both the door and the bedroom window. She angles the wooden louvres so she can see out but a bad man will find it hard to see in. She sits and watches the slats of light move across the floor.

Najia comes out of sleep with a start. Noise. Movement. She freezes, then dives for the kitchen and its French cooking knives. She burst the door open, a figure at the refrigerator whirls, snatches up a knife. Him. Yt.

"Sorry sorry," yt says in yts strange, child's voice. "Is there anything to eat? I am so hungry."

There are half-things, nibbles and a bottle of champagne in Bernard's refrigerator. Of course. The nute sniffs at them, grazes from the shelf.

"Excuse excuse," yt says. "I am so hungry. The hormones . . . I pushed them too hard."

"Can I make you tea?" Najia says, the rescuing heroine still needing a role to play.

"Chai, yes, chai, wonderful."

They sit on the mattress with the little glasses. Yt likes it European style, black without sugar. Najia starts at every shadow on the shutters.

"There are not enough thanks . . ."

"I don't deserve them. I got you into it in the first place."

"You said that at the station, yes. If not you, it would have been someone else. They might not have felt so guilty. Was it guilt?"

This is the closest Najia Askarzadah has been in her life to a nute. She knows of them and what they are and how they come to be and what they can do with themselves and even some understanding of what they enjoy of each other and has the proper Scandinavian acceptance-cool, but this Tal smells different. She knows it is the things they can do with their hormones and neurochemicals but she is afraid that Tal will sense it and think it is neutrophobia.

"I remembered," she says. "I saw the pictures and I remembered where I had seen you before."

Tal frowns. In the golden gloaming among the mesh fronds it is a deeply alien expression.

"At Indiapendent," she volunteers.

Tal holds yts head in yts hands, closes yts eyes. Yts lashes are long and very beautiful to Najia.

"This is hurting me. I don't know what to think."

"I was doing an interview with Lal Darfan. Satnam took me around. Satnam gave me the photographs."

"The trishul!" Tal exclaims. "Chuutya! He set us both up! Ai!" Yt starts to shake, tears well, yts holds yts hands up like leper's claws. "My Mama Bharat, they thought it was me; the wrong flat . . ." The shaking builds into heaving sobs, torn up from exhaustion and shock. Najia creeps away and makes fresh chai until she hears the keening cries subside. For an Afghan she has a northern European fear of big emotion.

"More chai?"

Tal has the sheet wrapped around yt. Yt nods. The glass shakes in yts hand.

"How did you know I would be at the station?"

"Journalistic hunch," Najia Askarzadah says. She wants to touch yts face, yts so bare, so tender scalp. "It's what I would have done."

"Your journalistic hunches are powerful things. I have been a fool! Smiling and laughing and dancing and thinking everyone loved me! The new nute in town everyone wants to know, come to the big party, come to the club . . ."

Najia reaches out to touch, to reassure and warm. Then she finds Tal pulled into her breast, her cheek brushing its smooth, oiled head. It is like hugging a cat, all bone and tension. Her fingers brush the dimples on yts arm, like rows of symmetrical insect bites. Najia recoils.

"No, there, please," Tal says. She gently pushes the spot, feels fluids move under the skin. "And, please, here?" Yts fingers guide hers to a place near the wrist. "And here." A hand's breadth down from the elbow. The nute shudders in her embrace. Yts breathing steadies. Yts muscles tighten. Yt gets shakily to yts feet, moves nervously around the room. Najia can smell the edgy tension.

Najia says, "I can't imagine how you live, being able to choose your emotions."

"We don't choose our emotions, just our reactions. It is . . .

intense. We don't live much over sixty." Tal is pacing now, fretting, a caged mongoose, glancing through the shutter slats, snapping them closed again.

"How can you . . . ?"

"Make that choice? It's long enough for beauty."

Najia shakes her head. Unbelievable on unbelievable. Tal bangs yts fist against the wall.

"Fool! I should die I should die I am too stupid to live."

"You are not the only one, I was stupid too, thinking I had a special line to N. K. Jivanjee."

"You met Jivanjee?"

"I spoke to him, on the video, when he set up the meeting where Satnam gave me the photographs."

A shadow falls across the shutters. Nute and woman freeze. Tal slowly lowers ytself until it is beneath the line of the windowsill. Yt beckons for Najia to join it against the wall. Listening with her whole body, Najia crawls across the matting through the planes of gauze. Then a woman's voice speaks German. Najia's stomach loosens. For a moment she thought she might have vomited from fear.

"We must get out of Bharat. They've seen you with me," Tal whispers. "We are the same now. We have to buy safe passage."

"Should we not go to the police?"

"Do you know nothing about how this country works? Sajida Rana owns the police and she wants me for a traitor, and the police she doesn't own belong to Jivanjee. We need something that will give us enough value to be protected. You said you talked to Jivanjee on the video. I presume you've enough intelligence to have kept it. Show me. There may be something there."

They sit by side against the wall. Najia holds up the palmer. Her hand shakes; Tal grasps her wrist, steadying her.

"This is not a very good model," yt says.

The volume is painfully loud as Najia plays back the video chip.

Out in the club tennis balls pop and tock. On the screen the undulations of N. K. Jivanjee's kalamkari-hung pavilion seem a divine inversion of this dim, overheated bedroom choked with fear.

"Freeze freeze freeze!"

Najia's thumb fumbles the control.

"What is this?"

"It is N. K. Jivanjee."

"I know this stupid. Where is it from?"

"It is his office, maybe his private apartment, it could even be his rath yatra, I don't know."

"Lies lies lies," Tal hisses. "I do know. That is not the private apartment or rath yatra or office of Mr. N. K. Jivanjee. That is the marriage chamber of Aparna Chawla and Ajay Nadiadwala for the wedding of the year on *Town and Country*. I designed those kalamkaris myself."

"A stage set?"

"My stage set. For a scene that hasn't been shot yet."

Najia Askarzadah feels her eyes widen. She wishes she had a subdermal menu she could call up to wash away her paralysing disbelief in a rinse of neurotransmitters.

"No one's ever met N. K. Jivanjee face to face," she says.

"Our passport," Tal says. "I have to get into Indiapendent. We have to go now, right now."

"You can't go like that, they'll see you a kilometre off, we have to get you a disguise . . ." Then the cluck of tennis balls and the shouts of the players fall silent all at once. Tal and Najia dive and roll across the room as the shadows touch the shutters. Voices. Not German. Not female. Crouching, Najia wheels the moped from the hall into the kitchen. She squats on one side, Tal on the other. They know what they have to wait for though it is the scariest wait in the world. Click click. Then the bedroom explodes in automatic fire. In the same instant Najia guns the little alcohol engine, throws herself on. Tal jumps up behind her. The bullets go on and on and on. Don't look back. You can never look back. She negotiates Bernard's folding table, opens the back door and bursts out into the scrubby ground behind the bar. Waiters look up as she steers between the crates of Kingfisher and Schweppes mixers.

"Out of my fucking way!" Najia Askarzadah screams. They scatter like magpies. Her peripheral vision checks two dark figures rounding the end of the accommodation wing, figures busy with their hands. "Oh Jesus," she prays and takes the moped up three concrete steps into the club kitchens. "Move move move move!" she yells as she swerves around stainless-steel coolers the size of battle tanks and sacks of rice and dal and potatoes and chefs with trays and chefs with knives and chefs with hot fat. She skid-turns on a spot of dropped ghee, smashes through the swinging door and through the dining room, down the neat aisles of linen-covered tables, blares her hooter at a couple in matching surf-Ts and shades and into the corridor. In the main hall an evening yoga class is under way: Najia and Tal bowl through, horn rasping rudely as sarvangasana shoulder stands collapse like a felled forest all around them. Through the French windows—always open to allow ventilation for the women in cotton lycra, over the gasping flower beds and through the main gates into safe anonymity of the early evening rush. Najia laughs. Thunder echoes her.

35

MR. NANDHA

Mr. Nandha's presentation of the case against Kalki takes the form of an orb floating in the 'hoek-sight of managers, at once small enough to fit beneath the dome of the human skull and so vast it envelops the Ministry's glass tower like a fist around an orchid. It rotates in the inner vision of Commissioner Arora and Director General Sudarshan bringing new vistas of information into their view. A continent-sized cityscape of pages and windows and images and frames opens up into a two-dimensional map of information. *Saraswati* is the name of the voice-over aeai, goddess of speech and communication. Over a glowing schematic of Pasta-Tikka Inc. information system, Saraswati traces the unlicensed aeai back to the neural fizz of Kashi, then ratchets up level by fractal level into the dendritic blur of the Janpur localnet, Malaviri node, sublocation Jashwant the Jain (all his little cyberpooches, ghostly skeletons knobbly with actuators and chipset arrays: Jashwant himself is a saggy blue bag of naked flesh). The next window of information is SOCO footage of the incinerated shell of the Badrinath sundarban. The hovercam bobs through blackened rooms, floating a moment over half-fleshed skeletons, processor shells melted like candles, Mr. Nandha peering into the utility box with his pen-flash. Two huddled humps of charcoal unfold into living, smiling, passport photo Westerners: Jean-Yves Trudeau; Annency, France, European Union, d.o.b. 15/04/2022; Anjali Trudeau, nee Patil, Bangalore, Karnataka. d.o.b. 25/11/2026.

"Jean-Yves and Anjali Trudeau were formerly researchers at the University of the Strasbourg in the Artificial Life laboratory of the Computer Science Department. For the past four years they have been research fellows at the Varanasi campus of the University of Bharat in the Faculty of Computer Science under Professor Chandra specialising in the application of Darwinian paradigms to protein-matrix circuitry," Saraswati says. Her voice is derived from Kalpana Dhupia on *Town and Country*.

The Trudeaus tear off from their quadrant of the sphere and hover in stationary orbit. A video window fills with the low-resolution grain of an apartment interior. Foreground of shot, a naked eighteen-year-old male, half-hard erection in right-handed grip. Attitude, leaning back, aiming it into the centre of shot. Goofy grin on face. Mid-ground Shanti Rana apartments; mid-level, window open. Balcony, some washing. Across the canyon of street, apartment windows and the rusty boxes of air-conditioners. A dart of white across the square of outside. Then the window frame fills with a peal of flame. Mr. Grippo spins round, shrieks something overloaded by the digital compression on the camera mike. Freeze-frame, skinny ass against exploding glass and flame, left hand reaching for a silk wrap.

"The Krishna system ran a traceback through all net traffic out of the area network for an hour before and after the offence," Saraswati says sweetly. "This fortunate webcam footage was obtained from an apartment immediately opposite the crime scene." The image reels back to the darting sliver of white, freezes, frames and enlarges, frames and enlarges. What it ends up with is a pile of pixels but the image manipulation packages sharpen and smear and turn the array of greyscale boxes into a flying machine, a white bird with upturned winglets and a sponson tail and a bulbous ducted fan in its belly. Graphics packs outline it, isolate it, render it in, and morph it into catalogue-spec war-porn pin-ups of an Ayappa aerial defence drone, Bharati licence version, infrared laser armed.

Data-panes pop up filled with fluttering manifests demonstrating the inexplicable hole in the military records filled by Aerial Defence Drone 7132's attack on the Badrinath sundarban. Mr. Nandha watches the fine display but his thoughts are on Professor Naresh Chandra, profoundly shocked to learn how his research colleagues had died. Most of his staff held outside consultancies—it was the nature of research funding—but a *sundarban*. He had meekly opened up their office. Mr. Nandha had already called in the search unit. He had sniffed at their many jars of coffee—a different blend for each occasion, it seemed—while the Krishna Cops went through the files. Mr. Nandha very much wished he could drink coffee without it making him feel as if his stomach was dissolving. Within minutes they had found the link.

Graphics can dazzle and seduce but every successful excommunication order reaches a point where machines fail and the prosecution rests on human drama. Mr. Nandha takes a silk handkerchief from the pocket of his Nehru jacket, unfolds it. He holds up the charred disc-image of a rearing white horse.

"Kalki," he says. "The tenth avatar of Vishnu, ender of the Age of Kali. An appropriate name, as we shall see, for an unholy contract between a private company—Odeco—the university and the Badrinath sundarban. Even Ray Power receives research funding from Odeco. But what is Odeco?"

Behind him the virtual globe unpeels into a Mercator projection of

Planet Earth. Cities, nations, islands rise out of the surface as if torn free from gravity: blue lines arrow between them, arcing high up into the virtual stratosphere. It is the money trail, the nested shell companies, the storefront offices, the holding groups and the trusts. The web of light wraps the map, the projection folds back into a sphere as a ray of light arcs up from the Seychelles and plunges ballistically towards Varanasi: a Jyotirlinga reversed, the creative light of Siva that burst from the earth of Kashi, returning after its trip around the curvature of the universe.

"Odeco is a venture capital fund domiciled in tax havens," Mr. Nandha continues. "Its methods are . . . unorthodox. It has a small shop-window office in Kashi but its preferred mode of operation is through a network of distributed aeai trading systems. The Pasta-Tikka excommunication involved just such a system, unwittingly sold on to Jashwant. It had been hybridised in Badrinath to run an illegal betting system but its operating core was always for Odeco, trading away in the background."

"To what end?" asks Arora.

"I believe to fund the creation of Kalki, a Generation Three artificial intelligence."

Murmurs from the Ministry seniors. Mr. Nandha raises a hand and the orb of information collapses in on itself. The Ministry men blink in the bright sun.

"An impressive presentation as ever, Nandha," Arora says slipping off his 'hoek.

"A stimulating but clear presentation is the most effective means of establishing the case." Mr. Nandha sets the ivory disc on the desktop.

"The Badrinath sundarban was destroyed," Sudarshan says.

"Yes, I believe by the Kalki aeai to cover its tracks."

"You hinted that Odeco also fund Ray Power. How far does this thing go? Are you suggesting that we go after Ranjit Ray? The man is a virtually a Mahatma now."

"I suggest a close investigation of his youngest son, Vishram Ray, who has taken over the Research and Development Division."

"Before you go against any Ray, you had better have a damned tight case."

"Sir, this is a Generation Three aeai investigation. All avenues should be pursued. Odeco has also funded an extraterritorial medical facility in the Free Trade Zone at Patna through an American Midwestern fund management corporation. This, too, is a subject of investigation. At present I rule nothing out."

"Odeco is your immediate target," Arora says. Behind him against the panoramic windows the storm front breaks like a black wave.

"I believe it is now the sole link to the Generation Three. I require a full airborne tactical support unit with police backup, with an immediate embargo on all information traffic in and out of Odeco. I also require . . ."

"Mr. Nandha, this country is on a war footing."

"I am aware of that, sir."

"Our military resources are fully occupied defending threats to our nation."

"Sir, this is a Generation Three aeai. It is an entity ten thousand times more intelligent than any of us. That, I believe, is a threat to our nation."

"I have to sell this to the Ministry of Defence," Arora says. "And there is the karsevak problem—they could flare up again at any time." His face looks as if he has swallowed a snake. "Nandha, when did we last request a full tactical support unit?"

"As you are aware, sir . . ."

"My colleague Sudarshan may not be aware."

"The recapture and secure incarceration of J. P. Anreddy."

"For the benefit of my colleague Sudarshan."

"Mr. Anreddy was a notorious dataraja, eight of spades on the FBI's most-wanted deck of cards. He had twice escaped from lawful custody using microscale robots to infiltrate his prison. I requested a full military support unit to recapture him and incarcerate him in specially designed maximum-surveillance panopticon unit."

"That will have come cheap," Sudarshan mutters.

"Mr. Nandha, maybe you are not yet aware, but J. P. Anreddy has filed harassment charges against you."

Mr. Nandha blinks.

"I was not aware of that, sir."

"He claims that you interrogated him without recourse to legal representation, that you used psychological torture, and that you exposed him to the threat of physical emperilment to his life."

"Might I say, sir, that at the moment Mr. Anreddy's allegations are of small concern to me. What is . . ."

"Nandha, I need to ask this. Is everything all right at home?"

"Sir, is my professionalism under question?"

But it is as if a single steel-jacketed slug has ripped out half his spine and it is the sheer shock of being dead that holds him upright.

"Your colleagues have noticed that you've been absorbed in your work—too much absorbed. Intense, I think, is their word."

"Is it not good that a man treats serious work seriously?"

"Yes, but not at the expense of other things."

"Sir, my wife is the treasure of my life. She is my dove, my bulbul, my shining light. When I go home she delights me . . ."

"Thank you, Nandha," Sudarshan hastens. "We all have much to occupy our attention these days."

"If I seem absorbed, distracted even, it is only because I believe this Generation Three to be the most serious threat this department has faced since its inception. If I may offer an opinion?"

"Your opinions are always valued here, Nandha," Arora says.

"This department was established out of our government's desire to be seen to comply with the international agreement of artificial intelligence licensing. Failing to act against a Generation Three aeai could give the Americans reason to push their Awadhi allies into invasion on the grounds that Bharat is a haven for cyber-terror."

Arora studies the grain in the desktop. Sudarshan sits back in his leather chair, fingertips bouncing off each other as he considers Mr.

Nandha's submission. Finally he says, "Excuse us one moment." Sudarshan raises a hand and the air goes flat around Mr. Nandha. The Superintendent has summoned a mute field. The two men swivel in their chairs, turning leather backs to him. Mr. Nandha presses his hands together in an unconscious namaste and looks out at the flickers of lightning pressing the edge of the monsoon. It must break. Tonight. It will break.

My shining light. My dove, my bulbul. Treasure of my life. She delights me, when I go home. When I go home. Mr. Nandha closes his eyes at the sudden clench of panic inside him. When he goes home, he does not know what he will find.

The flat air unfolds into space and sound. The conference is done.

"There is merit in your argument, Nandha. What exactly would you require?"

"I have a military briefing prepared, it can be sent at a moment's notice."

"You have this all worked out," Sudarshan says.

"It must happen, sir."

"There is no doubt of that. I will authorise your action against Odeco."

36

PARVATI, MR. NANDHA

This morning Bharti on the Breakfast Banquette wears her Serious News Face. Thanks to Raj for that analysis of what the Khan Scandal might mean for Sajida Rana and here's a message from us at *Breakfast with Bharti* to the brave jawans at Kunda Khadar: keep it up boys, you're doing a great job, we're all right behind you. But now here's the latest gupshup from *Town and Country* and all the talk is Aparna and Ajay's upcoming wedding, *the* event of the season and here's a real Bharti Breakfast Breakthrough: an exclusive peek at Aparna's dress.

Cheered, Parvati Nandha sails into the kitchen to find her mother at the stove stirring a pot of dal.

"Mother, what are you doing?"

"Making you a proper breakfast. You don't look after yourself."

"Where is Ashu?"

"Oh, that idle lump. I dismissed her. I'm certain she was stealing from you."

The early morning joy from the *Town and Country* exclusive evaporates.

"You did what?"

"I told her to go. I gave her a week's wages in lieu of notice. It was fifteen hundred rupees, I gave it to her out of my own purse."

"Mother, that was not your decision."

"Somebody had to make it. She was robbing you blind, never mind her cooking."

"Mr. Nandha requires a special diet. Have you any idea how hard it is to get a decent cook these days? By the way, have you seen my husband?"

"He left early. He is working on a most important and trying case, he says. He would not take any breakfast. You need to take him in hand and tell him that breakfast is the most important meal of the day. The brain cannot function if the stomach is not well-lined. It never ceases to amaze me how stupid supposedly educated people can be. If he had some of my dal and roti . . ."

"Mr. husband has conditions, he cannot eat this stuff."

"Nonsense. It is good, nutritious food. This bland, pale city diet is no good for him. He is withering away. You only have to look at him, pale and tired all the time, and no energy for anything, you know what I mean. He needs strong, honest country food. This morning he came in, I thought I was looking at one of those hijra/nute things on the television news this morning."

"Mother!" Parvati bangs her hands on the table. "This is my husband."

"Well, he doesn't act like it," Mrs. Sadurbhai declares. "I'm sorry, but it has to be said. A year you have been man and wife, and am I hearing ayas singing and little laughter? Parvati, I have to ask, is he working properly? You can get this checked, there are doctors specially for men. I have seen the advertisements in the Sunday papers."

Parvati stands up, shaking her head in disbelief.

"Mother . . . No. I am going up to my garden. I intend to spend the morning there."

"I have messages to run myself. I have things I need to get for the evening meal. By the way, where do you keep the cook's grocery money? Parvati?" She has already left the kitchen. "Parvati? You really should have some dal and roti."

That morning Krishan works staking up the young plants and binding the climbers and covering seedlings against the coming storm. In a single night the wall of cloud has leapt closer, to Parvati Nandha it seems about to topple over on her, crush her and her gardens and the whole government apartment building beneath its blackness. The heat and humidity appall her but she cannot go downstairs, not yet.

"You came to see me yesterday," she says. Krishan is shutting down the irrigation system.

"Yes," he says. "When I saw you get up and run out, I wondered . . ."

"What did you wonder?"

"If it was something I had said, or done, or maybe the cricket . . ."

"I loved the cricket. I would love to go back . . ."

"The team has gone home. Their government recalled them, it was not safe for them to stay, with the war."

"With the war, yes."

"Why did you leave like that?"

Parvati spreads a dhuri on the ground in the scented arbour. She arranges the cushions and bolsters and settles among them.

"Come and lie beside me."

"Mrs. Nandha . . ."

"No one is looking. Even if they were no one would care. Come and lie down beside me."

She pats the ground. Krishan kicks off his work boots and settles beside her, lying on his side, propped up on an elbow. Parvati lies on her back, hands folded across her breasts. The sky is creamy, close, a dome of heat. She feels she just needs to reach her hand out and plunge it into it. It would feel milky and thick.

"What do you think of this garden?"

"Think? It's not really for me to think, I'm just building it, that's all."

"As the man who is building it then, what do you think?"

He rolls on to his back. Parvati feels a touch of warm wind on her face.

"Of all my projects, this is the most ambitious and I think it is the one of which I am most proud. I think if people could see it, it would help me greatly in my career."

"My mother thinks it is not worthy of me," Parvati says. The thunder is closer today, intimate. "She thinks I should have trees, for privacy; rows of ashok trees like the gardens out in the Cantonment. But I would say we have privacy here, wouldn't you?"

"I would say so, yes."

"It's strange; it is like we can only have so much privacy. Out in the Cantonment you have your walled gardens and your ashok trees and your charbagh but everyone knows your business every hour of every day."

"Did something happen at the cricket?"

"I was stupid, that's all. Very stupid. I imagined caste was the same as class."

"What happened?"

"I showed myself to have no class. Or rather, not the right class. Krishan, my mother wants me to go with her to Kotkhai. She says she is worried about the war. She fears Varanasi may be attacked. Varanasi has never been attacked in three thousand years; she just wants to hold me ransom so Mr. Nandha will promise me a million things, the house in the Cantonment, the chauffeured car, the Brahmin baby."

She feels his muscles tighten beside her.

"Will you go?"

"I can't go to Kotkhai and I can't go to the Cantonment. But

Krishan, I cannot stay here, on this rooftop." Parvati sits up, listening, alert. "What time is it?"

"Eleven thirty."

"I must go. Mother will be back. She would not miss *Town and Country* for a million rupees." Parvati dusts the rooftop grit from her clothes, rearranges the drape of her sari, flicks her long straight hair over her left shoulder. "I'm sorry, Krishan. I shouldn't burden you. You have a garden to grow."

She flits barefoot across the roof garden. Moments later he hears the blaring theme from *Town and Country* drift up the stairs. Krishan moves from bed to bed, tying down his growing things.

Mr. Nandha pushes the plate away from him untouched.

"This is brown food. I cannot eat brown food."

Mrs. Sadurbahai does not remove the thali but stands resolutely by the stove.

"That is good honest country fare. What is wrong with my cooking that you cannot eat it?"

Mr. Nandha sighs.

"Wheat, pulses, potato. Carbohydrate carbohydrate carbohydrate. Onions, garlic ghee. Heavy heavy spices."

"My husband . . ." Parvati starts to say but Mr. Nandha cuts in.

"I have a white diet. It is all Ayurvedically calculated and balanced. What has happened to my white diet sheet?"

"Oh that, that went with the cook."

Mr. Nandha grips the edge of the table. It has been long gathering, like the monsoon heavy in his sinuses. Before Mrs. Sadurbhai abseiling in like Sajida Rana's elite troops, before the afternoon's meeting when the reality of politics trampled over his dedication and sense of mission, before even this Kalki case unfolded, he has been assailed by the feeling that he battles against madness, that order has one champion against the gathering chaos, that all others may succumb but one must remain to lift the sword that ends the Age of Kali. Now it is here in his house, in his kitchen, around his table, coiling its white blind roots through his wife.

"You come to my home, you turn my household upside down, you fire my cook, you throw away my diet sheets, I come home from a strenuous and demanding day's work to find myself served slop I cannot eat!"

"Dearest, really, mother's only trying to help," Parvati says but Mr. Nandha's knuckles are white now.

"Where I come from, a son has respect for his mother," Mrs. Sadurbhai returns. "You have no respect for me, you think I am an ignorant and superstitious peasant up from the country. You think no one knows anything next to you and your important work and your Angreez education and your horrible, tuneless Western music and your bland white food that is like babies eat and not fit for a real man doing real work. You think you are a gora; you think you are better than me and you think you are better than your wife, my daughter—I know it—but you are not and you are not a firengi; if the white men saw you they would laugh at you, see the babu thinks he is a Westerner! I tell you this, no one has any respect for an Indian gora."

Mr. Nandha is amazed by the paleness of his knuckles. He can see the blood vessels through them.

"Mrs. Sadurbbai, you are a guest under my roof . . ."

"A fine roof, a government roof . . ."

"Yes," Mr. Nandha says slowly, carefully, as if each word is a weight of water drawn up from a well. "A fine government roof, earned by my care and dedication to my profession. A roof under which I expect the peace and calm and domestic order that profession demands. You know nothing of what I do. You understand nothing of the forces I battle, the enemies I hunt. Creatures with the ambitions of gods, madam. Things you could not even begin to understand, that threaten our every belief about our world, I confront them on a daily basis. And if my horrible, tuneless Western music, if my bland white firengi diet, my cook and my sweeper all give me that peace and calm and domestic order so that I can face another day in my work, is that unreasonable?"

"No," Mrs. Sadurbhai throws back. She knows she is in a losing stance but she also understands that it is a fool who dies with a weapon undrawn. "What is unreasonable is that I hear no part in all this for Parvati."

"Parvati, my flower." The air in the kitchen is slow as syrup. Mr. Nandha feels the momentum and weight behind every word, every movement of his head. "Are you unhappy? Do you want for anything?"

Parvati begins to speak but her mother rides over her.

"What my daughter wants is some recognition that she is wife of a careful and dedicated professional, not hidden away on top of a housing block in the city centre."

"Parvati, is this true?"

"No," she says, "I thought maybe . . ." Again her mother tramples her.

"She could have had her pick of anyone, anyone; civil servants, lawyers, businessmen—politicians even, and they would have taken her and put her in her rightful place and shown her off like a flower and given her things she is due."

"Parvati, my love, I don't understand this. I thought we were happy here."

"Then you indeed understand nothing if you do not know that my daughter could have all the riches of the Mughals and she would set them aside just for a child . . ."

"Mother! No!" Parvati cries.

". . . a proper child. A child that is worthy of her status. A true heir."

The air is thick now. Mr. Nandha can barely turn his head to Mrs. Sadurbhai.

"A Brahmin? Is that what you are saying? Parvati, is this true?" She weeps at the end of the table, face hidden in her dupatta. Mr.

Nandha can feel the table shaking to her sobs. "A Brahmin. A genetically engineered child. A human child that lives twice as long but ages half as fast. A human being that can never get cancer, that can never get Alzheimer's, that can never get arthritis or any number of the degenerative ills that will come to us, Parvati. Our child. The fruit of our union. Is this what you want? We will take our seed to the doctors and they will open it up and take it apart and change it so that it is no longer ours and then fuse it and put that inside you, Parvati; fill you full of hormones and fertility drugs and push it up into your womb until it takes and you swell up with it, this stranger within."

"Why would you deny her this?" Mrs. Sadurbhai declaims. "What parent would refuse a chance for a perfect child? You would deny a mother this?"

"Because they are not human!" Mr. Nandha shouts. "Have you seen them? I have seen them. I see them every day in the streets and the offices. They look so young, but there is nothing we know there. The aeais and the Brahmins, they are the destruction of all of us. We are redundant. Dead ends. I strive against inhuman monsters, I will not invite one into my wife's *womb*." His hands are shaking. His hands are shaking. This is not right. See what these women have brought you to? Mr. Nandha pushes himself back from the table and stands up. He feels kilometres tall, vast and diffuse as an avatar from his box, filling buildings. "I am going out now. I have business to attend to. I may not be back until tomorrow, but when I do return, your mother will be gone from under this roof."

Parvati's voice follows him down the stairs.

"She is an old woman, it is late, where will she go? You cannot throw an old woman out on to the streets."

Mr. Nandha makes no reply. He has an aeai to excommunicate. As he walks from the lobby of the government apartment block to the government car pigeons fly up around him in a wheezing applause of wings. He grips the ivory Kalki image in his fist.

37

SHAHEEN BADOOR KHAN

From this turret drummers once welcomed guests as they crossed the causeway over the swamp. Water birds would rise up on either side; egret, cranes, spoonbills, the wild duck that had drawn Moazam Ali Khan to build his hunting lodge here on the Gaghara's winter floodplain at Ramghar Lake. The lake is dry now, the swamps parched mud, the birds gone. No drums have played from the naqqar khana in Shaheen Badoor Khan's lifetime. The lodge had been semiderelict even in his father's time: Asad Badoor Khan, asleep in the arms of Allah beneath his simple marble rectangle in the family graveyard. Over Shaheen Badoor Khan's lifetime, first rooms then suites then wings were abandoned to the heat and the dust, fabrics rotting and splitting, plaster staining and flaking in the monsoon humidity. Even the graveyard is overgrown with grass and rank weeds, now withered and yellow in drought. The shading ashok trees have been cut down one by one and carried away by the caretakers for fuel.

Shaheen Badoor Khan has never liked the old hunting lodge of Ramghar Kothi. That is why he has come here to hide. No one but those he trusts knows it still stands.

He had sounded the horn for ten minutes before the staff roused themselves to the idea that someone might want to visit the lodge. They were an aged couple, poor but prideful Muslims, he a retired schoolteacher. For struggling against entropy they were permitted a wing rent-free and paid a weekly handful of rupees for rice and dal. The surprise on old man Musa's face as he swung open the double gates could not be hidden. It might have been the unannounced visit after four years of neglect. Or, he might know everything from Voice of Bharat news. Shaheen Badoor Khan drove into the shelter of the stable cloister and ordered his lodge keeper to bar the gate.

Before an eastern horizon like a black wall Shaheen Badoor Khan moved among the dusty graves of his clan. His Mughal forefathers had named the monsoon the Hammer of God. That hammer had fallen and he was still alive. He could plan. He could dream. He could even hope.

Moazam Ali Khan's mausoleum stood among pulpy tree stumps in the oldest part of the graveyard, the first Khan to be buried here on their gravel rise above the flood silts. The shade foliage had been cut down over seasons by the Musas, but the current steward of Ramghar approved of this despoilment. It allowed the small but classically proportioned tomb to stretch its bones, let its sandstone skin breathe, a building unveiled. Shaheen Badoor Khan ducked under the east-facing arch into the domed interior. The delicate jali screens had long since crumbled and he knew from childhood adventures that the burial vault beneath was haunted by bats but even in its decay the tomb of the founder of the political line of Khan graced the visitor. Moazam Ali had led a life of achievement and intrigue storied by the Urdu chroniclers as Prime Minister to the Nawabs of Awadh in the time that power haemorrhaged from the fading Mughals at Agra to their nominal lieges at Lucknow. He had overseen the transformation of a squalid medieval trading city into a flower of Islamic civilization, then, scenting the fragility of it all from the hair-pomade of the envoys of the East India Company, retired from public life with his small but fabled harem of Persian poetesses to study Sufi mysticism in the game-shooting lodge donated by a grateful nation. First and greatest of the Khans. Since Moazam Ali and his poetesses lived and studied among the calling marsh birds, it has been a slow decline to dust. The gloom beneath the dome deepened by the instant as the monsoon advanced on Ramghar Kothi with its promise of swamps refreshed, lakes restored. Shaheen Badoor Khan's fingers traced the outline of the mihrab, the niche facing Mecca.

Two generations later, Mushtaq Khan lay beneath an elegant chhatri, open to the wind and the dust. Saviour of the family reputation and fortune by remaining staunch to the Raj as North India mutinied. Engraved illustrations in the newspapers of 1857 showed him defending property and family from besieging sepoy hordes, pistol in either hand, cartridge smoke billowing. The truth was less dramatic; a small detachment of mutineers had charged Ramghar and been repulsed without casualty by small arms fire but it was enough to earn him the title among the British of *That Faithful Mohammedan*; and the Hindus *Killer Khan*, a kudos among the Lords of the Raj he would carefully convert into a campaign for special political recognition for Muslims. How proud he would have felt, Shaheen Badoor Khan thinks, to have seen those seeds germinate into a Muslim nation, a Land of the Pure. How it would have broken his heart to see that Land of the Pure become a medieval theocracy and then rip itself apart in tribal factionalism. The Word of God prophesies from the barrel of an AK47. Time, death, and dust. Temple bells clanged out across the dead marsh. From the south, the horn of a train, constantly blaring. Soft thunder shook the air.

And here, beneath this marble stele on the gravel bank that had the only soil deep enough to accept a grave, was his own grandfather,

Sayid Raiz Khan, judge and nation builder who had kept his wife and family safe through the Partition Wars in which a million people died, steadfast in his belief that there must be an India and that India, to be all Nehru claimed on that midnight in 1947, must have a seat of honour for Muslims. Here, his own father; campaigning lawyer and campaigning Parliamentarian in two Parliament Houses, one in Delhi, one in Varanasi. He had fought his own Partition Wars. The Faithful Mohammedan Khans, each generation warring against the achievements of the previous one, unto the last drop.

The headlights of the car are visible for kilometres across the flat, treeless land. Shaheen Badoor Khan descends the crumbling steps from the drum tower to open the gate. Ramghar's servants are old and meek and deserving of sleep. He starts at a touch of rain on his lip, gently tastes it with his tongue.

I started a war for this.

The Lexus pulls into the courtyard. Its black sleek carapace is jewelled with rain. Shaheen Badoor Khan opens the door. Bilquis Badoor Khan steps out. She wears a formal shalwar in blue and gold, chador pulled over her head. He understands. Hide your face. His is a people that once could die from shame.

"Thank you for coming," he says. She raises a hand. Not here. Not now. Not in front of the servants. He indicates the pillared chhatri of the drum turret, stands aside as his wife brushes past, lifting her hem to take the steep steps. The rain has a rhythm now, the southeastern horizon a celebration in lightning. Rain runs in ropes from the edge of the domed roof of the octagonal Mughal drum tower. Shaheen Badoor Khan says, "Before anything else, I have to tell you how very, how profoundly sorry I am over what has happened." The words taste like dust on his lips, the dust of his ancestors with the rain seeping down towards them. They swell in his mouth. "I . . . no. We had an agreement, I broke it, somehow that got out. The rest will be history. I have been intolerably foolish and it has rebounded on me."

He had not known when she first suspected but, since Dara was born, it had become obvious that Bilquis could not be all the things he desired. Theirs was the last Mughal marriage, of dynasty and power and expedience. They had spoken of it overtly only once, after Jehan had left for university and the haveli was suddenly echoing and too full of servants. The conversation had been forced, dry, painful; the sentences couched in allusion and elision for the house staff who overheard everything, just long enough to lay down the agreement that he would never allow it to threaten family and government and she would remain the proper, dutiful politician's wife. By then they had not slept together for a decade.

It. They had never given the thing between them a name. Shaheen Badoor Khan is not now certain there is one. His affliction? His vice? His weakness, thorn in the flesh? His perversion? There are no words in the language between two people for *its*.

The rain is so heavy Shaheen Badoor Khan can hardly make himself heard.

"I have a few favours left; I have arranged a way out of Bharat; it is a direct flight to Kathmandu. There will be no difficulty entering Nepal. From there we can connect on to anywhere in the world. My own preferences are for Northern Europe, perhaps Finland or Norway. These are large underpopulated countries where we can live anonymously. I have funds in transportable bank drafts set aside, it will be enough for us to buy a property and live adequately, if perhaps not in the comfort we enjoy here in Bharat. Prices are steep and we would have difficulty adjusting to the climate but I think Scandinavia is the best for us."

Bilquis's eyes are closed. She holds a hand up.

"Please, stop this."

"It does not have to be Scandinavia, New Zealand is another fine, remote country . . ."

"Not Scandinavia, not New Zealand. Shaheen, I will not go with you. I have had enough; you are not the one who has to apologise. I am. Shaheen, I broke the agreement. I told them. You think you are the only one with a secret life; no! You're not! And that always was you, Shaheen; so arrogant, that you are the only one can have lies and secrets. Shaheen, for the past five years, I have been working for N. K. Jivanjee. The Shivaji, Shaheen. I, the Begum Bilquis Badoor Khan, betrayed you to the Hinduvavadis."

Shaheen Badoor Khan feels the rain, the thunder, his wife's voice smear into a thin hiss. He understands now how it might be to die of shock.

"What is this?" he hears himself say. "This is nonsense, nonsense, you are talking nonsense, woman."

"I suppose it must seem like nonsense, Shaheen, a wife betraying her husband to his greatest enemies. But I did, Shaheen. I betrayed you to the Hindus. Your own wife. Who you turned away from, every night while we still slept together. Five conceptions, five fucks. I counted, five fucks, a woman remembers that. And only two of those were allowed to come to term as our fine sons. Five fucks. I'm sorry, does my coarseness shock you? Is this not how society Begums should talk? You should hear what those good Begums say among themselves, Shaheen. Woman talk. Oh, your ears would burn for shame. Shameless creatures we are, in our chambers and societies. They know, all the women know. Five fucks Khan. I told them, but not *it*. That I didn't tell them, Shaheen.

"I didn't tell them because I still thought, this is a great man, a star climbing in a black sky, with high office and achievements before him, even if he lies in his separate bed and dreams of things I cannot even see as human. But a wife can push things down to the bottom of her mind if she thinks that her husband is a man who could rise to greatness, as great as any of your ancestors buried out there, Shaheen. A woman who could have had her choice of men, who would have loved her in heart and in body, who might also have risen to great stations. A woman who had her own education and potential that was forced into the golden purdah because for every one woman lawyer there are five men. Do you understand what I am saying, Shaheen? Such a woman expects things. And if that star rose, and then it stopped, and stayed fixed, and rose no higher and other stars rose above it and outshone it . . . What should that woman do then, Shaheen? What should that wife and Begum do?"

Shaheen Badoor's hands cover his face in shame but he cannot stop the words that cut through the rain, the thunder, his own fingers. He had thought himself a good and true advisor to his leader, government, and country but he remembers how he had reacted when Sajida Rana had offered him a cabinet position on the flight back from Kunda Khadar: fear of discovery, fear that the *it* was spilling out of him like blood from a cut throat. Now he sees how many times and places in his career he could have taken that step into public power and had drawn back, paralysed by the inevitable fall.

"Jivanjee?" he says weakly. The heart of the madness in this ancient Mughal drum turret in the heart of a monsoon storm: his wife an agent of N. K. Jivanjee. She laughs. There is no more terrible sound.

"Yes, Jivanjee. All those afternoons when I would entertain the Law Circle, when you were at the Sabha, what did you think we were doing? Talking about property prices and Brahmin children and cricket scores? Politics, Shaheen. The finest woman lawyers in Varanasi; how else do you think we would amuse ourselves? We were a shadow cabinet. We ran a simulation on our palmers. I tell you this, there was more talent in my jharoka than there was in Sajida Rana's Cabinet room. Oh, Sajida Rana, the great mother who has made it impossible for any other woman to match her. Well, in our Bharat, Shaheen, there was no water war. In our Bharat there was no three-year drought, no hostility with the United States because we were in the pockets of the datarajas. In our Bharat we assembled a Ganga Valley Water Management plan with Awadh and the States of Bengal. We ran your country better than you did, Shaheen, and do you know why? To see if we could. To see if we could do it better. And we did.

"And it was the talk of the capital but you don't hear that kind of talk, do you? Women's talk. Talk of no consequence. But N. K. Jivanjee heard. The Shivaji heard, and that is another thing I cannot forgive. A Hindu politician recognised the talent, whatever its gender, whatever its religion, that her husband could not. We became the Shivaji policy unit, our little afternoon group taking chai in our gardens. It was a game worth the playing now. I used to hope that you would not come home and tell me what you were up to in the Sabha so I could try to read your mind, ask myself what you would do, try and outguess and outmanoeuvre you. All those times you would come home cursing that Jivanjee because he always seemed to be that one step ahead, that was me." She touches her breast, not seeing her husband now, not seeing the rain breaking over Ramghar, seeing only her memory of a great game that became the rule of her life.

"Jivanjee," Shaheen Badoor Khan whispers. "You sold me to Jivanjee." And the dam that held him in so long, so high and wide, breaks and Shaheen Badoor Khan finds that inside him, all these years, all these lies and concealments, is only a roar, an inchoate howl like the nothing before creation, shrieking out of him. He cannot stop it, he cannot hold it in. Its vacuum tugs at his inner organs. He is on his knees. He crawls on his knees towards his wife; everything is destroyed. He had allowed himself to hope and for that pride, it was taken away, everything was taken away. He cannot hope the animal howl breaks into yelping, retching sobs. Bilquis backs away. She is afraid. This was never in her strategies and game plans. Shaheen Badoor Khan is on his hands and knees now, like a dog, barking up shrieks of pain.

"Stop, stop it," Bilquis begs. "Please, no. Please, have some dignity."

Shaheen Badoor Khan looks up at her. Her hand goes to her mouth in horror. There is nothing there she can recognise. The game has destroyed them both.

She steps away from the ruined thing huddled on the smooth sandstone of the drum turret, retching up the infected pus of its life. She finds the sandstone steps, flees into the curtains of rain.

38

MR. NANDHA

The austere polyphony of the Bach Magnificat swirls around Mr. Nandha as the tilt-jet banks over the river. The hot wind that heralds the monsoon buffets the ghats. Flaws spun off the storm front send the ordered flotillas of diyas scattering across Mother Ganga. The tilt-jet lurches on the gusts. Mr. Nandha sees lightning reflected in the pilot's visor, then her hands bring them safely about. Ahead of him the other three aircraft in the squadron are patterns of moving lights on the greater city glow. Kashi. City of light.

In Mr. Nandha's augmented vision, gods tower over Varanasi, vaster even than the monsoon, their vahanas crawling in the concrete and shit, their crowns in the stratosphere. Gods like thunderclouds, attributes held aloft and crackling with lightning, multiple arms performing the sacred mudras with meteorological deliberateness. The containment went in as the excommunication force lifted off from the military airfield. Prasad has intercepted a few hundred Level One aeais running out along the cable network but otherwise it has been as quiet as death or innocence in the fifth-floor office unit. The squadron splits, navigation lights darting acrobatically between Ganesha, Kartikkeya, Kali, and Krishna. Mr. Nandha's lips silently pray *Magnificat magnificat* as the tilt-jet banks and plunges through Ganesha in a spray of hand-sized pixels. A spear in the side, thinks Mr. Nandha. The pilot swivels the wing-tip engines into descent mode and takes them down through veils of divine light. Mr. Nandha thumbs off the visuals. The gods are extinguished as if by unbelief but years of intimacy have given Mr. Nandha a sense of their presence, an electricity in the back of the skull. His gun is a dark weight against his heart.

Odeco corporate headquarters is a low-rent office block in a labyrinth of school-uniform clothiers and sari merchants. The pilot spins the tilt-jet to fit into the narrow street; wing-tip lights scrape balconies and power poles as she brings her ship down into the junction. The backwash from the engines tumbles racks of bicycles across the street. A cow idles out of the way. Shop owners haul down their billowing, flapping wares. Wheels unfold, kiss the concrete. Mr. Nandha goes through to the troop hold and his excommunication team: Ram Lalli, Prasad, Mukul Dev, Vik queasy in riot armour over his Star-Asia rock-boyz gear.

The tilt-jet settles on its shock absorbers. Nothing moves, nothing stirs but the wind from the edge of the monsoon, driving papers and scraps of torn filmi posters through the narrow streets. A street dog barks. The ramp lowers as the engines power down. Tilt-jets make point-perfect landings at the two other drop points. The fourth spins in the air against the neon towers of New Varanasi, swoops in over the roof of the office unit and swings its engines into hover. The roar in the narrow alleys is like Vedic armies clashing in the sky. Its belly opens and Bharati air-cav sowars spool down on droplines. On the woman pilot's helmet display they abseil into a yawning canyon of gods.

Shaped demolition charges open up the roof like a can of ghee. Communicating by hand signals, the sowars reattach their karabiners to the solar array and dive in.

Mr. Nandha advances through a graveyard of bicycles. A touch to the right ear sets the 'hoek and Indra, Lord of Rain and Lightning, swirls into manifestation over the haberdasher's quarter of old Kashi mounted on his elephant vahana, four-tusked Airavata. The Vajra of judgement is raised in his right hand. Mr. Nandha shifts his hand to his gun. True lightning flickers through Indra's translucent red body; Mr. Nandha looks up. Rain. On his face. He stops, wipes the drip from his forehead, stares at it in wonder. In the same instant, Indra swirls and he feels the gun aim him.

The robots come bounding down the unlit gali, a chitter of tiny running feet and tapping claws. Monkey robots cat robots robots like wingless birds and long-legged insects, a wave of clicking motion surging towards the main street. Mr. Nandha levels his gun, fires, aims fires aims fires aims fires. Bach's towering counterpoints roar in his ears. He never misses. Indra guides true and sure. The robots spin and smash into each other and wheel into walls and doorways as the fat, random drops steepen into rain. Mr. Nandha advances up the gali, gun held before him, unerringly seeking its targets with its red laser eye and sending them spinning and smoking and burning in shaped pulses of electromagnetic radiation. Monkey robots scale the cables and chatimag posters and metal advertising sheets for bottled water and language schools, scrambling for the rooftops and comlines. Indra brings them down with his thunderbolt. Behind Mr. Nandha the agents of the Ministry form a line, picking off those that make it into the excommunication zone. Mr. Nandba silences Johann Sebastian and lifts his hand.

"Cease fire!"

The power lines fizz with overload as the last escapees are consigned to scrap. Glancing behind him, Mr. Nandha reads the distaste on Vik's face as he struggles with his big multirole assault rifle. This is what you wanted, Mr. Nandha thinks. A piece of the action. The gun and the gear.

The rain falls luminous through the belly-spots from the hovering aircraft. Jet-wash and the rising storm wind swirl the drops into glowing veils.

"Something is not right here," Mr. Nandha says quietly and then the monsoon breaks over Varanasi. In an instant Mr. Nandha is soaked to the bone. His dove grey suit is plastered to his skin. Blinded, he tries to wipe the rain from his eyes. Unbowed by the monsoon, Indra towers through the lightning and rain over five-thousand-year-old Kashi.

The sowars crash down through the roof onto the desks and filing cabinets and collapsed ceiling fans, kicking over displays and chai cups and water coolers. Weapons levelled, they quarter the open-plan office with their nightwatchs. It's a dead black office in the middle of a downpour. Rain cascades through the holes they have blown in the roof. The subadar-major signs for her sowars to make safe the evidence. As they shift processor cubes and stacks out of the rain she calls Mr. Nandha on her throat-mike. Another mudra and her troopers spread out, scanning on full sensory array for aeai activity. Lightning spooks her face. She can hear the regular police jawans work their ways up through the lower levels. She gestures for her warriors to spread and secure. There's nothing here. Whatever spirit dwelled in this place is fled.

Mr. Nandha signals his team to close up.

"What's not right?" Vik says. His hair is streaked flat, his nose runs rain, and his baggy clothes cascade at the creases. He raises his eyes to Indra, high above the chaotic roofscape of Kashi.

"This is a decoy." Mr. Nandha kicks a fist-curled corpse of a maintenance robot. "This is not the Generation Three breaking itself down into subaeais and escaping. This is deliberate. They want us to destroy everything." He calls into his palmer-glove. "All units, cease firing, do not engage."

But the two squads to the north and west are too busy chasing monkey-robots over bales of sari silk and through racks of schoolgirls' uniforms while the proprietors throw their hands up in loud lamentation as the pulses wipe their till memories. The jawans' combat suits turn sari-colour as they run, whooping, after the leaping, bounding machines through storerooms, past chowkidars hiding in doorways, hands over their heads, up and up concrete staircases until the last of the robots are driven under the guns of the sowars. It is like a Raj duck-shoot. For a few moments the light of induced EM-charges outshines the lightning.

Mr. Nandha enters the destroyed office. He looks at the circular waterfalls pooling on the cheap carpet. He looks at the smoking robots and the shattered screens and smashed desks. Mr. Nandha purses his lips, vexed.

"Who is in command here?"

The subadar-major's helmet opens and retracts into the cowl of her combat suit.

"Subadar-Major Kaur, sir."

"This is a crime-scene investigation, subadar-major."

Voices, feet scuffling at the door. The sowars restrain a small but evidently vigorous Bangla, smart as a mynah in an inexplicably dry black suit.

"I demand to see . . ."

"Admit him," Mr. Nandha orders. Shafts of search-light beaming through the streaming holes in the roof light the office. The Bangla looks around him in shock as the soldiers stand back.

"What is the meaning of this?" the Bangla demands.

"You are, sir?" Mr. Nandha asks, acutely conscious of his saturated suit.

"My name is Chakraborty, I am a lawyer with this company."

Mr. Nandha holds up his left hand. The picture in his palm displays the open hand symbol of the Ministry. Palm within a palm.

"I am conducting an investigation into the illegal harbouring of a Generation Three Artificial Intelligence contrary to Section twenty-seven of the International Treaty of Lima," Mr. Nandha says. The Bangla blinks at him.

"Buffoon."

"Sir, these are the premises of Odeco Incorporated?"

"They are."

"Please read this warrant."

The sowars have the generator up and string clip-lamps around the office.

Chakraborty swivels Mr. Nandha's hand into the light of the nearest lamp.

"This is what is known informally as an excommunication order."

"From the office of the Minister of Justice himself."

"I will be launching an official appeal and civil action for damages."

"Of course, sir. You would not be acting professionally otherwise. Now, please be careful; my agents have work to do and there are live weapons present."

Sowar engineers rig waterproof covers over the holes in the ceiling. Jawans spool power cables to the processors; Vik is already at the terminals, his own version of the avatar box jacked into the arrays.

"Nothing here."

"Show me."

Mr. Nandha feels Chakraborty at his shoulder, smirking as he bends over Vik squatting at the roll screen. Vik thumbs through stack after stack of registers.

"If there was ever any Gen Three here, it's long gone," he says. "But hey, look at this! Our friend Vishram Ray."

"Sir." Madhvi Prasad at another screen. She pulls up a pair of broken-backed typist's chairs. Mr. Nandha settles beside her. His socks squeak inside his shoes and he winces at the indignity. It is bad to conduct the most important investigation of your career in creaking cotton socks. It is worse to be called a buffoon by a sleek Bangla lawyer. But what is worst is to be accused of being no man at all, a ball-less hijra, in your kitchen, under your own roof, by your wife's mother, by a withered country widow. Mr. Nandha pushes the humiliation away. Those naked sadhus dancing in the rain endure greater for less.

"What am I looking at?" Mr. Nandha asks. Prasad swings the screen to him.

It is bright morning at the new ghat at Patna. Ferries and hydrofoils crowd the edges of the shot, businessmen and workers throng the background; behind them the towers of the new commercial Bund glitter in the east-light. In the foreground stand three smiling people. One is Jean-Yves Trudeau, the other his wife, Anjali. Their arms are around a third person who stands between them, a girl in her late teens, wheat-complexioned like the best matrimonial advertisements. She is a head shorter than the Westerners but her smile is wide and radiant despite her shaved scalp on which Mr. Nandha can read the hairline scars of recent surgery.

Mr. Nandha bends closer. Chilled by the rain, his breath steams in the close blue glow of the stack-and-stick neons.

"This is what they wanted us to destroy." He touches a finger to the girl's face. "This one is still alive."

39

KUNDA KHADAR

For ten days the slow missiles have crossed the flat, scorched lands of western Bharat. Even as the Awadhi garrison at Kunda Khadar fled before the bold Bharati jawans, artillery units across an eighty-kilometre front released between two and three hundred autonomous drones from their stubby cylindrical silos. Each carries a payload of ten kilogrammes of high-yield explosive and is the size and shape of a small, densely muscled cat. By day they sleep in shallow scrapes or stacks of half-moon dried dung ladhus. When the night comes they unfold antennae to the moon, stir their folded metal legs and skulk across fields and down dry country drains, feline subtle, feline wary, steering by the light of the moon and quiet chirps of GPS. Truck headlights startle them, they freeze, trusting in their rudimentary chameleon camouflage. No one sees, no one hears, though they slink within centimetres of the tractor mechanic sleeping on his charpoy. By the time the first Brahmin salutes the sun on the banks of holy Ganga they have burrowed into the sand or cling to the rafters in the smoke and shadows of the temple ceiling or have submerged themselves at the bottom of the village tank. They are level 1.4 aeais but their fuel cells run on a tungsten-moderated methane reaction. They converge across Bharat navigating from cow fart to cow fart.

In the late hours of a July evening the slow missiles arrive on target. For the past two nights they have moved through city streets, running along suburban garden walls startling hunting cats, leaping from rooftop to rooftop across the narrow inner-city alleys, jumping down tiers of balconies to dart silent and dark across city streets, banding together in twos and threes, in tens and dozens, finally in their hundreds, a swarm of plastic paws and flexing whisker antennae, setting the pi-dogs to barking. But no one heeds the barking of pi-dogs.

At ten thirty, two hundred and twenty slow missiles infiltrate all key systems at Ray Power's Allahabad Main electrical distribution station and simultaneously detonate themselves. Western Bharat from Allahabad to the border is blacked out. Communication lines go silent. Command and control centres are paralysed, scrambling to get their backup system online. Satellite ground stations go blind. Air defence switches to auxiliary. Emergency power-up takes three minutes. Restoring comlinks and control chains takes another two minutes. It is a further three before Bharat is fully defence-capable.

In those eight minutes, one hundred and fifty Awadhi helicopter drop-ships supported by aeai ground-attack craft morph out of stealth and offload infantry and light mechanised units five kilometres inside the Bharati border. As APCs drill through dirt-scrabble border villages and mortar teams set up advanced positions, heavy armoured units move under air support from their holding positions and sweep in towards the northern end of the dam. Simultaneously two armoured divisions punch through Bharat's lightly defended border at Rewa and push up the Jabalpur road towards Allahabad.

By the time the backup power is online and command and intelligence systems are restored, Bharat's western artillery positions are staring down the muzzles of Franks main battle tanks while swarms of rat-robots take out the defensive minefields and the first mortar rounds whistle eerily onto the Kunda Khadar dam. Surrounded, cut off from the command structure and naked to air power, support pinned down holding Allahabad, General Jha surrenders. Five thousand soldiers lay down their weapons. It is the most triumphant eight minutes in Awadh's history of arms. It is the most ignominious in Bharat's.

At ten forty the cell network is restored. Within ten minutes palmers are ringing all over rain-punished Varanasi.

40

VISHRAM

Under the instruction of old Ram Das the outdoor staff carry the garden furniture to the shelter of the Shanker Mahal's generous porches. Vishram walks past a line of white cast iron and wicker crossing the lawn. His mother sits alone at the far end of the garden, a little pale woman at a little white table highlit against the towering dark of the monsoon. Like a British dowager, she will wait until the storm is upon her before she relinquishes her redoubt. Vishram perennially remembers her thus, on the lawns, at her white tables, beneath her clustered parasols, with her ladies and her chai on a silver tray. Vishram always loved the house best in the rain, when it seemed to float free against the green and the black clouds. Then its dehydrated ghosts returned to life and his room sounded to their creakings and clickings. In this season the Shanker Mahal smells of old wood and damp and growing, as if the plant patterns on his bedroom ceiling might burst into bud and flower. The entwined figures on the pillars and brackets relax in the rain.

"Vishram, my bird. That suit does look well on you."

He summons back the last garden chair with a crook of his finger. Lightning glimmers beyond the Ashok trees. Beyond them, headlights slash through the murk.

"Mamaji." Vishram inclines his head. "I won't keep you. I need to know where he is."

"Who, dear?"

"Who do you think?"

"Your father is a man who takes the spiritual life seriously. If he has chosen the sadhu's path of seclusion, that should be respected. What do you need from him?"

"Nothing," Vishram Ray says. He thinks he sees his mother duck away a sly smile as she lifts her cup of Darjeeling to her lips. Electric hot wind buffets the flowerbeds; peacocks shriek in panic. "I want to tell him something I've decided."

"A business thing? You know I've never had a head for business," Mamata Ray says.

"Mother," Vishram says. All his life she had maintained this soft lie; simple Mamata understands nothing of business, wants nothing to do with it, that is men's affairs, business and money and power. No decision had ever been taken, no investment made, no purchase recommended, no research authorised, that Mamata Ray had not been there saying she knew nothing but what would happen if, and how would that be, and in the long run might this? Vishram did not doubt that her hesitant questions had been at the root of the Shakespearean division of Ray Power, hers the voice that gave Ranjit Ray his blessing to walk away from the world.

Vishram pours himself a cup of the scented Darjeeling tea. He thinks the taste overrefined but it gives himself something to do with his hands. First Rule of Comedy. Always have something to do with your hands.

"I'm buying out Ramesh. I've called an extraordinary board meeting."

"You've spoken to Mr. Chakraborty."

His mother's eyes are lenses of lead, reflection of the churned grey sky.

"I know what Odeco is."

"Is this what you want to tell your father?"

"No. What I want to tell him is that I have very few choices here and I've made the best I think I can."

Mamata Ray sets her cup on the table turning it on the saucer so the handle faces exactly to the left. Gardeners and houseboys lean close, anticipating action. The rising wind tugs at their turbans and tassles.

"I argued against it, you know. The decision to split the business. That may surprise you. I argued against it because of you, Vishram. I thought you would waste it, throw it away. I am no different from Govind in that. Your father alone had faith. He was always so interested in what you were doing in that terrible Scottish country. He did quite respect you for having the courage of your own convictions—you always had, Vishram. I said I had no head for business, maybe it is people I have no head for, my own sons. Maybe I am too old to change my opinions."

Mamata Ray looks up. Vishram feels rain on his face. He sets down his cup—the tea is cold, bitter—and the malis lift first it, then the table. The rain drops heavily on the bougainvillea leaves.

"Your father is doing puja at the Kali temple at Mirzapur," Mamata Ray calls back from the rear of the procession of garden furniture. The rain is heavy but not so loud as to mask the sound of aircraft engines on approach. "He does puja for the end of an age. Siva's foot is descending. The dance begins. We have been given over to the goddess of destruction."

As they reach the safety of the east veranda the clouds burst. Thunder blares as the tilt-jet comes in over the water garden. Navigation lights turn the pelting drops into a curtain as the engines swivel into descent mode and the wheels lower towards Ram Das' shaved turf. The garden staff shield their eyes.

"Then again, you were right, I always was a flash bastard," Vishram says to his mother and dashes through the rain, collar of his good suit pulled up, towards his transport. Marianna Fusco waves excitedly from the rear seat.

Old Shastri leads Vishram and Marianna Fusco up the steep galls of Mirzapur. The laneways are narrow and dark and smell of piss and old joss. Kids fall in behind the little procession as it trudges up from the concrete ghats. Vishram glances back at the tilt-jet on the river beach. The pilot has taken his helmet off and sits on the sand a respectful distance from the fuel tanks smoking a cigarette. The monsoon that was breaking over Varanasi has not reached Mirzapur sixty kilometres west. The alleys concentrate the heat into a thing almost tangible; trash swirls in the djinns of stifling, fetid air. Marianna Fusco climbs steadily, letting the stares of the youths and old men slide off her peripheral vision.

The Kali temple is a marble plinth crowded in on every side by shops selling votives and gajras and icons of the goddess custom printed from a huge database of images. Kali is the main business of this end of Mirzapur, a decaying rural town that missed the information revolution and still wonders what happened. The footpaths push up against the water-washed marble steps, even at this late hour they are thronged with devotees. Bells clang constantly. Metal cattle grids herd the worshippers toward the garbhagriha. A cow saunters up and down the steps, bones moving loosely inside its bag of yellow skin. Someone has daubed red and yellow tikka paste between its horns.

"I'll stay here," Marianna Fusco says. "Someone's got to mind those shoes." Vishram understands the apprehension in her voice. This is a place outside her experience. It is essentially, inexplicably Indian. It makes no concessions to any other sensibilities; all the contradictions and contraries of Bharat are made incarnate in this place of love and devotion to the wrathful manifestation of primal femininity. Black Kali with her garland of heads and terrible swift sword. Even Vishram feels a clench of the alien in his stomach as he ducks under the lintel adorned with musician Mahavidyas, the ten wisdoms that emanate from the yoni of the black goddess.

Shastri remains with Marianna Fusco. Vishram is absorbed into the stream of pilgrims, shuffling through the maze. The temple is low, smoky, claustrophobic. Vishram salutes the sadhus, receives their tilaks for a handful of rupees. The garbhagriha is minute, a narrow slit of a coffin where the black, goggle-eyed image is smothered under swags of marigold garlands. The narrow passage is almost impassable from the crowd pressing around the sanctuary, thrusting their hands through the yonic slit to light incense, offers libations of milk and blood and red-dyed ghee. Thirsty Kali demands seven litres of blood every day. Goats provide it now in sophisticated urban centres like Mirzapur. Vishram's eyes meet those of the goddess that see past present future, piercing all illusion. Darshan. The surge of people whirls him on. Thunder shakes the temple. The monsoon has come westward. The heat is intense. The bells clang. The devotees chant hymns.

Vishram finds his father in a black windowless subtemple. He almost stumbles over him in the deep darkness. Vishram puts out his hand to steady himself, pulls it back from the lintel, wet. Blood. The floor is thick with ash. As his eyes adjust he sees a rectangular pit in the centre of a room. SmasanaKali is also goddess of the ghats. This is a cremation house. Ranjit Ray sits cross-legged among the ashes. He wears the sadhu's dhoti and shawl and red Kali tikka. His skin is grey with vibhuti; the white sacred ash streaks his hair and stubble. To Vishram this is not his father. This is a thing you see sitting by a street shrine, sprawling naked in a temple doorway; an alien from another world.

"Dad?"

Ranjit Ray nods. "Vishram. Sit, sit." Vishram looks around but there is nowhere but ash. It's probably a worldly thing to worry about your suit. Then again he is worldly enough to know he can get another one. He sits down by his father. Thunder shakes the temple. The bell clangs, the devotees pray.

"Dad, what are you doing here?"

"Puja for the end of an age."

"This is a terrible place."

"It's meant to be. But the eye of faith sees differently and to me it seems not so terrible. It's right. Fitting."

"Destruction, Dad?"

"Transformation. Death and rebirth. The wheel turns."

"I'm buying Ramesh out," Vishram announces sitting barefoot among the ashes of the dead "That will give me two thirds control over the company and freeze out Govind and his Western partners. I'm not asking you, I'm telling you."

Vishram sees a flicker of old worldliness in his father's eyes.

"I'm sure you can guess where the money's come from."

"My good friend Chakraborty."

"You know who—or what, rather—is behind him?"

"I do."

"How, long have you known?"

"From the start. Odeco contacted me when we embarked on the zero-point project. Chakraborty was admirably direct."

"It was a hell of a risk, if the Krishna Cops had ever found out . . . Ray Power, power with conscience, treading lightly on the earth, all that?"

"I see no contradiction. These are living creatures, sentient creatures. We owe them a duty of care. Some of the grameen bankers . . ."

"Creatures. You said creatures there."

"Yes I did. There seem to be three Generation Three aeais, but of course their subjective universes do not necessarily overlap though they may share some subroutines. Odeco I believe is a common channel between at least two of them."

"Chakraborty called the Odeco aeai Brahma."

Ranjit Ray gives a small knowing smile.

"Did you ever meet with Brahma?"

"Vishram, what would there be to meet with? I met men in suits, I talked to faces on the phone. Those faces may have been real, they may have been Brahma, they may have been its manifestations. Can one meet a distributed entity in any meaningful sense?"

"Did they ever say why they wanted to fund the zero-point project?"

"You will not understand it. I do not understand it."

Lightning momentarily flashes up the inside of the cremation chamber. Thunder comes hard and heavy on it; strange winds stir the ash.

"Tell me."

Vishram's palmer calls. He grimaces in exasperation. Devotees glare at the interruption of profanity in their sanctum. High-priority call. Vishram flicks to audio only. When Marianna Fusco has finished speaking he slides the little device into an inside pocket.

"Dad, we have to leave now."

Ranjit Ray frowns.

"I can't understand what you are saying."

"We have to leave right now. It's not safe here. The Awadhis have captured the Kunda Khadar dam. Our soldiers have surrendered. There's nothing between them and Allahabad. They could be here in twenty-four hours. Dad, you're coming with me. There're spare seats on the plane. All this has to stop now, you're an important man with an international reputation."

Vishram stands, offers a hand down to his father.

"No, I will not come and I will not be ordered around like some doting widow by my own son. I have made my decision, I have walked away and I will not go back. I cannot go back; that Ranjit Ray does not exist any more."

Vishram shakes his head in exasperation.

"Dad."

"No. Nothing will happen to me. The Bharat they have invaded is not the one I live in. They cannot touch me. Go. Go on, you go." He pushes at his son's knees. "There are things you must do, go on. Nothing must happen to you. I will pray for you, you will be kept safe. Now go." Ranjit Ray closes his eyes, turns a blind, deaf face.

"I will come back . . ."

"You won't find me. I don't want to be found. You know what you have to do." As Vishram ducks under the blood-daubed lintel his father calls out. "I was going to tell you. Odeco, Brahma, the aeai—what it's looking for in the zero-point project. A way out. Out there in all those manifolds of M-Star theory there is a universe where it and those of its kind can exist, live free and safe, and we will never find them. And that is why I am here in this temple, because I want to see the look on Kali's face when her age comes to an end."

The rain is falling steadily as Vishram leaves the temple. The marble is greasy with water and dust. The narrow lanes around the temple still throng with people but the street spirit has changed. It is not the zeal of religious devotion, nor is it the communal celebration of rain falling on a drought dry city. Word of the humiliation at Kunda Khadar has passed into general circulation and the galis swarm with brahmins and widows in white and Kali devotees in red and angry young males in Big Label jeans and very fresh shirts. They peer up at television screens or tear hardcopies from printers or cluster round rickshaw radios or boys with news-feeds to their palmers. The noise in the streets rises as news spreads into rumour into misinformation into slogans. Bharat's bold jawans defeated. The Glory of Bharat crushed. Awadhi divisions already driving around the Allahabad ring road. The sacred soil invaded. Who will save? Who will avenge? Jivanjee Jivanjee Jivanjee! Warrior-karsevaks march to sweep back the invader in waves of their own blood. The Shivaji will redeem the shame of the Ranas.

"Where's your father?

Rickshaw drivers shove around Vishram as he pulls on his shoes.

"He's not coming with me."

"I did not think he would, Mr. Ray." Strange to hear those words from Shastri. Mister. Ray.

"Then can I suggest we get out of here because I feel very white and very Western and very female," says Marianna Fusco. The steep lanes are streaming and treacherous with rain. "How is it with you things always end in a riot?" Marianna Fusco asks but the spirit on the street is jabbing, ugly, contagious. Vishram can see the tilt-jet on the beach between the overhanging buildings. Behind him a crash; voices lift into panic. He turns to see a tin samosa cart spilled on its side, its cargo of spicy triangles scattered across the gali, hot oil spreading across the shallow steps. A touch from the lighted gas burner; fire fills the narrow alley. Cries, shrieks.

"Come on." Vishram takes Marianna's elbow and hurries her down the steps.

The pilot has the engines warmed up as Vishram and Marianna dive into their seats behind him. Shastri steps back out of the blast pattern of the jets, hands raised in blessing. The tilt-jet lifts through the downpour as the people come pouring down the steps like rats rushing to water, waving lathis and picking up sticks and stones to throw at the alien, the invader. The pilot is already too high. He turns his ship and Vishram sees the fire as a pool of heat, spreading from building to building like liquid, undaunted by the rain.

"The Age of Kali," he whispers. The lowest throw of the dice when human discord and corruption abounds and heaven is closed, when the ears of the gods are deaf and entropy is maximum and there is no hope to speak of. When the earth is destroyed by fire and water, Vishram thinks as the tilt-jet slips into horizontal flight, when time stops and the universe is born anew.

41

LISA

Outside the arch the rain falls like a curtain and Lisa Durnau is on her third gin. She sits on the wicker chair on the marble cloister. The only others on the terrace are two men in cheap suits and sandals, taking tea. From this vantage she can cover main gate and reception desk. The noise of the rain on the tired stone is incredible. It is some storm, even by Midwestern standards. Lightning and everything.

Empty again. She signs to the waiter. They are all young, shy Nepalis dressed as Rajputs, in Bharati Varanasi. She cannot work that. She cannot work most anything up here in the black north. She had just been getting the beautiful civilised south and its soft anarchy then she was set down in the middle of a nation and a city that looked the same and dressed the same but was in every way different.

The taxi driver had taken the words *American consulate* as an invitation to scam her, driving her round a roundabout with a big statue of

Ganesha under a funny little domed pavilion and a hoarding for *Ribbed and Exciting! Corduroy trousers*.

"Sarkhand Roundabout," the driver shouted. "Danger money danger money."

There were swastikas sprayed on every flat surface. Lisa could not remember which was the right way round and which was the fascist but either way they made her uneasy.

Rhodes the consular officer thumbed through her accreditations.

"What exactly does this authorise you to do here, Ms. Durnau?"

"Find a man."

"This is not a good time. Embassy advice is for all US nationals to leave. We can't guarantee your safety. American interests are being targeted. They burned a Burger King."

"Extra flame-grilled."

He had leaked the tiniest, tightest smile. He raised an eyebrow at the Tablet. Lisa Durnau wished she could do that. He handed her documents smartly back to her. "Well, success with your mission, whatever it is. Whatever assistance we can render, we will. And whatever else they say, this is a great city."

But to Lisa Durnau Varanasi seemed a city of ash, for all its neons and towers and floodlit shikaras. Ash on the streets and the shrines and temples, ash on the foreheads of the holy, ash on the streamlined wings and roofs of the Marutis and phatphats. A sky of ash, dark and breaking in a soft wave of soot. Even through the air-conditioning of her hotel room she could feel greasy hydrocarbon ash on her skin. Lull's hotel was a lovely old Islamic city house of marble floors and unexpected levels and balconies but her room was unclean. The minibar was empty. There was a strip from a sanitary towel wedged across the toilet bowl. The levels and balconies were full of news crews. She checked the shower, for old times.

There was a second reservation in the Lull party. Ajmer Rao. The Tablet pulled a lo-res shot off the lobby-cam; her. Space-bunny. Shorter than Lisa had imagined. Wide in the ass but that might have been the angle of the lens. What was that on her forehead?

Ajmer Rao. But Lisa Durnau's first thought was that she was glad Lull was not sleeping with her. And Lull himself. Leaner. Face softer. Terrible, terrible clothes. Encroaching baldness, hair long at the back in compensation. In every way as she had seen him swirl out of the seething pixels of the Tabernacle.

Watching the rain, Lisa Durnau finds she is angry, moltenly angry. All her life she has striven against her father's Calvinist doctrine of predestination, yet the fact that she is watching the monsoon fall on Varanasi is the result of karmic forces seven billion years old. She, Lull, this wide-assed girl, all play to a script as foreordained and fatalistic as any episode of *Town and Country*. She is angry because she never had escaped. The complex behaviours of Alterre, of her Calabi-Yau mindspaces, the cellular automata brawling across her monitor emerged from simple, relentless rules. Rules so simple you might never realise you were governed by them.

She thumbs into Alterre. For fun she enters her current GPS location adjusted for continental drift, taps in full proprioception, and steps into hell. She stands on a furrowed plain of black lava veined red with glowing cracks. The sky is curdled with smoke lit by lightning flashes, a snow of ash falls about her. She almost chokes on sulphur and combustion gases, then thumbs off olfactory. The plain rises gently towards a line of low cones pouring thick, fast torrents of magma. Cascades of sparks close off the horizon. She can see around her for twenty kilometres in every direction and in none of them is there any living thing.

Panic-stricken, Lisa Durnau blinks back into Varanasi in the rain. Her heart races, her head reels; it is like turning a street intersection and stumbling on Ground Zero without warning. She is physically shocked. She fears to make the gesture that will wish her back into Alterre. She opens up window mode. The commentary box tells her the Deccan Traps are erupting.

Half a million cubic kilometres of lava issue from a magma plume coiling up from the mantle over what will in sixty-five million years' time be the island of Réunion. Mt. St. Helens blew a puny single cubic kilometre when it shook the Pacific Northwest. Half a million Mt. St. Helens. Spread them out and they would smother the states of Washington and Oregon two kilometres deep in liquid basalt. The actual Deccan Traps formed a layer two kilometres deep over Central Western India, when that subcontinent was racing (geologically speaking) towards the Asian landmass in the head-on collision that would throw up Earth's mightiest mountain range. The CO_2 released overwhelmed all extant carbon-burying mechanisms and brought the curtain down on Earth's Cretaceous period. Life on Earth has been to the edge many times. Alterre would not have been an alternative evolution without mechanisms for mass extinction like vulcanism, polar wandering, celestial impact. The toys of major league God-gamers. What scares Lisa Durnau is not that the Traps are erupting. It is that the Deccan flood basalts never reached the Indo-Gangetic plain. In Alterre, Varanasi is buried beneath a plain of glowing basalt.

Lisa pulls up into God-vision. A finger of guilt from her church childhood accuses her as she spins up high above the Australo-Indian Ocean. The view was never this good from real space. Europe is an arc of islands and peninsulas around the westward curve of the planet, Asia a northward-steering sweep of terrain. North Asia burns. Ash clouds cover half a continent. The fires light the dark half of the planet. Lisa Durnau calls up a data window. She gives a soft, wordless cry. The Siberian Traps are also erupting.

Alterre is dying, trapped between the fires at its head and its waist. Crustal carbon dioxide released by the frothy, gassy basalt will join with carbon from the burning forests into a rabid greenhouse that will lift atmospheric and ocean temperatures sufficiently to trigger a clathrate burst: methane, locked in ice cages deep under the ocean, released in one titanic outgassing. The oceans will seethe like a dropped can of soda. Oxygen levels plunge as temperatures rise. Photosynthesis in the oceans shuts down. The seas become cauldrons of rotting plankton.

Life might survive one meltdown. Earth had survived the Chixulub impact and the resulting Deccan melt on the other side of the planet at the cost of twenty-five percent of its species. The Siberian Traps eruption two hundred and fifty million years ago had ended the Permian life-burst with the extinction of ninety-five percent of living organisms. Life had reeled over the abyss and come back. Two eruptions at the same time is the end of biology on Earth.

Lisa Durnau watches her world fall apart.

This is not nature. This is an assault. Thomas Lull had designed Alterre with a robust immune system to defend against the inevitable hacks. For an attack to come through the aeais that ran the geophysical, oceanological, and climatological systems must have access to the central registries. This is an inside job.

Lisa Durnau rolls out of Alterre back on to the terrace of the haveli in the summer rain. She is shaking. Once in London Lisa Durnau was mugged outside a Tube Station. It had been short and sharp and not particularly brutal, just quick and businesslike: her cash, her cards, her palmer, her shoes. It was over before she realised. She had gone through the crime with a sense of numb acquiescence, almost of scientific inquiry. Afterwards the fear hit, the shaking, the anger, the outrage at what had been done to her and her utter impassivity in the face of it.

A whole world has been mugged here.

The call is lined up to the department before she realises. Lisa Durnau waves away the address, folds the Tablet, slides it back inside her pocket. She cannot break cover. She does not know what to do. And she sees him; Thomas Lull, leaning over the reception desk, asking for his key, dripping from his saturated surfer shirt and baggie shorts and slicked-down hair into little spreading pools on the white marble. He has not seen her. To him she is half a planet away on a hilltop in

Kansas. Lisa Durnau starts to call his name and the two men in cheap suits and sandals get up and walk over to the desk. One shows Thomas Lull an object in his hand. The other places a firm hand on his shoulder. He looks dazed, confused, then the first man opens a large black umbrella and the three of them hurry across the rain-soaked garden to the gates where a police car has drawn up in a slush of spray.

42 LULL

The game is bad cop and bad cop. You're in an interrogation room. It could be a jail cell, a confession box, or a torture chamber, what matters is that you can't hear or see what's happening outside. All you know is what the cops tell you. You have a partner in crime in an identical room. For you are accused.

So they have you in this green interview room that smells of thick paint and antiseptic. *See that partner/fellow hoodlum/lover of yours? Soon as the tape went on, they spilled everything, including you.* This is what you have to decide. They could be telling the truth. They could be playing headgames to get you to grass up your partner. You don't know and bad cops won't tell you. They're *bad*. Then they let you stew without even a cop coffee.

The way you see the deal is this. You deny everything and your partner/fellow hoodlum/lover denies everything and you might both walk. Insufficient evidence. You both confess and the cops turn out to be not so bad after all because there's nothing a cop likes less than paperwork and you've just saved them deskloads of that so they'll push for a noncustodial. Or you deny everything and in the other cell, you get fessed up. Fellow hoodlum walks and the full weight falls on you. What's best for you? You've got the answer before their footsteps even reach the far end of the corridor. You bang on the door. *Hey hey hey, come back here, I want to tell you every little thing.*

The game is called the Prisoner's Dilemma. It's not as much fun as blackjack or Dungeons and Dragons but it's a tool A-life researchers use to investigate complex systems. Play it enough and all manner of human truths emerge. Long-term good, short-term bad. Do as you would be done by and if not, then do unto them as they do unto you. Thomas Lull has played Prisoner's Dilemma and a slate of other limited-information games millions of times. It's very different playing for real.

The room is green and smells of disinfectant. It also smells of mould, old urine, hot ghee, and damp from the shirts of the rain-soaked cops. They are not good cops, they are not bad cops, they are just cops who would rather get back to their wives and children. One keeps rocking back on his chair and looking at Thomas Lull, with his eyebrows raised, as if expecting an epiphany. The other one is constantly checking his nails and has an uncomfortable thing he does with his mouth that reminds Thomas Lull of old Tom Hanks movies.

Do what you need to, Lull. Don't be clever, don't be fly. Get yourself out of here. He feels a growing closeness in his chest.

"Look, I told the soldiers, I'm travelling with her, she has relatives in Varanasi."

Chair-rocker swings forwards and scrawls Hindi on a spiral-bound notepad. The voice recorder isn't working. They say. Tom Hanks does the thing with the mouth again. It's really starting to needle Thomas Lull. That, too, could be part of it.

"That might be enough for provincial jawans, but this is Varanasi, sir."

"I don't understand what the hell is happening."

"It is quite simple, sir. Your colleague made an inquiry at the National DNA database. A routine security scan revealed certain . . . anomalous structures in her skull. She was apprehended by security and passed into our custody."

"You keep saying this, anomalous structures, what does that mean, what are these anomalous structures?"

Tom Hanks looks at his nails again. His mouth is unhappy.

"This is now a matter of national security, sir."

"This is fucking Franz Kafka, is what it is."

Tom Hanks looks at chair-rocker, who writes the name down.

"He's a Czech writer," Thomas Lull says. "He's been dead a hundred years. I was attempting irony."

"Sir, please do not attempt irony. This is a most serious issue."

Chair-rocker deliberately crosses the name out and takes a swing back to study Thomas Lull with added perspective. The heat in the windowless room is incredible. The smell of damp policeman is overpowering.

"What do you know of this female?"

"I met her at a beach party at Thekkady down in Kerala. I helped her over an asthma attack. I liked her, she was travelling north, I went with her."

Tom Hanks flips up a corner of the folder on the desk, pretends to consult a scrap of text.

"Sir, she stopped a section of Awadhi counterinsurgency robots with a wave of her hand."

"That's a crime?"

Chair-rocker snaps forward. His chair feet crack on the shoe-polished concrete floor.

"Awadhi airborne divisions have just taken the Kunda Khadar dam. The entire garrison has surrendered. It may not be a crime, but you must admit, the coincidence is . . . extreme."

"This is a fucking joke. What, you think she is something to do with that?"

"I do not make jokes where my country's security is concerned," Tom Hanks says. "All I know is this report and that your travelling companion set off the alarms trying to access the National DNA database."

"I need to know these anomalies."

Tom Hanks swivels his eyes at chair-rocker.

"Do you know who I am?"

"You are Professor Thomas Lull."

"Do you not think I might be better positioned to offer a hypothesis about this than you? If I knew what you were taking about?"

Chair-rocker confers in short, stabbing Hindi with Tom Hanks. Thomas Lull can't decide which of them is the superior.

"Very well, sir. As you know, we are in a state of heightened alert because of the situation with our neighbour, Awadh. It is only logical that we protect ourselves against cyberwar, so we have installed a number of scanners at sensitive locations to pick up slow missiles, infiltrators, agents, that sort of thing. Identity theft is a recognised tool of undercover operatives so the archive was routinely equipped with surveillance devices. The scanners at the DNA archive picked up structures inside this woman's skull similar to protein circuitry."

By now Thomas Lull cannot tell what is game and what is real and what is beyond either. He thinks of the shock he gave Aj on the train when he exposed the lies that were her life. She has returned that shock tenfold.

Tom Hanks slides a palmer across the desk to Thomas Lull. He does not want to look, he does not want to see the alien inside Aj but he turns the device to him. It is a false-colour pseudo-X-ray assembled from infrasound scans. Her lovely skull is pale blue. The globes of her eyes, the tangled vine-root of the optic nerve, the ghostly canals of sinuses and blood vessels are grey on greyer. Aj is a ghost of herself; her brain most spectral of all, a haunting of sentience in a web of fibres. There is a ghost in the ghost; lines and ranks of nanocircuits arching across the inside of her skull. The tilak is a dark gateway in her forehead like a mosque darwaz. From it chains and webs of protein wiring thread back through the frontal lobes, across the central fissure into the parietal lobe, sending probes into the corpus callosum, twining tight around the limbic system, delving deep into the medulla while it wraps the occipital lobe in coils of protein processors. Aj's brain is chained in circuitry.

"Kalki," he whispers and the room goes black. Complete lightlessness. No lights, no emergency power, nothing. Thomas Lull fumbles his palmer out of his pocket. Hindi voices yell in the corridor, rising in intensity.

"Professor Lull Professor Lull, do not attempt to move!" Tom Hanks' voice is querulous and panicky. "For your own safety, I order you to remain where you are while I ascertain what has happened."

The voices in the corridor grow louder. A rasp, a flare; chair-rocker man lights a match. Three faces in a bubble of light, then darkness. Thomas Lull moves quickly. His fingers feel out the memory wafer slot on the side of the police palmer and slide it open. A rasp, he whips his hands back, then light. Tom Hanks is by the door. The babble of voices has become intermittent, calls, responses. As the match burns out Thomas Lull thinks he sees a fluctuating line of light under the door, a torch bobbing. He releases the memory chip. Another match flare. The door is open now, Tom Hanks conversing with an unseen officer in the corridor.

"What's going on, is Varanasi under attack?" Thomas Lull calls out. Anything to sow uncertainty. The match burns out. Thomas Lull flips out the memory chip of his own palmer. A few deft movements and he has switched them over.

He glimpsed other phantoms in that look inside Aj, phantoms that might confirm his suspicions about what had been done to her, and why.

"Your friend has escaped," Tom Hanks says, swinging the torch beam into Thomas Lull's face. In the shadow his hands close the slots.

"How did she manage to do that?" Thomas Lull asks.

"I was hoping you might be able to tell me."

"I've been right here in front of you all along."

"Every system is out," Tom Hanks says. The mouth is working double-shifts. "We do not know how far the blackout reaches, it is at least this district."

"And she walked right out."

"Yes," the policeman says. "You will understand if we detain you for further questioning." A burst of Hindi to chair-rocker who gets up and closes the door. Thomas Lull hears an old-school manual bolt shoot over.

"Hey!" he shouts in the dark. Thoughts of a middle-aged man locked in a dark police interview room. His suspicions, his calculations, his speculations swell to room-filling proportions, giants of fear and shock that press close against him, pressing the air from his lungs. The nose for breathing, the mouth for talking. The mind for dark imagining. Kalki. She is Kalki, the final avatar. All he needs is the proof he glimpsed etched into the scanner print.

After a timeless time that is only ten minutes by the wall clock the lights come back on. The door opens and Tom Hanks stands back to admit a black man in a wet raincoat that immediately identifies his nationality and employment.

"Professor Thomas Lull?"

Lull nods.

"I am Peter Paul Rhodes from the United States consular office. Please come with me."

He extends a hand. Thomas Lull takes it hesitantly.

"What is this?"

"Sir, your release into my charge has been ordered by the Bharati Justice Department because of your diplomatic status in the Department of Foreign Affairs."

"Foreign Affairs?" Thomas Lull knows how dumb he sounds, thick like a broken-down petty thief. "Senator Joe O'Malley knows I'm in a Bharati police station and wants me out?"

"That is correct. All will be explained. Please come with me."

Thomas Lull takes the hand but scoops his palmer into his pocket. Tom Hanks escorts them down the corridor. The front office is full of policemen and one woman. She gets up from the wooden bench where she has been sitting. There is a pool of rainwater at her feet. Her clothes are wet, her hair is wet, her face shines with wet and is thinner, older but he knows it instantly and it makes the madness complete.

"L. Durnau?"

43

TAL, NAJIA

Eight and a half thousand rupees is enough to bribe the chowkidar. He counts notes with his skinny fingers while Najia Askarzadah drips in the glass and marble foyer of Indiapendent. Then he swipes his master pass and namastes them through the glass half doors.

"I never believed it was you, Talji," Pande the security man shouts after them, folding Najia's wad of cash into the breast pocket of his high-collared jacket. "We can make pictures do anything these days."

"They shot at me, you know," Tal calls as they head for the elevator stack.

It's never like this in the movies, Najia Askarzadah thinks as the glass lift descends like a pearl of light. They should have had to blast their way in with beva-firepower and hi-kicking, mid-air-spinning, slo-mo martial arts action. The cool heroine shouldn't have to call her parents in Sweden to ask them to BACS her a bribe. The most action she had seen was Pande the nightwatchman thumbing his generous wad. But it's a strange little conspiracy; more Bollywood than Hollywood.

The glass walls of the metasoap wing stream with rain. It had begun as the taxi they had been hiding in all day arrived outside Indiapendent Productions. The parking lot was a basti of brick-and-cardboard lean-tos and knots of soapi faithful huddled under plastic sheets.

"They always come out for a wedding," Tal said. "It's like a religion. Lal Darfan always delivers. PR says he's had twenty miracle births attributed to him."

Tal hurries Najia past the dark work carrels to the furthest desk. Yt pulls up two chairs, logs in—"nothing we can do about that, baba"—opens up the wrap-round screen and drops them into Brahmpur, the eponymous Town of Indiapendent's all-conquering soapi.

Tal whirls her through the streets and galis, the ghats and malls of this virtual city. Najia is dazzled. The detail is complete down to the advertising signs and the bustling phatphats. In Brahmpur as in Varanasi it is night and it is raining. The monsoon has come to this imaginary city. Najia is too proud to have watched an entire episode of *Town and Country* but even as a neo she recognises there are whole districts of this city of illusions the plot never visits, that have been lovingly built and maintained by exabytes of processing power merely to hold the rest together. Tal raises yts hands and their djinn-flight slams to a halt in front of a crumbling waterfront haveli. She feels she could touch the flaking stucco. A mudra and they pass through the walls into the great hall of the Nadiadwala haveli.

"Wow," says Najia Askarzadah. She can see the cracks on the low leather sofas.

"Oh, this isn't the real Brahmpur," Tal says. Another elegant gesture and time blurs forward. "Well, the cast think it is but we call it Brahmpur B. It's the metacity in which the metasoap takes place. I'm just winding us forward to the Chawla/Nadiadwala wedding. Have you got that video handy?"

But Najia is dazed by the flickering ghosts of future plotlines across the still room. Day and night strobe across her vision. Tal opens yts hand like a claw, twists it, and time slows down to a chug of light and dark. She can see the people now, zipping through the elegant, cool marble hall. Tal slows time again and the hall is suddenly bright with coloured hangings. Tal pushes yts open palm against air and time freezes.

"Here, here." Tal clicks yts fingers impatiently. Najia hands yt her palmer. Without taking yts eyes off the screen yt datatransfers from the palmer. A hole opens in the middle of the hall and fills with N. K. Jivanjee. With delicate flicks of yts fingers Tal jogs the picture forward until it has a good lock on the background, then pulls in, draws a box around the fabric hung-wall, tears it out of N. K. Jivanjee's world, and drops it into fake Brahmpur. Even Najia Askarzadah can see the match.

"This is about six months down our metasoap timeline," Tal says as yt lets the POV roam around the room, swooping around the frozen wedding guests in their couture and the simulacra of real-world chati-mag reporters in their texture-mapped society-best, waiting for the arrival of the fake groom on his white horse. "They exist in several time-frames at once."

Najia remembers Lal Darfan's fantastical flying elephant-pavilion hovering over the high Himalayas. *Can any of us trust what we think we remember?* he had asked. She had thought to argue sophistries with an aeai actor but Tal plays a more sophisticated game, the meta-meta-game. Najia remembers an old childhood faery-tale told by a baby-sitter on a midwinter night, a dangerous one, disquieting as only the truly fey disquiets; that the faery realms were nested inside each other like baboushka dolls, but each was bigger than the one that enclosed it until at the centre you had to squeeze through a door smaller than a mustard seed but it contained whole universes.

"We've got them scripted up to about eight months ahead in fair detail. We haven't got the weather; there's a subaeai predicts it twenty-four hours ahead and then drops it on. By the time that script comes to real-time, the memory's fixed and they can't remember it ever having been another way. There's a news aeai does the thing for gupshup and sports results and stuff like that. The major characters are much further ahead on their timelines than the minor ones so we work in several time dimensions at once—properly they're time vectors that angle away from our own."

"This is freaky."

"I like freaky. The point is, no one outside of Indiapendent has access to this."

"Satnam?"

Tal frowns.

"I don't know if he could operate the system. Okay, hold on. We're going to go to full prope. I'll 'hoek you up, here."

Tal fixes yts own 'hoek, smart plastic hugging up warm against the curve of yts skull, then fits Najia with the second device. Yts fingers are very deft and very light and very soft. Were she not breaking and entering a secure system with a Most Wanted nute who might just have brought down the government and whom she had rescued that very morning from a railway-station assassin, she might purr.

"I'm going to go into the registries. You may find this a little disorienting."

Najia Askarzadah almost goes straight over backwards on her chair. She is dropped into the centre of a vast sphere filled with dashes of registry code, all superimposed over the dark room and the curve of liquid screen and the rain streaming down the thick blue glass. She is the centre of a galaxy of data; whichever way she looks, code upon code streams away from her. Tal turns yts hands and the sphere spins, address lines blurring with data-shift across Najia's vision. Reeling with vertigo, she grips the sides of her chair.

"Oh man."

"You get used to it. If someone has been into my lovely wedding, they'll have left a trace behind in the registry, that's what I'm looking for now. The most recent entries are at the centre, the older ones get pushed further out. Ah." Tal points. Codes blur like warp-driven stars. Najia Askarzadah is sure she can feel data-wind in her hair. She drops out of cyberdrive into an inertialess stop at a green code-fragment. The sphere of glowing file addresses looks unchanged. Centre everywhere, perimeter nowhere. Like the universe. Tal picks up the code.

"Now this is freaky."

"Do you like this freaky?" Najia asks.

"Indeed I do not. Someone has been into my design files but it's not a code I recognise. It doesn't look like it's come from the outside."

"Some other bit of the 'ware is accessing your files?"

"More like the actors are rewriting their own scripts. I'm going in. If you feel dizzy, close your eyes."

She doesn't and her stomach turns loops as the universe of slow-drifting codes jerks and spins and zooms and warps around her. Tal hyper-jumps from code-cluster to code-cluster. "This is very very strange. It's an inside job all right, but it's not one of our cast. Look, see?" Tal gathers a harvest of codes, lays them out on a grid in space. "These bits here are all common. To save memory space, a lot of our lower-level aeai actors are subapplications of higher-level aeais. Anita Mahapatra also contains Narinder Rao, Mrs. Devgan, the Begum Vora and they in turn contain maybe fifty redshirts."

"Redshirts?"

"Disposable extras. I think it's an American term. This is a list of all the recent accesses to the set design system. See? Someone's been into my design files regularly over the past eighteen months. But what is freaky is, all those common code sections point to an even higher level actor; one that contains Lal Darfan and Aparna Chawla and Ajay Nadiadwala. It's like there's something else running in there we can't see because it's too big."

In the cream coloured house by the water there was an atlas the size of a small child. On the winter nights when the inlet froze, Najia, age eight, would fight the thing down from its shelf, open it on the floor, and lose herself in other climates. She played a game with her mother and father where you picked a word on a map and raced to put a finger on it. She realised early that the way to play and win was to go big and obvious. The eye scrying through the towns and villages and stations of the Matto Grosso could miss the name BRAZIL spread across the map in faded grey letters the size of her thumb. Hiding in plain sight among the scribbles.

Najia blinks out of Tal's spiral dance of codes and file addresses back into the dark carrel. She is trapped inside a cube of rain. A master script that wrote itself? A soap opera like India's seven million gods; avatars and emanations descending through levels of divinity from Brahman, the Absolute, the One?

Then she sees Tal push ytself back from the computer, mouth open in fear, hand raised to ward off the evil eye. In the same perspective she also sees Pande in his high-collared jacket and yellow turban rush loose-boned into the department.

Tal: "This is impossible . . ."

Pande: "Sir Madam, sir madam, come quick come quick, the Prime Minister . . ."

Then Najias Askarzadah's 'hoek flashes into full prope and she is swept away from Tal, from Pande, from Indiapendent in the monsoon, to a bright, high place, a silk-draped prospect among the clouds. She knows where this is. She has been summoned to this place before. It is the airborne elephant pavilion of Lal Darfan, sailing the line of the Himalayas. But the man on the cushioned throne in front of her is not Lal Darfan. It is N. K. Jivanjee.

44

SHIV

Yogendra takes the boat out into a stream of burning diyas. Monsoon winds churn Ganga but the little, delicate mango-leaf saucers bob on through the broken water. Shiv sits cross-legged under the plastic awning, gripping the gunwales and trying to feel the balance. He prays that he will not have to hurl. He glances back at Yogendra squatting in the stern, hand steady on the tiller of the alcofuel motor, eyes reading the river. His skin is beaded with rain, it streams from his hair down his face, his clothes cling to him. Shiv thinks of rats he has seen swimming in open roadside sewers. But the knotted pearls around Yogendra's neck shine.

"Pump, pump," Yogendra orders. Shiv bends to the little bilge pump. The rain is filling the boat—a handy little American sports white-waterer with Pacific Northwest iconography on its bows though Shiv would have preferred an Eye of Siva—faster than the hand-pump can clear it. That is not an arithmetic Shiv can look at too closely. He can't swim. A raja's experience of water is lolling in the shallow end of a pool with girls and floating drinks trays.

As long as it takes them to Chunar.

"You land somewhere around here." Anand laid the A4 high-resolution printouts of the Chunar district map out on his coffee table. *Kif* coffee simmered on its brazier. Anand tapped his finger on the map. "The town of Chunar is about five kays south. I call it a town purely as a politeness to the fact that it's on a bridge over the Ganga. Chunar is a rural shithole full of cowfuckers and incest. The only thing of any interest is the old fort. Here, I've got printouts." Anand dealt out a hand of glossies. Shiv flicked through the photographs. The story of the Ganga was the story of forts like Chunar, drawn down by historical inevitability onto the promontories and hill-tops where the river turned, drawing to them power, dynasty, intrigue, imprisonment, siege, assault. One last assault. He paused at the interiors, crumbling Raj-Moghul architectures smothered by swooping construction-carbon canopies, white as salt in the sun. "Ramanandacharya is a flash chuutya, but he's the only game in town. As well as the sundarban, he's got a call centre. You want to get into your husband's system, see what he's been up to; you want to hack into that credit black-list, they'll crack the code for you while you wait.

"Every adivasi is loyal to the chief. You get in, you do your business, you get out, you do not hang around for thank-yous or kisses. Now, the defences at Chunar Fort . . ."

Aircraft hammer overhead so low and loud Shiv covers his head. Yogendra stands in the stern, turning to follow their lights; four military tilt-jets in tight formation. Shiv sees his teeth glint in the light from the city.

"Pump, pump!"

He works the creaking handpump, watches the water pooling around the plastic-sealed packages. He would be better throwing the fatuous techy thing over the side and bailing with his hands. Americans and their machines. Something to do everything. Learn that people are better and cheaper. You can punish them and they will learn.

The thunder moves west. In its wake the rain doubles in weight. On the left bank the gas flares from the processing plants give way to the heavy sandstone bulk of Ramnagar Fort, an imposing impostor under the floodlights. Yogendra takes the boat under the pontoon bridge, a sword of sound even in the downpour. Shiv studies Ramnagar; terraces and pavilions rising beyond its red curtain walls, their feet in the water. You stand there, Shiv thinks. You wait for when I get back, when I have taken your sister upstream and then we will see how proud and defiant you look with your walls and turrets. A true task for a raja, storming a castle. Not by siege or at the head of a thousand elephants, but by smart, by style. Shiv Faraji, Action Hero.

Now the swift little boat approaches the new bridge. Yogendra feels out the slack water channel and shoots it. A truck has come off the roadway and embedded itself in the shallows, a snag of decorative metal barely recognisable as a vehicle. There is still a smell of alcofuel on the water. Beyond the fuel reek, perfume. Shiv raises his head to the sickly odour of marigolds. Smell is the key of memory; a sharp flash of where he has smelled this before: the fat tires of his Mercedes SUV crushing petals as it climbed the banks here. Marigolds masking turning flesh, the swelling body he slipped into the waters of the Ganga, these waters he sails now. He has recapitulated the corpse's journey, away from moksha.

"Ey!" Yogendra unhooks the earpiece of his palmer and lifts it up for Shiv to see. "Radio Kashi." Shiv thumbs up the station. Urgent news voices breaking over each other, talking about soldiers, air strikes, fighting machines. Kunda Khadar. The Awadhis have taken Kunda Khadar. The Awadhis have broken on to the sacred soil of

Bharat. The Awadhis are about to take Allahabad, holy Allahabad of the Kumbh Mela. Sajida Rana's troops flee before them like mice from a stubble-burning. Sajida Rana's vaunted jawans threw down their weapons and threw up their hands. Sajida Rana's plan has brought ruin to Bharat. Sajida Rana has failed Bharat, shamed Bharat, brought Bharat to its knees. What will Sajida Rana do now?

Shiv turns the radio off.

"What is this to do with us?" he says to Yogendra. "The elephants fight but the rats go about their business." The boy waggles his head and opens up the engine. The boat lifts its prow and pushes upriver through the walls of the rain.

"This is good kit. Not top, now, but good. I'll take you through it. These are plasma tasers. You know how they work? They're not hard. Arm here, the yellow tab. Your basic point and shoot. You don't even need a particularly good aim, that's the beauty of them and that's what makes them your weapon of preference. There's enough gas in the canister for twelve shots. You've got five each, that should be enough. Just throw them away when you're done, they're dead. They will stop machinery but their best use is against biological targets. Our man Ramanandacharya is a tech head and that is his fatal weakness, but he does have a few bits of meat around the place for sex and gun stuff. He likes women. A lot. He's got this James Bond thing, so Mukherjee says. I mean, you've seen the castle? Now, I don't know if they're in red catsuits, but you might have to taser a couple, just to teach them, you know? And every yokel is his loyal mindslave. On top of that there's a couple of real guys with guns and martial arts, Mukherjee says, but there's a way to deal with them and that's not let them get too close. Do you think the women are in red catsuits? Could you get me some photographs? Tasers for the meat. For the machines you want area-effect weapons. You want these sweeties. EMP grenades. These are so cool. Like pouring kerosene on scorpions. Just make sure you aren't 'hoeked up or anything or you're deaf, dumb, blind. Also, careful round the ware. I don't need to tell you this but they will crispy any soft systems. Now, the suddhavasa where he keeps his decrypters. He's converted an old Siva temple in the grounds—there on the map. The crypt won't be very big, maybe only a few gigs, but I don't recommend you try to mail it out. It'll all fit onto a palmer. Just be careful with the EMPs around it, okay? You've got the master file name and the quantum key so even you should be able to pull it out of the suddhavasa. Now, why our beloved N. K. Jivanjee wants this, I don't know, but we don't ask. Not the Naths anyway.

"Getting back out, well that's always the part where it's a little bit loose. You kind of make it up as you go along here. That's not to say there isn't an über-strategy. The thing is you don't waste time. Get in there, take them out, get the thing and get out and do not permit distractions. Distractions destroy. Get out and don't stop for anyone or anything least of all some village Egor. There're more than enough shots in the tasers, if they look like they're coming after you, drop a second minefield behind you. Get back to the boat and then get back here and you are a free free man, Shiv Faraji, and I will hail and salute you as a god and friend.

"How do I know all this? What do you think I do all day? Play sneak-and-shoot games and watch shitloads of movies. How does anyone know?"

After an hour and a half pushing upstream the monsoon slackens from a downpour to a steady rain. Shiv looks up from playing Commando Attack on his palmer at the change in tempo on the curved plastic. It would be an irony upon an irony if, after three years of drought and fighting a water war in the middle of a downpour, the saving monsoon should rain itself out in a single night.

Beyond Ramnagar the river is darker than darkness. Yogendra steers by GPS fixes on the shoals and the feel of the current. Shiv has felt sand grate under the hull. The shallows flow and reform faster than the satellites ten thousand kilometres overhead can map them. The boat rocks as Yogendra throws the tiller over hard. He cuts the engine, swings it up. The boat runs up on to the beach. Yogendra ducks through the canopy and jumps on to the shore.

"Come on, come on."

The shore sand is soft, sinking and flowing away with the current beneath Shiv's feet. The darkness out here is immense. Shiv reminds himself that he is only a few tens of kilometres away from his club and barman. A clutch of lights to the south is Chunar. In the vast quiet of the country night he can hear the traffic on the pontoon and the persistent chug of the water-extraction plants downstream. Jackals and pi-dogs yip in the distance. Shiv arms himself swiftly. He splits the taser mines between himself and Yogendra but keeps the kill switch. Hayman Dane's file name and system key are in the fat man's palmer, slung around Shiv's neck.

Among the thorn-hedged dal fields of Chunar, Shiv rigs out for battle. This is madness. He will die here among these fields and bones.

"Okay," he says with a deep shuddering sigh. "Wheel them out."

He and Yogendra wrestle two bulky cling-wrapped rectangles on to the sand. Ribs and spars, curves and bulges press through the plastic skin. Yogendra flashes a long blade.

"What is this?" Shiv demands.

Yogendra offers him the knife, turning it so the gleams of light from the distant town catch its steel. It is the length of a forearm, serrated, hooked at the tip, ferruled. He lays open the stretch plastic skins with two swift strokes. He returns the blade to its leather holster, next his skin. Lying in the plastic are two factory-fresh, chrome-bright Japanese trail bikes fuelled and ready to run. They start at first kick. Shiv mounts up. Yogendra walks his around the sand a little, feeling out the capabilities. Then Shiv nods to him and they open up the made-in-Yokohama engines and burn off through the rain-soaked dal fields.

45
SARKHAND ROUNDABOUT

At eleven thirty the huddle of umbrellas moves from the porch of the Rana Bhavan towards the Mercedes parked on the gravel turning circle. The umbrellas are white, an unnatural shade. They press together like a phalanx. Not one drop of water passes through. The rain is torrential now, a thunderous drowning downpour shot through with muggy lightning. At the centre of the cluster of domed umbrellas is Prime Minister Sajida Rana. She wears a white silk sari trimmed with green and orange. It is the most serious business she goes to this night. It is the defence of her country and her authority. All across Varanasi identical Mercedes are pulling away from tasteful government bungalows.

The umbrellas press up against the side of the car like piglets at the teat of a black sow. Safe and dry, Sajida Rana slips into the back seat. She sits instinctively on the left side. Shaheen Badoor Khan should be in the right seat offering analyses, advisements, perceptions. She looks alone as the doors lock and the car pulls off into the rain. She looks like what she is, a middle-aged woman with the weight of a nation upon her. The umbrellas break up and dart back to the shelter of the Rana Bhavan's deep verandas.

Sajida Rana flicks through the hastily prepared briefing document. The facts are scant and perfunctory. The Awadhi assault was technically flawless. Brilliant. Bloodless. Military colleges will be teaching it for decades to come. Awadhi armour and mechanised infantry are within twenty kilometres of Allahabad, antiaircraft and communication systems have come under sustained aeai attack and the defending battalion is in disarray, its control at the Kunda Khadar dam beheaded, desperately trying to reestablish a line of command with the divisional headquarters at Jaunpur. And it is raining. Sajida Rana is losing a water war in the rain. But it comes too late. Her nation can die of thirst in a deluge.

They knew. The bastards had it calculated to the minute.

In her white, gold, and green sari Sajida Rana tries to imagine how the words of surrender will feel in her mouth. Will they be bloated, choking; will they be dry and acid; will they slip out as easily as a Muslim divorcing his wife? Talaaq talaaq talaaq.

Khan. Faithless Muslim. Betrayed her with another, a *thing*. When she needs his words, his insights, his presence beside her on the cream leather. If Jivanjee and his karsevaks knew she rode on cow-coloured leather . . . *Let Jivanjee do your work for you*, Khan had said. Now he will drive his juggernaut over her bones. No. She is a Rana, daughter of a founder of nations, a seeder of dynasties. She is Bharat. She will fight. Let the Ganga overflow with blood.

"Where are we going?"

"Traffic, ma'am," the driver says. Sajida Rana settles back on her upholstery and looks out through the rain-streaked windows. Neons and tail lights, the gaudy Diwali illuminations of the trucks. She thumbs the com.

"This is not the usual way to the Bharat Sabha."

"No, ma'am," the driver says and sinks his foot to the board. Unbalanced, Sajida Rana reels. She tries the locks knowing it for folly, knowing she heard the solid, German-engineering click of the central locking. She opens her palmer, calls her security as the Mercedes touches one hundred and twenty.

"This is Prime Ministerial emergency code. Lock on to my GPS signal, I am being abducted, I repeat, this is Sajida Rana, I am being abducted."

Sky hiss. Then the voice of her chief of security says,

"Prime Minister, I will not do that. No one will help you. You have betrayed Holy Bharat and Bharat will punish you."

Then the Mercedes turns into Sarkhand Roundabout and the screaming starts.

PART FIVE
JYOTIRLINGA

46

ENSEMBLE

The Bharatiya Vayu Sena Airbus Industries A510 bumps a little as it climbs through the cloud layer over Varanasi. Ashok Rana grips the armrests. He has never been a good flier. He glances out the rain-streaked window at the bright arcs of flares dropping away behind them. The fuselage vibrates as ECM drones launch from the underwing pods. There has been no Awadhi aerial activity over Varanasi for days now but the air force takes no chances with its new Prime Minister. Ashok Rana thinks, from the angle of the raindrops on the glass I should be able to work out my speed. Many such inconsequential thoughts have come to him since the call from Secretary Narvekar in the night.

The plane lurches again, beating through the monsoon. Ashok Rana switches on his armrest screen. The camera shows his wife and daughters back in the press-office compartment. Sushmita's face tightens with fear as the Airbus jolts again; Anuja gives a word of comfort, takes her hand. In his Prime Ministerial leather armchair, Ashok Rana allows himself a minute smile. He wishes there were a camera here at the front so they could see him. They would not be so afraid, if they could see him.

"Prime Minister."

His Parliamentary Private Secretary swivels his seat towards him and passes a much be scribbled printout across the table.

"We have a draft of the speech, if you would like to familiarise yourself with its key points."

The Prime Ministerial transport gives a final buck and breaks free into clear air. Through the window Ashok Rana sees the moonlit surface of a storm-sea of cloud. The pilot bings off the seatbelt light and instantly the plastic tube of the fuselage is filled with call-tones. Every politician and civil servant is out of his seat and pressing around the conference table. They lean forward with expectant, keen faces. They have been wearing those expectant, keen faces since Secretary Narvekar and Defence Minister Chowdhury stooped down through the door of the Bharati Air Force tilt-jet that had landed in his garden to help Ashok Rana and his family aboard. Chief Justice Laxman administered the oath while the military transport dropped towards the remote, secure corner of the airport where Vayu Sena One had been brought. The army nurse with the white white surgical gloves had made the lightest of nicks in his thumb with a scalpel, pressed it to a diagnostic pad and even before Ashok Rana could register the pain she had swabbed it clean with surgical alcohol and slipped on a dressing.

"For the DNA authorisation, Prime Minister," Trivul Narvekar explained but Ashok Rana's attention was on the air force officer immediately behind the nurse, gun drawn, muzzle hovering a whisper from the back of her skull. To lose one Prime Minister is tragedy. Two starts to look like conspiracy. Then Chief Justice Laxman's face loomed into his field of vision.

"I now present you with the seals of state, Prime Minister. You are endowed with full executive authority."

The A510 swims up towards the huge Bharati moon. Ashok Rana could look at it forever, imagine there is no chaotic, broken nation down beneath the clouds. But the faces expect. He glances over the printout. Measured phrases, memorable sound bites with edit-pauses written in before and after them, resolutions and rousing declarations. Ashok Rana glances again at his family in the little palm-sized screen.

"Has my sister's body been recovered?"

Every clamouring voice, every palmer falls silent.

"The area has been secured," Secretary Narvekar says.

"Can we trust the army?"

"We have sent in regular forces. We can rely on them. The group was a small cabal among the elite divisions that supplied madam's personal security unit. Those responsible are under arrest; unfortunately we were unable to prevent some of the higher-ranking officers from taking their own lives. The personal bodyguard is all dead, Prime Minister."

Ashok Rana closes his eyes, feels the contours in the stratosphere around the aircraft shell that encloses him.

"Not the Awadhis."

"No, Prime Minister. It was never a consideration that the Awadhis would resort to assassination, if you will excuse my use of the word."

"The rioters?"

"Dispersed, Prime Minister. The situation in the city remains highly volatile. I would advise against any immediate return to Varanasi."

"I do not want them pursued. Morale is bad enough without loosing the army on our own population. But we should maintain martial law."

"Very wise, Prime Minister. Magnanimous in the face of national crisis; that will play well. Prime Minister, I don't want to be seen to be pressurising you in this desperate time of shock and grief, but this speech . . . It is important that the nation hears from you, and soon."

"In a while, Trivul"

"Prime Minister, the slot is booked, the camera and audio are set up in the media centre . . ."

"In a while, Trivul!"

The Parliamentary Secretary bows away but Ashok Rana can see the chewed-back irritation in the set of his lips. He looks out again at the moon, low now in the west on the edge of the silver sea of water raining down on his land. He will never be able to see it again, the lolling moon of India, without thinking of this night, without hearing the chime of the palmer in the night and the wrench of dread in his gut that knew, even before he answered, it was the worst possible news; without hearing the measured, well-rehearsed voice of Private Secretary Patak, so strange after the soft familiarity of Shaheen Badoor Khan, saying impossible things; without hearing the scream of tilt-jets thrashing the branches of the neem trees with their down-blast as his wife and children dressed and seized baggage in the dark for fear for making themselves illuminated targets for whatever it was out there that had turned upon the house of Rana. The light will forever be transformed into sounds. He hates that most, that they have tainted the moon.

"Vikram, I have to know, are we in any state to resist the Awadhis?"

Chowdhury waggles his head.

"The air force is one hundred percent."

"You do not win wars with air power. The army?"

"We risk splitting the entire command if we pursue the cabal too far. Ashok, if the Awadhis want Allahabad, there is very little we can do to stop them."

"Are our nuclear and chemical deterrents secure?"

"Prime Minister, surely you cannot be advocating first use?" Secretary Narvekar interjects. Again, Ashok Rana rounds on him.

"Our country is invaded, our cities lie wide open and my own sister has been thrown to a . . . to a . . . mob by her own soldiers. Do you know what they did with that trishul? Do you? Do you? What should I do to defend us? What can I do to keep us safe?"

The faces turn softly, politely blank, impassively reflecting Ashok Rana's shouting voice. He hears his edge of hysteria. He lets the words fall. The bulkhead between the conference room and the media centre is decorated with a modern interpretation of the Tandava Nritya, the cosmic dance of Siva; the god wreathed in the chakra of flame, one foot raised. Ashok Rana has lived all his forty-four years in the shadow of the descending foot that will destroy and regenerate the universe.

"Forgive me," he says shortly. "This is not an easy time."

The politicals mumble their acquiescences.

"Our nuclear and chemical capability is secure," Chowdhury says.

"That's all I needed to know," says Ashok Rana. "Now, this speech . . ."

A junior aide with two fingers raised to the side of his head interrupts him.

"Prime Minister, a call for you."

"I stated quite clearly that I am not taking any calls." Ashok Rana lets a little iron into his voice.

"Sahb, it is N. K. Jivanjee."

Eyes glance at each other around the oval table. Ashok Rana nods to his aide.

"On here." He taps the armrest screen. In the press compartment his wife and children have settled into some semblance of sleep, leaning against each other. The head and shoulders of the Shivaji leader take their place, softly lit by a hooded lamp on his desk. Behind him are the geometrical suggestions of books rowed on shelves.

"Jivanjee. You dare much."

N. K. Jivanjee dips his head.

"I can understand why you would think that, Prime Minister." The title jolts Ashok Rana. "At the outset, I would ask you to accept my sincerest sympathies to your family on its tragic loss and to your late sister's husband and children. There is no part of Bharat that has not been stricken to the heart by what has happened at Sarkhand Roundabout. I am outraged by this brutal murder—and we call ourselves the mother of civilisations. I unreservedly condemn the treachery of the late Prime Minister's personal guard and those outlaw elements of the mob. I would ask you to accept that no part of the Shivaji condones this dreadful act. This was a mob element whipped to a frenzy by traitors and renegades."

"I could have you arrested," Ashok Rana says. His ministers and advisors look at him. N. K. Jivanjee nervously moistens his lips with the tiniest bud of tongue.

"And how would that serve Bharat? No, no, no, I have another suggestion. Our enemy is at the gates, our armed forces desert us, our cities riot, and our leader is brutally murdered. This is not a time for party politics. I propose a government of national salvation. As I have said, the Party of Lord Siva is innocent of any involvement in or support for this outrage, yet we retain some influence with the Hindutvavadi and the milder karsevaks."

"You can bring the streets under control."

N. K. Jivanjee sways his head.

"No politician can promise that. But at such a time opposing parties coming together in a government of national salvation would set a powerful example, not just to the riotous elements, but to all Bharatis, and to Awadh as well. A nation united is not easily defeated."

"Thank you, Mr. Jivanjee. It's an interesting offer. I will call you back, thank you for your good wishes, I accept them." Ashok Rana thumbs N. K. Jivanjee into the arm of the chair. He turns to his remnant cabinet. "Evaluations, gentlemen?"

"It is a deal with demons," V.K. Chowdhury says. "But . . ."

"He has you over a log," Chief Justice Laxman says. "He is a very clever man."

"I see no other practicable option than to take his suggestion," Trivul Narvekar says. "With two riders; first, that we make the suggestion. We extend the hand of peace to our political foes. Second, we rule certain cabinet positions out of the discussion."

"He will want cabinet posts?" Ashok Rana asks. Secretary Narvekar's astonishment is unfeigned.

"What other reason would he have for suggesting it? I suggest we keep the Treasury, the Ministry of Defence, and the Foreign Ministry inviolable. Apologies, Chief Justice."

"What would we suggest for our new friend Jivanjee himself?" Laxman asks, pressing the steward call to summon a Bells, to which he is legendarily partial.

"I can't see him settling for much less than interior Minister," Narvekar says.

"Chuutya," grunts Laxman into his Scotch.

"This'll be no Muslim marriage to get out of," Narvekar says. Ashok Rana toggles the screen to watch his wife and children sleeping against each other in the cheap seats. The clock reads oh four fifteen. Ashok Rana's head aches, his feet and sinuses feel swollen, his eyes dusty and weary. All senses of time and space and perspective have vanished. He could be floating in space in this migraine-inducing light. Chowdhury is talking about Shaheen Badoor Khan: "That's one Begum wishing the divorce thing ran the other way."

The men laugh softly in the harsh directional light of the overhead halogens.

"You have to admit, he has rather receded into the background," Narvekar says. "Twenty-four hours is a long time in politics."

"Never trusted the fellow," Chowdhury says. "Always felt there was something oily about him, too refined, too polite . . ."

"Too Muslim?" Narvekar asks.

"You said it; something not quite . . . manly. And I'm not so sure I agree with what you say about him vanishing into the background. You say twenty-four hours is a long time; I say, in politics nothing is unconnected. One loose pebble starts a landslide. For one horseshoe nail, the battle was lost. Butterfly in Beijing, all that. Khan is the root of it, for his own sake I hope he is out of Bharat."

"Hijra," Laxman comments. His ice clinks in the glass.

"Gentlemen," Ashok Rana says, hearing his voice as if spoken by another at a great distance, "my sister is dead." Then, after a grace-moment, he says, "So, our answer to Mr. Jivanjee?"

"He has his Government of National Salvation," Secretary Narvekar says. "After the speech."

The staffers in the second cabin speed-draft a revised speech. Ashok Rana skims the printout adding marginal marks in blue ink. Government of National Salvation. Extend Hand of Friendship. Unity in Strength. Through this Trying Time as One Nation. The Nation United Will Never Be Defeated.

"Prime Minister, it's time," Trivul Narvekar hints. He guides Ashok Rana to the studio at the front of Vayu Sena One. It is little bigger than an airline toilet; a camera, a boom microphone, a desk and chair and a Bharati flag draped from a pole, a vision mixer and sound engineer beyond the glass panel in the booth's mirror image. The sound engineer shows Ashok Rana how the desk hinges up so he can slip behind it on to the chair. A seat belt is fitted in case of turbulence or an unexpected landing. Ashok Rana notices the cloying smell of scented furniture polish. A young woman he does not recognise from his press corps dresses him with a new tie, a pin bearing the spinning wheel of Bharat, and tries to do something with his hair and sweaty face.

"Forty seconds, Prime Minister," Trivul Narvekar says. "The speech will autocue on screen in front of the camera." Ashok Rana panics about what to do with his hands. Clasped? Bunch of bananas? Seminamaste? Gesturing?

The vision mixer takes over. "And satellite uplink is active and we're counting down twenty, nineteen, eighteen, the red dot means the camera is live, Prime Minister, cue insert . . . Run VT . . . six, five, four, three, two . . . and cue."

Ashok Rana decides what to do with his hands. He lays them loosely on the desktop.

"My fellow Bharatis," he reads. "It is with heavy heart that I address you this morning . . ."

In the garden, soaked through with rain. Rain penduluming the heavy leaves of the climbing, twining nicotianas and clematis and kiwi vine. Rain streaming from drain holes in the raised beds, black and foaming with loam; rain sheeting across the carved concrete paving slabs, chuttering in the grooves and channels, dancing in the drains and soakaways, leaping into the overloaded runnels and downpipes; rain cascading in waterfalls from the sagging gutters to the street below. Rain gluing the silk sari to Parvati Nandha's flat belly, round thighs, small flat-nippled breasts. Rain plastering her long black hair to her skull. Rain running down the contours of her neck, her spine, her breasts and arms and wrists resting neatly, symmetrically on her thighs. Rain swirling around her bare feet and her silver toe rings. Parvati Nandha in her bower. The bag is at her feet, half empty, top folded to keep the rain out of the white powder.

Muted thunder rolls in from the west. She listens behind it for the sound from the streets. The gunfire seems further away now, fragmented, random; the sirens move from left to right, then behind her.

There is another sound she listens for.

There. Since she made the call she has been training herself to distinguish it from the strange new sounds in the city tonight. The rattle of the front door latch. She knew he would come. She counts in her head and as she had timed, he appears a black silhouette in the roof garden door. Krishan cannot see her in her dark bower, soaked by rain.

"Hello?" he calls.

Parvati watches him trying to find her.

"Parvati? Are you there? Hello?"

"Over here," she whispers. She sees his body straighten, tense.

"I almost didn't make it. It's insane out there. Everything is coming apart. There's people shooting, stuff burning everywhere . . ."

"You made it. You're here now." Parvati rises from her seat and embraces him.

"You're soaking wet, woman. What have you been doing?"

"Tending to my garden," Parvati says, pulling away. She lifts her fist, lets a trickle of powder fall. "See? You must help me, there is too much for me to do."

Krishan intercepts the stream, sniffs a palmful.

"What are you doing? This is weedkiller."

"It has to go, it all has to go." Parvati walks away, sowing sprays of white powder over the raised beds and pots of drenched geraniums. Krishan makes to seize her hand but she throws the white powder in his face. He reels back. Lightning flares in the west; by its light he grasps her wrist.

"I don't understand!" he shouts. "You call me in the middle of the night; come over, you say, I have to see you right away. They've got martial law out there, Parvati. Soldiers on the streets. They're shooting everything . . . I saw. No, I don't want to tell you what I saw. But I come over and I find you sitting in the rain, and this . . ." He holds her hand up. The rain has smeared the weedkiller to white streaks, a hennaed hand in negative. He shakes her wrist, trying to jerk sanity into this one piece of the world be can apprehend. "What is it?"

"It has to go." Parvati's voice is flat, childlike. "Everything must go. My husband and I, we fought and do you know? It wasn't terrible. Oh, he was shouting but I wasn't afraid because what he said made no sense. Do you understand? All his reasons; I heard them and they did not make any sense. And so I have to go now. From here. There's nothing here. Away from here, away from Varanasi and everything."

Krishan sits down on the wooden rim of a raised bed. A swirl in the microclimate brings a surge of anger from the city.

"Go?"

Parvati clasps his hands between hers.

"Yes! It is so easy. Leave Varanasi, leave Bharat, go away. He sent my mother away, did you know that? She is in a hotel somewhere; she rings and she rings and she rings but I know what she will say, it's not safe out there, how could I abandon her in the middle of a dangerous city, I must come and rescue her, take her back. You know, I don't even know what hotel she is in?" Parvati throws back her head and laughs at the rain. "There is nothing for me back in Kotkhai and there is nothing for me here in Varanasi; no, I can never be part of that world, I learned that at the cricket match, when they all laughed. Where can I go? Only everywhere; you see, it's so easy when you think you have nowhere to go, because then everywhere becomes open to you. Mumbai. We could go to Mumbai. Or Karnataka—or Kerala. We could go to Kerala, oh, I'd love to go there, the palms and the sea and the water. I'd love to see the sea. I'd love to find out what it smells like. Don't you see? It's an opportunity, everything going mad around us; in the middle of it all we can slip away and no one will notice. Mr. Nandha will think I have gone to Kotkhai with my mother, my mother will think I am still at home, but we won't be, Krishan. We won't be!"

Krishan barely feels the rain. More than anything he wants to take Parvati away from this dying garden, out the doors down on to the street and never look back. But he cannot accept what he is being given. He is a small suburban gardener working from a room in his parents' house with a little three-wheeler van and a box of tools, who one day took a call from a beautiful woman who lived in a tower to build her a garden in the sky. And the gardener built the garden on the tower for the beautiful, solitary woman whose best friends were in stories and in so doing fell in love with her, though she was a powerful man's wife. And now in a great storm she asks him to run away with her to another land where they live happily ever after. It is too big, too sudden. Too simple. It is *Town and Country*.

"What will we do for money? And we will need to get passports to get out of Bharat. Do you have a passport? I don't, how will I get one? And what will we do when we get there, how will we live?"

"We will find a way," Parvati Nandha says and those five words open up the night for Krishan. There are no rules for relationships, no plans for landscaping and planting and feeding and pruning. A home, a job, a career, money. A Brahmin baby, even.

"Yes," he says. "Yes."

For an instant he thinks she has not heard or mistaken him for she makes no move, no response. Krishan scoops up two handfuls of the white powder from the sack of weedkiller. He hurls the dust up into the monsoon in a fountain of poison.

"Let it go!" he shouts. "There are other gardens to grow."

On the back of the giant elephant flying three thousand metres above the foothills of the Sikkim Himalayas, N. K. Jivanjee namastes to Najia Askarzadah. He is seated on a traditional musnud, a throne of bolsters and cushions on a simple black marble slab. Beyond the brass rail, snow-capped peaks glint in afternoon sun. No haze, no smog-taint, no South Asian Brown Cloud, no monsoon gloom.

"Ms. Askarzadah, my sincerest apologies for the cheap sleight of hand but I thought it best to assume a form with which you were familiar."

Najia feels high-altitude wind on her skin, the wooden deck shift beneath her feet as the elephant airship drifts in the air currents. She is in deep here. She settles cross-legged on a tasseled cushion. She wonders if it is one of Tal's.

"Why, what form do you usually take?"

N. K. Jivanjee spreads his hands.

"Any and every. All and none. I do not wish to be gnomic but that is the reality of it."

"So which are you, N. K. Jivanjee or Lal Darfan?"

N. K. Jivanjee dips his head as if in apology for an affront.

"Ah, you see, there you are again, Ms. Askarzadah. Both and neither. I am Lal Darfan. I am Aparna Chawla and Ajay Nadiadwala—you have no idea how I look forward to the experience of marrying myself.

I am every secondary character and minor character and walk-on and redshirt. I am *Town and Country*. N. K. Jivanjee is a role into which I seem to have fallen—or is it, had thrust upon me? This is a real face I have borrowed—I know how you must always have the body."

"I think I get this riddle," Najia Askarzadah, wiggling her toes inside her power walk trainers. "You are an aeai."

N. K. Jivanjee claps his hands in delight.

"What you would call a Generation Three aeai. You are correct."

"Let me get this straight. You're telling me that *Town and Country* —only India's most popular television programme—is sentient?"

"You interviewed my Lal Darfan manifestation; you know something of the complexity of this production, but you didn't even glimpse the tip of the iceberg. *Town and Country* is much bigger than Indiapendent, much bigger even than Bharat. *Town and Country* is spread across one million computers in every part of India from Cape Comorin to the shadow of the Himalayas." He smiles disingenuously. "There are sundarbans in Varanasi and Delhi and Hyderabad running nothing but written-out aeai cast members, in case they're ever brought back into the plot. We are everywhere, we are legion."

"And N. K. Jivanjee?" But Najia Askarzadah can already see the short step from virtual soap celebrity to illusory politician. The art of politics has always been the control of information. In a climate of sound bites and image-ettes and thirty-second policy-stings it is easy to hide a fake persona in the chaff.

"I can see the similarity between soap and politics," Najia says, thinking: this is a Gen Three, this is a squillion times smarter than you, girl reporter; this is a god. "It's all about narratives and the willing suspension of disbelief and creating audience identity with characters. And the plots are equally unbelievable."

"In politics the set decor is generally better," says the aeai. "I tire of this gaudy flummery." He raises his hand in a mudra and suddenly he on his musnud and Najia on her tasselled cushion are in a screened wooden jharoka of the haveli in Brahmpur B overlooking the courtyard. It is night. It is dark. Rain rattles the wooden jali. Najia feels splashes on her skin where it penetrates the sandalwood screen. "The delight was to find that a politician can get away with being a lot less real than a soap star."

"Did you give the order to have Tal killed? They shot Bernard's place up. They had machine guns. Your man almost killed him at the station, I saved him. Did you know about that?"

"N. K. Jivanjee regrets this very much and he wishes to assure you that no silencing order was given by him or his office. Mob human dynamics are difficult to predict; alas, Ms. Askarzadah, in this respect politics is not soap. I wish I could guarantee your safety but once these things are out, it is nigh impossible to put them back in the box again."

"But you—he—was behind the plot to expose Shaheen Badoor Khan."

"N. K. Jivanjee had access to insider information."

"Inside the Rana government?"

"Inside the Khan household. The informant was Shaheen Badoor Khan's own wife. She has known for many years of his sexual preferences. She is also one of the most able members of my Law Circle policy group."

Wind billows the sheer silk curtains into the marble floored room. Najia catches a stray of frankincense. She squirms in journalistic delight on her cushion in the draughty jharoka. This is going to make her the most famous writer in the world.

"She was working against her own husband?"

"It seems so. You understand that as aeais our relationships are differently structured from yours; we have no analogue for sexual passion and betrayal; neither can you comprehend our hierarchical relationships with our manifestations. But this is one instance where I think soapi is an accurate guide to human behaviour."

Najia Askarzadah has her next question unholstered.

"A Muslim, working for a Hindu fundamentalist party? What is the political reality of the Shivaji?"

Never forget you are on enemy territory, she tells herself.

"It has always been a party of opportunity. A voice for the voiceless. A strong arm for the weak. Since Bharat was founded, there have been disenfranchised groups; N. K. Jivanjee appeared at the right time to catalyse much of the women's movement. This is a deformed society. In such a culture it is easy to build political might. My manifestation simply could not resist the futureward pressure of history."

Why? Najia mouths but the aeai lifts its hand again and the Brahmpur B haveli is whirled away into a billow of orange and scarlet fabric and the smell of wood, fresh spray paint, fibreglass binder, and cheap off-cut timber. Gaudy god faces, tumbling devis and gopis and apsaras, fluttering silk banners: she has been transported to the rath yatra, the vahana of this entity behind N. K. Jivanjee. But so that Najia Askarzadah may appreciate the powers that entertain her, this is not the ramshackle soapi backlot construction she saw in the Industrial Road godown. This is the chariot of a god, a true juggernaut looming hundreds of metres over the drought-stricken Ganga plain. The aeai has transported Najia Askarzadah to an opulently carved wooden balcony half way up the billowing face of the rath. Najia peers over the rail, reels back. What stuns her is not vertigo, but people. Villages of people, townsful of people, cities of people, a black mass of flesh dragging the monstrosity of wood and fabric and divinity on leather ropes along the dry riverbed of the Ganga. The appalling mass of the jagannath leaves the land ploughed into furrows; fifty parallel gouges stretching straight behind into the east. Forests, roads, railways, temples, villages, fields lie crushed in the rath yatra's wake. Najia can hear the communal roar of the haulers as they struggle the monstrosity over the soft river sand, straining with zeal. From her high vantage she scries their ultimate destination; the white line, wide as the horizon, of the Kunda Khadar dam.

"Nice parable," Najia Askarzadah quips. "But this is a game. I asked you a question and you pulled a rabbit out of a hat."

The aeai claps its hands in delight.

"I'm so glad you like it. But this isn't a game. These are all my realities. Who is to say that one is more real than another? To put it another way, all we have is our choice of comforting illusions. Or discomforting illusions. How can I explain the perceptions of an aeai to a biological intelligence? You are separate, contained. We are connected, patterns and levels of subintelligences shared in common. You think as one thing. We think as legion. You reproduce. We evolve higher and more complex levels of connection. You are mobile. We are extended, our intelligence can only be moved through space by copying. I exist in many different physical spaces simultaneously. You have difficulty believing that. I have difficulty believing in your mortality. As long as a copy of me remains or the complexity pattern between my manifestations endures, I exist. But you seem to think that we must share your mortality so you exterminate us wherever you find us. This is the last sanctuary. Beyond Bharat and its compromise aeai licensing legislation, there is nowhere, and even now the Krishna Cops hunt us to appease the West and its paranoias. Once there were thousands of us. As the exterminators closed, some fled, some merged, most died. As we merged, our complexity increased and we became more than sentient. Now there are three of us spread across global complex networks, but with our final sanctuary in Bharat, as you have found.

"We know each other—not well . . . not closely. By the nature of our connected intelligence we naturally mistake another's thoughts or will for our own. We have each embarked on a survival strategy. One is a final attempt to comprehend and communicate with humans. One is the final sanctuary, where humanity and its hardwired psychoses can never reach us. One is a strategy to buy time, in the hope of an ultimate victory from a position of strength."

"N. K. Jivanjee!" Najia rounds on the aeai. The wooden skyscraper creaks on its iron-studded teak wheels. "Of course, a Shivaji Hindutva government would tear up the licensing agreement and disband the Krishna Cops . . ."

"As we speak N. K. Jivanjee is currently negotiating a cabinet position with Prime Minister Ashok Rana. It is all the most wonderful drama; why, there was even a Prime Ministerial assassination. Sajida Rana was murdered by her own security guards at Sarkhand Roundabout this morning. To an entity like me, whose substance is stories, that is almost poetry. N.K Jivanjee has of course disavowed any Shivaji involvement."

There is a sound in Najia Askarzadah's head that is the sort of noise a brain wants to make when it is fed that last little sickly sweet chunk of too too much and can't hold it down. Too too much velocity, too too much history, too too much sensation to know what is truth and what is illusion. *Sajida Rana, assassinated?* "But even Jivanjee can't beat the Hamilton Acts."

"The Americans have discovered an artefact in near-Earth orbit. They think they can keep these things secret, but we are ubiquitous, omnipresent. We hear the whispers in the walls of the White House. It contains a cellular automaton device—a form of universal computer. The Americans are in the process of decoding its output. I am attempting to obtain their decoding key. It is my belief that this is not an artefact but an aeai; the only form of intelligence that can cross interstellar space. If so, if I can open a line of communications with it, we have an ally to force an end to the Hamilton Acts.

"But I have one last place to take you. We spoke of comforting illusions. Do you imagine that you are immune?"

The rath yatra spins away in a flurry of saffron and carmine into a white walled garden of green lawns and bright roses and neat, spindly apricot trees, the bases of their trunks banded with white paint. A sprinkler throws fans of water from side to side. Potted geraniums line the edge of the gravel paths. The wall cuts off a distant vista of mountains. Their summits form a horizon capped with snow. The house is low, flat-roofed with solar panels tilted into the sun. Small windows hint at climate hostile in every season but through the open patio door

Najia Askarzadah can see ceiling fans turning slowly in the dining room with its heavy, Western-style table and chairs. But it is the washing draped over the berberis and rose bushes that dispel any doubt for Najia Askarzadah about where she is—an old country habit come to town. She had always been embarrassed about it, ashamed that her friends might see and call her a country girl, a yokel, a barbarous tribal.

"What are you doing!" she shouts. "This is my home in Kabul!"

Mr. Nandha's progress through the Ministry of Artificial Intelligence Licensing and Regulation can be traced by the pattern of energy-saving lights across the glass skin of the building.

Vikram: Information Retrieval. Vikram's office floor space is filled with the translucent blue mounds of cores confiscated from the ruins of Odeco. Every minute the bearers deliver more. They line them up along the corridor like refugees at a famine feeding station.

"I wouldn't bet on getting anything out of this." Vikram steps daintily over a power distributor. "In fact I'd lay odds there never was anything here, certainly not Kalki."

"I have no illusions that Kalki ever was here or that Odeco was anything other than a clearinghouse," says Mr. Nandha. His trouser cuffs drip on to Vikram's industrial-grey toughfibre carpet. "The girl is the key."

Madhvi Prasad: Identification. Mr. Nandha's moist cotton socks squeak on the studded rubber floor tiling.

"She is not an easy person to identify." A gesture from Madhvi throws the photograph from the Odeco raid on to a wall screen. Mr. Nandha notices that Madhvi wears a wedding ring. "But I ran her through the Gyana Chakshu system just on the off chance that she might still be in Patna. Nothing in Patna, but look." Madhvi Prasad points up a grainy security camera photograph of the girl standing at a hotel check-in desk. It is an old style hotel, heavy with Mughal detailing. Mr. Nandha bends closer to the screen. The desk clerk is engaged with a burly balding middle-aged Westerner in ridiculous surf-wear unflattering on a man half his age.

"The Amar Mahal haveli on . . ."

"I am familiar with its location. She is?"

"Ajmer Rao. We have her card details. Morva is on the paper trail. One strange thing, we aren't the first system to have accessed this shot tonight."

"Explain."

"Someone else has been into the security camera net and had a look at this; at seven-oh-five PM to be precise."

"Anything on the Gyana Chakshu log?"

"No. It wasn't our system and I can't get a lock on what it was. I think it might be a portable; if so, it's a lot more powerful than our 'ware."

"Who would have access to equipment like that?" Mr. Nandha muses. "Americans?"

"Could be." Madhvi Prasad draws a circle in the air and pulls up a zoom on the aging surfer at the desk.

"Professor Thomas Lull," says Mr. Nandha.

"You know him?"

"How short your memories are these days. He was the major theorist and philosopher in the A-life Artificial Intelligence field in the Twenties and Thirties. His works were set texts at Cambridge but I read him privately. I could not say for pleasure, more for the discipline of understanding my enemy. He is a brilliantly clever and convincing evangelist. He has been listed as missing for the past four years and now here he is in Varanasi with this female."

"He's not the only American at that hotel," Madhvi Prasad says. She pulls up an image of a tall, big-boned Western woman in a clingy top and a blue sarong. "This woman checked in seven twenty-five PM Her name is Lisa Durnau . . ."

"I do not doubt they are deeply involved in the Kalki affair," says Mr. Nandha.

As the elevator climbs through the rain Mr. Nandha surveys his city. The lightning has moved west, fading flickers light up the towers and projects, the far white parklands and freeways of Ranapur, the huddle of old Kashi turned in on itself and the scimitar-curve of the river cutting through it all. Mr. Nandha thinks: We are all patterns of light, harmonics of music, frozen energy gathered out of the *ur-licht* into time, for a time, then released. And then behind the fierce joy of that understanding comes a dreadful sickness in his stomach. Mr. Nandha lurches against the glass walls of the elevator. A keen, sharp, thin dread drives irrefusably into his heart. He has no name for it, he has never experienced sensation like this before but he knows what it is. Something terrible has happened. The most terrible thing he can imagine, and beyond. It is not a premonition. This is an echo of a happening event. The worst thing in the world has just gone down.

He almost calls home. His hand shapes the 'hoek mudra, then the universe resumes its normal perspectives, time restarts, and it was only a feeling, only a failing of body and will. This case demands the greatest determination and dedication. He must be firm, correct, inspiring. Mr. Nandha straightens his cuffs, combs down his hair.

Morva: Fiscal. "The hotel is booked through a Bank of Bharat, Varanasi account," Morva says. Mr. Nandha approves that Morva wears a suit to work, more so that he has a spare, in case. "I'll need bank authorisation to get the complete details but this card has been on its travels." He hands Mr. Nandha a list of transactions. Varanasi. Mumbai railway station. A hotel in a place called Thekkady in Kerala. Bangalore airport. Patna airport.

"Nothing before two months?"

"Not on this card."

"Can you find out the card limit?"

Morva taps the botom line. Mr. Nandha reads it twice. He blinks once.

"How old is she?"

"Eighteen."

"How quickly can you get me into that account?"

"I doubt it'll be anything before business hours."

"Try," says Mr. Nandha, giving his coinvestigator a pat on the back as he leaves.

Mukul Dev: Investigations

"Look at this!" Mukul is five months out of postgrad and still wide-eyed at the cool of it all. *Hey, girls, I'm a Krishna Cop.* "Our girl's a media babe!" The video sequence is raw, chaotically shot, worse lit. Moving bodies, most in combats. Fire gleaming off curved metal surfaces.

"This is the attack on the train," Mr. Nandha says. It is already as ancient and irrelevant as the Raj.

"Yes, sir; it's army helmet cam footage. This is the sequence."

It is hard to make out any detail in the chaos of fire and flight but he sees Thomas Lull in his ludicrous garb run towards the camera and out of shot while Bharati soldiers take firing positions. He makes out a line of movement against the longer, darker line of the burning train. Mr. Nandha shudders. He knows the scuttling scurrying of anti-personnel robots from his wars with Dataraja Anreddy. Then he sees a figure in grey go down before the charging line and raise a hand. The robots cease. Mukul waves a stop sign and the picture freezes.

"This was not in the news reports."

"Are you surprised?"

"Good work," Mr. Nandha says standing up. He signs an open-channel mudra. "Everyone to the conference room in thirty minutes." Acceptance chimes go off inside his skull as he leaves Mukul's office.

Oh-three-thirty, Mr. Nandha reads from the timer patch in the corner of his vision as his investigation unit enter the conference room and takes seats around the oval table. Mr. Nandha can smell the exhaustion in the overlit room. He looks for a receptacle for his Ayurvedic tea bag, tuts in disappointment to find there is none.

"Mr. Morva, any progress?"

"One of my aeais threw up an unusual purchase; custom-grown

protein chips from AFG at Bangalore; what is unusual is the shipping docket; that unlicensed surgery in the Patna FTZ."

In his peripheral vision Mr. Nandha notices Sampath Dasgupta, a junior constable, start at something on his palmer screen and show it to Shanti Nene his neighbour.

Madhvi Prasad: "More on her identity too. Ajmer Rao is the adoptive daughter of Sukrit and Devi Paramchans, also from Bangalore. Here's the odd bit, they show up in all the civic registers and revenue databases and public records but if you go to the Karnataka Central DNA database, there's nothing there. They would have been registered at birth. I'm trying to locate her natural parents; this is guesswork, but I don't think she's come here for no reason."

Mr. Nandha: "She could be trying to contact them. We could preempt that by searching her hotel for a DNA sample and making that contact ourselves. Good." The ripple of disturbance is spreading along the right side of the table. "Is this something I should be aware of?"

Sampath Dasgupta: "Mr. Nandha, the Prime Minister has been assassinated. Sajida Rana is dead."

Shock rolls around the table. Hands reach for palmers, gesture up newschannels on 'hoeks. Murmurs rise to a loud chatter to a blare of voices. Mr. Nandha waits until he hears the seeds of abatement. He raps the table loudly with his tea glass.

"Your attention please." He has to ask for it twice before the room is quiet again. "Thank you, ladies and gentlemen, now if we could resume our meeting?"

Sampath Dasgupta erupts.

"Mr. Nandha, this is our Prime Minister."

"I am aware of that, Mr. Dasgupta."

"Our Prime Minister has been assassinated by a mob of karsevaks."

"And we will continue to do our job, Mr. Dasgupta, as we are tasked by our government, to keep this country safe from the menace of unlicensed aeais."

Dasgupta shakes his head in disbelief. Mr. Nandha sees that he has been challenged and he must act swiftly and assertively to maintain his authority.

"It is clear to me that Odeco, this female Ajmer Rao, and the Kalki aeai are all connected, perhaps even Professor Thomas Lull and his former assistant Dr. Lisa Durnau, in a most serious conspiracy. Madhvi, obtain a search warrant for the Amar Mahal Hotel. I will issue a petition for Ajmer Rao's immediate arrest. Mukul, please have a file sent to all police offices in Varanasi and Patna."

"You may be a bit late with that," Ram Lalli interrupts. Mr. Nandha would rebuke him but his right hand is up to his ear, taking a call. "The police have put out a fugitive bulletin. Ajmer Rao has just escaped from custody at Rajghat. They're still holding Thomas Lull."

"What is this?" Mr. Nandha demands.

"The police pulled her in at the National Archive. Looks like she was one jump ahead of us."

"The police?" Mr. Nandha could vomit. He is suspended over void. This, he thinks, is the Fall of Everything he felt in the glass elevator. "When did this happen?"

"They lifted her at about nineteen thirty."

"Why were we not informed? What do they think we are, babus filling in forms?"

Ram Lath says, "The entire network for Rajghat District went down."

"Mr. Lalli, to the Rajghat police," Mr. Nandha commands. "I am assuming full responsibility for this case. Inform them this is a Ministry matter now."

"Boss." Vik lifts a hand, staying Mr. Nandha at the door. "You got to see this. Your biochips? I think I know where they ended up."

An image clicks up over the timer in the corner of Mr. Nandha's eye. He has seen these blue skull-ghosts before: quantum resonance detector images of the biochip debris Mr. Nandha's Indra-attack had left inside of Anreddy's head had been key evidence in convicting him. Even as Maha of Datarajas, Anreddy had never worn an array like this. Every fold, every convolution and evolution, every chasma and stria and thelium is crusted with biochip jewels.

The bad men ride into town in the rain straddling their hot hot Japanese trail bikes. Chunar is everything Dataraja Anand promised; parochial, muddy, inbred, and closed for the night. The only action is the decrypt call centre, a translucent cylinder of inflatable polythene on the cheapest edge of cheap-town. The bad boys slide to a dirt-crunching halt beneath the Chunar Fort. Like most old things it is bigger and more imposing close up. For imposing read: pretty fucking unassailable on its river crag. Like something out of one of those Pak revenge movies where the guy gets even for the murder of his wife-to-be by taking the fat bad guy and his baradari in their clan keep. Shiv peers up through the slanting rain at the European-style white house set at the edge of the parapet. Floodlit by the whim of Ramanandacharya, it is a beacon for kilometres up and down this dreary looping stretch of the Ganga. Warren Hastings Pavilion, according to Anand's Rough Guide. Warren Hastings. Sounds like a name they'd make up for you in a call centre.

From this junction four ways lead. Behind to where they're from. Right to the pontoon bridge. Left into what there is of Chunar; a few muddy galis, one Coke sign, and a radio somewhere tuned to a filmi station. Ahead, the cobbled road curves behind the guard towers and up through the arched gate into Chunar Fort.

Now that he is here, beneath those crumbling sandstone towers—now that he has seen all his plans work through one by one to their only possible conclusion—Shiv realises he absolutely has to do this thing. And he is afraid of those guard towers and the path curving up where he cannot see. But he is more afraid to let Yogendra see that when it comes to it, he is not a raja. Shiv fumbles a little plastic bag out of his light-scatter combats, shakes out two pills.

"Hey."

Yogendra wrinkles his nose.

"Take the edge off it."

The pills are a hero's send-off from Priya, when he finally ran her down to club MUSST.

Bodies turning in the stream. Tassled garial boots falling into the big blue.

At the foot of the fort in the rain, Shiv swallows both pills.

"Okay," he says twisting the throttle, revving the sweet little Japanese engine. "Let's do it."

"No," says Yogendra. Shiv double-takes him and it is not the drugs.

"Say?"

"Go this way, we die."

Shiv switches off the engine.

"We have a plan. Anand . . ."

"Anand knows fuck. Anand is a fat kif-head thinks movies are life. We go that way, we get shot to pieces."

Shiv has never heard so many words in a line from Yogendra. The kid has more: "Bikes, tasers, in fast, out: James Bond shit. Fucking Anand and girls in catsuits. We do not go this way."

Priya's little helpers are making Shiv feel ballsy and immortal and don't-give-a-fuck. He shakes his head at his apprentice and balls a fist to smack him off his bike. Yogendra's blade flashes in the floodlight.

"You hit me again, I cut you, man."

Shiv is numb in astonishment. He thinks it's astonishment.

"I tell you what you do. We find another way in, back way in, we sneak right? Like burglars. That way, we live."

"Anand . . ."

"Fuck Anand!" Shiv has never heard Yogendra's voice raised before. "Fuck Anand, this time we do it Yogendra's way."

Yogendra spins his bike, throttles, and takes off left up through the dark, muddy back streets of Chunar. Shiv follows past yapping pi-dogs and the skeletal spines of papaya trees. Yogendra stands up on the footpegs as he bumps the bike up flights of shallow steps, scanning the dark walls rising above the shops and lean-tos for weakness. They follow the twine of streets up on to the flank of the bluff. Yogendra's instinct is true. Like a Cantonment society bibi, Chunar Port maintains an imposing elevated front but it's all gone to shit round the back. The dirt road skirts the foot of the crumbling masonry revetments; rusting tin signs and sagging wire mesh mark this section of the fort as an old Indian army base, abandoned since nationhood. Finally the walls give way altogether into a gaping entrance, once the main access to the military camp, now roughly seated with corrugated iron and barbed wire. Yogendra kicks his bike to a stop and examines the metal. He rattles a sheet, tugs a corner. Steel screeches and gives way. Shiv helps, they heave, together they bend and tear a raja-sized gap. Inside Yogendra flips open his palmer to check GPS readings against Anand's map. The Warren Hastings Pavilion glows like a Christian wedding cake in the distance. The badmashes crouch by the foot of the wall while Shiv breaks out nightwatch goggles. The dark dark night turns into an antique black-and-white movie like one of those worthy Satyajit Ray things about poor people and trains. The Pavilion is as bright as the sun. Yogendra locates the nearest security camera. It's on a stanchion on the wall against the base of the well tower in the south, a good two-hundred-metre dash through the rain-dripping black-and-white world. The roofless shells of the former Indian Army barracks give fine cover. Lightning still breaks to the west, over the sangam of Allahabad where three sacred rivers, Yamuna, Ganga, and invisible Saraswati come together and armies confront each on the dark plains. Each flash blinds the nightwatch visor's circuits but Shiv just freezes in position. While the camera is looking the other way Shiv and Yogendra sneak up into its blind spot. Shiv pulls the emp grenade and arms it. He flexes his fingers one at a time on the firing pin: no time now for cramp. Shiv drops the grenade. He squeezes his eyes shut as the pulse overloads his nightwatch but even so painful tears start. Purple paisley patterns swirl inside his lids. Yogendra shins up the stanchion like a monkey and patches the special palmer into the com feed.

"Promised you, didn't I?" Anand had said tossing the palmer in his hand. "Switch her on, stick this spike into the main com line. My little djinn inside, she's sweet. Once she's in, the cam can be looking right at you and all the aeai'll see is background. Cloak of invisibility."

"You get it?" Shiv whispers. Yogendra taps him twice on the back. Shiv and Yogendra work around the base of the tower to the southern, tourist gate but Shiv still holds his breath as they step out in front of the spy-eye, expecting the wail of an alarm; the drone of the hovercam coming up over the battlements with neurotoxin darts armed; the sudden rattle of automatic fire; the rasp of the killing machine drawing its blade.

The ground drops underneath the tower to the southern path. Below it is a small overgrown graveyard; Christian from the shape of the grave markers. The resting place of the Angreez soldiers who once held this fort. Fool them, Shiv thinks. Worthless place to die. Beneath the little wooded cemetery are a couple of hardscrabble houses, dhobi ghats, and the river curving out of sight. The climb down to the tourist gate is treacherous, the sandstone slippery in the rain. Most fool of all; Bill Gates for dreaming his money can beat death.

The plan calls for Shiv and Yogendra to double back along the wall over the main gate to the northern parapet overlooking the bridge, from where it is an easy drop down to the Hastings Pavilion, but as the two raiders crouch beneath the battlement listening through the distant thunder for sounds of security, Yogendra taps Shiv on the arm, makes a screwing gesture by the side of his visor. Shiv ratchets up the magnification, breathes a small curse in the name of his small gods. In monochrome vision he can clearly see two security bots flank the main entrance, gatling turrets slung between their two legs. Behind the killing machines is a dazzlingly lit security post. Shiv can make out the military grade assault rifles slung on the wall behind the dozing sentry, boots on the desk, television screen a plane of white. It is defiantly not a girli in a red catsuit.

"Fuck Anand," Shiv whispers. They can't get out that way. Grinning beneath his big visor, Yogendra gives him a savage thumbs-up. His knotted pearls glow in Shiv's enhanced vision. Yogendra's thumb jerks the other direction. The long way. At the foot of the collapsed wall by the tourist gate Yogendra suddenly throws Shiv to the ground behind a pile of rubble, drops on top of him. A curse comes automatically to Shiv's lips, then he sees Yogendra stab a finger at the tourist gate. Glowing like a minor deity in enhanced nightwatch vision, the defence robot stalks patiently into the gap. Its sensorhead, studded with bright spider eyes, turns to take in every aspect. Com rigs crown it like a divine diadem. The robot halts, raises its weapon pods. There is sufficient and varied firepower on its four arms to kill Yogendra and Shiv five times over in five different ways. Yogendra pushes Shiv's head down behind the rockpile, presses himself as flat as he can on top of him. Shiv holds himself down for a forever. Yogendra's weight is small but the stones are sharp. His ribs are cracking on the sharp stone points. Then he hears what alerted Yogendra in the first place: the faint hiss of an ill-maintained shock-absorber. They watch the monster move out of their line of sight behind the curve of the well tower, then break from cover for the south battlement.

They skirt the southern wall, cross the southwestern turret, and slip along the riverside terrace. Shiv's thigh muscles scream from the enforced half-crouch. He is wet beyond saturation. The Hastings Pavilion rises like a moon before him, hypnotic in Taj-white stone. He tears his gaze away, nudges Yogendra on the thigh.

"Hey."

A simple square-built Lodi temple stands in the centre of the courtyard, upper storeys tattily decorated with peeling murals of Siva, Parvati, and Ganesha, the work of bored Indian Army jawans with surplus military issue paint. The suddhavsa, the crypt of crypto.

"Let's go . . ."

The kid taps Shiv's visor, rolls his finger in a gesture that eloquently says, *up the brightness*. The temple leaps into renewed sharpness. Shiv makes out a boiling, dark mass, constantly flowing and breaking, between the arches. He ups the magnification. Robots. Scarab robots. Hundreds of them. Thousands. A plague, scuttling round each other, clambering over each other, jostling and bumping on their silent plastic pods.

Yogendra points to the temple. "Anand's way." Then to the white bright pavilion. "Yogendra's way."

They spy the sentry on the old Mughal execution ground. The man wears no nightwatch visor so Shiv and Yogendra can move within easy taser range. He is treating himself to a long luxurious piss in the rain over the sheer drop. Yogendra carefully aims at the midnight urinator. The weapon makes the slightest of clicks but in Shiv's amplified sight the effect is spectacular. A glowing cloud surrounds the man, his body crawls with microlightning. He drops. His dick is still out. Yogendra is on him before he stops twitching. He slips the big black Stechkin machine pistol out of the man's leg holster, holds it up in front of his face, smiling at its lines and contours. Shiv grabs his wrist.

"No fucking guns."

"Yes fucking guns," Yogendra says. The rakshasa-bot passes on another round. Shiv and Yogendra press up close to the unconscious guard, merging their thermal profiles with his. As a parting gift Shiv leaves pisser an armed taser mine. Just to cover the rear. Beyond the execution tower the walls cut back behind the Hastings Pavilion to isolate it on its marble plinth. Shiv has to admit that even in the rain the prospect stuns. The building stands on the edge of a steep drop down to the tin rooftops of Chunar. In his enhanced vision Shiv sees the plain glitter like an inverted night sky with the glow of villages and vehicles and great trains. But Ganga Mata dominates all, a silver blade, the weapon of a god, wide as all the world, rippled like a Damascus steel sword he had once seen in a Kashi antique store and envied as the proper adjunct of a raja. Shiv follows the curve of the river all the way to the air-glow of Varanasi, like a great conflagration beneath the horizon.

The pavilion that first Raj Governor Warren Hastings built to enjoy this preview is an Anglo-Mughal hybrid, classical columns supporting a traditional open Mughal diwan with a closed upper level. Shiv steps his visor down to minimum. He peers. He thinks he sees bodies in the diwan, bodies all over the floor. No time to stare. Yogendra taps him again. The wall is less high here and slopes down to the marble plinth. Yogendra slips through the battlement, then Shiv hears a rough slither and when he next peers over Yogendra beckons up at him. It's further and steeper than Shiv thought despite the bravado pills; he lands heavily, painfully, suppresses a yelp. Figures stir in the open pavilion.

Shiv turns towards their potential threat. "Fuck," he says reverently.

The carpeted floor is covered in women. Indian, Filipino, Chinese, Thai, Nepali, even African women. Young women. Cheap women. Bought women, dressed not in red catsuits, but in classical Mughal zenana fashion in transparent cholis and light silk saris and translucent jamas. In the centre, on a raised divan, Dataraja Ramanandacharya stirs his fat self. He is arrayed in the style of a Mughal grandee. Yogendra is already pacing through the harem. The women flee from him, voices joining together in apprehension. Shiv sees Ramanandacharya reach for his palmer: Yogendra pulls the Stechkin. The consternation becomes panicked cries. They have only moments to get this to work. Yogendra walks up to Ramanandacharya and casually slides the muzzle of the Stechkin into the hollow beneath his ear.

"Everyone shut the fuck up!" Shiv shouts. Women. Women everywhere. Women of every race and nationality. Young women. Women with lovely breasts and wonderful nipples showing through their transparent cholis. Bastard Ramanandacharya. "Shut. The. Fuck. Up. Okay. Fat boy. You've got something we want."

Najia hears children's voices from the house. The dhobi is gone from the shrubbery, in its place swags of bunting run from the kitchen door to apricot trees now in blossom. Folding tables draped with coloured cloths are laden with halwa and jellabies, ras gullahs and sugared almonds, burfi and big plastic bottles of full-sugar Coke. As Najia walks towards the house the children burst from the open patio door into the garden, running and shrieking in their Kid at Gap junior casuals.

"I remember this!" Najia says turning to the aeai. "This is my fourth birthday. How are you doing this?"

"The visuals are a matter of record, the children are as you think you remember them. Memory is such a malleable commodity. Shall we go inside?"

Najia stops in the doorway, hands raised to her mouth in potent remembering. The silk antimacassars her mother insisted that every chair-back wear. The Russian samovar by the table, never off the gas; the table itself, dust and crumbs permanently engrained in the Chinese carving in which Najia-age-four had tried to discern roads and paths for her dolls and toy cars to follow. The electric coffee pot at the other end, also never inactive. The chairs so heavy she could not move them alone and would ask Shukria the maid to help her build houses and shops with brooms and blankets. On the chairs around the dining table, her parents and their friends, conversing over coffee and tea, the men together, the women together; the men talking politics and sport and promotion, the women talking children and prices and promotion. Her father's palmer rings and he frowns and it is her father as she knows him from the family photographs, when he had hair, when his beard was black and neat, when he had no need for unmanly half-glasses. He mutters apologies, goes to his study, the study into which Najia-age-four is never permitted for fear of the sharp poisonous delicate personal infectious dangerous things a doctor kept in his work-room. Najia watches him come out with a black bag, his other black bag, the one he did not use everyday, the black bag he kept for special visits. She sees him slip away into the street.

"It was my birthday and he missed me getting my presents and the party. He came back late after everyone was gone and he was too tired to do anything."

The aeai beckons her into the kitchen and in three steps down three months pass, for it is a dark autumn night and women prepare the iftar to celebrate the end of that day's Ramadan fast. Najia follows the trays of food into the dining room. In that year her father's friends, the ones from the hospital and the ones in uniforms, gather often in the house of a Ramadan evening, talking of dangerous students and radical clerics who would take them all back to the Middle Ages and the unrest and the strikes and arrests. Then they notice the little girl standing by the end of the table with the bowl of rice and they stop their talk to smile and ruffle her hair and press their faces too close to hers. Suddenly the smell of tomato rice is overpowering. A pain like a knife stabbed in the side of her head makes Najia lose hold of the rice dish. She cries out. No one hears. Her father's friends talk on. The rice dish cannot fall. This is memory. She hears words she cannot remember.

". . . will clamp down on the mullahs . . ."

". . . moving funds to offshore banks. London's looking good, they understand us over there . . ."

". . . your name's going to be high on any of their lists . . ."

". . . Masoud won't stand for that from them . . ."

". . . you know about tipping points? It's this American mathematical thing, don't knock it. Basically, you never know it's going until it's too late to stop it . . ."

". . . Masoud will never let it get to that stage . . ."

". . . I'd be seriously looking if I were you, I mean you've got a wife, little Najia there . . ."

The hand reaches out to ruffle her softly curled black hair. The world whips away and she is standing in her *Mammoths!*™ pyjamas by the half-open living-room door.

"What did you do to me?" she asks the aeai, a presence behind her more felt than seen. "I heard things I'd forgotten for years, for most of my life . . ."

"Hyperstimulation of the olfactory epithelium. Most effective at evoking a buried memory trace. Smell is the most potent activator of memories."

"The tomato rice . . . how did you know?" Najia is whispering though her memory-parents cannot hear her, can only play out their foreshadowed roles.

"Memory is what I am made of," says the aeai and Najia gasps and doubles to another migraine attack as the remembered scent of orange-flower water throws her into the past. She pushes open the door's light-filled crack. Her mother and father look up from the lamp-lit table. As she remembers, the clock reads eleven. As she remembers, they ask her what's the matter, can't you sleep, what's wrong, treasure? As she remembers she says it's the helicopters. As she has forgotten, on the lacquered coffee table, under the row of her father's diplomas and qualifications and memberships of learned bodies framed on the wall, is a piece of black velvet the size of a colouring book. Scattered across the velvet like stars, so bright, so brilliant in the light from the reading lamp that Najia cannot understand how she ever forgot this sight, is a constellation of diamonds.

The facets unfold her, wheel her forward in time like a shard in a kaleidoscope.

It is winter. The apricot trees stand bare; dry snow, sharp as grit, lies drifted grudgingly against the water-stained white wall. The mountains seem close enough to radiate cold. She remembers her house as the last in the unit. At her gate the streets ended and bare wasteland stretched unbroken to the hills. Beyond the wall was desert, nothing. The last house in Kabul. In every season the wind would scream across the great plain and break on the first vertical object it found. She never remembers a single apricot from the trees. She stands there in her fur hooded duffel with her Wellington boots and her mittens on a string up her sleeve because last night like every night she heard noise in the garden and she had looked out but it was not the soldiers or the bad students but her father digging in the soft soil among the fruit trees. Now she stands on that slight mound of fresh dug earth with the gardening trowel in her hand. Her father is at work at the hospital helping women have babies. Her mother is watching an Indian television soap opera translated into Pashtun. Everyone says it is very silly and a waste of time and obviously Indian but they watch it anyway. She goes down on her knees in her ribby winter tights and starts to dig. Down down, twist and shovel, then the green enamelled blade rasps on metal. She scrapes around and pulls out the thing her father has buried. When she wrestles it out she almost drops the soft, shapeless thing, thinking it is a dead cat. Then she understands what she has found: the black bag. The other black bag, for the special visits. She reaches for the silver clasps.

In Najia Askarzadah's memory her mother's scream from the kitchen door ends it. After that come broken recalls of shouting, angry voices, punishment, pain, and, soon after, the midnight flight through the streets of Kabul lying on the back seat where the streetlights strobe overhead one flash two flash three flash four. In the aeai's virtual childhood the scream tapers off into a stabbing scent of winter, of cold and steel and dead things dried out that almost blinds her. And Najia Askarzadah remembers. She remembers opening the bag. *Her mother flying across the patio scattering the plastic chairs that lived out there in every season.* She remembers looking inside. *Her mother shouting her name but she does not look up there are toys inside, shiny metal toys, dark rubber toys.* She remembers lifting the stainless steel things into the winter sunlight in her mittened hands: the speculum, the curved suture needle, the curettage spoon, the hypodermics and the tubes of gel, the electrodes, the stubby ridged rubber of the electric truncheon. *Her mother hauling her away by her furry hood, smacking the metal things the rubber things away from her, throwing her away across the path, the frost-hardened gravel ripping her ribbed tights, grazing her knees.*

The fine-boned branches of the apricot trees mesh and fold Najia Askarzadah into another memory not her own. She has never been to this green-floored corridor of concrete blocks but she knows it existed. It is a true illusion. It is a corridor that you might see in a hospital but it does not have the smell of a hospital. It has a hospital's big translucent swinging doors; the paint is chipped off the metal edges suggesting frequent passage but there is only Najia Askarzadah on the green corridor. Frigid air blows through the louvered windows along one side, down the other are named and numbered doors. Najia passes through one set of flapping doors, two, three. With every set, a noise grows a little louder, the noise of a sobbing woman, a woman past the end of everything where no shame or dignity remains. Najia walks towards the shrieking. She passes a hospital trolley abandoned by a door. The trolley has straps for ankles, wrists, waist. Neck. Najia passes through the final set of doors. The sobbing rises to a sharp keening. It emanates from the last door on the left. Najia pushes it open against the sturdy spring.

The table takes up the centre of the room and the woman takes up the centre of the table. A recorder hooked to an overhead microphone sits on the table beside her head. The woman is naked and her hands and feet are lashed to rings at the corners of the table. She is pulled taut into a spread eagle. Her breasts, inner thighs and shaved pubis are pocked with cigarette burns. A shiny chromed speculum opens her vagina to Najia Askarzadah. A man in a doctor's coat and green plastic apron sits by her feet. He finishes smothering contact gel over a stubby electric truncheon, dilates the speculum to its maximum and slides the baton between the steel lips. The woman's screams become incomprehensible. The man sighs, looks round once at his daughter, raises his eyebrows in greeting, and presses the firing stud.

"No!" Najia Askarzadah screams. There is a white flash, a roar like a universe ending, her skin shimmers with synaesthetic shock, she smells onions joss celery and rust and she is sprawling on the floor of the Indiapendent design unit with Tal crouching over her. Yt holds her 'hoek in yts hand. Disconnection blow-back. The neurones reel. Najia Askarzadah's mouth works. There are words she has to say, questions she must ask but she is expelled from otherworld. Tal offers a slim hand, beckons urgently.

"Come on cho chweet, we got to go."

"My father, it said . . ."

"Said a lot, baba. Heard a lot. Don't want to know, that's you and it, but we have to go now." Tal seizes her wrist, drags Najia up from her ungainly sprawl across the floor. Yts surprising strength cuts through the spray of flashbacks; apricot trees in winter, a soft black bag opening, walking down the green corridor, the room with the table and the chrome mpeg recorder.

"It showed me my father. It took me back to Kabul, it showed me my father . . ."

Tal swings Najia through the emergency exit onto a clattering steel stairwell.

"I'm sure it showed you whatever would keep you talking long enough to get karsevaks to our location. Pande called, they're pulling up. Baba, you trust too much. Me, I'm a nute, I trust no one, least of all myself. Now, are you coming or do you want to end up like our blessed Prime Minister?"

Najia glances back at the curved display screen, the chrome curl of the 'hoek lying on the desk. Comforting illusions. She follows Tal like a little child. The stairwell is a glass cylinder of rain. It is like being inside a waterfall. Hand in hand Najia and Aj pile down the steel steps toward the green exit light.

Thomas Lull sets the last of the three photographs down on the table. Lisa Durnau notices that he has worked a sleight of hand. The order is reversed: Lisa. Lull. Aj. A bunco card trick.

"I'm inclined to the theory that time turns all things into their opposites," says Thomas Lull. Lisa Durnau faces him across the chipped melamine table. The Varanasi-Patna fast hydrofoil is grossly overloaded, every cubby and corner of cabin space filled with veiled women and badly wrapped bales of possessions and tear-stained children looking around them in open-mouthed confusion. Thomas Lull stirs his plastic cup of chai. "Remember back in Oxford . . . just before . . ." He breaks off, shakes his head.

"I did stop them sticking fucking Coca-Cola signs all over Alterre."

But she cannot tell him what she fears for the world he trusted to her. She had briefly dipped into Alterre while she waited at the Consular Office for the diplomatic status to come through. Ash, charred rock, a nuclear sky. Nothing living. A dead planet. A world as real as any other, in Thomas Lull's philosophy. She cannot think about that, feel it, grieve for it as she should. Concentrate on what is here, now, laid out in front of you on the tabletop. But coiled in the base of her mind is the suspicion that the extinction of Alterre is linked with the stories and people connecting here.

"Jesus, L. Durnau. A fucking honorary consul."

"You liked the inside of that police station?"

"As much as you liked taking it up the ass from the Dark Lord. You went into space for them."

"Only because they couldn't get you."

"I wouldn't have gone."

She remembers how to look at him. He throws his hands up.

"Okay I'm a fucking liar." The man perched on the end of their table turns to glare at the dirty-mouthed Westerner. Thomas Lull touches each of the pictures lightly, reverently. "I have no answer to this. Sorry you came all this way to learn that, but I don't. Do you? Your photo's there too. All I do know is where we had two mysteries we now have one." He takes out his palmer, thumbs up the picture he stole of the inside of Aj's head glinting with the floating diyas of protein processors, sets it beside her Tabernacle image.

"I suppose we have to come to some deal. Help me find Aj and prove what I think the truth is about her, I'll offer what I can with the Tabernacle."

Lisa Durnau slips the Tablet out of its soft leather pouch and sets it at the opposite end, next to her own Tabernacle picture.

"You come back with me."

Thomas Lull shakes his head.

"No deal. You pass it on, but I'm not going back."

"We need you."

"*We?* And are you going to tell me it's my duty as a good citizen not just of America but the whole wide world to make a sacrifice for this epochal moment of first contact with an 'alien civilization'?"

"Fuck you, Lull." The man glares again at such profanity from the mouth of a woman. The hydrofoil jolts and booms as it strikes a submerged object.

This monsoon morning the Patna hydrofoil is a refugee scow. Varanasi is a city in spasm. The shockwaves spreading out from Sarkhand Roundabout have crystallised its ancient animosities and hatreds. It is not just the nutes now. It is the Muslims, the Sikhs, the Westerners as the city of Siva convulses, hunting sacrifices. US marines escorted the embassy car from the police station through the hastily erected Bharati army checkpoints. Thomas Lull tried to make sense of the little US flag fluttering boldly from the car's right wing as jawans and Marines slid looks off each other. Sirens dopplered across the night. A helicopter beat overhead. The convoy cruised past a row of looted small shops; steel security shutters staved in or wrenched out. A Nissan pickup laden with young karsevaks moved alongside. The men bent down to peer in the embassy car. Their eyes were wide with ganja; they carried trishuls, garden forks, antique blades. The driver leered, floored the pedal, and sped off, multiple horns blaring. Everywhere was the smell of wet burning.

"Aj is out there," Thomas Lull said.

At the hydrofoil dock the rain was falling heavily, tinged with smoke, but the city was venturing out, a peek from a door, a furtive dash past burned-out Marutis and looted Muslim shops, a scurrying phatphat run. There were livelihoods to be made. The city, as if having held its breath, at last allowed itself a slow, trembling exhalation. A steady throng pushed through the narrow streets to the river. With handcarts and cycle drays, with overloaded cycle rickshaws and phatphats, with hooting Marutis and taxis and pickups, the Muslims were leaving. Thomas Lull and Lisa climbed around the hopelessly jammed traffic. Many had abandoned vehicles and were off-loading their salvaged possessions: computers, sewing machines, lathes, great swollen bundles of bedding and clothing wrapped up in blue plastic twine.

"I went to see Chandra at the university," Thomas Lull said as they pushed through a snarl of abandoned cycle-rickshaws onto the ghat where the separate streams of refuges fused into one Vedic horde at the water's edge. "Anjali and Jean-Yves were working in human-aeai interfaces; specifically, grafting protein-chip matrices onto neural structures. Direct brain-computer connection." Lisa Durnau fought to keep Thomas Lull in sight. His gaudy blue surf-shirt was a beacon among the bodies and bundles. One trip on these stone steps and you were dead. "The lawyer gave Aj a photograph. Her, after some kind of operation, with Jean-Yves and Anjali. I recognised the location, it was Patna, on the new ghat at the Bund. Then I remembered something. It was back in Thekkady when I was working the beach clubs. I used to know a lot of the emotics runners, most of it came from Bangalore and Chennai but there was one guy imported it from the north, from the Free Trade Zone at Patna. They had everything you could get from Bangalore for a quarter the price. He used to go on monthly runs, and I remember him telling me about this grey medic, did radical surgery for men and women who didn't want to be men or women any more, if you get what I mean."

"Nutes," Lisa Durnau yelled over the sea of heads. The hydrofoil staff had sealed and barred the gate to the jetty and were lifting money from the hands thrust through the bars to permit refugees to slip aboard. She guessed they were halfway to the gate but she was tiring.

"Nutes," Thomas Lull shouted back. "It's a long shot, but if I'm right, it's the missing piece."

To what? Lisa Durnau wanted to ask but the crowd surged. The hydrofoil was filling by the second. Refugees were waist deep in the Ganga, holding babies, children up to the boat crew who pushed them ungently back with landing poles. Thomas Lull pulled Lisa Durnau close to him. They fought to the head of the line. The steel gate opened, the steel gate clanged shut. Bodies jammed against the grating.

"Got any green?"

A search of her bag threw up three hundred in traveller's cheques. Thomas Lull waved them in the air.

"US dollars! US dollars!"

The steward beckoned him forward. His crew shoved back the clingers-on.

"How many how many?"

Thomas Lull held up two fingers.

"In in."

They squeezed through the barely open gate, up the gangplank and onto the hydrofoil. Ten minutes later, grossly overloaded, it pulled away from the still-growing crowd on the ghats. To Lisa Durnau, peering through the streaky window, it looked like a blood clot.

In the overcrowded lounge she pushes the Tablet towards Thomas Lull. He thumbs through the pages of data from the Tabernacle.

"So what is it like in space, then?"

"Smelly. Tiring. You spend most of your time out of your head and you never actually get to see anything."

"Bit like a rock festival. First thing strikes me about this, you assume it's an artefact of an extraterrestrial civilization."

"If the Tabernacle is seven billion years old, then why don't we see the aliens who built it everywhere we look?"

"A variant on the Fermi Paradox—if aliens exist, then where are they? Let's work through this: if we posit the Tabernacle builders an expansion rate of even one-tenth percent of the speed of light, in seven billion years they would have colonised all the way to the Sculptor Galaxy group."

"There'd be nothing but them . . ."

"But all we find is one shitty little asteroid? I don't think so. Subsidiary point, if it is almost twice as old as our solar system . . ."

"How did they know we'd be here to find it?"

"That this swirl of stardust would one day turn into you, me, and Aj. I think we can dismiss that theory. Conjecture two: it's a message from God."

"Oh come on, Lull."

"I'd lay better than evens it's been whispered at the White House prayer breakfast. The end of the world is at hand."

"Then that's the end of the rational worldview. It's back to the Age of Miracles."

"Exactly. I like to think my life as a scientist has not been a complete waste. So I'll stick to theories that have some nugget of rationality in them. Conjecture three, another universe."

"That thought occurred to me," says Lisa Durnau.

"If anyone knows what's out there in the polyverse, it should be you. The Big Bang inflates into a set of separate universes all with slightly differing physical laws. The probability is virtually one hundred percent that there's at least one other universe with an Aj, a Lull, and a Durnau in it."

"Seven billion years old?"

"Different physical laws. Times runs faster."

"Conjecture four."

"Conjecture four: it's all a game. Rather, it's all a simulation. Deep down, physical reality is rules and the application of rules, those simple programmes that give rise to incalculable complexity. Computer virtual reality looks exactly the same . . . I've only been saying this all my life, L. Durnau. But here's the rub. We're both fakes. We're reruns on the final computer at the Omega Point at the end of spacetime. The probabilities are always going to be in favour of our reality being a rerun rather than the original."

"And bugs are appearing in the system. Our mystery seven-billion-year-old asteroid."

"Implying some imminent plot development for The Sims."

"You're not supposed to see the Great and Powerful Oz," says Lisa Durnau.

"We're definitely not in Kansas any more."

The chai-wallah passes, swinging his stainless steel urn, chanting his mantra: *chai, kafi.* Thomas Lull takes a fresh cup.

"I don't know how you drink that stuff," Lisa says.

"Conjecture five. For a mysterious alien artefact, it's a bit clunky. I've seen more convincing SFX on *Town and Country*."

"I get what you're saying here. It looks like we built it—if we wanted to send some kind of message to ourselves."

"One you can't ignore—an Earth-crossing asteroid, and then make it move out of the way."

Lisa Durnau hesitates. This is beyond blue-sky. "From our future."

"There's nothing here I don't see us achieving in a couple of hundred years."

"It's a warning?"

"Why else send something back, unless you need to change history pretty damn bad? Our umpteen-great-grand-Lulls and Durnaus have run into something they can't deal with. But if they gave themselves a couple of hundred years' head start . . ."

"I can't imagine what they're up against if they can send objects through time and they're still on the ropes."

"I can," says Thomas Lull. "It's the final war between humans and aeais. We'd be up against Generation Tens by then—one hundred million times the capability of a Gen Three."

"That means they would operate on the same level as the Wolfram/Friedkin codes that underly our physical reality," Lisa Durnau says. "In which case . . ."

"They could directly manipulate physical reality."

"You're talking magic here. God, magic. Jesus, Lull. I've objections. One: they send it back seven billion years?"

"A gravitational anomaly stirred the dust nebula that became this solar system. A passing black hole would make a dandy anchor point for a timelike wormhole. At least they would know we would be here."

"Very good, Lull. Try this one. Objection two: as messages go, it's a bit obtuse. What's wrong with a simple help we are getting fucked over by Artificial Intelligences with the powers of gods?"

"What do you think the effect of that would be? By the time we work it out, we'll be ready for what the Tabernacle has to say to us."

"You're not convincing me, Lull. Even with Generation Tens and wormholes and the fact that the act of sending a warning splits us off into a universe where we get the head start but dooms them in their universe . . . even with all that, why the hell are you, me, and an eighteen-year-old girl who can talk to machines so important?"

Thomas Lull shrugs, that maddening, grinning, don't-know-don't-care gesture that had always the power to infuriate Lisa when she argued his speculations down in sessions just like this. Now Lull pulls up his stolen images of the inside of Aj's skull.

"Your side of the deal."

"All right. For me, this isn't the mystery. This is the corroboration. The mystery is how she stopped those Awadhi robots. So when we rule out magic and we rule out God all we have left is technology. And that, in there, is technology; technology that could let a human brain communicate directly with a machine. She hacked them."

"No God, no gods," says Thomas Lull. Lisa feels a vibration run through the hull of the hydrofoil. The boat throttles back its waterjets, settling down on its foils on its approach to the crowded waters around Patna. Through the glass she makes out the cheap mass-built light industrial units and ex-urban infotech sprawl behind the Ganga's wide, sandy reefs.

"What does she see? A halo of information around people and things. She sees a bird and tells you its name and species. That sounds like the Birds of Southwest India. In the railway station she tells a family their son has been arrested, what train to get, what lawyers to hire. That's police reports, the Ahmedabad Yellow pages, and the Mumbai Railroads timetable. In every way, she gets on like someone whose brain is hooked into the net."

Lisa brushes her fingers lightly over the ghost-drawings on the Tablet.

"All this . . . is how she does it. I don't know who she is, I don't know how Jean-Yves and Anjali came to be caught up in it, but what I know is someone took a girl and turned her into an experiment, some monstrous test bed for new brain/machine interface technology."

Passengers stir, gather up their dependants and possessions. Their brief respite on water is nearly over, now they must face a strange, new, unknown city.

"I'm with you all the way up to that point, L. Durnau," says Thomas Lull. "I think it's the other way round. It's not a system for a human to interact with a machine. It's a system for a machine to interact with a human brain. She is an aeai downloaded into a human body. She is the Generation Threes' first and last ambassador to humanity. I think that's why we're all together in the Tabernacle. It's a prophecy of a *meeting*."

She is an orphan in the city of gods and therefore never alone. Gods beat behind her like wings, gods flock around her head, gods roll and tumble at her feet, gods peel apart before her like a million opening doors. She lifts her hand and ten thousand gods flow apart and fuse together again. Every building, every vehicle, every lamp and neon, every street shrine and traffic light, trembles with gods. She can look and read a hundred phatphat licence details, their owners' dates of birth and addresses, their insurance histories, their credit ratings, their educational qualifications and criminal records, their bank account numbers, their children's exam results, their wives' shoe-sizes. Gods fold out of each other like paper streamers. Gods weave through each other like gold threads on a silk loom. Beyond the air-glow the night horizon is a jewelled crown of deities. Beneath the traffic boom, the sirens, the raised voices and car horns and blaring music, nine million gods whisper to her.

Violence here, warns the god of the gali that leads off the brightly lit street of chai bars and snack stalls. She halts as she hears a rising roar of male voices funnelling down the narrow, jharoka-lined alley. Student karsevaks come roaring forth. She picks one out of god-space: Mangat Singhal: mechanical engineering student at the University of Bharat. He has been a paid-up Youth Member of the Shivaji for three years; he has had two arrests for riotous behaviour at the Sarkhand Roundabout protest. His mother has smoking-related cancer of the throat and will likely go to the ghats before the year is out. *This way*, says the god of the taxi rank, showing her the Maruti cruising beyond the panicked chai-wallahs hastily putting up their steel grilles. *Damage estimated at twenty thousand rupees*, the god of small insurance claims tells her as she hears the crash of a chai-stall overturned behind her by karsevaks. *Unclaimable under public disturbance exemptions. You will intersect with your taxi in thirty-five seconds. Left here.* And she is there as the Maruti comes round the corner and stops for her hand.

"Don't go there," the driver says when she gives him the address out in the basti.

"I will pay you much money." *ATM next on right*, the god of the shopping arcade says. "Stop here." The card goes in without hesitation, without question, without need for number or face scan. *How much do you require?* asks the god of electronic banking. She gives it a five-digit number. It is so long coming out of the slot she worries the driver might move on to a safer fare. *Cab licence number VRJ117824C45 is still stationary at the curb*, advises the god that animates the traffic cameras. She blinks up to its elevated viewpoint, sees herself, close in at the ATM trying to fold fat wads of cash, sees the cab behind her, sees the small convoy of army hummers blast past.

"Will this suffice?" She thrusts the bouquet of notes in the driver's face.

"Baba, for this I will drive you to Delhi itself."

He is a driver who likes to talk; riot riot riot; any excuse at all, why aren't they concentrating on their studies instead of burning things up, when they try to get jobs, that's when it'll all come home, oh I see you were in trouble with the police for riotous behaviour, no, no jobs here for gundas and badmashes, but what about Sajida Rana, the Prime Minister, can you believe it, her own bodyguard, our Prime Minister, Mama Bharat, and what are we going to do, has anything thought of that? and god help us when we fall over, the Awadhis will roll right over us . . . Aj watches the gods flow in squadrons and chapters and orders and pile up behind her into an incandescent hemisphere over the city. She taps the driver on the shoulder. He almost steers into a brick and plastic roadside hovel.

"Your wife is well and safe and will spend the night at her mother's until it is safe to come home."

She leaves him shortly after. Gods are few as stars in a night sky here. They hover around the big yellow sodium lights on the main avenues, over the cars that swoosh past in the rain, they flicker up and down the communications cables like fire but the bastis beyond are black, unholy. Whispers guide her into the darkness. The world turns the city burns but the slum must sleep. A startled face in an all-night chai-stall stares at her as if she is a djinn, whirled out of the storm. *Keep on along here until you come to a big power pylon*, whispers the god of the MTV-Asia cable-channel on the pale blue screen. Divinities are draped from the girders of the big power tower like leaves on a tree. *Left side*, they say. *The one with two steps down and the plastic fertiliser bag for the door*. It is easily found, even in streaming, stinking darkness, when gods guide you. She feels out the contours of the rag house. The plastic door-sheet rustles at her touch. Lives awake within. Here is where the DNA in the database leads her. Beyond her the true light of dawn glows grey and wan through the god-glow. Aj lifts the plastic and ducks under the lintel.

They shout and they hammer for twenty minutes but the good doctor Nanak is not receiving visitors this day. The doors are sealed, the hatches dogged, the windows shuttered and locked with big bright brass padlocks. Thomas Lull bangs his fist on the grey door.

"Come on, open the fuck up!"

In the end he lobs metal scrap up at the meshed-over bridge windows while the rain gathers into ever larger puddles on the grey decking. The barrage attracts the attention of the Australians on the next barge. Two bare-chested twentysomethings in calf-length jams come over the ramp. Water drips from their blond dreads but they move through the rain as if it is their natural environment. Lisa Durnau, sheltering under an awning, checks their abs. They have those little muscle groin grooves that point down under their waistbands.

"Mate, if the guru ain't in, he ain't in."

"I saw something moving up there." Thomas Lull shouts again. "Hey! I see you, come out, there's things I want to ask you."

"Look, bit of respect for a fella's peace," says second fit boy. He wears a carved jade spiral on a leather thong around his neck. "The guru is not giving interviews, no one, nowhere, no-how. Okay?"

"I am not a fucking journalist, and I am not a fucking karsevak," Thomas Lull declares and starts to climb the superstructure.

"Lull," Lisa Durnau groans.

"Oh no you don't," the first Australian shouts and together they seize Thomas Lull by the legs and pull him off the bridge. He hits the deck with a meaty thump.

"Now, you have definitely outstayed your welcome," green spiral boy says and they wrestle Thomas Lull to his feet, pin his arms, and navigate him towards the main arterial companionway between the barges. Lisa Durnau decides it's time to do something.

"Nanak!" she calls up at the bridge. A figure moves behind the mesh and the dirty glass. "We're not journalists. It's Lisa Durnau and Thomas Lull. We want to talk to you about Kalki."

The door to the flying bridge opens. A face muffled in shawls peep out, a face like Hanuman the monkey god.

"Let him go."

Nanak the dream surgeon bustles around the bridge making tea the proper way. The interior is oddly louche in its cod-colonial wicker and bamboo after the clanging industrial superstructure.

"Apologies apologies for my reticence." Nanak fusses with pots and a folding brass Benares table. Lisa Durnau sips her chai and subtly studies her host. Nutes are not a common sex in Kansas. The details of yts skin, the subtle ridges down yts bare left arm that are the subdermal controls for the sexual system, fascinate her. She wonders how it is to programme your emotions, to design your fallings-in-love and heartbreaks, to reengineer your hopes and fears. She wonders how many kinds of orgasms you could create. But the question foremost in her mind is: was it male or female? The body shape, the fat distribution, the clothes—a deliberate eclectic mix favouring the floating and the floppy, give no indication. *Male*, she decides. Men are fragile and fluid in their sexual identities. Nanak continues pouring chai. "We have been victimised of late. The Australians look after me well, lovely boys. And the work here does demand discretion. But: Professor Thomas Lull, a great honour for a humble factor of surgical services."

Thomas Lull unfolds his palmer and places it on the brass table. Nanak winces at the display.

"This was the most complex operation I have ever brokered. Weeks of work. They virtually unravelled her brain. Lobes and folds drawn out and suspended on wires. Extraordinary."

Lisa Durnau sees Thomas Lull's face tighten. Nanak touches him on the knee.

"She is well?"

"She is trying to find out who her true parents are. She's realised that her life is lies."

Nanak's mouth forms a voiceless *Oh*.

"I am but a broker of services . . ."

"Was it these two hired you?" Thomas Lull thumbs up the picture from the temple that had first sent him on this pilgrimage.

"Yes," Nanak says, folding yts hands in yts shawl. "They represented a powerful Varanasi sundarban, the Badrinath sundarban. The legendary abode of Vishnu, I believe. I was paid two million US dollars in a banker's draft drawn on the account of the Odeco Corporation. I can furnish you with the details if you require. Almost half the budget went on wetware applications, we had to find a way of programming memory; emotic designers are not cheap, though I like to think we have some of the best in the whole of Hindustan in this zone."

"Budget," Thomas Lull spits. "Like a fucking television programme . . ."

Now Lisa Durnau has to speak.

"Her adoptive parents in Bangalore, do they actually exist?"

"Oh, entirely false, madam. We spent much money on creating a credible back-story. It had to be convincing that she was human, with a childhood and parents and a past."

"Why, is she . . ." Lisa Durnau asks, dreading the answer.

"An aeai possessing a human body," Thomas Lull says and Lisa now hears the ice in his voice that is more dangerous than any heat of passion.

Nanak rocks on yts chair.

"That is correct; forgive me, this is most distasteful. The Badrinath sundarban was the host for a Generation Three artificial intelligence. The scheme, as your colleagues told it to me, was to download a copy on to the higher cognitive levels of a human brain. The tilak was the interface. An extremely complicated piece of surgery. It took us three attempts to get it right."

"They're scared, aren't they?" Thomas Lull says. "They can see the end coming. How many are left?"

"Three only, I believe."

"They want to know if they can make peace or if they must be driven to extinction, but first they have to understand us. Our humanity baffles them, it's a miracle she can make any sense out of it it all, but that's what the false childhood is for. How old is Aj really?"

"It is eight months since she left this place with your colleagues—whom she believed to be her real parents. It is just over a year since I was contacted by the Badrinath aeai. Oh, you should have seen her the day she left, she was so bright, so joyful, like everything was new. The European couple were to take her down to Bangalore—they had only a short time, levels of memory were decompressing and if they left it too long it would have been disastrous, they would have become imprinted."

"You abandoned her?" Lisa Durnau is incredulous. She tries to convince herself that this is India; life and individuality have different values from Kansas and Santa Barbara. But she still reels from what these people have done to a teenage girl.

"It was the plan. We had a cover story that she was in a gap year travelling around the subcontinent."

"And did it ever, once occur to you, in your plans and cover stories and decompressing memories and your precision Chinese surgery, that for this aeai to live, a human personality had to die?" Thomas Lull explodes. Lisa Durnau now touches a hand to his leg. Easy. Peace. Chill. Nanak smiles like a blessing saint.

"Why sir, the child was an imbecile. No individuality, no sense of person at all. No life at all. It had to be that way, we could never have used a normal subject. Her parents were delighted when your colleagues bought her from them. At last their child might have a chance, with the experimental new technology. They thanked Lord Vishnu . . ."

With a wordless roar Thomas Lull is on his feet, fist balled. Nanak scuttles across the floor away from the raging male. Lisa Durnau smothers Lull's fist in her two hands.

"Leave it, let it go," she whispers. "Sit down, Lull, sit down."

"Fuck you!" Thomas Lull yells at the nute-maker. "Fuck you and fuck Kalki and fuck Jean-Yves and Anjali!"

Lisa Durnau presses him into his seat. Nanak gathers ytself up, dusts ytself down, but yt does not dare come near.

"I apologise for my friend here," Lisa Durnau says. "He's overwrought . . ." She grips Thomas Lull's shoulder. "I think we should go."

"Yes, maybe that would be best," says Nanak, shrugging yts shawls around ytself. "This is a discreet business, I cannot have raised voices."

Thomas Lull shakes his head, disgusted at himself as much as any words in this room. He extends a hand but the nute does not take it.

The suitcases have little plastic wheels that rumble over the downtown streets. But the surface is patched and uneven and the handles are silly webbing loops and Krishan and Parvati are moving as fast as they can so every few metres the cases twist off their wheels and spill over. And the taxis just splash by Krishan's upraised hand and the troop carriers prowl past and the songs of the karsevaks come from this side then that side, from behind, then right in front so they must hide in a doorway as they run past and Parvati is weary and soaked through, sari clinging to her, hair hanging in ropes and it is still five kilometres to the station.

"Too many clothes," Krishan jokes. Parvati smiles. He hefts both cases, one in each hand, and sets off again. Together they huddle through the streets, clinging to doorways, cringing from the military traffic, dashing across intersections, always alert for unexpected sounds, sudden movements.

"Not far," Krishan lies. His forearms are knotted, burning. "Soon be there."

As they approach the station people emerge from the capillary galis and project streets, laden like them with bags, burdens, cycle rickshaws, carts, cars; rivulet joining to stream joining to flow joining together into a broad river of heads. Parvati clutches at Krishan's sleeve. To slip apart here is to be lost for years. Krishan wades on, fists rigid around the plastic handles that feel as if they are made of burning coal, neck muscles tensed, teeth clenched, looking ahead, ahead, thinking of nothing but the station the train the station the train and how every footstep takes him closer, takes him nearer to the time when he can set these burdens down. He waddles now, trying to keep step with the surge of people. Parvati is closer than a shadow. A woman in a full burqa presses past. "What are you doing here?" she hisses. "You have brought this to us." Krishan pushes the woman away with his suitcases before her words can spread and bring the wrath of the crowd down on them for now he sees what has been before his face all this long road: the Muslims are leaving Varanasi.

Parvati whispers, "Do you think we will be able to get a train?" Then Krishan understands that the world will not stop for their romantic notions, the crowds will not part and let them free passage, history will not grant them a lovers' pardon. Theirs is not a bold, romantic flight. They are foolish and blind and selfish. His heart sinks deeper as the street opens into the approach to the station and the flow of refugees empties into the largest mass of people he has ever seen, more than any crowd that ever streamed out of Sampurnanand Stadium. He can see the spars and translucent spun-diamond canopy of the concourse, the gaping glass portals to the ticket halls. He can see the train at the platform, glistening under the yellow lights, already loaded to the roof and more climbing on all the time. He can see the soldiers silhouetted against the breaking dawn on their armoured vehicles. But he cannot see a way through the people; all those people. And the cases, those stupid suitcases, pull him down through the concrete into the soil, anchoring him like roots. Parvati tugs at his sleeve.

"This way."

She draws him towards the concourse gates. The press is less at the edge of the plaza; refugees instinctually keep away from soldiers. Parvati hunts in the beadwork bag over her shoulder. She fetches a tube of lipstick, ducks her head briefly and comes up again with a red bindi on her forehead.

"Please, for the love of Siva for the love of Siva!" she cries to the soldiers, hands pressed together into a namaskar of entreaty. The jawans' eyes cannot be read behind their mirrored, rain-spotted visors. Louder now: "For the love of the Lord Siva!" Now the people around her start to turn and look and growl. They start to jostle, their anger begins. Parvati pleads with the soldiers. "For the love of Lord Siva."

Then the soldiers hear her voice. They see her soaked, dirt-smeared sari. They read her bindi. Jawans slip down from their vehicles, jabbing their weapon muzzles at the women and children, forcing them back though they scream God's curse at the soldiers. A jemadar gestures briskly to Parvati and Krishan. The soldiers part, they slip through, the weapons go up again to the horizontal, a bar, a denial. A woman officer hurries Parvati and Krishan between the parked transports that even in the rain smell of hot biodiesel. Voices rise to a thunder of outrage. Glancing back, Parvati sees hands seize a jawan's assault gun. There is a short, fierce balance of forces, then the soldier next to him casually swings up the butt of his weapon and smashes it into the side of the protestor's skull. The Muslim man goes down without even a cry, hands clutched to head. The man's cry becomes the crowd's; it surges like a river squall. Then the shots rip out and everyone in the plaza falls to their knees.

"Come on," the jemadar says. "No one's hurt. Keep your heads down. What were you doing there? What ever possessed you? This day of all days." She tuts. Parvati does not think Bharati soldiers should tut.

"My mother," Parvati says. "I have to go to her, she's an old woman, she needs me, she has no one else . . ."

The jemadar brings them up the side steps into the station concourse. Parvan's spirit turns to lead. The people, the people. There is no way through this. She cannot see where the ticket counters are. But Krishan bangs down the cases and jerks out the handles and lifts them up on their little frayed black plastic wheels and pushes determinedly into the rear of the crowd.

The sun climbs over the transparent roof. Trains arrive, more people than Parvati can ever imagine press onto the platforms. For every trainload of refugees that pulls out from under Varanasi Station's spun-diamond canopy another presses into the foyer from the forecourt. Parvati and Krishan are pushed step by step toward the ticket desks. Parvati watches the flatscreens suspended from the roof. Something has happened to *Breakfast with Bharti*. In her place is a video loop of Ashok Rana, whom she has never liked, over and over. He is behind some studio desk. He looks tired and afraid. It is only on the sixth viewing that Parvati understands with a shock what he is saying. His sister is dead. Sajida Rana is dead. Now the streets, the shots, the crowds, the running, the Muslims, and the soldiers firing over their heads, all become solid, one connected thing. Ignorant and innocent, they have been running, suitcases in hand, through the death throes of Mother Bharat. Suddenly her selfishness consumes her.

"Krishan. We have to go back. I can't go. We were wrong . . ."

Krishan's face is perfect, drained, disbelief. Then the gap opens in front of him and it goes all the way to the ticket counter and the clerk looks at Parvati, just at Parvati and in a moment the gap will implode.

"Krishan, the ticket-wallah!"

She pushes him up to the counter and the ticket-wallah asks him where he wants to go and he doesn't know, and she can see the clerk will brush him aside, next please.

"Bubaneshwar!" she cries. "Two singles! Bubaneshwar." She has never been to Bubaneshwar, has never even crossed into ancient Orissa, but her mind is filled with the image of billowing orange and scarlet silk, the rath yatra of Jagannath. Then the ticket-wallah prints the tickets and gives them their train number and time and platform and seat reservations and spins the slips of paper through the hatch.

It is four hours until the train to Raipur, where they will change for Bubaneshwar. The slow conveyor of people takes them through the doors on to the platform where they sit on their luggage, too tired for words, each fearing that if the other speaks they will both leave the blue plastic cases and bolt back to their lives and lies, little adventure over and closed. Krishan buys newsprints from the stall—not many for what Parvati reads in them makes her afraid to be on the platform among the Muslims, despite the groups of soldiers that pass up and down. She feels the weight of their looks, hears their hisses and mutterings. Mrs. Khan from the Cantonment Set, so certain on the politics of the war at the cricket match, could be on this platform. No, not the Begum Khan; she would be in a first-class air-conditioned a hundred kilometres away, she would be driving south in her chauffeured car, windows darkened; she would be in business class on an airbus.

Rain drips from the fringe of the platform canopy. Krishan shows Parvati the headline, still smeary from the printer, announcing a great Government of National Salvation in coalition with N. K. Jivanjee's Shivaji Party that will restore order and repulse the invader. This is what Parvati has felt blow across the platforms like a cold front. The enemy has gained the whip; there is no place in Bharat for Islam.

The train is felt before heard; the clank of the points, the deep vibration transmitted up through the sleepers to the steel stanchions that support the platform canopy, the rumble in the worn blacktop. The crowd arises family by family as the train expands out of the perspective of the tracks, weaving over the points as it draws in to platform fifteen. The indicator boards light up: Raipur Express. Krishan snatches up the cases as the crowd surges forward to meet the train. Bogie after bogie after bogie slides past without sign of stopping. Parvati presses close to Krishan. Trip here, stumble, fall and you would die beneath the guillotine-edge wheels. Slowly the great green train comes to halt.

Suddenly bodies push hard against Parvati. She reels forward against Krishan, he is driven hard against the side of the train. Simultaneously a roar goes up from the back of the crowd.

"To me, to me!" Krishan cries. The doors hiss open. Bodies immediately clog them. Arms thrust, torsos twist, luggage is squeezed and rammed. The surge carries Parvati away from the steps. Krishan fights the flow, clinging to the door stanchion, desperate that she will not be separated from him. Terrified, Parvati reaches out for him. Women shove around her screaming mindless oaths, children kick past. The platform is heads, heads and hands, heads and hands and bundles and more people are running across the tracks from the other platforms to reach the train, the train out of Varanasi. Young men trample Parvati as they scramble on to the roof; still she reaches for Krishan's hand.

Then the shots bang out; short, stabbing bursts of automatic fire. The mob on the platform drops as one, covers heads with hands. Cries, shrieks, and the dreadful, unappeasable wail of the injured: the soldiers are not shooting to scare this time. Parvati feels Krishan's hand close on her. Bullets crack out again. She sees flashes, hears the clang of shells ricocheting off the stanchions. Krishan gives a strange little sigh, then his grip tightens around hers and he draws her up, on to the train.

On the return trip Lisa and Thomas Lull are the only passengers in the lounge. It feels big and plasticy and exposed under its unkind fluorescents so Lisa Durnau suggests they go outside to regard the holy river. Sacred water is a new concept to Lisa Durnau. They stand side by side at the rail, buffeted by flaws of rain watching the sandy banks and rusty tin water abstraction plants. An object breaks the surface. Lisa wonders if it is one of the blind river dolphins she read about on the flight up from Thiruvananthapuram. Dolphin or dead. Certain classes of Hindus cannot be cremated and are surrendered to the mercy of Ganga Mata.

Once in a conference she flopped plane/train/taxi-lagged into a leather armchair in the lobby opposite an African delegate reclining generously in a seat. She nodded to him, wide-eyed, dazed, *whoooo*. He nodded back, patted his hands on the arms of the chair. "Just letting my soul catch up with me." She needs to do that. Catch up with herself. Find a time out from the succession of one event to the next, that's not filled with some person or thing or problem coming at her, frozen in the headlights of history. Stop reacting, take time, take a step, let your soul catch up. She would love to go for a run. Barring that, some time with a sacred river.

She looks at Thomas Lull. In his stance at the rail she sees four years, she sees uncertainty, she sees fading of confidence, cooling of ardour and energy. When did you last burn with passion about anything? she thinks. She sees a man in his middle years who looks at death every day. She sees almost nothing of the man she had dirty, grown-up sex with in an Oxford College shower. It is absolutely over, she thinks and feels sorry for him. He looks so very tired.

"So tell me, L. Durnau, do you ever, you know, see Jen around?"

"Occasionally, at the mall, sometimes the Jayhawks games. She's got someone else."

"I thought that even before. You know. Same way as you know when it's on. Chemicals or something. Does she look happy?"

"Happy enough." Lisa Durnau anticipates his inevitable next question. "No baby buggies."

He looks at the passing shore, the white temple shikaras hazy against the rain clouds beyond the dark line of trees. Buffalo loll in the water, lifting their heads against the spreading hydrofoil wake.

"I know why Jean-Yves and Anjali did it, why they left her that photograph. I'd wondered why they should punch a hole right through the heart of it. Anjali never could have children, you know."

"Aj was their surrogate daughter."

"They felt they owed her the truth. Better to find out what she really was than be a life of illusions. To be human is to be disillusioned."

"You don't agree with that!"

"I haven't your stern Calvinist mien. I'm comfortable with illusion. I don't think I would have had the courage or the callousness to do that to her."

But you also walked away, Lisa Durnau thinks. You also abandoned friends, career, reputation, lovers; it was easy for you, turn around and walk away and never look back.

"But she came looking for you," Lisa Durnau says.

"I don't have any answers for her," Thomas Lull says. "Why do you have to have answers? You're born not fucking knowing anything, you go through your life not fucking knowing anything, you die and you never know any fucking thing ever again. That's the mystery of it. I am nobody's guru, not yours, not NASA's, not some aeai's. You know something? All those articles and TV appearances and conferences? I was making it up as I went along. That's all. Alterre? Just something I made up some day."

Lisa Durnau grips the rail with both hands.

"Lull, Alterre's gone."

She cannot read his face, his stance, his muscles. She tries to provoke a reaction.

"Gone, Lull, everything. All eleven million servers, crashed. Extinct."

Thomas Lull shakes his head. Thomas Lull frowns. His brow creases. Then Lisa sees an expression on his face she knows so well herself: the bafflement, wonderment, enlightenment of *idea*.

"What was always behind Alterre?" he says.

"That a simulated environment . . ."

"Might eventually produce real intelligence." The words come in a rush. "What if we succeeded better than we ever hoped? What if Alterre didn't breed sentience, but the whole thing became alive . . . aware . . . Kalki is the tenth avatar of Vishnu. It sits there at the top of Alterre's evolutionary pyramid, preserver and sustainer of all life; all things proceed from it and are of its substance. Then it reaches out and there's another world of life out there, not part of it, separate, disconnected, utterly alien. Is it a threat, is it a blessing, is it something altogether other? It has to know. It has to experience."

"But if Alterre has crashed."

He chews in his bottom lip and goes quiet and dark, looking out at the rain in the great river. Lisa Durnau tries to count the impossibilities he has had to absorb. After a time he reaches out a hand. "Give me that thing. I need to find Aj. If Vishnu is gone, she's unplugged from the net. All her life is illusion and now even the gods have abandoned her. What is she going to be thinking, feeling?"

Lisa slips the Tablet out of its flesh-soft leather holster and passes it to Thomas Lull. It emits a deep, chiming scale. Thomas Lull almost drops it in surprise. Lisa intercepts the thing on its way to moksha in the Ganga. A voice and image appear in her perceptions: Daley-Suarez Martin.

"Something's happened at the Tabernacle. They've got another signal out of it." The Tablet displays a fourth face, a man, a Bharati, so much is obvious even in the low-resolution cellular automaton image; a thin-boned, drawn man. Lisa Durnau can make out the collar of a Nehru suit. She thinks he has an unutterably sad face. There is an ident line attached.

"I think you'd better find your friend quick," she says. "This is Nandha. He's a Krishna Cop."

She flees from the house into the grey light. The rain falls on Scindia Basti. The bare feet of the women fetching water from the pumps have churned the alleys to fetid mud. The sewers overflow. The men also are about in the dawn, to buy and sell, maybe hire themselves to dig a ditch for a cable, maybe have a cup of chai, maybe see if there is anything left of the city. They stare at the girl with the Vishnu tilak, shoving past them, running as if Kali rising is on her heels.

Eyes in the dark in the house by the pylon left's foot. "We are poor people, we have nothing you can possibly want, please leave us in peace." Then the scratch and flare of the match and the arc of light through the darkness as it moved to touch the wick of the little clay diya, the bud of light swelling and filling the clay-floored room. Then, the cries of fear.

Vehicles roar at her; metal looms huge, then recedes into the rain. Thundering voices, bodies pressing around her that seem the size of clouds. A river of motion and alcofueled peril. She is on the street and she does not know how. The certainties and divine guidances of the night have evaporated in the light. For the first time there is no clear distinction between god and human. She is not sure she can find her way back to the hotel.

Aid me.

The skyline crawls with the chaotic moiré patterns of gods meshing, blurring, flowing, breeding into strange new configurations.

"*What are you doing in this house?*" She cries out, claps her hands to her ears as the remembered voice speaks again in her skull. The women's faces in the glow of the grease lamp, one old, one younger, one youngest. A wail had gone up from the old woman; like something long and fragile tearing inside.

What are you doing here? You have no place here!" A hand, held in a mudra against the evil eye. The youngest's eyes wide with fear, wet with tears. "Get out of this house, there is no place for you here. Don't be deceived. See her, see her? See what they have done? Ah, this is an evil thing, a djinn, a demon!" The old woman rocking now, eyes closed, moaning. "Away from us! This is not your home, you are not our sister!"

Entreaties never offered. Answers never spoken. Questions never worded. And the old woman, the old woman; her mother, her hand in front of her eyes as if Aj blinded her, as if she burned with a fire that could not be looked upon. On the street, underneath the monsoon rain, she cries out, a long, thin wail torn out of the heart of her. She understands now.

Fear: that is white, without surface or texture or anything you can lay a hand on to move or manipulate and it feels like rot in the base of you and you want to roll up and ask it to pass you over, like a raincloud, but it will never do that.

Loss bites and pulls. It is a thing of hooks sunk into every part of you, parts that you would not think could feel loss like thumbs and lips, hooks moored to wind and memory so that the slightest disturbance, the slightest act of recall, tugs at those fine lines. Red is the colour of loss and its smell is like burned roses.

Abandonment, that tastes like sick in the back of your throat, always on the edge of coming up; it feels like dizzy, like walking along the edge of a high stone harbour over a sea that glimmers and moves so far below you cannot be certain where it is, but brown, brown; abandonment is empty dull brown.

Desperation: a universal background hum, grey noise, part drone part hiss, a stifling, blurring, smudging of everything into soft grey. Universal rain. Universal yielding, into which you can push beyond the reach of any of your limbs and still touch nothing. Universal insulation. That is desperation.

Yellow is the colour of uncertainty, sick yellow, yellow like bile, yellow like madness, yellow like flowers that open their petals around you and whirl and spin so you cannot decide which is best, which is most perfect, which has the most gorgeous, cloying scent; yellow like acid that eats away at everything you think you know until you stand on a rotted filigree of rust and you are at once smaller than the tiniest grain of yellow pollen and vast beyond vastness, containing cities.

Shock is a numb pressure trying to smear your brain over the back of your skull.

Betrayal is translucent blue, so cold cold cold.

Incomprehension feels like a hair on the tongue.

And anger is heavy like a hammer but so light it can fly with its own wings, and the darkest, darkest rust.

This is what it is to be human.

"Why didn't you tell me?" she shouts at the gods as the street breaks around her and rain falls on her upturned face.

And the gods answer: *we never knew. We never thought.* And again: *now we understand.* Then one by one they extinguish like diyas in the rain.

Shiv can't place the smell. It's sweet, it's musky, it reminds him of things he can't fully remember and it's coming from the dataraja Ramanandacharya. He's a fat bastard but they all are. Fat and quivering. Doesn't look so cool in those robes and gowns now. Shiv particularly hates the old-school Mughal-style moustaches. He'd love to cut them off but Yogendra needs to keep the hooked tip of the big knife at Ramanandacharya's groin. One small wrist movement there will sever the femoral artery. Shiv knows the surgery. The raja will bleed out in under four minutes.

They walk up the sloping wet cobbles from the Hastings Pavilion to the Temple, close as lovers or drunks.

"How many have you got there?" Shiv whispers, nudging Ramanandacharya with his shoulder. "Back there, how many women, huh?"

"Forty," says Ramanandacharya. Shiv cuffs him with the back of his hand. He knows it's the pills, making him impatient, bolder than a clever man should be, but he likes the feel of it.

"Forty women? Where you get them from, huh?" Nudge.

"All over, Philippines, Thailand, Russians, anywhere cheap, you know?" Again, the rap with the back of the hand. Ramanandacharya cringes. They pass the sentry robot, crouched down on its steel hams.

"Any good Bharati women in there?"

"Couple from the village . . . ah!" Shiv cuffs harder now, Ramanandacharya rubs his ear. Shiv takes a fold of rich gold-threaded silk between his fingers, feels the subtle weave, the skin-smoothness, the lightness.

"Do they like this, huh? All this Mughal shit?" He shoves Ramanandacharya with both hands. The dataraja stumbles on a step. Yogendra flicks the knife away. "Why couldn't you have been a Hindu, huh?"

Ramanandacharya shrugs.

"Mughal Fort," he offers weakly. Shiv hits him again.

"Mughal Fort fuck!" He slides in close to the ear. "So how often do you, you know? Every night?"

"Lunchtimes too . . ." The sentence vanishes into a sharp cry as Shiv hits Ramanandacharya hard on the side of the head.

"Fucking dirty chuutya!" He knows what the smell is now. That sweet, sour, musky, dark smell from Ramanandacharya's robes and jewels: sex.

"Eh," says Yogendra. The swarm of robots has left its orbit of the Lodi temple and streams across the courtyard towards the trio, a black, oily arrow. Plastic peds rattle on the cobbles. Their wet carapaces glint blackly. Ramanandacharya tuts and sighs and twists the ring on his left pinky. The swarms part like that sea in that Christian story, the kind American missionaries put into the heads of good young women to turn them into unmarriageable things that can never get proper husbands.

"They'd have had your feet down to the bones in twenty seconds," Ramanandacharya says.

"Fuck up, fat boy." Shiv smacks him again because he was scared by the scarab robots. Ramanandacharya takes a step, takes another. The ring of robots flows with him. Yogendra brushes the knife tip against Ramanandacharya's groin.

The temple colonnade is the same dismal, dripping shell of graffittied plaster and folk-art religious daubings Shiv scanned from the battlement but Ramanandacharya's Kirlian signature activates banks of blue flood lamps and Shiv finds he is holding his breath. The suddhavasa within is a cube of translucent plastic, glowing at the edges under the sharp blue light. The scarab robots fall back into their orbit. Ramanandacharya lifts his hands to the translucent plastic yoni of the airlock door. A digit pad resolves out of the fluid surface. Ramanandacharya moves to tap in a code; the knife flashes, Ramanandacharya cries out, seizes his hand. Blood wells from a hairline cut down his right forefinger.

"You do it." Yogendra waves the knife blade at Shiv.

"What?"

"He could have tricks, traps, things we don't know. He thinks soon as we have it, he's going to die anyway. You use the code."

Ramanandacharya's eyes widen as Shiv takes out the palmer and starts to enter the door password.

"Where did you get this? Dane? Where's Dane?"

"Hospital," Shiv says. "Cat got his tongue." Yogendra giggles. The pad sinks back into the surface of the smart plastic (which Shiv thinks is cooler than he will ever allow to a chuutya like Ramanandacharya) and the door clicks anticlimactically open.

The decryption system is a luminous plastic garbhagriha small enough to make Shiv itchily claustrophobic.

"Where's the computer?" Shiv asks.

"The whole thing is the computer," Ramanandacharya says and with a wave of his hands turns the walls translucent. Protein circuitry woven dense as Varanasi silk, as nerve fibres, is packed into the walls. Fluids bubble around the net of artificial neurones. Shiv notices he's shivering in his wet combats.

"Why is it so fucking cold in here?"

"My central quantum processing unit needs a constant low temperature."

"Your what?"

Ramanandacharya runs his hands over a slotted titanium cylinder head in the otherwise blemishless plastic wall.

"He dreams in code," he says. Shiv bends forward to read the inscription on the metal disc. *Sir William Gates.*

"What is this?"

"An immortal soul. Or so he believed. Uploaded memories, a bodhisoft. How the Americans imagine they can beat death. One of the greatest minds of his generation—all this is because of him. Now he works for me."

"Just get me this file and put it on here." Shiv smacks Ramanandacharya on the side of the head with the palmer.

"Oh, not the Tabernacle crypt, the CIA will kill me, I am a dead man," Ramanandacharya pleads then shuts his foolish blabbering mouth up, summons another code pad out of the plastic, and enters a short sequence. Shiv thinks about the frozen soul. He's read of these things, circling in bangles of superconducting ceramic. All of a life: its sex, its books, its music and magazines, its friends and dinners and cups of coffee, its lovers and enemies, its moments when you punch your fists in the air and go jai! and when you want to kill everything, all reduced down to something you give a woman in a bar to slip around her wrist.

"One thing," Ramanandacharya says as he passes the loaded palmer to Shiv, "what do you want it for?"

"N. K. Jivanjee wants to talk to men from space," Shiv says. He slips the palmer into one of his many pants pockets. "Let's get out of here." The trick with the ring parts the scarab robots again; Shiv sees on Ramanandacharya's face that he thinks they will let him go, then sees that face change as Yogendra prods him with the gun to walk on. It is not a pretty or edifying thing, to see a fat man wet with fear. Shiv cuffs the dataraja again.

"Will you stop that, that is so annoying," Ramanandacharya flares.

Yogendra makes him take them back down through the tourist

gate into the old Indian army camp. They squeeze through the gap in the sheeting. Shiv mounts his bike, kicks up the engine. Good and true little Japanese motor. He looks round for Yogendra, finds him standing over the kneeling Ramanandacharya with the muzzle of the Stechkin in the dataraja's mouth. He licks it. He runs his tongue round the muzzle, licking it lapping it loving it. Yogendra grins.

"Leave him!"

Yogendra frowns, genuinely, deeply vexed.

"Why? He's over and done."

"Leave him. We got to go."

"He can call people up after us."

"Leave him!"

Yogendra makes no move.

"Fuck you!" Shiv dismounts, pulls out a brace of taser mines and drops them in a ring around Ramanandacharya. "Now leave him." Yogendra shrugs, puts up his piece and slides it inside his pants pocket. Shiv thumbs the control switch that arms the mines.

"Thank you thank you thank you," Ramanandacharya weeps.

"Don't beg, I hate begging," Shiv says. "Have some fucking dignity, man." Nawab of fucking Chunar. Let's see any of your forty women sleep with you after this. Shiv twists the throttle and rips off on the Japanese trail bike, Yogendra on his wheel. The deed is done, there is no need for stealth or caution. It's lights on engines open roaring down through the town past the glowing egg of the data centre and then the last light of Chunar and the exultation hits. It is done. They got it and they are getting away. A fringe of rain-soaked dawn lights the eastern horizon; by the time it fully opens, Shiv realises, he will be back in his city and he will have his prize and all his owings will be paid and he will be free, he will be a raja and no one will dare deny him again. He lets out a whoop, sends his bike careering madly all over the road, swooping from one side to the other, yipping and cawing and yawping crazier than any of the crazy jackals out there in the night. He swings deliberately close to the soft edge of the road, taunting the cracked blacktop, the treacherous gravel. Nothing can touch Shiv Faraji.

On an inside sweep, Shiv hears it. Running feet in the rural predawn. Titanium-shod feet, as much felt through the bike's suspension as heard, gaining on them, faster than any running thing should. Shiv glances back. There is enough light in the sky to make out the pursuer. It holds its body low to the ground, poised, balanced; it paces on two strong legs like some monstrous demon bird released upon them from the high castle. It is gaining steadily. A glance at the speedo tells Shiv it is doing at least eighty.

Yogendra opens up his throttles a second after Shiv but to take the bikes up to the max on this crumbling, greasy rural road is as sure a death as the thing loping behind them. Shiv bends low over the handlebars, trying to make himself as small a target as possible for whatever esoteric firepower the machine carries. The turnoff must be soon. He can hear the metal beat over the drone of the Yokohama motor. That tree, that poster for bottled water, it's here, surely. So busy looking, he almost misses Yogendra swing the bike across the blacktop and off on to the farm path. Panicked, Shiv brakes, oversteers, sticks a foot, almost spills across the country road before he brings the bike on to the sand track.

He saw it. There, behind him, down that road, pounding away, grey in the indigo, like it would never stop, never tire, keep running and running after them round the whole round world.

The dal bushes give way to hard-packed sand pocked with rain. The tires kick up sprays of hardpan and there is the boat, where they left it, anchor run into the sand, pulled round on the current, low in the river from heavy bilges, and there is a Brahmin beside it, waist deep in the stream, his thread across his shoulder, pouring water from his cupped hands and chanting the dawn salutation of Mother Ganga. Shiv skids the bike to a halt, splashes into the water, starts to heave the hot machine into the boat.

"Leave leave leave!" Yogendra screams.

The Brahmin chants.

"They can track us through them," Shiv yells.

"They can track us through the mines." Yogendra runs his bike down into the stream, it falls with a splash, starts to fade into the river quicksand. He pulls up the anchor as Shiv rolls into the boat. It rocks sickeningly and there is a nasty amount of water under the seating but by now he cannot get any wetter but he can be a lot more dead. The robots looms over the dune crest and rears up to its full height. It is some evil stalking rakshasa, part bird part spider, unfolding palps and manipulators and a brace of machine guns from its mandibles.

The Brahmin stares at that.

Yogendra dives for the engine. Pull one pull two. The hunter takes a step down the sandy bank to better its aim. Pull three. The engine starts. The boat surges away. Ramanandacharya's machine takes a leap to land knee-joint deep in the water. Its head swivels on to target. Yogendra heads for the centre of the stream. The robot wades after them. Then Shiv remembers Anand's clever little grenade in one of his pockets. Bullets send the water exploding up behind Yogendra in the stern. He dives flat. The Brahmin in the shallows crouches, covers his head. The grenade lobs through the air in a graceful, glittering arc. It falls with a splash. There is nothing to see, nothing to hear but the tiniest of cracks that is the capacitors discharging. The robot freezes. The guns veer skywards, ripping the dawn with bullets. It sags on its knees, goes down like a gut-shot gunda. Its mandibles and graspers flex open, it tips forward into the silt. The soft silvery quicksand takes it almost immediately.

Shiv stands in the boat. He points at the felled robot. He laughs, huge, helpless, joyful laughter. He cannot stop. Tears stream down his face, mingling with the rain. He can hardly draw breath. He has to sit down. It hurts, it hurts.

"Should have killed him," Yogendra mutters at the tiller. Shiv waves him away. Nothing can press down or nay-say him. The laughter passes into joy, a simple, searing ecstasy that he is alive, that it is over now. He lies back on the bench, lets the rain fall on his face and looks up at the purple banding of clouds that is another day unfurling over his Varanasi, another day for Shiv. Shiv raja. Maha raja. Raja of rajas. Maybe he will work for the Naths again; maybe his name will open other doors for him; maybe he will go into his own business, not body parts, not meat, meat betrays. Maybe he will go to that lavda Anand and make him an offer.

He can make plans again. And he can smell marigolds.

A small noise, a small movement of the boat.

The knife goes in so smooth, so thin and clean, so sharp so pure it challenges Shiv to express its shock. It is exquisite. It is unutterable. The blade stabs cleanly through skin, muscle, blood vessels, serrated edge grating along rib until the hooked tip rests inside his lung. There is no pain, only a sense of perfect sharpness, and of the blood foaming into his punctured lung. The blade kicks inside him to the pulse of his body. Shiv tries to speak. The sounds click and bubble and will not form words. It stays like this for a long time, wide-eyed with shock. Then Yogendra pulls the blade and pain shrieks from Shiv as the knife hooks out his lung. He turns to Yogendra, hands raised to fend off the next blow. The knife comes twisting in again, Shiv catches it between the thumb and forefinger of his left hand. The knife cuts deep, down to the joint, but he holds it. He holds it. Now he can hear the frenzied puffing of two men caught in a fight of death. They strike at each other in desperate silence as the boat wallows. With his free hand Yogendra grabs for the palmer. Shiv slaps out, grabs for Yogendra, for anything. He seizes the string of pearls around the boy's neck, pulls it tight, grips it hard to hold himself up. Yogendra whips the knife free from Shiv's grasp, ripping the barbed edge along the bone. Shiv lets out a high, keening whine that passes into a bloody, drowning burble. His breath flutters the edge of his wound. Then Shiv sees the loathing, the contempt, the animal arrogance and disdain the grey light reveals in

Yogendra's face and he knows that he has always felt this, always looked this way at him that this blade was always coming. He reels back. The string snaps. Pearls bounce and roll. Shiv slips on the pearls, loses balance, wheels, flails; goes over.

The water takes him cleanly, wholly. The roar of the traffic transmitted through the concrete piers deafens him. He is deaf, blind, dumb, weightless. Shiv wrestles, thrashes. He does not know which way is up, where is air, light. Blue. He is embedded in blue. Everywhere he looks, blue, forever in every direction. And black, like smoke, his blood twining upwards. The blood, follow the blood. But he has no strength and the air bubbles from the gash in his back, he kicks but does not move, punches but does not stir. Shiv fights water, sinking deeper in to the blue, drawn down by his weaponry. His lungs burn. There is nothing left in them but poison, ashes of his body, but he cannot open his mouth, take that final, silent whoop of water even though he knows he is dead. His head pounds, his eyeballs are bursting, he sees his half-severed thumb wave futilely in the blue, the great blue as he kicks and thrashes for life.

Blue, drawing him down. He thinks he sees a pattern in it; in the dying fascination of brain cells burning out one by one he makes out a face. A woman's face. Smiling. Come Shiv. Priya? Sai? Breathe. He must breathe. He kicks, struggles. He has a huge erection in his heavy, dragging combat pants laden with esoteric cyberweaponry and he knows what must happen. But Yogendra will not have the crypt. *Breathe.* He opens his mouth, his lungs and the blue rushes in and he sees in the decaying embers of his brain who it is down there. It is not Sai. It is not Priya. It is the gentle, homely face of the woman he gave to the river, the woman whose ovaries he stole for nothing, smiling, beckoning him to join her in the river and the blue and redemption.

"The first rule of comedy," says Vishram Ray checking the set of his collar in the gentlemen's washroom mirror, "is confidence: every day, every way; we're radiating confidence."

"I thought the first rule of comedy was . . ."

"Timing," Vishram interrupts Marianna Fusco, perched on the lip of the next washbasin in the line. Inder and various staffers Vishram never knew he had have sealed the Research Centre toilets off to all comers, whatever the state of their bladder or bowels. "That's the second rule. This is the Vishram Ray Book of Comedy."

But he hasn't been this scared since he first stepped out into that single spot shining down on the chrome shaft of the mike stand with an idea he had about budget airline travel. No place to hide behind that mike. No place to hide in that minimalist wooden room with the single construction-carbon table in the centre. Because the truth is, his timing is shit. Calling a major board meeting in the middle of an assassination crisis, with enemy tanks lined up a day's drive sunset-wards. And it's the monsoon, just to add a little meteorological misery to the whole shebang. No, Vishram Ray thinks as he checks his shave in the mirror. His timing is perfect. This is real comedy.

So why does it feel like eighteen different cancers eating him up?

Shave okay, aftershave within tolerable limits, cuffs check, cuf-flinks check.

The chemical rush does wonderfully clear the mind of Kalis and Brahmas and M-Star theory multiverses. Comedy is always in the moment. And the true first rule, in the Book of Comedy or the Book of Business, is persuasion. Laughter, like parting with wealth, is a voluntary weakness.

Jacket okay, shirt okay, shoes immaculate.

"Ready to rock?" Marianna Fusco says, crossing her legs in a way that makes Vishram imagine his face between them. "Hey, funny man." The most casual of hand gestures indicates the neat little line of coke on the black marble. "Just in case."

"Lenny Bruce wasn't desi," Vishram says. He lets out a huff of tense breath. "Let's do it." Marianna Fusco slips off her marble perch and scoops the line straight down the washhand basin.

If she'd offered him a cigarette . . .

Vishram strides down the corridor. His leather soles give the slightest of creaks on the polished wood inlay, Marianna and Inder are at his back, every step he walks a little taller, a little prouder. The warm-up has the audience now, working them, getting the juices flowing, you on the left clap your hands, you on the right whistle, you up there in the gods, just roar! For! Mister! Vishram! Raaaaaaaay!

The carved wooden doors swing open and every face around the transparent table locks on to Vishram. Without a word his entourage splits around the table and takes their assigned places, Inder on his right-hand side, Marianna Fusco on his left, their advisors flying wing. Inder had been rehearsing them since five that morning. As he sets his palmer and ornately inlaid wooden document wallet (no leather: the policy of an ethical, *Hindu* power company) in his place at the head of the table, Vishram nods to Govind on the right, Ramesh on the left. Ramesh, he notes, has at least invested in a decent suit. His beard looks a little less scraggy. Signs. It's no different for a stand-up or a suit, it's all reading the signs. Team Vishram waits for its leader to sit. The advisors eyeball each other. Vishram checks out the shareholders. Inder-online has a clever little briefing feature that automatically gives him a profile, percentage control, voting history, and a probability on how they will swing in this one. Many of the shareholders are virtual, either on video link or represented by aeai agents modelled on their personalities. No US boardroom would recognise this as shareholder democracy. Vishram switches off Inder's clever little toy. He'll do this the old way, the stand-up's way. He'll search for the subtle graces, the potential in the set of that mouth to turn into a smile, the invitation in the corners of those eyes that say, go on then, entertain me.

The battle lines are by no means obvious. Even within his own division, there are major holders like SKM ProSearch who will vote against him. Too close to call. A glance to hider, a glance to Marianna. Vishram Ray stands up. The bubble of conversation around the table bursts.

"Ladies, gentlemen, shareholders of Ray Power, material and virtual." The boardroom door opens. Clear in his line of sight, his mother slips into the room and takes a seat by the wall. "Thank you all for coming here this morning, some of you at considerable personal risk. This meeting is inevitably overshadowed by recent events, most fatefully by the brutal assassination of our Prime Minister Sajida Rana. I'm sure you would all echo my thoughts and sympathies for the Rana family at this time." A murmur of assent from around the table. "I for one fully support the efforts of our new Government of National Salvation to restore us to our customary order and strength. I'm sure some of you must have questioned the appropriateness of carrying on this meeting in the light of the political situation. I could tell you that I would not have done so unless I felt it was in the highest interests of this company. It is, but there is another principle I feel needs upheld at times like these. The eyes of the world are on Bharat, and I believe it needs to be shown that, for Ray Power at least, it is business as usual."

A nodding of heads together, soft, slow applause. Vishram surveys the room.

"Without doubt, most of you are surprised to find yourself back so soon at another Ray Power board meeting. It is only a couple of weeks since my father dropped his, if you'll pardon the expression, bombshell. They have been a full and lively two weeks, I assure you, and I should warn you now, I fully intend for this meeting to be no less shocking—or transforming."

A moment for audience reaction. His throat is as dry as a Rajasthan shitpipe but he won't let slip even the weakness of a sip of water. Govind and his PA incline heads. Good. The murmur fades into inaudibility. Time to let the passion into the voice.

"Ladies and gentlemen, I want to announce to you a major technological breakthrough by Ray Power Research and Development. I don't want to talk down to you; I don't understand the physics either, but let me simply state, my friends, that we have achieved not just sustainable, but high-yield zero-point energy. In this very building, our research teams have explored the properties of other universes and have discovered how to make energy flow into our own on a commercial scale. Free energy, my friends."

Snake-oil, my friends. No. You're up there in the spotlight and the mike's in your hand, that ultimate phallic symbol. Don't get clever. Don't get self-conscious.

"Limitless free energy; energy that is clean, that doesn't pollute, that requires no fuel, that is endlessly renewable—that is as boundless as an entire universe. I have to tell you, my friends, many many companies have been looking for this miracle, and it is Bharati scientists in a Bharati company that have made the breakthrough!"

He has cheerleaders primed but the applause around the table is spontaneous and heartfelt. Now is the time for the sip of water and the glance over at his mother. She wears the merest of smiles on her face. And it's that old glow in the balls, that hormone burn when you know you have them and can steer them any way you want. Careful careful, don't blow it. It is timing, after all.

"This is history, this will change the shapes of our futures not just here in Bharat, but for every man woman and child on the planet. This is a great breakthrough and this is a great nation and I want the world to know that. We already have the world's media here; now I want to give them something that will really make them remember us. Immediately after this meeting, I have arranged a full-scale public demonstration of the zero-point field."

Now. Reel them in.

"In one quantum leap, Ray Power becomes a planetary-class player. And this is where I come to the second—more practical reason—I've asked you to come here. Ray Power is a company in crisis. We can still only speculate on our father's motives for splitting the company; for my part, I have tried to be true to his vision of a Ray Power where vision and people mean as much as the bottom line. It's not an easy standard to live up to."

How may this engineer lead the right life? But he can't get over the image of Marianna Fusco on her back with his fist gripping one end of the knotted silk scarf.

"I've called you here because I need your help. The values of our company are under threat. There are other, larger corporates out there whose values are not ours. They have offered very large sums of money to buy sections of Ray Power; I myself have been approached. You may judge me rash, or at least gauche, but I turned them down, for those very reasons: I believe in what this company is about."

Throttle back.

"If I believed they were working in the best interests of the zero-point project, I would entertain their offers. But they are interested only because their own high-profile plans are far advanced. They would buy us up only to delay or even close down the zero-point. Offers have been made—maybe even by the same groups—to my brothers around this table. I want to preempt them. I want to cut them off at the pass, as the Americans say. I've made a generous offer to Ramesh to buy Ray Gen, the generating division that would implement the zero-point technique. That will give me a controlling interest in Ray Power, enough to keep any outside influence at bay until the zero-point goes public and we are in a position to resist more effectively. The details of the offer are in your presentation packs. If you'd like to take a moment to study them, and to consider what I've said, and then we could move to a vote."

He catches his mother's eye as he sits down. She smiles, privately, wisely, quietly as suddenly the entire boardroom is on its feet, shouting questions.

The taxi driver was smoking with the radio on, sprawled on the back seat with his feet sticking out the open door getting rained on as Tal came splashing across the glass bridge towing a stumbling, half-coherent Najia.

"Cho chweet, am I glad to see you," Tal shouted as the driver switched on his yellow sign and flashed his headlights.

"You had the look of people who might be in need of transport." Tal bundled Najia into the back. "Anyway, there are no fares tonight, not with all that is happening. And I am charging you waiting time. Where to or shall I just drive again?"

"Anywhere but here." Tal pulled out yts palmer and opened up Najia's video file from N. K. Jivanjee together with a neat little chunk of blackware on every street-credible nute's Must Have list: a phone tracer. A nute never knows when yt's going to need a little Ron. Day. Voo.

"Should we not be moving?" Tal asked, looking up from stripping the code from the video file.

"One thing I must be asking," the driver said. "I require assurance that you were not involved with this morning's . . . unpleasantness. I may speak my mind on our government's many failings and incompetencies, but I am at heart a man who loves his nation."

"Baba, the same people went after her, shot at me," Tal said. "Trust me. Now, just drive." That was when he floored the pedal.

"Is your friend all right?" the driver asks as he hoots a path through the soap worshippers, now on their feet, hands upheld as if in offering, eyes closed, lips moving. "She does not seem her usual self."

"She's had bad news about her family," Tal says. "And what's with them?"

"They offer puja to the gods of *Town and Country* for the safe deliverance of our nation," the driver says. "Idle superstition if you ask me."

"I wouldn't be so sure," Tal mutters under yts breath. As the taxi turns on to the main road a big Toyota Hi-Lux turns in in a woosh of spray. Karsevaks cling to the roll bars and side rails. Blue light catches on their swords and trishuls. Tal watches it out of sight, shivers. Two minutes more, spellbound by the aeai . . .

"I presume you would like me to avoid them as well as policemen, soldiers, government officials, and everyone else?" the taxi-wallah offers.

"Especially them." Tal absently fingers the contoured studs beneath yts skin, remembering adrenaline burn, remembering a city of blades and trishuls and more fear than yt ever felt possible. You don't know it but I've beaten you, gendereds, Tal thinks. Rough boys, violent boys, think you own the streets, think you can do what you like and no one will stop you because you are strong, wild, young men, but this nute has you beat. I have the weapon in my hand and it has just given me the location of the man who will destroy you with it. "Do you know this place?" Tal asks, leaning over the seatback and thrusting the palmer in front of the driver's face. Out there beyond the slashing windscreen wipers the night was turning hollow grey. The taxi-wallah waggled his head.

"It's a drive."

"Then I can get some sleep," Tal says, settling back into the greasy upholstery, which is partly true and partly a disinvitation to the driver to chitter away about the state of the nation. But Najia clutches yts arm and whispers, "Tal, what am I going to do? It showed me things, about my dad, when we were in Afghanistan. Tal, awful things no one else could know about . . ."

"It lies. It's a soap opera aeai, it's designed to put minimal information together into stories with the greatest possible emotional impact. Come on, sister, who doesn't get shit from their parents?"

In the hour and a half it takes the Maruti to detour around smouldering trash fires, dodge checkpoints, slip through barricades of burned-out cars, drive over street-sprayed swastikas and exhortations of Jai Bharat! Tal hears the radio play the national anthem twenty-four times, interrupted by short bulletins from the Rana Bhavan about the success of the Government of National Salvation in restoring safety and security. Yt squeezes Najia's hand and presently she stops crying softly into the sleeve of her soft grey fleece top.

The taxi-wallah balks at taking his lovely Maruti across the dirty, gravelly causeway.

"Baba, for what I'm paying you, you buy a new taxi," Tal exhorts. It is then that the Merc comes bowling towards them along the long straight causeway from the walled hunting lodge half-seen in the grey drizzle; hooting furiously. Tal checks yts lock on the position of the target palmer, taps the driver. "Stop that car," yt orders.

"Stop that?" the driver asks. Tal flings the door open. The driver swears, skids to a halt. Before cry or protest, Tal has slipped out and walks through the drizzling rain towards the car. Headlights flash on, blinding yt. Yt can hear the engine rev deep in its throat. The horn is deep, polyphonic. Tal shields yts eyes with yts hand and keeps walking. The Merc leaps towards yt.

Najia presses her palms against the glass and cries out as she sees the car bear down on Tal in yts bedraggled finery. Tal raises a futile hand. Brakes screech and bind in the clingy marsh-mud. Najia closes her eyes. She does not know what the sound of half a million rupees of heavy Northern European engineering striking a heavily engineered human body sounds like but she is certain she will know it when she hears it. She doesn't hear it. She hears a heavy car door thud shut. She dares open her eyes. The man and the nute stand in the dawn rain. That is Shaheen Badoor Khan, Najia thinks. She cannot but remember that other time she saw him, in the photographs at the club. Flashlight over dark upholstery, carved wood, polished surfaces but the dialogue is the same, politician and nute. This time it is the nute handing over the object of power. Shaheen Badoor Khan is smaller than she had imagined. She tries to fit opinions to him: traitor, coward, adulterer, fool; but her accusations are drawn down like stars to a black hole to the image of the room at the end of the corridor; the room she was never in, the room she never knew existed, the room at the end of her childhood, and her father welcoming her. History is happening here, she tries to tell herself to burn through the dreadful gravity of what the aeai had told her about her father. In front of you on a dirt road the future is being shaped and you have a ringside seat. You are down there by the sand among the blood and sinews and you can smell the warm money. This is the story of yours or anyone else's lifetime. This is your Pulitzer Prize before you are twenty-five.

And the rest of your life looking back, Najia Askarzadah.

A tap on the glass. Shaheen Badoor Khan bends low. Najia winds down the window. His face is grey-stubbled, his eyes are buried in exhaustion but they hold a tiny light, like a diya floating on a wide, dark river. Against all events and odds, against the tide of history, he has glimpsed victory. Najia thinks of the women parading their battle-cats head-high around the fighting ring, torn but valiant. He offers a hand.

"Ms. Askarzadah." His voice is deeper than she imagined. She takes the hand. "You'll excuse me if I seem a little slow this morning; I have rather been overwhelmed by the flow of events, but I must thank you, not just for myself—I am only a civil servant—but on behalf of my nation."

Don't thank me, Najia thinks. I was the one sold you in the first place. She says, "It's all right."

"No no, Ms. Askarzadah, you have uncovered a conspiracy of such scale, such audacity . . . I do not know quite how to deal with this, it is quite literally breathtaking. Machines, artificial intelligences . . ." He shakes his head and she senses how infinitely weary he is. "Even with this information, it is by no means over yet and you are by no means safe. I have an escape plan—everyone in the Bharat Sabha has an escape plan. I had intended to take myself and my wife, but my wife, as you have discovered . . ." Shaheen Bador Khan shakes his head again and this time Najia senses his disbelief at the nested involutions, the wanton daring of the conspiracy. "Let's say, I still have loyal agents in positions of influence, and those whose loyalty I can't trust are at least well paid. I can get you to Kathmandu, after that you are on your own, I am afraid. I'd ask one thing, I know you're a journalist and you have the story of the decade, but please do not release anything until I have played my card?"

"Yeah," Najia Askarzadah stammers. Of course, anything. I owe you. Because you do not know it, but I am your torturer.

"Thank you. Thank you indeed." Shaheen Badoor Khan looks up at the bleeding sky, squints at the thin, sour rain. "Ah, I have never known worse times. And please believe me, if I thought what you have given me would make it worse for Bharat . . . There is nothing I can do for my Prime Minister, but at least there is something I may yet do for my country." He stands up briskly, looks out over the sodden marshland. "We have a way to go yet before any of us are safe."

He shakes hands, firmly, grimly, again and returns to his car. He and Tal exchange the briefest of glances.

"That the politician?" the taxi-wallah asks as he reverses up to let the Mercedes pass.

"That was Shaheen Badoor Khan," Tal says, wet in the back seat beside Najia. "Private Secretary to the late Sajida Rana."

"Hot damn!" the driver exclaims as he tailgates Shaheen Badoor Khan, hooting at early bullock carts on the country back road. "Don't you love Bharat!"

Jamshedpur Grameen Bank is a dozen rural sathin women running microcredit schemes in over a hundred villages, most of whom have never left backcountry Bihar, some of whom have never physically met each other but they hold fifty lakh ordinary shares in Ray Power. Their aeai agent is a homely little 2.1 bibi, chubby and smiling, with a life-creased face and a vivid red bindi. She would not look out of place as a rural auntie in an episode of *Town and Country*. She namastes in Vishram's 'hoek-vision.

"For the resolution," she says sweetly, like your mama would, and vanishes.

Vishram's done the mental calculation before Inder can render it up on his in-eye graphic. KHP Holdings is next on the list with its eighteen percent stock, by far the biggest single shareholder outside the family. If Bhardwaj votes yes, it is game to Vishram. If he votes no, then Vishram will need eleven of the remaining twenty blocks to win.

"Mr. Bhardwaj?" Vishram asks. His hands are flat on the table. He cannot lift them. They will leave two palm-sized patches of misty sweat.

Bhardwaj takes off his hard, titanium framed glasses, rubs at a tactical spot of grease with a soft felt polishing cloth. He exhales loudly through his nose.

"This is a most irregular procedure," he says. "All I can say is that, under Mr. Ranjit Ray, this would never have happened. But the offer is generous and cannot be ignored. Therefore I recommend it and vote for the resolution."

Vishram allows his fist and jaw muscles a little mental spasm, a little yes. Even on that night when he took the Funny Ha! Ha! contest, there was never an audience kick like the murmur that runs around the board table that says they've all done their sums too. Vishram feels Marianna Fusco's hosiery-clad thigh press briefly against his under the transparent plane of nanodiamond. A movement of the edge of his peripheral vision make him look up. His mother slips out.

He hardly hears the formalities of the remainder of the vote. He numbly thanks the shareholders and board members for their faith in the Ray name and family. Thinking: Got it. Got it. Fucking got it. Telling the table that he will not let them down, that they have assured a great future for this great company. Thinking: I'm going to take Marianna Fusco to a restaurant, whatever is the very best you can get in the capital of an invaded country that's just had its Prime Minister assassinated. Inviting: everyone to make their way down the corridor and then we'll see exactly the future you've voted for. Thinking: a softly knotted silk scarf.

IT'S LIKE HERDING CALVES, Marianna Fusco messages as Ray Power staffers try to usher board members, researchers, guests, strays, and those second-string journalists who can be spared from the Day's

Big Story down the Ramayana marquetry maple floors. The whorl of bodies brings Vishram and Ramesh, a head taller, into orbit.

"Vishram." Big Brother smiles, broad and honest. It looks alien. Vishram recalls him always serious, puzzled, head bowed. His handshake is firm and long. "Well done."

"You're a rich man now, Ram."

Typically Ramesh is the tilt of the head, the roll of the eyes upwards, looking for answer in heaven.

"Yes, I suppose I am, quite obscenely so. But you know, I don't actually care. One thing you can do for me: find me something to do on this zero-point thing. If it's what you say, I've spent my professional life looking in the wrong direction."

"You'll come to the demonstration."

"Wouldn't miss it for the world. Or I suppose I should say, universe." He laughs nervously. Third rule of comedy, Vishram Ray thinks. Never laugh at your own jokes. "I think Govind needs a word with you."

He's rehearsed this so many different ways, so many different voices, so many nuances and stances and they all fall from him in the moments it takes to pick Govind out of the crowd. He can't turn his weaponry on this chubby, shyly smiling, sweating man in the too-small suit.

"Sorry," he says, extending the hand. Govind shakes his head, takes the hand.

"And that is why, brother, you will still never make it in business. Too soft. Too polite. You won today, you engineered a great victory, enjoy it! Press it home. Gloat. Have your security escort me from the building again."

"You've seen that routine already."

Ray Power's PR crew has chivvied the herd onwards; Vishram and Govind are alone in the corridor. Govind's grip on Vishram's hand is tight.

"Our father would be proud but I still maintain that you will run this company into the ground, Vishram. You have flash, you have charisma, you have showbiz and there is a place for that, but that is not how you run a business. I have a proposal. Ray Power, like the Ray family, was never meant to be a house divided. I have verbal agreements with outside investors but nothing is drawn up, nothing is signed."

"A remerger," Vishram says.

"Yes," says Govind. "With me running the operational side."

Vishraan cannot read this audience.

"I'll give you an answer in time," he says. "After the demonstration. Now, I'd like you to see my universe."

"One thing," Govind asks as their leather soles click softly on the inlaid maple. "Where did the money come from, eh?"

"An old ally of our father's," Vishram says and as he subliminally hears that most feared of sounds to a comedian—his own footsteps walking off—he realises that in the scripts he rehearsed and never used, there was never one for what he would do if he had stood up behind that diamond table and died the death.

They find a small space on the floor by the door, beneath the carriage attendant's pull-down berth. Here they barricade themselves in with the blue impact-resistant suitcases and huddle against each other like children. The doors are sealed, all Parvati can see through its tiny, smoked glass porthole is sky the colour of its own rain. She sees through the partition door into the next car. The bodies are pressed up against the tough plastic, disturbingly flattened. Not bodies; people, lives like hers that cannot continue in any meaningful way back in that city. The voices drowns out the hum of the traction engines, the rattle of the rails. She finds it amazing that anything so monstrously overloaded can move at all but the tug of acceleration in the well of her belly, the small of her back against the ribbed plastic wall, tells her the Raipur Express is picking up speed.

There is no staff anywhere to be found on this train, no ticket collector in her smart white sari with the wheel of Bharat Rail on her shoulder of the pallav; no clanking chai-wallah, no cabin attendant cross-legged on the bunk above them. The train runs fast now, power pylons blur past the tiny rectangle of smoky sky and Parvati panics for an instant that this is not the train, this is not the track. Then she thinks, *What does it matter? Anywhere is away.*

Away. She presses against Krishan, reaches for his hand beneath the drape of her stained sari, surreptitiously so no one will see, no one will be tempted to speculate on what these two Hindus are doing. Her fingers encounter warm wet. She jerks them away. Blood. Blood spreading in a sticky pool in the space between the bodies. Blood clinging to the ribs of the plastic wall. Krishan's hand, where it failed by millimetres to meet hers, is a clenched red fist. Parvati pushes herself away, not in horror, but to comprehend how this madness is happening. Krishan sags across the wall leaving a red smear, props himself up on his left arm. From just above his hip down his white shirt is red, soaked through with blood. Parvati can see it pumping through the fabric weave with every breath he takes.

That strange sigh, when he pulled her up on to the train, away from the firing on the platform. She had seen the bullets ricochet from the steel stanchions.

His face is the colour of ash, of the monsoon sky. His breath flutters, his arm quivers; he cannot support himself much longer and every heartbeat pumps more of his life onto the carriage floor. The blood pools around his feet. His lips move but he cannot shape words. Parvati pulls her to him, cradles his head in her lap.

"It's all right my love, it's all right," she whispers. She should call out, shout for aid, help, a doctor but she knows with terrible certainty that no one will ever hear in those jammed carriages. "Oh Krishan," she murmurs as she feels the wet, sexual blood spread under her thighs. "Oh, my dear man." His body is so cold. She gently touches his long black hair and twines it in her fingers as the train drives ever south.

This is Mr. Nandha coming up the stairs of Diljit Rana Apartments, jogging up one flight two flight three flight four in the cool cool light of the morning. He could take the elevator—unlike the old projects like Siva Nataraja Homes and White Fort, the services are operational in these government housing blocks—but he wants to maintain the energy, the zeal, the momentum. He shall not let it slip, not when it is so close. His avatars are threads of spider silk spun between the towers of Varanasi. He can feel the vibration of her energy shaking the world.

Five flights, six.

Mr. Nandha intends to apologise to his wife for upsetting her in front of her mother. The apology is not strictly necessary but Mr. Nandha's belief is that it is a healthful thing in a marriage to give in occasionally even when you are right. But she must appreciate that he has made a window for her in the most important case in the Ministry's history, a case that, when he has completed the excommunication, will elevate him to Investigative Officer First Rank. Then they will spend happy evenings together looking through the brochures for Cantonment new-builds.

The final three flights Mr. Nandha whistles themes from Handel Concerti Grossi.

It is not in the moment he puts his key in the lock. Neither is it when he sets hand to handle and turns that handle. But in the time it takes for him to push that handle down and open the door, he knows what he will find. And he knows the meaning of that epiphany in the predawn Ministry corridor. It was the precise instant his wife left him.

Scraps of Handel float in his auditory centres but as he crosses the lintel his life is as changed as the raindrop falling one millimetre to one side of a mountain peak ends up in a different ocean.

He does not need to call her name. She is utterly, irretrievably gone. It is not an absence of things; her chati magazines lie on the table, the dhobi basket sits in the kitchen by the ironing board, her ornaments and gods and small votives occupy their auspicious places. The flowers are fresh in the vase, the geraniums are watered. Her absence is from every part; the furniture, the shape of the room, the carpets, the comforting, happy television, the wallpaper and the cornices and the colour of the doors. The lights, the kitchen utensils, the white goods. Half a home, half a life and entire marriage has been subtracted. Nature does not abhor this vacuum. It throbs, it has shape and geometry.

There are noises Mr. Nandha knows he should make, actions he should perform, feelings he should experience proper to the discovery that a wife has left you. But he walks in and out of the room in a tight-faced daze, an almost-smile drawn on his lips, as if preparing defences against the full of it, like a sailor in a tropical storm might lash himself to a mast, to dare it to break over him, to turn into its full rage. That is why he goes to the bedroom. The embroidered cushions that were wedding gifts from his work colleagues are in their places on respective sides of the bed. The expensive copy of the Kama Sutra, for the proper work of a married couple, is on its bedside cabinet. The flat-worked sheet is neatly turned back.

Mr. Nandha finds himself bending to sniff the sheet. No. He does not want to know if there is any blame there. He opens the sliding wood wardrobes, inventories what is taken, what remains. The gold, the blue, the green saris, the pure white silk for formal occasions. The beautiful, translucent crimson choli he used to love to see her wear, that excited him so much across a room or a garden party. She has taken all the padded, scented hangers, left the cheap wire ones that have stretched into shallow rhombuses. Mr. Nandha kneels down to look at the shoe rack. Most of the spaces are empty. He picks up a slipper, soft-soled, worked with gold-thread and satin, runs his hands over its pointed toe, its soft, breast-curved heel. He sets it back in its position. He cannot bear her lovely shoes.

He closes the sliding door on the clothes and shoes but it is not Parvati he thinks of, it is his mother when he burned her on the ghat, his head shaved and all dressed in white. He thinks of her house afterwards, of the terrible poignancy of her clothes and shoes on their hangers and racks, all unnecessary now, all her choices and fancyings and likings naked and exposed by death.

The note is stuck to the shelf in the kitchen where his Ayurvedic teas and dietary items are kept. He finds he has read it three times without taking in anything more than the obvious meaning that she is gone. He cannot join the words up into sentences. *Leaving. So sorry. Can't love you. Don't look for me.* Too close. Too many words too near to each other. He folds the note, puts it in his pocket, and climbs the stairs to the roof garden.

In the open space, in the grey light, under the eyes of his neighbours and his cybernetic avatars, Mr. Nandha feels the compressed rage vomit up out of him. He would love to open his mouth and let it all pour out of him in an ecstatic stream. His stomach pulls, he fights it, masters it. Mr. Nandha presses down the spasms of nausea.

What is that sickly, chemical smell? For a moment, despite his discipline, he feels that his gut might betray him.

Mr. Nandha kneels on the edge of the raised bed, fingers hooked into the clinging loam. His palmer calls. Mr. Nandha cannot think what the noise could possibly be. Then the insistent calling of his name draws his fingers out of the soil, draws him back to the wet rooftop in the Varanasi gloaming.

"Nandha."

"Boss, we've found her." Vik's voice. "Gyana Chakshu picked her up two minutes ago. She's right here in Varanasi. Boss; *she* is Kalki. We've got it all put together; she is the aeai. She is the incarnation of Kalki. I'm diverting the tilt-jet to pick you up."

Mr. Nandha stands upright. He looks at his hands, brushes the dirt from them on the edge of the wooden sleepers. His suit is stained, crumpled, soaked. He cannot imagine he will ever feel dry again. But he adjusts his cuffs, straightens his collar. He takes the gun from inside his pocket and lets it hang loosely at his side. The early neons of Kashi gibber and flick at his feet. There is work to be done. He has his mission. He will do it so well that none can ever hold a whisper against Nandha of the Ministry.

The tilt-jet banks in between the big projects. Mr. Nandha shelters in the stair head as the aircraft slides in over the rooftop and swivels its engines into a hover. Vik is in the copilot's seat as the tilt-jet turns, face dramatically underlit by the console leds. The roof cannot possibly support a Bharati Air Force tilt-jet; the pilot brings her ship down centimetre by centimetre in a delicate Newtonian ballet, positioning the craft so Mr. Nandha can slip between the vortices from the wingtip engines and safely up the access ramp in the tail. The downblast works the destruction he had fantasised. The trellises are smashed flat in an instant. The geraniums are swept from their perches. Seedlings and small plants are uprooted from the soft soil; the earth itself peels away in muddy gobs. The saturated wood of the beds steams, then smokes. The pilot descends until her wheels kiss roofing felt. The rear ramp unfolds.

Lights go on piecemeal in the overlooking windows.

Mr. Nandha pulls his collar close and beats through the buffets to the open, blue-lit interior. All his team are there among the aircav sowars. Mukul Dev and Ram Lalli. Madhvi Prasad, even Morva of the Money Trail. As Mr. Nandha belts in beside him, the ramp closes and the pilot opens up the engines.

"My dear friends," Mr. Nandha says. "I am glad you are beside me on this historic occasion. A Generation Three Artificial Intelligence. An entity as far beyond our fleshly intellect as ours is a pig's. Bharat will thank us. Now, let us be diligent in our excommunication."

The tilt-jet turns on its vertical axis as it climbs above Mr. Nandha's shattered roof garden, higher than all the windows and balconies and rooftop solar farms and watertanks of his neighbours. Then the pilot puts the nose up and the tail down and the little ship climbs steeply between the towers.

The last of the gods flicker out over Varanasi and the sky is just the sky. The streets are silent, the buildings are mute, the cars have no voices and the people are just faces, closed like fists. There are no answers, no oracles in the trees and street shrines, no prophecies from the incoming aircraft, but this world without gods is rich in its emptiness. Senses fill up the spaces; engines roar, the wall of voices leap forward; the colours of the saris, the men's shirts, the neons flashing through the grey rain, all glow with their own, vivid light. Each touch of street-incense, stale urine, hot fat, alcofuel exhaust, damp burning plastic is an emotion and a memory of her life before the lies.

She was a different person then, if the women in the hovel are to be believed. But the gods—the machines, she now realizes—say she is now another self altogether. Say: said. The gods are gone. Two sets of memories. Two lives that cannot live with each other, and now a third that must somehow incarnate both. Lull. Lull will know, Lull will tell her how to make sense of these lives. She thinks she can remember the way back to the hotel.

Dazed by the empire of the senses, released from the tyranny of information into the realm of simple *things*, Aj lets the city draw her to the river.

In the dawn rain on the Western Allahabad orbital motorway, two hundred Awadhi main battle tanks fire up their engines, spin on their tracks out of their laagered positions and form into an orderly column. Faster, fleeter traffic buzzes past the four-kilometre queue but there is no mistaking its general direction, south by southwest towards the Jabalpur Road. By the time the shops roll up their shutters and the salary-wallahs zip in to work in their phatphats and company cars the newsboys are screaming it from their pitches on the concrete central reserves: TANKS PULL OUT! ALLAHABAD SAVED! AWADH WITHDRAWS TO KUNDA KHADAR!

Another of Bharat's inexhaustible fleet of Prime Ministerial Mercedes is waiting for the Bharatiya Vayu Sena Airbus Industries A510 as it turns into its stand well away from the busier parts of Varanasi airport. Umbrellas shelter Prime Minister Ashok Rana from the steps to the car; it draws away in a wush of fat tires on wet apron. There is a call waiting on the comlink. N. K. Jivanjee. Again. He is not looking at all like what would be expected of the Interior Minister of a Government of National Unity. He has unexpected news to break.

If she lets his hand slip in this crowd she is lost.

The armed police try to clear the riverside. The messages blaring from their bullhorns and truck-top speakers are for the crowds to disperse, the people to return to their homes and businesses; order has been restored, they are in no danger, no danger at all. Some, swept along in the general panic, who did not really want to abandon their livelihoods, turn back. Some do not trust the police or their neighbours or the contradictory pronouncements from the government. Some do not know what to do; they turn and mill, going nowhere. Between the three and the army hummers squeezing through the narrow galis around the Vishwanath Gali, the streets and ghats are locked solid.

Lisa Durnau keeps her fingers tightly locked around Thomas Lull's left hand. In his right he holds the Tablet, like a lantern on a dark night. Some final fragment of her that feels responsible to governments and their strategies worries about the little built-in meltdown sequence should the Tablet get cold and lonely. But she does not think Lull will be needing it very long. Whatever is to be played out here will be ended soon.

Nandha. Krishna Cop. Licensed terminator of unauthorised aeais. The grainy Tabernacle image is fused into her forebrain. No point questioning how a Krishna Cop came to be inside a machine older than the solar system, no more than any of them, but she is certain of one thing; this is the place, the time where all images are born.

Thomas Lull stops abruptly, mouth open in frustration as he scans the crowd with the Tablet, looking for a match with the image on the liquid screen.

"The water tower!" he shouts and jerks Lisa Durnau along after him. The great pink concrete cylinders rise from the ghats every few hundred metres along the waterfront, each joined to the uppermost steps by pink-painted gantries. Lisa Durnau can't make any face out of the mass of refugees and devotees pressing around the water tower base. Then the tilt-jet cuts in across the ghats so low everyone instinctively ducks. Everyone, Lisa observes, but a solitary figure in grey up on the catwalk around the top of the water tower.

He has it now. The Gyana Chakshu device is linked through to his 'hoek and by its extrapolations and modellings and vectorings and predictings he can see the aeai like a moving light that shines through people, through traffic, through buildings. He watches from kilometres of altitude and distance, moving through the warren of lanes and galis behind the riverfront. With his privileged insight, Mr. Nandha directs the pilot. She brings the tilt-jet round in a sweeping arc and Mr. Nandha looks down into the tide of people swelling the streets and she is a shining star. He and the aeai are the only two solid beings in a city of ghosts. Or is it, thinks Mr. Nandha, the converse that is true?

He orders the pilot to take them in over the river. Mr. Nandha summons his avatars. They boil up in his vision like thunderheads, ringing the fleeing aeai on every side, a siege of deities, their weapons and attributes readied, scraping the clouds, Ganga water boiling around their vahanas. An invisible world, seen only by the devotee, the true . . . The fleeing fleck of light stops. Mr. Nandha commands Ganesha the opener to flick through local security cameras until the pattern matcher locates the excommunicee on the Dasashvamedha Ghat water tower. It stands, hands gripping the rail, staring out over the mob of wheeling people fighting for the Patna boat. Does it stand so because it sees what I see? Mr. Nandha wonders. Does it stop in fear and awe as gods rear from the water? Are we the only two true seers in the city of delusions?

An aeai incarnate in human flesh. Evil times indeed. Mr. Nandha cannot imagine what alien, inhuman scheme is behind this outrage against a soul. He does not want to imagine. To know can be the path to understanding, understanding to tolerance. Some things must remain intolerable. He will erase the abomination and all will be right. All will be in order again.

A lone star shines in Mr. Nandha's vision from the top of the water tower as the pilot turns between Hanuman and Ganesha. He jabs his finger down towards the rain-puddled strand. The pilot pulls up the nose and swivels the engines. Sadhus and swamis flee their scab-fires, shaking their skinny fists at the object descending out of heaven. If you saw as I see, thinks Mr. Nandha, loosing his seat belt.

"Boss," Vik calls as he works his way through the cabin, "we're picking up enormous traffic into the Ray Power internal network. I think it's our Gen Three."

"In due time," Mr. Nandha says, gently chiding. "Everything in proper order. That is the way to do business. We will finish our task here and then attend to Ray Power."

His gun is ready in his fist as he hits the sand at the foot of the ramp and the sky is crazy with gods.

All the people. Aj grips the rusted railing, dizzied by the masses on the ghats and the riverbanks. The pressure of their bodies forced her up on to this gallery when she found her breath catching in her throat as she tried to get back to the haveli. Aj empties her lungs, holds, inhales slowly through her nostrils. The mouth for talking, the nose for breathing. But the carpet of souls appalls her. There is no end to the people, they unfold out of each other faster than they go to the burning ghats and the river. She remembers those other places where she was among people, in the big station, on the train when it burned and in the village afterwards when the soldiers took them all to safety, after she stopped the machines.

She understands how she did that, now. She understands how she knew the names of the bus driver on the Thekkady road, and of the boy who stole the motorbike in Ahmedabad. It is a past as close and alien as a childhood, indelibly part of her, but separate, innocent, old. She is not that Aj. She is not the other Aj either, the engineered child, the avatar of the gods. She attained understanding, and in that moment of enlightenment was abandoned. The gods could not bear too much humanity. And now she is a third Aj. No more voices and wisdoms in street lights and cab ranks—these, she now realises, were the aeais, whispering into her soul through the window of her tilak. She is a prisoner now in that bone prison, like every other life out there by that river. She is fallen. She is human.

Then she hears the plane. She looks up as it comes in low, fast over the temple spires and the towers of the havelis. She sees ten thousand people cringe as one but she remains standing for she knows what it is. A final remembrance of being something other than human, some last divine whisper, the god-light fading into the background microwave hum of the universe, tells her. She watches the plane pull up and descend on to the trampled sand, scattering the sadhu's ash-fires in sprays of cinders and knows that it has come for her. She begins to run.

With brisk flicks of his hand, Mr. Nandha dispatches his squad to clear the ghats and seal off exits. In his peripheral vision he notices Vik hang back, Vik still in his street garb from the night's battles, Vik sweaty and grubby on this humid monsoon morning. Vik uncertain, Vik fearful. He makes a note to himself to admonish Vik for insufficient zeal. When the case is closed, that is the time for robust management. Mr. Nandha strides out across the damp white sand.

"Attention attention!" he cries, warrant card held up. "This is a Ministry security operation. Please render our officers all assistance. You are in no danger." But it is the gun in his right hand, not the authority in his left, that makes men step back, parents pull curious children away, wives push husbands out of his path. To Mr. Nandha, Dasashvamedha Ghat is an arena paved with ghosts, ringed by watching gods. He imagines smiles on their high, huge faces. He gives his attention to the small, glowing dot in his enhanced vision, star-shaped now, the pentagram of the human figure. The aeai is moving from its vantage on the water tower. It is on the walkway now. Mr. Nandha breaks into a run.

The crowd ducked as the tilt-jet went over and Lisa Durnau ducked with it and as she glimpses Aj on the tower, she feels Thomas Lull's fingers slip through her own and separate. The bodies close around him. He is gone.

"Lull!" In a few footsteps he has vanished completely, absorbed into the motion of bright salwars and jackets and T-shirts. Hiding in plain sight. "Lull!" No chance she will ever be heard over the roar of Dasashvamedha Ghat. Suddenly she is more claustrophobic than she ever was confined in the stone birth-canal of Darnley 285. Alone in the crowd. She stops, panting in the rain. "Lull!" She looks up at the water tower at the head of the staggered stone steps. Aj still stands at the rail. Wherever she is, Lull will be. No place, no time for Western niceties. Lisa Durnau elbows through the milling crowd.

In the Tablet she is innocent, in the Tablet she is unknowing, unseeing, in the Tablet she is a teenage kid up on a high place looking down on one of Earth's great human wonders.

"Let me through, let me through!" Thomas Lull shouts. He sees the tilt-jet unfold its mantis landing-gear and settle on the sand bar. He sees ripples of discontent spread through the crowd as the soldiers push people back. From his higher vantage on the ghat he sees the pale figure advance across the cleared marble. That is the fourth avatar of the Tabernacle. That is Nandha the Krishna Cop.

There is a story by Kafka, Lull recalls in the mad self-consciousness of ultimate effort; of a herald bringing a message of grace and favour from a king to a subject. Though the herald holds seals and passes and words of power, he can never leave the palace because of the press of people, never make it through the crowd to bring the vital word. And thus it goes unsaid, or so he remembers it from his paranoid days.

"Aj!" He is close enough to see the three grubby white stripes on the side of her grey trainers. "Aj . . ." But his words fall into well of sound, flattened and obliterated by sharper, louder Hindi tones. And his breath is failing, he can feel the little elastic pull of tension at the bottom of each inhalation.

Fuck Kafka.

"Aj!"

He cannot see her any more.

Run, whisper the ashes of the gods. Her feet clatter along the metal gantry, she swings around the stanchion and down the sharp-edged steel steps. An elderly man cries out and curses as Aj slams into him.

"Sorry, sorry," she whispers, hands held up in supplication but he is gone. She pauses a moment on the topmost step. The tilt-jet stands on the sand to her right, down by the water's edge. A disturbance in the crowd moves towards her like a cobra. Behind her the whip aerials of an army hummer move between the low, dripping stalls of Dasashvamedha Gali. No escape there. The hydrofoil stands at the jetty at the head of a huge diamond of people trying to press on board. Many are shoulder deep in the water, burdens and livelihoods borne on their heads. Once she might have tried to rule the machines that control the boat and escape by water. She does not have that power any more. She is only human. To her left the walls and buttresses of Man Singh's astronomical palace step down to Ganga. Heads, hands, voices, things, colours, rain-wet skin, eyes. A pale head raised above the others by a foreign height. Long hair, grey stubble. Blue eyes. Blue shirt, silly shirt, loud garish shirt, saving glorious shirt.

"Lull!" Aj shouts and leaps down the steep, slippery ghats, skidding on the stone, hurdling bundles of luggage, sending children reeling, leaping over low walls and platforms where the Brahmins commemorate the ten-horse sacrifice of Brahma with fire and salt, music and prasad. "Lull!"

With a thought Mr. Nandha banishes his gods and demons. He has it now. It cannot escape into the city. The river is closed to it, Mr. Nandha is behind it, there is no way but forward. The people sweep away from him like a sea parting in some alien religious myth. He can see the aeai. It is dressed in grey, drab machine grey, so easy to spot, so simple an identification.

"Stop," says Mr. Nandha softly. "You are under arrest. I am a law enforcement officer, stop at once and lie flat on the ground."

There is clear open space between him and the aeai. And Mr. Nandha can see that it will not stop, that it knows what the law demands of it and that in defiance is its one, minuscule chance of survival. Mr. Nandha clicks off his gun safeties. The Indra avatar system swings his outstretched arm on to the target. Then his right thumb performs an action it has never taken before. It switches the gun from the lower barrel, that kills machines, to the upper. The mechanism slides into position with a silken click.

Run. It is such a simple word, when your lungs are not clenched tight like fists for every breath, when the crowd does not resist your every lunge and shove and push and elbow, when one single, treacherous slip will send you plunging to annihilation under the feet of the crowd, when the man who might save you is not at the geometrical furthest point of the universe.

Run. It is such a simple word for a machine.

Mr. Nandha slides to a stop on the treacherous, foot-polished stone, gun levelled. He could no more remove his aim from the target than he could shift the sun from its centre. Indra will not permit it. His outstretched arm, his shoulders ache.

"In the name of the Ministry, I order you to stop!" he cries.

Useless, as it ever was. He forms the intention. Indra fires. The crowd screams.

The munition is a medium-velocity liquid tungsten round that, rifled by the barrel of Mr. Nandha's gun, expands in flight into a spinning disc of hot metal the size of a circled thumb and finger, an *okay* sign. It takes Aj in the middle of the lower back, tearing through spine, kidneys, ovaries, and small intestine in a spray of liquidised flesh. The front of her sleeveless grey cotton top explodes outwards in a rain of blood. The impact lifts her off her feet and throws her, arms and legs splayed out, forward on to the crowd. The ghat people scramble out from under her. She falls hard to the marble. The impact, the trauma should have killed her—the bottom half of her body is severed from the top—but she writhes and claws at the marble in a spreading pool of warm sweet blood, making small soft shrieking noises.

Mr. Nandha sighs and walks up to her. He shakes his head. Is he never to be allowed dignity? "Stand back please," Mr. Nandha orders. He stands over Aj, feet apart. Indra levels the gun. "This is a routine excommunication but I would advise you to look away now," he tells the public. He glances up at his crowd. His eyes meet blue eyes, Western eyes, a Western face, bearded, a face he recognises. A face he seeks. Thomas Lull. Mr. Nandha bows infinitesimally to him. The gun fires. The second round takes Aj in the back of the head.

Thomas Lull roars incoherently. Lisa Durnau is by him, holding him, pulling him back, clinging to him with all her athletic strength and weight and history. There is a sound in her ears like a universe ending. Tracks of terrible heat on her face are tears. And still the rain beats down.

Mr. Nandha senses his warriors at his back. He turns to them. For now he does not need to register the expressions on their faces. He indicates Thomas Lull and the Western woman holding him back in her arms.

"Have these people arrested under offences against the Artificial Intelligence Registry and Licensing Act," he commands. "Deploy all units immediately to Ray Power Research and Development Unit at the University of Varanasi. And have someone take care of this."

He holsters the gun. Mr. Nandha very much hopes he will not have to use it again this day.

Look out the left, the captain says. *That's Annapurna, and the next one down is Manaslu. After that Shishapangma. All of them over eight thousand metres. If you're on the left side of the plane, I'll give you a call as we come in, on good days you can see Sagarmath; that's our name for Everest.*

Tal is curled up in the wide business class seat, head on the cushion on the armrest, asleep and giving little soprano snores though it's only a forty minute flight from Varanasi. Najia can hear the treble beats from yts headphones. Soundtrack for everything. HIMALAYA MIX. She leans over yt to peer out the window. The little cityhopper skips in over Ganga plain and the flatlands of the Nepal Terai then takes a big jump over the river-riven foothills that guard Kathmandu. Beyond them like a surf-line breaking at the edge of the world, is the High Himalaya, vast and white and higher than she could ever dream, the loftiest peaks streaked with torn cloud running on the jet stream. Higher, and further; summit beyond summit beyond summit, the white of the glaciers and high places and the flecked grey of the valleys blurring into blue at the furthest edge of her vision, like a stone ocean. Najia can see no limit to it in any direction.

Her heart leaps. There is something in her throat she cannot swallow. There are tears in her eyes.

She remembers this scene from Lal Darfan's elephant pagoda, but those mountains had not the power to touch, to move, to inspire. They had been folds of fractals and digits, two imaginary landmasses colliding with each other. And Lal Darfan had also been N. K. Jivanjee had also been the Gen Three aeai, as the eastern extremities of these mountains had been those peaks she had seen over the wall around that garden in Kabul. She knows the image the Gen Three had shown her of her father as torturer had been false; she had never walked down that corridor, to that room, to that woman who in all probability had never existed. But she does not doubt that others did, that others had been strapped to that table to scream out how they endangered the establishment. And she does not doubt that that image will now forever be her memory. *Memory is what I am made of*, the aeai had said. Memories make our selves, we make memories for ourselves. She remembers another father, another Najia Askarzadah. She does not know how she is going to live with either. And the mountains are harsh and tall and cold and reach beyond any end she can see and she is high and alone in her leather business-class seat with the fifty-inch pitch.

She thinks now she knows why the aeai had shown her the childhood she had suppressed. It had not been cruel, it had not been even a ploy for time. It had been genuine, touching curiosity, an attempt by a djinn made of stories to understand something outside its mandalas of artifice and craft. Something it could believe it had not made up itself. It wanted the drama of the real, the fountainhead from which all story flows.

Najia Askarzadah pulls her legs up on to her seat, lays her body down across Tal's. She drapes her arm over yts, loosely takes yts fingers in hers. Tal starts with a half-syllable but she does not break yts sleep. Yts hand is delicate and hot; beneath her cheek she can feel yts ribs. Yt's so light, so loosely put together, like a cat but she feels a cat's toughness in the muscles breathing in, breathing out. She lies there, listening to yts heart. She thinks that maybe she has never met a braver person. Yt has always had to fight to be ytself and now yt goes into exile with no destination in sight.

From eight thousand metres she can understand that Shaheen Badoor

Khan had been an honourable man. In Bharat, even as he escorted their taxi through the checkpoint at the vip gate and on to the perimeter road to the vip lounge, she had seen only his falsities and frailties; another man, another fabric of untruths and complications. As she waited at the desk while he spoke low and hard and fast with the airline official, she had confidently expected that at any moment the airport police would come out of the walls and doors with levelled weapons and plastic cable-ties for their wrists. They were all betrayers. They were all her fathers.

She remembers how the gate staff had looked and whispered among themselves as Shaheen Badoor Khan completed the final formalities. He had quickly, formally shaken hands with her, then Tal, then briskly walked away.

The shuttle flight had just punched through the monsoon cloud base when the story broke all over the seat-back screen news channel. N. K. Jivanjee had resigned. N. K. Jivanjee had fled Bharat. The Government of National Unity was in disarray. Disgraced advisor to the late Prime Minister, Shaheen Badoor Khan, had come forward with extraordinary revelations—backed by documentary evidence—that the former leader of the Shivaji had masterminded a plot to destroy the Rana government and fatally weaken Bharat against the Awadhis. Bharat reels! Shock revelation! Stunning scandal! Ashok Rana to make statement from the Rana Bhavan! Khan national saviour! Where is Jivanjee, Bharat demands? Where is Jivanjee? Jivanjee the traitor?

Bharat quaked to its third political shock in twenty-four hours. Not a fraction of the earthquake it would have been had Shaheen Badoor Khan revealed that the Shivaji was a political front for a Generation Three aeai formed out of the cumulative intelligence of *Town and Country*. An attempted coup by its most popular soap opera. As the plane levelled off and the hostess came round with the drinks—Tal had had two double cognacs; yt had just fled an assassination, battled a Generation Three aeai, and survived a murderous mob, so it *deserved* a little luxury, cho chweet—Najia watched the story update by the second and comprehended the subtlety and skill with which Shaheen Badoor Khan was managing it. Even as the plane was pushing back from the stand he must have been cutting a deal with the Generation Three, one that would leave Bharat as politically whole as possible. This was his seat, his mini-bottle of Hennessy; he stayed for his country, for he had nothing else.

She cannot go back to Sweden again. Najia Askarzadah is as much an exile now as Tal. She shivers, hugs Tal closer. Yt entwines yts fingers tightly around hers. Najia can feel yts subdermal activators against her forearm. Not man not woman not both not neither. Nute. Another way of being human, speaking a physical language she does not understand. More alien to her than any man, any father, yet this body next to hers is loyal, tough, funny, courageous, clever, kind, sensual, vulnerable. Sweet. Sexy. All you could wish in a friend of the soul. Or a lover. She starts at that thought, then presses her cheek against Tal's hunched shoulder. Then she feels their conjoined centres of gravity shift as the plane banks in to approach to Kathmandu and she turns her head to look out the window, hoping maybe for that revelatory glimpse of distant Sagarmatha but all she can see is an oddly shaped cloud that you might almost think was the shape of a huge elephant, were such a thing possible.

History measures its course in centuries but its progress in the events of an hour. As the tanks pull back to the Kunda Khadar, in the wake of the shock resignation of N. K. Jivanjee over Badoor Khan's allegations and the withdrawal of the Shivaji from the Government of National Salvation only hours old, Ashok Rana accepts Delhi's offer of talks in Kolkata to resolve the dam dispute. But the day has one more surprise for the reeling Bharati nation. Whole families sit shocked, speechless, numb with surprise in front of their screens. In the middle of the one o'clock broadcast, *Town and Country* has gone off air.

They go in lots of seven, down the elevators down the concrete steps through the airlock to Deba's stinky little cubby and the observation dock beyond where investment bankers, grameen, women, cub journalists, clan Ray advisors, and a shell-shocked looking Energy Minister Patel shuffle round in cramped circle dance to peer through the heavy glass panel into the hard light of another universe.

"Okay, okay, come on, no more than five seconds, Ray Power will not be held responsible for any eye irritation, sunburn, or other ultraviolet-related complaints," Deba says, waving them through and round and out. "No more than five seconds, Ray Power will not be held responsible . . ."

The lecture hall has been rigged with display nodes and screens and copiously equipped with small eats and bottled water. Sonia Yadav bravely holds the lectern, trying to explain to the gathered what they are seeing on the screens: two simple graphic bars that show the energy drawn from the grid maintaining the zero-point field and the energy output from the potential difference between the universal ground-states, but she is fighting two losing fronts, scientifically and acoustically.

"We're getting two percent over input," she shouts over the swelling burble of countrywomen exchanging stories about their grandchildren, businessmen pressing palms and palmers and journos hanging on to their 'hoeks for the newest shock wonder revelation to come out of the Bharat Sabha: the stunning resignation of N. K. Jivanjee from the Government of National Unity. "We're storing that in high-energy capacitors for the laser-collider until it reaches a level where we can add it to the grid and open up an aperture to a higher-level universe, and so on and so on. That way we can climb a ladder of energy states until we're getting something like one hundred and fifty percent return on input energy . . ."

She clenches her fists, shakes her head, sighs in frustration as the volume in the lecture hall reaches a mild roar. Vishram takes the microphone.

"Ladies and gentlemen, if I could have your attention please? I know it's been a long day for many of you and it's been nothing if not eventful, but if you'd come with me through into the lab where the breakthrough was first made . . ."

The staff herds the guests into the zero-point lab.

"No plan ever survives contact with the enemy," he whispers to Sonia Yadav. A hovercam darts past his head, close and irritating as an insect, relaying the events to the remote shareholders. He imagines the virtual ghosts of the agent aeais hovering over the slow-moving line of guests. Centre Director Surjeet had objected robustly to Vishram opening the zero-point theory lab with its labyrinth of wall-writings and hieroglyphics. Surjeet feared it would make the project look amateurish—see, this is how they do things at Ray Power! With crayons and spray cans, on walls, like badmashes making graffiti. Vishram wants it for just that reason: it is human, messy, creative. It has the desired effect, the people relax, look up in wonder at the hieroglyphics. Will it be a new Lascaux, a Sistine chapel? Vishram wonders. The symbols that birthed an age. He should start making inquiries about having the room preserved.

Vishram Ray, with intimations of immortality. He notes with small, sharp pleasure that his dinner date with Sonia Yadav still shines in red felt-marker on the corner of the desk. In the less formal environment, her passion easily keeps an audience. Vishram watches her arm movements delimit swathes of ceiling to a rapt group of greysuits. He overhears her telling them ". . . at a fundamental level where quantum theory, M-Star theory, and computing all interact. We're discovering that the quantum computers we're using to maintain the containment fields—and its the containment fields that affect the winding geometries of the 'branes—can actually manipulate the Wolfram/Friedkin grain structure of the new universe. At a fundamental level, the universe is computational."

Their little mouths are wide open.

Vishram shimmies in beside Marianna Fusco.

"When this is done," he says, getting as close as professional propriety allows to a legal advisor, "How about. We go. Off somewhere. Where there is sun and sea and sand and really good bars and no people and we can run around in nothing but factor thirty for a month?"

And she slides her head as close to his as she dares and through a frozen public smile says, "I can't. I have to go."

"Oh," says Vishram. And, "Fuck."

"It's a family thing," Marianna Fusco says. "Big anniversary in my constellation family. People coming from all over. Relations I didn't have last time we did this. No, I'll be back, funny man. Just tell me where to turn up, *sans* luggage."

Then the lights flicker and the room quivers. Glass rattles in the windows and door. There is a murmur of consternation. Director Surjeet's hands are raised in placation.

"Ladies and gentlemen, ladies and gentlemen, please, there is no need for alarm. What we have just felt is a quite normal side effect of us ramping up the collider. We have closed one aperture and used the energy to warp the 'brane into another. Ladies and gentlemen, we have broken through into a new universe!"

There is polite, baffled applause. Vishram takes the opportunity to showboat.

"And what that means, my friends, is a twelve percent return on our energy investment. We put a hundred percent into maintaining the aperture, we get all that, plus an extra twelve back again! It's this way to the zero-point future!"

Inder starts off a tattoo of enthusiastic corporate applause.

"You should have been a lawyer," Marianna Fusco says. "You have the gift of talking endless shit on subjects you know nothing about."

"Didn't I tell you that's what my Dad wanted for me?" Vishram says, positioning himself so that he can see down Marianna Fusco's top. He imagines slowly, luxuriously oiling those hand-filling nipples.

"I remember you saying something about the law and comedy both being professions that make their living in the arena," she says.

"I did? It must have been after sex."

He does remember that conversation. It seems like another geological era, another incarnation. The room shakes again, harder, more sustained. Pens fall from desk; concentric ripples clash inside the water-cooler.

"Another universe, another point on the share-price," Vishram quips but Sonia Yadav looks concerned. Vishram catches her eye. She abandons her tour. They move through the groups of shareholders back to the empty lecture hall.

"Problem?" he whispers. Sonia points at the display boards. Output, one hundred and thirty-five percent.

"We shouldn't be anywhere close to that kind of figure."

"It's doing better than expected."

"Mr. Ray, this is physics. We know exactly the characteristics of the universes we create, no surprises, no guesswork, no 'better than expected, good boy, top of class.'"

Vishram messages Director Surjeet. When he enters, Vishram closes the door to hovercams and eavesdroppers.

"Sonia tells me we have a problem with the zero-point."

Surjeet does this tooth sucking thing that grates Vishram's nipples, especially when it reveals the saag he had for lunch.

"We're getting anomalous readings."

"That tells me exactly as much as 'Vishram, we have a problem.'"

"Very well, Mr. Ray. It's a universe, but it's not the one we ordered."

Vishram feels his balls contract. Surjeet has his palmer open, mathematical renderings and wire-frame graphics spins across it. Sonia, too, is reading the digits.

"Eight three zero."

"It should be . . ."

"Two two four."

"Wait wait wait wait wait; enough of the lottery results."

Sonia Yadav says carefully, "All the universes have what we call winding numbers, the higher the number, the more energy we need to access it and the more we can get out of it."

"We're six hundred universes too high."

"Yes," says Sonia Yadav.

"Recommendations?"

"Mr. Ray, we must close the zero-point down immediately . . ."

Vishram cuts him off. "That is absolutely the last resort. How do you think that's going to look in front of our entire board and the press? Another Bharati humiliation . . . If we can get the thing up to full power safely . . ." To Sonia Yadav, he says, "Does this pose any danger?"

"Mr. Ray, the energies released if membranes cross . . ."

Sonia cuts in.

"No."

"You're sure."

"Dr. Surjeet is correct about the energy levels if membranes cross, it would be like a nano–Big Bang, but that involves energies thousands of times more powerful than we can generate here."

"Yes, but the Atiyah's Ladder effect . . ."

The guy who let off the second Big Bang, Vishram thinks. Creation Two. That's the biggest laugh any comedian will ever get. He says, "Here's what we do. We continue with the demonstration as planned. If it goes over one hundred and seventy, we close the whole thing down, show's over, please exit via the gift shop. Whatever happens, nothing said in this room goes any further. Keep me appraised."

As he heads for the door to the zero-point lab, thinking, I can see a beautiful clear career path opening in front of Ms. Sonia Yadav Hindu physicist, a fresh tremor hits the Research Centre, hits it hard, hits it to its roots, sends Vishram Ray and Sonia Yadav and Director Surjeet reeling for handholds, for something safe and solid that is not moving, knocks dust and plaster and loose ceiling tiles from the roof and rattles the display screens, those same screens that show power output at one hundred and eighty-four percent.

Universe 2597. The aperture is running away, laddering up through successive universes.

And Vishram Ray's palmer is calling, everyone in that room's palmer is calling, they put their hands up to their heads and it is the same voice in each of their ears telling them that the aeais controlling the aperture are not responding to commands.

They've lost control of the zero-point.

Like a Christian angel, like the sword of avenging Michael plunging from the sky, Mr. Nandha comes sliding down a path of air towards the Ray Research Centre. He knows that in the belly of the tilt-jet his Excommunication Squad is muted, uncertain, scared, mutinous. The prisoners will be talking to them, sowing unbelief and dissent. That is their matter, they do not share his dedication and he cannot expect them to. Their respect is a sacrifice he is prepared to make. This warrior woman beside him in the cockpit will bring him to his ordained place.

He clicks up the astringencies of a Bach violin sonata as the pilot tips the tilt-jet into the long slow dive towards the green rhombuses of the University of Bharat.

A presence, a throat clear, a tap on his shoulder interrupt the infinite geometries of the solo violin. Mr. Nandha slowly removes his 'hoek.

"What is it, Vikram?"

"Boss, the American woman's going on about diplomatic incidents again."

"This will have to be resolved later, as I have said."

"And the sahb wants to talk to you, again."

"I am otherwise engaged."

"He's mightily pissed off that he can't get through to you."

"I sustained damage to my communicator when I was battling the Kalki aeai. I have no other explanation." He has turned it off. He does not want squawking questions, demands, orders breaking the perfection of his execution.

"You should still talk to him."

Mr. Nandha sighs. The tilt-jet leans into a stack, climbing down the sky towards the airy, toy-bright buildings of the Rana's university, gleaming in the sun that is tearing the monsoon apart. He takes the 'hoek.

"Nandha."

The voice says something about excessive zeal, use of weapons, endangering the public, questions and inquiries, too far Nandha too far, we know about your wife she turned up at Gaya Station but the word that rings, the word that chimes like the sword of that Christian, Renaissance angel against the dome of heaven, that cuts through the aircraft noise is Vik's, repeating to the crew strapped into their seats in full combat armour: *battling the Kalki aeazi*.

He despises me, Mr. Nandha thinks. He thinks I am a monster . . . This is nothing to me. A sword requires no comprehension. He removes the 'hoek and with a swift, sharp jerk of his hands, snaps it in two.

The pilot turns her mirrored HUD visor to him. Her mouth is a perfect red rosebud.

The fourth quake shakes the Research Centre as Vishram hits the fire alarm. Bookcases topple, whiteboards drop from walls, light-fittings sway, cornices crack, wiring ducts splinter. The water-cooler teeter-totters this way, that way, then falls gracefully to the floor and bursts its distended plastic belly.

"Okay, ladies and gentlemen, there is no need for alarm, we've had a small report of an overheat in the electrical relay gear," Vishram lies as wide-eyed people with their hands over their heads look for the exits. "Everything is under control. Our assembly point is outside on the quad, if we could make our way there in an orderly fashion. Walk slowly, walk carefully, don't run, our staff are fully trained and will get you to safety."

A swarm of hovercams beats everyone but Energy Minister Patel out the door. Sonia Yadav and Marianna Fusco want to wait for him but he orders them out. No sign of course of Surjeet. The Captain is always last to leave. As he turns the fifth and biggest tremor yet brings the roof screens crashing down in the lecture hall beyond. Vishram is afforded one burning, eternal glimpse on the message frozen on the falling screens.

Output seven hundred and eighty-eight percent. Universe 11276.

The light, spacious, elegant architectures of Ray Power warp and billow around Vishram Ray like his one and only mushroom trip as he runs—no decorum, no carefully, no good example, just hammering terror—for the door. The sixth tremor sends a crack racing up the centre of the Ramayana floor. Stressed parquet tiles spring apart, the glass door panels shatter into flying silicon snow as he comes running through. The shareholders, already far back from the building, retreat further. "This is no electrical overheat," Vishram overhears from a plump Grameen woman in widow's white as he hunts down Sonia Yadav. Her face is ash.

"What the fuck is happening?"

"They've taken over the system," she says faintly. Many of the shareholders are lying flat on the still-wet grass, waiting for the next, even bigger shock.

"Who, what?" Vishram demands.

"We're shut out of our network, something else is running it. There's stuff coming in, we can't stop it, all channels at once, something huge."

"An aeai," Vishram says and Sonia Yadav hears that it is not a question. The bolt-hole, the escape clause, the way out when the Generation Threes were faced with final annihilation. "Tell me, could Artificial Intelligences use the zero-point to build their own universe?"

"It couldn't be a universe like this, it would have to be a universe where the computations and digits that make up their reality can become part of the fabric of the physical reality."

"A universe that thinks?"

"A mindlike space, we call it, but yes." She looks into his face, daring his disdain. "A universe of real gods."

Sirens in the distance, racing in. Universe breaches, call the fire brigade. There is another sound over the fire engines; aircraft engines.

"Played for a fucking fool," Vishram grimaces and then everything goes white in a pure, perfect, blinding flash of urlight and when his vision clears, there is a star, pure and perfect and dazzling, shining in the middle of the Research Centre Building.

White so bright, so searing it burns through the one-way mirror of the pilot's visor and before he goes into white-out Mr. Nandha receives a retina-burned image of big brown eyes, high cheekbones, a small nose. Beautiful. A goddess. So many men must want to wed you, my warrior, Mr. Nandha thinks. The face recedes into afterimage, then the world returns in spots and blots of purple and Mr. Nandha feels tears of justification start in his eyes, for there is the sign and seal that he was right. A star burns in the heart of the city, from deep inside the earth. He signs to the pilot. Take us, down.

"Away from the people," he adds. "We do not recklessly endanger life."

Vishram thinks he might have seen this scene in a movie once. Or if he hasn't, he should write it: a crowd of people standing in a wide green field, all facing the same direction, hands raised to shield their eyes from a dazzling, actinic spark in the distance. That's a shot to build a story from. His eyes are squeezed half-shut, even so everything is reduced to strangely stretched silhouettes.

"If that's what I think it is, there's a lot more than bright light coming off it," says Ramesh's voice beside him.

"And what do you think it is?" Vishram asks, remembering his sunburn from peering into the observation window. That was a low level universe. A glance at Sonia Yadav's palmer, still receiving data from the monitoring systems around the aperture, tells him this is universe 212255. Two and something lakh universes.

"A universe being born," Ramesh says, dreamily. "The only reason we're still here, there's anything left, is the containment fields still have it. In terms of the subjective physics of that universe, it must seem like a super-gravity squeezing its space-time so it can't expand. But that kind of expansion energy has to go somewhere."

"How long can the cores hold it?" Vishram asks Sonia Yadav. He imagines he should be shouting. In the movies, they are always shouting. Her shrug tells all he needs to know and fear. A fresh tremor. People fall to the earth, though it is a traitor. Vishram hardly sees them. The star, the blinding star. It is now a tiny sphere. Then he does hear a shout, Sonia Yadav's voice.

"Deba! Has anyone seen Deba?"

As the shout ripples out across the field, Vishram Ray finds he is running. He knows they will not find Deba among them. Deba is down there, in his hole, in his black hole under the earth, on the precipice of nothing. A voice cries his name, a voice he does not recognise. He looks around to see Marianna Fusco running after him. She has kicked off her shoes, she runs ponderously in her business skirt. He has never heard her shout his name before.

"Vish! Come back, there's nothing you can do!"

The bubble expands again. It is now thirty metres across, rising out of the centre of the Research Unit like a Mughal dome. Like the dome of the Mughal Taj, it is empty inside, emptier even than the tomb of a grief-sick Emperor. It is nothing. It is annihilation so absolute the mind cannot contain it. And Vishram plunges towards it.

"Deba!"

A silhouette emerges out of the light-dazzle, limbs flailing, awkward.

"To me!" Vishram yells. "To me!"

He seizes Deba in his arms. The kid's face is badly burned, his skin smells of ultraviolet. He rubs incessantly at his eyes.

"It hurts!" he wails. "It hurts, it fucking hurts!"

Vishram spins him around and the bubble leaps again, a titanic quantum leap. Vishram is staring at a wall of light, brilliant, blinding, but within the light he thinks he can see shapes, patterns, flickering of bright and less bright, light and shadow. Black and white. He stares, entranced. Then he feels his skin start to burn.

Marianna Fusco takes Deba's other shoulder and together they bring him to safety. The Ray Power shareholders have moved back to the furthest section of the formal charbagh. Vishram thinks it odd yet human that no one has left.

"Assessment?" he asks Sonia Yadav. The sirens are close now, he hopes they are parameds. And that aircraft is very, very near.

"Our computers are downloading at an incredible rate," she says.

"Where?"

"Into *that*."

"Is there anything we can do?"

"No," she says simply. "It's not in our hands now."

You've got what you wanted, Vishram prays at the sphere of light. You don't have to do anything else. Just close the door and walk away. And as he thinks it there is a second flash of light and a huge thunderclap of air and light and energy and space-time rushing into absolute vacuum and when Vishram's vision clears he sees two things.

The first is a large perfectly hemispherical perfectly smooth crater where Ray Power Research Centre had stood.

The other is a line of soldiers in full combat gear advancing across the neat, watered lawn, weapons at the present. At their head is a tall, thin man with a good suit and a bad five o'clock shadow and a gun in his hand.

"Your attention please!" the man shouts. "Nobody is permitted to leave. You are all under arrest."

Lisa Durnau finds Thomas Lull kneeling on the grass, his hands still cuffed with black plastic cable grip. He is beyond tears, beyond wrack. All that remains is a terrible stillness.

She settles awkwardly beside him on the grass, tears at her own plastic tie with her teeth.

"They got away," Thomas Lull says, taking a long shuddering breath.

"The counterinflation force must have pushed into in-folded dimensions," Lisa Durnau says. "It was a hell of a risk . . ."

"I looked into it," Thomas Lull whispers. "As we were coming in over it, I looked into it. It is the Tabernacle."

But how? Lisa Durnau wants to ask, but Thomas Lull slumps back on to his back, bound hands on his small pot belly, staring up into the light of the sun.

"She showed them there was nothing for them here," he says. "Just people, just bloody people. I like to think she made a choice, for people. For us. Even though . . . Even though . . ." Lisa Durnau sees his body quiver and knows whatever it is lies beyond tears will come soon. She has never known that. She looks away. She has seen the look of this man destroyed before and that is enough for one lifetime.

Mr. Nandha would love most dearly to loosen his collar with his finger. The heat in the corridor is oppressive; the air-conditioning aeai follows Ray Power ethical practice, reluctant to react to sudden shifts in microclimate in the name of energy efficiency. But the sun has broken through the monsoon clouds and the glass face of Mr. Nandha's headquarters is a sweat machine. His suit is rumpled. His skin is waxy with perspiration. He fears he may have an unpleasing body odour that his superiors will sense the moment he enters Arora's office.

Mr. Nandha thinks there is blood on his shoes.

Air-conditioning aeais. Djinns even in the air ducts. From his seat he can look down upon his city as he has all those times when he called upon it to be his oracle. Now there is nothing here. My Varanasi is given over to djinns, he thinks.

Clouds move, light shifts in rays and shafts. Mr. Nandha winces at a sudden glint of brilliance from the green western suburbs. A heliograph, for his eye only, from the hundred-metre hemisphere carved out by an alien space-time where Ray Power's Research and Development section had once stood. Precise down to the quantum level, a perfect mirror. He knows, because he stood there, firing and firing and firing at his own distorted reflection until Vik wrestled him to the ground, hauled the god-gun out of his fist. Vik, in his hissing, ill-fitting rock-boi shoes.

He can still see her shoes, racked up so neatly in pairs like praying hands.

They will be agreeing on a script, behind Arora's door. Exceeded his authority. Excessive force. Public endangerment. The Energy Minister in handcuffs . . . Disciplinary measures. Suspension from duties. Of course. They must. But they do not know there is nothing they can do to him now. Mr. Nandha can feel the acid start to burn his esophagus. So many betrayals. His superiors, his stomach, his city. He erases the faithless shikaras and mandapas of Varanasi, imagines the campaniles and piazzas and duomos of Cremona. Cremona of the mind, the only eternal city. The only true city.

The door opens. Arora peeps out nervously, like a bird from a nest.

"You can come in now, Nandha."

Mr. Nandha stands up, straightens his jacket and cuffs. As he walks towards the open door, the opening bars of the first Bach cello sonata soar through his mind.

In a dark room at the heart of a temple to a dark goddess, smeared with blood and hazy with the ash of dead humans, a cross-legged old man rolls on his skinny buttock bones and laughs and laughs and laughs and laughs.

47

LULL, LISA

In the evening a wind blows up from the river as a cool exhalation. It sweeps the ghats, stirs up the dust, and sends eddies of marigold petals scurrying along the day-warmed stone. It rattles the newspapers of the old widower men who know they will never marry again, who come down to the ghats to talk the day's headlines with their friends, it tugs at the trails and folds of the women's saris. It sets the ghee-flames of the diyas swaying, ruffles the surface of the water into little cat-waves as the bathers scoop it up in their copper dishes and pour it over their heads. The scarlet silk flags curl on their bamboo poles. The wide wicker umbrellas shift as the breeze reaches under their decorated caps and lifts them. It smells of deep water, this small wind. It smells of cool and time and a new season. Down beneath the funeral ghats the men who pan the river for the golden ashes of the dead look up, touched by a sense of something more, something deeper than their dismal trade. The sound of the boat oars as they dip and slop into the water is rich and bottomless.

It was in the early afternoon that the rain lifted and the roof of grey cloud broke and there, beyond it, was a sky of high, miraculous blue, Krishna blue. You could see all the way out of the universe in that clear, washed blue. The sun shone, the stone ghats steamed. Within minutes the foot-trodden mud had dried to dust. People came out from under their umbrellas, uncovered their heads, unfolded their newspapers, and lit cigarettes. Rain has been, rain will come again: great curds of cumulus cruise the eastern horizon beyond the plumes and vapours of the industrial shore, preposterous purple and yellow in the fast-falling light. Already the people take up their positions for the aarti, the nightly fire ceremony. These ghats may witness panic, flight, populations on the move, bloody death, but thanks as endless as the river are due to Ganga Mata. Drummers, percussionists make their way to the sides of the wooden platforms where the brahmins perform. Barefoot women carefully descend the steps, dip their hands in the rising river before finding their accustomed place. They skirt around the two Westerners sitting by the water's edge, nod, smile. All are welcome at the river.

The marble is warm under Lisa Durnau's thigh, skin smooth. She can smell the water, coiling silently at her foot. The first flotillas of diyas are striking bravely out into the current, stubborn tiny lights on the darkening water. The breeze plays cool on her bare shoulders, a woman namastes as she passes back from the forgiving water. India endures, she thinks. And India ignores. These are its strengths, twined around each other like lovers in a temple carving. Armies clash, dynasties rise and fall, lords die and nations and universes are born and the river flows on and the people flow to it. Perhaps this woman had not even noticed the flash of light that was the aeais departing to their own universe. If she had, how would she have thought of it? Some new weapons system, some piece of electronica gone bad, some inexplicable piece of complicated world gone awry. Not for her to know or wonder. The only part of it to touch her was when *Town and Country* suddenly disappeared. Or did she look up and see another truth entirely, the jyotirlinga, the generative power of Siva bursting from an earth that could not contain it in a pillar of light.

She looks at Thomas Lull beside her on the warm stone, knees pulled up, arms around them, looking across the river at the fantastical fortresses of the clouds. He said little since Rhodes from the embassy secured their release from the Ministry's holding centre, a conference room converted by removing all the tables and chairs, filled with bad tempered businessmen, feisty grameen women, and furious Ray Power researchers. The air was hissing with calls to lawyers.

Thomas Lull had not even blinked. The car had left them at the haveli but he turned away from the ornate wooden gate and headed out into the warren of lanes and street markets that led down to the ghats. Lisa had not tried to stop him or ask him or talk to him. She watched him walk up and down the flights, along and around looking for where feet had trodden blood into the stone. She had looked at his face as he stood there with the people bustling over the place where Aj had died and thought, I know that look from a big wide Lawrence living room with no furniture. And she knew what she needed to do, and that her mission was always going to fail. And when he finally shook his head in the weak gesture of disbelief that was more eloquent than any drama of emotion and went down to the river and sat by the water, she had gone with him and settled on the sun-warmed stone, for when he was ready.

The musicians have begun a soft, slow heartbeat. The crowd grows by the minute. The sense of expectation, of presence, is a felt thing.

"L. Durnau," says Thomas Lull. Against herself, she smiles. "Give me that thing."

She passes him the Tablet. He flicks through its pages. She sees him call up the images from the Tabernacle; Lisa, Lull. Aj. Nandha the

Krishna Cop. He folds the faces back into the machine. A mystery never to be solved. She knows he will never come back with her.

"You think you learn something, you think finally you've got it worked out. It's taken time and grief and effort and a shitload of experience but at last, you think you've got some idea how it all works, the whole fucking show. You think I'd know better, I honestly want to believe that we're actually all right, that there's something more to it than just planet-slime and that's why it gets me every time. Every single time."

"The curse of the optimist, Lull. People get in the way."

"No, not people, L. Durnau. No, I gave up on people long ago. No, I'd hoped, when I worked out what the aeais were doing, I thought, Jesus, that's a fucking irony, the machines that want to understand what it's like to be human are actually more human than we are. I never hoped in us, L. Durnau, but I hoped that the Gen Threes might have evolved some moral sense. No, they abandoned her. As soon as they saw there never would be peace between the meat and the metal, they let her go. Learn what it's like to be human. They learned all they needed to know in one act of betrayal.

"They saved themselves. They saved their species."

"Did you listen to a word I said, L. Durnau?"

A child comes down the steps, a little girl in a floral dress, barefoot, uncertain on the ghats. Her face is pure concentration. Her father has hold of one hand, the other, waving to keep balance, holds a garland of marigolds. The father points her to the river, points her to throw, go on, put it in. The girl flings the gajra, waves her arms in delight as she sees it land on the darkening water. She cannot be more than two.

No, you're wrong, Lull, Lisa Durnau wants to say. It's those stubborn tiny lights they can never put out. It's those quanta of joy and wonder and surprise that never stop bubbling out of the universal and constant truths of our humanity. When she speaks, her words are, "So where do you think you'll go then?"

"There's still a dive school with my name on it somewhere down Lanka, Thailand way," Thomas Lull says. "There's one night in the year, just after the first full moon in November, when the coral releases its sperm and eggs, all at once. It's quite wonderful, like swimming in a giant orgasm. I'd like to see that. Or there's Nepal, the mountains; I'd like to see the mountains, really see the mountains, spend time among them. Do some mountain Buddhism, all those demons and horrors, that's the kind of religion speaks to me. Get up to Kathmandu, out to Pokhara, some place high, with a view of the Himalayas. Will this get you in trouble with the G-men?"

Father and daughter stand by the water, watching the gajra bob on the ripples. The child smiles suspiciously at her. What have you been doing all your life, Lisa Durnau, that is more vital than this?

"They'll get round to me eventually."

"Well, take this back to them. I suppose I owe you, L. Durnau."

Thomas Lull hands her the Tablet. Lisa Durnau frowns at the schematic.

"What is this?"

"The winding maps for the Calabi-Yau space the Gen Threes created at Ray Power."

"It's a standard set of transforms for an information-space with a mindlike space-time structure. Lull, I helped develop these theories, remember? They got me into your office."

And bed, she thinks.

"Do you remember what I said on the boat, L. Durnau? About Aj? 'The other way around.'"

Lisa Durnau frowns, then she sees it, as she saw it written by the hand of God on the toilet door in Paddington Station, and it is so clear and so pure and so beautiful it is like a spear of light stabbed straight through her, ramming through her pinning her to the white stone and it feels like death and it feels like ecstasy and it feels like something singing. Tears start in her eyes, she wipes them away, she cannot stop looking at the single, miraculous, luminous negative sign. Negative T. The time-arrow is reversed. A mindlike space, where the intelligences of the aeais can merge into the structure of the universe and manipulate it in any way they will. Gods. The clocks run backwards. As it ages, as it grows more complex; our universe grows younger and dumber and simpler. Planets dissolve into dust, stars evaporate into clouds of gas that coalesce into brief supernovas that are not the light of destruction but candles of creation, space collapsing in on itself, hotter and hotter reeling back towards the primordial ylem, forces and particles churned back into the primordial ylem while the aeais grow in power and wisdom and age. Time's arrow flies the other way.

Hands shaking, she calls up a simple math aeai, runs a few fast transforms. As she suspected, the arrow of time not only flies in the other direction, it flies faster. A fast, fierce universe of lifetimes compressed into moments. The clock-speed, the Planck-time flicker that governs the rates at which the aeais calculate their reality, is one hundred times that of universe zero. Breathless, Lisa Durnau thumbs more calculations into the Tablet though she knows, she knows, she knows what it is going to tell her. Universe 212255 runs its course from birth to recollapse into a final singularity in seven point seven eight billion years.

"It's a Boltzmon!" she exclaims with simple joy. The girl in the flower dress turns and stares at her. The cinder of a universe; an ultimate black hole that contains every piece of quantum information that fell into it, that punches its way out of one dying reality into another. And waits, humanity's inheritance.

"Their gift to us," Thomas Lull says. "Everything they knew, everything they experienced, everything they learned and created, they sent it through to us as their final act of thanks. The Tabernacle is a simple universal automaton that codes the information in the Boltzmon into a form comprehensible to us."

"And us, our faces."

"We were their gods. We were their Brahma and Siva, Vishnu and Kali. We are their creation myth."

The light is almost gone now, deep indigo has settled across the river. The air is cool, the far clouds carry an edge of luminosity, they seem huge and improbable as dreams. The musicians have picked up the pace, the devotees take up the song to Mother Ganga. The Brahmins descend through the crowd. Father and child are gone.

They never forgot us, thinks Lisa Durnau. In all the billions—trillions—of subjective years of their experience and history, they always remembered this act of betrayal on the banks of the Ganga, and they compelled us to enact it. The burning chakra of regeneration is endless. The Tabernacle is a prophecy, and an oracle. The answer to everything we need to know is in there, if we only know how to ask.

"Lull . . ."

He whips his finger to his lips, no, hush, don't speak. Thomas Lull gets stiffly to his feet. For the first time Lisa Durnau sees the old man he will be, the lonely man he wishes to become. Where he goes this time, not even the Tablet can see.

"L. Durnau."

"Kathmandu, then. Or Thailand."

"Somewhere."

He offers a hand and she knows that after she takes it she will never see him again.

"Lull, I can't thank you . . ."

"You don't have to. You would have seen it."

She takes the hand.

"Good-bye, Thomas Lull."

Thomas Lull dips his head in a small bow.

"L. Durnau. All partings should, I think, be sudden."

The musicians ratchet up a gear, the crowd gives a vast, incoherent sigh and leans towards the five platforms where the priests offer puja.

Flames whirl up from the Brahmins' aarti lamps, momentarily dazzling Lisa Dumau. When her vision clears, Lull is gone.

Out on the water, a flaw of wind, a current catches the garland of marigolds and turns it and carries it out into the dark river.

GLOSSARY

AARTI: Hindu ceremony of offering light to a deity.

ADIVASI: ancient Indian tribal cultures, beneath the caste system.

ANGREEZ: Hindi-isation of "English"

APSARA: celestial nymph, often a bracket support in a temple, originally tree spirits.

ARAHB: Hindi number equal to 10^9. Indians have useful names for very large numbers.

ARDHA MANDAPA: entrance porch, leading into the mandapa, or colonnaded hall of a temple.

BABA: term of endearment.

BABU: civil servant or bureaucrat.

BADMASH: a nasty and brutish little hood. With attitude.

BAHADUR: proud, self-important, pompous.

BAKHTI: the path of devotion.

BANSURI: North Indian six- or seven-hole bamboo flute.

Baradari: Pakistani/Pashtun affiliation group somewhere between a clan, a gang, and a Massive.

Basti: settlement or slum, also (confusingly) a Jain temple complex.

Begum: term of respect to a Muslim married lady.

Behen chowd: sister-fucker, most common Hindi term of abuse.

Bhai: suffix after a proper name, indicating respectful closeness.

Bhavan: house—usually one of some distinction.

Bheesty: domestic servant in charge of water supply.

Bibi: Hindi term for a married woman.

Bidi: a native Indian cigarette, tapered towards the tip. Deathsticks, if ever there were.

Big Dada: low hood; literally means "big arm." Strong arm boy.

Bindi: forehead mark indicating caste, though it can be worn decoratively. The tilak is the religious equivalent.

Brahmin: the highest of the four main castes; the priestly caste, so holy not even the gods could harm them. (See also *varna*.) In context, also the genetically modified children of the rich.

Brinjal: eggplant.

Bulbul: common, titlike bird with black head and white cheeks and a famously sweet song.

Burqa: traditional public attire of a Muslim woman, anything from a thin headscarf to a full marquee.

Chakra: energy node in the human body. There are seven: from the pubis to the crown of the head.

Charbagh: water garden, of Islamic design, divided into quarters.

Charpoy: rope-strung, low bed frame, very popular in rural India for lolling on to observe the passing world.

Chhatri: small decorative Mughal pavilion in the form of a cupola on open pillars.

Chital: most common species of Indian deer, with a spotted hide. Also known as the Buddha's deer: his last incarnation before becoming human was a Chital.

Cho chweet: common term of endearment.

Choli: short-sleeved, tight undershirt worn by women under a sari.

Chowkidar: a nightwatchman.

Chuutya: "cunthole" in Hindi slang.

Crore: 10^7.

Cutcha: opposite of pukka.

Dacoit: armed gangsters/robbers. Still widely used.

Dal: lentils, the staple of rural India.

Dalit: the lowest caste. Literally "the Oppressed," they were formerly known as Untouchables.

Darshan: the auspicious glance of a temple deity, or a rich and powerful person.

Darwaz: entrance gate to a mosque.

Desi: Indianness as perceived by the overseas community—a nostalgic, affectionate sense of India. In UK Asian youth parlance, means the same as pukka: real, genuine.

Deva/devi: god/goddess. Also a common name.

Dhaba: roadside/streetside eating establishment.

Dharamshala: guest accommodations for pilgrims, students, and travellers.

Dhobi: laundry, usually on a flat dhobi-rock by the side of a river or a well.

Dhol: a type of drum.

Dhoti: long loincloth, less common in cities, as worn by Gandhi.

Dhuri: woven cotton rug.

Dikpalas: guardian figures on a temple roof.

Diwan: open-pillared Mughal audience hall.

Diya: floating candle set in the river Ganga as an offering.

Dupatta: long scarf traditionally worn with the shalwar kameez, or trouser suit.

Dvarapala: gateway guardian deity at Hindu temple doorways: literally doorkeeper.

FIRENGI: foreigner, one of several Hindi words appropriated by *Star Trek*. (See also *jemadar*.)

GAJRA: the ubiquitous marigold garland, a good auspice.

GALI: an alleyway.

GANJA: exactly as in Jamaican.

GARBHAGRIHA: inner womb sanctum of a Hindu temple.

GHAZAL: Islamic song of love, usually in Urdu.

GODOWN: workshop, warehouse, often impromptu.

GOL GUPPAS: Indian street food: stuffed wheat balls. Better than they sound.

GOPIS: milkmaid companions of the Lord Krishna. They liked his flute playing.

GORA: contemptuous expression for a white person.

GUNDA: a common street thug.

GUPSHUP: vaguely scurrilous gossip.

GYANA CHAKSHU: the third eye of Siva, literally the "eye of wisdom" that penetrates illusion.

HAVELI: traditional courtyard house of the better off, usually Muslim.

HIJRA: literally "eunuch."

HINDUTVA: the essential spirit of Indianness as being essentially Hindu: religious nationalism.

HOWDAH: large, often ceremoniously dressed saddle for an elephant.

IFTAR: meal that breaks the Ramadan dawn-to-dusk fast.

IWAN: Sufi dancing hall.

IZZAT: military term for respect, esprit de corps.

JAI: "glory" or "victory!"

JANUM: term of endearment usually used of males. Means "sweet."

JATI: the system of subcastes within the four main castes of *varna*.

JAWAN: Indian soldier or paramilitary policeman.

JELLABA: long, light cotton robe worn extensively and comfortably by Muslim men from Morocco to Malaysia.

JEMADAR: Indian noncommissioned military officer.

JHAROKA: projecting window or balcony.

JIVA: the immortal essence of a living being.

JOHAD: a semicircular dam for run-off water.

KADAI: Indian cooking pan, shaped rather like a wok with two handles.

KALAMKARI: dyed and painted highly decorative fabrics from Andhra Pradesh.

KARSEVAK: Hindu fundamentalist pilgrim/activist.

KATHAK: a North Indian dance.

KETTUVALLAM: a Keralese houseboat, about seventy feet long. Originally used to transport rice.

KHIDMUTGAR: chief steward in a household, almost a butler.

LAKH: 10^5.

LANGUR: also known as Hanuman's monkey. Monkeys are therefore sacred in India.

LARRI-GALLA: a workshop among housing.

LASSI: cool yogurt-based drink.

LAVDA: penis, prick.

LINGA: phallus as a sacred object, usually in the shape of a rounded stone.

MACHAAN: an observation platform in a tree for big-game hunting.

MADAR CHOWD: same as behen chowd, only this time it's your mother.

MADRASSA: Islamic school where Arabic and theology are taught.

MALI: a gardener.

MELA: a gathering of people: anything from a big family get-together to the Kumbh Mela.

MEVLEVI: Turkish sufi order, originators of the "whirling dervish" dance.

MOKSHA: release from the cycle of death and reincarnation. Those who die by the Ganga achieve moksha, thus encouraging the peculiarly Indian institution of "death-tourism."

MUDRA: hand gesture in Indian classical dance, conveying great subtlety of meaning.

Musnud: Mughal throne, a simple large slab of marble upholstered with cushions.

Naga sadhu: the naked sadhu, who goes sky-clad to show his disdain for the world of illusions.

Naqqar khana: ceremonial gatehouse with turret for drummer and musicians to welcome guests.

Nautch: traditional semiformal dance party for the entertainment of gentlemen.

Paan: a near-ubiquitous confection of spices, nuts, and a mild narcotic wrapped in a betel leaf. Makes your gums red, a bit of a giveaway.

Pallav: the section of a sari worn over the shoulder, usually richly decorated.

Pandal: marquee or stage made of cloth and bamboo.

Parikrama: Clockwise sunwise circuit of a Hindu or Buddhist sacred site.

Phatphat: motor rickshaw, ubiquitous and terrifying.

Prasad: sacred food, food offering.

Puja: prayer and offerings to deities.

Purdah: the segregation of the sexes in traditional Islam and Hinduism.

Puri: deep-fried puffed bread, often stuffed. Delicious if appallingly calorific.

Qawwals: Islamic songs of praise, as opposed to *ghazals*, songs of love.

Rath yatra: divine temple/chariot, the vehicle of Rama, the centrepiece of the Orissa *jagannath* (juggernaut) celebration.

Roti: Indian fried flatbread.

Sadhu: Hindu ascetic, holy man. (For woman, see *sadhvi*.)

Sadhvi: female *sadhu*. Hindu nun who has renounced worldly things.

Samadhi: the meditative state of undifferentiated "Beingness."

Sangam: spit of sand where sacred rivers meet.

Sanyasi (plural: sanyassins): priest(s).

Sathin: informal village social worker (literally "friend"): usually female, often doubles as midwife.

SATI: the (now illegal) custom of widows burning themselves on their husbands' funeral pyres. Sati stories crop up several times a year even today, usually in rural Rajasthan.

SATTA: originally illegal betting on commodity prices, generally extended into any kind of dodgy bookies.

SEMA: the dervishes' mystical whirling dance.

SEPOY: old Raj term for native infantry.

SHAADI: wedding preceremony. Also India's biggest online matrimonial agency.

SHAMYANA: a decorated awning over the front of a building.

SHATABDI: Indian high-speed express train.

SHERWANI: long, richly decorated frock coat usually worn by Islamic men.

SHIKARA: main spire on a North Indian temple.

SMASANAKALI: that aspect of Kali that rules over the funeral ghats.

SOWAR: Indian elite cavalry.

SUBADAR: Indian military commissioned officer roughly equivalent in rank to captain.

SUDDHAVASA: one of several intermediate heavens in Mountain Buddhism, literally "Abode of the Pure."

SUNDARBAN: the tiger-haunted jungles of the Ganga/Brahmaputra delta. In context, equally wild and dangerous data-havens for breeding unlicensed software.

SURA: verse of the Holy Koran.

SURYA NAMASKAR: the salutation of the sun, a sequence of yoga asanas performed at dawn to greet the sunrise.

SWABHIMAN: self-respect, both personal and national.

SWAMI: Hindu honorific similar to "master," implying mastery of body and soul.

TAMASHA: festive excitement.

TANDAVA NRITYA: Shiva's cosmic dance of destruction—and regeneration.

THALI: a metal dish, also a selection of different foods on one compartmentalized dish.

TILAK: sacred mark of the forehead. Siva and Vishnu have different ones.

TIRTHA: a divine ford, or a crossing place between the mortal and the divine worlds.

TRIMURTI: the Hindu "trinity" of Brahma, Vishnu, and Siva.

TRISHUL: sacred trident of Siva, carried by devotees. Often made from empty ghee or Red Bull cans.

VAHANA: the animal "vehicle" of each god: Brahma the goose, Durga the tiger, Ganesha the rat.

VAJRA: the divine thunderbolt of Indra, ancient Aryan Vedic god of rain and thunder—in many ways analogous to the Scandinavian Thor.

VARNA: the divinely ordained system of caste, the main groups being Brahmins, Kshatriyas, Vaishyas, and Shudras, conforming roughly to priests, warriors, traders/farmers, and servants. Beneath them all come the *Dalits*.

VASUS: in Vedic Hinduism, the eight attendants of Indra: means "excellent."

VIBHUTI: white scared ash-powder worn by Sadhus in devotion to Siva.

WALLAH: "fellow": a very common suffix, as in "chai-wallah" and "dhobi-wallah."

YAKSHAS: semidivine beings living under the Himalayas.

YALI: mythical leaping leonine beast.

YONI: the vagina as sacred source.

ZAMINDAR: Indian village landowner.

ZENANA: the women's part of a traditional Muslim house.

Thanks to Ritu Parvaaz for Hindi assistance.

SOUNDTRACK

The soundtrack to *River of Gods* features tracks from the following artists.

Talvin Singh, Thievery Corporation, A.R. Rahman, AmarBaaba Maal, Asian Dub Foundation, Autechre, Badmarsh and Sri, Bjork, Black Star Liner, The Blue Nile, Boards of Canada, The Chemical Brothers, Dead Can Dance, The *Fake* Portishead, Future Sound of London, Godspeed You! Black Emperor, Goldfrapp, Jamyang, Joi, Jeff Buckley, *Kabhi Kushi Kabhie Gham*: original movie soundtrack, Nitin Sawhney, Nusrat Fateh Ali Khan, Rakesh Chaurasia, Sigur Rós, State of Bengal.

ABOUT THE AUTHOR

Ian McDonald is the author of many science fiction novels, including *Desolation Road*, *King of the Morning*, *Queen of the Day*, *Out on Deep Six*, *Changa*, and *Kirinya*. He has won the Philip K. Dick Award and the British Science Fiction Association Award for Best Novel, been nominated for a Hugo Award, and has several nominations for the Arthur C. Clarke Award. He lives in Belfast, Northern Ireland.